BLIND GUIDES

BLIND GUIDES

Scott R. Stahlecker

iUniverse, Inc.

New York Lincoln Shanghai

Blind Guides

iUniverse, Inc.

For information address:
iUniverse, Inc.
2021 Pine Lake Road, Suite 100
Lincoln, NE 68512
www.iuniverse.com

This book is a work of fiction. The names, characters, places and incidents are either products of the author's imagination or are used fictitiously. Any resemblance to actual events, locals or persons living or dead is entirely coincidental.

ISBN: 0-595-27009-3

Printed in the United States of America

To my wife Gena, who has endured my creative impulses for the past two decades. May we experience another century of life in the next twenty years.

What The Mind Sees The Eye Believes.

Preface

In my relatively short life I have had the opportunity to live for periods of time in Asia and Europe, and have traveled through all of the United States with the exception of Alaska. I can think of no better education than to walk and live with cultures that are different from my own. What I have learned is that human nature is similar anywhere I go, but more importantly, that people act and conduct their lives according to the cultures they have been born into. I have often thought that if I had been born within a different place in time and subject to a different set of circumstances than I have experienced, I would no doubt be a different person than the person I am now. How would I treat this new version of myself? Would I value his life as much as I my own? If not, what would be the reasons to treat him differently?

As we grow older we learn that culture, societal beliefs, education, experience, and religious and spiritual beliefs differ from person to person and from one distant culture to the next. Attitudes towards the nature of good and evil, the concept of God and the afterlife, sex, art, the freedom of expression, and the freedom to choose one's course in life, vary as well. We are prone to believe, quite naturally, that what we have been taught in our own cultures is the most valid and that those values are worth fighting and dying for. I would venture to say that every disagreement, to every war, is begun over differences in ideologies or religious beliefs. This has been from the beginning and I suspect it will be so in the end.

I am a citizen of the United States of America. I did not choose this country, in as much as I did not choose life itself, but I am grateful to have been born within its borders and to have been born period. Like all Americans there are aspects of my society and government which I do not like or subscribe to, and for the very reason that I am allowed to verbalize and print such a statement, is the reason why I cherish it as my homeland. In all my travels and through all my self-education, I have not lived in or discovered a country which grants me the freedom to choose and express myself as much as the United States Of America. Fortunately, I have not lived in or experienced a culture that tramples on the basic rights of its citizens, which all humans should possess, and the fact that you have this book in your hand tells me you enjoy your freedom as much as I.

They say that truth is stranger than fiction, but I would also add, that fiction sometimes mimics reality. In writing and rewriting *Blind Guides* over the past six years, I am amazed at how certain scenarios and characters reflect some of my own thoughts about life. Writers write and readers read for various reasons, and the original intent of my writing this particular piece has not changed through the years. What I value most in life is the freedom to think and express oneself, because it is directly linked to tolerating the ideas of individuals and accepting people of different cultures. The greatest threat to tolerance and freedom of expression has historically been organized religion, or politically forced ideologies. I still believe this to be true. Even as I write, news stories of religious extremist factions in the Middle East and terrorist activities in the "homeland" are daily occurrences. We stand from a distance and enjoy our freedoms, while shaking our heads after witnessing the examples of intolerance and lack of personal freedoms in distant lands.

In a free society there are many other factors that deter freethinking. We have the luxury of not having to fight for survival for our basic necessities. This gives us the time to discuss over cappuccino what is happening in other parts of the world, perhaps overlooking conditions that exist in our own countries and weaken our ability to think clearly. *Blind Guides* is a novel that touches on a number of these factors namely: religion, political and societal influences and artistic expression. It may raise a few eyebrows and set people shifting in their chairs. The book is, however, a work of fiction, with a timeframe set in the not so distant future. My hope is that you will find it enjoyable as well as thought provoking.

The Author

PROLOGUE

▼

"To Mr. Rick Forstein," the letter began, but quickly ended with a discrete admonition, "We urge you to take the responsibility of your position seriously and consider the long term ramifications of the council's vote." The preceding contents of the letter were equally direct. "We do understand that matters relating to the students of Marbel University rest in the hands of the student council, nevertheless, it has come to our attention that some of the work being presented at the annual art exhibit has already received strong objections from a number of students and faculty. While we encourage the creative accomplishments of our students, it's our belief that material which is offensive can be rejected as a matter of principle, thus leaving space for more appealing pieces."

He stood and walked over to his desk, folded the letter back along its creases, shoved it into the envelope and slid it under the corner of his desk calendar leaving just a corner exposed. Looking over the numbered squares of the calendar that lay before him he quickly found Saturday, April 24, 2009 where the words "Art Exhibit" were scribbled and highlighted in yellow. "Damn," he mumbled, "just two weeks away." The show would be the last major task of his elected position and it was proving to be the most difficult task he'd faced all year.

Rick was beginning to feel a bit claustrophobic. He found himself staring out of the tiny window of his room, overlooking the northern part of campus. Summer had arrived, the winter-rye grass seeded in the fall by the Grounds Department had died out and the bermuda was sprouting. The crepe myrtles lining the walk to the women's dorm would soon be budding watermelon red and lavender purple. This year, however, he would not see them bloom. Resumes had been sent to all the major computer firms in the state. Landor Inc. and Secur-ComE had already requested interviews and in a few short weeks this would all be behind him.

"What's with Stace? I know he has more photographs he could be showing, but why those!" He shook his head ever so slightly in annoyance, while the knots of muscle in his jaws flexed under his smoothly shaven face. Looking back through the window, he saw the glass doors of the science building fling open with the force of a single student. Moments later, an exodus of students flowed out of the building, signifying the last period of the day had ended. Rick watched until the stream of students slowed to a mere trickle. The council would meet again on Thursday and the vote on the final entries of the show would be taken. He was willing to concede the outcome of the meeting rested entirely upon him, but whether or not the exhibit was a success, would not affect his future. He understood the intent of the letter—that he had to at least try and appease the faculty—but that was all. In a few months, whatever the outcome, the whole episode would be history.

"Stace Manning!" Mrs. Colton screeched above the grinding of chairs and the shuffling of feet as her students got up to leave. "I need to speak with you before you go." Her tone was irritating like gavel on steel and Stace looked up from the sketch he was working on to see her peering over her bifocals at him. He slipped the sketch into his backpack. There was nothing he could say. He suspected this moment would come, but hoped it wouldn't. He'd not gotten sick. He just ran out of time. He should have felt guilty, but he didn't. The big round clock on the wall above her desk read 3:04. In the Rigby building, Mr. Salter would just now be turning the key on the photo lab door and he was determined to get there as soon as he could.

"You didn't turn your final report in on Tuesday when it was due. Is there any particular reason why?"

He thought quickly of an excuse, but Mrs. Colton was a veteran. She'd never fall for it. He hoped to defuse her with old-fashioned honesty. "I've been working on my photographs for the Art Exhibit. I guess time got a way from me."

She leaned back into her chair. The spring holding the tension to the backrest squeaked like a rusty door hinge. She stopped looking at him long enough to glance around the empty room. It was not the first time a student had failed to complete her final Texas Government report. Nor, was it the first time a student had disappointed her. She'd been teaching this class a full thirteen years and found herself provoked that such callousness amongst the younger generation towards their country still existed. "You do realize I'll have to drop you one letter grade for failing to meet the deadline?"

"Yes," he said timidly.

"If your report isn't in by next Tuesday I'll have to drop you another letter grade. You're currently looking at a *C*. If I don't see your report by next week your grade will drop to a *D*. I suspect you don't want that?"

"No."

"Then you're excused."

Stace lifted himself out of the chair and shuffled with a rattled expression towards the door. "You'll have your report by Tuesday," he said as he passed her desk.

Once outside, Stace picked up his pace and moved across campus, passing the women's dorm and the administrative offices, the ancient Oakly building and the science complex, then across Dutch street past the theology department on the left, and within a few minutes he reached the walkway of the Tindale building, which housed the fine-arts department. A century ago the Tindale building had been constructed of bright red brick, but its color had now dulled by years of harsh Texas winters and summers. The entrance stood carved into a patch of oak trees and it was in the process of being swallowed in an overgrowth of English ivy.

Stace did not fail to notice the abusive aromas hanging in the air of the building as he entered. The rank smell of paints and oils and adhesives and photographic chemicals seemed to ease the tension caused by his scuff with Mrs. Colton. Here lay his passion. He grabbed a hold of the cold steel handrail to the stairs and yanked himself over the two flights of steps to the second floor. At the top he stopped for a drink at the water fountain hiding in the crème colored tile wall. Wiping a trickle of cold water off his goatee he stopped and listened. From the room down the hall came the indiscriminate noises of someone working in room twenty-four, like the shuffling noise of a stool on the tile floor, followed by the familiar sound of a spinning table used for rotating clay pottery. He waited longer, until the muffled sound of young woman's humming told him it was Maria.

He tiptoed down the hallway, stopped at the second door to the left, and peered around the doorframe. Maria sat at one of the large laminated tables working a mountain of clay. Born of Mexican ancestry, her hair was long, dark and flowing, her complexion luxurious. He watched her hands drop toward the table and turn a plywood platform to get a better view of her work from different angles. Stace noticed the piece resembled the face of a woman. Maria reached up with the backside of her hand to rub her nose, and as she did, her hair fell in the direction of her tilted head, leaving the unobstructed view of her face. Stace imagined himself reaching for her delicate chin and caressing her neck, which eventually disappeared into her lose fitting tee shirt.

Feeling more than a little self conscious, He stepped back behind the doorframe and quietly walked back to the water fountain to get another drink. Did she see me?" he wondered. "She must have heard me this time." After a cool drink, he took a deep breath and decided it was time to hit the photo lab. Making himself more obvious than the first time, he proceeded back down the hall hoping she wouldn't notice him.

"Hi Stace," she blurted out as he passed by the doorway. He stopped and looked at her. "How you doing?" he asked reaching up and scratching his nose.

"Fine. I'm just working on a piece for the exhibit."

He took a few steps into the room. "Looks like it's coming along." The bust of the unfamiliar head looked like a character out of horror flick.

"Slowly," she said, scratching the itch on her nose again and leaving a film of moist clay on the tip of her nose. "An abstraction," she continued, "I'm not exactly looking for perfection."

"'Course not, that would be too easy. Anyone I know?"

"Not unless you know my aunt Sylvia," she said smiling. Her smile was gloriously white and surrounded by full, pink lips. "She lived with my parents and I before I came to school."

"I guess I'll have to wait until you're finished. You can introduce me to her."

She responded to his attempt at wit with a slight smile. "Sure."

"Let me know when you're done." He backed out of the room and headed down the hall.

Stace turned the handle of the oak door of the photo lab and flicked up the switch on the wall. The florescent light on the ceiling flickered on and off for a few moments before flooding the room in white, sterile brightness. He walked to the far corner of the room and sat on the old couch Mr. Hollister had brought in to make the place feel more like home. Removing his backpack he dug deep into the bottom and pulled out a black film canister. Opening the top he slid out a roll of 24 exposures of colored print film. He looked at the roll and smiled, remembering the photo session with a young eager model named Rebecca that former weekend. The session had cost him a letter grade in Texas

Government and he hoped it had been worth it. Leaving his backpack on the couch, he walked into the developing room.

Rick didn't hear the approaching steps that stopped at his door. The knocking startled him. "What!" he yelled.

"Phone call!" the voice shouted back.

"Be right there." The phone was still swinging from its cord when he grabbed it.

"This is Rick."

"Hi Rick. Is something wrong?"

"Hi Julie. No, not really. How's your day going?"

"Fine. Pat and I have been reviewing for Hernandez's final."

"Exciting," he said sarcastically.

"I need the grade you know. We've covered so much material over the semester I've forgotten most of it."

"What does the test cover?" he asked, staring down the long hallway.

"Nineteenth century writers. Even though it's an elective I've got to take it seriously. I can't afford a lousy grade in it and jeopardize my chances for graduate school."

"I wouldn't worry about it. This time last Year we both thought you were going to bomb several classes and you aced them, remember?"

"I know, but now it's getting down to the wire."

Rick let it go. Julie was a perfectionist. She probably already knew the material, but frantic studying eased her anxiety.

"Tonight at the library?" She asked.

"Sure, but I'll be running late."

"What's up?"

"I've got to meet with Professor Alkins."

"From the ethics department?"

"Yeah. We have an upcoming vote for the art exhibit and I'm having a problem with Stace Manning."

"His photographs?"

"You've heard."

"Who hasn't?"

"Right. Well, anyway, we have to make a decision on the final entries. He insists on showing a couple of newer photos, which are bothering some of the faculty members."

"Students too," Julie added.

"Like who?"

"Just some of the girls in the dorm. I also overheard a couple of the theology students talking about them."

"Have they seen the pictures?"

"I don't think so, just rumors."

"Well, I shouldn't be long. I hope to catch him in a few minutes. I'll meet you around 6:30."

"All right," she said, dragging the words out and exaggerating her disappointment. "See you then."

Rick hung up the phone and reached for the school directory on the shelf. The cover had been ripped off and there were doodles on every page. He looked up the number to the humanities department and dialed the number. A woman answered the phone.

"Katherine, humanities."

"Hi, this is Rick Forstein. Is Professor Alkins available?"

"He's not here, but you can probably find him in the Slater building."

"Thanks. I'll try there." Rick said.

Professor Alkins had received his tenure with the University back in 1992. While most of the students knew him, few of the faculty members understood him. They found his logic rather intimidating at times. With the students, however, he was approachable and personable. He was the only ethics professor on campus, but since money is rarely earned in the real world through an over abundance of ethics, he earned his salary by teaching philosophy. When Rick finally found him the professor was wearing dark blue cotton slacks and a solid yellow dress shirt. He carried an old leather briefcase in his left hand. The kind you can't buy anymore, the kind that are passed along through generations from father to son until the handle breaks off. His hair had long since frosted gray and looked as though he'd missed a hair cut in the last few months.

"Professor Alkins?" Rick knew who he was, but asked just the same. The professor looked up, hesitated, and acknowledged Rick saying, "Yes, can I help you?"

"My name is Rick Forstein, I was wondering if you had a few minutes?"

"Have we met?" he asked.

"No sir," Rick said respectively, "but I have a problem and I'd appreciate your insight."

"Insight," the old professor thought to himself. "I certainly give out a lot of counsel, but rarely insight." He glanced at his watch. "All right, I have a few minutes. Let's borrow one of these tables and I'll see if I can help you."

They walked over to an open area near the doors where a few tables and chairs had been placed as a break area for students. Once the two were seated, Professor Alkins set down his briefcase, folded his hands in front of himself on the table, and proposed to give Rick his full attention. What he saw was an intent young man with busy brown eyes. The student's dirty colored blond hair was neatly cut and parted on the left side—a dead giveaway for a right handed person—which meant Rick might think in analytical terms, but that was never a guarantee. The golden wire frame glasses pinched high on the young man's nose lent him an aura of intelligence.

"I don't know if you were aware of it, but I'm the Social Secretary for the student body this Year," Rick opened.

"I was aware of the position, but I didn't know you held the position." The professor quickly judged him to be articulate and capable of the position.

Rick continued. "One of my responsibilities is to oversee the committee that pre-judges the work of the students for the art exhibit."

"Pre-judges?" the Professor inquired.

"Yes. We look over art submitted by the students to make sure certain standards are met."

"What kind of standards?"

Rick took a moment to answer. Only a few written standards were outlined, but for the most part they dealt with the physical requirements of the entries. There were for instance, certain size and weight restrictions, as well as a limit to the amount of entries each student could show. As to the kind of standards the professor was alluding to, those were yet unwritten. "I guess I'm talking about certain standards of decency and morality."

"I was unaware the university had set those kinds of standards for the exhibit," the professor responded.

"They haven't. Perhaps they didn't need to set any in the past."

"And they need to now?" the professor probed.

"Some members of the faculty and the student body seem to think so."

Professor Alkins sensed the underlining tone. "The members of the faculty, have they expressed their concern to you?"

"Yes. This afternoon I found a letter in my mailbox signed by three faculty members who expressed their concern. It wasn't a threat in any way, they were just voicing their opinion and wanted to make sure I considered the issue thoroughly."

The professor leaned forward and set his chin in his hand. His fingers swirled across his tightly cropped silvery beard. In all his years at the university, he could remember many instances when the students and the faculty had been at odds with one another. This kind of tension was expected, given the generational differences. Rarely, could he recall, however, when both students and faculty expressed concern for the same issue. For the most part, the traditions of the university had remained unchallenged. In fact, only one faculty member attended the student council meetings and acted as an advisor. The elected students of the council were encouraged to function entirely on their own. "If you don't mind me asking, who are the faculty members?"

Rick glanced towards the door and pinched his glasses. Professor Alkins sensed he was uncomfortable with the request. "I can respect you wanting to keep their identities silent. Can you tell me which departments they represent?"

"Well," Rick started, but stopped abruptly with obvious concern. He leaned back against his chair and folded his arms across his chest. The pen in his polo shirt nearly popped out. He unfolded his arms to secure it and straitened out his collar all in the same motion.

The professor locked the fingers of his wrinkled hands together and leaned forward in his chair. "Who the faculty members are is really not important to me Rick. It would be helpful, because I know most of the faculty and I have some understanding of their characters. If I knew which departments they belong to I might be able to better understand their cause for concern. I take it the letter didn't convince you of reaching a decision on your own. Am I right in assuming you came to me to help you in making a decision?"

Rick prided himself in being a decisive thinker, and the professor's question suggested Rick lacked the resolve to make his own decisions. He rebounded by saying, "as head of the committee it's my responsibility to evaluate all the concerns expressed by students and faculty alike. The letter I received made me realize there was enough objection to the work being presented to warrant additional guidelines." He took a deep breath then continued, "I was hoping you could give me a more balanced perspective."

"I see," the professor said. He leaned back in his chair. "What's the source of the objection?"

"A student wants to exhibit photographs that many consider to be pornographic. Some of the female students have raised objections, as well as the faculty members I've referred to."

"As I understand, there's really no written standards or guidelines that would have previously disqualified the entries?"

"That's correct," Rick said smartly.

"Just moral objections to the nature of the work in question?"

"Yes sir."

Throwing his shoulders back Professor Alkins took a deep breath. For a moment, he turned his head away from Rick, looking out of the glass doors admiring the pleasantries of the coming summer. The Ash trees just beyond the door had a new set of bright green adolescent leaves, which would darken in the coming weeks. The leaves of the Oaks beyond them had emerged as well. The light from the sun was still bright in the sky and fell through the trees leaving globs of shadowy patches on the grass. Having taken in the scenery, he returned to his conversation with Rick. "What's your opinion of the photos?" He asked.

"I haven't seen them yet."

"Then perhaps this conversation is premature."

"Perhaps, but my real concern at this point is knowing how I might be able to sort through the objections that are going to arise."

"Very well. My advice to you is this; since no written guidelines were presented to the artists, in terms of the nature of the work they could submit, you, as well as the committee, have no authoritative grounds to dismiss this particular artist's work."

"Even if some of the faculty members oppose the work?" Rick questioned.

Professor Alkins chuckled. His chest quivered and his fingers danced. "Rick, I'm a member of the faculty, let me assure you, we are no different than students in many ways. Sure, we are set in our ways and perhaps old fashioned in our values, but nevertheless, similar. How people have reacted or may react to this student's art is not the question. The fact remains; no restrictions have been placed on the artists beforehand. On that basis alone the committee can't discriminate against any one of the artists."

Professor Alkins sensed his advice had little impact. "Are you worried that if the committee allows the pictures to be exhibited it might reflect negatively on you?"

Rick thought of his relationship to Julie and the consensus of her friends towards the photos. He thought about the three faculty members, one of which taught his upper level accounting class. "I can't imagine any repercussions," he said, lying. There would undoubtedly be repercussions. Someone would have to save-face in the fallout.

"Then it comes down to doing what is ethically right. Think of it in those terms and you and the committee shouldn't have any trouble making the right decision."

"Perhaps," Rick said, feeling that Professor Alkins hadn't fully grasped his dilemma. The advice had been oversimplified. The professor was bouncing between ideals and principles somewhere in the cosmic properties of his mind, which was easy for him to do, but he didn't have the pressure of making the decision. Rick stood up. "I appreciate your help professor. Thanks for your time. I won't keep you any longer."

"It was my pleasure Rick. I hope you are able to resolve your conflict." Professor Alkins eased himself out of his chair and grabbed his briefcase. Rick opened the door for him as they left the building.

At her cluttered desk located in a dinky office at the Zebra Gallery of Modern Art, Chelsea Barter had just finished a telephone conversation with Paul Prine, the owner of the gallery. She reviewed the notes she'd scribbled during the conversation: "Cover the upcoming Marbel University Art Exhibit. Arrange to display the winning entries at the Zebra." This event would be a first. The Zebra Gallery was by far the most influential gallery in the city. Located amongst a string of galleries and shops along the River Walk in San Antonio, it had a reputation for housing the most unique works of art from both well-known and local artists. Each year, Chelsea spent the bulk of her time considering pieces from dozens of artists to display. By and large, only exceptional pieces from professionals were chosen and only a handful of less reputable artists were ever considered. To "hang in the Zebra," some had said, "is to hang with the best of them," The fact that the winning entries from the students of the university would be housed there for a short period, would prove to be a phenomenal boost on their reputations as artists.

In the red glow of the university photo lab the soft contours of Rebecca's body were revealing their exquisite architecture. As each eight by ten photo completed its bath in the chemical solution, Stace carefully hung them on the line to dry. He was methodical to the point of boredom, reviewing each photo mechanically, concerning himself with only the technical aspects of their development and composition. He would save the critical analysis for later, when all twenty-four photos were processed and lay before him in the proper light. Several hours later, as the lamp posts of the university began to brighten in the coming darkness along the sidewalks outside, he was still working eagerly within the photo lab. The report for Texas Government class could wait. Before him, on the giant workbench of the lab, Rebecca's nude body appeared in the photos like bits and pieces of a dismantled doll. Not one single picture captured her entire body, rather, each photo contained isolated aspects of her delicate structure. Stace was pleased— though not entirely aroused—for the photos awakened within him the sense that he'd passed into the world of the gods, by capturing the power of creation in some small, albeit satisfying way.

Yet, out of the entire stack of photos only one particular photo captured his attention. In it, Rebecca was reaching toward an object with her left hand, while her right hand rested on her right hip. Taken from behind, the photo extended from the tip of her fingers on her left hand to just below the darken valley indicating the separation of her buttocks. A faint reminder of one of her breasts was exposed. Her dark brown hair, black in the colorless photo, waved angrily towards the sky. What Stace liked most about the photo was the tension arising between her hands. The hand that was raised was tensely searching for an unknown object. The other hand, resting on her thigh, seemed completely satisfied and content. It reminded Stace of the confused state of mind that arises when people, who are usually content with their fate in life, reach for something more to life then what lies just beyond their reach. The snaking twist in Rebecca's spine also reminded him of another photo in his arsenal. He strutted over to the file cabinet, opened the second drawer and located a portfolio of tree photographs. He set the file next to Rebecca's photo and immediately immersed himself in dozens of photographs, which to a person with no artistic imagination might look more like a collection of wasted film. After minutes of looking through dozens of photographs, he stumbled on a particular photo that seemed to match the twist in Rebecca's back. He set it next to the photo of Rebecca to compare the possibilities. With only a minimal amount of lab work, the two photos could be easily superimposed upon one another. As only an artist can see, Stace saw the finished composition even before he set to work on it. Eventually, Rebecca's half nude form would be emerging out of the canyon walls where the photo of the tree had been taken. Her hair would be blowing about in the breeze. She would be reaching for the heavens, or towards some imaginary goal she'd set for herself, and the new photo would symbolize man's attempt to reach for the unattainable. Would it be Stace's best work? Probably not, but if it succeeded in involving the viewer it would at least be a partial success.

Julie found an isolated study desk in the back of the library and flipped through the pages of her thick biology book. She waved a bright pink highlighter pen above it, constantly snapping the cap on and off and looking for important sentences to underline. Rick eventually located her, but instead of going directly to her, he took a left into the forest of bookshelves and followed an isle all the way to the back so he could sneak up behind her. She'd come to anticipate and enjoy the tactic, but still jumped when he slipped behind her unnoticed and grabbed her neck.

As she turned towards him her blond hair slipped over her shoulders and across her book. "Hi Rick!" she whispered eagerly.

"What are you studying?" He took her hair in his fingers and swept it back over her shoulders.

"Biology, but don't ask, my brain's jelly."

"Then take a break," he said.

"What have you got on your mind? The closet in the Oakly building?" she asked with anticipation.

"Actually, I've got something I need to talk about."

"All right, let's take a walk."

Twenty minutes earlier the sun had set over west Texas. The sky was coated in a dusty, orange glow. The afternoon breeze had settled into a nearly imperceptible flow of air carrying the aroma of Purple Mountain Laurels that were planted in clusters on the university grounds. Rick and Julie joined hands and headed in no particular direction along one of the dozens of sidewalks crisscrossing the campus. "Did you meet with Professor Alkins?" she asked after a few minutes of silence.

"Yeah. That was a waste of time."

She waited for him to continue.

"You'd think as long as he's been around he'd be a little more—"

"Traditional," she said.

"I understand there are no written rules that would help exclude Stace's photographs from the exhibit, but there are other things to consider. I'm not talking about tradition here, because that changes in time. I'm talking about certain values that should be looked at. The question is, whether an artist can display any kind of material no matter how offensive people think it is."

"I don't think they should."

Rick continued, "I know that Stace has a right to do what he wants, but this exhibit is going to be seen by students and faculty, not to mention the community. It reflects the ideals of the students and the university. I've got nothing against Stace. I don't even know him."

"Do you suppose he's purposefully showing those photographs just to make a little noise? Maybe, he's trying to upset people and get a little attention for himself."

"That's what I'm trying to understand and that's what's so upsetting. He's got every right to be in the exhibit, but why not show something people want to see?

"So what can you do about it?" Julie asked.

"Nothing, according to Professor Alkins."

"Nothing?"

"He said, since there are no written rules to disqualify the artists, then it wouldn't be right create guidelines at the last minute."

"That's oversimplified."

"I thought so. It means any artist's could submit anything they wanted to."

"So what are you going to do?" she asked.

"I'm not sure there's much I can do. I'll have to put it on the agenda for the meeting and call it to a vote. I might not have to do anything if the committee supports Stace, but if they don't."

"You should worry about it so much," Julie said. "Let's talk about something else."

Rick didn't respond.

"Did you bring anything to study?" she asked.

"Not in the mood to study."

"Let's head back inside anyway, I'm chilly."

The drop off point for entries in the exhibit was on the third floor of the Oakly building. Normally a rehearsal room for the university band, by evening the room was littered with works of art represented by various artistic mediums. When dropping off their entries, the artists had staked out their territory and the result was a dizzying array of twisted metal sculptures, pieces created of mixed media like wood, glass, and plastic, and along the walls were ink sketches, pastels, watercolors, oils and photographs. At precisely 7:00 p.m., in a room down the hall, the student council meeting was set to begin. Usually, one or two of the members were absent, but this evening all six members of the council were present including Rick, chairman of the group, which brought the number to seven. The group sat around four conference tables that had been placed together in a square, so they could all face each other.

Rick had decided earlier, that despite the rumors and the letter he'd received from the faculty members concerning Stace Manning's entries, he would not focus on the pieces in question. The meeting agenda he now passed around the room consisted of only two items. The first was in reference to making the exhibit a competition. This had never been done in the previous years. The second item was to review the participating artists entries to make sure they conformed to the size restrictions. Attempting to avert the controversy, Rick had decided to take Professor Alkins' advice after all. Since the council really had no authority to exclude any artist's entries based on the current guidelines, he reasoned the subject would be better left unmentioned. If he was lucky, he might be able to entirely sidestep the issue. But as he directed the committee's attention to the agenda, he was interrupted by four raps on the door. He could only guess who that might be. In walked Hugh Capshaw and Kate Donaldson, two of the faculty members who had sent him the letter.

"I hope you don't mind if we meet with you tonight?" Mr. Capshaw framed the question as statement.

Rick looked around at the other members, who seemed a little perturbed by the intrusion.

"We're sorry to interrupt, please continue," Mr. Capshaw said. He escorted Kate across the room and they took a seat in the row of chairs lining the wall.

Rick acted as if they were non-existent. "We have a lot to do this evening. First of all, let me begin by saying that I spoke with Chelsea Barter yesterday who represents the Zebra Gallery on the River Walk."

"The Zebra gallery is one of the best galleries in San Antonio," Jose interrupted.

Rick continued. "As you know the administration frowns on any type of competition, but in light of the interest of the Zebra Gallery we may need to consider a selection process for the artists. The Zebra Gallery doesn't have the space to display everyone's work, so I'd like to hear discussion on the matter."

Jose jumped right in. "I think it's a good idea. It will give the university and the artists good exposure. I'm sure that most of the artists in our exhibit would kill for a chance to display their work in the Gallery."

Andrea spoke next. "But how do we get around the event not turning into a competitive fiasco? Personally, I don't have a problem with competition in sports, but art is subjective. Who's to say what's good and what's bad? If you've seen any of Van Goths' paintings you know what I mean. He'd cut off his ear to get someone to notice his work. If we can get around the exhibit being a competition I'd be willing to support the idea."

"I think we can," Rick said after a pause. "I told Miss. Barter there would be objections to a competition. It just won't happen. No ribbons, no trophies, no prize money, nothing of that sort would be tolerated. But she came up with a good idea we should consider. She suggested that she attend the exhibit discretely and view the artwork herself. She would be the judge and decide which pieces to display in the gallery. After she made her selections she would simply contact the artists and arrange to have their work moved to the gallery."

"I don't see a problem with that," Jose added.

"Should we tell the artists?" Andrea asked.

"At this point who can it hurt? The entries have already been submitted. We'll just let the students know the gallery is interested in attending the exhibit and it's possible they might select a few pieces to display. Rick waited until he was sure there were no further comments regarding the discussion. He called it to a vote and the decision passed.

"The next item on the list is pretty straightforward. I have a list of the twenty-three students who have submitted work for our consideration. They have submitted three entries each and I suspect they met the size requirements, but we will need to go and look just to make sure. If you look at your list you'll see the name of the artist followed by a number. Each one of you has a number and each piece is marked. Take a look at each piece and see if they meet the size restrictions. If they do, put a check by the name of the artist and make note of the piece. Any questions?"

There were none and the members of the committee walked down the hall to view the entries. Rick remained in his seat for a few moments waiting to see what Mr. Capshaw and Kate Donaldson would do. He looked down over his list of names, one of which included Stace Manning, number 22.

"Do you mind if we take a look Rick?" Asked Mrs. Donaldson.

"By all means." He stood up and they preceded him down the hall.

The other counsel members were already busy looking over the entries. Some paired up like Susan and Carrie. The two of them were chuckling and exchanging comments over one particular sculpture of welded trash can lids that stretched from the floor to ceiling in a spiral. At the top of the sculpture the artist had tied long pieces of red ribbon that swirled down towards the floor. "No measuring to be done here. It'll take up the whole hallway in the Tindale building and probably flop over and kill someone," Susan said giggling.

Most of the work on display was really quite exceptional. It was obvious the artists had taken a great deal of time in preparation and in selecting their best work. "I wouldn't mind taking some of this stuff home with me," Jose said to Thomas, who'd been standing near by. It's as good as any work I've seen."

To Rick, however, the ominous task of reviewing Stace's three entries fell upon him. He'd hoped to review the other entries on his life first, but Mr. Capshaw, Kate Donaldson, Marsha, and several of the others were already huddling around Stace's photographs. Rick came up behind them and peered over their shoulders. The old floor creaked beneath them as they jockeyed for the best view.

The largest photograph, about the size of a poster and neatly framed, was the piece Stace had completed over the weekend. In it, he'd successfully transposed Rebecca's twisted torso on the trunk and limbs of the old Oak tree. The two seemed fused together into one fluid motion; each characteristic of the tree was captured in the expressions of the model. Rebecca's' buttocks were only partly exposed. The deep brown, crust of the trunk had been perfectly grafted and superimposed into an area just below her hips. From that point upwards, the rest of Rebecca's photograph had not been altered. The faint reminder of her left breast was still visible and erect against a violet colored sky. The other two photographs were similar in theme and composition. In one of them, Stace had superimposed the frontal portion of a giraffe with the frontal faced shoulders of a woman. The result was a fully nude woman with the neck and legs of a giraffe. Somehow Stace was able to retain the spotted fur of the giraffe, which helped to conceal the outline of the woman's breasts and vaginal area. The other photo was of a lion and an African American man. It consisted of the proud face of a male lion with a majestic mane, but the rest of its body, from the neck down, was that of the African American, standing on his hands and knees and poised on the top of a smooth, round bolder.

Mr. Capshaw had seen enough. "Surely you don't intend on allowing these photographs to be in the exhibit?" he asked Rick.

"Fantastic!" Jose exclaimed. "Look at the way the parts of the tree flow into the body. It's almost as if the two are one creature."

"You're kidding", Susan anxiously replied. "It's offensive, especially the giraffe photo."

Feeling a sense of responsibility and obligation, Thomas, the student chaplain had something to say. "I don't think it's appropriate to associate animals with the human form. There's something disturbing about it. It's as if the artist wants to bring man down to the level of the animals. Personally, I have a problem with all three of them."

"What do you think about the photos Rick?" Mrs. Donaldson asked.

Rick glanced at the others, who waited to hear his response. "I think we should discuss it in the conference room. Has everyone completed their list?" There were a few "yeses" and a few affirmative nods. "Good, then let's head back."

Once seated, the council members sat quietly in their chairs. Thomas fiddled with his pen on the table and Susan looked frustrated and gazed out the picture windows into the night sky.

Rick began by gurgling his words nervously. "I realize Stace's photos offend some of you. You may not even like his photographs altogether" He paused and took a deep breath. "Our responsibility is not to decide what we like or dislike. Our job is to verify that each artist has submitted three pieces for the exhibit and that the entries meet the size restrictions."

Susan spoke up. "Don't we have any guidelines for the artists to follow? Or, can they present anything they want to no matter how offensive it is?"

Rick had been debating the question for a week. "According to the bylaws, there are no other guidelines except those pertaining to size restrictions."

"Then we need to come up with other guidelines quickly," Thomas added.

"It's too late to create any guidelines for the exhibit," Carrie said looking at the others.

Jose agreed. "Carrie's right. The artists have submitted their work based on the requirements that were given and we can't come along after the fact and single out any particular artist based on our objections."

"But I think the circumstances dictate we do something about Stace's photographs before they cause serious problems," Thomas said, raising his soft voice a notch or two just to be heard.

"The fact is—"

"I wonder if I might be allowed to speak?" Mr. Capshaw interrupted.

Rick feared this moment would come. As the department head for the theology department, Hugh Capshaw had a great deal of persuasion. He personified the conservative religious tone of the university. Few would dare to question his counsel or challenge his influence. Out of respect, Rick granted him the floor.

"I know it seems a little unorthodox for myself and Kate Donaldson to be here this evening and I appreciate the opportunity to address you."

It seemed as if he was settling into one of his long sermons and the committee members eased back in their chairs.

"Mrs. Donaldson and I are here because we have been concerned for several years about the quality of the work being presented at the exhibit. We've always supported the exhibits, but lately the entries appear—well to put it bluntly—immoral. Quite frankly, they do not speak of the Christian nature that we all strive for and which characterizes this institution. Now, I had heard through the grapevine of these photographs and had to see for myself whether the rumors were true. Now I have nothing against Mr. Manning, but I do object to his methods of expression. Furthermore, I'm under the impression that most of the students would be offended by his work as well. I'm pleased that the Zebra Gallery is going to consider showing the work of some of our artists at their gallery. This will be good for the university and for those who will be selected. I would be greatly disturbed, however, if Mr. Manning's photographs happen to be those that are selected to be shown. Again, we represent at this university a certain level of morality and decency. Mr. Manning's work is not the best representation of the reputation we seek to uphold. I think we must consider the damage we'd cause to ourselves and to the university if we were to continue to support this kind of art."

There was a long period of silence following his oration. Even if one of the committee members chose to speak in rebuttal, their comments would be trivial. Rick recognized that any attempt to vindicate Stace would be useless. "Very well, does anyone have any suggestions?" he reluctantly asked.

"We can't change the current guidelines. Any attempt to do so would be censorship. If you do, then Stace will know he's been singled out," Jose said.

"The only way to get around that is to amend the bylaws to include all the artists," Susan said.

Jose countered. "It's still censorship. Sure we can extend the new guidelines to all the artists, but we'd still be creating them to exclude Stace's work.

"What about the rest of you?" Rick asked.

"Rick, I make a motion that we amend the current guidelines for the exhibit. The motion will be to add a third guideline stipulating that nudity of either the male or female body is prohibited in the works presented for the exhibit." Thomas said.

"And just who's going to monitor that?" Jose asked indignantly. "Art is completely subjective. Some of it's what you might call, modern art. Who's to say that a certain curve or a certain painted form does or doesn't represent nudity?"

Steven Daley, the senior class president, had been silent throughout the course of the discussion, but now felt obligated to say something. He raised his hand in keeping with the rules of parliamentary procedure and waited for the chair to acknowledge him.

"Steven has the floor," Rick said, grateful that at least someone recognized the diplomacy that the procedures offered.

"This is my last year here and I agree with Mr. Capshaw. Each year the entries seem to get worse. Call them immoral; call them un-Christian, I'd call them downright embarrassing. And I would think the university would be embarrassed at having them hanging in the Zebra Gallery as a representation of the university."

"We don't know if they'd be chosen for the gallery though." Jose blurted.

"But they could be," Steven said.

"That's not our concern. It's not a question of whether we like the photographs or how they make us feel. It's a question of whether we have the right to modify the guidelines after the fact and single out the work of any particular artist." Rick admonished.

"But we do have a moral obligation and a Christian responsibility to restrict what appears to be contradictory to what we believe as individuals and as a student body," Thomas said.

"You mean what you believe to be decent," Jose said, challenging him.

Thomas gave no reply.

"Mr. Chairman, there's a motion on the floor that requires a vote," Steven said, to end the discussion.

At this point there was really nothing more Rick could do except call the motion to a vote. Deep down, he agreed with Thomas and Steven and even with Mr. Capshaw. If they did not make an attempt to curb what seemed to be a growing trend towards immorality and decency, where would it end? What kind of photographs and sculptures would be presented next year? Jose was right as well. It would be unfair to single out Stace's work. What would be right would be to allow all the artists to show their work, then make the amendment to the guidelines for next year's exhibit. That's what Professor Alkins would if he was here. "But he's not here," Rick thought to himself, "and I must call the motion to a vote."

"Carrie will you get us some paper so we can have a concealed vote?" Rick asked.

She reached into her notebook and took out a sheet of notebook paper, ripped it into six pieces and passed them around the room.

"Alright, if you are in favor of the new guideline, that will disqualify Stace Manning's photographs from the exhibit, then write 'yes'. If you are opposed to the guideline, write 'no'. When you're done, fold them over and pass them up to me," Rick said.

The council took only seconds to decide. Rick stared at the two stacks of votes in front of him in disbelief. There were three for the amendment and three against. As chairman of the committee he was not required to vote, unless a vote ended in a tie. It was not over yet. Not one of the committee members asked what the outcome had been. They had watched Rick open each vote and divide the votes between the two stacks. They squirmed in their seats for a revote. Carrie was already ripping up seven sheets of paper and sending them around the room. Mr. Capshaw and Kate Donaldson were poised in their seats. Rick called for the second vote, and the count was tallied....

CHAPTER I

▼

Several years later...

Reverend Jeremiah Eisner walked across the plush magenta carpet of his office in Munich, Germany towards the mirror hanging over a cherry wood dresser as he'd done six days a week for the past thirteen years. He worked his fingers up the last two buttons of his creased dress shirt that was in all practicality, white. After adjusting his collar, he pulled the knot to his red silk tie with its splash of gold flakes up to his neck and with effort managed to secure the points of his collar with the two pea-sized buttons. More than once he'd thought about taking the scissors to the buttons, for his arthritic fingers had long since lost their dexterity. Running his thumbs along his waistline, he tugged at his suit pants and pulled them up over his bellybutton. Extending each arm in turn, he plugged the holes of his sleeves with modestly sized, fourteen-karat gold cuff links. Nearby, resting over the back of the burnt amber leather chair lay the vest to his three-piece suit. He slid it on and picked up a lint brush, stroking it down the length of his slacks as far as he could bend over.

On his way into his private bath, he paused as always at the painting of the man that endowed him with his daily dose of legitimacy. The reverend, a descendant of the late Kurt Eisner who was a socialist and assassinated through civil unrest over seventy years ago, gloried in the illusion of his heritage and his potential for greatness. He liked to think that his own ambitions were free of political idealism and he was chosen to preach his version of eschatology for the salvation of the masses. He was a man on a mission.

He walked into his private bath and stood before the frameless mirror instinctively feeling for his bath comb. Reaching up towards the ceiling like an off-balance ballerina, he suddenly stopped, for upon further examination he found that his receding lump of titanium-white hair looked quite satisfactory. He stretched for the hair spray and swirled the can over his head, then backed out of the perfumed fog. When the air cleared, he checked his teeth, nose and ears for unwanted distractions, then peered into the deep canyons extending from the corner of his lashes down through his cheekbones, all the way down into the edge of his frosty beard. He wasn't overly distracted by his signs of age, but the routine had become habit, giving him something to do while he waited for show time. Content with his appearance, he walked out of the bathroom and took a seat at his desk.

His library, gathered in enormous shelves built into two walls of his office, consisted of no less than one thousand, three-hundred and sixteen books, as well as hundreds of documentary films and subscriptions to over twenty-three magazines and newspapers. He'd devoured nearly all of the contents of the library. He was well versed in history, theology, social and economic theories, political movements and philosophy. Coupled with this knowledge, he had the ability to analyze these various avenues of thought into a cohesive whole, so that each aspect of their individual components could be seen as a steady stream of eschatology. This gift gave him the uncanny ability to predict the outcome of almost any situation with prophetic intuition.

As if these abilities were not enough, he was a supreme orator in both physical and mental presence. Tall and imposing, handsome—though not to the point of distraction—and sincere in his beliefs, the reverend's messages seemed to carry with them the will of God. Yet despite his vocabulary and intellect, he wasn't one to flaunt his abilities on his congregation, but formulated his speeches into simple phraseology, so that his theological discussions could be understood by the common man. As such, his influence could be felt throughout the Anglo-Saxon world. Indeed, his audio and video productions of his daily two-hour show were broadcast in nearly every modern country of the globe. His book, *Our Global Community*, had been published in thirty-seven languages and dialects. Assisting him with the disbursement of his vision was a staff of over one hundred individuals, most of them working directly out of the International Christian Coalition's Munich offices. In addition, he had an army of representatives working in many countries negotiating the furtherance of his work.

But the reverend had his enemies and his share of vices. Some even went so far as to say he was Hitler reincarnated as a bishop. Even so, leaders within many political arenas sought him for enlightenment. Such meetings were often secretive, for while these leaders valued his input, they weren't prepared to stake their reputations by association with him. Nor were these leaders isolated to the geography of Germany alone, but influential people throughout Europe and other countries around the world, valued his insight to such a degree that in some causes he influenced religious and political policy. In his younger years, the reverend was oblivious to the obsequious manner in which others sought his wisdom, but now coveted their glorification of him like a good pat on the back.

What had occurred recently within his mind was nothing short of a paradigm shift, a complete realignment of his understanding of the Christian faith. Central to this shift was the realization that the Christian faith was not to be the passive display of ethical and moral virtues, which draw men and women into its fold by those who lead by example. Rather, Christianity should be the vehicle that dictates political and sociological change. He was overwhelmed with the notion he'd reached a new plateau in his faith and that God was calling him on to bigger and better things. In fact, just hours ago, he'd learned of another reason to substantiate his self-glorification.

The letter was full of possibilities. Under normal circumstances he wouldn't have even seen the letter, but Mildred, his cheerful secretary in her late fifties, handed it to him just that morning, because she'd recognized its importance. Neatly presented, typed and signed by Frederick C. Watson, the CEO of Trojan Security, Inc., it now lay flat on his polished mahogany desk and read:

To Reverend Jeremiah Eisner:

Several years ago, I was approached by a colleague of mine with your book, and several video sermons you had preached. I was for the most part skeptical, but out of respect for my colleague I agreed to look over your material. The result of that fateful event has been nothing short of a complete transformation of my faith.

I'm particularly interested in your concept of the role Christians have in these final days of earth's history. You're justified in confronting the evils of our time and in insisting that the political and social leaders of our governments must adhere to the basic tenants of the Christian faith. I support you in the judgment that leaders who are not able to verify their faith should be relieved of their responsibilities and be replaced by individuals who are morally grounded. I believe, like you, that God can't bless a nation, whether it is Germany or America, when its leadership continues to support the humanistic agenda.

I'm the CEO of Trojan Security, the world's largest computer security corporation. We're located in Austin, Texas, but have corporate distributing offices in fifteen other cities around the globe including one in Heidelberg. Our main emphasis is in designing and implementing computer security systems for major corporations and organizations. My purpose for writing to you is not grounded towards financial gain. Our corporation has considerable resources and as for myself, God has provided me with more than an adequate standard of living.

Trojan Security has from time to time supported both churches and charities, but I would like to take our support to a new level. I think my ideas and suggestions would be worth your time. I will be in Heidelberg between July 5th and the 12th. If it is at all possible, I would like to set up a time that we may visit. I will have my secretary call your organization next week to arrange a convenient time.

Sincerely,

Fred Watson
CEO, Trojan Security, Inc.

The reverend stepped out from behind his desk and rocked to a stop in the middle of the floor. There was a short knock on his door and in walked Joseph Stautzen, the reverend's right hand man. With a discerning eye, Stautzen quickly ascertained the color of the reverend's suit and walked into the wardrobe closet, where he pulled the matching jacket to the reverend's suit off the hanger. This task wasn't too difficult, for the reverend wore only two colors of silk suits, sapphire-blue and sable-black. Stautzen spread the jacket open and slipped it through the reverend's outstretched arms.

"Any problems I need to know about?" the reverend asked.

"No sir. Everything's ready as usual."

Stautzen escorted him to the elevator and down to the bottom floor. When the elevator opened, Neli, the production director, met them and briefed them on the final details of the show. The three of them then proceeded across the grounds of the ICC's complex and into the production studio. The reverend positioned his body behind the crystal podium and placed his bible next to his typed sermon. In the few minutes remaining before airtime, he briefed himself on the notes regarding the weekly guest to the show. The guest, a councilman for the city of Augsburg, fidgeted in the adjacent lounge as though he was awaiting a summons by the high court. From somewhere behind the TV cameras Neli called out the last ten seconds before airtime. The reverend collected his thoughts, adjusted his notes, took a deep breath and began.

In a manner that maintained his support of Germany's political leadership, the reverend began by comparing the current political and religious setting of the European continent with that of the United States. It was his opinion that beginning in the late 1980's and continuing into the next two decades, the United States underwent dynamic policy changes that occurred by the influence of evangelical Christians. These evangelicals, otherwise known as the Christian Right Movement, had been able to successfully influence many politicians to support their ideologies and most notably, they had obtained enough influence to vote their own candidates into office.

After the turn of the millennium, the extent of the Christian Right Movement became more pervasive and the reverend cited examples: Producers and leaders of the media and television industries were forced to generate wholesome, family orientated material free of sex and violence, and objectionable cable programming was sliced in half. Laws against pornography become more severe, and coupled with successful boycotting campaigns, had put most of the companies in the sex industry out of business. Schools, colleges and universities, under fear of loosing federal financial aid, were obliged to promote creationism and downplay evolutionist ideologies. Archeological research projects, which did not seek to verify biblical interpretations of creation, lost their funding. A crackdown on the illegal use of drugs and criminal activity became paramount. Harsh penalties were imposed and prison inmates were required to attend religious services on condition of parole. Even the artistic world fell under their scrutiny. Libraries were cleansed of objectionable books; musical bands rated by content; even art galleries and museums were presented with strict guidelines dictating the type of material they could present, or their business permits and grants were yanked. "All of these changes and many more," the reverend assured his audience, "were a result of the collective repentance of the masses. God had given America success and prosperity as a nation because they had in the face of a humanistic agenda, chosen to unite under the Christian flag."

Bubbles of perspiration had collected on the reverend's forehead and were trickling down his cheek. He took out a white handkerchief from his back pocket, but before he could wipe himself dry, a makeup artist came running up to the podium to assist him. "That was outstanding," she said, with a serious expression, "now lift your chin." She patted his face with a dry towel then powdered his forehead to eliminate the shine.

"Twenty seconds!" Neli yelled from the shadows. The reverend walked over to one of the two chairs to the right of the podium and shook hands with the councilman, Hans Friedhof. The original intent of the councilman was to answer the recent allegations of impropriety within the Augsburg City Hall by two of his staff members, but the reverend's sermon had impressed him. He was also aware that the eyes of millions were upon him. The interview concluded with the councilman promising that the allegations would be seriously looked into and if proven to be true, the "responsible party—or parties—would be appropriately dealt with."

At the completion of the two-hour program the reverend returned to his office to consider the ramifications of the letter still lying on his desk.

CHAPTER 2

▼

Meanwhile, in Frankfurt...

Stace caught his sweating bottle of *Dopplebock* beer just as it tipped towards the frayed blanket he'd brought from his apartment to lay across the shag of grass spreading around the *Freibad* public swimming pool. Kissing the hot coppery glass, he sucked the last dregs of the yeast-infected brew over his tongue then spit it out. Disgust rattled his face as he swiped the dribble from his whiskers. It had been over an hour since his last swig. The balmy sun of September had cooked its contents into a revolting concoction.

His arms bowed as he leaned back and tipped his face towards the sky, enjoying the sensation of white-noon heat burning through his eyelids. Across his chest, beads of salt-ripened perspiration beaded into drops and ran through the dark curls of chest hair like infantrymen descending a hill through overhead brush. He rolled his head back and forth, massaging his shoulders with the brushing tips of his long black hair, listening to the orchestration of noises reaching his ears. He heard the tinkle of a breeze passing through the leaves above, the rumble of a car passing by the outside fence, and a father calling to his toddler, who was chasing a ball. Down by the pool, children were jostling for position behind the diving boards, and the metal springs of the boards croaked like frogs as children bounced on them. Nearby, people were laughing around the concession stand eating *pomfrits* and drinking beer. Closer to him, two young women were gossiping. Was it about the night before or the coming evening? Stace couldn't tell. He had learned little German in the past year he'd spent in Frankfurt.

What was her name? He held his breath and listened for her movements. He'd not heard her leave since he'd finished his confession and had closed his eyes. Never in his life had he dared to reveal so much to anyone, especially a woman. He felt stupid and awkward, as if he'd taken a knife and sliced open his mind, exposing his most ghastly secrets. Was she still seated on the corner of his blanket facing him, her feet folded to the side, sandy hair falling across the left side of her face? "She's probably bored stiff! I've been the pitiful American and played upon her sympathies," or so he thought.

"*Hallo*," she said, in a way that was characteristic of Germans calling people out of a daydream.

He dropped his head and opened his eyes slowly. "*Es tut mir leid.*" I hope I haven't bored you."

She looked at him amusingly with a slight smile twitching underneath her erect nose, her expression begging for more. It wasn't her habit to walk up to complete strangers, especially the men whom she knew were just scrutinizing her. Those men who looked over their books and newspapers, or lay with their heads propped over their folded arms stealing glances at the sunbathing women. She'd rather they just look once and got their fill, instead of concealing their lust under the pretext of nonchalance. Stace had looked as well. But she noticed in his glances a look of unspoiled curiosity. As if he was looking not only at her, but into her, with an unquenchable thirst to know. She sensed him to be foreign. His long curly hair clean and combed, a well-trimmed beard, and the unmistakable lack of custom that set him apart as a foreigner. At twenty-seven, she'd seen her stein full of the predictability of German men and the thick presence they wore about them like cologne. Almost unknowingly, she had found herself walking towards this stranger as though wrapped in the expectation of an unfolding romance.

"No," she said, "you don't bore me. I'm sorry to hear about your art exhibit."

Well, it really wasn't *my* exhibit," he said, hoping she wouldn't see through to his disappointment. But it was to be *his* exhibit. It would have given him the edge he needed to jump-start his dreams. He'd spent the last four years living through the reality of being rejected from the exhibit and he was surprised the pain of its memory played out today, just as much as it did when it happened.

A moment passed between them; one in which time anticipates and regrets then anticipates again.

"Would you like to go for a swim?" he asked.

"*Ja.*"

As they walked towards the pool she reached behind her and unfastened the bow around her back. He caught her movements out of the corner of his eye, turning his head just as the long strings from the bow fell to her side. She reached up to loosen the tie behind her neck, and her breast leaped from the cup and settled into a noble curve upwards. Timidly, he looked the other way. She tossed the top near her bag as they walked by her spot and continued towards the pool.

Stace, perplexed by her interest in him, walked ahead of her onto the first step leading into the center of the pool. Icy water, cold as the mountain streams of New Mexico, lapped across his ankles. Skin turned to goose flesh as he froze. Eva quickly caught up and stepped in, impervious to the chill. She descended the steps and dove in, moments later reappearing. He stood there admiring her tenacity, her head bobbing along the water as her body contorted below the surface, pushed and pulled by the hallucinogenic effect of the waving water.

"Come in!" she yelled at him.

"*Alles kalt!*" he protested.

"It's nice once you get used to it."

"I bet." Not wanting to appear like a total coward he dove in.

His body went numb with shock, but he resisted the urge to surface and swam past her into the deep end. Upon opening his eyes, he found himself as it seemed in another world. The depths awaited his exploration. He surfaced, took in a giant breath and dove for the bottom. Down and down he plunged as the pressure cramped his ears until he touched the crusty bottom. Then pressing his feet firmly on the bottom, he shot back up through the icy liquid until his head broke the surface. After spinning the water out of his hair he searched for her. There she was! gliding along the surface, head rhythmically swaying to the music of the water. He waited, arms swaying in suspense, until she moved in closer, then he disappeared again.

The underwater world exhilarated his spirit. Somewhere the pains of the world lay...somewhere above the surface the memories stung, but here was a world without walls and without the need to conform. Instinctively, he turned towards Eva and found her swimming along the surface directly above him. Her eyes were wide open and her hair was glowing in backlit sunshine, extending like an aura around her head. Diamond shaped ripples of light danced across her skin and her breasts greeted him with hazel-colored nipples. He joined her at the surface and she followed him back down into the depths. They swam side by side at times, or encircling each other like otter's out to play. Time seemed non-existent; words useless, but an occasional touch between them revealed their wanting to discover each other.

After their swim, they strolled up to where Eva had spread her blanket. She grabbed a towel and began to dry off and he just stood, searching for words.

"That was fun," she said, turning her head and squeezing the water out of her hair. "Are you doing anything tonight?" she asked without looking at him.

"No. I'm not. Would you like to get together?" he asked quickly.

She smiled.

Was it an affirmation? He wondered.

She finished drying her hair and left it wild. From a plastic bag she brought out a pair of denim shorts and pulled them up her unshaven legs. After snapping the button, she looked over to him as if expecting something.

The idea was not his. He was still searching for words. She pulled out a pink tank top from the bag and as she reached towards the sky it fell over her breasts. Having dressed, she put her hands playfully on her hips as if to say, "well?" then asked what she'd intended to ask all along. "Would you like to come over for dinner tonight?"

"Yes I would."

She fumbled for her wallet and took out a business card. "Here's my number. I live nearby. Call me around 6:00 and I'll give you directions."

He was ecstatic, but managed to conceal it. His response was formal, as if he was used to this sort of thing. "I look forward to it." He glanced at the card. "Eva Burtman, Investigative Reporter," it said.

She finished packing her things and walked towards the main gate.

CHAPTER 3

▼

Thousands of miles away in Austin, Texas, Julie peers into the bedroom as twilight slips of blue filter through the Venetian blinds and lap across Rick Forstein's sleeping body like plowed rows in a field. She lays the breakfast tray on the dresser and sits at the edge of the bed. Reaching over, she turns on the table light, and ushers in the reality of a new day. Rebecca their daughter, who'd followed her upstairs, pushes open the door and runs towards her father like a prancing fawn.

"*Shhhhh!*" Julie whispered, zipping her lips.

Rebecca hopped up on the bed and sat on her mother's pillow near her father's warm face and giggled.

"Daddy, daddy, time to wake up," she squealed, tugging at the blanket covering his shoulders. "Daddy, time to eat!"

Rick stirred and growled at her like a monster. She leaped from the pillow and landed on his chest. "Ugh!" he grunted, wrapping his arms around her tiny form like a grizzly and going "*aarrrrr!*" she screamed with delight and leaned towards him chomping on her bottom lip. He buried the back of his head in the pillow and tried to focus on her plump round face. "What do you want munchkin?"

"Me and mommy made breakfast," she beamed. "I made the toast. You gonna love it!"

"Is that right?" He shook her wildly and she giggled more. "Then I better get up."

"No! You eat in bed," she demanded.

"I can't eat in bed, the ants will come and get me."

She looked under the covers searching for the little critters.

"Just kidding," he said, hugging her again.

Little Rebecca was twenty-one months old. She was conceived in love and fell into the future plans of the Forstein's expectation of marital bliss at just the appropriate time. She was in all respects flawless; a creation formed in the bosom of angels. She first walked at eleven months, knew her primary colors by thirteen months and had developed a blossoming vocabulary. Her skin was silky white and vibrant, as plump as a porcelain doll, yet still concealed the mysteries of just what features she'd inherited from her parents. Happy, innocent and curious, she'd enjoyed a life up to this point void of trauma or neglect, having been the object of Julie's undivided admiration by day and the prize that awaited Rick at the end of his busy day.

"Today it's breakfast in bed," Julie interrupted. She reached over and picked up the neatly dressed tray of morning delights, along with Rebecca's offering of burnt toast saturated in butter, and slipped it over Rick's legs as he sat up.

"Ah yes. Thanks a bunch," he said, offering her a kiss. "Looks great."

"I made the toast all by myself," Rebecca insisted.

"I can see that, and you did a fabulous job," he said, reaching for his glasses and curled the wires behind his ears to secure them in place.

"By the way Rick, Kelly called yesterday. The church nominating committee met last week and they'd like you to serve as elder again this year. I told her I'd better check with you first."

"I don't think that'll be a problem. Call her back and tell her I accept."

"Sure," she said as she stood.

Rick watched her cotton robe slip off her shoulders and down to the floor. His eyes followed her as she walked towards the bathroom.

"What have you got planned today?" he asked, suspiciously eyeing the piece of burnt toast moving towards his lips.

She turned on the light and stood before the mirror. Grabbing a plastic shower cap hanging on one of the towel racks, she flipped it over her head and stuffed her hair into it.

"Susan's coming over at about 11:00 and the three of us are going shopping at the mall." "Ready to spend my hard earned money?"

"I've earned it too don't you think?"

He glanced at Rebecca, who was trying to put on her mother's robe. She'd finally found the sleeve holes and rammed her hands inside, but the sleeves were far too long and they flopped on the floor. She raised her hands into the air to keep them up and ran around the side of the bed. The hem of the robe dragged across the carpet behind her.

"Look daddy!"

"Yeah, you've earned it," he said to Julie, but she'd already started the shower and didn't hear him.

"You look very pretty munchkin."

"Like mama?" she asked, wiggling her fingers.

"Just like mama," he said. "Are you going shopping today?"

"Yes!" she yelled, the final "s" long and slurred.

"Mommy says she's gonna buy me new dress."

"Isn't that great!"

Rick thoroughly enjoyed the husbandry of his family life. He was particularly proud that his wife didn't need to work and his daughter didn't have to spend all day at the daycare. As far as he was concerned everything was as it should be. Within an hour he'd eaten, showered, and was headed off to work, fully intoxicated by the simple pleasures of his life.

At 10:30, Julie's older sister Susan arrived a half hour earlier than expected. Her marriage to her husband Greg ended abruptly when she turned forty. They had two children together when they were young and after they'd separated she'd raised the children on her own. When her youngest daughter left for college last year she was left alone, suffocating in the confinement of a spacious home in the West Lake Hills subdivision she'd earned in the trial of her divorce. Consequently, she spent as much time with Julie as she could.

As Julie finished putting the morning dishes into the dishwasher, Susan dressed Rebecca for the mall. After sliding yellow panties over Rebecca's rump, she propped her up on the edge of the couch. "You're so precious," she said, holding her chubby little hands. "Now lift your arms up high and touch the moon." Susan took her dress, gathered it around the collar, and slid it over Rebecca's head. "Now stick out your feet." Rebecca locked her knees and Susan capped her toes in ruffled socks and baby Nikes. "There. Now you're all ready to go." She leapt off the couch and Susan patted her on the butt as she ran towards the kitchen.

"She's absolutely beautiful Julie. I'm so proud of you and the life you've made for yourself."

"It's kind of scary don't you think?"

"What do you mean?"

"Things are going almost *too* well. Even I understand the laws of probability. Sooner or later *something* is bound to upset the balance in my life."

Susan watched Julie scrub away at a completely clean plate in the sink. "I've never known you to worry about things."

"Not worried, just expectant," she replied.

"Just because things didn't work out between Greg and I doesn't mean it's going to happen to you. Is there anything that would lead you to believe otherwise?"

She thought long and hard about Rebecca, about her and Rick and about the fact that she didn't have clue what Rick did at Trojan Security.

"No. Not really," she finally replied.

"Then let's go spend some money."

CHAPTER 4

▼

The sun was still poised over the trees as Stace walked towards his apartment from the *friebad* pool later that afternoon. He enjoyed the scenes along the aquaduct, which to him were fresh and exhilarating and had not yet lost their charm. But perhaps it was the way Stace looked at life—his artistic sixth engaging itself—for things which might appear normal to others were not normal to him. Children who passed by on their bikes laughed just like other American children, but their speech was different and to him, intriguing. And the old man walking towards him was like any old man who walked for his health, but he thought the man's olive green knickers, pinned just below the knee and held up by suspenders, rather silly. In the field he saw two young lovers in their teens embracing under the shade of a tree. Here too, young love was no different than what he was used to seeing. Yet, to him it seemed more pure. Not like kids smoking and kissing in front of a corner store. Here they were rather like Romeo and Juliet, nourishing a forever kind of love. Whether he realized it our not, this is why he loved Germany. It was surreal, mystical, and romantic.

He lived about ten minutes from the pool, on the top floor of a quaint German home on *Wiesenfeldstrasse*, a country road originating in *Sossenheim*. He rented the upstairs apartment from the owners, the Summersheims, who lived in the home on the ground floor. Although the house was relatively new, it reflected the architecture of old. Like most of the homes nearby, it was a square, two-story home graced with a red tile roof. The sides were constructed in stucco and painted white. The window frames were made of wood and dressed in planter boxes bursting with bright red geraniums Both the front and backyards were beautifully landscaped. Now retired, Mr. Summersheim spent his entire weekend maintaining them, and like a good painting, there was nothing more that could be added to them, nothing more that could be taken away, which was all Hanzel and Gretal to Stace, and suited him just fine.

At precisely 5:30, he took out Eva's card from his pocket and gave her a call. On the third ring she answered. He determined from the directions she'd given him that she lived about a thirty-minute walk from his apartment to her home in *Hochst*. When he turned onto *Loreleistrasse* forty minutes later it was nearly dark. He walked to the end of the street and stood for moment under the glow of a rusty lamp-post on the corner, its light faintly illuminating the building in which she lived in a dirty cream color. The building was nondescript. It sat on the corner of a small lot a few feet above street level. Surrounding the lot was a short cement wall. On top of the wall was a two-foot, cast-iron fence, which like the wall, continued all the way down the street. Eva's dull orange Opel was parked near the corner were she said it would be. He unlatched the handle of the gate and walked up the cracked walkway leading to the first of two sets of doors. Once inside the foyer, he knocked on the apartment door to the left.

Eva's German Sheppard sent barks of alarm under the door. "Sheeba! It's ok girl!" he heard Eva yell. The dog stopped barking, but growled for effect.

"Come on in," Eva said, opening the door.

He entered cautiously as Sheeba sniffed him over. Her back grizzled with specks of gray and brown fur. Sheeba sniffed his outstretched hand and checked in her simple mind for any verification that he was not a threat. "She's a good looking shepherd." Stace said.

"I'm just finishing up," Eva answered, walking towards the kitchen.

The round table in the dining room had been modestly set for two; white ceramic plates, fork and knife over paper napkins and two slim wine glasses. A wicker basket of bread wrapped in a pink and white-checkered flannel cloth steamed with the aroma of fresh bread.

"Can you open the wine?" She asked, handing him a bottle of red.

"Sure. Where's the cork screw?"

"Over there." She pointed to the first drawer near the sink.

"I'm afraid this isn't going to be fancy. I don't often get a chance to cook," she said, hovering over a frying pan on the stove.

On the counter between the refrigerator and the sink he saw a pile of shredded lettuce, sliced tomatoes and onions, and an open can of diced mushrooms. Next to the lettuce rested a bottle of cucumber sauce and a bag of pita bread. "What are you making?"

"Gyros. I'm just finishing frying up the lamb."

"Sounds good. Don't think I've ever had homemade gyros."

She smiled and flipped the strips of lamb over. He sat down at the table where he could watch her and opened the wine. Now was as good a time as any to ask her. "Your business card...what kind of work do you do Eva?"

She hesitated for a moment, pita bread in one hand, strips of lamb dangling off the end of a fork in the other. In actuality, she had expected the question to come sooner or later. It always did. The problem was, she could never be entirely honest about what she did. Not just to potential boy friends, but to many of her other friends as well. She always had to be careful she didn't to reveal too much and yet, do it in a manner that didn't raise suspicion.

"I'm a reporter," she said simply.

"Yeah, your card gave that away, but not with the Frankfurt paper, right?"

"No." Had it been any other person she would have tried to change the subject, but somehow she felt the need to say more. "I work for the *Schwarz Monatlich*."

"Don't believe I've heard of them."

"No. You probably haven't."

"What's it about?"

"My boss started the paper decades ago. He named it after himself. *Schwarz*, is Deutsch for black. *Monatlich*, simply means, monthly."

"The *Black Monthly*, sounds ominous."

"It fits."

She laid the strips of lamb into the pita pockets and stuffed them full of veggies, then dressed them with the cucumber sauce. Stace wasn't sure if she was ever going to elaborate.

"Well…primarily we investigate people and organizations—sometimes even companies—which you might say, work underground."

"Underground?"

"Not in the true sense of the word. They are organizations which have a political or ideological agenda."

"You mean hate groups?"

"In a sense."

"Are they still allowed to operate here in Europe?"

"Yes."

"That's good."

"Good?" she asked, walking towards the table with a perturbed look in her face.

"Not that I agree with most of them, but it's good they are still allowed to have a voice. You know they changed all that a few years ago in America."

"I know. Dig in."

He grabbed a gyro and set it on his plate. "So why them? Do you monitor them or something?"

"You might say the paper's a bit of a contradiction. We watch a few organizations very closely, but every now and then one of them steps over the line and we see to it that the public knows about them."

"Steps over the line?"

"Sure. Every once and a while some organization or company goes a little too far. Could be anything, like someone paying off a politician for favors…a big company lobbying for certain laws that favor another group's ideological slant—those kind of things."

"And you try and catch these people?"

"Sometimes we uncover enough evidence to shut them up for a while. Sometimes we just publicly expose their activities. We do what we can."

She changed the subject and they finished dinner.

"Would you like some coffee?" she asked, rising.

"That would be good."

"Have a seat on the couch and I'll bring it out to you."

He got up and went into the living room. Since his conversation had been cut short at the table, he looked for additional clues to her personality in her surroundings.

Directly across from him were windows dressed in white lace curtains. A soft breeze was blowing through the open window panel on the left. It slowly filled the curtain, raising it up towards the ceiling like a sail. He watched it fill and collapse under its own weight, only to refill again. A granite ledge ran across the length of the windows and held a few potted plants. Under a hanging lamp in the far right corner was a gigantic wicker chair with floral patterned cushions tied to its bamboo braces. Near the chair was an end table resting on a welded iron frame. On the table was a stack of magazines. The one on the top of the stack was *Paris Match*.

"You speak French?" he asked raising his voice.

"A little," she said from the kitchen.

Up against the wall to his right was a thick oak cabinet. It was lined with doors of various sizes with brass handles. A shelf in the middle held a dozen or so ceramic plates propped up on stands. At first he thought they were a collection of dishes, but none of them matched. Each one was unique, having either a picture or a painting on its face and German words written across it. His eyes dropped to the floor where Sheeba lay curled with her head poised on her front limbs. Her tired dark eyes peered at him indifferently. Down the short hall he could see photographs of friends or relatives hanging on the walls. In the left hand corner of the room a desk sat rammed into a corner with a computer monitor on top of it and a mountain of newspapers and correspondence. Stacked on the light brown carpet in front of the desk were several cardboard boxes sealed with packing tape. Resting on top of one of the boxes was a slim file. The label was clearly visible and read, "Christian Reform Movement."

Eva quickly blocked his view. She handed him a mug and walked over to the wicker chair. She took a moment to compose herself, tucking her feet up under her and balancing her mug in the fabric of her dress between her thighs.

"I was looking at your plates." He glanced towards the glass shelf. "What are they for?"

"I've earned them," she said proudly and immediately jumped up. "Have you never been to a *volksmarch*?"

"Can't say that I have."

"A *volksmarch* is like a hike. Some are short…say five kilometers, others are longer, like ten or more. You pay a few *marks* to register, and then you walk the distance. Some *volksmarches* are in the city, some in the country. When you finish the walk you get a little souvenir, usually a plate."

"So they're like trophies?"

"*Ja.* They have the name of the march and the date. The first one here is from the *Buga 99 volksmarch*. They hold it every year here in the city in late April when everything starts to bloom. This one is from a march I went to in *Feldberg* in the *Hochtaunus*."

"Sounds like fun."

"Lots of fun. Fact there's one coming up in *Treiburg* in a few months. Would you like to go?"

"I'd love to."

She was suddenly struck by her frivolity and jumped back in her chair reeling in thought. "*Schieza!* Meet him at the pool, invite the stranger to dinner, and three hours later I'm asking him to practically spend the weekend with me!" Like all the other men in her life, she fully expected that within a few days he'd be gone too, never to return her calls. She felt stupid.

But while Eva scolded her thoughts, Stace imagined her impulsivity to be just a confident expression of her will. And it was a confidence she wore well, giving her an attractive disposition of independence.

After a few minutes of silence she looked across the living room at him with a serious gaze. He felt comfortable with her facial embrace. "I enjoyed listening to you this afternoon," she said finally.

"I unloaded on you," he said, slightly embarrassed. "I didn't mean to take advantage of you. I haven't been in this country long. I still don't have many friends and if I'd expected we might become friends I probably would have kept my mouth shut."

She watched him cope with his embarrassment by brushing off imaginary dust flecks from his shirt. "So you didn't expect to become friends?" she asked, teasing him.

"No. And well…yes! I'm just not in the habit of sharing those kinds of things with anyone. Sometimes it's easier to tell things to a stranger than to a friend—right? I mean, there are no repercussions with a stranger."

"That's true. But consider me a friend now. I would really like to know more about you."

"Why?"

"Why consider me a friend, or why do I want to know more?"

"Why do you want to know more?"

"Because I think you're interesting, and well, I like you." But now she was being dishonest with herself and her insincerity troubled her. Actually, she liked him a lot, but she was just getting over feeling like an idiot and didn't want to relive the moment. "I just think we might be able to become good friends."

He smiled. She saw her honesty was received. She was quiet again for a moment, then picked up their conversation where it had stopped earlier in the day at the *freibad*. "What happened to you after the exhibit?"

"You don't give up too easily."

"I'm a reporter remember?" She smiled and rocked in her chair. Even Sheeba, who'd been resting peacefully, looked up at the unusual tone coming from her master.

"And you will not run when I tell you?"

"I promise."

He sipped his coffee and forced his mind to go back to the experiences surrounding the art exhibit. This wasn't easy. The mental act of rethinking through the event distressed him. The event had significantly changed his life and most of those changes had not been for the better. For the last four years he'd been living in the vacuum of his own thoughts. He didn't like emotional pain, refrained from social contact, hated commitment, and otherwise, considered himself a loner and doomed to it. Consequently, he viewed everything philosophically, because it allowed him to approach his relationship to the world with detachment. This line of thinking had suited him well, but he was now sensing it had robbed him of the very thing he wanted most, to be a participant in life. He'd become sick of his isolationism. Try as he may to reason the painful events of the exhibit out of his life, they still remained fresh in his mind. He was now ready more then ever to welcome the joy of human contact back into his life. It just so happened that now there was a willing listener.

"To be honest with you, I've never experienced anything more painful in my life," he began, "and I've never been able to forgive Rick Forstein for allowing it to happen." Indignation filled his eyes.

"You said this afternoon it was the nature of the photographs that caused the university to disqualify your entries," she said sympathetically, encouraging him to speak.

"So they said, but I never believed it."

"Do you think it was personal?"

"Yes I do. I've always thought art to be above the jurisdiction and limitations of—" he paused for a moment, recognizing he was reverting back to a theoretical analysis of art, which he didn't want to do. "What I'm trying to say is, "they had no fucking right to expel my work from the exhibit! None whatsoever!"

Eva was astonished by his anger, but since she was emotionally removed from the event, she had to wonder if the university had some legitimate grounds for rejecting his work. She wanted to believe him, but she had her own questions that needed to be verified before she would allow herself to side with him. "You said the exhibit was to be held at the university?"

"Yes, in the fine arts building," he replied, miffed by her question.

"And it was open for everyone to see?"

"Students, faculty, and perhaps even a few people from San Antonio might have come to it. More importantly, one of the most influential galleries in the city was going to cover it. Why do you ask?"

She'd not heard what she needed to hear and didn't respond. "Were children going to be allowed into the exhibit?"

"Doubtful," he blurted out, but upon reflection said, "maybe some of the faculty member's children. But I still doubt it." How many children do you know would like to go see an exhibit of modern art?"

She hesitated, trying to determine if the university's rejection of his work was based on whether it would be exposed to children. If that was the case, their argument might be grounded. In reality, nudity in art was not an issue with her. All across Germany and Europe thousands of paintings and sculptures of nude women and men were on display to the public to adults and children alike.

"Did they say your material was pornographic?"

Her own feelings about pornography were mixed, but she was intrigued by the freedom of eroticism and envied those who had the capacity to explore their desires free of restraint. Almost forgetting the question, she looked at him with renewed fascination, wondering if he possessed the creativity to assist in her own explorations.

"No." He was adamant. "They never said they were pornographic and they were nowhere near pornographic. My photographs contained simple representations of the human form. I intentionally withheld portraying the erogenous zones because it suited my purpose. I very much like—" he stopped short, realizing he was about to lapse into abstractions, and when it came to speaking about his creative passion—his reason for existence—he must choose his words more carefully. "I like creating the element of desire. When somebody looks at my photographs, I want their mind to travel to a place where the source of their pleasure is."

The wind picked up, sending the curtain sailing into the living room again. She was impervious to it. He knew he had her attention and the juices of his creative self began to flow.

"Does pornography and sex have anything to do with it?" he asked abruptly. She seemed incapable of reasoning at the moment.

"Think about it. There's something entirely primal about it, don't you think?" he continued. "I portray the human form because to me— as I believe to everyone—it brings out our most basic instincts. What the human mind seeks is that transcendental state where it can escape the suffering and pain of life. We have found that state in the expression of love. I'm not talking about sex here. I'm talking about the bond which exists between lovers, that magical place where a person forgets about himself, about the world, by caring for the needs of their lover. So, when someone looks at my photographs it's not sex that I want them to think about. What I want them to think—no, that's not it—I don't want them to think at all, I just want them to be carried off to a place where they're overwhelmed with the emotion of love."

Eva no longer wanted to debate his motives. She understood his photographs were rejected not because of their content, but through the refusal of the university to accept the vision behind their creation.

In that sense, they'd rejected not the photographs, but the man behind the camera.

In an attempt to empathize with him, she searched for an experience in her own life that had violated her person as much as the rejection of his work must have violated him. She got up and shut the window, then sat back down and sipped at her coffee. She could think of no specific experiences. She did discover, however, that her work as a reporter presented a wide range of injustices that were often left unsettled. She tried to count the dozens of individuals and organizations she'd tracked, which continually got away with crimes through their political and financial power. In her own way, she fought against those injustices tenaciously and with a vengeance.

At the present time, her energies were directed towards an organization known as the Christian Reform Movement. It was an investigation she started only a few weeks ago, handed to her by her boss. What she did not know, but would later discover, was that the CRM was once an underground terrorist organization based in Berlin. Their primary objective during the 1980's was to nullify the efforts of the East German Communist Regime. After the two countries reached agreements in the early 1990's, the East German Communist Regime effectively merging with the Federal Republic of Germany, the CRM's political criteria had been met, but they wanted more. Somehow the organization, or an offshoot of it, had established itself in Frankfurt. The ideological temperament of the group was always based on the objective of unifying the German people, but now their ideologies had evolved to promote the fundamentals of anti-Semitism. What alarmed Mr. Schwarz most about the organization was that they were promoting their ideologies under the banner of Christianity.

"*Hallo*," Stace said, yanking her out of her thoughts.

"Oh, sorry. I was thinking about what you were saying," she replied. "I can only imagine how you must have felt to have been rejected like that."

He was surprised at her comment. In a way it was connected to what he'd been saying and in a way it wasn't. "I should have the right to create and express what I damn well please and damn those who disagree," he blurted.

Those whom he felt had trampled on that principle were many. At the top of the list was Rick Forstein, followed by the committee members and finally, the university's administration. Born with some deficit in character that rendered him incapable of confronting conflict, Stace had been living with the regret of not having fought the university's decision ever since. He thought himself a coward for not standing up for what he believed in. Bullied and robbed of his voice, he'd made no attempt to face the injustice. He'd been a staunch advocate of passivity all his life, believing that the injustices of life had a way of working themselves out to those who possessed an honest heart. Trouble was, the problem had never worked itself out. This presented him with a moral dilemma. In the absence of justification he found that his heart contained emotions he'd rather not claim as his own. How he now wished he could go back in time and discredit the pious reputation of the university! How he had fantasized that the most horrific and catastrophic circumstances would befall the charmed life of Rick Forstein! Ironically, he was unable to determine if he was more enraged by his own inadequacies or by the actual injustice that had been served him. Time had compressed the two distinct situations into one. Both of them produced the same emotion; hate, and the emotion produced the same resolution; vengeance. After four years the unresolved conflict still tormented his mind like the stench of a dead armadillo flattened on the road somewhere in West Texas.

"I don't like to think about it," he said.

Eva thought he looked a bit frazzled. "Would you like to go for a walk?" she asked.

"That's probably a good idea."

Along *Loreliestrasse,* two rows of sleek European cars edged the street like lumpy caterpillars hugging the curb. The apartments and homes sitting beyond them were devoid of personality and had square-cut windows that appeared to be crying for the history they'd seen. For from the corners of each window the rust, soil and paint of yesteryear, wept like tears streaking the weather torn plaster.

They took a left onto *Gebenschusstrasse* and headed straight for McNare Kaserne. Left over from the Second World War, the Kaserne was now a US Army installation housing the 32nd Signal Battalion, along with a small infantry unit. As they approached the installation, one of its four-story buildings came into view, painted in the color and texture of an orange peel. Surrounding the installation was an eight-foot high, chain-link fence. The top of it curved inwards and several strands of barbed wire ran along its course. Stace wondered if it was designed to keep people in or out. From the third floor window of a barrack came the rumbling base line of one of U2's latest releases.

"I wish they'd all go home," she said, as they walked along the fence line towards the front of the Kaserne. "Not you of course...."

"Ah, you don't like the capitalists," he joked.

"Of course, I like Americans. I just don't like the memory of W.W.II popping up in my face all the time."

He understood. Americans were all over Frankfurt. He admired their misplaced loyalties, wondering how sane rational human beings could be moved under the guise of patriotic idealism to sell their souls to a higher power. The truth be told, it wasn't the American soldiers he hated, it was the idealism to which they surrendered. Granted, the America to which he was indigenous to marketed well the idea of an individual's right to succeed, but it had failed to disclose the fine print. To the not so exceptional and intellectually inferior, capitalistic success was for a select group.

What solidified his emotions was uncertain. He knew only that he sided with the unfortunate misfits of the world, who lived under a different set of values. So in a sense, one might label him either a rebel or downright stupid. He was fully capable of yielding; of cooperating with the ways of the world, but his sense of justice wouldn't permit it. He was born to that unique breed of mankind; of those rare individuals hopelessly infected with the inability to live in the present. They don't shake hands with greatness or success through the normal process of introductions and contacts. Rather, they come upon it through a stroke of luck. Their lives are often overlooked...their work obscured...their vision unnoticed. One only reads about their uniqueness in history books if they somehow manage to connect to practicality.

"I know what you mean," he said minutes later. "I guess after nearly seventy years you'd get tired of seeing them around."

They continued towards the front of the installation, stopping briefly at the entrance on *Konrad Glatt Strasse*. It was marked by a circle drive paved in black cobblestone. The night had turned misty and the cobblestone looked like polished flint. The drive led up into an archway cut out of the main administrative building. It was guarded by a virtually impenetrable iron gate and a pimple faced soldier dressed in full war gear brandishing an empty M-16.

"You still haven't told me that much about yourself," he said.

"There's not much to tell. "I've lived in Frankfurt all of my life. My father owns a *backerei* in downtown *Hochst*."

"*Backerei?*"

"Bakery."

"He and my mother, along with my brother, live above the *backerei* in a little apartment. I used to work for him in the mornings greasing pans for bread and pastries before going to school."

"Have they always owned the *backerei?*"

"They started it from scratch many years ago. My father used to work as a city representative."

"A politician?"

"You could say that, but you'd never hear him claim the title."

"And you brother?"

"Alfred's his name. He works for the phone company. I don't see him too often." Which was true, he and Eva kept their contacts to a minimum, meeting on occasions in busy cafés over coffee. What she left unsaid was that he also worked for the *Schwarz Monatlich*, setting up audio and video surveillance devices for the paper to assist with investigations.

"Your mother?"

"My mother works with my father at the *backerei*. She takes care of the books and works behind the counter with the customers."

He tried to picture her father leaning over a counter pounding dough into bread, while his wife, wearing a white cotton apron around her waist, served customers. He saw them waking long before the sun rose, working throughout the day and into the evenings, then collapsing late at night on a couch or something to spend a few minutes alone with each other. He envied the heritage of the woman who walked beside him, having lost his mother to breast cancer when he was young and growing up with his father whose gestures of love came sporadically after the long hours he worked as a house framer.

They said little on the way back to Eva's home after rounding the Kaserne, choosing rather to meditate on their attraction to each other. Eva's wholesomeness and warmth radiated from her presence, even though she was only willing to share a few words with him. They brushed up against each other several times during their walk and he felt the urge to take hold of her hand. But despite the urge he resisted. To him, the hours of the afternoon and evening had passed like months. He'd disclosed more to her about himself in that short time then he'd ever spoken to another woman. He walked her back up the sidewalk to the outside door of her apartment and stopped.

"I had a great time," he said, not wanting to overstay his welcome.

"Me too," she said.

"Can I call you again?" he asked.

"I'd like that."

CHAPTER 5

▼

By means of correspondence, the reverend agreed to meet with Fred Watson on Saturday morning July 11th at a cafe around the corner from the main entrance to the University of Heidelberg. Watson would arrive by plane into the Frankfurt *Flughafen* on the 5th to begin a week of meetings with his office staff at the Heidelberg branch of Trojan Security. As it was, the reverend couldn't break away from his daily programming until the weekend. Late Sunday afternoon, he steered his licorice black Mercedes out of Munich and headed north on the autobahn at a comfortable speed of 145 km/h. By 9:00 p.m., he'd checked into a local bed and breakfast. He preferred the more quaint method of lodging, because he'd become such a public figure that finding privacy at the larger hotels had become impossible. Once in his room, the reverend settled into a comfortable chair and read himself to sleep. He awoke at 2:00 with a familiar pain in his neck, turned off the lights and crawled into bed.

At 9:45 the following morning, the reverend took an outside table at a cafe fifteen minutes prior to his guest's arrival. On the sidewalk in front of him, young men and women walked proudly towards an uncertain future full of naiveté and expectation. He envied their zeal, but not their intellectual deficit. He had once been a professor of Theology at the university in Munich, until he was excused from the position from what he would later justify as, "differences in beliefs." The administration claimed, however, it wasn't his theology that was in question, but rather, his methodology.

"Reverend Eisner?" Watson asked enthusiastically.

Pulled out of his thoughts, the reverend stood up and faced the sharply dressed gentleman.

"Yes."

"I hope you haven't been waiting long. I know you're busy and I appreciate your time."

"It's my pleasure. Please, take a seat Mr. Watson."

"Thank you and please call me Fred." Watson removed his sports coat before sitting down.

A gold emblem stamped with the initials F.W. cinched a paisley tie to Watson's shirt. The reverend never judged a man by the clothes he was wearing, so he searched the man's face for any telltale signs. What he saw was a smoothly shaven man with an early forties complexion. His black hair had only just begun to gray in frosted highlights over his temples. His eyelashes were tailored and styled to meet a nose, which ran a straight line to a sharp point over his upper lip. As for his mouth, both lips were of equal proportion, so that they neither smiled nor frowned until the situation dictated so. Whether he was handsome or not, the reverend didn't care, for he'd determined long ago that a man's character was not revealed by such minor details.

"Have you eaten, Mr. Watson?"

"Please, it's Fred, and yes I have.

"I ate as well, but I'll order us more coffee. *Herr Ober!*" the reverend cried out to a young waiter standing by. The waiter, who was a student working between classes, dashed over wearing a pressed white shirt and a black bow tie.

"Are you ready to order now sir?" he asked, thrusting two menus at him.

"*Bitte. Zwei tasse kaffee.*"

"*Zer gut,*" said the waiter.

"So, you've been to Germany before?" the reverend asked.

"About once a year I get out this way. Trojan Security has several locations around the world and I try to visit them at least once a year. I never miss the opportunity to come to Heidelberg."

"It is a beautiful city!" the reverend proclaimed. "There's quite a history to this place.

"Afraid I've never stayed long enough to discover it."

"That's too bad. During the Reformation this university was the hub of Calvinistic theology. In 1563 the theologians here drew up what's called the Heidelberg confession. The confession laid the foundation for many Christian denominations existing today."

"I didn't know that," Watson replied. What he understood about the reformation was a vague understanding that Luther, the father of the Lutheran church and many others like him, broke away from the Catholic Church under great persecution. "I can only imagine what this city must have been like during those times," he replied.

It's all a question of what one perceives, don't you think?" asked the reverend. Watson didn't respond. "Take these students for instance..." the reverend gestured to the hordes of students passing by their table. "I venture to say, ninety-five percent of them are totally unaware of the more important dynamics of life."

"If you're referring to their lack of spirituality, I understand where you're coming from."

The reverend's eyebrow twitched towards the pastel blue sky. He was struck by the young businessman's intuition.

"I'm under the impression we're truly living in the last days," Watson continued, looking mystically at the reverend.

"That too, is also a question of perception," the reverend replied, pleased with the direction of the conversation. "In America that's the consensus, but here in Germany—indeed, all of Europe!—our people still live in ignorance. We've failed in our responsibility to walk in our faith and have allowed ourselves to be lead by leaders who don't serve God."

Watson listened intently. He'd traveled many miles to meet this man whom he'd only known by his words. He thought the reverend to be even more dynamic in person, speaking with a charisma that had to be witnessed.

The waiter returned with two tiny porcelain cups of coffee centered on a silver tray.

"*Danke*," the reverend said, turning silent and looking out into the street.

What was he thinking of now? The future or the past? Perhaps his mind was walking the ancient streets of Heidelberg much like the reformer Calvin. If that was the case, his countenance didn't reflect the triumph of that time. Rather, it appeared defeated and sorrowful, much like a man who'd suddenly realized he was fighting a losing battle. The reverend shook his head slightly, breaking free from the grip of his thoughts. "So, what can I do for you, or as your letter suggested, what do you think you can do for me?"

Before answering, Watson took a packet of sugar and swirled it into his coffee. "As I mentioned in my letter, I've watched your ministry for several years." He took a sip of coffee and continued. "During that time my faith has grown tremendously. I have thus far, had a good life and the Lord has provided me with everything I needed and wanted. But lately, I've become aware that I've not done enough to thank God for all of His blessings. I believe He's leading me to change that situation."

Looking over to Watson with pastoral concern the reverend asked, "and what might that be?"

"Well, it hasn't been all that easy for me to define. I've listened to your preaching and often wonder what it would be like to have been a preacher."

"It's never to late."

"I think it is, or at least, I don't feel it to be my calling. I have a responsibility towards the individuals within my company. If I were to just walk away it's quite possible my business would lose its competitive edge. The result could be disastrous. I don't even want to think about the prospect of dismissing hundreds of workers who have given me so much of their time. It could ruin many families."

"I can understand your position."

"Anyway, as I mentioned, I support your work and have come to feel akin to it. I'm especially impressed with your coalition's success within the political arena. Are you familiar with the American Christian Broadcasting Network?"

"Yes, and also with Pastor Tim Raymond. I've spoken to him many times."

"Their organization has been instrumental in changing much of the American political agenda for the past decade."

"I'm aware of that and admire the work they've done."

Watson sipped away at his coffee and glanced out into the street. He was silent for quite some time. As minutes slipped away the reverend looked at him with concern. Watson was hesitant for one simple reason; he'd met with Pastor Raymond last year and had proposed to him the same idea he now wished to share with Reverend Eisner. When Pastor Raymond refused him, he'd felt personally rejected. Although he still supported the ACBN in spirit, he'd withdrawn his financial support from their ministry. Despite that rejection, he was still thoroughly convinced the Lord had not only given him the idea, but that the idea would work. He just needed a man in the right position to carry the plan through.

"Yes, Pastor Raymond is a good man," Watson at last proclaimed, "but that's not why I'm here. I should begin by saying first of all, if for some reason you find no merit in my idea, then this conversation between us never happened."

He waited patiently for the reverend to respond to his terms.

The reverend looked questionably into Watson's optimistic face. Doubts crowded the reverend's mind, muddling his usual clarity of thought.

"Are we talking about something illegal here?"

"That would depend on your perception," he replied, offering a smile to release any building tension.

"I think at times the Lord has used mysterious ways of accomplishing His work. He often acts in ways completely contrary to popular wisdom. The furtherance of His work has never been dependent upon the rules of the land. He does what He does because He is God and the world has always adapted itself to His actions. Wouldn't you agree?"

"I couldn't disagree with such a statement."

"God doesn't say for instance, 'it's time to do this or that now, but I'll have to wait because man has created a law that I can't break,' does He?"

"Again, I'd have to agree."

"He's really not concerned about such insignificant matters. He has the right at any given time to do whatever seems right for Him, because He sees the bigger picture, the end from the beginning. Man's laws are of little consequence. Like you have said, 'it's all a matter of perception.' How you receive what I have to say will depend on your estimation of whether or not you believe God his given you a work to perform. It also depends on whether you feel an obligation to follow man's laws. I know you well enough to say, that your heart is in the Lord's work and if presented with an idea to further that work the laws of man wouldn't stop you from proceeding."

The reverend had wisdom enough to recognize when someone was patronizing him. Having confronted the distasteful gesture many times during his ministry, he'd learned to excuse it as a simple error in human judgment. He prided himself on the fact that he had the ability to look beyond a person's choice of syntax and to listen to what people were actually saying, and although he didn't yet understand the point Watson was leading to, he still couldn't find a reason to discredit him. There was in this businessman from America, sincerity to his logic. The fact remained; the reverend did believe his ministry to have the providence of God and he never once considered his work to be impeded by man-made laws. "Are you sure you wouldn't have made a good preacher?" he asked, whimsically.

Watson smiled. He was beginning to win the confidence of his new friend. "My expertise as I've mentioned is in running a business, a computer business to be specific. Guess I'm a born salesman."

"I must say, I'm not all that familiar with computers. I still do things the old fashioned way. About all I use them for is word-processing to write the rough drafts of my sermons. Everything else is done by my secretaries or by my audio-visual staff. It allows me to focus on what I do best, which is preaching."

"Are you familiar with the Internet?" Watson asked.

"I'm aware of it, but don't use it. The ICC has a web site, but other people on my staff handle it. It's my understanding the site has significantly increased our material sales."

"Are you aware that approximately 2 billion people now use the Internet every week? That's almost half of the modern world. Those who don't use it are affected by it in one way or another. For instance, you don't use it, but your secretaries do. The information they receive affects your ministry."

"Again, I'm at a loss. I'm not that familiar with it."

"Understood, but follow along with me."

"I'll try."

"Now, when you preach, what has to happen in order for you to get your message across?"

The reverend lifted his head back raising his eyebrows. Spinning his empty coffee cup on the napkin, he seemed hard pressed to answer a question so obvious. "Well, I suppose someone has to read my book, or listen to a tape, or view one of our videos."

"How do they get that information?" Watson pressed.

"They either buy them or they get them from a friend, 'spose there are other ways."

"That's only half correct, but you recognize the other half deals with marketing, or in getting your materials into the hands of people who will distribute it to your membership."

"True."

"What if I told you there was a way to by-pass that system. Think of it as a way to cut your advertising expenses, or a way to get your message to more people."

"Suppose I'd have to look into it," he said with a chuckle. "But money isn't the issue with me. Like you, I'm quite satisfied with what God has provided for me. But in answer to your question, I'd be very interested in getting my message to as great a number of people as possible."

"The Internet is utilized by many people, or at the least, has an impact on everyone. People use it in their homes, as well as organizations like businesses, governments, ministries, universities, schools, and even underground elements of society such as crime and drug rings. What's on the Internet is public information. Anyone can tap into it and get the information they need. From a security standpoint, the internet is like an enormous telephone party-line with hundreds of millions of people on it at any given time."

The waiter returned with a silver pot full of coffee and filled their cups, then disappeared again.

"All I know is that it's worked for the ICC. We move a lot of material through our web site."

"But people still have to get to your web site correct?" Watson asked.

"As I understand it. We have a listing of our materials and people can order what they want from it."

"But they still have to know where to find your site correct?"

The reverend was getting tired of the circular conversation. "That's correct," he said, with a slight tone of frustration.

Watson recognized the tone and sped things up. "I won't go into details Reverend Eisner, but how people actually get to your site is done in a variety of different ways. To make a long story short, with all the advertising and garbage that's on the Internet now it's a miracle people can actually find your site."

"So we're missing requests for materials?"

"You're probably missing a significant amount of sales, but that's not what I want to discuss with you."

"What exactly is it you're trying to explain to me?"

"To put it bluntly, we've discovered a way of reaching people with information without them even asking for it."

"I'm not sure I understand. Are you talking about controlling computers?"

"In a sense, yes. The program we're working on will be able to insert bits of written and photographic information onto the screen of anyone using the Internet without them knowing about it." Watson looked hard into the reverend's eyes to see if he'd understood the possibilities of such a tool. He looked lost.

"Explain."

"Take your book for instance, even if someone reads it they still have the ability to reject its contents don't they?"

"I suppose so," the reverend replied, although the idea that someone could reject his book seemed preposterous.

"That's the reality of the situation. It's like the Bible. When someone reads it there's always the chance they won't understand it. The reason for this is that their mind is distracted from receiving the message. The minute they've read a passage, they're thinking about the bills they haven't paid, or the dog needs a walk, or its time to put dinner into the oven. We have found a way that will allow people to by-pass those distractions."

"Are you talking about imprinting ideas into people's minds?"

"That's exactly what I'm saying. The subconscious is like a pool holding all the memories and impressions of the soul. From that pool of information the mind makes everyday decisions. If that pool is full of the things of this world—full of evil you might say—then a person will automatically make bad decisions. But if that pool has the necessary information to make good choices, than it can change the way a person acts. It gives them the necessary tools to make good decisions."

"And you're saying the Internet possesses this technology?"

"Not the Internet itself. That's the medium, but the technology exists to build a program that could do it."

"You've done this. You have this in place?"

"Not yet, but I'm in the process of putting a team together that will make it happen."

"Than it's just a theory."

"Not a theory, but when it's time for wheels to turn then wheels will turn," he replied.

There were few things that escaped the reverend. That turn of logic did.

"When it was time for the wheel to be made then someone invented the wheel. That's all I meant. Let me put it another way. If the ideas of the reformation hadn't come from Calvin in Heidelberg, they would have come from another person in another city. I take it Calvin wasn't the only one thinking about breaking from the Catholic Church during the 1500's." The reverend nodded and Watson continued "Present technology has reached the point where building such a program is possible. This program will be built by someone, better Trojan Security than someone else. And this program will be used by someone, better Reverend Eisner and the ICC than someone else, because I can tell you for a fact, if such a program were to be used by the wrong group—say Muslim extremists or terrorists—it would have catastrophic results."

The reverend parted his lips, but Watson didn't let him reply. "I know what your thinking. I've thought it through already a thousands times. It's not a question of *if* such technology exists—it does. It's not a question of *if* someone will use this technology to their advantage—they will. As far as I'm concerned there are only two arguments that need to be thought through." Watson shifted in his seat and leaned over to the reverend like he was about to close a multi-million dollar deal. The only two arguments you need to consider are these…. First of all, is what I propose to you ethical and legal? Secondly, if you're not the one to use this technology to further the work of the Lord, are you willing to accept the possibility that the technology will be used by the agents of Satan?"

"I don't see how that's possible," the reverend replied.

"That's understandable. I've had much more time to consider the ill effects of such a program. The reason it will affect so many people is because of the influence of the Internet. You know as well as I do that people are followers. They will follow anyone with vision who gives them something better to hope for than their present life affords. History is full of madmen who have used their influence to lead millions of people astray. Imagine a person, a person such as a modern day Hitler; imagine if he could get his hands on a program that could alter the way people think. One that could actually make people want to follow him by manipulating their minds instead of trying to just convince them of an idea. Imagine if such a person didn't have to rely on the ignorance of the masses, that they could instantly influence the leaders in government, in businesses, in institutions of higher learning. How? By targeting the Internet, the most accessible place to get information. Just imagine, millions of people suddenly and unexplainably acting in ways you could only describe as demonic. There would be utter chaos. It could postpone the second coming of Christ for hundreds of years." Watson leaned back into his chair, but never took his eyes away from the reverend's. "Now, if you can imagine all that, then you can imagine the possibility of having such a program utilized by the Church. In the right hands, it could help convert millions of people to Christianity who might never have a chance."

While he waited for the reverend's response, he extended a shaking hand towards his cup of coffee. He'd worked himself up into a frenzy. What irritated him most was that he was incapable of carrying out the idea himself. He could have the program designed, he could see to it that it was built, but he needed a charismatic religious figure such as Reverend Eisner, who had both the skills and the religious network established to make it happen.

Within the reverend's mind the words Watson said screamed like asteroids bouncing in mirrored sphere. As though negotiating the next move of a chess piece, he analyzed each word and phrase, as well as the expressions and tone of the American. He combined them with his own assessment of the political and religious state of the world, taking into account what he understood to be the overall present state of the human predicament. He considered his ministry and the International Christian Coalition he'd established and how the Lord had let him in the past and blessed the work of his hands. Through it all, he'd been able to lead thousands of individuals to the Christian faith. He understood the implications of each argument presented by Watson. He believed him. If such a program could be built than it would be built. And if it had the power Watson suggested it did, then it should be used by the Christian Church. Who was he to question that such an idea had not germinated in the mind of God? Perhaps the program was in God's plan all along. After all, this was the age of communication and technology. Who could doubt God wouldn't use such a medium to finish His work? The more he thought about it, the more he entertained the idea he had been chosen to help in the implementation of such a plan. And if the furtherance of the Gospel set him against the political and religious laws of the land, then so be it!

"If you need time to think, we can talk in a few weeks—"

"I don't need any time," the reverend responded. "I think it's rather fitting, that in such a city as this, where the reformation forged the present state of our world, that the plans of God for the final events of earth's history should also be initiated."

The implication of the reverend's statement rattled in Watson's mind like his first big sale, the one he thought he'd totally blown, until he himself was blown away when the client agreed to buy. The reverend had bought the idea. Their union was forged. He leaned across the

table and speaking in a low tone said, "you do realize any future communication we have will have to be done with extreme discretion. The
likelihood that some will misunderstand our motives is almost certain."

The reverend's mind flashed back to the many situations in the gos-
pels where Jesus was extremely secretive about some of his activities.
Not wishing to awaken any hostilities prematurely, Jesus often told his
disciples to keep his actions secret. "I understand," he said.

CHAPTER 6

▼

Eva sat at her petrified wooden desk watching shadowy forms pass in front of the windows to the basement office of the *Schwarz Monatlich*. The dinky windows, set in aged charcoal colored brick and protected from the outside by corroded iron bars, were covered with a crying layer of greenish paint. The forms passing beyond them were ghostly, lapping across the bars and flowing across the windows in a rhythmic flow seeking to lull her back to sleep.

Her weekend with Stace had been uneventful, which to her, was monumental in its simplicity. She'd learned more about the American in one day than she'd learned about her previous boyfriend in months. When she awoke that morning, she recognized her attraction to him had been an attraction based on pity. She recounted the story of his last year in college and the events surrounding the art exhibit. She envied his ability to simply pick up and move to another country far away from the pressures of his past. But having given all this some thought, she'd decided he was just a coward. He was on the run and when someone is on the run it's nearly impossible for that person to come to a sudden and decisive stop. More than likely, he'd be soon passing on. She'd probably never hear from him again.

"*Guten morgen,* Eva," came the raspy voice of her boss, Mr. Schwarz. "It's too early for you to be thinking so heavily," he said from the door of his office, which was really not an office, but a cutout in the corner of the basement with a window peering into the main office.

She turned to face him. Mr. Schwarz was the type of man to which clothes served no purpose, other than to cover the body. It was quite possible what he now wore had been a hand-me-down from his own father; unpolished black leather shoes, the same gray cotton slacks he always wore and a wrinkled, white cotton shirt. Forget the tie. He never met anyone important enough to impress. What he lacked in dress he made up for in the zealous pursuit towards the monthly publication of his paper. He'd lost two wives through the pursuit of his vision and didn't seek a third. What he had to show for his life was a rented basement, a handful of eager young visionaries and the diminishing circulation of a small newspaper with the outdated ideals of reform. Now aged to fifty-three, he looked more like seventy, with signs of hardship chiseled into the contours of his face like cracks in granite.

She called him by his first name, "Dexter, how long have you been here?"

"You mean, when did I ever leave?" he asked, a smile wrapping around the ends of his nose. "Always," he replied. Which was true to a certain extent. His skin was as white as flour for want of sunlight.

A jiggle at the door signaled the arrival of Shelly LeBlanc with a bag full of pastries followed Ruben Thanasouk. "And where's *de* coffee?" Ruben asked, in his thick Liberian accent, rising in pitch and ending with an overemphasized "*eee*" sound." He sniffed the air like a hound. "We brought *de* breakfast and you haven't made *de* coffee yet?"

"*Es tut mir leid*," Eva apologized. She walked across the office to the coffee maker and started a pot.

"Now you know it's our job to bring the breakfast and yours to make the coffee," Shelly said. She cleared a spot on the table next to Eva and tore open the bag of pastries.

"That's a cute top," Eva said. "Is it a one piece?"

"No, two." Shelly backed away from the table and took hold of the peachy seam of the outer sweater and pulled it up so Eva could get a good look at the matching top underneath. The blouse barely covered the bottom of her ribs.

"Aren't you cold?" Eva asked, looking at her pierced belly button.

"*Ja*, but fashionable don't you think?" she replied, with a whimsical grin flashing across her freckled face. "It'll warm up by lunch."

Eva never had the courage to ask Shelly about her genealogical background. In Eva's best estimation she suspected Shelly to be French, but she may have been English. She was definitely not German. Her complexion was fair and sprinkled with freckles, which were not visible from a distance, but at close range distracted from her otherwise, pretty face. Her hair had a slight brown pigment to it and always looked frazzled. This morning she had it pulled tightly around her bony head and secured in the back with a juvenile looking barrette. The bangs of her hair were not long enough to reach the barrette and they buzzed around her face like teased wires.

At twenty-two, Shelly was the youngest member of the paper. Eva disliked most of her choice in apparel, which she considered to be childish. She also thought Shelly's flippant disposition unbecoming of the seriousness of their work. Quite frankly, there were times when they didn't need a child buzzing around the office like a loose bee in a flower shop. But despite her demeanor, Shelly's administrative and secretarial skills were impeccable. She'd saved Eva's neck more times than Eva could count. Since Eva was the prominent writer in the office, her duties were stretched and she often didn't have the time to rewrite or edit her stories. In the last six months that responsibility had fallen on Shelly. She not only assisted Eva, but also orchestrated all the correspondence, hunted down advertising possibilities for the paper, filed whatever needed to be filed, answered phones, did most of the computer work and even managed to stop by the nearby bakery every morning.

Ruben Thanasouk had immigrated to Germany from Liberia when he was twenty-six in 1995. His parents had been killed during the military dictatorship in Liberia that same year. He was as black as pitch. His thin long features popped out of his face like a Braille photograph highlighted in sterling. The only part of him darker than his skin was the tightly packed crop of hair on his head. He also sported a matching goatee, which leaped out from his chin like a toothbrush. Like Eva, he was an investigative reporter, although his stories were confined to happenings in Germany alone. Having once worked for Amnesty International, he was adroit in uncovering human rights abuses.

"Ruben, Eva, I need to have a word with you two in my office," Mr. Schwarz said, poking his head out of his door.

Ruben finished making his cup of coffee and they walked into his office.

"Close the door behind you," Mr. Schwarz said to Ruben.

Eva took a seat on the couch backed up against the flimsy wall opposite Mr. Schwarz's desk and crossed her legs. Ruben remained standing by the door.

"How's the story coming on the Christian Reform Movement?"

She knew the look. Mr. Schwarz had his moments of light-heartedness, but he also had a war face.

"Not much I'm afraid. As near as I can tell they work out of an apartment over on *Hugelstrasse* near the *Ginnheim* tower. They've got a number of churches and a following throughout Germany. I haven't checked with Alfred yet, so I don't know the extent of their incoming and outgoing calls. Mechtild with the *Bundespost,* says they run a lot of packages through the post office."

"Maybe *dey've* got a tape ministry going or *someding,*" Ruben said.

"How many of them are there?"

"I figure about three people, two men and a woman. There's one other thing though," Eva surmised.

"What?" Mr. Schwarz questioned.

"I doubt there's anything to it, but they all come and go at different times."

"Like *dey* have jobs?" Ruben asked.

"I think they do. And the woman walks her dog twice a day in the park across the street."

"The one between the American housing area near *Paquetstrasse?*" Mr. Schwarz asked.

"*Ja.*"

"You're right. I don't see anything to it."

"It just makes me wonder how threatening the group really is. They don't seem to be hiding their activities or their identities," Eva said.

Mr. Schwarz reached over and picked up a pamphlet on his desk. "I found this on my windshield this morning. There may be only three of them, but it seems they've got quite a following." He handed the pamphlet to Eva. "Take a look at page two."

"*New Objectives Of The International Christian Coalition,*" was the article's heading.

"Familiar with them?" Mr. Schwarz asked.

"Who isn't?" said Ruben, reading what he could over Eva's shoulder. "Non-threatening, like *de* American Christian Broadcasting Network—"

"Is that what you think?" Mr. Schwarz asked.

"I claim ignorance!" Ruben replied. "I was dealing with my own revolution at *dat* time."

"Well, let me refresh your memory. To recap, the ACBN, along with other formidable Christian organizations in America at the time, became so powerful they were able to place their own candidate in the White House in 2008. Then they cleaned house. They started with the government, then moved to private industry, then checked in the closets of every American household. They stuck their puritan hands into everybody's business. Christ! They even sealed up their borders to immigrants. Oh, they'll still let you in, as long as you claim Christianity as your religion!"

"But—"

"Save it. I know what you're going to say. Violent crime dropped forty-six percent. They won the drug war. Militarily, they're still the most powerful nation. And they've come pretty damn close to wiping out poverty right? All fluff!" Mr. Schwarz fell back in his chair with a long sigh. "Can you imagine?" he mumbled to himself. "Listen you two, you know me. I call it like I see it."

"There's no need for you to explain anything to us Dexter," Eva said. "We know you, and you know us. That's why we work for you. We all understand that no force, no matter how good the motives or intentions, has any right to dictate conscious. Prosperity under those circumstances is only a pretense."

Mr. Schwarz smiled approvingly at his apprentice. She reminded him of himself, only younger. "My concern is that Germany, like so many other nations blinded by the false sense of prosperity in America, will soon follow America's lead. I've followed the International Christian Coalition ever sense I heard of them twelve years ago. They've become extremely influential and frankly...what is it Eva?" Mr. Schwarz noticed she'd flipped to the back of the pamphlet and was fixated on the last page.

"Perhaps nothing, but this name's familiar, Joseph Stautzen. He's listed as the Executive Secretary of the CRM under Reverend Eisner. It seems like I've seen his name floating around in the material I've collected on the CRM."

"Are you sure?"

She tweaked her head to the side as if rattling a memory loose. "Yeah, I'm sure."

"Then that's a problem. If The International Christian Coalition and the Christian Reform Movement are connected, then we need to find out the extent of their involvement with each other."

Ruben looked at Eva discretely with an expression of bewilderment. He failed to see the point.

"Eva, I want you to drop whatever your working on and focus strictly on the ICC and the CRM. Ruben—"

"*Ja.*"

"Assist Eva with this one."

"Sure. *Whateva* you want. But what about *de* next month's publication?"

"We'll have to rely on some of the older stories we've tabled, Shelly can handle that, at least until we know what's going on with these two organizations. And Eva, get Alfred into the CRM's apartment. We need something substantial to go on."

"I'll get him right on it," she replied. "Anything else?"

"No. That's it for now."

They walked back out of his office. "I don't know about you, but I fail to see *de* importance of *dis* story," Ruben whispered under his breath.

Eva didn't reply, but her expression mirrored his thoughts. She opened up her top desk drawer and flipped through a file consisting of previous notes she'd taken about the three members of the CRM. The information amounted to little more than brief notes of the CRM member's physical descriptions and patterns of their behavior that were given to her by *Frau* Becker, the apartment landlord who owned the apartment they were living in.

"Shelly!"

"*Ja.*" She hopped over to Eva's desk.

"Here are three names. I need you find out everything you can about these people. Find out if they work and where they work; their family backgrounds and nationalities, you know, everything."

"Sure." She snatched the file out of Eva's hands.

Eva then placed a call to the telephone company and was transferred to the service department. She left a message with the dispatcher to have her brother Alfred give her a call later that evening at home.

"I don't see much here," Ruben said, after browsing through the pamphlet. "Typical young radicals bent on saving *de* world. Any intelligent person can read *trough dis. Noting* rational or organized, just disjointed extremism."

"Just the kind of people stupid enough to be dangerous," Shelly said from her desk.

Ruben and Eva looked at each other simultaneously, realizing she could be right.

"Ruben, you ready for a little old fashioned surveillance?" Eva asked.

"Will it do any good?" he asked, thinking of more productive and less boring things he could be doing.

"We'll take two cars. I want to show you where the apartment is and have you watch it. Then I'm going to do a little research at the library and find out what I can about the International Christian Coalition."

CHAPTER 7

▼

Rick glided up the stairs to the second floor of Building D in the Trojan Security complex located at 16700 Research Boulevard. Having spent a three-day weekend with his family in the canyons of Big Bend National Park in Southwestern Texas, he was anxious to return to work. Walking down the long corridor, he took out his pass-card and slid it into the sleeve of the security system on the wall outside the computer lab. Behind the door, he could hear the familiar sounds of the mainframe humming its mechanical mantra. The security system processed his request for entrance and sounded with a buzz of rejection. He tried again and had the same result. The LED lights moving in a repeating pattern across its screen read, "Access Denied."

"That's strange," he mumbled. "Maybe Trish knows what's going on."

He walked down the hall to his office. The nameplate on the door had been pulled. Checking the door, he found it unlocked. To his amazement, the office had been cleared of all his personal belongings. The bookshelves were empty, except for dust, which had settled behind what was once there. His desk was cleared, except for the computer and a few Post It notes slapped to the side of the monitor. The three-drawer filing cabinet was empty and sounded of cheap tin as he opened and closed each drawer. Even the few personal pictures and calendar that once hung on the walls were missing. He stood in the middle of the floor dumbfounded.

"Hi there!" Trish said from the doorway. "How was your trip?"

"Trish. What the hell's going on?"

"You've been promoted," she replied with a delightful smile.

"Promoted? You're kidding."

"Would I kid you about something like that? The maintenance crew boxed your stuff up over the weekend and took it to your new office in Building A."

"And what about you?" he asked.

"Sorry, can't go with you. It's my understanding you won't need a secretary where you're going. Pity isn't it?"

"Yeah," he mumbled, still clueless.

"Come now, it's no big deal. I'll walk you on over there—card please," she said, holding out her hand and blocking the door. He handed her his security card that he'd been gripping tenaciously.

They exited Building D and walked down a long sidewalk past a glassy pond with ducks wading in the water in the shadow of a cluster of pampas grass, then onto the main sidewalk leading up to Trojan Security headquarters. The front lobby opened into a waiting area with a chest-high counter wrapped in strips of walnut wood and capped with pink and white marble. Behind the counter sat the receptionist.

"Rick Forstein," he said to the receptionist.

"Hold please," she said to the caller on the line, then addressed Rick directly. "Mr. Forstein, we've been expecting you." Pressing a button somewhere on the control panel to her switchboard, she spoke to a phantom voice on the other end. "Mrs. Tallon, Betsy. Mr. Forstein's here…yes ma'am, I'll send him right up."

"This is where I leave you," Trish said. "You won't forget about me will you?"

"If I ever get the chance to escape you'll be the first person I come to see."

"Mr. Forstein," the receptionist interrupted, "take the elevator up to the third floor. When you get there you'll find an empty room and a set of double glass doors. Go though the doors and Mrs. Talon will let you in."

Rick did as instructed. He entered the first set of doors and into the security zone, but another door, which seemed impenetrable without its handle, stopped him from proceeding. "Hello, Mr. Forstein," came the amplified voice of a woman.

Rick looked up into the corner and into the camera hanging next to the speaker. "Hi," he said in a serious tone.

From behind the thick door came two loud clicks and the door swung slowly open.

"Sorry about the inconvenience," the woman said from behind a desk against the far wall. "I'm Mrs. Tallon," she said, rising.

A quick glance around revealed nothing. Her desk was the only piece of furniture in the room. To the right and left of her desk opened two parallel corridors. He approached her and took her hand.

"Nice to meet you," he said. She looked to be in her fifties and oriental.

"I'm sorry I don't have a chair for you to sit on, but this will only take a minute."

She sat back down, turned her chair to the right, bent over slightly and spun the dial of a safe. Moments later, a small steel door opened. Extending a steel drawer, she pulled out a white, five by seven envelope. After slicing open the flap of the envelope, she pulled out a familiar looking security card. From the safe drawer she also pulled out a clipboard and after laying the card onto the board she handed it to Rick face up. "You'll need this to get into your office. Please read and sign this form." When he'd finished, he handed the clipboard back to her and she placed it back in the safe.

"Now, if you'll step this way." She stood up and he followed her to the door he'd walked in a few moments earlier. She pressed a red button on the wall and the door clicked open. "When you leave this area this button will open the door."

"I see." He followed her through the door and it shut tight behind them.

"You probably noticed this security system when you came in. To get through these doors you must first enter your own five-digit number then have your handprint read. Now, please place your hand flat on the glass." He laid his hand across the glass and she entered a series of numbers. A flash of light like the strobe of a camera lit up his hand. "I've instructed the computer to read your hand print. Now if you would, enter five numbers of your choosing then press the enter key." She turned so that her back was facing the system. He thought for a moment then entered five numbers. "This goes without saying, but please remember your numbers," she said.

"Understood." The door swung back open and she walked him to the corridor on the right and stopped. "It was nice meeting you, Mr. Forstein."

"Please. Call me Rick."

"As you wish Mr. Forstein," she said with a smile. "Your office is down this hallway, fourth door on the right. The security system at your door works just like those in building D. On your desk you'll find an envelope with information pertaining to you. It should answer any further questions you may have."

He discovered his new office to be much larger than the cubicle he'd come from. The desk was on the right. The name Rick Forstein, etched in white on a simulated wood plaque sitting on his desk, faced two formal visitor chairs. Behind the desk along the right wall was a series of empty bookshelves. In the far left hand corner of the room were two sets of filing cabinets. The wall on the left hand side of the room was clear, but at the end of the office was a window overlooking undeveloped wooded hills. Underneath the window sat a plush couch and a coffee table. On the table were three boxes full of his personal belongings. There were even a few generic oil paintings hanging in the open spaces on the walls. As he'd been informed, he found the envelope on his desk and as he fumbled to open it there was a knock at the door.

"Come in!" he yelled. In stepped Mitch Pruitt.

"Hey Rick. How ya doing?" Pruitt asked in his jovial manner, extending his hand.

"Great! I guess. Did you have anything to do with this?" Rick asked taking his hand.

"Everything! What do you think?"

"Are you kidding? This is heaven, but I'm more concerned with whether I'll like the new job."

"It's not a job. It's a position. You're moving up. There will be a lot more expected of you. You're no longer just a whiz in the design lab, you've got executive privileges."

"Why me?"

"Simple, you're the most qualified and the most gifted. I've been watching you and so have the others. You have energy and drive—but even more so—you've got the integrity required for the position."

Rick was flattered and intrigued. "What's it all about?"

"We're forming a new team for a special project and I want you to be a part of it. But if you don't want the position I think I can still get over to finance and have them reduce your next payroll check…."

"Wait just a minute. How much are we talking about?"

"Finance has authorized $89,000, plus perks."

"Perks?"

"Sure. Travel expenses, better stock options, access to the health club, this nice office—"

"And my team?"

"Nothing will change there. Your old department will remain intact and proceed as usual. I'm going to bump Chris up to fill your empty slot."

"He's the best choice," Rick replied. He thought of his friends for a moment, then back to the details of his new position.

"Who will I be working with?"

"Don't worry about that just yet. You'll get filled in at the briefing. Did you have a chance to look over the material?" Pruitt asked, pointing to the envelope.

"No. I was just—"

"Minor stuff," Pruitt said. "You know how to get in and out of the building right?"

"Yeah."

"Look, I've got to run. I'll let you get settled in. We've got a meeting scheduled for 10:00 a.m. in the conference room. That's in the other hallway. Watson's office takes up the whole east end of this floor, so you can only get there by going around Mrs. Tallon's desk."

Pruitt walked back to the door, but spun around as he reached it. "By the way, Mr. Watson will be there."

Rick waited a few minutes until Pruitt had cleared the hallway then reached for the phone. The phone rang at the other end once, then twice. By the third ring, he was beginning to wonder. On the fifth ring the answering machine clicked on. "Crap!" he complained. He listened to his own polished recording. "Hello. You've reached the Forstein's residence. We're unable to…" he smiled in frustration. Such good news was better shared in person anyway and with a bottle of good champagne.

At precisely 9:55 he left his office and headed towards the conference room. "Is it always this quiet around here?" he asked Mrs. Tallon as he passed by.

"Always."

The conference room was near the end of the hall on the left. The door was unlocked and the room, full of strangers. They eyed him with a slight expression of acknowledgment as he took a seat and said, "good morning." The two women on the other side of the table returned his gesture. The brunette smiled back at him, pushing a strand of curls away from her face that had fallen over her eyes. The woman with the light complexion cracked a shy smile. To her left sat a younger looking man in his thirties. He carried a foreign manner and said nothing. Next to Rick was an older gentleman, perhaps in his late forties. A thick mane of dusty, white hair curled over his ears. His skin was sun-stricken and rough. He reached over and shook Rick's hand. Like birds on a wire, each member of the team had taken every other seat at the table, establishing their own comfort zones. Rick wondered if they knew as much about the project as he didn't know. At that moment another door to the room opened and in walked Pruitt followed by Mr. Frederick Watson.

"Good morning ladies and gentlemen," Watson said authoritatively.

Rick had never met the man personally and was instantly impressed with his commanding disposition. Pruitt took a seat next to Rick as Watson moved to the head of the table and took off his coat, taking a moment to roll his shirt sleeves up as though he were ready to get down to work. When he'd finished, he looked at the group respectfully.

"My father began this company over twenty years ago and through his leadership has made Trojan Security the leading producer of security system software. I've been with the company since graduating from Texas A&M. I started as a programmer, later working my way up through the executive side of the house. When my father retired seven years ago, I was given the unique opportunity to keep his dream alive. Since that time, we've experienced a remarkable margin of growth even by industry standards. Yet, in all we've accomplished, in all the projects we've taken on, none of them are as important as the project we begin today."

"Each one of you has been hand-picked and bring to the table a unique combination of skills. I know you don't know each other, but you must learn to work with one other." He moved to the edge of the table, placed his palms flat on the surface and leaned over. Before he spoke again, he looked at each member of the team with a significant twinkle in his eye. "I ask just one thing from you, that you do not underestimate the significance of this project." After he was sure his comment had sunk in, he stood up and continued.

"If there was ever a need for security, that time is now. The implications of this project have the potential to cause literally, global panic. If the technology we're going to create were to fall into the wrong hands, it could threaten the political stability of our world. Each one of you has signed on with this company with the understanding that the work you perform here is highly classified. Due to the sensitive nature of this project let me forewarn you, any information regarding the creation and implementation of this project shall not be passed onto anyone outside of this room. You will not discuss it with any other Trojan Security employee, with any friend or relative, not even with your spouse. This is for their own safety as well as yours." He looked around the room at each participant, studying their faces for any signs of misunderstandings. "Ladies and gentlemen, are we clear on this issue?" To that everyone nodded.

"Folks," his tone was now endearing, "you're all familiar with the Internet. You know that despite the most advanced security measures which have been constructed to safeguard it, it's still a relatively unsecured method of distributing information. Even today, classified military and governmental files, as well as business related information, can still be hacked into by anyone with a moderate degree of computer sense. You know as well, there are perhaps a hundred other ways the integrity of the Internet can be breached. To this end, we at Trojan Security have designed a host of security programs to combat these possibilities. What we begin today will not deviate from what we've always done here, however, you will have to stretch your imaginations just a bit to fully grasp the importance of this project.

What we're going to do is design two programs. I make that clear from the start. The first program we're going to design is to simply verify the fact that such a program can be built, because if it can be built, then other people can build it, and that would be a frightening possibility. Like I said, this is really nothing new. We're in the computer security business. Every program we build is to safeguard information from known and unknown threats, and we build programs sometimes years in advance of the threat. Essentially, what we are going to do is build a virus, a virus so potentially threatening, as to necessitate the need for a security program with the capabilities to stop it. Once we know such a virus can be built, then our next goal will be to design the actual security program, which we will then be able to market with the rest of our programs and services."

As Mr. Watson spoke, his hands flipped about in front of him with subtle gestures on relative points. Not one person in the room was without his eye contact for more than thirty seconds. "Does anyone have any questions at this point?" None were solicited. "Good, because once you get into the meat of this project, some of you may have doubts. Some of you may question the program's legitimacy. And I just want to make it clear from the start about why we do things here at Trojan Security. Should you have any doubts about the virus, please remember that the ultimate goal is to build the security program to stop it."

Again, no questions or comments were offered.

"I'm sure all of you are also familiar with a phenomenon known as subliminal influences?" He posed it as a question and looked around the room for affirmation.

"Sure. Subliminal influences are bits of information that typically enter the subconscious mind without any other sensory perception," said the brunette.

To which Pruitt added, "well actually, they can be seen, or heard, and even felt, but any physical effect they have on the body is so minimal that the mind perceives the influence on a subconscious level."

"Exactly," the brunette said. "I wouldn't say that the influences are hypnotic, but the mind perceives the influence as an original thought. Once those thoughts are in the mind, then the mind acts upon them."

Watson looked thrilled to see some discussion and continued. "Now influencing individuals through subliminal messaging has been around for some time. Advertising agencies have been guilty of deceiving the public by this method of marketing. Film companies have also received careful scrutiny, since it is so easy for them to edit pictures or messages into the filmstrip. The point I'm leading to is this, if it hasn't been done on the Internet, than it's only a matter of time before it is used. If we can find out how it might be done, then we can create a marketable security program that will safeguard against this kind of thing happening. Such a program would be extremely lucrative—Pruitt!"

Pruitt stepped out of his chair as Watson took a seat.

"As Mr. Watson has mentioned, each one of you is a specialist in a particular area. Each one of these areas is important to the dynamic of this group and we believe, essential to the building of this program. Let me take a few moments to introduce you to one another."

"To my right, is Rick Forstein. Rick has been with us for a little over three years. He's extremely knowledgeable in the area of programming. If there's a new product on the market or a new piece of equipment or software, he's not only heard of it, but he can tell you everything about it. In my estimation he's got a complete grasp of what is or isn't possible. If it's not possible, then he'll find a way to make it possible. Isn't that right Rick?"

"I do my best," he said modestly.

"The gentleman to the right of Rick is Dr. Peter Loran. Dr. Loran previously worked as a neurosurgeon for many years. He's now actively involved in research and the writing of various books all centered on the complexities and capabilities of the human mind. More recently though, he has done extensive studies in an attempt to discover the human mind's relationship to this technology we call the Internet. I know absolutely nothing about it, but it's my understanding Dr. Loran has opened up an entirely new area of research, something that has to do with the relationship between neuro-space and cyberspace. But I'll leave it up to him to fill you in on all of the details."

"Next to Mr. Watson is Joseph Stautzen. Mr. Stautzen is on loan to us from the International Christian Coalition based in Munich, Germany. As you may or may not know, or whether you would like to believe it or not, the power of belief has a profound effect on the receptivity of the mind to accept information. Mr. Stautzen will be working with us to help us integrate this human dynamic into the program."

"We thought it appropriate to involve the expertise of the female gender into this scenario, so we hired the first two women we could find." Pruitt said, chuckling at his own humor.

The two ladies smiled nervously together. "Actually, that's not entirely true. "Davia Reese," he continued by motioning to the woman to his immediate right, "is a linguist. She's holds a Ph.D. in linguistics and has spent the majority of her life working freelance for businesses and governments translating their material into various languages. It may come as a surprise to some of you, but English isn't the only language in the world. Any program we create will also need to be translated into some of the world's most influential languages. It will be Davia's job to take our completed project and translate it into those various languages. Next to Davia, is Jeanette Thompson. Call her Jean. She's a graduate of the National Defense University in Washington. The NDU is the military's answer to training and equipping individuals to help America win the information war. She's our one stop source when it comes to understanding the intricate details of how the Internet works. You don't need to salute her, even though she's a retired Air Force Colonel."

Rick glanced over the table at Jean. If she was a retired Colonel, then she must be near forty. She didn't look a day over thirty-five. "She must be pretty damn smart to be here," he thought. "Definitely beautiful."

"As for myself, my name is Mitch Pruitt, I've been with the company eleven years. For the most part, you will answer to me and there should be no reason for you whatsoever to contact Mr. Watson. I'm sure you can appreciate he's a busy man. I will be keeping him abreast of your progress. If I'm not around, then Rick will be the lead man." As Pruitt concluded, Mr. Watson rose to add a few words.

"I think you can ascertain by the makeup of this group that we're very serious in our objective of creating this software. I want to personally thank each one of you for your participation and the sacrifices you've made to be here. I look forward to hearing of your progress. Let me also state, we have rather unlimited resources for this project, so if you need anything specific please let Pruitt know and he'll see you get it." After concluding, he walked back through the door he came in.

"I think we should all get to know each other before we begin. I've arranged for us to have lunch at the Pavilion in the Arboretum. Shall we," Pruitt said, gesturing towards the door.

CHAPTER 8

▼

In a private room of the Pavilion in the Arboretum a table awaited the Trojan Security team. Apparently, the arrangements hadn't been done according to Pruitt's specifications. While the others sat down, he discussed the discrepancies with the headwaiter. A pretty Mexican waitress was quickly summoned carrying baskets of hot tortilla chips, followed by another who poured iced tea. Minutes later the salads arrived. The team had driven to the restaurant in one of the company's green vans. The fifteen-minute drive had been silent. Perhaps by nature of their individual backgrounds, each member of the team had decided to keep their thoughts within themselves. But during the salad course, the oppressive silence of the group showed signs of relenting.

"Mitch said, you're involved with the study of neuro-space and cyberspace. Cyberspace I know, but I'm not familiar with neuro-space." Rick said to Dr. Loran.

"Please call me Peter." He pushed his salad bowl to the side and continued. "Cyberspace as you know, is a computer term that constitutes the invisible dynamics of the Internet. In the Internet, technology, knowledge, ideas, philosophies, etcetera, all mingle together into one. These dynamics are floating around in technical space, so to speak. Through a network of telephone lines that information becomes accessible to us with a few keystrokes on the computer. Neuro-space on the other hand, is its organic equivalent. Within our minds we possess the same range of ideas and knowledge, but on a more limited scale. Our brains, through what are called neurotransmitters, pull that information back out into logical thought."

"How are the two similar?"

"The connection between the two has to do with what's called ascendancy. All human beings have the desire to rise above the physical properties of their lives and to become—if I might use the term—to become like gods. In the past, we've sought to accomplish this through religion, philosophy, knowledge and even drugs. We've looked within our own minds to acquire this ascendancy. Today, however, we have the Internet, which is really an extension of the human mind, though on a grandeur scale, because the Internet collectively possesses all we know about life. Which is precisely why it's such a fascination. Millions of people log onto it every day looking for fulfillment. Think about it, you're sitting on a park bench with your laptop one minute and a few moments later you're in Belize looking over the shoulder of an anthropologist brushing the dust off a caveman's femur. Or you've got a few extra minutes in your office with your computer and you take off to a university library and pull a book on the secrets of ancient Rome. It's incredible! Everything you always wanted to know about life is just a few key strokes away!"

"With knowledge like that available who needs a god?" Rick added.

"Precisely, the Internet has become a god."

"Forgive me for interrupting, but I think we still need God." Stautzen said from across the table.

Rick felt a little offended by the intrusion. He flipped his fork over and thought of a response. Dr. Loran beat him to it. "I can't speak for Rick, but I believe in a god. What we need to remember is that all we know about God comes through information."

"Information?" Stautzen asked, tweaking his head to the side.

"Sure, information in the form of stories, or if you prefer, the ideas of religious people through the ages that have been passed on to us.

Prior to the computer age, all that information was written in books, but now we can call up the same information on the Internet. Everyday, more people add to that information base by exchanging their own thoughts about what god is. The Internet isn't a substitute; it's a storehouse of information. Wouldn't you agree Rick?"

Stautzen didn't give him the opportunity. "You're forgetting about the spiritual dynamics of life, that God speaks to everyone individually."

"I haven't forgot about anything. I'm saying people use the Internet like a cosmic fortuneteller's ball. They look into it for many different reasons, even for spiritual guidance. Perhaps you misunderstood. What you're hinting at is precisely what I'm trying to say. The Internet is a substitute for God for some people. Not in the sense they worship it, but in the sense it provides them with the information which enables them to make logical decisions about things even as deep as their belief in God."

Pruitt felt compelled to speak. "Personally, I think religion is one of the strongest motivational factors known to man. It supersedes any philosophy or ideology. Considering the program we need to build, it might be a good idea to incorporate some religious dynamics into it. I know Stautzen agrees with me, but do you think that's possible Dr. Loran?"

"Sure it's possible. I'd prefer to call it a belief factor though, which is to say, people are more drawn to their inner beliefs than to mere information. Don't quite know how it'd fit into the program, but if our goal is to build a program that will appeal to the greatest amount of people, then that would be a good starting place."

"Well, I think we can table this discussion for a later time. Would you excuse me for a moment?" Pruitt asked, rising out of his chair.

He walked through the swinging double doors of the room and addressed the attendant in the hallway. Within moments, a handful of waitresses entered carrying silver pans filled with a Mexican feast; beef and chicken enchiladas wrapped in red flour tortillas, Spanish rice, a tray of crispy beef tacos, another tray of beans seasoned with chunks of bacon, and bowls full of guacamole sauce, sour cream and the restaurant's special salsa. Moments after the buffet had been set, the main entrée arrived on a charcoal sheet of cast iron, upon which sat a heaping pile of marinated beef and chicken fajitas grilled with onions and green peppers. The aroma in the clouds billowing above it saturated the entire room. "Ladies and gentlemen, lunch is served," Pruitt said.

Halfway though lunch, Pruitt thought it time they got to know one another a little better. "Why don't you tell us about yourself Jean," he asked cordially.

She took a moment to finish swallowing and took a sip from her sweetened ice-tea. "Well, I just recently retired out of the Air Force after twenty-one years. I was anxious to get into the private sector."

"And you've spent some time at the National Defense University?" Pruitt pressed.

"I went there for a six month training course in 1999, was stationed in a few other locations after I'd finished my training, but later came back to the NDU to teach."

"I suppose most of what you know is classified?" Rick asked.

"Most of it, but not all."

"What other kind of work did you do in the service?" Dr. Loran asked.

"Actually, I wouldn't call it work. Much of what I've been doing has been in the area of research or consulting. When I first joined the service, I worked with the Advanced Research Projects Agency. The Internet as you know, began with the military back in the sixties under the ARPA. Later, I worked mostly as a civilian with National Science Foundation."

"Who are they?" Davia asked.

Rick answered for Jean. "The NSF represents a host of universities and educational institutions. Back in the seventies and eighties they started using the Internet established by the military to share information between their institutions."

"I'm impressed," Jean replied, glancing over at Rick and continued. "By the nineties, the Internet became the playing ground for anybody with a computer and a phone line. For the military, it had become a security nightmare. For one thing, the military had relied on the Internet to conduct its own business. The problem with this was, not only was the Internet an unsecured environment, but it relied on the civilian world for its support and maintenance. Which meant of course, any classified information transferred through its lines could fall into the wrong hands. But this was also a plus, since other countries and terrorists began using the Internet. In short, nothing was secure. Our military could also use the Internet to obtain information, as well as sabotage the military communications of other hostile governments. My work with the National Defense University in Washington centered around creating a system that would make our military less vulnerable to attack. We also spent a great deal of time building programs that would destroy the communication networks of our enemies."

"Did you succeed?" asked Rick.

Jean thought for a moment before answering. "It's an ongoing project," she answered appropriately.

"You mean you can't say," Pruitt said.

"I can't say at this moment, but three years from now, you'll be able to read about it in the local library."

Her response brought a smile to everyone.

"I will add this to my defense. I stay one step ahead of the competition. Only a handful of individuals in the world know what I know. Even fewer, have the connections or the capacity to stay at the cutting edge. When out in front I stay in front."

Rick was impressed with her assertiveness. It was an attraction that would be impossible for him to resist. He looked beyond her formidable nose, the only feature of her appearance that seemed placed, and into her eyes, which seemed to dance in thought as she spoke.

"Which is why you're here," Pruitt said, recapping her comments He was pleased the luncheon was turning out the way he'd planned.

What Pruitt may have lacked in intellectual superiority, he made up for in his talents as a facilitator. Once assigned to a project, he had the inert ability to see to its completion. Watson understood the talents of Pruitt as well. The two shared an unspoken loyalty to one another. The present project was unlike any other they'd ever attempted to build. They both understood that if Trojan Security didn't create the program someone else would. With that belief, Pruitt had correctly ascertained what the dynamics of such a program would require. If one could create such a weapon, it would not only require sophisticated technological expertise, but it would also utilize the most refined forms of psychological manipulation. It must also be able to reach inside the minds of perfectly rational human beings and have the ability to completely alter their belief systems. Pruitt was excited about the program from the start and had been chiefly responsible for pulling the team together. It was his baby.

Joseph Stautzen fully understood his role in the program as well, because as far as he was concerned, it was *his* baby. It agitated him that such a noble work was being carried out through the agency of a business corporation. Over the years he'd developed an acute enmity towards all corporate identities. What he despised most of all, was that the American ideal of prosperity and success had been embraced around the world. The almighty dollar had created an economic jungle, embodied in neon signs reaching into the most remote portions of the globe. But Stautzen was little more than a businessman impersonating a monk. A true Christian socialist, he worked towards the establishment of the kingdom of God on earth, looking forward to a time when the present way of life would be destroyed and replaced by a utopian existence in which God would make every man and woman equal, but not entirely equal, for those who had worked hardest to establish that kingdom, would be more adequately rewarded for their efforts. Furthermore, Stautzen was a human parasite, for he idolized Reverend Eisner with disturbing adoration. To him the reverend was John the Baptist reincarnated, if not in body than in message. In Stautzen's eyes, the reverend was the last hope for man and his proximity to the reverend, as a position of power, would surely land him a good seat in the kingdom to come.

"What about you Davia?" Pruitt asked, who'd said little since they left the office.

She was slow to respond, looking around the room as though she were a specimen in a laboratory. Her face was the color of milk. As a child growing up, her hair had once been bleached white, but now, after countless hours in the darkness of study it had reverted back to its original straw color. Her features were fine, delicate and elongated, as though they'd been outlined with an ink pen.

"My expertise is in languages," she managed to say.

The rest of the group waited for more details. Not one to wait, Pruitt coaxed her into saying a little more. "How many languages do you speak?"

"Fluently?"

He nodded.

"Seven. I can translate another five or so."

"Davia is quite modest as you can see. Isn't it true, you can translate just about anything you set your mind to?"

"If I have the resources…probably," she replied, just above a whisper.

Pruitt decided not to press her any further and stood up with his cell phone in hand. "Folks, I need to step out and make a couple of phone calls, then I think we should be heading back to the office. There's still some background information I need to fill you in on before we get started. If you would do me the favor and finish up, and I'll meet you outside in the van in ten minutes."

CHAPTER 9

▼

Eva didn't have a clue what to look for when she walked through the doors of the university library, except the information provided to her on the pamphlet given to her by Mr. Schwarz. She didn't expect to find any information on the CRM, so she made a mental note to contact her source at the *polizei's* office about them later. The main thrust of the pamphlet appeared to be a promotion for the International Christian Coalition. It offered some generalities along with two names, the Reverend Jeremiah Eisner and Joseph Stautzen. If the ICC was as large and influential as Mr. Schwarz suggested, then the library should have something on them. After only a few minutes of looking, she found more than she'd expected. Looking up the name of the ICC and its founder Jeremiah Eisner, she discovered four book references and a host of newspaper and magazine articles concerning their activities. In the *Guide To Germany's Religions* book, the ICC was listed as a nondenominational evangelical church with a countrywide membership of over 1.5 million and an international membership of 4.6 million. *The Financial Synopsis Reference Of Commercial and Private Institutions,* listed the ICC's annual budget to be approximately sixty-seven million *marks*. There was even a reference to the ICC in the *Media Manual,* which lists the various television and cable production studios. The manual listed the ICC as the forth largest Christian broadcasting Network in the world, and also, that their shows were viewed by approximately thirty-two million viewers a week. Her most productive reference was the discovery of Reverend Eisner's book entitled, *Our Global Community*. She checked it out and slipped it into her bag. To save time she discretely made photocopies of nine magazine articles on the ICC to read later.

On her way back to the CRM's apartment, she stopped at a corner deli and picked up a turkey sandwich, a Coke and a half-liter tub of Maya peach yogurt. Since the day had nearly ended, *Hugelstrasse* was lined with cars and she had to park along a side street. She walked up the sidewalk and spotted Ruben's white Fiat where she'd left him earlier in the day, some seventy-five meters from the apartment. "*Guten abend!*" she yelled, sticking her head in his window.

"*Scheisse* Eva!" he fired back.

She went around to the passenger door and hopped in.

"Brought you something." She tossed the bag in his lap and set the Coke on the dash.

"What *de* hell did you do *dat* for?" he asked, irritated.

"What? Bring you dinner."

"No. Scare the shit out of me."

"Thought you could use some excitement."

"I told you *dis* was a waste of time."

"Got any pictures?"

"Sure, I got pictures, but of what? I've seen four people come and go all day. One was of a *moder* taking her little girl on a walk. The other person was an old lady picking roses from *de* bush out front."

"That's three. The one picking flowers was probably the landlord. What about the other? Eva asked.

"Great shot of *de* back of some guy's head as he went inside."

"Could be one from the CRM."

"Yeah, and it could be *de* husband from one of *de* other five apartments in *de* building coming home from work." He cocked his head towards her. "And what'd you find out?"

"Found out I got a lot of research to do. Seems Reverend Eisner of the ICC is a busy man. He's a preacher, philanthropist, directs a number of different ministries, friend to all kinds of important people. He's also written a bestseller."

"Well just don't get fanatical on me," he said, eyes fixed on the front door of the apartment and juggling an old Pentax in his lap.

"You know me better than that. I'm too logical and cautious. Besides, I wouldn't let anything near me that might cause me to loss my head."

"Not like *de* men in your life," he teased.

She went silent and looked up at the apartment on the third floor with the curtains drawn.

"I suppose *dis* means I'm going to be here for a while," he said, pointing to the bag of food.

"Look. I know this seems like a waste of time, but it's all we can do at the moment. Why don't you stay here until 7:00 or so? It will be too dark to shoot after that."

"You know we really could use more help. I could sit here for weeks and not catch *anyting*. Did you get a hold of Alfred?"

"Not yet. I'll talk with him tonight."

"Even if I do manage to get some pictures of *de* occupants, we still won't know what *deir* up to until we get inside."

"I know."

Ruben poised the camera across his thigh and reached for the bag. "At least you got me some food, *tanks*."

"I'm going to head back to the office and see what Shelly's found out. By the way, I need you here in the morning at 5:30."

"Why so early?"

"Because I know you can't stay here around the clock. Morning and evening are the best times."

"Now you tell me. I've been sitting here in *de* sun all day."

"And I do appreciate it." She stepped out of the door and was nearly hit by a passing car. It's horn faded in the distance. She poked her head back in the window.

"You should be more careful," he said grinning.

"I'll bring you breakfast in the morning."

"Sure you will. Now get *de* hell out of here before you give me away."

Back at the office, Eva laid her briefcase across her desk and flopped down. "Shell—" She started in, but Shelly was already on the way to her desk with a file in hand. She laid it on Eva's briefcase.

"This is all I could come up with so far."

Eva glanced down and read the first name. Tasha Matyastick. "Czechoslovakian?" she asked.

"*Ja.*"

"Curious, don't you think?" Shelly asked.

Eva glimpsed at the other two names, Neil Usher, Derrick Sachs.

"German," Eva surmised. Below each name were a few additional notes.

"You're amazing Shelly. I'll check the rest of this out at home." She stood up and shoved the file into her briefcase. "If anyone wants me that's where I'll be. I've got some reading to do and Alfred is supposed to drop by my place later this evening."

CHAPTER 10

▼

The sun was licking the tips of the hills of *Bad Soden* as Eva headed out of *Sachsenhausen* and into the heart of Frankfurt. She crossed over the *Rhine* at the *Main-Neckar Brucke* and connected with the autobahn near the main train station, the *Hauptbanhof*. After merging into the far left lane, she picked up speed. At *Griesheim*, she pushed her Opel past 140 km/h. Seven minutes later, she exited at *Main Taunus*, took a left at the light, crossed under the autobahn and headed southeast into *Hochst*.

At the corner of *Bolongarostrasse* and *Konigsteiner*, she inched her car halfway up on the curb and left it running. She jumped out and walked over to the door at the corner of a building with candy and ice cream decals pasted all over it. The door buzzed as she entered, which summoned an elderly lady from the back room.

"*Ah, vie geht's* Eva!" Mrs. Dortmund said from behind the counter.

"Not much. Can you slice me a half kilo of ham please? I'll also need some coffee and a carton of eggs."

"*Ja Gut*. I'll slice the ham and you know where to find the rest." Mrs. Dortmund said, hobbling over to the meat section behind a glass counter.

Eva walked between the clustered isles to the back of the store. She slid open the door of the cooler and pulled out a carton of eggs, then walked over to the next isle for a bag of coffee beans. On her way back to the register she picked up a hazel nut candy bar. Mrs. Dortmund was already waiting by the register with the ham wrapped in butcher's paper.

"Can I get you anything else Eva?"

"*Nein.* That'll do for today."

Mrs. Dortmund cracked a slight smile. Wrinkles around her face responded instantly like ripples in a pond of water. "*Sieben marks und vierzig pfennings,*" she said, holding out her hand. Eva gave her eight marks, but refused the change.

"*Danke!*"

Eva returned the smile. She pulled her hair back over her shoulders then cradled her groceries in her left arm. She nearly lost the eggs at the door.

"*Vorsicht!* Here let me get the door for you. By the way, how's Gunter?" Mrs. Dortmund asked.

Eva stopped at the threshold. What she really wanted to say about Gunter she couldn't. "He's gone. I haven't seen him for weeks."

"I'm sorry. I didn't know."

"Don't be. It's for the better. You have a nice evening Mrs. Dortmund."

At *Konigsteiner street,* Eva passed the revelry of middle-aged men leaning half drunkenly on the counter of an *imbiss* sipping beers and munching on salty *pomfrits* seasoned with powdered red pepper. Moments later, she turned onto *Loreleistrasse* and started looking for a place to park.

She cruised slowly up her street between the two rows of tightly packed cars. At the corner, she took a right and spotted a space just down the road. Forget parallel parking, she darted into the space head-first. Her right front tire jerked as it jumped the curb, steering wheel spinning out of her hands. She got out, checked to see that her tail end was far enough off the street and walked back towards her apartment.

Once inside, she flipped the switch on the wall and the hanging lamp in the far corner above her favorite chair bathed the room in warm yellow glow. Sheeba whimpered and followed her to the dining room table where Eva set her briefcase and groceries down. At her desk, the buzz of the phone rang like a sick bell.

"*Hallo.*"

"What's up, Eva?"

"Alfred. Thanks for calling. Can you drop by this evening?"

"Sure. Any special reason?"

"We'll talk when you get here."

He knew better then to press her.

Forty-five minutes later, he arrived slightly winded from his brisk walk. "I had to park over on *Wausgaustrasse.*"

"Tell me about it." She kissed him on the cheek. "Good to see you again."

Eva and Alfred Burtman were separated by only two years in age. She was the elder of the two. They both shared their mother's nose; elongated and flanging outwards at the tip into a delicate round bump hanging over puffy, round lips. They had their father's eyes, striking in their gravity, and his eyebrows as well. On Alfred, they gave him a trace of intelligence. On Eva, they came off as earthy.

"Are you ever going to call me sometime when you don't need me for anything?" he jested, throwing his dusty cap on the sofa beside him. She sat down in her chair and didn't answer him for a few moments. "How's mom and dad?"

"They are fine. They keep asking me to take over the *backerei* for them and I keep telling them they should sell it and retire. "Father keeps talking about the government. Says they're all a bunch of communist Christians with their head so far up in the clouds they couldn't smell a coming inquisition if it reached over and yanked the Bible out of their hands."

"And mama?"

"She keeps asking about you and wondering when you're going to stop by."

Eva scooted to the edge of her chair and leaned towards her brother. "*Wie gehts,* sister?"

"I don't think it's anything serious, but Mr. Schwarz—"

"If Mr. Schwarz thinks it's serious than it probably is."

"We've been doing a story on an organization called the Christian Reform Movement."

"Never heard of them."

"We discovered today they might be tied in with another organization called the International Christian Coalition. You familiar with them?"

"You're not?"

"When have you ever know me to be religious?"

"You do watch television don't you?"

"I don't have time to watch television," she replied.

"If you watched TV, then you'd know what they're about."

"Why's that?"

"Because there's nothing more precarious than a religious organization with political motives. Or nothing more dangerous than a political power spearheaded by a religious organization. The ICC's either one or the other."

"You sound like dad."

"Do I? I'll take that as a compliment. Why the sudden interest in the ICC?" he asked.

Eva looked perplexed, while Alfred waited for a response. He looked around the room to reacquaint himself with his sister's life. "Eva!" he blurted, after giving her enough time.

"What?"

"The coalition. Why the interest?"

She walked to her briefcase, pulled out the pamphlet and tossed it to him. He took a quick look and handed it back to her. "It's not unusual the CRM would support the ICC. I can think of at least half-dozen organizations that support them. I guess my only concern would be if they were hostile. You know…radical."

"That's what I'm trying to find out."

"You need some help?"

"*Ja.*"

"What do you need?"

"Everything. The movement works out of an apartment on *Hugelstrasse.*" She glanced at her watch. "Ruben's been there all day watching the place."

"And at that rate you'll know something in late November, 2015, right?"

"We need a few bugs and a couple of video cameras inside the apartment." She made the request slowly with obvious hesitancy.

"Eva, how long have we been doing this together?" he asked, sensing her fear.

"About six years."

"Then you know I'm with you don't you? You know I'd do anything for you don't you?"

"*Ja.*"

"And you know I share the same concerns you do right?"

"*Ja.*"

"Then you know not to worry."

"I guess so," she said, the words drifting.

"What's the address and do you have any photos of the occupants?"

She reached for the file in her briefcase and copied the address of the apartment on a slip of paper. "I don't have any photos yet. All I know is there are three people living in the apartment and I don't even know when they come or go."

"I'll need some photos and a few specifics."

"Give me a few days."

The doorbell rang and Sheeba came running out from a room down the hall barking and setting both of them on edge.

"Expecting anyone?" Alfred asked.

"No," she replied and opened the door.

"Hello, Eva!"

"Stace!"

"I was going to call, but thought I'd just pop on over."

She stood in the doorway—startled and surprised—blocking his way.

"I hope you don't mind." Stace said, reading her expression.

"No…come on in."

Stace noticed the young man lounging on the couch. "I didn't realize you had company. I should come back another time." He started towards the door.

She grabbed his wrist and stopped him. "No! Please stay. This is my brother."

"Your brother?"

"Alfred's my name."

"You didn't tell me you had a new friend Eva." Alfred said, glancing at her.

"Actually, we just met. This weekend, at the *freibad* pool."

"It's was nice to meet you," said Alfred. "I was just leaving." He glanced at Eva to reaffirm they had an understanding.

"Tell mom and dad I said hello. I'll stop by as soon as I can."

"Sure, by the way, almost forgot to tell you. Dad's got something he wants to show you."

"What is it?"

"Can't say. It's a surprise."

Eva locked the dead bolt behind Alfred as he left.

"This is unexpected," she said.

"Are you sure I wasn't interrupting something?"

"Not at all. Alfred was on his way out. I'm glad you two had the chance to meet."

"You could be twins you know, except for a few subtle differences."

"I'm glad you noticed."

"How was your day?" he asked.

"Busy. Same-same. I came home a little early and brought work home."

Stace looked as if he were getting ready to apologize again for coming.

"Don't worry. What I need to do can wait. Have you eaten?"

He followed her towards the kitchen, but stopped short at the table. "No, but if you're going to make something, I'll eat."

"Great," she said, with her head in a cabinet.

His eyes flowed over the names of the three members of the CRM and the few notes written about them on the sheet of paper. The hand-written note was clearly visible on the bottom of the page; "Investigate connection between CRM and ICC."

"Heavy assignment?" he asked, holding up Reverend Eisner's book.

Stace's words pinned anxiety in her eyes as she looked towards him. "How stupid of me to leave my work out!" she thought to herself. "But I'll raise more suspicion if race on over there." "Not really. Normal stuff," she said, backing up towards the refrigerator eyeing him suspiciously, noticing he'd cracked the book open. "What was he doing reaching in my briefcase?" She'd have to do something about it. She walked to the table as if she were going for the groceries. "Here, let me get this stuff off the table so we can eat." She took the book out of his hand and tossed it into her briefcase along with the file. She closed the lid and took the case over to her desk.

"You mind putting the eggs into the fridge for me?"

"No problem."

"You know Stace, you never told me where you work," she said, diverting his attention.

"I haven't? Yeah, come to think of it, I guess I didn't. Told you everything else though didn't I?"

She smiled. "Well, almost everything," she replied, bringing plates and silverware to the table.

Stace told her all about his job developing film and his efforts to break into the freelance market. Took him all of three minutes. "I really am a photo nut. I take at least one of my cameras with me everywhere I go."

"Even to the pool?"

"Afraid you got me. That would be a little too obvious wouldn't it?"

She had her head stuck in the refrigerator and didn't see him pull his Nikon from his backpack. He focused on her belt. When she turned and stood, the auto-winder advance two frames.

"Hey! That's not fair." She stuck her bottom lip out in a mock display of annoyance.

"Everywhere, huh? Not the *freibad*, and I bet you don't take it into the shower with you."

"Depends on who's in the shower with me."

His bullet hit its target. The response he was waiting for crossed her face.

"I'm sorry. I didn't mean to say that," he said innocently.

"Ah, but you did."

They snacked on a plateful of sliced ham and potato salad and moved into the living room for coffee.

"Would you like to go out for dinner sometime?" he asked.

"I would like that very much."

"I have to admit, I'm a little embarrassed," he said softly, looking out the living room window.

"Why's that?"

"I don't have a car."

"So what. You and half of Germany don't own a car. We can take mine if we need to—Stace…"

"Yeah?"

"You say you take a lot pictures. Are you any good?"

He laughed full-heartedly, which caught her by surprise. "I got my first good camera, a real 35 mm, when I was twelve. That was fifteen years ago. I own three Nikons and about nine lenses. I also have a large format camera. I'll shoot anything that moves." He thought he'd stop there.

She thought that anybody with that much equipment had to be at least serious. "Can you develop film as well?"

"Anything you want. Why, anything you need done?"

"Maybe."

"I really could use you. Every day and all day." She thought to herself. They were severely understaffed at the paper. They could always use another set of eyes. But there was a reason they were understaffed. First of all, they couldn't afford another person and secondly, they couldn't just hire anybody. Most of what they did was legal, but some of it, positively insidious. She really had no idea who Stace was anyway. She didn't know whether she could trust him and if she could, would she want to put him at risk?

"I don't know Stace, but there are times we could use someone with your skills."

"Shooting or developing?"

"Both."

"I could use the extra work," he replied.

"Tell you what, if something comes up we'll see."

"Fair enough."

She resolved to drop the subject, but was enticed by the possibility of using him for at least some minor projects. And now that he'd come to see her again, she reconsidered how she might have taken him for a coward. She already sensed he was different than the average man. Not everyone has the courage to leap into an entirely different culture than the one they were raised in.

"I'm curious Stace, do you consider yourself to be religious?"

He was astonished by the seriousness of the question. It suddenly occurred to him he had no idea where she stood when it came to religion. He calculated a response. "If I say, I am and she's not, then she'll probably think I'm a fanatic. If I say, I'm not and she is, then she'll think I'm an atheist."

"I consider myself to be a spiritual man," he replied, nice and neutral.

"Is there a difference?"

"Sure there's a difference, to those who know there's a difference."

"Stace! Do I look like a toaster to you?" she asked with agitation.

"Ok, strait-up."

"Straight-up?"

"Means, no bullshit. But first you tell me. Why such a deep question?"

"I've got my reasons."

"Something to do with that book and those organizations you're investigating?"

"Something like that."

"And you promise not to hold it against me?"

"Why would I hold it against you?"

"Because I can't promise you what I think is exactly on center. I've got my own ideas."

"I won't hold it against you. Now spit it out," she said smiling.

"I know one thing...I'll have nothing to do with organized religion."

"Why's that?"

"Because I think being spiritual boils down to how you treat those around you, like your neighbors and your enemies. But it's more than that. It's giving people the freedom to discover God, or to discover what is evil, without a standard set of rules to go by. Religion seems to have it backwards. Religion tells you what it thinks is right and wrong and if you disagree with what it teaches, you're an outcast. Most people spend all their energy trying to fit into a religion, instead of trying to find out what life is all about."

She looked into his eyes trying to decipher his abstractions into images she could understand. He noticed her confusion. "I know... you're not as stupid as a toaster."

He continued, "I just don't like to see God brought down to my level. I'd rather keep Him on a pedestal. I think God is deliberately ambiguous to keep us humble. He wants to keep us guessing, wants us to keep asking questions. Religion spoils the mystery, because it always insists it has the right answers. That would be ok…but instead of leaving it at that, religions often insist on forcing their beliefs on other people."

"Then you don't believe in a personal God?" she questioned.

"You mean like a God that would give me directions if I asked for them? Or, that would help me win a baseball game if I prayed the right prayer?"

"Well, sort of."

"Absolutely not!"

"Why?"

"Because there's not one shred of evidence in my life to support the fact that God is walking around behind me with His hands on my shoulders and when I step in the wrong direction He immediately shoves me in the right direction. I've made too many mistakes in life to believe that."

"Maybe you were not listening."

"Do you believe He tells you what to do?" Stace asked.

She thought hard, "No. I guess I was just trying to understand what I believe. Maybe we're just not close enough to hear Him."

"So you don't hear Him, but your neighbor does. Your brother Alfred may hear Him, but your mother may not." Stace was fishing for examples. "Like I said, I believe God is above that kind of discrimination. Either He's the same with everyone and consistent, or He's nothing more than our imagination. Let's say, He does listen only to those that are good, then you have to define what is good. I've known many individuals whom I considered to be good, but life still came along and kicked them in the ass just like everyone else. And those were the ones that were trying. Then there are those that don't even try and all the good things in life just get handed to them. I tell you, there's just too many inconsistencies."

"But what if you ask for help?"

"You mean praying?"

"*Ja.*"

"From the little I know about religion and the Bible, I've yet to see the connection. The Bible, for example, is full of promises Christians can expect to receive as rewards for behavior, like special healing powers, or not having to worry about food, but the promises in the Bible don't pan out in reality. On the contrary, it's contradictory. On the one hand, it says you can pray for help, but on the other hand, it says bad things will happen to good people. A promise is a promise, and if the Bible talks about Christians being able to have extraordinary power, then the rest of the world should be able to see that evidence."

"I've never thought of it that way."

"I guess if I saw, one indisputable miracle, I might be more quick to believe. But even when I witness something that could be a miracle, I always find circumstantial evidence that could disprove it."

"Some people believe in miracles," she said.

"I know. Funny how people think that if you question something about God, you're automatically an atheist."

"I didn't say that you were—"

"I know you didn't, I just didn't want you to think, since I haven't quite figured out God, that I'm not entirely immoral," he replied.

Eva found his depth of thought refreshing. "All right, so what's it like to be spiritual?" Her question was not an attempt to just keep the conversation going. Something was stirring within her, which she didn't quite understand and Stace had a way of prodding her soul. "You really want to know what I think?"

"Sure. Why?"

"I find it a little unusual."

"Because it's not what you expected to be talking about?"

"It's just that few people are interested in going into some depth on the subject."

"Let's just say, I'm curious. So, how is being spiritual different from being religious?"

"To be spiritual is to first recognize that God is simply, beyond explanation. To me, He's beyond definition. We might be able to put a few pieces of His puzzle together, but I think we have to realize, what we know about Him is only a fraction of what He really is—if He is."

"Seems kind of hopeless the way you put it. Why even try to know Him?"

"On the contrary, there's a great deal of expectation in granting Him that respect and power. Gives you a certain depth of humility, because once you realize He's beyond explanation, you're not as quick to make rules to keep you on the strait and narrow."

Eva looked a little perplexed.

"Most people want to be *like* God rather than learn about Him."

She appeared to Stace even more confused.

"All I'm saying is this. Many religious people seem more interested in following steps, which they think will help them attain some like-ness to God. So they invent rules and ways of determining who God is. What happens next is, they try and mimic in their own lives, who they think God is. And when they think they've got it right, they assume this empowers them to judge the actions of others. That produces dangerous consequences."

"Like wars," she responded.

"It often ends there, but intolerance is where it all starts…. Look if a person chooses to believe in God, they first have to recognize any information about God comes at best, by secondhand knowledge. In other words, religions are formed and perpetuated by people sharing their ideas about God—nothing more."

"Doesn't seem to be much order in that way of thinking."

"You mean control, because there's a difference between order and control. Humans need a certain amount of order in their lives. That's a given. But most people mistake order for control. When it comes to religion, the rule should be to question everything, because when people don't question what they believe, they end up doing just about anything their religion tells them to do."

"But isn't that why people look for God? Because they want order in their lives?"

"I think most people look for God for two reasons, to get them somewhere in this life and to get them some place in the afterlife."

"Somewhere?"

"I'm talking about the idea that if you do what is right in this world, then success will come naturally. Biggest farce I ever heard of!"

"But, even I expect some good to come of my work, that I'll make a difference in this world," she said.

"The difference is you're hopeful, not expectant. Most of today's religions teach that your actions cause God to favor you more, which will in turn, bring you a reward either now or in the future."

"The afterlife?"

"Sure, the big payoff—heaven."

"And is there something wrong with that?"

"Other than the fact, no one has been to heaven and back and can explain it?"

"*Ja.*"

"Let me ask you this. Would you question someone giving you a million dollars if you knew they wanted something from you in return?"

"Sure."

"Then does it make sense that God would create a world inhabited by people, where He has to promise people heaven to win their allegiance?"

"Well—"

"Sound a little weak to you?"

"Actually, it sounds rather nice to me."

"Of course it sounds nice! I'd like to go to heaven myself, but the whole concept of good people go to heaven seems juvenile. The same goes with the idea of hell. Let's say, for example, you're the most evil person on earth and someone just killed your parents. You might be mad enough to kill them for what they did right?"

"That goes without saying, I'd want some kind of revenge."

"Granted, but how far would you take that revenge? Would you be willing to not only kill that person, but watch that person burn forever and ever?"

"Forever?"

"Right, like the Bible says, 'forever.'"

"No. At worst, I'd want to see the person dead."

"Now, take God, for example, and use the same illustration. This person, who has just killed your parents, is God's own creation—His own flesh and blood. Can you imagine God wanting to watch this person burn forever?"

"Seems a bit unbelievable when you put it that way, Stace."

"Because it makes no sense Eva. If we can't stand the thought of seeing a stranger burn forever—and we're human—how can it make any sense that God would want to see one of his own children burn forever? When we get to heaven, will we somehow have the capacity to be more cruel than we are now?"

Eva was thinking.

"Which brings me back to being spiritual. There are a lot of things being said today and being taught by so-called, 'men of God.' Most of what they are saying is related to rules created to affect outward religious behavior and appearances, which may or may not have anything to do with God."

"Makes you wonder what people religious leaders are teaching people," she said.

"Blind guides," he said. "But the scary part is, perfectly rational people can be lead to do just about anything, if they believe what they are doing is sanctioned by God."

Eva had seen enough of the world to know people could be astonishing cruel."

Stace continued, "Being spiritual, on the other hand, is different. It's questioning everything and yet, being open to everything. It's also recognizing what you learn today may change tomorrow. It allows you to be tolerant of yourself and other people's ideas."

"But how do you know where you stand?"

"I'll tell you where you stand. You're alive, and you have the wonder of knowing you're alive, and that's enough. Anything else is pure speculation."

"But what about right and wrong?"

"You mean sinners and saints?"

"*Ja.*"

"Don't give it a second thought. When in doubt, follow your heart and do what you think is right."

"Is that how you cope, Stace?"

"Call it the way you see it, but the way I see it is this…since God doesn't talk to me, I've got room to screw up and learn from my mistakes. Since I don't follow any particular religion, I'm not disappointed when God fails to meet my expectations, and I don't have to be angry at Him when He takes something away from me, because I don't believe He has a hand in my every day affairs. I don't even have to feel guilty when I question His existence. His silence will forever perpetuate that mystery. I find comfort in the fact that He's so far above my comprehension that all I can do is imagine how powerful He might actually be."

"I think what you do is very spiritual," Stace said, after a few silent moments.

"What do you mean?"

"You pursue justice. You defend the rights and freedoms of others."

"I don't know…it's all so confusing. Sometimes I don't know if I'm defending the right cause," she replied, her current investigation notwithstanding.

"It doesn't matter who's right or wrong. It's a basic freedom to have the right to choose. And it's spiritual to defend that basic right. You may not consider yourself to be religions, but you're answering to higher principles."

"I don't think I've ever thought of life in those terms."

"Well, you should, and you should feel good about what you are doing."

"It all seems so strange to me. I've always avoided religion, yet lately, I've felt something was missing in my life. Now you're telling me I've been religious all along?"

"Spiritual, is what I'd say."

"Is that why you left America?" she asked pointedly. "Was the atmosphere too religious for you?"

"I left because I'm a coward. Not like you," he responded.

"You're not a coward," she replied. "I think you made a stand by leaving."

"You make a stand by standing. I ran. I've never considered myself to be a fighter. I wanted to create—to think."

"You fight when you choose not to succumb. Not everyone can be an activist."

The compliment escaped him. He was thinking about the way he'd handled the decision surrounding the exhibit and not confronting Rick Forstein at a time when he could have.

"Listen, I know I've interrupted your evening, so I'm going to take off," he said rising. "I'd like to see you again though. How does your weekend look?"

"The paper shuts down on the weekend and I try to give it a rest. Give me a call later in the week and we'll make plans."

"I'll do that."

She opened the door for him and he stood in the doorway for a few moments with a blank look on his face. He wanted to kiss her, but instead, just reached out and touched her hand before leaving.

CHAPTER 11

▼

Throughout the night, Eva twisted on her bed dreaming indecipher-able dreams that produced within her a pleasant state of euphoria. She'd slept in, she was sure of that, for her room was bright with day-light and the sounds of midmorning. As she opened her eyes, Sheeba licked her face and spun circles wagging her tail.

"Get away girl!" Eva objected, wiping her face with the sleeve of her pajamas.

Eva rolled onto her back and studied the swirls in the plaster above her head, looking for the familiar faces and animals she'd marked, but the last image of Stace before he left the previous evening was all she could see. She pulled the comforter around her breasts and folded her hands across her stomach. For as long as she could think back, she couldn't picture another man who left her feeling as powerless as he did. His memory numbed her. She thought about Shelly in the office making the coffee she should be making. She could almost hear her pager going off in her bag, as Shelly tried to contact her. But they were mere whispers of annoyance, barely audible in her careless frame of mind. Her lack of initiative amused her. She couldn't help but smile with the realization something powerful had seized her; something more gripping than the passion she found in her work. She thought more about Stace, then more about work, considering the extremes that separated the two. The one extreme, work...typified by the mechanics of detachment for the sake of survival, and at the other end, Stace...typified by excluding those mechanics and chasing the hope of love. She smiled again, a healthy smile, blooming with the possibilities of romance.

Sheeba came back in the room, but Eva dodged her wet tongue. Methodically she rose, dressed in sweats and took Sheeba downstairs for a walk. When she got back, she placed a call to the office and told Shelly she had a little research to do. She brewed a pot of coffee, took a long hot bath, dressed and reluctantly opened her briefcase. She took out the reverend's book and read the back cover. "A must read for Christians in these last days," stated a quote from one of his contemporaries. She suspected its contents to be a heavy theological treatise and set it aside to wrestle with later. Then she opened the file Shelly had prepared on the three known individuals of the CRM.

Tasha Sibrina Matyastick:

Female. Age 25. Born 1988, in Klatovy, Southwest Czechoslovakia. Immigrated to Stuttgart, Germany in 2005. Studied Engineering at the university for one year and dropped out during the summer following her freshman year. Arrested March, 2006 in Stuttgart for organizing a student protest of the United Nations International Army's invasion of Albania. Served a three-month sentence at the Woman's Correctional Institution in Gaggennau, near the border of France. After release from prison drifted to Frankfurt. Currently resides at 1342 *Hugelstrasse*, apartment 3-B.

Present status: Employed as a clerk by the Schnell Department and Pharmacy near the corner of *Miquellallee* and *Hansaellee* in Frankfurt.

Derrick Burford Sachs:

Male. Born 1965 in Dessau, East Germany. Age 48. Immigrated to Frankfurt, West Germany on October 6, 1993.

Present status: Employed with Salter Imports, an import/export firm located in the *Niederrand* district.

Currently resides at 1342 *Hugelstrasse* apartment 3-B.

Neil Thomas Usher:

Male. Born 1966. Age 47. Born in Beescow East Germany, near the eastern border of Poland. Immigrated to Frankfurt, West Germany on October 6, 1993.

Present status: employed with the Gunter Group since 1997, a privately owned accounting firm.

Currently resides at 1342 *Hugelstrasse* apartment 3-B.

"Shelly was right, not much here," Eva mumbled to herself. She did, however, notice the possible connection between Derrick Sachs and Neil Usher. Both had immigrated to Germany on the same day and their original citizenship was from East Germany. After the fall of the Berlin wall in 1989, there was a mass migration of East Germans into West Germany. Thousands had crossed the borders during that time, many traveling as friends to begin a new life. Tasha Matyastick appeared to be the only one of the three with a questionable history. Evidently, she'd traveled to Germany to escape the political climate in Czechoslovakia with the intention to embark on a new life. Her arrest undoubtedly, cut short that goal.

Eva tossed the file into her briefcase, disenchanted with the mediocrity of its contents. What she had thus far was a list of three people who left the political horrors of their own countries for the freedom of the west. Individuals, who probably wanted nothing more than to live without the hassle of government breathing down their necks.

She took a sip of coffee and fingered the corner of the reverend's book. What bothered her now, was that in all the years she'd worked for the *Schwarz Monatlich,* she'd never been involved with an investigation that focused on a religious organization. Most of her investigations targeted the misuse of political and governmental power. At times, she covered stories about corporate organizations and white-collar crimes. Her role in those investigations was clear-cut; the laws were stated in black and white and it was just a matter of uncovering enough evidence to break a story and get a conviction. There was always a certain satisfaction in bringing down those of wealth and power; those who'd trampled on the common citizen to get to the top, so she never questioned the nature and purpose of her work. Her investigation of the ICC and the CRM would require an alteration of protocol. The more she thought over her new role, the more she suspected she was crossing over a yet, undefined line. Who's to say she wasn't in danger of encroaching on the very principles she stood for, that people had a right to believe what they wanted to believe? Taking a deep breath, she determined any further investigation of the two groups must be done with the utmost objectivity.

The first chapter of the reverend's book established his principle for motivation, fear. He began by highlighting the evils and horrors of the modern world and concluded with the Christian's responsibility to resist such evils in a united front-line offensive. With words backed by historical and biblical significance, his portrayal of the evils sizzled in Eva's consciousness with relevance. The reverend was a man of generalities and abstractions, not targeting his verbal arrows at any particular world leader or regime; rather, he focused on themes and sociological influences. It was a tactical maneuver, designed to introduce the reader to recognize the prevalence of evil, which ran through the world and bound it together in darkness. He assumed political and governmental institutions were in general, lead by individuals who sought office for the sake of power alone. He cited the trend of global leaders who had embraced the idealism of capitalism as an indication the end of the world was near. Such materialist goals signaled the end of culture and initiated a race for financial superiority that wouldn't end until all the natural resources of the world were used up. This led him to his next point and the next few chapters; an assault on the rampant spread of violence and crime. His overall objective in these chapters; to show that the ideals of capitalism had supplanted the necessity for spiritual morality. And in the absence of spiritual morality, the human race had deteriorated to the point where the laws of survival dictated behavior. In the middle of the book, he spoke about the movement of the global masses towards a humanistic agenda and the unnatural reliance on technology to solve humanity's need for immortality. He cited recent advances in DNA cloning and the proliferation of scientific measures to prolong life. He called to point the United Nations recent move towards space exploration and its attempt to find other inhabitable planets. To the reverend, this revealed a pathetic epitaph to the existence of mankind. It proved mankind had lost its ability to conscientiously curb its assault on the natural resources of the world; that mankind was no longer able to control its greed even when confronted with global catastrophes and the possible extinction of the human race. He even covered at length the results of global warming. Scientist's had predicted as early as the nineties that the oceans of the world could rise as much as eighteen feet should there be a massive meltdown of ice in the Polar Regions. He claimed recent scientific studies had shown the oceans had indeed, risen an unprecedented six feet and the shorelines of the world were already rippling with disaster.

His conclusion and solution to all of these crisis's was the institution of faith in Christianity around the world, for it alone could purge the human spirit of its incessant greed and at the same time force a universal healing of the nations. He called for the spiritual awakening of mankind to repent of their evil deeds, demanding that the oppressed forgive their oppressors and that the oppressors have compassion on the oppressed. Such a change must be initiated from those in positions of power, and then embraced by common men and women of every nation. For if it was to be embraced by those in power, then its benefits would trickle down into the lives of the masses. Nothing short of a complete global repentance would bring about the favor of God. Nothing short of a spiritual awakening of every soul on earth could awaken God's favor of the human race and allow God to work His miracle working power. In the reverend's interpretation of theology, the final days of earth's history would be marked by such a revival of the Christian faith. In his summation of the book, he appealed to all, for the time of revival was now knocking on the door of the human heart.

It was 2:35 in the afternoon when Eva finally laid the book down. She searched desperately for an excuse that would allow her to disbelieve the words she'd read. She walked into the living room and looked out the window. Across the street, a woman was pulling in the comforter from the window, which she'd laid on the window ledge earlier that morning to air out. Beyond the corner, on raised tracks running above the side street, a *U-Bahn* whizzed by on its way to *Niedernhausen*. The sky was a rich blue. A gentle wind pushed swirling clouds across the sky. Everything was normal and yet, extraordinarily different. Hidden in the normalcy of life was a disquieting calmness, not unlike the hours before an approaching storm. True to their intent, the words of Reverend Eisner had reached their target.

CHAPTER 12

▼

"Folks, if I could please have your attention," Pruitt said, after entering the conference room. Davia and Jean ended their conversation at the coffee pot and joined the others seated around the table.

"Before we get started, I need to fill you in on more details of the project and instructions on how I think you should proceed. As Mr. Watson alluded to, the ultimate goal of this project is to design a security program with the ability to detect and kill a virus we're going to create. I'm sure Jean can confirm, the Internet is a hostile environment susceptible to any number of potential threats. On any given day, any nut with a PC can cause havoc with just a few strokes on the keyboard. It's vitally important then, that the virus we create goes beyond the everyday, run-of-the-mill virus normally designed by hackers. In other words, it should be more dangerous then anything previously conceived to be possible."

"Most security breaches on the Internet occur when hackers break into existing systems. For instance, banking systems have been known to have loopholes that allow unauthorized money transfers. The military is in danger of having classified material leaked into the wrong hands. Even corporations and business are susceptible to industrial espionage and having their secrets leaked to competitors. Most hackers target these holes for various reasons, some for money, but most for the

simple pleasure of seeing just how far they can get. But to my knowledge, no virus has ever been designed for the sole purpose of disseminating propaganda from a hostile group, at least from the perspective
of cloaking their information in the form of a virus."

"It has long been thought that some advertisers and individuals in
the movie industry have used what is known as subliminal influences.
It's really quite a simple process, but let me give you an example.
Advertisers know the more a person thinks about a given product the
more likely they are to buy that product. When you stop at the corner
store to buy a soda, you pretty much know what you're going to buy
before you go into the store. You have a picture of the product in your
mind and you find the product on the shelf based on your mental picture. So let's say a company like Coca Cola wants to sell its product.
One way to do it is to use commercials. The more commercials you see
of Coca Cola, the more you'll take the image of that product to the
store and buy it, as opposed to another soft drink. However, some
companies have been known to use more seductive methods, a method
known as subliminal influencing. One way of doing this is to hide the
image of the product in a picture. Either the name of the company or a
picture of the product can be hidden in a photograph so effectively,
that the person viewing the photograph never sees the image, but their
subconscious mind sees it. Another way to do it is by inserting images
into a filmstrip. When the film is being edited for viewing, individual
pictures of the product can be inserted into one or more frames in the
overall filmstrip. What happens is, the eye views the filmstrip as a
whole and never notices the image of the product inserted into the
film."

"And you know this as fact?" Jean asked.

"It's a proven fact. I've seen it happen myself."

"When?"

Pruitt looked around the room nervously, "Actually, I'm a little
embarrassed to say, but if it'll help me prove my point what the hell."

"I was watching one of those romantic comedy's at my home one evening. You know, one of those class B productions that carries the plot by using flashes of the female anatomy." He looked over at Davia and Jean. They didn't seem to be offended, so he continued. "Well, during one section of the film, which I found particularly…interesting, I rewound the video and set it on slow motion. I was advancing past a scene I wanted to see again and happened to notice an out of sequence frame. It was still moving too fast for me to see, so I rewound the tape, taking it frame by frame. When I got to the out of sequence frame, I hit the pause button."

Pruitt stopped again, hesitant to continue.

"And?" Jean insisted.

"And there was a few isolated frames of a man performing oral sex on a woman."

The room was silent for a moment until Rick spoke up, "It had nothing to do with the subject of the film?"

"Nothing whatsoever. The scene was about a couple sitting on the sofa watching TV. The man in the scene reached over and took off the woman's top. That frame I just described was inserted while her top was being removed, and I hasten to add, the people within the inserted frames were two entirely different people."

"What was the purpose?" Stautzen questioned.

"I thought about it later and the only thing I could think of was it was an R-rated film. The scene, however, was definitely X-rated. So in the editing room someone inserted this other scene. I suspect it was to increase the arousal performance of the film. How much the scene affected me I don't know, but I did stop to rewind. I did notice. Fact, I checked all the sex scenes to see if any more frames had been inserted, but that was the only one. Anyway, evidently it slipped right past the ratings committee."

Pruitt smiled with uneasiness. "You see, even in this case, the obvious intent of the film makers was to increase the marketability of their film and they used a subliminal message to do it. Subliminal influences don't have to involve the sale of a product. In fact, the most effective ones target the emotions. They attempt to manipulate behavior by touching on points of the human psyche which influence behavior."

"Now, what I want you to consider is this. Let's suppose the PLO wants to make the Jews more sympathetic to its cause. Or let's suppose one of the Russian socialist leaders wants to convince the Russian people to believe in his socialistic ideals. Take it a step closer to home and say the Republicans in the coming election want to convince the American people they were the party to vote for. How would they go about doing this?"

"Commercial...advertising," Rick answered.

"But they'd still have to convince the people they were right. People would have to watch them or read about their ideas correct?" asked Pruitt. "And based on how much information people were already wrestling through, would determine whether people wanted to believe them. You see, people don't make decisions based on information necessarily; they make decisions on how they feel. If I could make you feel good about the terrorist organization that killed thirteen people in Rome last week, I might be able to get you to support them—right?" He looked around the table waiting for a response. In the absence of one, he pressed his point. "At the current rate, the present way of disseminating information changes public opinion only after a long period of time and only after a barrage of information. But what if there was a way to by-pass this system?"

"You mean by developing a way that affects the thought processes of the mind?" asked Dr. Loran.

"What if there was a way to give people information and a way to alter the way they feel about any given subject without them even knowing about it?"

"Given that this could be done utilizing the Internet, I'd say you could effectively rule the world," Jean concluded.

Her comment effectively silenced the group for the next few moments.

"I'm joking," Jean added to soften her outburst.

"Perhaps only slightly." Pruitt said. "I wish I could tell you we're ahead of our time and we're the only company considering the possibilities of such a program. But I don't think so. It's a bit like Thomas Edison inventing the light bulb. He may have been the first one to do it, but the technology existed within his time for such an invention. If he didn't invent it, someone else would have. It's the same with this program. Either it's already built, or it will soon be built and our task is to not only build it, but to create a security program that can identify it and destroy it."

"I can think of at least a half-dozen ways in which someone could use the Internet and project onscreen pictures or messages." Rick spoke up.

Jean nodded in agreement.

"I could even program a key on the keyboard to randomly throw images up on the screen. As the monitor recycled itself you'd never even see it." Rick continued.

"I think on a small scale it would be a simple task. But this virus must be able to effectively interface with the worldwide web. It must be able to infiltrate any computer system accessing the Internet." Pruitt said.

"Ok. Then we'll design a program that can pass through all the major search engines used by the Internet. Anyone looking for information over the web has to use any number of search engines to find information. When they lock onto the search engines, a virus could be designed that would infiltrate their PC or office systems." Jean suggested.

"Great, and who's going to break into these systems?" Rick asked. "Personally, I like the view from the backyard of my house. I wouldn't want to exchange it for bars at the local penitentiary."

"It's really not our intention to carry the program that far. We could simulate the dynamics of the Internet on-sight." Pruitt said.

"Pruitt, do you know what that would involve?" Rick asked.

"Yes, and we have the resources to do it."

"Let's say you could simulate the same conditions here. How are we going to know the program will actually work in the real world? Dr. Loran insisted. "Let's say we're able to pull it off from the technical standpoint. How are we going to know the program will produce the necessary affect on the human mind? I mean, you're going to have to test the psychological aspects of the program as well."

"So we'll test it on individuals," Pruitt replied.

"How?" asked Rick.

"That will be an easy process. We simply solicit volunteers from the community to see how the program is changing their thinking."

"Like rats?" Dr. Loran asked.

"No, volunteers. Medical, drug and research companies do it all the time. They pay volunteers to test their medicines and therapies. We'll do the same. We'll have volunteers sit at a computer and play on the Internet. We test their responses to see how they process the information. When the program's fine-tuned and working, we'll make them aware of the impressions we've placed on their minds. Should be totally harmless. Once they're aware of those suggestions, they'll just simply disregard them."

Dr. Loran ran his hand over his head and sighed.

"It's not like we'll be hypnotizing them to go out and shoot the president, Dr. Loran." Pruitt said whimsically.

"What kind of information do you suggest using?" Dr. Loran asked.

"Something that will be universal and have an affect on all races and backgrounds."

"Like sex," Jean said.

"Well, that would definitely have an impact and get everyone's attention. But sex is a basic instinct. If we flash images of the opposite sex on screen, we will get a response, but it won't be the one we're looking for. We have to keep in mind that we will be trying to influence a persons internal belief system, which might involve getting a person to change their political allegiance, or their moral and ethical standards through manipulation of their religious beliefs. The program we design should work within these same parameters."

Pruitt reached down and picked up his briefcase. He set it on the table and pulled out Reverend Eisner's book. Stautzen watched the book slide across the conference table towards Dr. Loran and looked at Pruitt in shock.

"*Our Global Community*," Dr. Loran read for the group to hear.

"Consider it a working example of a religious regime in the making. Stautzen is the author's right hand man." He looked at Stautzen. "I would like you to work with Dr. Loran and make the contents of this book come alive. You need to make these words so convincing that an atheist would follow Reverend Eisner anywhere he wanted to lead them."

"You're kidding?" Dr. Loran asked.

"No and yes. Whether or not you believe what the book teaches is up to you."

"I know, I'm familiar with the man," Dr. Loran said.

"Then you've seen a few of his shows?" Pruitt asked.

"I've seen enough."

"Then you know he has a profound affect on people?"

"I see your point," said Dr. Loran.

"Like I said, it's a working scenario. I've read the book and—"

"Do you believe it?" Dr. Loran interrupted.

Pruitt shot a glance back at Stautzen. "It doesn't matter what I believe. What matters is that we use something that can legitimately alter people's lives, and his ministry is definitely having an impact."

Stautzen spoke up. "I think what Mr. Pruitt is trying to say, is the reverend has one of the fastest growing ministries today. He's obviously touching people's lives. This doesn't necessarily mean what he says is right or wrong—"

"I'll grant Mr. Eisner this, he does use the psychology of religion effectively." Dr. Loran insisted. "Nevertheless, if the book is able to produce a change in human behavior, then by all means, it could be used as a model, especially if our intent is to build a security program that will stop its influences."

Pruitt held up his hands, sufficiently silencing the debate. I respect your differences of opinions. Obviously, there may be more debate as you continue and I look forward to your progress."

Rick glanced up at Pruitt.

Let me know if there's anything you' all might need."

CHAPTER 13

▼

"Three bear claws, Mrs. Seiler? Here you go. A loaf of *weizenkeimbrot,* Mrs. Kantrel and half dozen glazed? Just a second. Let me ring up George on the register and I'll get right back with you." And so it went six days a week. The traditional rush for morning pastries, leaving the *Burtman's Backerei* in downtown *Hochst* in crumbs and their owners frazzled.

By 6:00 a.m. every morning except Sundays, Leda and her husband Kermit would lay out the treasures of their craft behind the glass display counters in the front room. Nothing was left undone, not even the full tray of pretzels placed on a table outside the door for children to help themselves to on their way to school. By 9:00 a.m. the pretzels, along with most of the other pastries and bread would have disappeared. It was a labor of love they both shared; Kermit mixing, pounding, rolling, baking, Leda dressing each donut and roll with pastel colored creams and icings, and bagging the seven different types of bread they made. While Leda cleaned up in the aftermath, Kermit would begin preparing the late afternoon selections of *brot.* Through the years he'd mastered the art, producing masterful sculptures of flour and water, which would earn a place in the heart of any food critic.

It was late afternoon when Eva came walking up the cobblestone sidewalk. Kermit was in the kitchen baking the next day's supplies of cakes and pies and Leda was busy sweeping the crumbs out the front door towards a cluster of pigeons.

"Eva! Leda cried out.

"*Hallo,* mama."

Leda clung to her as though she were making up for lost time. She held Eva's cheeks with her cramped and tired hands and looked into her eyes. "Its been too long Eva. Too long!"

"I know mama."

"Kermit! It's Eva!" she yelled to her husband in the kitchen.

"*Was?*" he yelled back, over the drone of the large mixer.

"It's Eva!"

"*Augenblick mal!*" he laid down his frosting knife, wiping his hands across his stained apron.

Eva couldn't wait. She stuck her head through the crack in the door separating the kitchen from the display room, "hi!"

"Ah, Eva!" he said coming towards her. He wrapped her in his arms then stepped back. "It's so good to see you!"

His hug was as warm as the ovens and sweet as frosting. "I've missed you too," she said. "I've missed both of you," she said again, now looking at her mother, who'd leaned against the wall and taken a saintly pose.

"Young lady, where have you been?" he asked.

"Busy. You know."

"*Ja, ja,*" he said, joyfully mocking her. "Is there anything you need?"

"Nothing. I just wanted to see how you two were doing."

"How long can you stay?" he asked, backing away to shut the mixer off.

"About thirty minutes."

"Good. Just let me catch up in here and I'll be right out."

"Come, let us sit down and talk," Leda said, taking hold of her daughter's arm and escorting her to a table in the corner behind the counter. "Can I get you some coffee?"

"*Ja bitta.*"

She returned with two cups of coffee and lemon crème donuts.

"*Danke.*"

"They used to be your favorite."

"They still are."

"You know, if it wasn't for Alfred we'd never even know you were alive."

"Now you know that's not true mama," she said, knowing full well it was.

"Alfred says you have another boyfriend."

"Word gets around fast."

"Can't blame him for that. He said he saw you last night and we begged him to tell us how you were doing."

"What else did he tell you?"

"Just that the man was an American."

"You disapprove?"

"Disapprove! Come on Eva, when where you ever concerned with whether I approved of what you were doing? She spoke as to a friend and not to a daughter. "I'm much too old and you're an intelligent young woman now. All I want is for you to be happy."

"Thanks mama—"

"But do tell."

"Well, his name's Stace Manning. He's an American, but you know that already, and he came to Germany last year."

"Where does he work?"

"He's a photographer. Right now he's working for a film developing company in *Hattersheim*, but he does some freelance work."

"Is he stable?"

"I just met him last weekend mama."

"Sorry, just curious."

Eva had few friends while growing up and fewer girl friends that were her age, because she said, "they just like to play make-believe-family with their dolls all day." She took that autonomy with her into high school and completely by-passed the stages of young love and sexual discovery. As time progressed, her impressions of the world took on a more serious nature, and the questions she raised about life were those that might be better discussed in collegiate philosophical classes. Still, she'd been and would always be a daddy's girl, because throughout her school years, she spent whatever time she could with her father. Kermit recognized in his little girl the disturbing pulse of his own nature; an above average dose of insight combined with an acute sense of justice, which had rattled in his mind like the voice of a lunatic for as long as he could remember. He knew those who possessed such insight could take only one of two paths through life. Either they learned to capture and use that insight in a constructive way, or they would wind up an eccentric mumbling idiot. And it scared the hell out of him to see this characteristic forming in his young daughter.

"What's he like?" Leda asked.

"He's a passionate man...artistic."

"Have you slept with—

"No! Of course not mama. He's not like other men I've known. He's open like a book. Honest, you know."

Kermit appeared in the doorway behind Eva. Leda looked up at her husband intuitively. "Eva's got a boyfriend, an American—and passionate!"

"Mama!" Eva said, raising her voice and slapping her mother across the shoulder.

"*Gut*. Very *Gut!*" he said, taking it as a sign of normalcy in her life. "How's work? Alfred said you were investigating the ICC."

"*Ja*. Familiar with them?"

"A little," he said with disinterest. His impressions of the ministry were mixed and he didn't want to influence her one way or the other.

The bell above the door to the *backerei* chimed and Leda jumped up.

"*Guten tag, Frau Necklen!*" she said. "What can I get you today."

"I need a loaf of *vollkornbro*t and *roggenbrot*."

Leda reached for a sheet of transparent wax paper and removed the loaf of whole-grain bread first.

"Just a small loaf of the *roggenbrot* if you don't mind."

Seeing that his wife might be busy for a few minutes, Kermit said to Eva, "Come upstairs, I want to show you something."

She followed her father into the kitchen and up a stairwell into the apartment. Being in the stairwell reminder her of the many times she and Alfred would sneak downstairs into the *backerei* and eat left over pastries while their parents were sleeping.

"I remember when you and Alfred would sneak down stairs at night and steal pastries," he said suddenly.

"You knew?"

"You'd be surprised what I know about you two," he said, turning towards her at the top of the stairs with a twinkle in his eyes.

He entered his study beyond the living room and sat down behind his desk, the same desk he inherited after his father passed away four years earlier. The room used to be hers. When she moved out her father waited two years to make it his own. He'd anticipated and even hoped, she would move back in, but she never did. The study now doubled as an office where Leda did the books every night.

"It looks good. You did a good job," she said, admiring the refinished walnut desk with its fresh coat of stain and varnish.

"*Danke*, but I didn't bring you up here to see the desk. No. No. Something much more important."

He pulled open the top drawer and carefully brought out a wrinkled envelope bearing the name of the *Deutsch Geschaftlich* Bank of Frankfurt.

"What's that?"

"It *was* the mortgage on the *backerei*. Your mother and I made the last payment in August, two years and seven months early!"

He opened the envelope and brought out the document. Holding the bottom of it, he ran his right hand across its length to flatten it and hold it in place. At the top was a red stamp mark reading, "Paid in

Full," followed by the date "August 28, 2013." She looked at her father, who was fixated at the stamp as though he still couldn't believe it. It was a late-blooming victory in his life, which he'd worked sixteen years to win. Up by 4:00 a.m. and finishing by 8:00 p.m., everyday except Sundays, doing everything from sweating near the heat of the ovens pounding dough, to scrubbing pots after dinner time. It was the certificate that had come to justify his existence.

"I don't know what to say."

"I know. I almost didn't believe I'd live to see the day."

"How'd you manage to pay it off early?"

"Your grandfather left us a little. I applied it to the balance and we've been making double payments for the last three years."

"He'd be happy to know he helped."

"Yes" Kermit said reflectively, folding the document back up and slipping it into the envelope.

"I guess it's time to file it away now. I wanted to wait until you had a chance to see it."

She came around behind him and wrapped her arms around his stout shoulders. "I'm proud of you and mama."

"Come now, it's just a mortgage note—paid off mind you—but a note just the same." He stood up and looked into her eyes. Something wasn't right. "What's wrong?"

"Nothing," she replied.

"I know you better than that. Let's go into the living room and have a talk."

She sat down on the living room couch and ran her hands along the new fabric she'd never seen before.

"Looks nice don't you think? Gives the room new color and life."

"You really should consider buying a new couch."

"What for? You're not here. A few guests occasionally, thanks to you. But really, the only person that sits on it is Alfred."

He was right of course and she was glad. She remembered the many times she'd fallen asleep on it watching TV. It was still as comfortable as ever.

"Now, what's wrong Eva?" he asked, perched on the edge of his favorite chair across from her.

"Nothing really, papa." Which was a typical analytical response for her. Then she thought about all of the events that had transpired in the last week and looked at each one in turn. She had met a man, had a new assignment, was worried about Alfred, there was a host of other insignificant items demanding her attention and most particularly, she was confused about the contents of Reverend Eisner's book. Alone, they were not unusual or significant matters, but together they seemed overwhelming.

"I just have a lot of things on my mind lately."

He looked at his daughter sympathetically, thinking of the many times she used to tug on his pant legs as he worked in the kitchen. She was still the same little girl, but now she clung to him for encouragement in different ways. "You have a new friend?" he asked, hoping to isolate her problem.

"A friend, but I think we could be more than friends."

"Then that's good news. Any trouble at work?"

"No. Just the usual workload."

"What are you working on now, something about the ICC? Alfred wasn't very specific."

"Mr. Schwarz thinks there's a connection between the International Christian Coalition and a smaller group called the Christian Reform Movement."

"That's a little different than what you're used to investigating, isn't it?"

"It is."

"You say that like it's a problem."

"Could be."

"Why's that?"

"Because I'm used to chasing down the bad guys."

"You've always enjoyed that haven't you?" he asked, admiring what his daughter had made of herself.

"*Ja.*"

"And there are no bad guys here?"

"None that I can see."

"From what I know, the ICC's just another Christian ministry, but I've never sat through one of its shows. Wouldn't have time or interest for that, but I know they provide the funding for a few sizable charities."

"That's just what I mean, I don't see a story in it."

"What about the other group? The Christian...what did you call them?"

"The Christian Reform Movement. CRM. It's an underground Christian ministry. They've got a following."

"A real fizzler right?"

"Exactly." She thought of her brother Alfred. She couldn't help thinking her instructions to bug the group's apartment had been premature. It could be an unnecessary risk. Problem was, it wasn't her call. She and Alfred both worked for the same man and he'd proven time and again that his hunches were worth checking into.

"Dad. I've been wanting to ask you something...."

"Ask."

"How come we never went to church together as a family?"

He turned his head away from his daughter and looked out the window. Through it he could see the image of a young girl dressed in a flowing dark blue dress, talking to three other friends under an imposing archway of the school dormitory building of the St. Katherine Academy for Girls. The three of them standing together they were an impressionistic painting of innocence and virginity. The face of one of the young women shone more than the others; the face of his first and only love, Leda. They'd fallen in love before exchanging words. Nearly everyday on his way to and from the public high school in *Sossenheim,* he'd stood holding onto the iron railed fence surrounding her academy, searching the courtyard and windows for the vision of the only one who could heal the disturbing impulses of his emerging manhood. He wouldn't leave until he'd seen her and she was always faithful to their silent courtship; either standing under the archway, or appearing in the window of her dormitory room.

It was not a time for lovers, less than ten years after the Second World War, when the world was going through the aftershock of a madman who, tormented by the nature of his crimes, released himself from his fate by committing suicide in an underground bunker. The city of Frankfurt was still in partial ruins. The process of restoration had begun, but the jagged memories of the war seen in its blown up buildings divided the inhabitants of Frankfurt by culture and religious persuasions. Leda's father was a stoic Catholic. Kermit's parents, Lutheran, and after the order of those fiery Protestant fathers who gripped their faith with the zeal of the early reformers. Neither Leda or Kermit would dare contradict the authority of their parents, nor could they forever revolt against the magical and higher authority of love. Something had to give. Towards the end of their senior years, when their resistance against the authority of their parents was at its height, they broke their silent engagement and wed in words and touch.

It was a simple and symbolic gesture. Kermit had returned after the sun set one evening to the corner of the outer courtyard. From where he stood he could see the lights of Leda's room and waited for her silhouette in the window. When he saw her face searching for him, he lit a cigarette. Leda saw the faint glow of the match paint the sidewalk and the underside of the canopy of tree over his head. Descending two flights of stairs, she crept out the front door and made her way through the shadows towards him. When she reached the edge of the building, she stopped and looked for the sisters. Knowing she'd escaped unseen, she moved towards the outer wall where the cover of trees was greatest. She followed the wall down to the corner where it met up with the iron fence and where Kermit stood waiting at the corner. She was more beautiful than he'd imagined, more radiate than he'd anticipated, the drag of his cigarette painting her face in campfire orange. Flipping his cigarette into the night sky, they were instantly shrouded in darkness. Before speaking a single word to each other they joined hands, stood as close to each other as fragrance is to flower and kissed.

This became a nightly ritual until the month of May when they both realized they would have to proclaim their love to their parents. This would be difficult for Kermit, but for Leda, the prospect of telling her father filled her with fear, because she understood that her mother's tragic death still affected her father's decisions. Leda's mother had been killed in the war on her way home from evening mass. She had refused the demands of her husband to remain in the safety of their apartment during the evening hours, for she vowed that no matter how desperate the situation was it would not affect her worship. She was struck down by the fragments of a bomb, which destroyed the Schreyer's home barely fifty meters down the street from the church. After the war, her father had gone to work in Bremen in the north to help rebuild the shipyards. He'd left his only daughter Leda in the care of the nuns to educate and raise her until his return. Leda and her father communicated through letters. She and Kermit agreed that she would send notice to her father in Bremen of her love for Kermit and wait for his response. Thirteen days passed since she'd sent her letter and in the afternoon of the fourteenth day came his reply.

That evening, as Leda crept along side the outer wall to meet Kermit at the corner post, Kermit searched for an answer to her letter, which he hoped would be written on the expression of her face as she approached. When she approached, the most desperate moment in his life had been realized. Her face was swollen, eyes puffed and red from crying. Even the soft, dark contours of her bangs were damp and hanging limp from the moisture of her tears. Her father had written he was returning home on the train and as long as he lived, she would not dishonor her mother's death by an infatuation with a young Protestant boy. If she cared at all for her late mother, she would never see Kermit again. Kermit vowed to never tell his parents about Leda. He would not risk losing his love by allowing them to interfere with his plans to marry her.

After graduation, Leda moved back into the apartment with her father and she and Kermit made secret plans to elope. Early one July, they met in the depth of night and from the *Hauptbanhof* in Frankfurt traveled by train south to *Freiburg*. Kermit took a job working in a factory, which made iron-works and Leda worked in a textile mill. They returned to Frankfurt four years later after Leda's father passed away and only then did Kermit reveal the true reason for his departure to his parents. It would be years before he and his parents came to speaking terms.

"So it was by religion you might say, that your mother and I came to meet. A meeting that was both bitter and sweet. You could even say, our love for one another has been our religion. Your mother and I made a joint decision years ago that you and Alfred would be raised in the principles of that religion."

She'd never heard the story of how her parents had met and fell in love. As he related the story to her, she sat on the couch considering her own emptiness and needs. She felt she was at the threshold of something much more meaningful and powerful than anything she'd ever experienced. But it was coming too fast for her. She'd spent a lifetime encircling herself in a cocoon of systematic actions which had kept her warm and secure. This shell was now threatened with the onslaught of emotions brought on by her attraction to Stace, and chiseled away by the awareness of her own spiritual needs. Things were beginning to unravel and she wasn't sure where to place the longing or the blame. Her father had substituted his need for religion with love, a love purified in a world saturated with ideologies and warheads. A love, which surpassed the loftiest of theological ideals.

Around the corner and down the hall the door to the kitchen opened and the voice of her mother bounced upstairs.

"Kermit! The bread!" she yelled.

Her father jumped out of his seat and stopped in the foyer looking at Eva.

"That's all right papa. I've got to get back to work now anyway."

She followed him downstairs and out into the front room where her mother was serving another customer. "I have to go now," Eva said.

"So soon?"

She looked into her mother's eyes with a renewed appreciation for her and kissed her on the cheek.

CHAPTER 14

▼

From his vantage point, Ruben picked at his goatee and watched as a young woman approached the walkway leading up to the apartment. She had straight black hair sitting on her head cut in an oriental cap, curling just below the ears and tapering to points beside her cheeks. Bangs hung high over her forehead. He was too far away to make out her facial features, with the exception of noticing that those features where sharp and defined like the crease of mountain peaks, and her eyes were as sleek as an Egyptian's with mascara. Her denim skirt buffed her black boots as she walked, and she carried an ivory cloth bag stuffed with groceries. Before she made the turn up the walkway, Ruben lifted the Pentax to his right eye and held the 300mm lens as steady as he could. The auto lens focused on her face giving credibility to his assumptions. She was indeed beautiful and the auto-winder clicked off four rapid shots.

Tasha was just returning from her shift at the department store. After the short ride on the *S-Bahn* from *Miquelalle,* she'd stopped at the corner grocery store and picked up a few things. The walk from the corner had taken about fifteen minutes. Exhausted and winded, she wasn't looking forward to making dinner.

"*Abend,*" Derrick said, from the worktable where he was busy dubbing audiotapes of the sermon Neil preached the weekend before. His inflection was lifeless, a mere courtesy. He didn't even look up as she passed by and set the bag of groceries on the kitchen counter.

"Hello, Derrick."

"Is he still out there?" Derrick asked her.

"*Ja.*"

"Since yesterday," he said.

"What do you suppose he's after?" she asked, removing a loaf of bread out of the bag and laying it near the refrigerator.

"What they always want."

"Who do you suppose he's with?"

"Definitely not *polizei*—too obvious," he replied.

"Detective?"

"No reason for that. Probably just a reporter. Nothing to worry about Tasha."

She walked into the living room and stood at the corner of the window, pulling the edge of the curtain and peering outside. Ruben hadn't moved; his black form clearly visible through the reflection of the windshield.

"He's a nigger," Derrick said, like he'd been sucking on an ice-cube. "It's a shame isn't it? Probably came here on the first boat out of Africa."

Tasha paid no attention to him. She went back into the kitchen and finished putting away the groceries then went to her room. When she'd disappeared behind her door, Derrick got up and went to the window to have another look. Same beat up white Fiat parked eighty meters down the street. Same nigger. He watched the man raise a camera to his face then lower the camera towards the seat beside him. A minute later, the lock on the front door popped and in walked Neil Usher.

"The son of a bitch is still there," Derrick said from the window.

"I know." Neil set his briefcase on the table and walked over to Derrick. While they watched, the Fiat pulled out from around the silver car in front of it, entered the roadway and drove past the apartment.

"Where's Tasha?" Neil asked.

"In her room," but as he spoke she came out. They waited. The door to the bathroom closed and the sound of water from the shower chugged through the pipes in the wall.

"What does she know about him?" Neil asked.

"Nothing. Other than he's watching the place. I've been playing it off."

"What can you tell me about him?" Neil asked. They sat down at the dining room table across from each other.

"Not much more than you already know. He showed up yesterday morning sometime and stayed to early evening. Got here sometime around 6:00 this morning."

"So, he was here all day?"

"Near as I can tell. If he left this morning sometime I don't know. I woke up about 3:00 this afternoon."

"All right. Guess all we can do is keep our eye on him."

"You want me to follow him?" Derrick asked.

"Not yet. We'll wait a while. If he's still around next week then we know we've got a problem. Then you can follow him. We don't need this crap in the equation right now. Not a word of this to Tasha. She doesn't need to know."

Neil Usher and Derrick Sachs were two men who existed in the opposite spectrums of the prism of life, but shared the same ambitions. Neil was clean-cut, educated, cautious and calculating. Derrick was wild, simple-minded, careless, and ruthless. They operated together as one, like the minds of a schizophrenic, with more cohesion in two men than could ever be possible in one. Neil was the right hand and Derrick was the left. Rather than despise or deny the existence of the other, they seemed to have merged together into the purpose of one, being perfectly content with the discrepancies and inadequacies of the other. But like one character in the mind of a schizophrenic is bound to emerge as the dominant voice, Neil had taken on the commanding role. This suited both of them, because Derrick was a man who liked to be led and he could be led to perform the dark deeds with an unnatural disassociation to law and order.

They'd met while serving in the Berlin underground where they, along with two-dozen other radicals, began the Christian Reform Movement. The ideological temperament of the group revolved around three objectives: Their primary concern was the reunification of the German people under one flag and with one purpose. To this end they personified the reincarnation of the Third Reich's assumption that the German race was superior to all existing nationalities. Secondly, though they sided with the Federal Republic of Germany and its democratic ideals, they were inherently, socialistic. They pushed for an equal distribution of economic resources within the country, so that every German could enjoy the same freedoms and opportunities. Thirdly, and most extraordinarily, they laid claim to the Christian faith as their governing force. Using the biblical Old Testament as a model, they thought themselves and their ideals to be invincible and those that stood in their way, expendable. But when the two countries united, the CRM dissolved. After nearly a decade of nourishing themselves on the milk of dissension and revolutionary aspirations, Neil and Derrick looked to the west and the challenges that presented themselves there. In October of 1993 they'd immigrated to Frankfurt. Upon their arrival in Frankfurt they immediately reactivated the CRM. Not one of the prior objectives with the original CRM had changed, although there were modifications to be made. For example, the existence of social inequality in the west was different from that of the east. Under communism in the east, the dreams of the individual had been supplanted by the good of the state and equality was the result of the abuse of political power. In the west, inequality had surfaced as a direct result of capitalism. The race for political and economic power was given into the hands of the strong, the healthy and the intelligent. Due to the west's obsession with greed, it had become virtually impossible for the poor and unfortunate to succeed. There was no hope for the common man who lacked money, or contacts. Neil and Derrick viewed the pursuit of capitalism as a demon in need of an exorcism.

If their Christian perspective in the east had been fanatical, they took it to an extremist level in the west. For where there's a proliferation of social freedom, there's also the proliferation of ideological, philosophical and theological thought. In the east, those who exercised the Christian faith, worshipped in secret places and in the cramped cavities of their minds. There, religion was more primal in nature, feeding on the existence of oppression, which had a way of breathing relevance into the faith. In the west things were different. There, freedom encouraged the expression of spiritual thought beyond its primal level. It had given rise to the merging of thousands of ideas and teachings from a variety of differing religions. Neil and Derrick believed those ideas had eroded the pure teachings of the Christian faith, and they felt it was up to them to set things straight.

But in Frankfurt, the inclusion of others into their ecumenical fold proved difficult at first. The people of the cosmopolitan city, having laid hold of the traditions and aspirations of the North Americans, were uninterested in pursuing any belief seeking to drag them back into the dark ages. The time was one of prosperity and there's no room for self-sacrificing when times are good. In fact, the general consensus of most Christians across Germany and Europe at that time was that God was in the process of blessing his children with material and financial success. The proof of those blessings could be seen everywhere, but most noticeably in the prosperity of the United States, were the political leadership had collectively subscribed to the Christian faith. Indeed, the twenty-first century had witnessed the mass migration of ordinary heathen to the Christian faith; people who now saw Christianity as an answer to their physical and materialistic oppression.

At first, Neil and Derrick didn't buy into the concept that God rewards his faithful with success and position in the present life, but as time progressed and they began to drink from the cup of that idealism, they became more intoxicated by its potential. Eventually, they would come to see in the ministry of Reverend Eisner a spokesman who could usher in the times of prosperity they believed to be prophesied in the Bible. The reverend taught that the reward of the faithful came in the form of prosperity and success. That God would bless those who subscribed to His will. A Christian was not to seek materialism, but rather, receive its blessings as a testimony of their personal connection to God. It was an old idea wrapped in modern day terminology. An idea born on the assumption that God rewards the faithful, so he can tease the heathen into submission. Neil and Derrick had felt such a passage into God's favor when their revolutionary efforts helped to bring down the Berlin wall. As a reward, God had led them to the west and had introduced them to the greater work of the International Christian Coalition. There was not a doubt in their mind that the joining of the ICC and the CRM was providential.

Tasha Matyastick, however, was another story.

She was two years old when she and her mother immigrated to Germany. The year was 1988, and her mother thought it time she learn the circumstances surrounding their departure from Czechoslovakia.

Nikoli Matyastick, her father, had been planning his escape from Czechoslovakia since he was a teenager, but the volatile political climate of the seventies and eighties made escape from his native land a necessity. He'd attempted many times to obtain the necessary papers for he and his family to immigrate to any free country within Europe, but the government made it virtually impossible for all but a few to leave. Furthermore, any individual who even dared to obtain the necessary papers to leave became immediately suspect as an enemy of the state.

Nikoli, however, was in a better position than most. He was a commercial pilot, whose flights on occasion took him to other destinations in the free world. During one particular flight into Frankfurt, he'd come into contact with a man named Gerund Hershel, an individual who worked for the German office of immigration. Hershel also had acquaintances with one of the Czechoslovakian ministers of foreign affairs. Hershel had agreed to help Nikoli and his family to immigrate to Germany and contacted the official in Prague concerning the matter. After nearly a year and through secret correspondence between Herschel and the Czechoslovakian minister, the minister consented to help, although he required 225,000 crowns, or roughly $15,000 to secure the proper documentation. It would be another thirteen months before the Matyastick family could save or sell what they could sell to come up with the money. Once they obtained the money they re-contacted Hershel and prepared to leave. Their hope of liberation, however, was quickly extinguished. The official in Prague now demanded a higher price to be paid for all of the Matyastick's to leave. The 225,000 crowns would only provide safe passage for two and he wanted an extra 70,000 crowns for the entire family. The Matyastick's had by this time sold all they could sell and it would be another year before they could come up with the extra amount needed. Their desperation forced a cruel and necessary decision.

Nikoli, through the assistance of Hershel, arranged for his daughter and wife safe passage to the west. On one of his trips into Frankfurt, he handed a crinkled brown envelope full of 225,000 crowns to Gerund Hershel. Five weeks later on a subsequent visit, Hershel handed back to Nikoli the necessary documentation for his wife and daughter to leave Czechoslovakia. Their parting was one of anticipation, rather than farewells, for the Matyastick's had a plan.

His wife Kasarla and daughter Tasha arrived successfully in the west and through Hershel's continued support found residence in Stuttgart where Hershel had family who could acclimate them into German society Months dragged on through winter, then spring, as Nikoli waited for his opportunity, but the security forces of the Socialist regime monitored his every move. In an attempt to confine him to Czechoslovakia, the regime arranged with the airlines that he should only be given flights within the country. His wife Kasarla began to doubt if she'd ever see her husband again.

Nikoli didn't plan the exact day of his escape, but the events on the day on November 17, 1989 required a swift decision. Since September, there had been an unusual amount of civil unrest building amongst the citizens of Prague. It was a nightly occurrence for Nikoli to hear sirens echoing in the distant streets. By day, the normal hustle of pedestrians along his street had diminished to a trickle. The only citizens venturing outside were those who had to go to work. On this particular day, Nikoli was scheduled to fly out of Prague to Ostrava, just south of the southern border of Poland in Northwestern Czechoslovakia. After cinching up the last few buttons on his uniform coat, he looked around the apartment he'd never see again. Kasarla had taken just a few memorabilia, but she'd left the majority of the souvenirs of their twenty-three years of marriage displayed around the tiny, two-room apartment. Nikoli grabbed a faded black and white photograph of his wife and daughter off the fireplace mantel and stuffed it into his flight bag. After closing the front door behind him, he descended the cement staircase leading out to his car. He'd always been aware of the presence of the security officers and had been careful not to encourage them with a glance. Today was different. As he started his car, he looked for them in the alleyway behind him to his right, then up the street to the corner where they sometimes stood. Adjusting the mirror on the windshield he searched for them in the parked cars behind him and across the street. They were nowhere to be seen and Nikoli was set on edge wondering where they might be. He planned his moves based on them following him and their absence might force him to readjust his plans, possibly at a moments notice.

He lived on the southwest side of Prague. The airport was out on the north side of the city. Depending on the time of day, he would take either the expressway though town or the back roads around the city. It was 4:30 p.m. and traffic would be at its worse, so he decided to take the country roads. Even these roads were prone to having some traffic, but as he drove through the suburbs they were almost deserted. He checked his rear view mirror often, but the only motion he saw were leaves skidding angrily across the road behind him kicked up by the tires of his car.

Arriving at 5:15 into the employee parking lot, he made his way up the escalators into the pilot's lounge, where there, huddled around a dusty black and white television, were a handful of pilots and two supervisors watching a breaking story on television. Throughout the day, tens of thousands of demonstrators had invaded the city streets, and random images were flashing through the TV's snowy reception depicting thousands of Prague's citizens moving like a herd through the streets surrounding the capital. Determination sizzled in their eyes and fury in their fists as they yelled slogans encapsulating years of frustration. Hundreds of army troops were being mobilized with tanks and weapons to stop the civil unrest. Nikoli checked the flight schedule. His flight to Ostrava was scheduled to depart at 7:05 and he had up until 6:50 before his absence in the cockpit would be expected.

Walking briskly through the terminal, he took another look down the corridor before moving to gate three where Flight 17 to Frankfurt was just finishing boarding. He sat down for a moment and looked over the top of his newspaper for the security forces, which had been following him like a pilot fish for half a year. Still, no sign of them. It was quite possible they were busy with the situation building in Prague, so he knew he'd have to make the most of his sudden advantage. Stuffing the newspaper under his arm, he pulled his black cap with its stiff shinny visor down over his forehead and made his way out the door, across the tarmac and up the lift into the plane. He raced into the cockpit and shut the door. He knew the captain, but greeted them with a seven-inch kitchen knife. Nikoli was no villain. He simply held the knife out for display like a boy showing his friends a pet bunny. There were two other men in the cockpit, the copilot and the navagator. Any one of them could have taken him down without resistance. They looked at each other and then at their friend Nikoli. Moments passed. Finally, Captain Vaclav spoke, "You will be traveling with us today to Frankfurt, Nikoli?"

"Yes."

"Then you will join us for coffee," the captain said, pouring some from a thermos into a mug. He passed the mug over to Nikoli and took the knife out of his trembling hands.

"It will be nice to have you on board for the flight," said the copilot.

There was not a pilot, stewardess, or supervisor in the company who wasn't aware of the events surrounding the life of their friend, Nikoli. Sure, some of them sided with the communist regime, but they were not in the cockpit that afternoon. He was amongst friends. They spoke little during the flight and the door to the cockpit remained closed, despite attempts by the stewardesses to bring the crew refreshments. Nikoli knew full well that his seat for the flight to Ostrava had been taken by a standby pilot and his absence would be reported to the authorities. The manhunt would already be in full swing.

Captain Vaclav gave the last instructions to his crew before their final approach into Frankfurt International and turned to his friend.

"When we shut down you're going to have to tie us up. There's electrical tape in the compartment above your head. Realistically, we can give you about five minutes before reporting you. Leave the knife."

Nikoli thanked his friends after tying them up and locked the cockpit door behind him. He greeted the stewardess—whom he surprised—and joined the rest of the passengers entering the terminal. He quickly made his way up to the third level and hid in a maintenance closet through the night. The German *polizei* had far better things to do then hunt for another disenchanted Czechoslovakian. Then next morning he slipped unnoticed out of the airport wearing a maintenance uniform. By nightfall, he was reunited with his wife and Tasha in Stuttgart.

Six years passed as Nikoli and his family created a new life for themselves in Germany. Nikoli never flew commercially again, but he still liked to fly. About once a month he'd rent a single engine plane for half a day, often taking his wife along with him. On one fateful day, however, Tasha's parents were found dead in the wreckage of a rented plane. The authorities concluded the accident had been caused by a problem with the electrical system. Gerund Hershel knew better.

After the accident, the Hershel's raised Tasha as one of their own, but she would always remain adrift. Embedded in her mind were the many fragmented stories of the oppression in Czechoslovakia and how her parents had devoted the better part of their life in seeking freedom from it. What she heard, she didn't want to believe. What she remembered, she didn't want to forget. Her parent's sacrifice in reaching a new world had cost them their lives. It had also given Tasha her own life and the freedom to find herself and for that, Tasha could never forgive herself. She left the Hershel's a week after her seventeenth birthday.

As she grew into a young woman, her absence of roots would become more profound. She'd been unable to successfully merge into the mainstream of the German society, choosing rather to live within her profound sense of imagination. If asked who she was, she would fall silent. If asked what she believed, her expression would draw a pathetic blank as she wandered through the empty rooms of her mind where those beliefs had failed to take up residence. Her world was a river, bordered on one side with disbelief and on the other side with impossibilities. The world had robbed her of justice at an early age and as a consequence, she didn't know how to channel her anger or how to find what she was looking for—but at least she was looking. Many years later, the flow of her river carried her downstream where a sheet of paper blew across her path announcing a revival meeting of the Christian Reform Movement. She'd been walking home in the early evening from her job as a waitress at a local pub in Stuttgart, when the bright yellow announcement brushed her ankle and blew into a puddle on the cobblestone street where it floated face up. She reached down and picked it up by the corner and while it dripped drops of oil and dirt-stained water she read it. The announcement spoke of a Christian gathering to be held that evening on a nearby street. It would begin at 6:30. Her watch ticked 6:13.

She entered the dinky theater on *Guerickestrasse* fifteen minutes later with all the mental caution of a dehydrated sponge. The ancient theater's wooden seats were nearly filled to capacity. The taped organ music blasted out of the PA system and rippled the crimson curtains along the walls. In the cathedral ceilings above, the liturgical music bounced back down towards the congregation like a gentle rain. When the song ended in a high-pitched sustain, goose-bumps spread across her body. She watched as a handsome young man approached the podium. The lights were dimmed and the features of Neil's face were highlighted from a hidden light positioned somewhere below the microphone.

Neil spoke clearly and precisely. He read and knew his audience well, and spoke words that touched every heart in the place that was either absent of purpose or cast in the despair of loneliness. To Tasha, Neil seemed magical, possessing a sense of purpose she'd never before seen in a person. Her experience was like that of lovers; when communication becomes telepathic. She couldn't even remember the exact theme of Neil's message, but the warmth of his presence had extended their long tentacles across the theater and penetrated every oracle of her soul.

She had to meet him, had to be with him. It was a strange infatuation; one rather like flame is to oxygen and how the two need each other in order to exist. In this case, Neil was the flame; a burning life-sucking force, feeding off the adoration of his converts, and Tasha was the oxygen, feeding his fire through her own lack of origin and direction.

The magic of relationships is how each participant shares their individuality with the other. It's two people building a puzzle together. They have no idea what the final picture might be, so they carefully lay pieces of their individuality on the table to discover what the picture of their life together might be. The pieces of Tasha's puzzle were all out of focus. Neil's pieces were out-of-this-world. The result would be a relationship of codependence on Tasha's part and one of psychological abuse on Neil's.

CHAPTER 15

▼

Ruben parked his Fiat down the street from the CRM's apartment for the fifth day in a row. The morning was cool and the steam from his breath fogged the windows in the tiny compartment. After the sun rose, the mist in the windows condensed into beads of moisture. In his boredom, he watched the life of one bead grow to the size of a tear and begin a mad dash downwards. Zigzagging along the face of the window, it sought out other beads of condensation, absorbed them, picked up additional speed, and finally disappeared into the rubber slit at the top of the door. The processed amused him and he watched as others fell. It was now Friday. He'd seen no new faces enter or exit the apartment since Wednesday and he had sixteen shots in his camera to prove it. With frustration, he cleared his windows with an old tee shirt and failed to notice the faded blue Mercedes van, with the stone crack in the windshield, park thirty meters behind him.

Throughout the week, Eva's brother Alfred had been doing his own reconnaissance, and his actions had gone completely unnoticed, even to Ruben. For several days he parked his utility van at various locations around the apartment and even behind the apartment along *Kurhessenstrasse*, where he had a view of the back parking lot. Yesterday, he did a little footwork by entering the building though the back door with this tool belt hanging around his waist and a roll of cable encircling his shoulder. He counted steps, made note of the exits and examined the lock of the door on apartment 3-B. By his own estimation he had the place thoroughly cased, but the details of the occupants of the apartment were still a mystery. He couldn't make his move until the apartment was empty and he couldn't know if it was actually empty until he knew who lived there and when they left the building. He was relying on Eva to provide him with that information.

Although it was still morning, Ruben decided to call it quits at five minutes to nine and headed down *Eschersheimer* towards Frankfurt. He pulled into a fifteen minute parking slot in front of Strickland Photography at ten after. He set the dial on his parking placard to read 9:15 and tossed it on the dash, giving him twenty minutes before the parking *polizei* could give him a ticket and plenty of time to turn in the roll of film for developing. Another person who had gone unnoticed to Rueben was Derrick, who'd followed him from the apartment in his own van, and who now waited across the street watching him. After placing the film canister in the envelope and pressing it shut, Ruben handed the package to the man behind the counter and told him he'd be back after lunch to pick it up.

Back in his Fiat, Rueben traveled through Frankfurt and over the river and into *Sachsenhausen*. Derrick watched him park in front of a three-story, two hundred year old brick building marked with the name, Ansel Insurance Company. "Where the hell's he going now?" Derrick mumbled to himself and wrote the name of the insurance company in a note pad he kept in the top pocket of his flannel shirt. He watched as Ruben ducked under the low arch of what appeared to be an entrance to the basement and noticed a sign that said, *Schwarz Monatlich*. "Well, I'll be dammed," he whispered and pulled his van into an open slot across the street.

Ruben descended the stairs and entered the dank hallway. The brick along its walls had once been a rich charcoal color, but time had given it a sooty appearance with patches of lime-green algae forming in the corners near the cement floor. He fumbled for his keys to the steel door, and Eva glanced in his direction as he entered the office.

"What? he asked her.

"Nothing, I just didn't expect you back so soon."

"I'm just getting back from Strickland's—turned in *de* film."

"You took it to Stricklands?"

"Where was I supposed to take it?" They always took their film to Stricklands.

"Stricklands I guess," she replied, annoyed they still had to trust their surveillance film to a commercial developer. "When will it be done?"

"After lunch," he said, sitting down at his desk. "And *dat* should be it. I've been there everyday since Monday—not including last Friday mind you—and have good shots of everyone who lives in *dat* apartment. Hell, I've got their front, back, profile, and even a picture of the mailman."

"And how about the—"

"I've got my notes too." He tossed his pad on her desk.

She looked over at him and smiled at his frustration. "Good work."

"Now what?"

She reached into her briefcase and pulled out the file on Derrick, Neil and Tasha and tossed it on his desk. "We know these three people are involved with the CRM. I want you help Shelly find out all you can about Neil and Derrick."

"What about the other one?"

"Leave her to me."

At noon, Eva and Ruben broke for lunch. They drove through *Sachsenhausen* and *Oberrad* and into the northern part of *Offenbach* where the river turns north around *Fechenheim,* another suburb of Frankfurt. Along *Nording Strasse* they pulled into the parking lot of a street cafe. The cafe, about the size of Eva's living room, served a greasy selection of hamburgers, wieners, *wurst, pommes frits,* and of course, beer.

Derrick had followed them to the cafe, and was now parked in a cut out along the street close enough to see the ketchup dripping from their hamburgers. His own notes consisted of a list of names and addresses where he'd been that morning, as well as an accurate description of Eva and Ruben's physical appearances. Judging from the mannerisms of the woman, he thought the woman to be the black man's superior.

The two finished eating, jumped in Eva's Opel, made a u-turn in the street and headed back towards Frankfurt. Eva couldn't find a parking space near the entrance of Stricklands and dropped Ruben off to pick up the film. Derrick followed her around the block a couple of times as she killed time. After picking Ruben up they headed towards the *Schwarz Monatlich*. When they pulled into a slot near the entrance, Mr. Schwarz greeted them with a soda in his hand and take out pizza he'd gotten from the Pizza Hut down the street. The three of them talked on the sidewalk for a brief moment, just enough time for Derrick to sketch a few notes in his pad about the old man.

Approximately forty-five minutes later, as Derrick waited, a utility van bearing the name of the Frankfurt telephone company parked directly in front of him. A lean young man in his twenties got out of the van and starting walking directly toward him. Derrick sat up nervously and prepared himself for the encounter, but the young man turned between the two vans and opened up one of the cargo doors. The man grabbed his utility belt and snapped it around his waist, then took out two orange cones. After closing the door, he set one cone on the street near the rear bumper and looked up. The two exchanged glances and nodded a casual greeting. Alfred set the other cone near the front bumper of his van and walked across the street towards the *Schwarz Monatlich*. He rapped on the door three times and waited for it to open. Shelly was near the door filing paperwork and let him in.

"Alfred! So good to see you again," Shelly said. She'd been attracted to Alfred since the first time they'd met, but he never responded to her flirtations.

"*Guten tag.*"

Shelly understood by the intonation in his voice he wasn't going to respond today either. She backed away and let him pass.

He walked to his sister's desk. "Are you aware one of the men from the apartment is parked across the street?"

"You're kidding," she replied in a sudden state of anxiety.

"In the blue van."

She jumped out of her chair and wove her way around the desks to the windows along the wall. Ruben and Shelly were right behind her. In the middle window overlooking the street was a clear spot where Eva had once scraped off the paint so she could look outside. She put her eye to the hole and looked across the street. People were scurrying about on the sidewalk and cars were whizzing by obscuring her view. But there he was…wind blown hair, wrap around sunglasses, flannel shirt rolled to the elbow and hanging over the doorframe of the van.

"Let me take a look," Ruben said. He had his hand on Eva's shoulder and nudged her away, "*Dat's* one of *de* guys I've seen. I've never seen him leave, only come, at about 7:30 every morning."

"We still don't know why he's there. Maybe he's waiting for his girlfriend to take her to lunch." Shelly said, after looking out the window herself.

"I think it's safe to say he's not parked outside enjoying the weather. They know we're on to them." Alfred said.

"He's right," Eva said. "He's either Neil Usher or Derrick Sachs."

Shelly said, "we know that Neil is employed with the Gunter Group. He's probably clean-cut and has a day job. Derrick works an all night shift in an import/export business, so it doesn't really matter what he looks like. If you ask me, I'd say this man is Derrick Sachs. Definitely not clean cut and he has the time to run around during the day.

"Question is…how did he find out about us? Why's he here?" Alfred asked.

The only one in the group who had the possible answer was Ruben. "He could have followed me back from *de* apartment *dis* morning."

Mr. Schwarz came out of his office and looked at the group huddled around the window. "What's going on?" he asked with his hands on his hips.

"Derrick Sachs is parked out front watching the place," Eva said.

"Who is Derrick Sachs?"

"A member of *de* CRM."

They cleared a path for Mr. Schwarz as he walked towards the window. "Where?"

"In the blue van across the street." Alfred answered.

Mr. Schwarz took a long hard look at the man in the van and shook his head from side to side. "I don't like the looks of this. What are you all doing about it?" Without waiting for an answer he continued. "Listen Eva..." he began, looking at the group formed around him, "I want all of you to take these people seriously." He checked to see if they understood him. "Keep me informed, you got it?"

Eva was the only one that answered. The rest of them nodded. He walked back into his office and shut the door behind him.

"I take it you haven't been able to get inside their apartment yet." Eva said to her brother.

"No. Too risky. Haven't you got some photos you can show me? I need to know who these people are and when they come and go."

"We were just getting to *dem* on my desk." Ruben said. They moved to his desk and he opened the package and lined up the photos.

Alfred looked through the line up and picked up the picture of Derrick Sachs. "Ok, here's one of them," he said and set the photo on the desk below the others.

"We know that Tasha's a young woman in her late twenties and Neil is pushing fifty, so I think we can safely exclude these others," Eva said, plucking up a number of photos and setting them off to the side. This bought the number of photos down to eleven.

Ruben picked up two photographs of a couple and tossed the photos in the discard pile. "*Deese* two are probably married. I saw *dem* taking their baby for a walk in *de* stroller."

Nine photos left. Several of them were of the same individuals taken at different angles. There were three men and a female.

"These must be of Tasha then," Eva said, sliding three photos down near Derrick's picture. "Not bad Ruben."

"I've seen her *de* most. She walks her dog in *de* park across *de* street in the morning. She's a pretty one she is."

"All right, three left," Eva said, looking up at Alfred and Ruben.

"This one here…" Alfred began. He lifted the picture up to his face. "He has a uniform on." He'd seen the uniform around town, but it took him a few moments to remember where. "Garbage man? Utility company?" he thought to himself. "I've got it," he said. "This man works for the parks department." After looking at the lunch box the man was holding, he reaffirmed his guess. "Definitely parks department." He tossed two photos onto the discard pile.

The four remaining photos were of two men. Eva picked out the two clearest shots and put the other two in the pile. That left two photos of two different men beside Derrick's photo. Both men were dressed in suits and ties. One of them held a briefcase and had a sports-coat folded over his left arm.

"Shelly, I want you to enlarge these two photos along with the photos of Tasha and Derrick."

"At Stricklands?"

"No. Just use the copy machine."

Shelly took the photos, enlarged them, made copies and gave them to the others.

"I *tink* I'll park myself outside *de* Gunter Group and see if I can identify *dis* Neil Usher," Ruben said. He stood up and grabbed his windbreaker.

"Wait!" Alfred said. "We don't know what Derrick is after yet. What if he follows you?"

"*Den* I loose him."

"Let me go ahead of you. I've been spending as much time around that apartment as you have. It's possible he may know who I am as well. I want to check his reaction as I leave."

"When are you going to be able to get inside the apartment, Alfred? Eva asked as he headed for the door."

"I'll have to wait until next week. Probably Tuesday. I'll let you know."

As he slipped out the door Eva went to the window to watch. He crossed the street and headed for his utility van. She focused on Derrick's reaction. Derrick glanced casually at Alfred then back towards the building. She watched Alfred pack his cones and bag then drive away. Derrick never gave him a second thought.

"What do you think?" asked Shelly.

"I think Alfred's in the clear."

Alright," she said, turning towards Ruben. "Now you."

Ruben folded the copies of the two men, slid them into his back pocket, then walked out the door. Eva heard him ascending the stairs and watched him move towards his Fiat parked a few slots down the road. Ruben kept his eyes in front of him, giving no indication he was aware Derrick was watching him. Derrick glanced towards Ruben several times as he got into his car and backed out of the space into the street. Derrick brought his arm inside the window and for a moment Eva thought he was going to follow Ruben. Instead, he reached for a note pad from his top pocket and jotted down a few notes. When he finished writing he got out of the van.

"Shit!" Eva yelled, as he jogged across the street towards the stairs. "He's coming."

She pulled away from the window and raced to Ruben's desk snatching up the photos and shoving them into her briefcase along with the reverend's book. She stood at her desk waiting for either a knock on the door or for him to come charging in. Her head swelled with thoughts of what she would say or do. Shelly waited behind her computer as quiet as a rat that had just been spotted by a cat Except for the hum of Shelly's computer and the clop of pedestrian's shoes passing the basement windows, the office was unbearably silent. A minute passed, then another. Shelly looked over to Eva and shrugged her shoulders. She frowned as if to say, "Well, where is he?" As she did, they both heard the slamming of the paper machine dispenser on the sidewalk. Eva ran over to the window and peeked through the hole. Derrick was nowhere in sight. Then she shifted to the right to get a better view of the entrance and saw him.

"He's buying a paper Shelly. One of our papers!" Shelly jumped up to have a look. By the time she reached the window he'd crossed the street.

"We forgot about the papers," Eva said. Of course, she was right, but there was nothing she could do about it now. She was a reporter and reporters work for papers and papers get distributed and people can find out all kinds of information in papers. Eva shuddered when she thought of the editorial page, where every member of the paper's staff would be listed along with their titles and responsibilities. Derrick didn't need to barge into the office. All he had to do was look at the editorial page. From the list of names it would be no problem for him to find addresses and any other type of information he wanted. It could be only a matter of days before he'd know practically everything about her.

CHAPTER 16

▼

Throughout the week the Trojan Security team had tossed around a handful of ways in which it would be possible to send hidden messages though the Internet. The term they used for the program was that of a virus, which insinuated that the implementation of such a program would be potentially deadly element. In its biological form, a virus attacks a living organism with the intent of disrupting the healthy flow of life. In the computer world, the same destructive properties of a virus exist, although in mechanical form. Every member of the Trojan Security team was comfortable with the idea of creating a virus that affected the mechanical components of a computer, but what they were expected to create was something far more disastrous. It would be a virus that would not only affect the cold, metallic components of a computer, but one that could forever alter the psychological temperament in the minds of those who used the computer.

To pacify the team's probability that they would be intelligent enough to understand the potential impact of the virus, CEO Watson had decided to appeal to the team member's sense of responsibility and avarice. Each member of the team had been chosen because of their expertise, but Watson went a step further and offered them a healthy compensation package as a motivational incentive. Apart from being the son of the creator of Trojan Security, Watson was particularly adept in the art of motivation. The dynamics of his art centered around his ability to recognize and take advantage of the talents of his workers, as well as to treat them with dignity and respect. The later, usually falling into the realm of financial compensation.

Watson was correct in assuming that a misguided group of individuals would be willing to use a program similar to what they wanted to create, and it was even possible such a program already existed. Appealing to the team's good nature, he took the incentive much further in implying the Trojan Security team had a moral responsibility to create a security program that could destroy the existence of such a program. Still, for some of the team's members, especially Rick, his participation in the project took him through a circular pattern of ethical arguments, which played in his mind like the cranking of a jack-in-the-box. There was certainly good reason to build the program and good reason not to. If the program already existed, it would be morally right to create a security program that could destroy it, but if the program didn't exist, they were walking on a thin sheet of ice and using their skills to create something that was better left in the graveyard of ideas, along with all the other inventions of destruction.

In his mind, Rick thought of a time decades ago when a team of scientists created and developed the mechanics of nuclear fusion, which led to the hydrogen bomb. Who could argue its creation caused both massive destruction and ironically, a certain degree of security, at least for those who possessed the technology. Had the technology been created by radicals and not by a civilized world, it's quite possible America might not be the super power it is today. But since it was created by rational and civilized human beings, who possessed a relative understanding of right and wrong, that same technology was used to forge a slogan known as "peace through strength." That same technology had kept many uncivilized and radical governments from imposing their ideological slavery upon others. How was this different?

In his attempts to reconcile these questions, Rick downplayed his role and lost himself for the time being in a quiet place in his mind where he could work without the distractions of the ethical implications of the project. "Hell, I'm just one man working for a computer company in a city. One man in seven billion who goes to work and gets a pay check in order to feed his family. I'm not special. In fact, there are probably a thousand other individuals in the world who have my skills and could build this project. Fact I wouldn't doubt it if a few of them are engaged in building something just like it. Yeah, that's it. Somewhere in China or Uganda there's a team just like us building this same damn software—so who cares? We build the program and we design the software that will destroy any chance of it getting into the wrong hands! Sounds good to me! And the day after we do, I'll drive to work in my Miata and take on another project. Maybe I'll get another raise and buy a new ride." So it was, through some asinine self-talk, that Rick was able to jam the gears to the jack-in-the-box and get down to work.

But the fact remained, talent and technology had reached such a level and it was impossible to keep such a beast of a program from being born. That's to be expected from the race we know as human beings. For man is a creation fastened with enormous drive for change and stimulation, as well as an erroneous sense of his own mortality and potential to err. It's not unlike the blind, who despite their blindness, fail to judge the future catastrophes of their day and still roll out of bed, grab their walking stick and proceed beyond the door into life. Past civilizations will testify that the greatest error of the human intellect is its failure to grant people the right to be different and the right to accept these differences as gifts of potential unity. Therefore, such a program was from its inception inevitable, and after being created would need to be destroyed, if indeed, it could be destroyed.

The team had divided the program up into two essential components. The primary component was what they referred to as the, "psychological stimulus element." This part of the program dealt with the elements of the power of suggestion. Above all, this element would have to target those areas of the human intellect that affect a person's ability to think and reason, beyond their established moral framework. In other words, it must be able to take an otherwise normal individual, one who possesses the ability to reason at a cognitive level, and completely alter their belief structure, so that they might act in a way that was previously impossible for them to act. At its most simplistic level, this might involve causing a person who believed in a supreme God to suddenly become an atheist. At its most extreme level, this element would be able to cause a person to kill another person, when they previously respected the sanctity of life.

The other component of the program was what they referred to as the, "technical element." It would apply the psychological stimulus element into a working environment by utilizing the properties of computer hardware and the Internet. Where Rick and Jean Thompson were concerned, the technical aspect of the program was a given. It was not a matter of *if* the program could be built; the problem would be how to nail a possible handful of scenarios down to one working solution. When the psychological stimulus element could be worked out, it could then be merged into the technical medium.

Once the team had been able to obtain a reasonable assessment of what would be required to build the program, they spent the rest of the week brainstorming. To this end, all five members of the team solicited a treasure of input based upon their own beliefs and how their beliefs prompted them to act in certain given situations.

From the outset, Stautzen resented the fact that the primary element of the program had been labeled as the "psychological stimulus element." To him, there was nothing psychological about it. There was only one aspect to life that prompted people to believe what they believe and to act the way they act. That aspect centered on religious beliefs. All good and evil stemmed from a person's religious background. If what a person believed was in error, then what a person did was in error.

Dr. Loran then proceeded to give a detailed account of how beliefs really stem from a person's sociological and geographical upbringing.

He agreed with Stautzen on the assumption that religious beliefs did influence behavior, but that was only because religion was an existing sociological dynamic, which already existed. He argued, that a person is religious simply because their parents and grandparents were religious and those beliefs were passed on from generation to generation. Stautzen of course, disagreed, refusing to believe he was a Christian simply because his parents were Christian and that his most treasured beliefs were nothing more than hand-me-down habits.

Davia had been one of the most silent participants in the group, but thought her input might be helpful to the discussion. She spoke shyly, but with clarity, in a high pitched voice that added to the tension in the air. First of all, she claimed she was neither Christian nor a believer of any organized religion and that as an atheist, she still possessed an able set of values and beliefs.

Stautzen was quick to attack her logic much to the embarrassment of the others. He could not believe she was really an atheist, nor did he believe there was such a thing.

Dr. Loran prepared to speak again by leaning forward and raising his hand. He carried an air of authority, which captivated everyone's attention. He considered himself to be a man of great intellect and thought Davia's frailty needed some defending. He proceeded again by emphasizing his point, by stating Davia had simply given up the religion she'd been raised on due to a sequence of unfortunate circumstances. After loosing her religion, she latched on to another set of beliefs, which emphasized the non-existence of God and had therefore, brought comfort into her life. None would argue his point, except Davia, who didn't feel the least bit vindicated, yet she was too shy to press her point. Dr. Loran seemed pleased, twisting the ends of his mustache between his fingers as he leaned back in his chair.

Stautzen fumed with indignation.

Jean spoke up, "and what of your beliefs, Dr. Loran?"

"What about them?"

"I guess we can assume that all religious beliefs are to you like a vapor, neither here nor there. It all comes down to whether we sat on daddy's knee and were told stories of God, Mohammed, or Darwin."

He stroked the chin of his beard formulating a response. He didn't even look bothered—just challenged. He thrived on debate and arguments that challenged his wit, and there would be no emotional contact with arguments of scientific debate.

Jean grew frustrated by his silence. "If we're to believe what you say, then what even you believe is a learned response to stimuli. Even if you could verify your assumptions with scientific evidence, you're simply repeating what others have said before you. Belief is either real or not. Correct?"

Dr. Loran was quite comfortable with the fact that his own beliefs were learned and that even he was advocating a point others had taught before him. He didn't claim to be original, but he did feel that if people know why they believe what they do, it is far better than believing something simply because somebody told them to believe it. "You're right Jean, what I believe I have learned. I suppose that makes my beliefs just as...let's say...as not as valid as anyone else's beliefs. However, people should know why they believe what they do, rather than simply swallowing what others tell them is true. He looked around the group to ascertain if he was getting his point across and saw he wasn't. "Belief is just a vapor, if it's not relevant to the physical world. For instance, I can tell you how and why alcohol affects the mind. I can tell you it impairs judgment, why it causes a person to loose their inhibitions, how with continued use it begins to cause irrefutable damage to the cells of the brain. To me this is useful information. It's an understanding based on physical evidence that can be tested for relevancy. On the other hand, it's my understanding religion leads some to believe alcohol is more than a drug, it's a concoction conceived by demons and that whoever consumes it falls under the control of those demons. Such beliefs are mere fabrications to illicit fear in believers. It's heresy and not based on any scientific analysis. Now in this case, both religion and scientific investigation have arrived at basically the same point; that consuming alcohol can lead towards inappropriate behavior. But in many other cases involving religion, people arrive at the most whimsical and erroneous conclusions about anything!"

"Wait just a minute Dr.—"

"Please, let me finish. My point is this. Most religious beliefs are based on stories and superstitions. That doesn't make believing in something less important, it just means you should have confidence in what you believe. And you can only get that through scientific evidence or by personal experience."

"And what of death, Dr. Loran. To what purpose does science give us concerning life after death?" Stautzen asked.

"There's no life after death," he replied calmly, though his response seemed uncertain.

"Then your scientific argument is impotent. In those areas that concern the human soul, it comes up short. Sure, science can tell me the color of an apple is red because it absorbs every other color other than red. It can tell me how the flavor of an apple rests on the tongue and is absorbed by taste, which depending on some genetic structure, will tell me whether I like the flavor or not. But on the other hand, I don't have to give you a reason for why I like the apple. Furthermore, I have the pleasure of knowing that a Supreme Being created that apple for my delight, which is a pleasure in and of itself," replied Stautzen.

"You don't know that for sure," Dr. Loran insisted.

"And you, Dr. Loran, can't tell us how the apple descended from that chunk of microscopic matter you scientific minds affectionately refer to as the primordial matter that existed shortly before the big bang." Stautzen blurted back.

Throughout the discussion, Rick had failed to comprehend the passion to which Stautzen and Dr. Loran espoused their views. Rick had searched desperately to find any situation in his own life where he could find the origins of his own convictions, but came up empty. This puzzled him greatly. Not being able to identify any particular event that would give substance to his beliefs, made him wonder if he actually believed in the Christian traditions in which he were raised. The fact remained; he'd never really questioned his beliefs because he never really had to. For him, the Christian traditions he was raised on had worked. They'd provided him with a working set of values to conduct himself, and the proof of their relevance could be found in the success of his life. Having thought through this dilemma and considering himself to be the leader of the group, he knew it was time to put an end to argument and turn the group towards more pertinent issues.

"We need to recognize that the nature of belief is not as important as knowing that belief works. By this I mean, that regardless of what one believes, whether that be Christianity," he said addressing Stautzen, "or scientific analysis," he said, looking towards Dr. Loran, "belief is what gives people relevance and substance. It provides them with answers to their questions about life."

Dr. Loran silently agreed with him. He thought Rick had understood him well and he cracked a slight smile.

Stautzen on the other hand, had a vested interest that the project target individuals who were seeking God and some form of spirituality. The program would be worthless to him without this particular dynamic and he realized he would have to adjust his line of reasoning. "Mitch Pruitt brought up the suggestion we look into building the program around what we have been discussing. I'm willing to consent to Dr. Loran, the world revolves around religious beliefs, or erroneous beliefs, and perhaps even…superstitions."

Dr. Loran looked up from the table towards Stautzen, completing the smile he'd begun a few moments earlier.

Stautzen kept the momentum going. "We should play up this part of the program. The people who will be most affected by this program will be those who rely on religion with its mystical and mind controlling influences. The more scientific a person is, the less likely they will be to recognize the subliminal affects of the program. Anything we tell them to do might be simply reasoned away. Lord knows," he said jokingly, "there are definitely more superstitious people than there are practical people in this world."

Everyone seemed to agree with him, but perhaps no one more than Dr. Loran.

"Good, we're finally headed in the right direction," Rick said.

The team then focused their attention on isolating the specific components of the psychological stimuli element. Their purpose was to find those dynamics of belief that have the greatest impact on the intellectual and emotional mechanisms of the human mind. Dr. Loran and Stautzen shot off various suggestions. Davia played the part of secretary and was thorough in summarizing their findings into a readable format. She listed their points into a series of "rules," which would provide them with a working model.

Rule1. *Belief is central to action.* People act in harmony with their beliefs, regardless of whether those beliefs can be proved to be right or wrong, justifiable or unjustifiable.

Rule 2. *Messianic Complex.* This rule states that the more a believer conceptualizes their own beliefs as superior to the beliefs of others, the more likely that person will act in a manner outside the conventional boundaries of society.

Rule 3. *Fear.* Fear is the greatest motivational factor. For the believer, the loss of salvation and immortality will keep the believer focused on their beliefs. They will not deviate from traditional teachings, for even questioning them might mean the loss of eternal life.

Rule 4. *Safety in numbers.* This rule states that people are more likely to succumb to and follow a particular set of doctrinal beliefs as the number of believers who share their beliefs increases.

Though simplistic in its design, the team was pleased with the list they'd created. Their four rules encapsulated the most important dynamics of belief and read like a resume of the psychological backgrounds of all believers, regardless of their cultural and sociological backgrounds.

Originally, each member had been hired and given very few specifics as to what the program was all about, except Stautzen. Watson had hired him through the recommendation of Reverend Eisner. Watson and the reverend had been adamant that the creation of the program be used to further the religious and political goals of the ICC. They were counting on Stautzen's powers of persuasion and zealousness to get the job done, but cautioned him that in leading the group to accept the ICC's agenda as a working model, he should not give them the impression this aspect of the program had been fixed. Which is precisely why Stautzen was completely surprised that Pruitt, while at lunch on Monday, had immediately informed the team that the program was to be built around the ICC as a model. He could now see Pruitt's logic in tossing Reverend Eisner's book on the table. It streamlined the brainstorming and allowed the group to swallow the idea early on. Stautzen could tell, however, there were still doubts lingering in some of the members.

"Some of you are concerned the program will be built around the ideologies of the ICC. Perhaps I can ease your fears and help you see the logic in proceeding that way. We really have only two possible options anyway. One option would be to make up our own religion. The other option would be to use one already in existence; hence, the ICC." Before the others could speak, he quickly emphasized to the team the drawbacks in creating their own religion.

"It's quite possible for us put something together which would allow us to test the effectiveness of our program. In fact, I would consider it a challenge and a thrill to do so. I guess it would be a little like Dr. Loran being given a chance to test one of his own theories. Religion and belief are what I consider to be my areas of expertise. I've always been fascinated by their nature, wanting to understand more about why people believe what they do. Since I've spent a great deal of time thinking about it, I've come up with some of my own conclusions and I'd welcome the opportunity to test my conclusions."

The rest of the group remained attentive as Stautzen continued in his thick German accent using a commanding display of English.

"But as much as I would like to do this, it would be best to utilize a system already in existence. Here's my reason. This part of the program must be precise. We don't have the time to develop some new idea or philosophy that people *might* follow. This could take decades. We are going to have to rely on short informational bleeps to try and get people to swallow something much bigger, which is why our focus should be on the program and getting people to follow a religion that already exists. This means, they are going to have to be somewhat familiar with the concept we're trying to get across to them."

"I don't think it would take that much time at all. People can become unbelievers almost overnight, with just the right chain of circumstances and information," Davia interrupted.

Stautzen looked out the conference room window for a moment doubting her comment.

"I'd have to agree with Davia. I was not always so scientific in my approach to life. I grew up a Southern Baptist in Athens, Georgia and I was as much a believer as anybody until I reached the seventh grade," Dr. Loran said.

I don't think you lost your faith over the course of a week," Stautzen said addressing both of them. "But there may have been a series of small events that triggered your agnosticism. This is precisely what I'm talking about. I'm just guessing Dr. Loran, that your method of scientific investigation has played an enormous part on how you came to answer life's questions. Who knows, maybe it was that one book you read on the *Origin of the Species* that changed your life."

"Actually, it was my father. He was a chemist and an archeological hobbyist. He hid a lot of books up in the attic of our home in Athens. I found them one day in an old cardboard box and started reading them. You know you can't find the *Origin of the Species* in any library these days."

"Well, there you go! You didn't wake up one morning suddenly changed, but through the course of studying and investigation you slowly suppressed what you now refer to as religious superstitions."

"Perhaps," Dr. Loran replied, lost in a childhood memory.

Stautzen continued, "We all realize we're not going to be able to convert a Jew in Jerusalem to suddenly accept the teachings of the Roman Catholic Church. We're not going to be able to convince the average German or American to suddenly promote the ideals of a Muslim extremist. Give me twenty years and I might be able to convert a Jew to Christianity, but I think it will be impossible to do this with just a few subliminal influences coming across a computer screen. If I understand the potential of the program correctly, it will be best utilized by leading a person who accepts one particular point of view, to expand their thinking and accept another point of view. Those two points must be similar in some way."

"But I thought we were to work under the guidelines that the program might be used by extremists, by fanatics trying to persuade rational people of their ideologies," Jean said.

"Stautzen's right. There's a big difference between inviting someone to listen to you and trying to invade their mind with unnatural ideas. If you've earned someone's trust, you might be able to get that person to read a book or go to a meeting with you. This program will have to implement highly suggestive information capable of passing any level of detection. That information will have to appear onscreen without a user being aware of it, then disappear without a trace. Given that scenario, the user will have to instantaneously relate to the subliminal influence." Rick said.

"I think it could be done, if it's done right, but it seems to me you'd have to present a lot of information in order to change someone's way of thinking. A fanatical group might use such a program, but the greatest danger lies with the bigger religions. With just a little bit of urging, they could effectively convert thousands to their beliefs." Dr. Loran suggested.

"And maybe they wouldn't have to spend a great deal of time presenting a lot of information to do that." Stautzen said.

"What do you mean?" asked Rick.

"It may just be a matter of getting someone's attention, then leading that person to welcome outside sources," Stautzen continued.

"Explain," said Dr. Loran.

"Just that it might be as simple as getting a person to read a book, or watch a cable program, or even visit a web sight. Such a program could be highly effective. By flashing the name of a book or a certain television station on screen, it's possible people would subconsciously turn to that station at the prescribed time. It would be a voluntary decision. A person would then be eased into following a different set of beliefs."

"I see some possibility there. Fact, it's simple enough to meet the criteria." Dr. Loran said. "It's possible the message could also get much more suggestive over a period of time. Let's say we flash a simple message on screen like, "Turn your TV to channel 23 now!" and you place behind that phrase some type of suggestive image. I guess for religious purposes that might be the picture of Jesus, or someone else. Or it might even be a beautiful nature scene, anything that invokes an emotional response. If that message was effective enough, it could cause a person to go to the TV and turn to channel 23. After a period of time, the intensity of the message could be increased."

"Exactly," agreed Stautzen. "In order for the program to work there should already be a connection between where the user is and where we want them to be. Let me give you an example. Say the Roman Catholic Church has this program and they'd like to convince all Protestants of their universal authority. Now they could knock on a few doors and hand someone a doctrinal dissertation supporting their position and of course, they'd get very little response. But if they could get Protestants to watch one of their video productions, they'd be much more effective. They wouldn't even have to start with a controversial point, but with something much more enticing. Slowly over a period of time, they would begin to break down the walls that Protestants have built against the Catholic Church. It may sound simple and the participants might not be very threatening. I mean, we don't see Protestants or Catholics as a terrorist group, but the fact remains, any type of mental manipulation should be considered extremely harmful."

"But we have to recognize as well the limitations. You may not agree with me Stautzen, but religion has certain cultural and language dynamics that will limit the scope of this program. Reincarnation for example, is a religion that is for the most part centralized in Asia. It's rooted in the culture and traditions of that geographical area. There's simply no way reincarnation could be accepted on a global scale. Therefore, a program of this sort wouldn't be of much use to them. It would be the same with any terrorist group. They have a limited agenda usually stemming from their political environment and does anyone in say...Austin, really give a damn about whether the PLO meets their political agenda?" Dr. Loran said.

Rick felt the need to disagree. "I agree in part with what you're saying, Dr. Loran. True, if the program was to be used by Buddhists trying to convert Americans to their beliefs, it would never work. But on a smaller scale, the program could have a profound impact in a particular geographical area."

"This is why we need to target the program in the interest of those who are most likely to use it; towards those big enough to cause the most damage," Stautzen quickly added.

"Like the ICC, right?" asked Dr. Loran.

Stautzen answered Dr. Loran by way of a question. It was important the team feel they'd made the decision on their own. "Who would stand to gain the most in using this program?" "Big business," Jean said smiling "Like Trojan Security."

The group chuckled at the obvious.

"True, Trojan Security will profit and so will we, but seriously—who?"

"Anyone with a warped political or religious agenda," said Rick.

"You're close. Historically speaking, the greatest powers on earth evolved when religion and political ambition united together under one force. The Medes and Persians, the Romans, the Middle East during the crusades, Jerusalem, and today America. Everyone of them were forged in religious idealism, which acted like a social magnet, drawing citizens and leaders towards one purpose."

Dr. Loran said, "You forgot about Russia, Austria, Africa and—"

"Great countries, true! but not superpowers. So, if you looked around today, which countries maintain the strongest level of idealism with the military power to advance their superiority?"

"America. China, but if you're considering power in the form of idealism, I'd say some of the players in the Middle East. Perhaps even—"

"America is a good example." Stautzen interrupted him. "Can you think of any other country in the world which in less than two-hundred and fifty years has been able to accomplish what they have?"

No one spoke up.

"From a military standpoint, it's still the world's foremost superpower. But aside from that, its democratic principles, combined with its strong Christian heritage, have had more influence on the world than any other nation in history. America is strong because of its religious fundamentalism. In general, its people abide by the teachings of the Bible and rely on God for their source of strength."

"I don't mean to knock you off your box preacher, but it seems to me you have got your viewpoint on history a little mixed up," Dr. Loran said. "Just seven years ago, I was engaged in a research project with a team from the University of Louisiana. We'd been working on a project involving euthanasia. Some of you may remember that at the turn of the millennium there was an enormous movement by professionals in the medical field that entertained the concept of euthanasia. They argued that due to the advances in medicine and medical procedures, the medical community was causing the elderly to live much longer than nature intended. At that time, modern medicine had the capabilities to keep the physical body performing, but advances in keeping patients functioning mentally had fallen behind. In short, we were keeping people alive who had long since lost the mental capacity or desire to live. We were studying the moral and ethical implications of this dilemma and were being funded by a secular organization that believed in euthanasia. This organization was also pushing legislation through that would have granted the elderly the option of ending their life based purely on their own choice or those who cared for them. But under the new "fundamentalist government" you speak so highly of, they created laws which ruled research toward any aspect of euthanasia illegal."

"I didn't mean to offend you Dr. Loran. I guess we all see events a little differently," Stautzen said.

"Apology accepted."

"I only wanted to illustrate that the United States at this moment in history is a prime example of the type of nation which might benefit from exploiting such a program."

"Why do you say that?" Dr. Loran questioned, again on the defensive.

"Because it's a nation with perhaps the greatest sense of idealism. I mean that in a positive way. If we're going to put this program to the ultimate test, we should target it towards this type of idealism, or one that resembles it."

"Are you suggesting we build a program that will persuade Americans to agree with the religious pursuits of the present administration? Because I don't think the majority of Americans agree with the course our government has chosen to follow."

"No. What I'm suggesting is we capitalize on the emotional intensity to which America influences other nations." Stautzen said. He knew he'd been successful in generating Dr. Loran's interest and by the expression of Jean and Rick, guessed he had their interest as well. He didn't want to blow it at this point.

"All of you recognize your government is extremely powerful and much of their power comes from their sense of religious superiority. Some call it idealism, some call it democracy, some even call it providential, but the fact remains, the American way of life has perhaps the most influential ideals the world has ever known. Yet, all of you, being Americans, may not realize the influence America has in the affairs of other nations and in particular, that of Western Europe. I live there. I know.

"I've had the opportunity to live in both a communist and a democratic society. I grew up in Eastern Germany where the rumors of freedom drifted over the walls like a mist. You could see and feel it, but the moment you tried to think it, that sense of freedom would disappear back into your mind, because you sure didn't voice it. When the wall came down, I was one of the first to leave and made my way down to Munich where I studied theology. Now, you may not be able to understand this in America, but in East Germany, the mystical qualities of religion provided me with a source of unseen freedom. I first learned about Christ from a pamphlet that drifted over the wall into East Berlin. It was carried by a balloon, which popped in the atmosphere and sent literature down from the skies. When I immigrated to western Germany, I began to see that the rumors I'd heard about were true. That people had work and lived in nice homes and had enough food to eat. When their children got sick there was medical care. All off these things I associated with the impact of the Christian faith upon the government. To me the two are one in the same. Every good thing has been the result of the Christian faith and when people live in a country where that faith is exalted then the entire nation is blessed as a result." Stautzen stopped for a moment to catch his breath and collect his thoughts. He was speaking form the heart now, but he was still choosing his words to reach his objective.

"I realize of course, that there's a flip side to my point of view. America is no longer the land of freedom it once was. The first Europeans who settled here were looking to escape the taxation and governmental oppression of their homelands, but more importantly, they were trying to escape religious oppression. They succeeded by instituting a method of government that separated church and state. As a by-product, they forged a new sense of idealism. That idealism was based on the consensus that the pursuit of individual freedom and opportunity should be given equally to everyone. This new idealism took a long time to come into practice. The first Europeans that landed here were still deeply rooted in their conservative natures imposed by years of religious practice. However, over a period of time the government and the people settled into their new role. The 1950's through the 1990's were a time of incredible change within America and the rest of the world looked on as America became a superpower both militarily and spiritually. I doubt even the founders of your country had any idea the extent to which the American people would embellish on their freedom. Almost overnight, Americans found that abortion, gay and lesbian rights, divorce, gun control, the use of drugs, and even criminals and crime, were all protected under the constitution. It seems ironic that the most profound declaration of individual freedom established by a government would eventually emerge as a contradiction."

"You all know what happened next. God-fearing people outraged that America was becoming another Sodom and Gomorra starting advocating a return to morality. Eventually they succeeded in either amending or suspending the areas of the constitution they believed encouraged decadence. And I don't think anyone in this room can deny the fact that to a large degree they succeeded. America is much safer, less crime ridden, far more decent and moral, than it has been in a century. What you're experiencing now is a backlash of the changes in your government, which were implemented through the fundamentalist Christian movement. Some of you suspect a return back into the dark ages and some of you are content with the positive changes you see going on around you. You can only sit back and watch and hope that everything will turn out well."

"Europe is now at the point where America was in the late 20th century. We have our factions and divisions, but for the most part Europeans are still embracing the qualities of American idealism. Since Europeans have always watched the United States, they have seen that the changes imposed by your government have resulted in a greater increase in the political and economical powers of your nation. One can't argue with results. Today, Germany has once again emerged as the most influential political power in the region. Christian fundamentalism has entered mainstream politics and has begun to influence the election process as well as the legislative process. There are organizations that promote this trend as well as organizations that oppose it. For the time being, those organizations opposing the government are still legal and are generating much debate. I expect that to end much like it ended in America. But Europeans are more acutely aware of the evils associated with power that is controlled by a religious institution. History has repeated itself too many times in European continents with the evils associated by religious dominance. Religious persecution for us is very real and it looms around every corner. We have followed the Americans into embracing the tenants of freedom and are just now realizing like Americans, that it's impossible for people to handle that freedom without destroying themselves and threatening the human race. Now you seem to be on a road back to the middle ages, yet your economic and political influence is still on an upswing. It's all rather confusing to Europeans. Some of them like myself, believe it's God ordained, but that's beside the point, either way you look at it, the situation in Europe is rather explosive at the moment."

"I guess what I'm trying to say is, if there were such a program in existence today, then the most logical and dangerous place for it to be implemented would be on the European continent. So why should we waist time considering that some small terrorist organization or religious minority might use it, or that a corporation might use it to sell their soft drinks? If we don't stretch the program to its outer limits we'll only be able to create an inadequate security system. We will fail.

We know the technology exists and at this very moment such a program could already be in use. In light of the hideous crimes that have historically originated from Europe, it seems to be the best proving grounds for our security program."

"Which brings us back to the ICC," Dr. Loran said.

"Yes. Think of them as representing the Christian fundamentalist movement here in America—but much more powerful. They're not the biggest, but certainly one of the most influential. In light of what we've been discussing, they have a tremendous impact upon the political arena in Europe. They're fully capable of duplicating the same changes and conditions that occurred in America. That should be enough reason in itself."

"I don't get it Stautzen. You work for this organization. Why would you want to have a program built around their ideologies? It seems in your best interest to—"

Dr. Loran cut Rick off. Stautzen was grateful he did. "Then our best course of action would be to develop a program that would destroy their influence upon the masses in Europe." With one statement he had taken the creation of the program from an idea into reality.

"We can't do that. That's not our job," Rick said, disagreeing with the direction that the discussion had turned.

"Why not? We're not playing around here. This is a real opportunity to invoke positive change." Dr. Loran said appealing to the entire team.

"Because it's not our place," Rick countered.

"Sure it is. Personally, I can't think of anything more threatening and potentially dangerous than the infringement of individual liberty. It's a universal dilemma and should be considered as one of the essential ingredients to the program. The worst-case scenario is for this technology to get in the hands of either a political or religious power and then used to influence unsuspecting people into subscribing to their way of thinking. If there is a villain to this whole scenario, it would seem to me to be that of the Christian fundamentalists. Historically, their purpose has always been to control. It's not the humanists we need to worry about, because they could really care less about what people think. The most decadent forms of human rights abuses have always occurred when religious institutions have been in power. Targeting the ICC is a perfect starting point. If we can build a program to stop them, then we'll be building a program that has a good chance of stopping anybody."

"Dr. Loran's point is a good one," Jean startled the team by saying. "Target the ICC. I'm sure Stautzen can tell us all about them and specifically, how they approach and win new converts to their cause. We design our program with the assumption they're building a program themselves. We ask the same questions they would ask and we implement the same methods and tactics they would use. It may not be exact in every detail, but if and when the time comes when an organization of their magnitude where to use such a program, then our security measures should be able to stop them."

There was little more Stautzen needed to say. He listened to their silence as an indication of their acceptance.

Rick, however, was still skeptical. He wasn't entirely opposed to the plan. Focusing on the fundamentalists provided them with a working model. Given the fact that they were a potential threat, added a new dimension to the program. It gave the program a sense of realism that took it beyond the experimental stage. Even so, something didn't seem right. He thought it might have something to do with his own belief of the fundamentalist influence on American politics as a good thing. He didn't find it to be a personal threat and could think of more than a half-dozen examples where their agenda had made positive changes. Maybe it had something to do with the idea being introduced by Stautzen—a foreigner. Perhaps Rick was simply suspicious of the German, whose presence in the group seemed suspect. Or maybe it had something to do with the psychological stimuli element itself. Frankly, it just plain bored him. His real interest was in the technical creation of the program. After he'd given it some thought, he determined he was happy the week was drawing to a close and that this portion of the program had been settled on. He didn't like committees and certainly didn't like discussions centering on theology, abstract theories and psychological fluff.

Next week the team would be splitting up. Jean and Rick would begin working on the technical aspects program. Dr. Loran, Stautzen and Davia would begin their research and synopsis of the ICC. Rick was confident they would succeed despite the nature and intensity of the team members. He was anxious as well to work with Jean, whom he found stimulating from more than an intellectual standpoint. He'd suspected for sometime there might be others who knew more than he did about the world of computers, but he'd never met one as attractive as Jean.

CHAPTER 17

▼

"He still out there?" Shelly asked.

Eva was at the window again. She was beginning to feel a bit claustrophobic. "*Ja*, but I've got things to do and I sure the hell can't stay cooped up in here all day."

"Where you headed?"

"Out! Call me if you need me."

She reached for her briefcase and bag and nervously walked up the stairs leading up to the street. Without even glancing at Derrick she hopped into her Opel and headed toward the *Untermain-brucke* towards Frankfurt. She thought she'd lost him for a moment, but as she cleared the bridge on the other side of the river she saw the top of his van cresting the curve of the bridge about a half-kilometer behind her. After crossing the bridge, she started wandering aimlessly through the tight city streets. Right at the *Theaterplatz*, past the *Romer*, left on *Haseng*, a short zigzag past the corners of *Holzgraben* and *Schaferg*. He was still behind her. Just up the road was a five point intersection centering on the congestion of *Eschenheimer Tor*. One street banked off to the right and a choice of three streets darted off to the left. She veered left and opted for *Hochstrasse* at the last possible moment. When she came upon the *Alte* Opera a minute later, he was still in her rear view mirror.

Indignantly amused, she chuckled. She'd always been able to justify her own methods of surveillance, but found it ironic that her methods were now being used to track her. This seemed to defy logic. She was used to being the hunter not the hunted. She knew of course, that since Derrick was following her, the CRM was fully aware of her investigation, but this was beside the point. It still gave him no right to follow her around. Her attitude originated from the fact that up to this point all of the investigations she'd done were clear-cut and without any personal threat to her life. Once she began an investigation, she wouldn't stop until she thought there was enough evidence to convict. By the time her enemies knew what was happening, they were under the merciless hands of the media or the law. Now, for the first time in her career her investigation had been compromised. The vision of the man in her rearview mirror shook her confidence, rattling loose another emotion she rarely experienced; fear.

She was not accustomed to the depths in which this fear now plunged her. She quickly found the A-66 and drove out towards *Hochst*. She thought about going back to the *backerei* to see her parents where she could feel safe. Fortunately, she had the presence of mind not to lead Derrick there. Going home was not an option either. So, without even realizing it, she'd driven beyond *Hochst* into *Hattersheim* and parked in front of Stroof's Photo where Stace worked. Fumbling for her bag on the seat, she leaped out of her car, hurrying up the short flight of stairs leading into the front office. She stepped inside the glass door then turned around and looked up and down the street.

"Can I help you?" a woman behind a counter asked in German, thinking she needed directions.

"I need to talk with Stace."

"Who?"

"Stace Manning," she persisted, looking out the door.

The woman behind the counter picked up an intercom microphone standing next to the phone. Eva heard her voice blast into a warehouse beyond a closed door. "Stace Manning, please come to the front lobby," the woman said. Her second request was more of a directive.

In the warehouse Stace was busy cutting 5 by 7's of blurred shots of the old train station in Frankfurt. It was the first time he'd ever heard his name called over the loud speakers and he wondered why. Mr. Paterson's office was up that way. He stalled for a moment and finished cropping the poorly taken photos as best he could. He shoved them into a package along with the original negatives. He sponged the package shut and slid them into a crate with other packages he'd been working on since lunch. Placing his hands flat on the workbench before him he hung his head, and couldn't think of anything he'd done wrong. For months he'd worked this same table, fine-tuning the monotonous sequences of movements of his work, which he could now do with his eyes closed. He'd pressed the foreman for a new position, but always got the same excuse. He was too fast and thorough to replace. "A victim of my own efficiency," he muttered.

Slowly and deliberately, the van crept down the street towards Stroff's photo like a metallic blue cat stalking, wheels turning like flipping paws searching for a flash of orange, a sign of Eva's car. She caught sight of the van and backed away from the door, falling into one of the chairs along the wall. Her heart throbbed like a water balloon bouncing along the pavement.

"Eva! What are you doing here?" Stace asked, popping his head through the door of the warehouse.

She jumped out of her seat. "I thought you might need a ride home."

"I'd rather take the *S-Bahn*," he said bluntly.

Her face paled like sunlight brightening a brown-faced wall.

"Only kidding."

She raised her eyes back up to his face and smiled tensely.

"Are you ready to go?" she asked.

"Not yet." He pulled back his shirt sleeve and checked his Swatch. "Can you wait about twenty minutes? My shift ends at 5:00."

"*Ja.*"

"*Gut!* You can wait here if you like."

"I think I will."

She sat down folding her hands around her knees, glancing around the lobby nervously trying to ease her anxiety. No doubt Derrick had spotted her car in the parking lot and was waiting for her to resurface. Time passed sluggishly on the huge clock on the wall, a Fuji promotional giveaway. Its face was a blown up photo of a giant box of film. Out of the dot in the "i" of the name Fuji, the long black hour and second hand converged. The minute hand lurched forward every sixty seconds. The woman behind the counter shuffled through orders she'd written up and cracked a smile of indifference towards her.

Stace finished fifteen minutes later. They jumped into her Opel and headed up the street out of *Hattersheim*. Neither one of them spoke until they approached the *Main Taunus* exit on the autobahn. Eva was busy looking into her rear view mirror and Stace was watching her movements with suspicion.

"Are you busy tonight? she asked.

"No, not really. There was that show I wanted to catch…or—"

She slapped him in the shoulder. At the *Main Taunus* exit she traveled north towards *Bad Soden* into the *Taunus* Mountains. About a kilometer up the road she swerved at the last moment into the far right lane then onto the access road. Stace seized the handle of the door, but said nothing. At the light she took a hard left, went over the overpass and entered the parking lot of a shopping center.

"You hungry?" she asked.

"No," he said, distracted by her actions.

She veered into the back parking lot and Stace expected her to park, but she kept circling and circling, up one isle, down the next, up another, all the while keeping her eyes in the rearview mirror. It finally occurred to him she wasn't looking for a place to park. Suddenly, she dashed around the side of the building into the front parking lot. She found a spot at the end of one of the rows and doubled parked across two lines. She still wasn't offering any information and he wasn't about to ask. They sat there a full three minutes before she shoved the Opel into drive and just barely missed a car coming down one of the rows. She headed towards the exit, went over the overpass and continued north towards the *Taunus* Mountains.

"Well...since you weren't hungry, I thought we'd go for a little ride," she said.

"I ride, huh? Ok. Sounds good to me."

Meanwhile in the parking lot, Derrick drove towards the front of the mall and slammed the van into park. He was still uncertain whether they'd parked or whether they'd left the area. He surveyed the front parking area, but couldn't spot her Opel. Shifting the van into drive, he circled the mall and ran through the back parking lot again. Seeing no trace of the car, he slapped his hands across the steering wheel and headed out of the parking lot. Driving as slow as a snail over the overpass, he looked in both directions over the road passing under him. They were nowhere in sight. "Crap!" he grumbled.

"So where are we headed?" Stace shouted above the roar of the wind whipping through the windows. A sharp ninety-degree turn loomed ahead.

Eva took her foot off the gas and stood on the brake pedal. Tires screeched and Stace held on as the Opel nearly flipped over into the ditch on the right side of the road. Eva quickly regained control and they came to a sudden stop at the first traffic light in *Bad Sodden*.

"Sorry about that Stace. We had a lot happen at the office today and I'm having trouble getting it out my mind."

Stace loosened his grip on the door handle.

"Have you ever been up this way?" she asked.

"No," he said. It didn't matter what he said. She wasn't listening to him anyway.

"When I was younger my father used to take my brother and I up this way."

The light turned yellow and she eased the Opel into the intersection just as it turned green.

They drove through the quaint town and she turned right onto a thinner road that began winding up through the *Taunus* forest.

"We don't see a lot of mountains in Texas. In the hill country we have some hills they try to call mountains, but nothing like this."

After five kilometers, she took a left and pulled into an unpaved lot. She parked next to a silver Audi, the only other car in sight. They got out of her car and stood for a moment in the silence. Above them loomed a canopy of enormous pine and fir trees. These rose like spears thrust into a forest floor of field grass speckled with sprigs of wood ferns. Their leaves and branches hung like Spanish moss.

"It's beautiful isn't it?" she asked, but again, she was just saying words. Her mind was elsewhere. Stace followed her as she headed up a hiking trail speckled with loose stones.

"Beautiful," he thought to himself, for a moment dropping his suspicion of her behavior. He hiked for a few minutes, stopped, taking in a breath of fresh air. The atmosphere within the forest carried with it no particular aroma, or at least one in which he could identify, but it was sharp and cool, invigorating his senses. He took in another deep breath then ran up the trail, joining Eva at her side.

"It'll be dark in Frankfurt by 7:00," she said. "It'll be dark here in another forty-five minutes."

He looked up through the trees. Their tips were sprinkled with flecks of sunset. As they continued, the depth of the forest floor darkened with each step.

"Have you ever felt like giving it all up and running away," she asked without turning towards him.

"Giving what up?"

"The charade…you know, the rat race," she replied.

"Sometimes."

"I forgot. You're a bit on the run yourself aren't you Stace?"

"I don't think you can ever run away. You can leave one place for another, but all you really end up doing is trading one set of circumstances for another. You still wake up as yourself in the morning no matter where you lay you head."

She slipped on a loose stone and he caught her elbow and held her up.

"Sure, I may have swapped countries for a while, but I still have to earn a living. I still have my hobbies and interests. Still have the same troubles on my mind." He stopped rambling for a moment and glanced at her. She'd not looked at him since they started up the trail and he wondered if she was even listening to him. "And I'm still looking for that one person to share my dreams with."

She kept hiking and they said nothing until they crested the top of the ridge. The trees along the edge were coated in the diffused orange light from the setting sun. Just over the ridge was an open meadow stretching downwards into a shallow valley. Clumps of wild grass and sprigs of violet flowers dressed it. Adolescent pines encircled its border. Beyond the meadow was a series of overlapping ridges and valleys, gradually descending in the distance towards *Wiesbaden*. At the edge of the world the sun appeared like a cotton ball dyed in burnt orange, nesting in an ocean of cream on the horizon.

"Let's sit here," she said.

He sat down next to her and looked behind him towards the parking area. He could still see the silver Audi, now dulled to the color of a forty-year-old nickel. "Besides, it's not really running away. I prefer to see it as maturing. Sometimes you have to let go of the things in life you can't change and move on."

"What's America like," she asked, for the first time looking at him.

"It was wonderful—still is wonderful. There are places in America where you can get lost. Places like here in the mountains where you can be who you are and the world can be the way it is. Places where you discover what you thought was important was really not important."

"What do you mean?

"That there are other things in life to think about rather than making a living, and sometimes you have to be willing to walk away from the past in order to notice them."

"It's not so easy as you make it sound."

"It's as easy as you want it to be. Remember when you were a child? Didn't you and your brother fight?

"*Ja*, but not often."

"What'd you fight about?"

"Alfred used to take my hair brush and hide it from me."

"A real crises!"

She shrugged her shoulders. "It was at the time. He'd bug the crap out of me!"

"It's not so important anymore is it?"

"Of course not, we grew up."

"And now you have bigger problems?"

"Yeah…I do. Problems I won't grow out of."

"So that means you have to fight them all your life?"

She leaned back against her arms. The sun had set, but her face was still lit in a soft glow. How he wished he could creep inside her mind to listen to what she was thinking.

"As hard as I try they just keep coming. No sooner than I finish one investigation, I have another one sitting on my desk." She sighed in frustration.

"That's because there are more criminals then you could ever hope to stop."

"Is that why you left Stace? Did you not have the will to fight the university's decision, or because you didn't want to even try?"

He looked over the plains towards Wiesbaden. The edge of the horizon was no longer visible, obscured by an impenetrable haze of darkness. Only a hint of pink remained in the sky above. "I think there's more to life than fighting, even fighting for what you believe in. I don't think it has anything to do with being a coward."

"I didn't say you were a coward."

"Not in those words, but call it the way you see it. I just think there's a point where you need to settle in and enjoy life. Even old soldiers have to retire at some point and leave the battle for the younger ones. It doesn't mean you quit fighting altogether, it just means you…well, you just fucking let it go!"

He was standing now and Eva was startled by his outburst. She reached for his hand. He was looking away from her, fixed on some point in the darkness, fidgeting. She touched his hand delicately at first, but he didn't respond. She gripped it with conviction then tugged on it gently. "I didn't mean to upset you, please, sit down."

"You didn't upset me. I upset myself. Everything is as serious as you make it to be, or as comical as you want it to be. I would like to believe life is wonderful. There are too many things to enjoy and experience without having to focus on the injustices twenty-four hours a day. At least, that's what I keep telling myself. But even though I'm in Germany, I can't seem to let go of my past. It's as if I'm dragging behind me this huge steel ball on a chain and until I reconcile the past I'll never be able to move forward." He was calm now, his words softer, blending into the swirl of the breeze flowing over the ridge.

"Was it the university's decision or something more personal that—"

"Tell you the truth it's all running together now. As an artist I understand my work might be rejected. I expect it and I guess in a certain way I work towards it. I don't just shoot pictures to try and make a living. I shoot as an expression of who I am. I'm always conscious of the impression I would like to leave on the world. When I was young, I was much more egotistical about my work. I don't know if I can explain this accurately without you misunderstanding me, but I thought I had some special gift, that my work would make some profound impact in the world…"

"But—"

"But, I was wrong. Just because you think you're something special doesn't mean others think so."

She knew that he was thinking about the individuals responsible for excluding him from the art exhibit. They not only succeeded in banishing him from the exhibit, but they had affectively altered the course of his life. What they had done may have seemed incidental to them, but for Stace, the significance of their actions replayed themselves over and over in his mind, undermining his confidence and rendering him creatively impotent.

"I know who I am as an artist, is much more important than what a few people may think of my work. Any real artist creates from an unspoken need to create and not through a need to be accepted."

She knew now, that he was lying to himself. In an effort to forget his pain, he was reasoning away the injustice done to him and he was looking for a reason to continue his work. He was stuck in a theoretical nowhere land, striving to maintain his identity as an artist, but couldn't, as long as there were people like Rick Forstein in the world.

Stace knew full well that artistic greatness came to those, who with a wild sense of recklessness overlook any objection to their craft. It was their lot to be misunderstood and in some cases rejected. Though he understood this, he had a difficult time living by it. This perplexed him and gave him good reason to doubt his own commitment to his craft. He couldn't accept the fact that no matter how much creative energy he put into his photographs, the possibility existed that his work would never be appreciated. He wanted to be recognized. He wanted to change the world in *his* time, not the world three hundred years from now. This would mean he'd have to compromise and that he was unwilling to do.

As Eva listened to him and imagined what the source of his troubles were, she tried to put them into the context of what she was going through. It occurred to her, that here was a man with deep convictions similar to hers and that they shared in struggles the average man or woman wouldn't consider as important. Through art, he wrestled and expressed his understanding of the greater issues of life. Though his impressions may have seemed impractical and perhaps even abstract, they were nevertheless, relevant. She understood as well the importance of art, that in its abstraction and mystical manner it also had a way of being brutally honest about life. She, on the other hand, was practical in her desire to change the world for the better. Due to that practicality, she was forced to face head-on those who abused the laws and to hold them accountable for their actions.

She gazed into the sky above. It was taking on a mud puddle diffusion of approaching blackness. The forest still had detail to its elements, but behind them in the direction of her car was nothing but blackness. She thought of Derrick and wondered if he was lurking somewhere, then looked at Stace, the last thing she wanted tonight was to be alone. But there was more to it than that. She liked this man...she more than liked him.

In his weaknesses she discovered a peculiar strength, a man who had the courage to face his vulnerabilities. She'd not seen this quality in men. The extent of his confession revealed he lived well above the testosterone challenges other men associate with their own rites of passage. And he had said something to her that continued to impress her. He'd said, "there's more to life than fighting—even fighting for what you believe in." As she thought about that statement, she wondered what it would be like to give up her own fight, to begin focusing on other things in life beyond her work at the *Schwarz Monatlich*. The thought was totally foreign to her, but acknowledging it as a possibility electrified her with a sense of hope. He'd given her that hope and she wondered if there were other things he could awaken within her. She was beginning to realize her attraction to him was substantial and it was based primarily on his openness and not hers. She knew that if their relationship was going to continue—if she was to one day know this man—then she would have to be much more honest with him than she'd been. A full disclosure of her work was not warranted, but he would have to be made aware of the possible dangers.

"Stace..."I haven't been totally honest with you."

He tentatively looked towards her. She was starring out into the distance with an expression he'd never seen.

"I haven't been entirely dishonest with you, but there are things you should know."

"I'm all ears."

"We were followed by someone into the shopping center."

"Followed? Are you sure?"

"*Ja*. The man showed up outside my office this morning. He followed one of the other reporters there. He waited for me to leave then followed me to *Hattersheim* where you work. I lost him in the mall parking lot."

"Are you sure he's not still around?" Stace asked, glancing back towards the car.

"Pretty sure."

"Do you know who he is?"

"His name is, Derrick Sachs. He's a member of an organization called the Christian Reform Movement in Frankfurt."

"Christian? What would they be following you around for?"

"I don't know."

"I think we should head back to the car," he said jumping to his feet. He gave Eva his hand and pulled her up.

"Are they dangerous?"

"I have no reason to believe they are, but then again, we haven't discovered what they're all about."

"So this sort of thing is common in your line of work?"

"Not really. I've had threats in the past few years from people I've investigated, but never a situation like this."

He had a picture in his mind of when she picked him up at work. The fact that she'd even come seemed unusual to him and the episode in the parking lot was well, bizarre. But that was before he knew why. He felt concerned for her safety, but now wondered about his own. Whoever had followed her now knew where he worked and worse, might jump to the conclusion he was working with her.

She stopped and faced him. "I didn't mean to get you involved with this. I was scarred this afternoon and without even thinking about it ended up at your work."

"Don't worry about it. It's probably nothing."

He didn't believe this, but thought she needed to hear it. Eva didn't believe it either. They found the car and wound their way down through the mountains.

"Do you know what this guy looks like? What was he driving?"

"An old Mercedes van and yes, I know what he looks like."

"Do you have a photo of him?"

"*Ja,* in my briefcase, along with a photo of some of the other members of the CRM." She waved her thumb towards the back seat.

He took that as permission and yanked the briefcase onto his lap. "Do you mind?" he asked clicking the locks open.

"Actually I do, let me get them."

He opened the case towards her and flipped on the dome light. She pulled out the envelope with the prints. "Here."

He spread the four photos out in his hand like cards. "Three men and one woman. Which one's him?"

"That one."

He brought the picture up to his face and leaned into the light. "Are you sure this is the same man that was following us today? I can barely see him."

"I'm sure. I still have to get it enlarged."

"I can do it for you."

"You can?"

"Sure."

"I don't really think you should. I don't want you involved. Besides, I can't let the negatives out of my sight."

"You won't have to. I've remodeled my bathroom. It doubles as a make-shift photo lab."

"You have a photo lab in your apartment?"

"It's what I do. Would you expect anything less?"

"I just don't know. Like I said, you don't need to be involved."

"Seems to me I already am. We can do it right now, take less than an hour and you can watch. Besides, I'd feel better if I didn't let you out of my sight. What do you say?"

CHAPTER 18

▼

Tasha slipped a cotton glove over her left hand, grabbed a wooden spoon with the other, bent over the pot of *kartoffelsuppe* simmering on the stove, and carefully lifted a spoonful of broth up to her lips. The potatoes were perfect, soft and chunky. They mingled well with the diced celery and onions. The dill and salt were fine, but the pepper was lacking. She sprinkled in a few dashes, speckling the creamy surface with freckles. Satisfied, she moved the pot over three bowls and poured. At that moment the oven buzzed and she pulled the *huh-nerkeule* out of the oven. She knew about five ways to prepare chicken, but thought it best roasted. Within a few minutes, she had it sliced onto three plates, garnishing each plate with a fork full of relish and two dinner rolls.

Through the door of the kitchen she saw Neil, working out of his briefcase as usual on the dining room table. She never asked about his work, even though he performed the ritual every night. As his custom was, he would finish the work he brought home from the office around 7:00, before turning his attention to the work of the ministry. She'd learned from experience there was only one thing he could be inter-rupted with from the moment he got home to the time he retired at night, that was dinner and he liked it hot. So, without hesitation she carried a plate in to him and set a bowl of potato stew above it. She smiled, even though she didn't expect him to return the gesture, but she liked to believe he appreciated dinner just the same, as well as all the other things she did for him and Derrick and for the cause. She returned to the kitchen and ripped off a sheet of aluminum foil, folded the edges around the lip of Derrick's plate and wondered what could be keeping him. She debated on whether to put his dinner in the fridge or to leave it covered on the counter. Either way, there would be consequences if she failed to make the right choice. The door handle turned, making her choice an easy one.

Derrick had reason to be in a good mood. He'd had a productive day following the black man in the Fiat to the *Schwartz Monatlich*, then following the woman in the Opel around. He would not tell Neil he'd lost her in the parking lot of the mall, but rather, that the hour had gotten late and he thought he should return to the apartment. Since Tasha was present at the table, he would sit on his report until later.

While Tasha and Derrick ate silently, Neil returned to his work behind his briefcase. This routine had become nearly unbearable to Tasha. Every evening Neil scribbling figures and shuffling papers behind his briefcase, and Derrick saying little if anything, grunting and slurping his way through dinner, as she quietly listened to the rhythm of her own food crunch and slide down her throat. Tonight was no different, except that Neil suddenly collected his papers, tossed them into the briefcase, closed the lid with a slam and dropped the case with a thump on the floor beside him. He moved so quickly even Derrick stopped chewing and looked up.

"*Was?*" Neil asked. "I'm sick of working for these people. They suck the living life out of you—you know?"

Tasha and Derrick glared at him. He never lost control. No matter what the circumstances, he was always calm and proper, like the surface of a lake at dawn. Actually, Tasha was wondering why Neil even bothered to work in the first place. Like other ministries, the CRM regularly solicited for donations. These donations were sufficient enough to allow all three of them to quit their jobs and devote their entire energy towards the ministry. But Neil insisted they run the ministry like a business. What income they received from donations was returned back into it, so they could continue to reach even more people. It was a labor of duty. Tonight however, his attitude was different. Perhaps he was finally considering it time for him to resign his position, so that he could more actively pursue what he considered to be the Lord's work. This coming Monday evening, he would be expecting a call from Stautzen in the United States. He looked forward to this call with great anticipation. If the news from Stautzen were good, if the program could be built, then it would signal a turn for the better in the CRM's ministry, and it would be irresponsible for him to continue working. If that were the case, he could finally sever once and for all his connection to the world. But work wasn't the only thing on his mind. For he believed that his ministry, in conjunction with the ICC, was designated by God to carry on the final work of bringing the gospel to the world. He knew satan and his angels would do anything to stop them. That assault had already begun. He could tell from the expression on Derrick's face that he was anxious to fill him in on the details of the assault.

He turned to Tasha. "Tasha, that was good. I know I don't often say so, but I appreciate the meals you make and all the extra work you do around here."

She smiled coyly, enjoying the moment and thought the gesture sincere.

"If you don't mind, Derrick and I need to discuss something."

Tasha missed the hint.

"Do you mind?" Derrick said raising his voice slightly.

"No, I'm sorry. I'll just start on the kitchen."

"Why don't you wait on that until later."

"Well, ok," she whispered and backed into the hallway.

"So what did you find out?" Neil asked after hearing Tasha's bedroom door close.

Derrick recapped for him everything he'd found out about who was watching their apartment, giving him detailed descriptions of the black man and the German woman. Then he reached inside his coat pocket and pulled out a folded copy of the *Schwarz Monatlich* and tossed it across the table.

"What's wrong?"

"You don't know?" Neil explained to him that the *Schwarz Monatlich* was notorious for its success when investigating corrupt organizations. Derrick understood. The danger was clear. If the *Schwarz Monatlich* had begun an investigation of their ministry, then their entire plans regarding the implementation of the program was in jeopardy.

"What else?" Neil asked.

"I also followed the woman into *Hattershiem*. She picked up an American at a place called Stroof's Photo."

"An American…are you sure?"

"Not entirely. He may have been European, but he definitely was dressed like an American, blue-jeans, white high-top tennis shoes, long hair pulled back into a ponytail, English words on his shirt—"

"I see what you mean. Let's assume he's an American. What's his interest in the woman, or more specifically, his connection to the *Schwarz Monatlich*?"

Derrick was silent.

"Stroof's Photo…the developing company?"

"I think so. Probably works there, but maybe developing film from—"

"I don't like it," Neil said, stabbing his chicken with his fork. "Where'd they go?"

Derrick thought of the excuse he was going to use but it escaped him. Neil would probably know if he wasn't telling the truth anyway. It was one of Neil's many gifts. "I followed them to the shopping center just outside of *Hochst*. The *Main Taunus Einkaufszentrum*."

"And?"

"I lost them in the parking lot."

Neil took a deep breath. He twirled his knife in his fingers then balanced it carefully on the edge of his plate. "I see."

"Do you think they discovered you were following them?" His words came sharp. He expected the truth.

"I don't know."

"We're going to assume they know we're on to their investigation. I expect they'll move even quicker now, because they'll expect us to be covering our tracks."

"You suppose they know about Stautzen and the program?"

"I doubt it, but we don't know what the American knows. We don't know who he's working for. He could be assisting the paper with their investigation. He could even be working with Trojan Security."

"You think he might be after the program? This is not good Neil."

Neil picked up the knife again and spun it in his fingers, thinking. Derrick pushed his plate away and looked past Neil towards the dubbing machines. "Why the investigation? Who was the American? Had the program been compromised?" Both of them turned the ramifications of these questions over in their minds, and both arrived at the same conclusion; the program was God ordained. There might be a few setbacks, but it was destined to succeed and with that as their only assurance, they must do everything in their power to ensure that it did.

"What do you suggest?" Derrick asked Neil. He made few decisions on his own, especially one of this magnitude.

"To start, you should quit your job."

"What should I tell them?"

"Tell them anything you want, except that you have obligations with the ministry. The paper will be checking on our employment and activities."

"Then what?"

"Tomorrow, go directly to *Hatteshiem* and Stroff's Photo. If the American does work there, follow him after he gets off. Find out where he lives if you can. Stick with him until you're sure he's down for the night."

"What about Tasha?"

"We leave her out of this. The less she's involved the better, but I'm going to tell her to quit her job too. We need someone here at the apartment in case they try something," he said decisively.

Derrick asked, "What about you?"

"I'll hand in my resignation Tuesday. I should give them at least a month, but I'll give them a week. I can't just quit on them. If the paper comes sniffing around, I want them to know I left on good terms and that I'm not in a rush to get out of there."

"Maintain the appearance?"

"Exactly. Everything's business as usual, as if we know nothing about the paper's investigation."

CHAPTER 19

▼

"Just follow *Wiesenfeldstrassa* around the corner," Stace told Eva.

She followed the single lane asphalt road as it curved to the right. Towards her left was the *Nidda* Canal, running black as night.

"Last house on the right, under the street light. See the BMW parked along the curb?"

"*Ja.*"

"Park behind it."

"I didn't realize you were so close to the pool. They'll be closing this weekend for the winter.

Stace stuck his hand out the window and felt the chill on his fingers. Up ahead near the streetlight stood an old poplar tree. Most of its leaves had already fallen. Those that remained, spun in the breeze of a cold front blowing in from *Bremerhaven* to the north. In the headlights of her car a flurry of leaves danced across the street. "No. I didn't know that. I still can't read most German signs. I probably would have showed up next weekend and been the only stupid American standing in front of the gates waiting for them to open."

She smiled.

"Come on. Let me show you the place."

He walked her down the cement pebble driveway running along the right side of the house. Next to a downstairs window on the lower level was an opening lit by a light on the wall. Beyond the opening, a skinny staircase led up to the second floor and his apartment.

"Let me take your coat and I'll show you around," he said, once they stepped inside.

"This of course, is the kitchen," he said, pointing as he walked.

She stopped at the open door and looked at the window, which faced north and was dressed in white-laced curtains. On the wall to her left was a wooden table cluttered with a toaster, a half loaf of wheat bread and a jar of strawberry jam. Three chairs bordered the table and looked as though they'd never been moved. On the opposite wall was the sink, which sat in the middle of a counter top painted in frog green. Below the counter was a row of waist high, darkly stained cabinets, with matching cabinets running the length of the wall above it. Unwashed dishes filled the sink. A black microwave filled in the left corner. The refrigerator to the right was rippled in a surface simulating leather. Almost everything, fridge, stove, counter tops, even the electric can opener, were painted a variation of green.

"Very nice," she said. "Everything looks new."

"I was the first to move in after they remodeled the place. Can't complain."

"Laundry room," he said, turning around and opening the first door on the right.

"Looks like you keep up with it."

"I don't have a lot of clothes, so I wash every few days." He closed the door and they continued down the long hallway.

"Bedroom one." She looked inside. "Nothing in here but extra photo equipment and some of the work I've done. I'll show you them another time. And here is the master bedroom." He swung the door open and flipped the switch on the wall. Light from a glass bubbled ceiling fixture lit the room.

"The furniture's beautiful."

"Ancient."

"Antique anyway. Walnut?"

"No idea. Walnut, Cherry—it came with the place. I need a ladder to get up on the bed.

"I can see that. They don't make headboards like that anymore."

Eva watched the red glow of digitized numbers on the alarm clock switch from 6:47 to 6:48. "What's in the shoe box," she said, nodding to the shoe box on the dresser.

"Knickknacks. Keeps the cluster out of sight." He turned off the light and they backed into the hallway.

"This end of the apartment is the living room." He slid open a sliding door built of fogged glass set in a wood frame.

She stepped over the threshold. The most impressive feature of the room was a series of windows built into the far wall. Rectangular panes, as tall as Stace, took up the bottom portion and above them, filling in the arch of the ceiling and coming to a point in the center, were additional triangular shaped windows and a sliding glass door. Creamed colored curtains synched with a bow filled in the corners.

"I spend a lot of my time here, excuse the mess," he said, gesturing towards the left half side of the living room, where an oversized, leather couch dominated the area. On the couch lay a couple of People magazines, as well as a novel by Leo Tolstoy. The paperback lay flipped over to hold a page. Before the couch sat an obtrusive coffee table topped with tinted glass. It was covered with photography magazines, a stack of USA Today newspapers, dirty dishes and a half full ashtray.

"Have you read it? he asked, noticing she was fixated on the novel.

"No."

"Don't recommend it, unless you like trudging through the lives of aristocratic Russians. It reads like an ancient soap show, but the history of the time is interesting. People falling in and out of love. A little too mushy for me I'm—" he stopped short, looking at Eva and hoping he'd not given her the impression that falling in and out of love wasn't a worthwhile topic to read about. "The books about relationships. Some good, some bad."

"I see." She crossed her hands behind her back and smirked.

He walked to the stereo and found something he thought she might like. "I got this CD at a concert my brother took me too when I was thirteen. Just three guys, Al Di Meola, Jean Luc Ponty and—"

"You said you had a photo lab?"

"Almost forgot. Down the hall in the bathroom." She followed him out of the living room.

"Nothing fancy here," he said, turning on the light to the toilette room. "Interesting concept you Germans have of separating the toilet from the bathroom." He switched off the light. "But you wanted to see the lab." He walked to the next door and flipped the switch. "Here it is."

She had no idea what a photo lab might light like, but this one looked like it had it all. In fact, she completely overlooked the bathtub to her right as her eyes drifted towards a conglomeration of stuff to her left. Most of the equipment lay on the long table against the wall. An enlarger stood in the far corner. Along the front of the table was a neat row of charcoal colored plastic pans full of liquid. Behind the pans were four or five coffee cans filled with strange utensils as well as several gallon sized metal containers listing ingredients like sodium thiosulfate and other unrecognizable names. There were brushes and rags, stacks of paper, a roll of paper towels and dozens of tiny plastic containers used for storing 35 mm film.

"I still prefer the old methods of developing and still haven't gone digital.

From the light fixture set in the wall, Stace had spliced into the existing wires and rigged up a red bulb. He reached for the wall switch at the door, then with his fingers found the other switch. The bathroom filled with a warm reddish glow. It took Eva's eyes a few minutes to readjust.

"Crude, but effective. Everything I need is here. I can develop black and white as well as color."

He switched the red light off and the room was swallowed by darkness. She felt the heat of his body move past her towards the door. For a moment she wondered what he was up to. Actually, he'd become so accustomed to the tools and fixtures in his lab, he was just as comfortable in the dark as in the light. When the lights went back on he was at the door.

"Do you have the negatives? he asked.

"*Ja*, but I forgot them in the car."

"Why don't you run back downstairs and get them?"

While she ran out to the car, Stace headed for the kitchen. From a wine rack on the floor under the table, he grabbed a bottle of apple wine, and picking two of his fancy jelly glasses, he poured. When Eva returned he handed her a glass.

"Here you go."

"What's this?"

"Exactly what it looks like. You've had an exciting day. Are these the negatives?"

"*Ja.*"

"Hold onto them for a second."

He went back to the kitchen and brought back a chair. "I'm not used to visitors. You'll be more comfortable sitting."

She followed him into the bathroom and he shut the door. "This shouldn't take too long. So, tell me...if you can, about the investigation you're working on."

"The assignment was Mr. Schwarz's idea."

"And you don't think it's exciting enough for you?" he asked, removing several sheets of developing paper from its light proof container.

"I'm used to investigating less ambiguous topics, white-collar crimes I guess you'd call them. But I wouldn't go so far as to say any of those investigations have been dangerous."

He listened to her synopsis with great interest. She was far from dull. Fact, she was borderline mysterious. One would never guess from the way she looked and carried herself the type of work she was involved in.

"This religious organization…what did you called them?"

"The Christian Reform Movement."

"Kind of dull? Same old run of the mill, save the world kind of stuff right?"

"So far, yes. Until Derrick, one of their members started following me today."

"Us you mean."

"But you've got nothing to do with it."

He held two thin strips of negatives to the light and examined the faces. "You and I know that, but do they?"

For a moment she considered how it must have looked to Derrick when she picked Stace up at work. "I didn't really think—"

"Don't worry about it. What's the worse they could do? Chase us down on the street, force us into a corner and shove religious literature down our throat?"

"That would be embarrassing."

"Seriously though, there must be more to their interest in you, otherwise, they wouldn't be following you."

"Could be. The movement might be linked to another organization known as the International Christian Coalition."

"The ICC? he asked, looking at her for the first time since he'd set to work.

"Yeah. Why? Have you heard of them?"

"Who hasn't? I don't know all the details about them, but they're well known in the states. Based out of Munich I believe."

"How'd you know?"

"Common knowledge. They advertise that after every broadcast."

He completed preparing the negatives for enlargement. "Tell you what, the bottle of wine is on the kitchen table. Do me a favor and refill my glass. I have a couple of things left to do, then we'll have to wait a few minutes until these are ready to look at. Have a seat in the living room and I'll be right out."

Twenty minutes later he came out of the bathroom.

"Finished?" she yelled.

"Almost." He poked his head into the living room, "hungry?"

"Starved."

"I'll get something and be right with you."

She started to rise.

"I'll get it. Relax."

He dropped a few copies of the prints off in the storage room, then went into the kitchen. A few minutes later, he'd whipped up a couple of tuna sandwiches and set them on a plate along with crackers and Swiss cheese. After removing a six-inch serrated knife from the dish drainer he headed down the hallway.

"That was quick."

"Eating's a necessity. What I buy makes up fast and just keeps me moving. The tuna should go great with the apple wine," he said, twisting his lips around in disgust.

"You have quite a CD collection."

"You're joking, right? They've been out for what, twenty, thirty years? Think I've got about fifteen or so at last count. My real love is in the storage room where I keep my photos."

"Small collection but a good one. I like your taste in music, but there are a few artists I'm not familiar with."

Her use of the word "artists" struck him. Most people consider an artist to be someone who paints. Some might go so far as to call a musician an artist, but to Stace her choice of the word indicated the depth to which she understood the nature of those who create. "Artist..." he thought silently to himself. "I like how that sounds."

They stuffed themselves and polished off the bottle of wine, discussing insignificant details of life in which words were only foreplay to their discovering deeper possibilities of their relationship together. Hours passed. Stace ceased to be distracted by the way her nose had a slight bend to the right. She disliked the fact that he smoked. "The prints!" she suddenly blurted, but giggled as if they were as relevant as the weather.

"Let's go check them out," he said jumping up.

The eight by tens were hanging on a thin wire stretching over the bathtub. He'd clipped them at the corner and they'd long since dried. He was pleased with the results from a technical standpoint and she was grateful to see the figures blown up to a larger size. She swayed ever so slightly in front of each picture, studying the details of the faces and trying to get a read on the characters behind the faces.

"Who's who?" he asked. He was staring at the photograph of the young woman coming out of the apartment walking a dog.

"This is Derrick Sachs," she said, making Stace focus on another print. "The one who followed us today."

Regrettably, he took his eyes off the woman and looked at the shot of a man coming up a sidewalk approaching an apartment. He was slouched over as though he was counting cracks in the sidewalk. Though the angle was a little off, Stace could still make out the features of his rugged face.

"This is, Tasha Matyastick."

"I noticed."

"Thought you would."

He turned and smiled. They were as close as breath. "And what makes her so mysterious?" he whispered to her.

She turned towards the picture. "That's the problem. We know very little about her—much less the rest of them. Just minor biographical details that don't amount to didly. Derrick seems to be the one in charge, or perhaps, he's the gofer who takes care of the details. Tasha…well, I just don't know. She works at a department store in the daytime and she's from Czechoslovakia. In fact, they are all immigrants to Frankfurt."

"Which one's Neil?" he asked, looking at the two photos on the end.

"Don't know that either. Got to be one of these two."

"But you don't know for sure." He stated as a matter of fact. Both photos were of men in their late forties taken as they were exiting the apartment. Both men were wearing suits. One of them was holding his coat and a briefcase.

"What does Neil do?"

"He works for a computer accounting firm by day."

"But you know nothing about his work?"

"No. Why?"

"Only that some businessmen are more busy than others. The dedicated one's bring their work home, hence the briefcase. But since you know nothing about his work, then—"

"I'm not too worried about that at the moment. Another day or two and I'll know. I'm more interested in finding out what they're up to. We also think there's a forth person involved, Joseph Stautzen. He works for the ICC, but we think he's connected to the CRM as well."

"So what you have so far is your boss' intuition...these pictures, and a hunch."

"Correct. If it wasn't for the hunch, I'd say I've got nothing."

"Except for the cat and mouse routine this afternoon."

"So they know I'm on to them."

"Which doesn't give you a lot of time does it?"

She reached up and took the photos off the wire.

"What's your hurry?"

"I thought I'd get back to my place. I think better there."

"Now? It's 9:30 already. Don't you ever stop? Look, why don't you stay here tonight."

A curious expression rippled her face.

"I'll sleep on the couch and you can sleep in my room. Or, if you think you'd be more comfortable you can sleep on the couch."

Before Eva could answer, he voiced his concern. "Does Derrick know where you live?"

"I...I don't think so, but I don't know what he knows." She imagined him sitting in his van across the street from her house plotting who knows what. "I'm not going to run from these people. I told myself years ago that I will not live in fear."

"I'm not asking you to hide. I'm just asking you to relax and stay a while. Tomorrow you can reevaluate the situation."

She considered the idea. The hour was late and she felt a bit too tipsy to drive anyway. "I think I'd be more comfortable on the couch."

CHAPTER 20

▼

At precisely 6:30 the following morning, Alfred drove his utility van along *Hugelstrasse* and crept past the CRM's apartment. He took a hard right onto *Kurhessenstrasse*, which cut into *Hugelstrasse* like a blade opening out of a jackknife. A steady mist had fallen across Frankfurt through the night, which glazed the roads like a heavy coat of corn syrup. The wheels under the van slurped as he continued down *Kurhessenstrasse* behind the apartment, took a right on *Ricarda Huch* and parked. Grabbing a set of binoculars, he walked down the street and into the park. A hint of dawn was forming in the surrealistic oranges and grays glowing low across the sky. From where he stood, propped on the side of a monstrous cypress, he watched the lights in the buildings across the street flicker on one by one, like squares on a yellow and black checkerboard.

He stood there for nearly an hour, turning over the photos Eva had given him of the CRM members until he could no longer stand to look at them. As dawn came and went, the traffic along Hugelstrasse increased to the point where the cars and buses seemed linked together like railroad cars hooked together as one. He expected to have seen Tasha walk her dog by now, but perhaps she'd done it earlier. Finally, at 7:20, Derrick emerged from the front entrance followed by a man he suspected to be Neil. After exchanging last minute words, Derrick left to continue another day of stalking Eva and Neil returned inside. Alfred grew frustrated, thinking he might miss his opportunity, but several minutes later he saw Neil in his BMW take a right onto *Hugelstrasse*. Last to go would be Tasha and he knew she left for work at 7:45. This morning she was two minutes late. She'd have to hurry to catch the U-3 into town. He walked back to his van, then drove to the front of the apartment. By the time he'd set his cones, grabbed his tool belt and the devices he'd be installing, it was 8:05.

Tasha had caught the 8:00 *U-Bahn* and at that moment was exiting the train under the intersection at *Miquel Adickesallee*. She made her way up the underground corridor onto street level and walked along *Miquel Allee* towards work with apprehension. She hated confrontations. Meanwhile, Alfred ascended the stairs up to the third floor and knocked sharply on the door of apartment 3-B. If anyone was still in the apartment he could easily act confused, as if he'd knocked on the wrong door. After a moment of waiting and getting no response, he reached into his bag and pulled out a tool of his own making. One that could penetrate even the most sophisticated of locks. Forty-five seconds later he was inside.

Tasha turned right onto *Hansaallee* and walked into Schnell's department store. The night before, Neil had asked her to quit her job under the pretense the ministry was growing and they needed her around the apartment to help with the increased workload. She'd been anticipating that news from Neil for a long time, but confronting Mr. Schnell with the news wasn't going to be easy. Mr. Schnell, the son of the store's founder, was an exacting man who ordered his employees around like a disgruntled varsity coach. The preceding month he'd reluctantly given her a raise. He did it to shut his wife up, who'd begun to pester him that Tasha was due for one. Upon informing Tasha of the extra one mark per hour, he made it clear to her that he thought she didn't deserve it. Truth be told, she hated the man, but needed the work. In the back of the store, Mr. Schnell kept a cubbyhole of an office. She didn't waver in her task, but slowed with every step as she made her way down an isle towards the back.

When she knocked, he was seated at his desk facing the door unwrapping a crumpled piece of paper. Filbert's distributing had over-charged him for a case of toothpaste. He had made three inquiries to the company the day before, but no one returned his calls. His first call this morning would be less diplomatic. He would demand a hearing with their general manager.

"Mr. Schnell?" she asked timidly, tapping the doorframe.

"What is it?

"I need to talk to you about something." She hesitated, taking a half step in his direction.

He'd been running the store for the past twelve years, the filing cab-inet behind him was full of employee files of workers which had been fired, quit, or just never came back after the first day. He read the tone of her voice and knew what she was going to say even before she spoke.

"Today's my last day. I'm sorry, but something's come up and I can't work here anymore after today."

"Why work today?" he asked, pushing his swivel chair away from his desk.

She was taken back by his response and didn't know what to say. "I don't—"

"Why work today?" he repeated and stood up.

She lurched backwards into the hallway.

"If what you need to do is so important then let me just give you the rest of the day off!" His voice tweaked another notch higher. "Just go home now and do what it is you've got to do!"

Mrs. Schnell had been lining up bottles of vitamins on a shelf nearby. She heard the roar of her husband's voice and was moving towards them.

Mr. Schnell had stopped just outside of his office, legs parted like a fighter bracing for a blow. Contempt wrinkled his face. He caught sight of his wife moving down the isle towards them, but never took his eyes off Tasha. Her mouth hung open and void of words. Deep within her she could feel something terrible and involuntary moving through her body. She managed to break free of his gaze and turned around. Through her tears the tidiness of the products on the shelves lost their shape and form, swirling into a blur of color. She didn't notice Mrs. Schnell walk past her. She didn't hear her raise her voice at the brute. She could barely find the door. When she did, she stepped outside into the nip of the morning overwhelmed with embarrassment. She leaned back against the glass front door and patted her eyes with the sleeve of her red blouse. Suddenly feeling the urge to flee, she didn't collect herself until she sat down on a plastic chair gazing over two parallel tracks at the *U-Bahn* station.

It took Alfred only a few minutes to find the phones. One was in the living room sitting on the windowsill. The second was located in one of the back rooms on the nightstand near the bed. He returned to the one in the living room. Unscrewing the plastic cap of the mouthpiece, he laid it on the windowsill next to the phone and took out a tiny audio device from a pocket in his tool pouch. The miniature transponder, shaped like a crescent moon, slid neatly into the uncapped part of the handset, which he secured with two strips of electrical tape, so it wouldn't rattle inside the receiver when someone used the phone. He screwed the plastic cover back on and walked down the hall.

The phone in the back room was a much older model. When he unscrewed the cover of the mouthpiece, he discovered it to be full of dust and fuzz. Holding the handset over the rug, he vigorously blew into it. Particles of light gray dust floated to the floor, but the fuzz remained. He removed a rag from his pouch that was already soaked in a solvent solution, and swirled the rag around the plastic housing to clear off enough residue so that the transponder could be secured into place. Blow, swirl, blow, swirl…the delay cost him a precious four minutes. Tasha was halfway home on the U-3 when he'd finished with the phone. She'd be home in sixteen minutes.

His next task was to place other audio bugs in a few choice locations around the apartment. One in the living room and one in the dining room would suffice. In the living room, he ran his hand along the bottom of the windowsill and found a small lip. He could put one here, but the device was taller than the lip and it might be spotted if someone was sitting on the couch. He thought of attaching the device on one of the mounts of the curtain rods. But from what he understood, they never opened the curtains. The bug would certainly be concealed, but the curtains would act like a filter, possibly sealing out important conversations. The bottom of the couch was another option, but the adhesive he used to attach the device wouldn't hold to the fabric. Under the kitchen table would have been an ideal spot except anyone of them might discover it simply by bending over and picking up a scrap of food.

The best location he could find was underneath a table pushed against the back of the couch. On top of the table was a vase of half dead wild flowers. Next to the vase was a stack of brochures about the CRM and a laser printer. Directly underneath the printer was a half-inch stack of printing paper. He knelt down and peered at the underside of the table. It was smooth and dark with a three-inch border. This looked like a good spot. The table was also centered between the living room and the dining room and would pick up any conversations occurring in both rooms. He removed the bug out of his tool bag and curled his fingers around its edge. It was round like a quarter and as thick as a pencil. The bottom was capped with a sheet of aluminum and on the top side a metal screen protected the inside components. With his other hand, he removed a pre-cut piece of two-way adhesive tape from his top pocket. Carefully, he removed one of the paper seals on the tape and attached it to the bottom of the bug, then shoved the paper seal into a pouch on his tool bag—or so he thought. The piece sailed onto the back of his pant leg. Once the tape had been secured to the backside of the bug, he pealed off the other seal and shoved it into his tool bag. In the far corner of the table he located a dark cavity between two bolts and leaned over and pressed the bug in place. When he stood up the paper seal from the adhesive tape perched on his pant leg fell to the floor near the printing paper.

Tasha was five minutes away.

Walking quickly into the back bedroom he moved towards the other phone. The accordion style closet doors were open and he took a quick look inside, then rummaged though the dresser against the bed. He glanced over the desk and bookshelves taking a mental picture of everything in sight. With the same manner of precision, he took an inventory of the contents of the other two rooms and within three and a half minutes had returned to the living room. Along one of the walls were two cheap office tables placed side by side. On the tables were two computers and a color printer. Computer books, papers, brochures, a can of pens and pencils, and everything one might expect to find in a homemade office, littered the tables. He removed a video and an audiocassette tape from a box under the tables and slid them inside the top of his overalls. In the dining room was a similar arrangement; three identical office tables lined the left wall. On top of the tables were stacks of audio and videocassette dubbing machines. He reached inside his tool pouch and this time pulled out a small black aluminum box. Inside the box was a transmitter, and protruding out of the box was a video camera lens. The device was capable of transmitting video data slightly over five miles. Despite its size, it was still large enough that hiding it would take creativity and planning. The quickest he'd ever installed one was just under thirteen minutes.

He checked his watch. The longer he stayed the greater the risk. Even though he suspected the occupants of the apartment to be gone for sometime, he found himself experiencing an unpleasant sense of anxiety. It was a familiar feeling to him; one he usually worked around, but an inner voice told him something wasn't quite right. Walking over to the far side of the window, he pulled the curtains back and peeked outside. He first looked down the length of *Hugelstrasse* towards the U-3, but something at the bottom of his peripheral vision alarmed him. There was a flash of a person passing underneath the cement overhang of the main entrance to the apartment. When he looked down it was too late. The form was no longer visible. He closed the curtains and held his breath, listening for sounds. Deep down in the stairway, he heard the muffled sound of the outer door. Before it closed, the second door opened and he heard a shuffle of footsteps, as if someone was kicking the dust off their feet by stamping them against the floor. Someone was coming but whom? His mind rapidly replayed the flash of the form over and over and he recognized in the sequence the shinny, black short-cropped hair of a woman. Whether it was Tasha or not, he didn't know, but the same voice that told him to look out the window was now telling him to get out. He raced to the door and stepped into the foyer. The footsteps of the woman were just stepping onto the first flight of stairs. Anticipating the door of their apartment might close with a pop, he faked a cough to cover the sound. Tasha heard the cough and remembered the telephone van out front. Safe in the landing between the two doors, he made no attempts to conceal his presence, descending the staircase with more noise than necessary. He met Tasha on the second floor landing. The two exchanged glances. Since she'd been crying and knew she didn't look her best, she dropped her face towards the floor.

"*Guten morgen,*" he said. She didn't respond.

Relieved to be outside, he tossed his stuff in the back of his van and headed for the *Schwarz Monatlich.*

CHAPTER 21

▼

Reverend Eisner awoke on Saturday morning with a renewed sense of determination. He'd received a call late Friday evening from Stautzen, who'd confessed to him that the most important aspect of the program had been set in motion. The program would be built using the ICC as a model. If all went well, the program should be complete in less than two months. Stautzen's admonition to the reverend was that he should prepare his ministry for a dynamic explosion in growth.

Despite the excitement of the news bubbling within him, the reverend felt compelled to carry out his morning ritual of reading from the word of God. While an undergraduate student in theology classes over forty-two years ago, he'd gotten in the habit of reading a specific number of chapters from both the Old and New Testaments daily. He was not selective in his approach, reading five chapters from the Old Testament and five chapters from the New Testament in sequence. So it was, that when he'd finish reading Malachi he would begin again at Genesis, and having completed the last chapter of Revelation, he'd start fresh with the gospel of Matthew. To date, he'd read though the entire Bible sixty-three times. He kept a tally of his progress in the cover of his worn, leather bound King James, which he carried in his heart and hand for more years than he could remember. Whether he was bored with the reading or not he would still read, resigning to the task every morning between 6:00 and 6:30, seated in the high back chair behind his desk in the study of his home. After competing his daily reading, he would fill his pipe, ignite it with a blue-tipped match and as the tobacco sizzled and snapped he'd watch the smoke rise in a curling stream into the stillness of his study. As dizziness began to cloud his mind, he'd push his chair away from the desk, turn slightly in the direction of the window and ponder the words he'd read.

What the reverend reflected on most were the individual characters played out in the Bible. He studied those characters ferociously, admiring those who should be admired and despising those who should be despised, while keeping in mind that each character had their place in God's plan and each one of their lives was therefore, justifiable. Although one would never catch him saying it, he thought the character of Christ to be somewhat wimpy and passive. He was much more impressed with the patriarchs and prophets of old, who seemed to him to represent more of the true nature of God. They were quick and decisive, ever ready to do battle against the enemies of God. Over the years, the reverend had selected from their personality traits all of the most important qualities to duplicate in his own life, purposely overlooking the more subtle qualities of the life of Christ, which made the reverend, little more than a patchwork of the characters he idolized.

He was of course, oblivious to this deficit and had a strange way of covering it up, believing every person who had ever lived was involved in a divine chess game played between God and the devil. "People were like pawns," he often said, and "moved by the whims of angels under the command of God." In his own mind he knew the game to be fixed from the beginning. That is, that God would eventually win, but in the meantime, every player on the board was predestined to fulfill a specific role to the overall outcome of the game. His relationship to Watson verified his thinking on this point. From the start he disliked the American, primarily, because the American was simply, a Capitalist. Watson was a highly successful businessman and in the reverend's mind one can't serve both God and money. Even so, Watson had a plan to promote the cause of God, and although the reverend might have considered him to be evil, it was not beyond reason that God could manipulate the ideas of Watson to assist the reverend in God's overall plans.

The reverend was also no stranger to the art of compromise. He knew his lavish lifestyle resembled little in comparison to the example of the patriarchs. He recognized this weakness, but justified it under the assumption that his true call from God to him had not yet come. For the reverend understood the limits of toleration that twenty-first century heathen give to those who proclaimed to be ministers of God. They were expected of them to be wealthy and successful, for what other justification was there that God was blessing their lives? The facts were simple; he'd devoted his life to God and God had blessed him for it. Who was he to deny those blessings? He lived in one of the finer mansions in southern Munich with a splendid view of the Austrian Alps. His handsomely furnished home rested on seventy-six acres of untouched land speckled with flowering meadows set in a lush forest—not to mention a charming lake. Although the reverend didn't fish, he kept a rowboat and in times of great stress would row out into the middle of the lake and refill his hectic life with tranquility. He needed only one automobile but had three. The one he drove into Munich and back everyday was a Mercedes he exchanged every year for the newest model. He also owned a late model BMW and an antique Jaguar. He possessed a thick and well-diversified financial portfolio, but only he and his private accountant knew the exact value.

Even so, the reverend was acutely aware of the fact that before the second coming of Jesus he must give those riches up and completely forsake the world. But this must be a give and take situation. God must provide him with overwhelming evidence that such a time had come. The last thing he wanted to do was give up his lifestyle prematurely. The worst thing that could happen to him at this point in life would be for him to misread the signs. If he gave it all up and Christ delayed his coming, then it was entirely possible he could end up a poor and bro-

ken man, embarrassing himself before the world, and history was riddled with the lives of men who died and left nothing more than the
example of what over-zealousness and fanaticism can do.

Having considered all of these ramifications and consequences, he
tapped the crusty ashes out of his pipe. It was now or never...do or
die...put up or shut up...a time when great men of great faith
act...the stuff of history books...and he was the man of the hour.

CHAPTER 22

▼

In the Summersheim's garden, earthworms were still dozing in the crust of topsoil. Faded yellow broccoli blossoms, left in the ground over the course of the summer were laced with frost. Not even the birds had risen. The rainbow snapdragons along the driveway had yet to swallow a bee. Stace had spun all night, like a snake wrestling free of its outer skin. The night, still hanging in his room, awaited the enlightening rays of the sun.

Sometime after 4:00 a.m., he tiptoed into living room. In the blue light filtering in from the street light he admired Eva's shape beneath the flimsy, evergreen blanket. She lay on her back with the blanket pulled up under her chin, her arms gracefully folded over her stomach, fingertips barely touching. Her head was nestled in a pillow and cocked towards the stereo. A halo of mangled blond hair sprang madly around her face. Her lips begged for his. The rise of her bosom…the traceable, circular peaks of her nipples, took him back to the memory of their exquisite form when he first met Eva at the pool.

He'd never met a woman like Eva. She wasn't preoccupied with the millions of inconsequential details of life as other women might be, who focus on following the latest in fashion or social etiquette. What he admired most about her was her passion towards her work, and whether he realized it or not, it was her passion that was reacquainting him with his own buried dreams. To say it was lust he had towards Eva, would not do justice to his wanting. Neither would admiration or worship. Words that describe such wanting have not been breathed. They have not been written and forever remain unspoken, like a thought from the gods, so sacred that mortal men can only wonder how the miracle of love begins and where it ends.

He leaned over and stroked her cheek with the backside of his hand. She didn't seem to mind. He caressed the form of her jaw and moved his finger over the fullness of her lips. This time she stirred and he withdrew, and she rolled over onto her side and extended her legs, which allowed the blanket to slide off her breasts. Then like child, she brought her knees up into a fetal position, leaning them towards the back of the couch. She was wearing one of his old tee shirts and in the soft light he could see the darkened flesh of her nipples and the weight of her bosom stretching the cotton fabric. Involuntarily, he reached out again—but stopped short. If and when the time came, the sharing of their bodies would be one of mutual consent. His hand still outstretched over her bosom, he contented himself by feeling the heat of her body, as though he were warming himself in the flames of a fire. He whispered good night and went back to his room.

Eva had been tossing and turning all through the night. The couch was short and the cushions soft. Each time she moved, the cushions would separate from themselves or pull away from the back of the couch, leaving some portion of her body slipping between the cracks. She'd heard a noise at Stace's entrance, like she'd heard many strange noises that night in the unfamiliar apartment, but the shuffle of footsteps across the living room carpet was unmistakable. She continued to sleep play, even as the creaking of the coffee table suggested he was sitting just inches from her. She was fearful and anxious at his presence. Not fearful in the sense that she was afraid of what he might do, but fearful of her own reaction to his advance. So she pretended to be asleep, frozen in a state of anticipation. She'd known him now for just a couple of weeks, and she was confused by the trust she placed in him.

She'd known few men, but never had she wanted one as much as she felt she needed one now. She'd not yet discovered anything negative about him, except his unbridled sincerity, which was a quality so rare in her experience with men, that it alarmed her. As much as she longed for his embrace, she couldn't help wonder if everything was moving too quickly and yet at times, not fast enough.

She didn't hear the movement of him leaning towards her and when his first touch graced her cheek it was barely perceptible. The tender stroke of his creative hands seemed to be stroking her innermost soul. Then he withdrew. Why? Before she had her answer, he touched her once more with a stroke that desired much more than a mere touch of her flesh. From her earlobe, down her jaw line, over her chin and across her lips, he caressed. She had a knee-jerk reaction. Suddenly he stopped. Then she heard his heavy breathing. Would he try again? She had her answer when she heard his footsteps shuffle lightly down the hallway.

A few hours later, Stace awoke for a second time and with a quick glance out the window saw a subtle change of lightness in the sky. "Is she awake yet?" he wondered. He thought about going in see to her, but didn't want to startle her. "How would that look? me standing over her gawking." He was feeling a little ashamed for sneaking in to see her earlier that morning. He hopped out of bed and drifted down the hallway towards the kitchen to make breakfast. With breakfast made and the morning half broken into a blossoming glow, he walked down the hallway carrying a tray full of coffee, eggs, toast and sausage links. From the door, he summoned her up by saying, "good morn-ing," but she didn't move as he set the tray on the coffee table.

"Eva, it's time to wake up," he said again. She stirred and slowly opened her eyes. Seeing him seeing her, and wearing the disarray of a morning face, she yanked the blanket over her face. He bent over and snapped the blanket down.

"I'm going to jump in the shower. Have some breakfast while it's still hot."

When he returned from showering, she was dressed and had finished eating.

"You cook too?" she asked as he walked into the living room.

"I try. The bathroom's free if you need it."

"What time is it?" she asked, looking around the cluttered coffee table for her watch.

"Still early, about 6:45. Do you need to get going?"

"I usually get to work around 8:30, but my schedule's flexible. They won't start missing me until the afternoon. Why don't you let me give you a ride into work? It's the least I can do."

"Sure, sound's good. Hey! Since we have some extra time, would you like to take a look at some of my photographs?

"I'd love to. Give me a few minutes," she said, heading into the bathroom.

Like an excited boy, he snatched his portfolio out of the storage room and hurried back into the living room. His portfolio consisted of a number of large photographs wrapped within protective envelopes of see-through plastic. He carefully pulled them out and started laying them across the couch, over the coffee table, against the stereo and across anything else that would prop them up. By the time Eva returned a few minutes later, he'd created a gallery.

"My goodness!" she exclaimed when she returned.

He stood apprehensively in the background while she studied each photograph. She looked over a third of his work without saying a word. Anxious for some response, he stepped up beside her as she was looking over a photograph of scene he'd captured a year before he'd gone to college. It was during a visit to see a friend who was serving in the army at Fort Huachuca in Sierra Vista, Arizona. He remembered taking the photo like it was yesterday.

"What do you think?" he asked.

"I think it's beautiful," she replied genuinely.

His heart dropped a notch. "Just beautiful?" he thought.

She quickly elaborated, "Stace, I don't consider myself to be an expert, so I couldn't begin to give you a professional opinion of your work. I can only tell you how they make me feel. Take this one for instance; when I look at it, it's as if I've been transported into the scene. Kind of like last night when we sat on the ridge in the *Taunus* Mountains, except I find this picture much more stimulating…. And this one," she continued, backing up to look at a photograph of two monkeys. "How'd you get them to do that?"

"I didn't. They did it on their own."

The photograph was a black and white of two monkeys that shared adjoining cages. The cages came together at a point and were separated by a cement beam about a foot in diameter. In one cage, an adult monkey was standing near the beam holding a piece of apple. It was sitting with its profile to the camera and reaching out of its cage around the barrier as far as it could. In the other cage a baby monkey was standing in the corner with his back facing the camera. The baby monkey was bending over and reaching around the barrier with his left arm tucked between his legs.

"I could see what they were trying to do. The adult monkey was trying to share the apple with the baby monkey, but the apple piece kept falling on the ground outside the cage. I waited twenty minutes until they succeeded. At the moment when the baby monkey finally managed to grab the apple, I snapped the shot. I submitted the photograph to the local paper and the next Sunday it came out in the *Around Town* section.

She drifted over to the photographs submitted for the exhibit. He'd purposely stood the three next to each other, propping them up against the window on the floor.

"Let me guess, these are what got you thrown out of the exhibit."

"Very perceptive," he replied.

"Frankly, I don't see what the fuss was all about."

"Then you like them?"

"I don't dislike them," she replied. "I mean, I don't think they're offensive, if that's what you mean. I've seen far more revealing and suggestive art than this. What was their objection again?" she asked, having forgotten the details.

"I believe their exact response went something like this…'Mr. Manning, while we appreciate your talent and creativity, we regret to inform you that the committee finds your photographs unsuitable for public viewing. We feel your work runs contrary to the values held by the university. It has always been the objective of the administration to promote decent Christian virtues to the students given under our trust. We regret any inconvenience this may cause you. Should you desire to resubmit work of a different nature, please contact Rick Forstein no later than April 20th.'"

"And that was that."

"Downhill from there."

"To be honest Stace, I don't understand them."

"The university?"

"Your photographs." She looked at him cautiously, gauging his reaction.

"I—"

"Wait. I'm not finished. You asked me what I think about them and I'll tell you, but I'm not sure you're going to like it, so I'm treading lightly."

His face crinkled, waiting for the verdict.

"I find them very stimulating. Perhaps that's why the committee rejected them. I don't consider myself to be a religious person, but I know from experience that religious people are usually conservative and they're not looking for this kind of stimulation. I think the photographs are tastefully done—though obviously sexual and erotic."

He smiled.

"But, I still don't understand them."

Stace had prepared himself for the usual reaction people had toward his work. He'd expected her to be evasive, then reluctantly agree that she enjoyed them. It was what most people did. But she didn't respond in the usual way. Quite the contrary, she was forthright and because of this, believable, and since he believed her, he was ready to accept her opinion as genuine. He could overlook the fact she didn't understand them. This he welcomed, because he was perfectly comfortable with being original.

Eva was only half-truthful of her response. The rest was unspeakable. For if Stace had this much passion for his art, how much more passionate could he be towards her?

He pointed to the photo of Rebecca and the tree. "This is the last really creative project I completed."

"Why's that?"

"When I found out I was excluded from the exhibit, I lost my desire."

"That was years ago Stace!"

"I know."

"What about your photo lab?"

"I use it of course, but not for anything I'd consider serious."

"Don't you think it's high time you begin again?"

His eyes shifted over to a floor lamp in the corner and he analyzed its trunk of brass, which curled at the top like candle wax. At the curl was a frilly, corrugated paper lampshade. A fly was smacking itself between the light bulb and the lampshade. Stace reached over the couch and knocked it out of its self-imposed prison. "Actually, I think its time to go."

During the drive to *Hattersheim* the two sat in silence. When they were near Stroof's photo she broke the silence. "You're off this weekend aren't you?"

"I am."

"Why don't we get together tomorrow?"

"I don't know, why don't we?"

"No," she began, then realized he was at it again.

He looked at her with a silly grin. She smacked him in the thigh.

"Let's do," he replied.

"Do what?"

"You know, get together."

She didn't answer.

"I'm glad you stayed last night," he said, after they arrived at his work and he got out of the car. "What time?"

"I'll pick you up in the morning around 9:00."

CHAPTER 23

▼

Rick never questioned the legitimacy of his promotion until now. His reason was primarily based on his understanding of how Trojan Security filled its positions. Policy dictated that programmers would be moved up when Trojan Security had room in the ranks to promote. Turnover was minimal. The privileges and perks of working for the company were far above industry standards. They were constantly reinventing the wheel and maintained a creative edge. Any new idea or concept for future programs was encouraged, then debated vigorously for its merit. When the company made decisions to move on, those ideas were always handed to one of the existing programming teams. Never, had the formation of a new team been established to carry out that objective, and under no circumstances was any program with any reasonable security implications given to a handful of strangers. Rick tried to focus on the fact that it was his talent and skill as a programmer that earned him the position. He didn't know all of the other programmers and their skills, but he did know he was one of the company's best. Perhaps it was a combination of his skills and personality? Perhaps it was his relationship with Mitch Pruitt? As much as he considered the obvious, there was a sinking feeling within him giving rise to his suspicions.

The most pressing suspicion was the nature of the project itself. It occurred to him as highly unorthodox. Most of the security programs built by Trojan Security were built out of necessity. Programs begin with the understanding that there is a perceived threat and are built to combat this threat. Of all the programs he'd worked on, most of them for large-scale commercial conglomerations, none of them even come close to the working format presented to the team. Furthermore, this program would be different, because they were acting on an unknown threat and building the program through radical assumptions. He could understand that someone might want to create a program designed for psychological warfare. There were certainly enough "kooks" in the world willing to do just about anything to get their point across, but the idea still seemed to him as too far-fetched.

Another thing bothering him was that Trojan Security was completely bypassing their own criteria, time proven guidelines that form the prerequisites to any security program. For prior to any program being built, normal operations call for the designers to meet with the responsible parties within the contracted corporation. Countless hours, which sometimes span months of talks and negotiations between the corporation and Trojan Security, are logged. Before a single line of program is written the programmers obtain from the executives an exhaustive list of the concerns, perceived threats, and other variables that must be incorporated into the design of the program. These steps were absolutely essential. If the programmers don't know the exact areas needing to be safeguarded, then they have no working basis in which to begin. The psychological stimulus element, coined by the others in his team, provided no working background information to building any worthwhile security program. It was a flimsy, half concocted list of imaginary ideas designed to stop a perceived ideological threat.

His second cause for concern was the team players. He knew absolutely nothing about them, least of all the German, whose position on the team seemed extraordinary. While they were hammering out the details of the psychological aspects of the program, Rick couldn't help but sense that the entire outcome of the meeting had been prearranged. For a time he dismissed his thoughts, thinking his concerns stemmed from Stautzen's charismatic ability to dominate the conversation. Rick thought he'd been designated the leader of the group, but that assumption was quickly shattered and Stautzen had emerged as the unspoken leader.

By far the strangest idea Rick kept turning over and over in his mind was that Trojan Security had no intention of building the secondary security program to over-ride the virus. Neither Watson nor Pruitt gave any indications they wouldn't carry through on the intent, but was the security program ever in the overall plans?

"Good morning ladies and gentlemen," Pruitt said as he entered the committee room. "You've accomplished a great deal this week."

Rick looked at his longtime friend with renewed suspicion. Throughout the week Pruitt had been absent from their meetings, so how could he know how they'd been progressing?

"Mr. Watson is also pleased you've been able to cover so much ground in so little time. Today we'll begin phase two of the project. We'll be splitting into two groups. Dr. Loran, Joseph Stautzen and Davia will work on one team and Rick, you and Jean will work together in putting the technical mechanics of the program down on paper."

"I'm still not exactly sure how we are going to proceed," Rick stated, concealing his frustration.

"Understood, but that should become clear to you in a moment."

"Stautzen and the other's will continue to work on the psychological stimulus element. Their main objective will be to outline the specific teachings and doctrines of the International Christian Coalition. They'll be using the Reverend Eisner's book to get their information. It will be their job to gleam from the book any relevant material the ICC uses to obtain converts. Especially the psychological elements they use in leading others to follow their particular belief system. Dr. Loran, I want you to work closely with Stautzen. You are the best qualified of all of us to determine which teachings have the greatest psychological impact. I need you to determine first of all, why the reverend says what he says, then figure out why what he says works so well. I want you to break it all down to the bare bones."

"Easy enough," Dr. Loran replied.

"And when you and Stautzen think you've got the crux of the matter, you need to figure out the best way we can use this information to persuade users of the Internet to want to know more. It may be that you will simply want to devise a plan that will motivate the general public to look at the reverend's book or to watch the ICC's broadcasts. You may even find a way to get his teachings on screen, so that they become accustomed to his slant on theology. Use your creativity and imagination, but remember, whatever you decide to do has to work within the slim specifications of the program. Simply reprinting his book on screen will not work. Ideally, Internet users should have no idea they're being bombarded with subliminal messages—Davia?"

"Yes."

"After Dr. Loran and Stautzen determine the messages or phrases that might be used, it will be your job to translate their work into different languages. Start with the more common ones like German, French, Italian, Spanish, etc. Focus on languages central to Western Europe."

"It was my understanding we were first going to test this program on some volunteer subjects here in Austin first?" Rick questioned.

"We will," Pruitt replied, "but in order to gauge the effectiveness of the program we'll have to test other individuals as well. What may work on Americans may not work on Europeans. Different cultures and such."

"Will we be testing this program out in Europe as well then?" Rick persisted.

Pruitt and Stautzen glanced at each other.

"Yes," Pruitt replied, as if it had been in the plans all along. "Like I said, it's important we test the relativity of the program with people of different cultures and who speak different languages." He paused for a moment. "It's my understanding were are going to test the impact of the International Christian Coalition on the general public. They're based out of Munich, Germany correct?"

Several nodded in affirmation.

"Then it's a given. We must test the ICC's influence on people of German descent, hence, the people we test the program on will be in Germany." He was speaking now not as a facilitator, but as the man in charge.

He turned to address Rick and Jean specifically. "Rick, you were uncertain how to proceed. In the most simplistic terms, you'll be taking the information provided by Stautzen and designing a way to disseminate this information on the Internet."

"But—"

"I have complete confidence in you. You know how things operate here. You're familiar with our equipment and resources. This afternoon, we'll be bringing in all the equipment you may need and setting it up in your office…Jean, you're the expert on Internet protocol and have a good working knowledge of the scenarios that may be unfamiliar to Rick. So work together."

"We really have no time frame to work with, but I can tell you Mr. Watson is anxious to see the program completed. I've indicated to him it might take as long as two weeks. Does that sound about right?"

"Two weeks!" Rick exclaimed.

"Just kidding. I was thinking more along the lines of four."

"Months?"

Pruitt said nothing.

Rick thought the time-frame ridiculous.

"Possible, correct?" Pruitt asked him.

"Perhaps."

"I'll take that as a yes. Just one more thing," he paused to close his briefcase, "keep your Saturday's open."

Rick was even more certain now that his suspicions were justified. Judging from the demeanor of Pruitt, Rick felt he was in some way involved in the deception. If he was involved, then Watson was involved. He glanced around the room to ascertain who else might have full knowledge of the program's purpose. Dr. Loran was a possible candidate, but he had no interest in religion of any form. In fact, he was diametrically opposed to it. If anything, Dr. Loran would be more interested in preventing such a program from ever coming into existence. But then again, that was the whole purpose of the program wasn't it? Rick reasoned. Perhaps they were all being misled in a similar way? What of Jean Thompson? In many respects she was the expert, especially when it came to understanding the workings of the Internet. Her brilliant military history proved nothing. The military was full of patriots as well as traitors. For all he knew, she might have had a grudge against the military and this was her way of getting back at them. The knowledge she learned through her military training would certainly be potent in the wrong hands, but was it classified? Was she in it for the money?

His suspicions turned again to Stautzen. Rick couldn't dismiss the week's proceedings as merely coincidental. Stautzen had deliberately led the group towards focusing on the ICC as the potential identity that might use the program. The premise he used in his argument was lethal. The program, in the hands of any ideological nutcase could in theory, weaken and cripple the psychological makeup of anyone it came into contact with. Stautzen proposed a worthy goal; built a model program around the ICC, since it had great potential to cause a lot of damage. Sounded good in theory, but what if the ICC actually used the virus?

About the only person Rick could rule out was Davia. Her only function was to translate whatever Dr. Loran and Stautzen asked her to translate. Besides, she seemed so overly introverted that she probably had trouble ordering a cup of coffee at a coffee shop.

Shortly thereafter, Watson sat in his leather bound chair twirling his monogrammed silver pen nervously over his thumb. 360 degrees one way then 360 degrees back the other way. He could perform the sequence every second flawlessly, perfecting the habit through years of sitting at his desk reviewing and signing paperwork.

"Do you think he's on to this?" Watson asked Pruitt, who sat complacently in front of his desk.

"I don't think so, but then again, Rick's a pretty sharp guy."

Watson had considered there might be set backs to his objective, but now that he was confronted with the obstacle, he was unprepared to deal with it. "I knew we should have hired an outside man to lead the group."

"We would have still run the same risks. You know we needed to keep the program in-house as much as possible. Rick may not be the best, but he's certainly capable of building the program. He's perfect, capable and expendable, should the occasion arise."

"But what if he resigns or worse?"

"I wouldn't worry about that. The files will show our main objective all along was to build the security program. That's clear on paper. Rick and the others were fully informed this was our objective. As far as the law is concerned, we are in the clear. If it did go to court, you know we have the resources and legal staff to back us up. Rick's smart enough to figure that out."

"True, but what about after the program's complete?"

"Then it's out of our hands and halfway around the world. There are only four people who know about the program and its purpose; you, me, Stautzen and the reverend. I don't expect any of them to say anything. Even if they were caught, the records will show the overall objective of the program, and if anyone doubts our objective, our lawyers can prove that we did nothing wrong. We are in the computer security business. We saw a security threat and we designed a program to stop it. If all else fails, we'll begin building the security program as proof of our original intentions."

"And the ICC?"

"I know how you feel about them Fred, but ultimately, they run their own risks. If it comes down to it, we'll tell the authorities the program was copied and stolen by, well…any one of them. Again, the records will show we did everything possible to safeguard the program didn't get into the wrong hands."

"Nevertheless, I'm still worried about Rick, or for that matter, any of the others. What if they decide to walk?"

"I agree. Right now their input is essential to building both the psychological and technical aspects of the program. I think the program can be built in as little as four weeks—six tops. Jean and Rick know more than anyone does about putting this thing together. They'll all hold out for the bonus. It's doubtful they'll walk. As far as Rick's concerned, that may be another story. We need him to build the program, but as long as he's around we run the risk of him discovering more. Rick's no private eye and all the information about the program is right in front of him already. The only thing hidden is what the four of us involved know and that's all locked up in our heads."

"Nevertheless, I want you to get in touch with security so that they can watch him. I want to know where he goes, who he talks to, and what he's doing until we've completed the project—understood?

"I'll put a man on him twenty-four-seven.

CHAPTER 24

▼

Eva's arrival at the *Schwarz Monatlich* shortly after 9:00 am went unnoticed. On a corner table against the wall, Alfred and Ruben were busy hooking up cables and power cords to Alfred's equipment. Earlier that morning, he'd brought in a receiver to pick up incoming audio signals from the CRM's apartment, an encryption device, an amplifier to boost the signal and a CD recording machine to document any traceable conversations. Alfred was an electronic genius, who could build just about anything the newspaper needed from scratch. They'd been using this particular set-up for the last three years. No one knew exactly how it worked except Alfred, who tried to explain the system to them others years ago, but every time he set up the equipment he had to explain the process all over again.

"The bugs in the apartment are powerful enough to pick up whispers of conversation. They send these conversations a short distance to a receiver in the trunk of my car parked around the corner from the CRM's apartment. Now, the last thing we want is for someone else to pick up these conversations, so I designed a piece of equipment that scrambles the conversations into digital garbage. That signal then leaves my car through the radio antenna and is picked up by a dish I've installed on the roof of this building. The signal travels by cable into this amplifier. The amplifier boosts the signal and sends it to the receiver. These two pieces of equipment basically work together. Tied in with them is this de-scrambler unit. It changes the scrambled digital signal back into an analog signal. This off course, all happens instantaneously. The conversations can be heard though this speaker or through the headphones. The CD recorder is for backup."

"We'll take your word for it Alfred," Eva said.

"*Guten morgen,* Eva. We are making some progress," Mr. Schwarz said. He walked up to her desk.

"Did you find out who Neil Usher is?" she asked.

"I spotted him as he was getting off work last night," Ruben said, power cord in hand.

"Good, which one is he?" She took the four glossy eight by ten's out of her briefcase and laid them across her desk.

"*Dis* one," Ruben said, pointing to the man holding the briefcase. "Where'd you get *de* photos?"

Alfred interrupted. "We're all set to go here." He flipped on the switches and set the frequency on the receiver. His fingers spun over five gear-like dials on the encryption device as he locked in a sequence of numbers. The CD recorder hummed.

"From a friend. A photographer."

"A friend?" Shelly asked. The others took note of her tone.

"Yes, a friend, and he's quite a handsome fellow," she added.

Shelly seemed pleased. Eva matched her expression with a smile.

"How long have you known the man?" Mr. Schwarz asked.

"A couple of weeks," she responded, rather bothered by his inquiry.

"Two weeks?" he questioned.

"Seems like a decent young man, an American," Alfred said, coming to her defense.

"You've met him?" Ruben questioned.

Eva turned her miffed gazed towards Ruben.

"In passing," Alfred said.

"What does he know?" asked Mr. Schwarz.

"Nothing. I just asked him to enlarge the negatives I had."

Mr. Schwarz kept silent, but stewed.

"That's all!" she persisted, raising her voice.

Mr. Schwarz didn't twitch. "Two weeks? You don't know anything about the man."

"Look. He enlarged a couple of negatives. We've been taking our stuff to commercial developers for years."

"Less eyes the better...seems to me," Alfred said. His words were convincing enough to stop the inquisition.

Eva took the forth photo and threw it in the trashcan next to her desk. "Shelly, do me a favor and post these on the board."

"All right, we need to divvy up shifts to monitor the CD recorder. Any volunteers? asked Mr. Schwarz.

"No need! Alfred said.

"What do you mean 'no need?'" asked Mr. Schwarz.

"I've done some modifications, and if I might say so, you seem a bit on edge."

"Spare me the advice."

"Two CD's. When one finishes the other engages. If there's been no audible signals of voice communication on either machine, they'll rewind themselves for another session."

"And what happens when they both run their length?" Mr. Schwarz asked.

"The CD's run for six hours each with continual audio signals. That's a full twelve hours of recording time. You don't need anyone here to watch the equipment run, you just have to make sure the CD's get exchanged every twelve hours."

"Thank God!" Shelly said.

"But, we still have to arrange a schedule over the weekend to change out the CD's correct?" Mr. Schwarz sought to verify.

"Correct."

"That's what I needed to know. Shelly, I want you to make out a revolving schedule for the weekend. I want a one-hour window. That way, if there's any trouble with the equipment—"

"There won't be sir," Alfred interrupted.

Mr. Schwarz looked at him comically. "As I was saying, just in case there's any trouble we can page Alfred and he'll run right over."

"Can't think of anything else I rather do this weekend sir."

"You can put me on the list too Shelly," Mr. Schwartz said.

"Ok."

"Now, about the apartment Alfred," Eva said.

"There are books, files and stacks of paper everywhere. Also, boxes full of brochures and pamphlets, along with hundreds of audio and videotapes. I took a few samples." He reached into his toolbox and pulled out a couple videotapes, then tossed them onto Eva's desk with a handful of brochures. "Maybe you'll find something in here that will help you out. They have a regular production studio in there, a whole string of dubbing machines. Top of the line."

"*Anyding* interesting in *de* bedrooms?" Ruben asked.

"Not really."

Mr. Schwarz snorted in disappointment.

"Maybe it's what you didn't find that's important," said Shelly.

"What do you mean?" Ruben asked, but Alfred answered for her.

"Well, I expected to find three bedrooms, which I did, but everyone of them was being lived in. With all the equipment they have, you'd think they'd use one of the rooms as an office. Apparently, Neil, Derrick and Tasha each have their own room."

"What's *dat* supposed to mean?" Ruben asked.

"Only that Tasha's probably not sleeping with Neil or Derrick," piped in Shelly.

"Relevance please," Mr. Schwarz said.

"Just that, it's hard for me to imagine the three of them leading separate lives. You'd think as long as they have been together Tasha would be close to one of them."

"So *dey* practice abstinence." Ruben said.

"Still doesn't mean they're not all in this thing together." Mr. Schwarz said. "We know Neil and Derrick were friends long before they met Tasha, but I see no reason to believe she's an outsider."

"I doubt she is either, but for the sake of argument, let's say she just rents a room from them. Maybe she's only there to give them a hand with the office details," Eva added.

"And if *dat's de* case, she may not be too involved with *deir* cause. We might be able to get some information from of her," Alfred said.

"I think you're all drawing straws," Mr. Schwarz concluded. "Do you remember anything else unusual about their rooms Alfred?"

Alfred tried to remember everything he saw. There was nothing special about Tasha's room. Her furnishings were simple and lacked femininity and frill. The room with the phone was well kept. It was the only room of the three with a desk. On the desk was an open Bible. Beside the Bible was a writing pad scribbled with notes. Beside the desk was a chest high bookshelf stocked with religious titles. The last room, the one nearest to the living room, was the most unkempt of the three. The bed was unmade and dirty clothes were piled in a corner. The trashcan in the corner was empty, unlike the one in the other room with the desk where it was full. The dresser was stuffed with unfolded clothes. From a bar in the closet, hung a few sport shirts and a couple of suits.

"Look folks, I've got to take off." Alfred said. "If you have any problems with the equipment page me."

"You didn't get the chance to slip in a video camera did you?" Eva asked.

"No I didn't. Actually, I just made it out the door before Tasha came home."

"I thought she worked through the day." Shelly said.

"So did I," Alfred said, ticked by the memory of just having escaped before she came back. "Well, she's home now."

"Did she see you?" Eva said with some concern.

"Yes, but she didn't catch me in the apartment if that's what you mean. I'd already started down the stairs. We made eye contact. She didn't look happy."

"Let's just hope she didn't get *dat* good a look at you," Ruben said.

Alfred looked at him. "Seems that I recall Derrick followed you to this office."

"Point taken."

"Be careful," Eva said as he walked towards the door.

"You too big sister."

"What's next Eva?" Ruben asked.

Mr. Schwarz spoke up. "Eva, I think you should focus your attention on the ICC. Have you finished reading the book?"

"Not yet." She lied. She just didn't want to ague with him and she was still digesting the contents.

"Read the book. Pay particular attention to what that man doesn't say."

"Reverend Eisner?"

"*Ja.* There's a lot a radicals in this world. Most of them are just out to get attention, so they make a lot of noise. Some of them back their words up with action. See if you can find out what the ICC is capable of doing. You may even need to take a trip down to Munich. In fact, plan on it. Next weekend. You don't have plans do you?"

"No."

"Good…and Alfred."

"Yes sir."

"I want you to focus on the CRM. Shelly can help you."

"Should we keep watching *deir* apartment?" he asked.

"We already know what they look like, so don't worry about that for now. Let's wait and see what the CD's reveal over the weekend."

"Yes sir."

CHAPTER 25

▼

"You have to think like a criminal," Jean said, from the couch in Rick's office.

They had been brainstorming throughout the morning on the possible ways the program might be built. He was accustomed to thinking along conventional lines, because all of the programs he'd designed for Trojan Security utilized a specific sequence of priorities. First you define the threat, which had yet to be defined as far as he was concerned, then you outline the specific dynamics of the program to guard against those threats. Next, you design the program line by line. Finally, you test the program and implement it.

"What we have to do is imagine how someone else might use the program, not necessarily how you might use it. This someone would have basically one concern," she continued.

"Getting caught," he said.

"Exactly." She sat up, straightened her back and shifted toward the edge of the couch. Her hands lifted off her lap to help her explain. "Seems to me, the main concern is for it to not be traceable."

"Then you're thinking of a Telnet operation."

"That's what I'd do. I'd use a remote pay phone and tap into the Internet to distribute the virus. Completely anonymous. The authorities might be able to locate the phone and the time it was used, but that's all they'd have."

"I see what you mean." His expression was long and drawn out. He had never considered such protocol. He was also wondering how Jean just jumped right into the topic. If she was trying to be discrete, she could have been less obvious. Had she been prompted? Or was she as excited about building the program as she acted?

"Of course there are other ways, but I've essentially ruled them out because they're far too complicated."

"Doesn't hurt to suggest them," he suggested, rocking backward in his chair.

Her hands flew off her lap and began flipping about as though she needed them to help her talk. "One way would be to infect the operating systems of computers such as DOS or Windows. Ninety-five percent of all computers in the world operate on these two systems. But you would have to get into the labs where they're produced, an amazing security feat, or have someone working on the inside who could infect the systems for you. Possible, but highly unlikely. A step down from that would be to infect components like keyboards, mouse units or other hardware, but again, you'd run into the same security obstacles. You'd have to bribe in-house workers to do the work for you. Both of these ideas are useless because they'd require either a lot of money or people. The more people involved the more likely you're going to get caught."

As she voiced her ideas he watched her mouth form around words and phrases. She'd stroked her lips with a dash of cherry flush that morning, nothing too loud or obnoxious, just a trace to bring out the contours, which begged for a taste. The green patterned sweater dress she'd slipped into that morning was cut modestly above the knees, but at the present time, was pulled up near the middle of her thighs. Her crossed legs were wrapped in neutral colored panty hose, which she wore only to conceal the slight variations of tone in her otherwise, tanned legs. He'd never seen her hair up and this morning it fell as usual over her shoulders; mahogany brown with streaks of highlights.

"Whoever is going to build this program, much like ourselves, will likely be a single person or a small group of people. They'll lock themselves in a lab and figure out how to do it by eliminating all the risks," Rick said.

"But the virus could also be spread by hiding it in an specific program," she said.

"A software package?" he questioned.

"It would have to be a software program that everyone wanted to buy—"

"Or needed to buy."

"Anyone of the major spreadsheet or word processing programs would do. Or, the program could be slipped into a program that enhances the speed of existing modems. People would buy it because they wanted to access the Internet faster."

"Virtually any software program would do, but that would be a bit too complicated don't you think?" he asked.

"Complicated, risky, not to mention passive. The last thing you'd want is your virus sitting on computer software stores around the world waiting for some hack to discover it."

"There's no guarantee anyone would want to buy those programs either. The damage the virus would cause would be limited to the amount of programs sold. Only those people who unknowingly bought the program would be infected by the virus," she said.

"Pruitt was right. I don't really see anyway around it. The Internet is the most viable option. It reaches the most people in the quickest amount of time," he said.

"And it's the cleanest. The risks are extremely low in getting caught. Like I said…'you have to think like a criminal.'"

"But if you ask me, I think it's an impossibility. Granted, on a small-scale people throw viruses into the Internet on a daily basis. But this has to be much bigger in scope to be able to work."

At that moment Pruitt, followed by two service technicians dressed in tan work overalls and carrying a folded office table, interrupted them. In the course of the next ten minutes, they'd filled Rick's office with boxes of new equipment.

"The latest and the best. You'll be looped through the mainframe computer in Building G. I've been giving this a lot of thought and I think the toughest thing is going to be integrating this program into the Internet," Pruitt said.

Rick and Jean glanced astonishingly at each other.

"So, by this afternoon you'll have twelve new phone lines. That will give you access to all the major Internet providers and if you need more lines let me know."

"There's one more thing we'll need," Rick said.

"Name it."

"I'll be needing an Internet I/O HTTP. Retrieving Device."

"Never heard of it."

Jean looked puzzled as well.

"Ah, perhaps they don't make them yet, but then again, they'd be illegal even if they did." He turned towards Jean. "Guess we'll have to build our own." She tried to look as though she knew what he was talking about.

"Just what is this device?" Pruitt asked.

"I'll fill you in on that later, because we've got to have one before we can start building this program," Rick said.

"Well, I'll be back first thing tomorrow," Pruitt said leaving.

"I think it's time for lunch," Rick said to Jean. "It'll be a while before we can get down to work." The tech's had already starting opening boxes, turning Rick's office into a trash heap of papers, plastic bags and Styrofoam molding.

"I'll drive," she said.

"If you insist."

"You like barbecue?" he asked, once they were outside and heading for the parking lot.

"Depends."

"I know a nice little place where they serve great barbecue briskets. Nothing fancy, but the food's good.

"All right."

He followed her to her new Lexus, gold with a hint of metallic flake, parked at the far edge of the lot.

"New?"

"Off the shelf. Picked it out before I drove down from Colorado Springs."

"When do you plan to park it a little closer?"

"When it gets its first scratch."

"So, home's in Colorado?"

"For now. When I was in the Army I went there for several AIT courses at the Air Force Academy. Liked it so much I stayed."

They got in the car and drove under a canopy of old scrub oaks lined along the main entrance until they came to the access road. "Go right onto Research. I'll tell you when to get off."

"What's an AIT Course?" he asked.

"An additional training course for Army personnel. I've been to dozens of them. When the Army isn't able to provide the training for what they need you to know, they send you to a place that does. Most of the time it's at an Air Force Base."

"What did you take there?"

"Classified," she said pointedly.

He didn't press the question. There were a lot of questions he'd like to ask her, but didn't want to appear too obvious. Jean, however, wasn't being serious and when he failed to press her she glanced over at him. "You give up easy don't you?"

He smiled...thoughts elsewhere.

"So what's this HTTP thingamagigger?"

"I'm surprised. A woman with your obvious skills and expertise?"

She grinned. "I'm sure I know what you're talking about, I just don't know what you're getting at."

"Well, you did such a fine job of assessing the possible ways the program should or shouldn't be built, I thought you would atleast have a clue—"

"Let me guess, since we have to go through the Internet, we'll have to get the virus into the main hubs responsible for the most Internet traffic."

"And those places are?" he asked, enjoying the game.

"We have to target the major corporations that provide gopher services and Internet access."

"My goodness you are sharp aren't you? Now, take the next exit at Duval."

"I get paid for my brains just like you."

"By the way, if you don't mind me asking, how much are you getting paid to work on this program?" he asked.

"I don't mind, but they might."

"Classified, right?"

"Something like that."

"You see that brand new building made to look like it's falling over?"

"Rudy's?"

"That's it. Next driveway."

"Now, getting back to the thingamagigger."

"Pleasure before business," he replied.

They stepped onto the boardwalk off the parking lot and through the front door.

"Order for me," she said, "and where's the ladies room?" He pointed her towards an opening in the back where an rusty Texaco sign was nailed to the wall over the doorway.

The cashiers were just ahead of him, at the end of a series of stainless steel rails that ushered patrons up to the counter like cattle. A handful of people stood in front of him. Within minutes they were rapidly served by two teenage cowgirls dressed in jeans, boots and bright red, western-style shirts, the kind with pointed pockets and buttons.

Behind the girls, young studs in white tee shirts worked the open flame broilers cooking brisket and chicken. Rick didn't know what to get Jean, so he ordered a pound of brisket and a half chicken. The studs wrapped his order in crispy white butcher's paper. The cute young girl at his register grabbed the package from the counter behind her and tossed it into a plastic basket. She reached into a loaf of white bread and threw in six dry slices.

"Anything to drink?" the girl asked, her hand poised over the cashier waiting for his answer.

Reaching behind him, he grabbed two bottles of Pepsi swimming in a livestock tank full of ice water. After paying, he took a seat at one of the long rows of picnic tables in the dining area. Jean came up behind him, thought to scare him, decided not to, and sat across from him.

"You were not kidding," she said flatly.

"Told you, nothing fancy, but the food's good. I've got beef or chicken, what do you want?"

"Little of both thanks…now business."

"Like I was saying, the best way to do this is to build a virus that will infect the various Internet servers."

"All of them?"

"No! No. There must be hundreds of mom and pop companies. I'm talking about the big corps."

"The ones Pruitt's hooking up for us."

"Yeah, makes you wonder doesn't it?"

"About what?"

He opened the wrapper of the brisket and chicken and slid them to the center of the table, dishing a little of each out onto paper plates. He slid her a plate, "enjoy."

"But you're talking about accessing the mainframes of these corporations," she said, then looked around and brought her voice down to a whisper. "First you'd have to break into them, then you'd have to find a way to download the virus into their system." The thought excited her.

"Hence, the need for a program that will reach inside of their computers and get the information we need."

"That would be the thingamagigger," she reasoned.

"Precisely. Think about it. If we can make a virus that will attach itself to the home-page of say, the AOL or Netscape browser, then whenever somebody pulled up that home-page they'd be infected by the virus."

Jean was gnawing on a drumstick. The pupils of her eyes raced back and forth in the whiteness.

"But of course, that's just an idea," he said, as though it were a joke.

"No, it's a good one," she said, bulge of chicken in her cheek, drumstick pointing at him. "It's worth looking into."

Brainstorming was one thing, implementation was another. His idea was certainly plausible, but he would have never considered actually doing it. He was after all, an expert and knew just about any system could be infected with any virus he could think up. But the idea was highly illegal. He took a swig of Pepsi and read over the multi-colored flags of NFL teams hanging from the ceiling, struck with anxiety.

Jean pressed on. "I really think you've got something here—attacking the web browsers that is. It would infect the greatest amount of people. It's also a program that could be done by any hacker worth half the price of their equipment. More importantly, it fits neatly within the restrictions. A few disks, one hacker, a few isolated telephone locations…whammo!"

"You actually believe it could be done don't you?"

"Yes I do. And it will be done. By you and me."

He sunk his teeth into a slab of brisket to buy himself time, eventually swallowing and wiping his mouth with a paper towel. "I know I asked you about the money before, but let me ask you in a different way. Just why did you decide to hire yourself out to Trojan Security for this project?"

She wasn't the slightest bit disturbed by his assault on her ethics, and set her drumstick down to free her hands. "I gave the best years of my life to the Army. I joined when I was seventeen. The Army put me through college and I did my time." She paused for a moment, as though she were recalling a speech she'd memorized. "When I joined, I believed in what the military was being used for. We were in Iraq at the time fighting against Saddam Hussein, helping to keep the Iraqis free and combating terrorism. You know, that kind of patriotism gets your engine running. Shortly after that, we were back in Bosnia again, fighting Serbian forces, which were still genocide was the solutions to their problems. Still in South Korea, fighting against the communist interests of the north. Still cleaning up Afghanistan" Her hands were flying now, like two frazzled parakeets. "We were in Panama, Honduras, Germany and dozens of other places, keeping the world safe for democracy. And you know what happened after 9-11, all hell broke lose. Terrorism became our new war. America at that time was still free. With that freedom came power. The kind of power that makes every other nation either quake in its soil or covet our prosperity. Those who coveted that prosperity were pledged the blood of our young men and women. Those who opposed us ran the risk of sanctions or military force. And through it all I learned every bit of electronic and computer warfare I could, so I could share in the pride of being an American. I believed all that, do you understand?"

She took a deep breath. Rick cringed when she continued.

"Then came the changes. No one saw them coming except a few isolationists, which most Americans excused as humanists and pessimists. Those isolationists made a stink about every piece of legislation they claimed violated the First Amendment. I hated them. It was so obvious. Crime was out of control and legislation demanded tougher crime bills and gun restrictions. They fought that legislation and lost. But, laws were finally implemented and crime shot way down. They opposed school prayer amendments. They lost. And grade school children across the country became more obedient and compliant. They promoted laws for the legalization of drugs. They never won that war from the start. With legislation calling for more law enforcement and harsher penalties against drug abusers, the streets eventually began cleaning up. They opposed restrictions against pornography and the censoring of literature, art and the media. They lost there too. Then later, they even opposed mandatory church services for prison inmates. Can you imagine? Who wouldn't want our criminals converted? Everyone thought they were crazy back then. By the year 2007 everyone knew they were crazy. But who could argue with the results?

It's amazing how fast things can turn. People can change. I certainly did. If you were alive during that period and lived in America, which you were, you know from all outside appearances America had been the Babylon of decadence. Within a short period of time, we'd completely reversed that perspective. We became the model for all other nations to follow. We became the most ethically and morally balanced nation in existence. But living in that environment today is another story. Almost every freedom we had has been taken away. Some governmental agency or law restricts almost everything we want to do now. We've become a nation of mice living in a spotless cage running a circular path of existence. We can only move and think within the limitations of the walls of our maze. Climbing the walls is unthinkable. In fact, anything thinkable is unthinkable! And we owe this sterilization of thought to all the Christian conservatives who took control and took away our freedom. I have only one way to thank them, by putting myself in a position to make sure the power of their influence never takes root in another country. If this program can do that, then I'd do just about anything to see it's built."

The chicken was cold. The brisket was like brick. The Pepsi's were warm and swimming in a puddle of condensation. The slices of bread had turned to stone. Rick sat poised with plastic fork in hand ready to devour, but had suddenly lost his appetite. He didn't know what to say and furthermore, didn't want to respond to what she'd said, because he didn't believe her. She'd over exaggerated the situation and it wasn't his intent to prove her wrong. Only one thing was for sure, she'd dissolved any fears he had that she was involved with Watson's creation of the program to use it for yet unknown reasons. Time for a subject change.

"Why didn't you quit the Army when you no longer believed in them?"

"The goals of the military never changed. They never do. We were sent to more countries than ever before with the same objective, to protect American interests and to make the world safe for democracy. As I was alluding to, no one can argue the military succeeded in carrying out that objective. Where I began having a problem was when I finally began to disagree with the political goals and ambitions of Washington. Suddenly, I found myself employed by an institution I loathed and forced to subscribe to its ideologies. By the time I reached that decision, I'd been in for eighteen years. I could retire in another two, but I really didn't have all of my thoughts together and hadn't made any emotional decisions until I was in my twenty-first year. I stuck around a couple more just to make sure I was doing the right thing."

"And now you have a new mission in life?"

"I'm through with missions. To be honest with you, I was offered good money to work on what I saw to be a worthwhile project," she confessed.

"But you seem to be really into this program."

"Well…don't think too highly of me. In the end we all serve ourselves, don't we?"

CHAPTER 26

▼

A quilt of woven clouds had been loitering over Frankfurt since the day before, obscuring the sun, yet bringing no promise of rain. That evening, a warm front of clear skies had crept its way up from Austria and had pulled the clouds northwards towards *Bremerhaven*. Saturday bloomed a glorious day, unusually warm for October and clear, with a blazing sun hanging half way to noon as Eva drove to Stace's home to pick him up.

"Did you bring your camera?" she asked as he hopped in her car.

"Right here in my back pack." He set the pack down on the seat between them and felt for the bulge just to make sure.

"What's on the agenda?"

She thought about it for a moment and rolled her window down. "I thought we'd drive up to *Bad Homberg*. There's a house on a hill I'd like you to see. After that, the museum will be open."

"What kind of museum?"

"The *Frankfurter Kunstverein*. It's a museum of contemporary exhibitions. This month it's exhibiting work by a few prominent photographers. I thought you'd like to see it. Later this evening, we'll take a walk around *Sachsenhausen*. There's a lot of clubs and excitement down that way on Saturday night."

He'd been through *Sachsenhausen* by day and tried to imagine what it might be like at night. "You picked a good day."

"I did. Then tomorrow—"

"Tomorrow?"

"It's supposed to be even warmer tomorrow, so we'll drive out to *Rudesheim* and take a boat ride on the *Rhine.*"

"Intriguing."

"Yes, intriguing," she repeated, wishing he'd said, romantic. "*Rudesheim* lies along the *Rhine* River and curves through the hills. Along the river are dozens of castles. They grow a lot of grapes in the region for wine. It's really quite beautiful."

An hour later, they parked along the curb on a side street in *Bad Homberg* and walked through the town towards the house. A winding crushed gravel path scattered with sightseers led them up to the entrance.

"Quite a house," he said.

"I exaggerated a little, but it's not near as large as some of the other castles."

The home of the nobleman was an enormous sprawling estate resting in the foothills of the *Taunus* Mountains. The nobleman's wealth had been incalculable and it was doubtful whether he knew how much he possessed. For him to even ponder such a minute detail would have been demeaning. He paid his accountants handsomely for seeing to this nightmare, which gave him time to do what he liked doing best; hunting and more precisely, discussing the details of his wealth with other noblemen, and how his accountants kept track of his wealth so he didn't have to.

The home was a palace, simply because it lacked all the delightfully crude elements of a castle, like the unfinished, precisely cut, weather worn exterior of castles typically built of quarried stone. It also lacked the cold drafty interiors of castles, with their intricate nooks and crannies and irregularly shaped rooms. Pains had been taken by the German government to make sure the palace in the present age maintained its 1000 year old authenticity. The main hallway on the third floor reeked of the hunt. Running seventy-five feet in length, it was decorated with the stuffed animals of the nobleman's many kills. The lifeless eyes of deer, bears and dozens of other furry creatures, peered over the hallway. The palace contained about thirty rooms, most of them dressed in silk wallpaper. The floors were crafted of intricately laid wood polished to a mirror shine. There were ceilings carved out of imported hardwoods and sporting intricate engravings. Enormous egg-tempura paintings scattered throughout the palace could have been on loan from the Louvre in Paris. Off the master bedroom was located what was believed to be the first indoor toilet in Germany.

Architecturally speaking, the palace was laid out like an immense *L* shaped letter about four to six stories high, depending on whether one included the basement and attic. At the juncture of the *L* was an archway, leading out into a cobblestone reception area. Here the servant's quarters and kitchen were located on the bottom floor, well away from the palace's aristocratic owners. The outside of the structure was plastered in the color vanilla. Identically shaped square windows with emerald green shutters were lined around the palace in neat horizontal rows. The palace was capped in traditional ceramic roofing of square-cut panels cast in tarnished steel. Just beyond the servants' quarters, the lawn gave way to a sharp descent into a low lying forest of trees and brush, but only for a short distance, for the ground quickly leveled out into a small lake.

After Stace and Eva had their fill of the palace and surrounding gardens, they walked down a secluded path towards the unpretentious lake, where its surface seemed as if it had been sliced from a chunk of cerulean blue ice that had been laid on its side by a giant's hand. A family of swans stroked effortlessly across the surface, cutting three lines of rippling waves like piercing arrows. Stace and Eva sat on the banks at the far end of the lake, so they could view the palace on the hill. Reminiscent of a boy attempting his first efforts at romance, Stace finally gained enough courage to reach out and take Eva's hand. It was a moment suspended in days of wanting.

"I live for moments like this," he said, his neck stretched back, face soaking in the rays of the sun.

"They're too few and far between," she replied looking at him. "In fact, sometimes I avoid these experiences, because I don't want to suffer the let down of going back to work on Mondays."

"I know what you mean."

"I used to enjoy what I do, but lately, I'm losing interest. Scares me in a way."

He took his eyes off the sky and turned towards her. "Why's that?"

She thought long and hard before responding, so long in fact, that Stace no longer expected an answer. "Because my work is so much a part of who I am, but the energy I once had for doing it is no longer there. I guess in a way, I feel a part of me is dying off."

"Maybe you take things too seriously. You're too intense."

"Tense?" she asked.

"No, intense. I don't think you're capable of being tense. You're the most composed woman I've ever met. What I meant to say was perhaps you're too driven."

"You think so?"

"I do. Or maybe you're just changing. Change is good. I know I've certainly changed, compared to what I was like in my early twenties."

"And you don't think you've lost anything? she asked"

"Hell no. Do you miss adolescence?"

"No, but my adolescence wasn't like my early twenties."

"Mine were."

"So how'd you get around it?"

"Guess I settled into life. I stopped worrying about what everyone was thinking about me and started doing what I wanted to do."

"But what about your work, your photography?"

"I came to the conclusion I wasn't God's gift to the world and my work wasn't the most important aspect of my life. I haven't quit shooting for my dreams. I'd still like to become a renowned photographer. I just stopped pushing the idea upon myself. I think in due time it will all come together."

She had a difficult time understanding his logic. He'd never see his dream come true with that kind of wishy-washy attitude.

"I'm not sure how all that applies to me. Take my boss Mr. Schwarz, he hasn't lost any of his zeal and he's sixty-seven."

"But what does he do?"

"He runs the paper. Without him nothing would happen."

"Sure about that? Does he go out on assignments? Does he even write any of the stories?"

"Not any more. He orchestrates everything from his desk."

"And if he died today would the paper cease to exist?"

"I doubt it. Ruben and I would probably pick up where he left off."

"You'd probably have to stay back in the office and run the show then, wouldn't you?"

"Maybe."

"You'd probably have to hire another reporter just as energetic and capable as you are, right?"

"I suppose," she said, wondering.

"Mr. Schwarz may still be providing the vision, but it sounds like you and the others are doing all the leg work."

"I don't understand your point." She straightened herself up and wrapped her arms around her knees.

"Just that you really never lose what's inside you. You may have to slow down, change the way you do things, but the passion is always there."

"All right, I concede your point. But I wouldn't know the first place to begin."

She suddenly jumped up and ran to the water's edge. One of the swans had waddled onto shore near them and she felt like chasing it back into the water. The swan saw her coming and at first held its ground, reeling its pointed head back in defiance and letting out an awkward *squawk*! Its cry bounced across the lake and into the ears of a boy walking along the banks on the other side. Eva shrieked back at it and chased the swan into the lake. Stace was standing when she came back.

"Get it out of your system?"

She didn't answer.

Despite the differences in the issues facing them, Eva had found room in her clouded mind to accept the possibility Stace might be right. One thing was for sure, she couldn't continue working at her present pace. Sooner or later she had to slow down. Was there anyway she could redirect her energies into a more leisurely line of work? She didn't have an answer to that question at the moment, but she was willing to look into the possibilities.

"Let's catch a bite to eat in *Bad Homberg* and head to the museum," she said.

It was rounding 2:00 in the afternoon when they walked up to the entrance to the *Frankfurter Kunstverein*. Near the entrance, people clustered around a woman that looked to be in her early forties.

"I see you standing in that crowd," she said.

"Who is she?"

"My guess, she's one of the photographers of the exhibit."

Stace was taken back to the final day of the Marbel Art Exhibit when he'd slipped into the auditorium to watch the presentation of the winners. At the last minute, and due to the interest of the Zebra gallery, the committee had decided to turn the exhibit into a contest. The grand prize had gone to Maria. She'd completed her sculpture of her aunt Silvia, which he'd watched her working on down the hall from the photo-lab. His great disappointment at having been pulled from the exhibit was only offset by the joy that his friend Maria had taken the first place prize. Maria was greeted on stage by Chelsea Barter, the representative of the Zebra gallery, which promptly displayed a collection of her work in the gallery. Within a few months time, Maria had secured an agent who'd been successful in getting her work into other notable galleries within Texas. Maria later received a scholarship to begin a master's program at the University of Houston. Stace lost touch with her when she left to study in the fall.

The museum was a three-story structure located near the *Roemer*. Now a famous tourist stop, the *Roemer* was once the center of the Frankfurt city government. The bottom two stories of the museum were reserved for its most prized collections of paintings, sculptures and mixed media presentations. The works had been purchased and collected over the years and had a permanent place of residence there. The third floor was used for revolving exhibits and about once a month the work on display would pass on to another gallery and the museum would acquire a new exhibit. Stace and Eva wandered the hollow halls and rooms of the first two floors before checking out the photographs upstairs.

"Take this one for instance. I could have painted that and done a much better job." Eva said. They were standing in front of an enormous fifteen by ten foot canvas, which could have been painted by a chimpanzee. Stace found no use for the painting either, but tried to imagine the inspiration that went into it.

"Perhaps the artist was just experimenting with differing variations of color."

"Or practicing brush strokes," she added. "I'm not impressed. What makes it so good? Why is it even hanging in here?"

He found the name of the artist in the brochure he'd picked up at the door. The life of the artist had spanned four decades. The particular painting they were standing in front of had been painted when he was seventy-four years old. "The artist, probably become so well known that everything he painted was being snatched up." The brochure also had two other pictures of the artist's work done earlier in his career. The technique and style were the same. "On second thought, must have been his vision."

"Right," she responded doubtfully.

They moved on to the next painting.

"Now this I can understand, but only slightly. It's similar to that one over there, but at least you can make out the impression of a face of a man who seems to be in torment. He's surrounded by walls—I think. I don't like it, but at least I can make something out of it. Even having just a little portion of the painting recognizable is helpful don't you think?" she asked.

"I agree. Even when the rest of the painting is chaotic you're still driven by the expression of the man."

"It's something to relate to anyway. There's emotional contact with the painting. It seems to me, that art needs to have that in it."

"Emotional contact?" he questioned.

"*Ja*. I may not like it, but it has to reach out and grab somebody."

"I know when I shoot pictures it's important for me to connect with the viewer. Sure, I might be able to dazzle them with technique and style, but to me that's an introverted way to approach art. Technique can be taught. Simply coming out with a new variation of an artistic form doesn't qualify one to be a great artist. People have to enjoy your work. It must touch them in some way."

They made their way up the escalator to the third floor in silence. Stace was bubbling inside with the resonance of creativity. Eva was content with his expression. Stace was thinking and more importantly, imagining.

The third floor was swarming with people shuffling about and murmuring amongst themselves about the relevance and beauty of the work being shown. Three prominent photographers and one, young and upcoming photographer were being spotlighted. Each photographer's work was displayed in a separate room.

"I know some people don't consider photography to be an art form. Why is that?" Eva asked him. She was standing in front of a photograph of the Frankfurt city skyline taken at dawn.

"Because most people think the camera does all the work."

"And it doesn't?" she questioned, trying to draw him out.

"It can do most everything, except the creative part. My first camera was a Minolta. A P.H.S. camera."

"P.H.S.?"

"Push Here Stupid."

She laughed.

Anyway, it was one of the first auto-focus cameras on the market. Did practically everything for you. Chose the aperture and speed and even focused the lens. It made it easy for anybody who could point and shoot to take good pictures."

"And that's not a good thing?"

"Sure, it's great, especially for the amateur photographer or the tourist who wants good pictures of their vacation. Before they came out with the auto-focus cameras it was quite a task just to get the camera to take a decent photograph. The older cameras were far less sophisticated. Lens choice was minimal and you had to calculate the correct aperture and speed of the shutter. Even simple shots required a lot of skill. But technology changed all that. Nowadays, you can buy a camera right off the shelf, run outside with it, trip on the curb and drop it, and if it doesn't break and snaps a shot, it might end up in this room."

Eva yelped with laughter and had to put her hand over her mouth to shut herself up. "So, what makes a good photograph?"

"Basically the same dynamics that go into making a good painting. You need a decent subject, and you have to compose the subject matter to bring out the elements you want. From that point, there are literally thousands of variations of light and focus considerations, lens choice and film choice, to bring out the proper mood. Timing is essential, not to mention having a vast memory of experience to tell you what you see may be beautiful, but the camera may not record the image as you see it. This requires adjustments."

"What's the most important part?"

"Everything. You screw up one element and the picture is just a picture."

"Aren't they all the same? This picture of Frankfurt is just like the one I saw in a travel agency before."

"I doubt it."

"So explain the difference."

"Did you ever go out a buy a camera at the store when you were a child?"

"No, but I was given one for my birthday one year."

"Me too, except mine was for Christmas and I took pictures of everyone opening their gifts. Thirty-six shots of blurred faces and wrapping paper."

"That was your Minolta?"

"No, that was a toy camera. It took pictures all right, but I quickly graduated from that thing and got me a real camera, the Minolta. Anyway, what did you take pictures of?"

"My gifts…the neighborhood."

"How'd they come out?"

"I had eight or ten blurry and dark shots of my birthday party, six or seven pictures of my house and—"

"I bet they didn't come close to capturing the mood of the party did they?"

"No."

"And the pictures of the house were all the same weren't they?"

"Yeah, everyone of them taken from the front of the house. Two of them were clear enough to keep."

"If you looked at the pictures of the house today could you tell me what kind of day it was? Was it windy? Temperature?"

"Probably not."

"And the pictures of the party, did they capture the excitement in the eyes of your friends?"

"I remember a great shot of my friend Frieda's teeth. She was laughing."

"Do you remember the photo of the mountain scene I took in Arizona?"

"*Ja.*"

"Let me tell you what went into that shot."

"When I'm shooting nature shots I like to do it in the morning. It's the best time because everything's waking up. If I'm lucky, there's an early morning mist, which provides some unique opportunities. On that particular shot, I got up at about 5:00 and drove into the mountains. After I parked, I hiked another two miles into the mountains to a place where I'd been before, but it had been during the middle of the day and that's the worse time to shoot."

"Why's that?"

"Because when the sun is high the shadows are at their minimum. Contrast between the light and shadows are at their peak. No drama. I hiked to the top of the ridge before the sun peeked over the horizon. I couldn't see it, but I knew it was rising because above me the clouds were turning color. First they were just a dull yellow, but as the sun rose higher the clouds began to catch on fire, filling the entire sky with a warm orange glow slowly brightening into vibrant reds. I knew the composition I wanted, so I set my tripod up near a stand of trees overlooking a valley and a cliff of rocks."

"Why use the tripod?"

"It keeps the camera absolutely steady. Anyway, I was lucky that morning and a mist was moving up the valley towards me. I set the camera on the tripod, locked it on the composition I wanted then waited. Timing was everything. I sat there for thirty-five minutes, checking the composition, wiping the lens clean of mist, rubbing my butt—"

"Your butt?"

"I was sitting on this pointed rock and well, never mind. I was watching the sky because Arizona has some of the most brilliant sunrises in the country. They build in color and intensity until they reach their maximum and collapse. I knew I had about ten minutes remaining to get my shot in, but now the mist wasn't cooperating. The sun was heating the atmosphere and causing a breeze to kick up. The mist kept coming towards me and covered the view. I kept waiting, one eye open and pressed to the camera and my legs were beginning to cramp. I wiped the lens for the last time and adjusted the aperture. Then I got lucky. There was a hole in the mist and I was able to focus on a distant ridge. I rechecked all my setting and "*click*."

"I see what you mean," she said. "A once in a lifetime shot."

"Well, I could always go back, but nature never duplicates itself. There will never be another shot like it. Come on, let's take a look at the other photos."

They walked towards another photographer's work. Most of the photos were portraits of people, some were of children playing in a playground, and a few nudes.

"You shoot a lot of photographs of people don't you?" she asked, admiring a shot of two children playing on a swing. In it, a young boy about ten years old was pushing his friend on the swing. The photographer had caught the girl at the highest point on the swing. She was having the time of her life.

"I do, but I don't think I shoot any more pictures of people than I do of wildlife or nature scenes. Shooting people is less demanding."

"How so?"

"For one thing you don't have to drive and hike for hours and most people are anxious for you to take their picture."

"Why nudes?" she asked.

"I'm not sure I can give you the answer you're looking for. In reality, I find the female form interesting and sensual. I could lie, tell you I'm a professional and only interested in things like form, shadows and texture, but I won't. I find nothing wrong with my attraction as a man towards women. Aside from that, there is the artistic challenge of creating a good photo from an already good subject."

"You make it sound simple."

"It should be. As a man I'm attracted to women…women are attracted to men, so any photo of a nude man or woman is bound to create a reaction. I don't understand how this basic instinct can be labeled as evil by some people."

"You mean sex?"

"Sex, but more than sex, it's also the desires that lead to sex. It's the way people find fault with their own desires and actions, as if these desires are demonic. Take desire…or lust. We're told from day one that it's wrong to want something we don't have. But can you think of anything mankind has done that wasn't caused by a person desiring to have something better? Can you imagine a world where people run around not wanting to do or accomplish anything? To get anywhere in life you have to first want it. And lust…lust is really just another term for desire, and a way of describing desire for companionship and sex. Can you imagine any relationship without it? Hell, you might was well choose a lover out of box a cereal. Every relationship begins with lust and desire, and it's lust and desire that keeps the relationship going— don't you think?"

"I'd hope so."

"I know I'm talking terminology, but I know what I'm saying. I take pictures—not all my pictures—but some pictures of the human form, because I enjoy doing it, and I think the women I've taken pictures of wanted to have their picture taken in the first place. You've seen my work, do you find it tasteful?"

"I'm really not sure where 'tasteful' begins and ends, or where offensive begins or ends. If you are asking whether I get the same response with your female nudes as you do, I'd have to say no. But that one of the male…"

"Greg was his name."

"Is interesting."

"Would you say I've succeeded at making an emotional connection?"

"I'll grant you that."

"I wish I could accurately describe how my photographs make me feel. I mean, beyond what may be stimulating about them, they seem just as natural as taking a picture of a naked mountaintop or a naked shoreline. To me, anything in nature is stimulating. We see just the simple forms or curves, even patterns, but behind it all there's a dynamic intelligence. So who can say one form or another form is less important than another. Who can say in their right mind that 'I can't look at this or that, because of the way it makes me feel.' Or, who can say one representation of nature is more diabolical than another? It's ridiculous. I can take a picture of an armpit and the back of a woman's head and it's acceptable. Drop the camera down a notch and catch the exposed portion of a breast and suddenly, I'm a pervert with a camera. Same body, same woman, and if you believe it, same creator who made them both, yet one particular curve is deemed more offensive than the rest. Frankly, I find that kind of thinking offensive!"

Right before her eyes Stace was coming alive. Up until that moment, she'd only seen him from a distance, as if he'd been communicating to her through a glass bubble, concealing his true feelings. She liked that first impression of the man, but the Stace that was now surfacing was much more alive than she'd imagined. His soul was bottomless and whether she knew it or not, the journey she was taking into his soul was also rejuvenating her. She was finding answers to questions she'd never even thought to ask herself. She was discovering the woman she was and not the woman she'd made herself out to be.

"You hungry?" she asked.

"A little."

From the museum, they walked a few blocks to *Mainzer Gasse* where she knew of a great restaurant perched on top of the eighth floor of a classy department store. She chose a table near the window overlooking downtown Frankfurt and *Sachsenhausen*. At 4:30 in the afternoon, the fest halls and bars had not yet come to life. They wouldn't be in full swing until after 11:00. Stace and Eva would never make it to them.

Much of what they said to each other over the course of the next few hours would not pass in words. With thoughts carried by fairies between their unspoken desires they discovered another meaning to their existence together. It has been said, that people fall in love with each other, but that distinction rests with those who consider love to be demanding. For with them, love is like a precious commodity, dispenscd only when all the possible risks have been eliminated. But others, carry the joy of love with them like a bouquet of flowers. It's not a question of how little love they have to give, but the realization that they can't give and express love fast enough, for fear that it might wilt before it's exchanged. Stace and Eva understood this kind of love, and it was inevitable that the two would find themselves together, alone.

She had just finished sliding a CD into Stace's stereo, propped her feet up on the coffee table and laid her head against the back of the couch. Her next sensation was an almost imperceptible touch. He'd walked across the rug and without a sound had dropped to his knees behind her and touched her neck. Then he reached up again with both hands, running them down over the contours of her head and shoulders. Leaning closer, he buried his nose into the aroma of her hair. Delighted with the sensation, he clawed his fingers into her hair taking in fistfuls, whispered her name and sucked the nape of her neck as if the taste of her flesh was ointment to his soul. He'd not shaved since Friday morning and strands of her hair were getting caught up in the rakes of his whiskers. She could feel his hot breath lingering over her hair, the song of his panting increasing. A race of goose bumps traveled at lightning speed down her spine, over her thighs and down to her toes still wrapped in socks. She let her head fall forwards towards her chest. With a finger he parted her hair in the middle of her head, then reached up with both hands over her earlobes, fingers stretching like cat paws in parallel rhythm over the line of her jaws towards her lips. With one of his fingers he found the flesh of her lips and caressed the outline. Then, the tip of his finger on teeth. Lips wrapping around the knuckle entombing his finger in seas of warmth. Tongue swirling, pulling his finger down deeper. A twitch of pain as her teeth lock down. He, taking her neck into his mouth like a vampire, gripping, nearly penetrating. Her moan, mouth parting, as the *pop* of his finger passes through her lips. He would show no mercy now. Diving again, teeth exposed, starting below the collar of her blouse, moving swiftly up the sides of her neck devouring earlobes, numbing sensations all the while rippling over her body, pricking the nipples of her breasts into submission. Slide of hand around her throat dropping down over her collarbone. The hesitation…as if electricity were housed somewhere beyond the first button of her blouse.

CHAPTER 27

▼

"No Pruitt! We can't do it and I won't do it! Just think about it!" Rick said fuming with anger, jugular veins in his neck popping out like ropes. He'd never spoken to Pruitt in this manner, but right was right and there was no possible way he was going to hack into the files of major web browsers, which would allow them to unleash the virus.

"Then how in the hell are we going to do it?" Pruitt asked.

"We'll have to find another way."

"How?" Pruitt asked, trying to think of a reason not to fire Rick on the spot.

"We'll have to simulate…simulate the conditions somehow, but we certainly can't hack into those systems."

"Rick's right," Jean said. She looked directly into Pruitt's glaring eyes. "I can tell you from first hand experience you don't want to screw around with those companies. Nothing can save you if you get caught. And all the money in the world couldn't get me to risk the next forty years of my life in jail. Either we find a way to simulate the same dynamics of the browsers and the Internet, or it's just not going to get done, because we've looked at all the other options and they won't work."

Pruitt took a few deep breaths and composed himself. He had sense enough to understand Jean knew what she was talking about. If there were other options she would have known about them. He looked at Rick, who was at that very moment working out the details of a resignation letter in his head. Pruitt knew Rick was the still the best man for the job. He needed him.

"Look, I'm sorry Rick. I didn't mean to assault you like that. It's just that we've got a lot riding on this project. You're right of course, legally and ethically there's no reason we should have to steal some of their programming information. I was wrong for asking you to do it." He was lying. He'd do anything possible to get the information needed.

Rick didn't budge. He stood by the window looking outside into the hill country imagining the sound of the wind blowing through the oak trees, but all he could hear was his own heart throbbing in his ears.

"I have a lot of confidence in you Rick. As far as I'm concerned you're the most capable programmer at Trojan Security." He put his hand around Rick's shoulder and drew him close to his side. They were facing the window now and Pruitt dropped his voice down to a whisper. "I mean that Rick, you're the best we've got, and we go back several years." Pruitt took a deep breath and considered his next choice of words. "I'm going to recommend to Mr. Watson we give you a bonus when this is completed. I should think $25,000 is a workable figure. I know you're a man of principle and we can't buy your support, but what else is a company to do?" He grinned and gently shook Rick's shoulder. "We pay for performance, that's business and there's nothing unethical about it. I want you here and I want you to be happy with us. I can promise you, I won't ask you to do anything illegal again or jeopardize your standards. Ok?"

Rick hesitated a few moments before answering. "All right," he replied. Then to himself he said, "it better be the last time."

"Great!" Pruitt said. He turned around and faced Jean. "I've got confidence in both of you. If you've got to simulate what needs to be done then so be it."

When Pruitt left, Jean was the first to speak, "I can't believe it! He actually pressed us on the idea. I believe in what we're doing, but I'm sure not going to risk jail time for it!" Her words bounced off Rick like a splash of water in a frying pan. He was still at the window considering his options. Jean left him alone. She walked over to the new equipment and fired it up. The hard drives clicked on with a whine.

In a way it seemed like yesterday, the passing of time obscuring events and faces like dusty images in the broken mirror of a ghost town saloon. He remembered the name, Stace Manning, but the only detail he could recall of Stace's face was the rage in his eyes when Rick had told him about the committee's decision to not let his work be shown at the exhibit. It took Rick over a year to convince himself it was the committee's decision and not entirely his own. But doubts lingered. Deep down, he knew he should have supported Stace. No matter how he analyzed the event from an intellectual standpoint, Rick couldn't absolve himself from the feeling he'd skirted his responsibility. He'd overlooked an important principle. But principles are often a matter of perspective, and as the years passed those principles were replaced by more important issues, like making a living—and what ever happened to Stace anyway?

Rick wasn't at all impressed with the offer to buy his cooperation for $25,000, but it could buy a little tolerance and quite possibly, justification. Maybe it was the way the transaction went down, which he didn't like, like the way Pruitt expected him to just shut up by waving numbers in his face. Maybe it was the sick feeling in the pit of his stomach that made him feel superficial when he thought about what he could do with the extra money. Or maybe it was this same old version of himself that kept rearing its ugly head at him every time he turned around.

What perplexed him most was that he really couldn't give a shit about the program from an ethical standpoint. After all, he was comfortable with the overall aim of the program. If it was to leak out and get into the hands of someone like the ICC then so be it. As far as he was concerned, the world was a much safer place than it was ten years ago thanks to organizations like the ICC and the American Christian

Broadcasting Network. More importantly, he agreed in the basic political agenda of those organizations.

The truth be told, Rick was a man of wavering contradictions. One
of those contradictions stemmed from his Christian faith and his need
to make a living. His church environment had kept him on the straight
and narrow up to this point in his life, but now he was confronted with
a dilemma, which his church and its traditions had yet to provide an
answer for. He sided with the program, because in general it would
promote the Christian faith. He opposed it, because of the possibility
that it might fall into the wrong hands. He was for the program, when
he considered a man—such as himself—must work and provide for his
family. The large bonus just thrown in his face would seem to justify
that argument. He was opposed to the program, when he considered
Trojan Security was using him and they might have other ideas for the
program. But then again, "it's what companies do," Pruitt had said and
"it's what employees do," he thought to himself. After all, who was he
to question Trojan Security's reputation? He just worked there. Of
course, this was in complete contradiction to his quest to get to the
bottom of why the program was being created. Needless to say, he was
just plain tired of thinking about it.

Meanwhile, at a distant northeast country club in Austin a golf caddie answered the phone…"Fred Watson, please." Pruitt said through
his speakerphone as he sat behind his desk.

"I'm sorry sir, Mr. Watson has given specific instructions he's not to
be disturbed."

"Tell him this is Pruitt. He'll talk to me."

"I'm sorry sir, but—"

"Listen! What's he doing now?"

"He's on the seventh sir and shooting from thirteen feet for a birdie.
Are you sure you want to interrupt him?"

"No, not just yet, but hold the line. When he sinks the putt and
hands you the club give him the phone."

The seventh green sloped gently to the right about three degrees. Just beyond the tee it tapered about five degrees into a sand pit. Watson's putt called for him to perform a feat just beyond his skill of expertise. He must drive the putt slightly up hill to the left and calculate the power without error. Too much power and the ball would be pulled into the sand pit. The last six holes had put him two over par. Not the best he'd done, but a promising start nonetheless. If he finished the front nine with less than seven over, he would pocket a token $20.00 from his competition, Jeff Mitchell, an executive with Dell.

The air was still, the green soggy. A thunderstorm had rolled through the night before dropping an inch of rain on the course. Watson's cleats swished as he walked across the green and approached the ball. Squatting, he held his putter as a pendulum, lining the ball up with the hole and analyzing the slopes of the green. The sand pit loomed like quicksand in the background. Rising, he moved in just behind the ball and took a few practice swings. Black crows sitting in a nearby mesquite tree cocked their heads and held their throats. Mitchell and his caddie were motionless.

Pruitt cracked his knuckles until his patience gave out. "Well?" he shouted. The caddie shoved the speaker against his pants to muffle the sound. He dare not answer.

Satisfied, Watson stepped over the ball, gripped the handle and made a few last second calculations. A crow squawked, but it didn't faze him. He would not be denied. One last look at the hole and he drew his putter back. A smooth even swing struck the ball with a *prick* and sent it shooting off towards the hole. Mitchell grinned. Too much power. Even Watson thought he'd hit it too hard. The ball bounced three times then rolled, water spinning off of it in a symmetrical spiral like the flares from a whirly bird firecracker. Three feet from the hole it slowed down drastically, crept to the lip, hung for just a moment, then rolled in.

"Is that Mr. Pruitt on the phone?" Watson asked his caddie nonchalantly, as if he expected to make the putt all along.

"Yes sir. Outstanding shot sir!"

The caddie exchanged club for phone. Watson moved to a stand of trees beyond earshot.

"Watson!"

"What's going on Pruitt?"

"We almost lost Rick this morning."

Watson waited for an explanation.

"He and Jean have come up with some good ideas, but it was going to require—"

"Is he staying, Pruitt?"

"I believe so."

"Is the program still on line?"

"Yes sir."

"Then the only thing I need to hear about is if we're running into some of those problems we discussed."

"No sir. Nothing like that."

"So we're still on schedule?"

"Yes sir. But I had to twist his arm with a bonus."

"Under fifty grand I hope," Watson replied, looking over to the green so that he wouldn't miss Mitchell's putt.

"Yes sir."

"Good."

"And what did security find out."

"They've got photos of he and Jean having lunch together."

"And how often do employees have lunch together?"

"Often sir." Pruitt understood the implication.

"Then we really don't have much to convince him not to walk if he decides to—do we?"

"No sir. I'm not sure we ever will with Rick."

"Well, you just make sure that if and when he and Jean mix it up we get something substantial."

"Yes sir."

Back at Trojan Security Rick had managed to lay aside his doubts for the moment. He sat next to Jean, who was tossing computer manuals back into one of the empty boxes.

"What?" she looked at him "You don't need these do you?" she asked.

"If I do, we're in a lot of trouble."

She spotted another manual on the other side of his computer monitor, and as she reached for it her arm slid across the back of his hand. The warmth of her skin through her cotton sleeve enchanted him. She was wearing a thin, lightly colored blouse, and as she backed into her seat he saw the form of her breasts dangle momentarily in the light cast from his monitor. The aroma of her perfume followed, mingling with the warmth of her body. Her action seemed deliberate. When she settled in her seat, the unpleasant thoughts associated with Pruitt's visit had escaped him.

Their most pressing dilemma at the moment was how they might simulate the dynamics of the software programs used by major web browses. Much of their time was spent in close proximity to one another, so close at times that their knees often brushed together, discussing some possibility or another, or an inticate programming detail that would have to be built. They spent as much time discussing the program as they did thinking about each other, though the conversation stayed within the boundaries of technical jargon. Hidden video cameras concealed in Rick's office recorded every subtle touch, every nuance of their gestures, and even the moment when Jean brushed off a crumb from Rick's lips with her fingers, which was left over from a sandwich he'd just finished. Before they knew it, it was 5:00, then 6:00, then 6:20. At Rick's home, Julie was just now setting the table with little Rebecca tagging along behind her holding two spoons in her dimpled fingers.

"It's late and I need to get going," he said reluctantly.

Jean put her hand on his knee. "I know. Would you like to get together tomorrow?" she asked.

"To work on the program?"

"Yes, of course. We made good progress today. I'd hate to break the rhythm."

"I know what you mean. But I can't tomorrow," he replied, for the first time regretting the dawning of Sunday, church, and an afternoon with the family.

"I understand." She sucked in the corner of her bottom lip.

"I've got other plans," he said quickly, sparing her the details of his matrimonial commitment.

"Another time perhaps."

"I'll see you on Monday then," he said, as he reached to shut down her computer.

"I'm going to stay a little longer."

"You sure?"

"I've got nothing better to do tonight."

He grabbed his briefcase and didn't turn around at the door. She watched him leave.

As he drove home that evening, he couldn't shake her lingering memory from his mind. Curiously, he found this infatuation, stimulating. Throughout his short married life the thought of even considering another woman was unthinkable, not because it was beyond his capability, but because the sanctity of marriage had brought him great comfort, like the fit of a fir lined glove in winter. Certainly her actions were deliberate? Like when she reached for the manual, hovering over him like a flower waiting to be plucked. Then later, the bone and muscle of their knees rubbing together and the pull of his slacks across her pantyhose as they brushed together. She didn't wait long to pick the crumb from his lip. Her gestures were sensuous, not a figment of his imagination. He leaned his head towards the window and let the breeze suck at his hair.

What intrigued him most about her memory was the way it peeled away the layers of his conscious and sent it drifting like a feather over the asphalt. Things significant now seemed minute and undefined, like obligations dropped at the edge of a forest of possibilities. Things familiar, like his wife, his daughter, the mortgage and work, now seemed blurred at their edges. Even the confinements of his religious faith seemed unrealistic and harsh, as though they were merely ancient beliefs with no bearing on the present. As he pulled into his driveway and set the parking brake, his thoughts and actions turned mechanical.

As usual, little Rebecca waited for the signal of her cocker spaniel, Muffin. He lay curled on the tile floor in the kitchen near the heat of the oven where the baked chicken had just been removed. Between trips to the table with her mother, Rebecca would return to the kitchen to watch her furry friend. She couldn't understand how Muffin knew exactly when her daddy came home, but he always did, acknowledging the exact moment when her daddy's car bumped the curb at the bottom of the driveway. Today was no different. Suddenly, his right ear mysteriously peaked, then the left. He raised his head, cocked it over to one side and when he was sure, jumped up and barked. Then his little paws started moving frantically, their nails clicking across the tile like the steel wheels of a locomotive engine slipping across polished rails, When he reached the carpet he shot onto the couch like a gazelle, pushed the corner of the curtains aside with his short wet nose and barked furiously. Rebecca never made it to the couch in time to watch her daddy get out of the car. By the time she reached the couch, Muffin was running towards the front door and she was still in hot pursuit, giggling and wobbling right along behind him.

"Hello munchkin!" her daddy said entering the foyer. He set his briefcase down, pulled her up to his chest and gave her a big bear hug.

"Mommy made chicken," she said, her eyes just inches from his. "I set the table!" she beamed proudly.

"Well, aren't you a big girl." She nodded clumsily three times and smacked her lips.

Julie arrived moments after he'd set her down on the floor next to Muffin. Normally, she would have welcomed him home from where she always stood cooking in the kitchen, but he was late and she was just as anxious to see him as Rebecca. "Good to see you," she said warmly, reaching over to kiss him and letting him take her in his arms.

"Sorry I'm late."

"We missed you today."

"Me too, I'm not used to working on Saturdays."

"Do you have to work tomorrow?"

"No, not this week. Smells good." He tossed his coat on the chair and walked into the dining room. After dinner, he read a quick story to his daughter then went to help Julie out in the kitchen.

"You already know about my day, so how was yours?" she asked, rinsing a dish and putting it into the dishwasher.

"Busy as usual. We've just started designing another program and we're not sure how to proceed. What about that doctorate program you were thinking about doing? When does it start?"

His change of subject caught her off guard. She rinsed another dish before answering. "Starts up again in the spring. Why?"

"Was that a one year program or two?"

"Two, to get the discipline I want."

He was embarrassed to ask what that discipline was. He'd forgotten. "I think you should go for it."

She turned off the water and started wiping down the counters with a dishrag. "I thought you wanted me to wait," she said without looking up.

"Well, it's your decision really. I just thought with Rebecca being so young you wanted to wait until she got older. But I know you've been anxious to start."

She turned around and moved towards him with dishrag in hand and brushed up against him. He stepped to the side, so she could clean the counter behind him.

"I think it would be good for you," he said.

"I've been trying to figure out how I can make it work. Rebecca's old enough to take to a day-care now and I'd have to work around your schedule. They have night classes, but I'd rather go in the daytime, so we can still have our evenings free. Then there's the money…"

"I've got that covered."

"How so?"

"Seems this project is so important they've offered me an immediate bonus."

"A bonus?" She stopped wiping and looked at him. "They've never offered you a bonus before have they?"

"No."

"Why this time?"

"Don't know."

Julie didn't look convinced. She'd always known little about his work and he hadn't shared any details about the present project. "Do they think you're going to quit or something?"

"Maybe."

"Did you lead them to believe that?"

"Not that I'm aware of."

"Are you going to quit?"

"No, and believe me, if they didn't want me they wouldn't have offered the bonus, nor would they have promoted me. So don't worry."

She rinsed the dishrag in the sink. "I guess you're right. How much?"

"Twenty-five grand. Can you believe it?"

"$2,500?"

"No, two, five, zero, zero, zero. That should pay for your tuition and then some."

She turned back at him in disbelief. "I guess that's one way of saying they'd like to keep you around!" She leaned over and kissed him with one of those long and grateful kisses.

"I told you, nothing to worry about."

"Well, in that case, I'll be glad to help you spend some of the money."

He smiled. "I thought you would."

CHAPTER 28

▼

The first thing Eva did upon awaking was to suck in a mountain of Stace's atmosphere then exhale with a complete sense of satisfaction. Deep within her the world was blooming like the first day of spring; when the flush of love is blooming everywhere and there's not enough time to run from one place to another and enjoy the aroma. What spawned her euphoria was her surrender to a new and worthy cause; that of devotion to the man she loved. Everything in her life suddenly become secondary, as though she were mysteriously flipped around and pointed in a different direction. She didn't sense any repercussions to her actions from the evening before, because there were none. No guilt, no fear, not even a hint of impropriety. Those obsessions had been swept away like darkness banned to the outskirts of the universe.

The alarm clock next to his bed read 5:40 in bright, blood red numbers, painting the room in a faint, scarlet glow. Stace lay curled behind her, their bodies molded together as one. He stirred as she rolled over to face him, but didn't wake. His long inky hair sprawled frantically across his face and pillow, the rhythm of his breath was deep and hard. He was somewhere far away, lost in dream. She looked at him intently. The ridge of his nose promenading out of his face. Strong square jaw speckled in whisker. The sliver of his eyes set behind black curling lashes. Not pretty, he was rather, unique, possessing the kind of face that invites inquiry as to the origin if its sensitivity. She would no longer question his interest in her, that question being satisfied. In fact, she wouldn't allow any doubts of any kind to surface, choosing rather to simply believe and trust.

After a few moments, she slipped away from him. In the living room she dressed, having found her clothes contorted on the floor where they'd been left the night before. She switched off the stereo, grabbed her bag and tiptoed down the hall and almost made it past his room.

"Will you be back?" he asked.

She peered into the glow towards the bed. "How long have you been awake?"

"Just a few moments."

"Sorry I woke you. I've got to run to the paper this morning. There's some equipment I need to check on, but I'll be back in about an hour."

"I'll have breakfast ready by the time you get back," he said, rolling out of bed.

She watched him move towards her and take her hand.

He walked her down the hall and grabbed his coat from a hanger near the door. "Wear mine this morning. It's cooler now than it was last night."

"Thanks."

After helping her into it, he gently turned her around by the shoulders and began buttoning her up. She stood silent and compliant like a toddler being dressed. When he finished he bent over and kissed her on the forehead, then pushed her loose bangs behind her ears. "You hurry back now."

"I will."

At work she quickly changed out the CDs, setting them on the stack of others that had been recorded over the weekend. She had no intention of running them through the scanner to listen to any conversations they might have recorded. She hopped in her Opel and headed back to Stace's apartment.

By 8:30 they were headed northwest towards *Rudelsheim*, the quaint romantic city laced along the banks of the fertile *Rhine* River. Tourists from the surrounding areas were beginning to arrive and strolled along the spotless mercantile streets. They found a place to park near one of the many ports along the river built for the Brandenburg's massive seventy-five foot touring yachts. Eva purchased tickets and they boarded one of the yachts, landing a table on the upper deck overlooking the lower deck, where they could watch the bow cut a path through the calm, silent waters of the river.

The day had dawned just as spectacular as she'd predicted. The sky was clear and blue, of the variety in which one can scan from the horizon up into the heavens and witness the gradual wash in color of pale blue to imaginary blackness. The sun was mildly threatening, warming everything it touched, dispelling any illusion of an approaching winter. In the clear skies hung aromas seen only through smell, such as the waft of fresh river water soaked in mountain fragrance, and co-mingling with churning diesel smoke as the yacht backed out and broke free of port. From *Rudelsheim*, a stream of civilized smells poured out of restaurants and bakeries and coffee shops, converging with the already present aromas. Further along, the aromas of remnant grape blossom and harvest, intermixed with the musty smell of turned soil, broken twigs, and rotting grapes that had bloomed too late for picking. And each one of these smells eventually mingled into one, pouring over the bow of the ship and threatening to blow the napkins out from under their coffee cups.

Stace sat opposite Eva, holding a cup of coffee between his hands, wondering just where heaven began and earth ended. Behind her, he watched the scenery drift by like the journal of an ancient countryside lost in the culture of a forgotten time. Around every corner a fortress or castle pierced the sky. It was scenery that would cause even the most practical of men to wonder, but for an artist like Stace it was breathtaking. He reached into his backpack and pulled out his Nikon and snapped a few pictures of the hills for the sake of remembrance. This was rather unnecessary for him to do, because once having taken in a scene it was locked in his memory forever. He swung the camera around and adjusted the focal length of the 135 mm zoom lens on Eva. She sat compliantly looking at him and confirming in her own mind what she already knew to be true, that his attraction to her was genuine. The camera's auto-winder shot four frames, capturing her face as it changed from a curious look into a self-conscious smile.

"If you had the choice Stace, where would you really like to be?"

He thought for a moment…"here with you," he said, setting his camera on the table.

"Thank you, but that's not what I meant."

"It's what I meant."

She smiled warmly.

"I'm really not too concerned about where I'll be in the next few years or the next ten years for that matter. I'm more interested in what I can experience in life at the present moment. In America, we call it drifting, and I couldn't think of a better place to drifting than here with you right now."

"So you don't have any future plans?"

"Certainly, I've got plans. But if you mean specific ones like where I'd like to live or what kind of job I'll have until my photography pays off, then no. But you know, there are two things in life that really irk me. Work for one. I hate it. But don't get me wrong, I could shoot pictures twenty-four-seven if I had the option. Problem is, the opportunity hasn't presented itself yet."

"And the other?"

"Sleep. It's a waste of time."

A silent waiter holding two silver pots interrupted them. A foot-long stream of coffee poured out of the tips of both pots as he filled their cups.

"What about you Eva?"

"Be honest with you, I never imagined myself doing anything other than investigative work, but if I really had the option, I'd rather be doing something else."

"If everyone in the world was as honest as you Eva, you'd be out of job."

"Never saw it like that, but it gets a little depressing focusing on the bad elements of life all the time. I envy the freedom you have Stace."

"I'm not entirely free. True freedom is for those without a conscious. I seem to have been blessed with an unusually active one."

"I'm not sure what you mean," she said.

"It may seem like I don't have a care in the world, but I work hard at focusing on the bad elements just as much as you might."

"Why on earth would you do that?"

"It's part of the artist's burden."

"Burden?"

"Sure. I compare the artist's burden to baking a cake. You take all of life's pain, sorrow, injustices and ironies, and put them in a bowl. Then you capture all the beauty in life, the emotions of the human spirit and throw them into another bowl. Then you take all of the spiritual qualities of life, such as the ideas and dreams of mankind and put them into another bowl. After you have all these ingredients, you pick an artistic medium such as painting, music, poetry—or in my case photography—and create something that will enrich the lives of others."

"I had no idea the process was so complex," she replied dumbfounded.

"It's not, if you're an artist. Fact there is no process, just the frantic desire to express yourself and the faint hope that your expressions will connect with others."

"Imagine that…and all this time I thought you were just a lazy son of a bitch!" she said sarcastically.

Suddenly, the tables behind them began clearing as the other passengers stood. The bow of the yacht started making a gentle turn to the right towards an open port and its engines slowed.

"Are we getting off?" he asked.

"Look to your right."

His eyes wandered up to an ancient castle on the hill.

"*Ehrensfels'* Castle," she said. "I think you'll enjoy it."

After debarking and crossing the street they came to a wide up-hill path lined in overgrown trees. Ten minutes later at the top of the hill they came upon a circular cobblestone entrance graced with a three-tier fountain. The cobblestone shimmered in the sun, having been buffed to a high gloss over the centuries by the sandals of noblemen, the boots of soldiers and modern day tennis shoes. The castle walls zigzagged in ninety-degree angles around the circular entrance. In the far right corner was an outdoor cafe.

She took his hand and led him up a skinny wooden staircase along one of the outside walls. Joined by walkways along the top of the castle were a number of observation points bordered with waist high walls of stone fingers, which made them look like rooks on a chessboard. In ancient times these were guard posts, where warriors would slide their archery bows between the fingers and fire at intruders below. Each guard post overlooked a different angle into the surrounding countryside, providing a three hundred and sixty degree view around the castle. After half an hour or so of exploring each one of them, Stace and Eva returned to the main walkway running parallel with the river below. They stood leaning up against the wall, arms dangling over the edge, gazing at the magical world below them.

"Do you ever wonder what it would have been like to have lived during another period in history?" he asked her.

"Sometimes."

"Do you believe in fate?" he pressed.

"I don't know what I believe," she responded without looking at him.

He said, "I don't believe in absolutes. It always amazes me the way people order their lives around an imaginary destiny, like the rest of the world is supposed to conform their lives around them."

"I think we all do a little of that don't you?" she asked, taking her eyes off the coal barge pushing its way upstream in the river far below them and looked at him.

"It's important to know who you are, but when you start to force yourself or your beliefs on other people, then you've stepped over the line."

A younger couple holding hands walked by. Eva waited until they passed. She was considering the conversation she had with her father earlier in the week. Had her parents completely subscribed to the wishes of their own parents, her father and mother may have never married, and she would have never been born.

"Have you always just floated through life Stace?"

"Actually, I think I'm rather grounded."

"When it comes to religion you're not."

"Seems like we've had this conversation before." He stepped behind her and wrapped his arms around her stomach, resting his chin on her shoulder. She tipped her head towards his face and their cheeks pressed together. "You and I live in two different worlds," she whispered.

"I think we are very much alike," he reassured her.

"I don't know how to say what I would like to say without frightening you."

"I don't think you can frighten me."

"I've never met a man like you," she said softly and tucked her head underneath his chin. He wrapped his arms around her and stared across the *Rhine* at the distant hills. With her ear pressed against his chest she listened to the sound of his pounding heart, feeling secure in the warmth of his presence. After a few minutes, she looked into his face and searched his eyes intently. "I would like what we've begun to never end. I would like to know you Stace, like no one else has ever known you. But I'm afraid...afraid I'm not enough for you."

"Why would you think that?"

"Because you're an intense individual, deeper than any man I've met."

He stepped back slightly and took her face in his hands, searching for the reason for her lack of faith. "You're the intense one Eva. I drift around hoping I might find a way to connect to this world and whether I crawl out of bed each morning makes no difference to anybody. Your work is very important. I can only dream of making half the impact in this world that you've already made."

She turned her head to the side again and buried it in his chest. He held her tightly, then sighed deeply. She could feel his hot breath penetrating her scalp. Moments turned to minutes. Finally she whispered, "I love you Stace," but her words were carried away in the breeze and barely reached his ears. She waited.

For a flash of time he was uncertain of what she'd said. He wanted to believe—but disbelieved—and had to know, so he reached down and gently took hold of her face and looked into her eyes.

"What did you say?" he questioned eagerly.

"I love you," she repeated without delay.

She could see he was confused. For a moment she doubted. "But if—"

He stopped her words with a kiss and pulled away.

"There is no 'but if.' I was looking for a way to return what you said that wouldn't seem trivial. You are a special woman Eva. I knew that from the first moment I met you, and it seems like I've known you for years. I've never felt the desire to protect and care for anyone, such as the way that I feel impelled to care for you—"

"I'm not asking anything from you Stace...I just wanted to let you know how I feel."

"I know Eva. And I don't know what the future might hold for us, but I do know that what we've have started together has been wonderful, and I would like to continue."

CHAPTER 29

▼

Julie Forstein's night had been full of Cinderella dreams, where the subconscious rehashes though the images of a perfect life and scrambles them into broken images. She rolled the switch of the lamp near the bed and set in motion another day. Rick lay curled up beside her, his chest curved around her back, knees tucked behind her thighs, right arm hanging over her waist like a propped up puppet arm. She ran her hand back and forth along his arm, the tips of her fingers tunneling through the long wiry curls of his hair.

"*Ummmm*," he moaned.

"Time to get up," she said, twisting her neck around.

"Let's skip church today," he grunted.

"Can't. It's my week to teach and you've got platform duty."

"Again? What is it this time?"

"Scripture reading. If you don't show up they'll wonder where you're at."

"Tell them I'm sick."

"They might believe it. You're never sick."

Rick didn't respond. His mind was beginning to slowly engage itself and reality was overtaking him like a screaming computer processor. There was work, the program, Jean…the evasive act he used last night to skirt his wife's advances, and the fact that within a few hours he'd be standing before a thousand people at the Fellowship Church reading a testy piece of scripture. He felt Julie take his hand and press it reassuringly. She rolled out of bed and let his arm fall across the mattress, and he followed her blurry form with his eyes as she shuffled into the bathroom. He rolled onto his back and reached for his glasses on the nightstand. Above him the beads from the acoustic ceiling hung like creamed perspiration. He pushed the bedspread off his chest and folded his hands underneath his head, then stared into space and thought. The toilet flushed, immediately followed by the swish of water from the shower, and he imagined Julie emerging from the tentacles of her pink nightgown and it falling haphazardly around her ankles, followed by her panties dropping like a feather on the floor. There was a popping sound as the glass shower door opened and a metallic *click* when it closed, and her body would be silhouetted against the sea colored tile on the shower room wall.

Although the night had removed him a safe distance from the seductions of the day before, the sensations were still as keen as they were the previous evening. His memories took feverish proportions, swelling strange desires within him. To squelch the fever, he immediately thought of his responsibilities at the church and throwing the covers aside wrapped himself in a flannel robe and tied the belt around his toned abdomen with a snap. He paced nervously across the bedroom floor, purposely avoiding his image in the full-length mirror on the wall, until he heard the shower stop, and after a showing and dressing he drove his family to church.

As was the custom, Pastor Mitchell and the three elders who would accompany him to the podium, met for a brief moment before the service in the church office. Greetings were exchanged and Rick was given a slip of paper with the morning's text inscribed on it, which had been selected by the pastor from the book of Ecclesiastics. When the service began, the four men walked humbly to the front of the congregation, where Rick sat next to Elder Cramer and waited for his moment at the podium. When prompted, Rick read the text with sobering responsibility, then sat back down to listen with intent at the opening lines of this Sunday's sermon. True to form, Pastor Mitchell used the scripture reading to spawn his discourse. "Ecclesiastics, the preacher," Pastor Mitchell began, "spoke of the reality that in this world there was a time for peace and a time for war." Manipulating the text to his advantage, Pastor Mitchell quickly entered on a discussion of the duty of the American government to assist in anyway possible the government of Uganda, which was at the present time fighting off tribal rebels seeking to overthrow it.

Out of boredom and to avoid the appearance of complacency, Rick reopened his Bible to the book of Ecclesiastics. He had read the passage many times before, but this morning discovered its far-reaching ambiguities comforting. Not only was there a time for war and peace, but also a time for love and hate; sowing and reaping; coming together and parting with one another; a time for wealth and poverty; and more pointedly, a time to embrace and a time to refrain from embracing. Like his thoughts, the text was neither here nor there, and delightfully refreshing in its philosophical innuendoes. It seemed to suggest in detail that not all of life is carved in the rigid harness of cherry wood, but that some things and certain situations might as well be whittled out of balsa. He had of late been considering just that very dynamic to life…that there was room in his ordered and managed life for harboring at least some degree of waywardness.

Of one thing he was certain; a division of purpose had risen within him. He was well aware of his responsibilities to church, as well as his work and family obligations, but he was also infatuated with exploring the sensations of the day before and his feelings toward Jean. What intrigued him most about his attraction to Jean was the sense of euphoria associated with it. This euphoria wasn't limited to the sexual attraction he had for her, but rather, it was the enchanted and detached mood it set him in. Something about the feeling gave him the ability to remove himself far away from his present responsibilities, and seemed almost as if he'd found a spiritual door. On one side of the door was reality, but on the other side, a more pleasurable sensation. Obviously, *reality* could be performed merely out of habit, and curiously, that which was *pleasurable*, could be enjoyed without the other side of life needing to know about it. He felt like an enormous ship floating on the ocean of fantasy, yet at the same time, anchored to the depths of sanity.

But if Rick cared to think about it, there was a nagging prick in his soul originating from his position amongst the faithful in the church, because he'd been trained to resist such feelings of pleasure. All prior experiences told him his newly found awareness of his infatuation towards Jean was in direct contradiction to his understanding of a Christian's way of life. The tension however, caused between what he knew to be right and what he knew to be wrong, lent to the moment's alluring qualities. He couldn't argue the fact that nothing had changed from a physical standpoint. Anyone looking into his life from the outside would see the same old dedicated Rick Forstein, family man and spiritual leader. And after all, while even in the midst of having such fascinating thoughts, he'd not been struck by lightening on the podium, and felt as composed and secure as he'd ever been seated among the congregation. He smiled and looked out into the crowd.

He looked at his wife Julie seated near the front on the right side of the church. Rebecca was kneeling on the floor beside her, coloring book propped on the chair, chubby hands clutching a crayon and carefully coloring within the lines just like he'd taught her. Julie seemed to be enjoying the sermon. She listened when she could, often directing her attention to Rebecca and glancing towards Rick from time to time with a reassuring expression. "She has no idea," he thought to himself, considering for a few moments all of the wonderful qualities she added to his life, but suppressing them with thoughts of Jean. But what Rick had only just now been discovering about himself, Julie had suspected for sometime and her intuition would surface again later that afternoon.

After church, Rick and Julie made a quick stop at home to change out of their church clothes and after packing the cooler with lunch they drove out to McAurther Park on the east side of lake Travis.

"Is everything all right at work?" she asked, after setting the table with plastic plates and forks.

Rick was conveniently distracted. The tablecloth on the cement table was flapping in a gust of wind and threatening to pitch their lunch into the dirt. Julie held the cloth down while Rick steadied the plates until the wind settled.

"Why do you ask? Got that bonus didn't I?"

"You seem a little preoccupied."

"Not really, you know work keeps me busy. I'm always planning or building one program or another. I just can't automatically shut down on the weekends."

Julie cranked off the tie to the sandwich bag and pulled out a turkey-on-wheat sandwich for him. She pealed off the top of a plastic container and after spooning up a heaping mound of potato salad slapped it down on his plate.

"Julie, I wish I could tell you more about the program I'm working on, but I can't, even though I know it might alleviate some of your concern."

"I'm not concerned about the program or whatever else you've got going on at work. I'm concerned about you. But since we are on the subject, what can you tell me?"

"Not much more than I've already have."

"Can you tell me when you'll be finished with this one?"

"About four to five weeks if we're lucky."

"Lucky?"

"The program's a bit complex."

"Why so hush-hush?"

"The technologies a little out of the ordinary."

"You still working with the same crew they threw together?"

"Yeah, but we've split up. The doctor, the German and the linguist are working on one aspect of the program. Another person and I are working on the technological side of it."

"What other person?"

He took a bite of his sandwich and washed it down with a swig of Dos XX's beer. Skirting the issue wouldn't help, so he exaggerated the point. "The pretty brunette of course. Wouldn't have it any other way."

Julie smirked while scooping potato salad off Rebecca's cheek.

"Actually, it wasn't my call. She was hired because of her Internet skills. The others know absolutely nothing about programming."

"But of course, you don't mind her assistance do you?" she stated flatly, picking crust off her sandwich.

"Of course not. She's gorgeous! But a little rich for my taste."

"I bet," Julie said, hurling a chunk of crust at him. He closed his eyes as it hit him smack in the forehead.

"Must be torture going to work every day now."

"Absolutely!" He frowned painfully, eyes twinkling.

"If you're worried though about—"

"I'm not."

"But, if you were," he held up his finger as though lecturing on a specific point, "yesterday was the first time we worked together. She'll be gone in a month."

"Good. I'll be glad when you're finished with this one, then maybe things will settle down to normal. I miss talking to you about work."

"You hate talking about my work."

"I thought I did, but now I don't know what you're…well, never mind. I'll just be glad when you're done."

"What you're up too. That's what you meant to say, right?" Rick asked, finishing her broken sentence.

"A month is more than enough time," Julie mumbled, then asked, "what's her name?"

"Who?" he asked smiling. "Jeanette, Jane, maybe Jean. Yeah, that's it, Jane—I think. Like I said, we just started working together yesterday." He changed the subject. "Swimming is out of the question. Too cold. I should have checked the weather channel last night. Look's like everyone else did." The campsite was deserted with the exception of one other couple. They were pulling mountain bikes out of a pickup truck.

Julie smirked tensely and wiped Rebecca's runny nose. She pulled away and whined. Julie held the back of her head and told her to blow.

"Let's take a hike along the lake after eating. Might as well enjoy what we can," he said.

Twenty minutes later they'd packed everything into the Explorer. He grabbed the baby backpack and strapped it on. Julie adjusted Rebecca's cap on her head and retied her tennis shoes, then lifted her into the backpack and pulled her legs through the openings. They dangled for a second until she started kicking her daddy. "Go! Go!" she squealed.

"Hold on honey," Julie said, pulling down one of her pant legs, which had bundled up leaving her knee exposed.

"She'll be all right," he said.

Julie ignored him and finished checking Rebecca's clothing to make sure everything was covered. "Ok, we are ready."

"Sorry, time to go home now," he joked.

Rick's newly learned ability to redirect Julie's concerns reaffirmed what he'd been thinking about throughout the morning, that it was possible for him to perform his domestic obligations with the same manner of wit and charm he'd always used. He was with Julie in body, but not in spirit and enjoyed the sensation of slipping from one reality to another.

They took a footpath out of the parking lot and found a trail along the limestone cliffs thirty feet above the lake. Rapidly sweeping cumulous clouds spun overhead churning the surface of the lake into an angry, convulsing complexion. Only two brave sailboats negotiated the stiff breezes, but a herd of wind-surfers swarmed all over the lake, their sailboards cutting long smooth trails behind them.

Julie followed Rick from a distance, which continued to lengthen the further they hiked. She couldn't help but admire his fatherly presence as her daughter's feet continued to kick against his back urging him to go faster and faster. She had only a name to go on. Jane. "Sound's like a comic book hero. Probably just as gorgeous as he said." She could point to no action on her part that might cause him to stray from her, but that brought her no comfort. She could only assume the fault rested in her own deficiencies or lack of appeal. "And why the sudden interest in me finishing my Doctorate degree?" The more she considered the influx of the disjointed thoughts crowding her mind, the further and further she lagged behind.

▼

On Monday, October 15th, at precisely 7:00 in the evening, Stautzen placed a call to Neil in Frankfurt. Neil was awake and sitting at his desk, the heat from the florescent desk lamp illuminating an open Bible and a stack of notepaper. The outline of next week's sermon would not be written that night. He sat, eyes tracing the scratches covering his secondhand desk, pondering a new set of problems, while waiting for Stautzen's call. He picked it up on the first ring.

"*Guten abend,*" Stautzen said.

"*Gut morgan.*"

"We're about four weeks from completion. Are you making all the necessary arrangements?" Stautzen inquired.

"We've begun the preliminary preparations. I've been working on a series of messages to be sent out to our churches. The transition of our members to the ICC should go smoothly. We should have everything finished about the time the program's complete."

"*Gut.* I'll be speaking with the reverend later. I'll let him know everything is on schedule."

"What do you know about the *Schwarz Monatlich*?" Neil suddenly asked.

"Never heard of them. Why?"

"Because they're doing on investigation on my ministry or the ICC."

"How'd you find this out?"

"They've been watching our apartment."

Stautzen sat up on the edge of his bed and propped his elbows on his bonny white knees. "How much do you think they know?"

"How much could they know? Only Derrick and I know what's going on."

"What about Tasha?"

"She knows nothing and never will. I'm concerned though about the American."

"What American?"

"The one we've seen tagging along with one of the reporters. You sure nothing's going on in Austin?"

"I've seen nothing out of the ordinary."

"If I was you I'd look into the members of your team more closely."

Stautzen took a mental inventory of every participant on the team. He'd check with Pruitt first thing in the morning. "I'll look into it."

"There's too much at stake not to."

"Call if there are any changes," Stautzen said.

"Likewise."

Stautzen spent the next hour fuming about the untimely involvement of the *Schwarz Monatlich*. He propped a few pillows against the headboard of the bed and searched for clues in the sterile implements of his apartment. The apartment had been decorated to such an extent that it lacked any charm. It reminded him of the lobby outside the production studio of the ICC where visitors waited to catch a tour of the ICC's production methods. There, like his room, the furniture was modern and all the fixtures new, but everything was designed to appear antiquated as though they'd just been dug up from an archeological expedition in Cairo. Even the paintings hanging on the light green pastel wall in the living room were prints of the old masters like Renoir and Monet. They were selected with care, because they matched the ivory bound leather couch sitting on the floor beneath them, and the nude hanging in the bathroom coordinated with the soap dish and the toothbrush holder.

He was at a loss for reasons as to why an investigative paper would be looking into the ICC. Its reputation was impeccable in the community and its extensive global assistance programs were helping thousands of needy individuals. As for the CRM, they were similar in mission with the ICC, though on a much smaller scale, and there was really no connection to the two on paper. Still, the fact persisted like a canker sore; the *Schwarz Monatlich* was doing an investigation and there were only two logical explanations for it. The most pressing conclusion he could come up with was that the paper had discovered the existence of the program and was building a case against both the CRM and the ICC. The presence of the American was disturbing and seemed to verify that a member of the team might have leaked information to an outside source. The program however, was still weeks away from completion and the only danger would come when it was put into operation. The other possible explanation was that the paper was doing an investigation strictly on the CRM, because his relationship to Neil Usher and the CRM had begun on a questionable event.

Stautzen had met with Neil personally, when he'd visited the ICC compound just less than four years ago. Such meetings with strangers were common to Stautzen, since the ICC received daily offers by many individuals and organizations who would like to work with the ICC, and Stautzen had to formally and tactfully decline their backing and support. He did, however, appreciate their financial contribution. After meeting with each representative of the various organizations, Stautzen would promptly call on his secretary to print a form letter for him to sign indicating his decision about their requests. Every letter had the same last paragraph…"We thank you for your interest and willingness to support the goals of the ICC, but regret it is against ICC policy to mingle our common interests together in a way that lends to collusion. We appreciate the gesture and pray the Lord will bless the results of your ministry." Stautzen had grown tired of responding to such inquiries. He knew they were just attempts by smaller organizations to use the name and power of the ICC to boost their own donation base. While such networking might be common practice in the business community, Stautzen wouldn't allow the practice to infiltrate the work of God.

On the fateful day that Stautzen and Neil met, the two exchanged cordial greetings and sized each other up quickly. Neil absorbed the excesses of Stautzen's office with indifference, and that of the man himself, sitting poised, wearing a vested suit with the sleeves of his starched white shirt cinched with cuff links. Stautzen judged Neil's appearance as far too common, and thus, could not consider Neil with any serious attention, especially since Neil had failed in his introduction to solicit any praise towards the ICC's ministry. This alarmed Stautzen, simply because it was so out of the ordinary. He eyed Neil suspiciously across his desk and wondered what the abnormally handsome young man wanted.

"I've driven down from Frankfurt to visit with the reverend personally. I was told by his secretary he was unable to accept visitors," Neil said.

"Did you tell them the purpose of your visit?"

"No, except it was urgent and I needed to speak with him."

"That's our policy." He glanced at the card his secretary had given him bearing the name of the visitor, "Mr. Usher?"

"Correct."

"The reverend is, as I'm sure you're aware, a very busy man. He sees people, but usually by appointment only. If you wish, I could arrange for a time for you to meet with him on another day."

"I'm afraid that won't do," Neil said firmly.

"What is it that you wish to ask him?"

"I wish to ask nothing of him. But I've something I'd like to discuss with him."

"Perhaps I could relay the message to him."

"Are you sure there's no possible way to have just a word with him?"

Stautzen leaned back against his seat and folded his hands in his lap, searching for the most appropriate words in which to excuse the persistent young man from his office. "I'm afraid that's impossible without an appointment," he replied, bringing his arm up in a grand sweeping motion to check his watch.

"I see." Neil replied, quickly assessing the situation. He started to rise.

"If you wish though, you may jot down what it is you want to tell him and I'll see that he gets it." Stautzen reached into a desk drawer and pulled out a sheet of stationary and an envelope.

Neil scribbled a short note and sealed it in the envelope.

"Will that be all?" Stautzen asked rising.

"No. That will not be all. I must have your word you will put this in his hands before he leaves work today."

Stautzen thought the request so odd he failed to answer. He reached to take the envelope from the man, but Neil held onto it. The envelope drew taunt as a guitar string between their fingers.

Neil looked deep into Stautzen's eyes. "I must have your word on this."

Stautzen gazed at the man intently, looking for weakness, but saw only determination. He knew in an instant that should he not agree to deliver the letter the man would find another way to confront the reverend. It was his job to ensure that sort of thing never happened. "I'll see that he gets it."

The envelope snapped in Stautzen's direction.

"Thanks for you time," Neil replied.

"Always a pleasure," Stautzen responded diplomatically, extending his hand. He escorted Neil out of his office and past the secretary who glanced at Stautzen knowingly. The corridor leading to the elevator was bright with sunlight that shown against the opposite wall in distorted squares of light. Neil appeared to flicker on and off as he passed each window and Stautzen thought it rather odd that on a day like this the man was clutching an umbrella.

Wishing to rid his mind of the unfortunate meeting, Stautzen headed directly for the reverend's office holding the envelope. He greeted the secretary and walked through the reverend's open door. The reverend stood looking out the window with his back towards the door.

"I've just spent ten minutes with a man who drove all the way down from Frankfurt to see you."

The reverend cocked his head to the side to hear his executive secretary more clearly.

"What did he want?"

"Wouldn't say, but wrote a note. Said it was urgent you read it before you leave for the evening."

The reverend chuckled and turned around. "Urgent, eh?"

"Yes sir—like everything else right?"

They enjoyed a snicker between themselves.

"Right, and if I had a *phinning* for every time that happened…well, never mind. Just drop it on the desk if you would." He turned back towards the window. "Exceptional day, wouldn't you say?"

"Outstanding."

Stautzen tossed the envelope on the desk and left the reverend to his thoughts.

Within an hour a fall storm blew in over Munich with all the swiftness and fury of a Bangladesh tiger chasing a victim. The reverend was in mid-sentence answering a question on the Apostle John's exile on the isle of Patmos with a tour guest, when the lights of the auditorium flickered twice then evaporated into darkness. The rest of the audience murmured in the horror of the moment until the backup lights came on two seconds later. The tour quickly concluded and the guests were escorted to their cars and busses just as the claws of the storm were bearing down on the complex.

In the administrative offices computers were unplugged and employees were huddling by windows or glass doorways watching the approaching clouds within the safe confines of the building. Reverend Eisner stood in front of his office window, curtains pulled open wide so he could witness the spectacle in all its glory. Angry clouds moved swiftly overhead licking the tree tops into curls like the tops of ice-cream cones. Flashes of brilliant light ignited the sky, igniting everything in electrifying splendor. The once tranquil fountain in the center of the park below looked like a raging sea. The walls hummed, the cracks in the seams of the windows wheezed. As far as the reverend was concerned this was as close to the nature of God as one could get. To get even closer one would have to venture directly out into His breath. Without a moments hesitation he grabbed his coat and briefcase and headed outside. Mechtild his secretary looked dumbfounded at his departure, but said nothing.

Once in his Mercedes the reverend drove south towards his home. Ten kilometers later he took a fork in the road, which led him onto a two-lane country road twisting even further into the Alps. The rain fell like arrows slapping against the windshield as the wipers flapped frantically back and forth driving huge sheets of water off the glass. The reverend was amused by his sense of confidence, surging headlong into the fury without misgivings. He'd driven this road thousands of times before and knew he could negotiate the curves in blind faith if he had to, but suddenly, he passed through a curtain of ice electrified by millions of marble sized hale. They danced around the surface of his car like huge pulsating atoms, producing the ungodly sound of dry bones crunching between two sheets of steel. The noise sent terror to his soul. Visibility dropped to zero. He panicked, slamming his foot down on the break pedal. The sensation of weightlessness and spin followed. Then all went black.

He awoke minutes later to the sickening smell of rubber and the sound of flowing water somewhere nearby. When he gathered the courage to open his eyes he first caught sight of the deflated airbag

hanging over the steering wheel. A feeling of cold wetness ran across his
ankles. Was he bleeding? He looked down. Water was spilling in under
the dashboard! He looked out the windshield and saw he'd sailed strait
into a ditch gushing with runoff water, which now flowed over his
hood, pushing and tugging at his car. Frantically, he opened the door
and stepped into the pounding hail. With hands over his eyes and sting
on his head he located a tree fifty meters down the road and ran over to
it. Huddling against the trunk he waited for the storm to pass. After
the hail fell more rain followed, and when the rain died down to a mere
trickle he walked back to his car. He found it flipped over in the ditch
and jammed like a log. Only the wheels and the black twisted pipes of
the undercarriage were visible above the rush of water still flowing
though the ditch.

Fifteen minutes later he spotted a car coming around the curve. He
waved it to a stop and asked the woman inside to give him a ride to his
home. He'd been shaken but not injured and returned to work the second day following the accident. Two weeks later, while drudging
through delinquent correspondence, the reverend came across the
unopened envelope and the note scribbled by the madman from
Frankfurt. He read the note in silence, sat quietly for a moment, then
paged Stautzen.

When Stautzen arrived a few minutes later the reverend peered over
his bifocals at him and sighed deeply.

"Remember that visitor you spoke with a couple of weeks back,"
asked the reverend.

"There were many. Which one?"

"The persistent one from Frankfurt with the urgent message."

"Sure I do. Why? Has he come back?"

"No, but I'd like him to. Do you know how to get in touch with
him?"

"I believe I still have his card."

The reverend handed the note to Stautzen and he read it aloud.
"Rev. Eisner, I drove down from Frankfurt to see you today and was

detained. Mr. Stautzen has ensured me that he will put this note in your hands before you leave this evening. Last evening I had a dream in which I saw you behind the steering wheel of your car. You seemed possessed with a look of terror. I was not shown the reason for that terror, but remembered it may have had something to do with a severe storm approaching. I don't often have such dreams, but when I do they normally have some significance. I can only recommend to you that you proceed today with great caution."

"You remember what happened that evening," asked the reverend.

"Yes," Stautzen replied, barely audible.

"Now, I'm just as much a skeptic as you, but when this sort of thing happens to you, you take notice. We're in the business of expecting these kinds of things to happen."

"Sir, this could have been merely circumstantial. Anyone can watch the weather reports and predict the weather, especially within a twenty-four hour window."

"I know, but just the same—find him will you!"

The reverend credited Neil with the dubious distinction of saving his life, despite the fact that he'd read Neil's note two weeks too late. He could use a man like Neil on his side. When they met a few weekends later, the reverend warmed up to him quickly. He was particularly impressed with the scope of Neil's reform movement and that he'd practically built the organization on his own. He saw in Neil one like himself; a man determined, a man with a mission running through his blood. The reverend also become mesmerized by Neil's concepts on the apocalypse and thought him particularly adept at merging prophetic insights with the signs of the times. His understanding of the political climate of Europe was equally impressive. In time the two would spend hours discussing those details and formulating ideas together on how and in what way the Lord would use the political processes of the world to hasten a second coming of Christ. It was inevitable then, that the ICC and the CRM would become inextricably intertwined with each other.

Stautzen watched disenchanted through the course of the next few years as the reverend began to rely more heavily on Neil. Stautzen had given the reverend nine years of his life. He'd been his counselor, his friend. He was an asset. He provided much of the background research for the reverend's weekly broadcasts and in some cases, much of the reverend's messages were laden with his own theological insights. He'd hoped that one day the burden of the ministry would be transferred to him, but with the untimely introduction of Neil, the likelihood of that taking place was becoming more remote.

Then came the day when Reverend Eisner disclosed to Neil and Stautzen his meeting with Fred Watson of Trojan Security. The three of them discussed the idea in the reverend's office behind closed doors.

"I think it's one of the most risky—not to mention unethical—ideas I've ever heard," Stautzen stated flatly.

The reverend and Neil remained silent, possessing the same relative amount of indifference towards Stautzen.

Stautzen continued. "I think it's against the Lord's will to work with a secular organization in spreading the gospel. You would be jeopardizing this entire ministry by doing so."

After some silence Neil spoke up. "I think you need to be careful, Jeremiah…but God works in mysterious ways. If He's using Trojan Security to further His work, you need to be receptive to that fact."

"Those were my thoughts as well. We have to look at the big picture."

"But manipulating people's minds? Surely the Lord doesn't work in that manner?" Stautzen pressed.

"Doesn't He?" Neil interrupted. "Is it not the work of the Holy Spirit and angels to interfere with the consciousness of man?"

"But by deception?" Stautzen asked.

"I don't see it as deception. As far as I'm concerned the Lord has the right to use whatever means He wants to reach sinners. Throughout the course of every individual's life God drops hints to let them know He's alive and trying to speak to them. And the only way He does this is through common everyday events. He uses what's available to His advantage." Neil said.

Stautzen remained silent.

"I think we also have to consider that satan and his demons are trying to influence people. Can we not assume that satan himself would use such a method to his advantage if given the opportunity? He'd use the program, so why not beat him to it?" Neil asked.

"With all due respect Neil, I still don't think that makes it right."

"Your point is taken," the reverend responded quickly and decisively. "I'm not so sure there is a right or wrong here. There's seems only to be a possibility to further God's work."

"I have to agree with you, Jeremiah. We don't often know the way in which to proceed with our responsibilities. It helps to stay focused on the primary objective; saving sinners. The question is always, "will our actions further that cause or will they take us away from it?" It is no different with the decision on whether to use this program," Neil concluded analytically.

"I believe in providence gentlemen. I think the ICC is what it is today through the hard work of dedicated individuals led by the Spirit of God. We've succeeded because we've listened to His guidance. I admit, there may have been a time at the beginning of our ministry when I wondered if God was with us, but I do not for one instant, doubt He has been with us through every step of the way. Millions of people use the Internet on a daily basis. I would suspect many of them are not saved. So, we use a method of getting their attention, of bringing the Gospel to them. I can only come to the conclusion this would be a good thing." The reverend was now absorbed in one of his many moments when his logic becomes indisputable. "Ethical? Ethical questions are reserved for philosophers. Gentlemen, we're not in the business of philosophy. As ministers of God we possess what philosophers only dream of obtaining." He paused for a moment…"Yes! there's only one thing to consider. Will this program save sinners? If it has even the slightest possibility of accomplishing this mission, than it must be done."

He turned towards Stautzen and addressed him warmly. "Joseph, I appreciate your concern and respect your opinion. That's why you're here and why I want you to be personally in charge of this project from the start. I'm not telling you that you should go, but I'm asking you as a friend, would you to meet with the Trojan Security team that will be putting this program together."

"Where sir?"

"America. You leave in a week. If during the course of putting this together you feel it's not in the best interest of the ICC to proceed than you have my full support to pull out."

"I'm still not sure on how to proceed."

"I've spoken to Fred Watson at length about this. He's made it clear to me the program is to be designed specifically to assist in the ICC's ministry. It will be your responsibility to help steer the team you'll be working with in that direction.

"I'm still concerned about the legalities."

"I've considered them as well. Mr. Watson has explained to my satisfaction that the program will be built in the most secure of environments. I assure you, I would not ask you to do anything which your conscience would lead you to think unjustified."

Stautzen considered the doubts in his own mind and the recommendation by the reverend and Neil to proceed. He had a great deal of respect for both men and a humble realization that the two held a position in the work of God that far exceeded his. This insecurity brought him some degree of comfort, his own inferiority giving way to a strange relationship of codependence with them. The Reverend's urging that he should be in charge of the development of the program gave him a fresh sense of confidence, and he was able to reconsider his position and follow their lead.

CHAPTER 31

▼

"Ruben! Listen to this!"

Shelly spun the CD back to the point where the conversation between Neil and Stautzen had been recorded early that morning. Ruben took the headphones from her and slipped them over his ears.

"One more time," he said, his eyes twitching with anxiety.

"Where's Eva?" he asked.

"She hasn't been in all day. Hasn't called either."

"Page her."

Eva arrived about forty-five minutes later. Ruben, Shelly and Mr. Schwarz were seated around the equipment discussing the recording. At her arrival they ceased talking. Mr. Schwarz walked up to her while the others avoided her eyes.

"What's wrong?" she asked, setting her bag on her desk.

"We've got something."

"That's good."

"No it's not. You need to hear this."

He escorted her to the old olive coated swivel chair sitting in front of the equipment. She sat down slowly and he helped her put the earphones on. He flipped the switch and the CD lurched forward. He stood behind her, resting his hands on her shoulders.

Shelly watched for her reaction through slanted eyes. Eva sat motionless and compliant, listening through the preliminary exchange with composure. She flicked back a stand of hair that had fallen across her nose and adjusted the headphones, then set her arms over the ripped armrests of the seat. A moment passed. Her hand twitched, a forefinger extending tensely into the air. She clenched her left fist. Her eyes fierce now, then confused—then fierce again. Suddenly she leaned forward, her hands catching the fall of her face as she bent towards the table. And there she remained.

Mr. Schwarz's hand slipped away from her shoulders. Shelly came to her side and leaned towards her. She placed her hand on her head and stroked it reassuringly.

"Are you ok?" Shelly asked.

Eva didn't respond.

Everyone waited for her to breakdown, but she didn't.

"Will you be all right," Shelly asked a second time in whisper, leaning towards her friend so the others didn't hear her ask.

"I'll be all right," she sighed, breath whistling through her flattened hands across her face. "I always am aren't I?" she muttered.

"Yeah, you are," Shelly agreed somewhat relieved, and handed her a tissue from the box that Ruben had gone to retrieve.

Eva refused it. Instead, she defiantly wiped her tears with her fingers.

Mr. Schwarz spoke. "What do you know about this man you've been seeing?"

She took a deep breath and for the first time since she'd met Stace she felt she knew nothing at all about him. She looked at Shelly, who'd backed against the equipment and stood looking down at her. Eva expected her to be indifferent, but her face showed nothing but understanding. She seemed to sense she'd fallen in love with the man. "I know very little about him," she said regrettably.

"Then we've got to find out more about him," Mr. Schwarz said quickly.

She turned in her chair and gazed at him in disbelief.

Mr. Schwarz realized the impulsiveness of his comment, but didn't take it back. "If he is involved with the CRM, the ICC, or this program as they refer to, and I'm afraid it looks like he is, then we must find out who he is and what he knows.

"Do you have any idea what you're asking me to do?" Eva pleaded, her voice trembling. Mr. Schwarz remained silent, but looked to Shelly for backup support. Shelly looked at him in a state of momentary confusion, but understood his intent. She dropped one knee on the floor towards Eva and looked into her sullen face. Eva's hair had fallen around her head providing a natural covering from all the shame and she refused to push it back. Shelly pulled some of it behind her ears. Looking into Eva's twisted face she said, "Mr. Schwarz is right Eva. If this American is involved with the program we need to know."

She glanced at Shelly incredulously, the bottom of the whites in her eyes glistening with tears.

"More importantly Eva," she said calmly, "you need to know."

Eva knew she was right.

"Let's talk about what we do know," Mr. Schwarz began, after enough time had lapsed for Eva to regain her composure. "We know there's a definite connection between the ICC and the CRM. We know they're working with a company named Trojan Security to build some kind of a program." Raising his voice a notch or two he added, "If any of you have doubted the purpose my concern in the past it's time to lay those doubt to rest. The tone of the conversation in the recording reveals they are planning something significant."

There was no opposition to his comment.

Mr. Schwarz looked at Eva sympathetically, "Are you sure you don't know anything more about the American?"

"His name's Stace Manning," she said, "and no, I don't."

Mr. Schwartz looked at the others. "Does anyone have any suggestions regarding this American, assuming of course, he's not a victim of circumstance?"

They were silent for a moment, not wishing to offend Eva with any further suggestions the man she was seeing might have other reasons for getting involved with Eva.

"Very well," Mr. Schwarz said, "then I see only several possibilities. He might be working for one of the Christian groups or he might be working for an outside agency.

"Perhaps he's with another paper." Shelly said.

"Or *de* law," Ruben added.

"Or he's with some other group," said Mr. Schwarz.

"Like who?" Eva asked.

Mr. Schwarz was hesitant to conclude. "Well, we really can't assume anything until we know more about this program."

"If he's working with *de* ICC or *de* CRM in implementing *de* program, we can only assume he's using Eva to distract us from *dis* investigation," Ruben said avoiding Eva.

"That's impossible!" Eva erupted.

"Why Eva?" Mr. Schwarz asked.

She was almost too embarrassed to say it, "because I approached him, he had no interest in me until—"

"Where?" Mr. Schwarz asked.

"At the *Horst freibad*. He was sitting up the hill from me. After a few hours I went to him and introduced myself."

"But if he knew who you were Eva, it's possible he could have been following you for weeks. You may have initiated *de* contact, which might have saved him a lot of trouble." Ruben said.

The thought of such a deception was unbearable to her. She couldn't bring herself to imagine everything she'd experienced with the man had not been real. Had it all been a lie? She felt like a fool.

"If that's the case, then it would be dangerous for Eva to consider seeing him again," said Shelly.

"There's still *de* possibility he's working for an outside agency. He might just be trying to get some information from us," Ruben said.

"Then again...there's the other possibility," Mr. Schwarz reminded them.

A few minutes lapsed while everyone considered who Stace was and what he might want. Eva was the first to break the silence. "There's only one way to find out what he's up to."

They all understood what she meant.

"There's still a lot that we don't know," Mr. Schwarz continued in his previous mode of thought. "Let's assume for the sake of expediency that he's working with one of the Christian groups. More than likely, he has already told them about our investigation."

Eva thought it ironic that Stace had been willing to help her enlarge the negatives of the members of the CRM. She wondered why it took him so long in bathroom when he was working with her negatives.

Mr. Schwarz continued. "Since they know we're watching them, I suspect they'll try to cover their tracks. So we'll have to work fast. Let's find out what Trojan Security is and what they do. We need to know what this program is about. We also need to dig a little deeper into the backgrounds of the CRM members. Who were they and what did they do in East Berlin? The woman is still a mystery. How does she fit in? We might be able to get information out of her.... Shelly, I want you to get with our contacts at the phone company and find out if they can trace the origin of the phone number that originated to Neil last night. That could lead us to Trojan Security."

"Eva, I know this is going to be difficult for you, but we need you on this," Mr. Schwartz paused.

"I know," she said, "I know what to do."

"Are there any questions?"

"Good, I've got an old friend I need to talk to."

CHAPTER 32

▼

Silly with despair, Eva spent the next three days submerged in despondency. At every waking moment she thought of Stace and at every waking moment she tried to push those thoughts of him aside. More than once over the course of the days following her hearing of the recording she laughed. It was a tense sort of laugh at the sheer irony of it all. That irony being, it was entirely possible he was in no way involved. In which case, her despondency would have been self-induced. But if he was involved, then his love towards her was a mockery.

Stace had called Monday evening, then Tuesday, then Wednesday morning, and just now, late Wednesday night. Her answering machine recorded his swelling distress, this evening's message sounding more desperate than all. But Eva wasn't emotionally equipped to decipher the tone in his voice, which to her seemed at times to express genuine concern for her whereabouts, but may have just reflected his frantic attempt to obtain more information from her. An hour after his call she was somehow able to wrestle stability into her thoughts. She knew what she must do and knew for the sake of her own happiness and sanity she must glue the shattered fragments of the situation together. She picked up the handset and dialed his number.

"Hello," his voice sounded on the other end.

She considered its sweetness, remembering for an instant its power to lure her.

"Hello!" He said louder.

"Hi Stace."

"Hi Eva! I've been worried about you. Where are you?"

"I'm at home."

"I've called several times. Did you get my messages?"

"I did, but I've been working late at the office the past few nights and didn't want to wake you up. Fact I just stepped in, so thought I'd call you."

"I'm glad you did. It's good to hear your voice again."

She didn't reciprocate his compliment, considering the deception she was engaged in and how much it hurt.

"Listen Stace, if you aren't busy this weekend I need to drive down to Munich. I was wondering if you'd like to come along."

"Work or pleasure?"

"Work," she said flatly, "but we may have time to do some sightseeing."

"The ICC's down that way isn't it?"

"Yes. How did you know?"

"You told me once remember?"

She thought about it for a moment and couldn't remember. "Yes, I remember."

"Sure, sounds like fun. Can I see you tomorrow night?"

"I've got too much to do this week."

"I see. Any way, I can help you out?"

"I don't think so, but thanks for asking."

"I'm worried about you, you know."

"Yes I know."

"What about Friday night?"

"I'd like to, but I've got to prepare for the weekend. I'll pick you up around 9:00 Saturday morning."

"All right—hey Eva!"

"*Ya.*"

"If you need anything please call."

"I will. See you Saturday." She managed a quick "good-bye" and hung up the phone.

He let down the receiver sluggishly.

One can never know a person fully, nor can one make any judgments about a person without the benefit of evidence. Yet, one can tell to some degree within a matter of time whether a person is inherently evil or by nature reasonably good. What Eva lacked was evidence and the benefit of time. Throughout the week she had relived every moment, every conversation, every touch she'd experienced with Stace hoping she might find evidence of his dishonesty. She also looked for clues in the unspoken expressions of their time together. She could only conclude Stace was definitely not evil—deceptive perhaps—but not evil. By Saturday morning she felt confident she could suspend any emotional connections she had to him. She also understood she would still have to maintain the appearance she cared for him. To get the information she needed she'd have to play his game. Saturday morning, five after 9:00, she pulled up along the curb in front of his place and waited in the car.

He'd been watching from the window. When she didn't come up to the apartment he grabbed his coat and backpack and walked out to the car. He slid into the front seat and without saying a word leaned over and kissed her cheek.

"Good morning," she said, interrupting his passion.

"Same to you."

They said little to each other as they drove south through Frankfurt on the A66. When the autobahn opened into four lanes she pulled into the second lane on the left and picked up speed.

"Have you been down this way?" she asked, trying to appear comfortable.

"I've been as far south as Worms, but no further."

"You'll like the drive. When we get down south it gets more mountainous."

He looked out his window and watched the tall pines at the edge of the autobahn drift by in a blurry unbroken wall.

"What did you go to Worms for?"

"For my father. He's a history nut, especially when it comes to religious history. I shot nine rolls of film there. Got all the cathedrals inside and out. Pictures of the old wall and gate. Close-ups of every reformer in the statue in the main square. Ever been there?"

"No, but I studied the history in school. It's a Mecca for Protestants."

"Yeah, he got a real kick out of the photos."

"You've never mentioned your parents."

"Are you sure? Must have slipped my mind. Not much to say really."

"Where do they live?"

"He lives in Oklahoma, Oklahoma City."

"And your mother?"

"She died when I was young."

"Was it an accident?"

"Breast cancer."

She ceased the interrogation momentarily. South of Worms the autobahn squeezed into two lanes. She took the far left lane and picked up speed to 155 km/h. In the right hand lane trucks and busses zipped by as though they were going backward.

"What does your father do?"

"He's in construction."

"Like building homes."

"Yes, but he doesn't swing a hammer any more. He works for a housing developer as one of their supervisors. Most of the time he sits in an office trailer scheduling contractors."

"Are you close?"

"Not really."

"I'm sorry."

"Don't be."

"He never remarried?"

"No. Swore he never would and never has. Doesn't even go out."

"Got any brothers or sisters?" She was genuinely curious about his history, but at the same time she hoped she might be able to trip him up. She was looking for the slightest bit of hesitancy in his responses; anything that might lead her to believe his past was as phony as he was.

"A younger sister."

"How old?"

"Let's see…she'd be twenty-four now."

"So she was thirteen when your mother died."

"Something like that."

"How'd she take it?"

"Not very well—I think. I don't know. We were doing our own thing at that point. She was going in one direction and I was going in another. We were both trying to deal with the situation as best as we could."

"Where is she now?"

"She still lives at home with my father. She's a junior at the university, working on a degree in physical therapy."

"What's her name?"

"Samantha. I've always called her Sam."

The interrogation was going nowhere. Either Stace had everything memorized or he really did have a family somewhere. She tried to picture his family, imagining his deceased mother, his weathered father, his sister and the house he grew up in. She took what little she knew of his character and attempted to analyze his behavior with the history he'd given her, but all she could come up with was a confusing set of images. She could find nothing concrete to either believe or disbelieve. In the absence of proof she could feel the love she had for him stirring in her heart again, looking for a way out.

A few hours later as they were climbing the steep hills just outside of Stuttgart, Stace had a few questions of his own.

"Your brother seems like a serious fellow. What kind of work does he do again?"

She weighed her answer. "He works for the telephone company."

"Not an operator correct?"

"A technician."

He was looking out the window again. When he turned to ask her another question she snapped her head towards the road.

"What's so interesting about the ICC?"

"Why do you ask?"

"Just curious," he said, but having reconsidered the question he proposed it another way. "I'm just trying to understand what the ICC has to do with us."

"I don't understand," she said looking over to him.

"You've been avoiding me all week. I'm hoping it has something to do with the ICC and not with me. That's all."

"It's the ICC and then some. I just haven't had time to think about us."

"Have you had a breakthrough in your investigation?"

"Yes, nothing important, though. This week has just been busier than I'm used to."

"And it has nothing to do with me?" he persisted, speaking into his window.

"No. Sorry if it seems that way."

He recognized her deception, but decided not to confront her about it.

"Has the ICC got anything to do with Derrick who was following us a few weeks ago?"

She was becoming uncomfortable with his line of questions. Was he making conversation or trying to get information from her? Avoiding his questions would surely raise his suspicions. "It's possible."

"Are you expecting him to be there?"

"No."

"Oh, and all this time I thought I was tagging along to protect you."
He smiled.

"You are."

"What does the ICC have to do with your investigation?"

"I'm not sure," she replied evasively. "But it's a part of our investigation, so I'm doing a little background work on it."

"What's the plan?"

"The ICC has a show this afternoon. I thought we would see it then take a tour of the place."

"And then?"

"We'll play that one by ear."

By 1:40 they'd entered the outskirts of the Munich. Stace sat up and took notice of the mixed array of buildings, some modern, some ancient, but everything clean and tidy just like a typical German city should be. The autobahn they'd been traveling on split into more lanes to accommodate the volume of traffic. It wove its way through the heart of the city; an antiquated path paved over to accommodate the modern age. Passing the central business district, marked by long tall rows of buildings cut into the geography like slices of pizza, Eva found the road she was looking for. She headed south towards the Southern Alps towards Austria. She stopped once to look at a map and check her notes. She'd not anticipated the ICC to be located this far out in the country. She found the right turn she was looking for and within ten minutes they'd reached their destination.

The entrance to the ICC was marked by a fifteen foot tall cement impersonation of Christ struck in a serene pose holding a baby lamb within the folds of his arms. The statute stood isolated in deep green grass and from the angle at which it stood from the road it towered above the backdrop of the mountains to the south. Below the sandals of Christ was an inscription bearing the name, "The International Christian Coalition. Peace Be With You." Eva turned left onto a recently paved asphalt road boarded on each side with rolling mounds of flowerbeds in full bloom. Behind the flowerbeds was a row of young apple trees, which had lost their leaves. Their young shoots twisting crankily into the clear sky looked like bundles of forks wrapped together.

The complex appeared to be surrounded entirely by a six-foot high, white plastered wall. It ran parallel to the entrance road both to the right and the left about 200 meters in each direction. In the far right corner Stace could see the tops of giant satellite dishes. Within moments they'd reached the main gate where a security post rested in the middle of the road. They were greeted promptly by a security guard, who was dressed in a white uniform cinched at the waist by a thick black belt with a pistol holster. He handed Eva a visitor's guide and pointed towards the direction in which she should park.

The immense parking lot was half full. Split in two, it was divided by the entrance road and both sides contained rows and rows of bright white outlines for parking spaces. At the end of each row was a light pole with a sign bolted at the top bearing a number. There were fifty-two rows in all. Eva parked on the right side in the middle of row thirty-four, guided into her space by a young man dressed in white and waving an orange flag.

Stace took a moment to look at the brochure Eva had tossed on the front seat. In it, there was a brief synopsis of the ICC's history, color photographs of the complex and on the back panel an artistic rendering of the grounds. The rendering was more like a landscape layout. It showed the outline of the major buildings in the complex and their position. It had obviously been designed and painted before the complex had been completed, because it portrayed the surrounding landscape as mature. The baby apple trees lining the front drive were full grown in the picture. He ran his fingers along the edges of the buildings on the pamphlet and looked out the windshield. Other cars blocked his view, but from what he could see everything seemed in its place.

"Ah! The donations of the faithful hard at work," he said, folding the brochure back up and slipping it into his coat pocket for future reference. "My dad would really enjoy seeing this place. He's a big fan of the ICC. Guess I'll take some pictures and send them to him."

She reached for her purse and got out of the car. The breeze blowing in from the distant Alps chilled her. She opened the back door of the car and removed her coat. He met her by the trunk and they walked towards the center of the parking lot where they met up with other visitors. The tops of the main three buildings of the complex loomed in the distance. Most significant was the sanctuary in the center of their view. To the left of the sanctuary was a long three-story building seen from its side, and towards the right, a flatter two-story building, which housed the production studios. An invitation to experience the beauty of the ICC complex lay ahead. Before the sanctuary was what appeared to be a small park.

They reached the end of the lot and stepped on to an enormous, skillfully laid out area paved in brick of various designs and colors. It reminded Stace of the outer patio of El Campo's Mexican restaurant, though on a much grandeur scale. This patio measured a stone's throw in depth and twice that far in width. Fully-grown trees grew out of holes in the brick providing shade. Beneath the trees were raised bedding plant areas full of geraniums, pansies and assorted colors of carnations. All the flowers were set in flowing patters amidst boxwood hedges, all the boxwoods sheared with precision as if a military barber had pruned them. Eva immediately noticed this area was unusually warm and still. The bricks had soaked up the heat from the sun, making the area feel more tropical. There were benches to sit on everywhere; both in shade and sun and many of the visitors were already enjoying them. By far though, the most impressive area of the park was at its center.

It measured at least forty meters in length and fifteen meters wide, an enormous fountain by any means and exceptionally beautiful. Its shape was like a crescent moon, although its corners were rounded instead of coming to a fine point, and it was filled with water contained by a waist high stone wall. On the outside, the wall was built of charcoal colored, triangular shaped stones set in white mortar. The inside of the wall was fashioned with thousands of aquamarine colored tile. Though the pool was only two feet deep it looked bottomless. Dozens of tiny fountainheads scattered just above the surface of the water delivered a fine midst across the surface. It resembled a thick layer of fog hovering above a mountain lake. Above the midst twelve life-size figures appeared to be walking on the water. Each figure was cast in bronze and represented the personification of each of the twelve apostles. Each statue was evenly spaced along the width of the pool, six on one side and six on the other, all turned towards the center. What arose out of the center, as though floating on the surface of that mist-coated lake, was a small fishing boat sculptured in cement. From the center of the boat extended a mast and from the mast two sails of sand colored fabric snapped in the slight breeze. In the bow of the boat stood another bronze figure. This one was of Christ, standing with outstretched arms beckoning his disciples to do the impossible, walk on water. Even Stace had to admit it was one of the most beautiful statues he'd ever seen, however, sarcasm got the best of him. "Check out the pigeon sitting on the mast pole," he said to Eva. Sure enough, a speckled pigeon had just alighted at the tip of the pole and was trying to regain its balance. Stace quickly took out his camera and took a picture just before it gave up and flew off. The mast was coated with hardened, white bird excrement.

Stace swung his camera left and opened the lens on the administrative building. Measuring about 200 feet in length and three stories high, its sides were coated in a thick layer of off-white stucco. Large windows dominated the face of the building to give an overview of the park. At the bottom of the third floor a narrow outside balcony ran the entire length and was bordered with a wooden railing. Isolated tables and chairs were scattered across its length. The roof was capped in a traditional red tile producing a striking contrast between the blue of the sky above it and the white stucco below it. After Stace had taken several photos of the building he turned around to snap a shot of the sanctuary.

He was not at all impressed with the church, which is to say, it was much too excessive for his taste. The walkway leading up to the sanctuary, lined with cypress trees, gave one the mood of being ushered up to the very house of a God. Stace refused the sensation, thinking it a little over dramatic. The entire structure was built of a cream colored stone. It was concave in the front, opposing the crescent shape of the fountain like two boomerangs flipped in opposite directions. The entrance resembled the leading edge of a flying saucer tipped at an angle, higher in the center, then tapering off towards the sides and sweeping around the back. The roof was layered with giant sheets of aged copper turning various shades of green. Like a French artist's cap, it bowed in the center and hung out over the front, and was supported by five-foot diameter, white roman-style columns. Directly below the canopy, just under the lip of the copper roof, was a series of glass-stained windows. They too, were longer and wider to the front of the building, eventually tapering off into smaller sizes. Stace and Eva stopped at the base of the church where circular marble steps rose up towards the main entrance.

"You look baffled," she said.

"Not really, just thinking about something. Actually, I find the whole thing rather depressing."

"I'm impressed," she said.

"Extreme is the word. But if you prefer a more sophisticated term, how about the fleecing of the faithful."

Eva started up the marble staircase.

"Let's not go in just yet. I want to take a few more pictures first," he said.

"Of what?"

"Just around."

She stepped back onto the path and followed him around the right side of the church. The air was calm and reeked of freshly mown grass.

Most of the trees around the sanctuary were native pines, saved during the construction when the complex was built. A couple walked by and greeted them. Nearby, where the sun lit the lawn, a family enjoyed each other's company. He led Eva towards the back.

"Where are you headed, Stace?"

"Just looking and we have a little time before the show starts. This place is much bigger than I thought," he said, catching a glimpse of the southernmost wall off in the distance. "They're certainly well equipped. Check out the satellite dishes over there." She followed the lens of his camera as he snapped shots of the five dishes pointing into the sky.

Directly behind the church was an employee parking lot with about thirty cars parked in it. In the far northeast corner was a maintenance building. Next to it was another building running along the eastern wall that looked like storage units. A road ran from the parking lot, past the storage units and back towards the front parking lot.

"Let's get back," she said.

"You sure you want to go?" he asked, as they rounded the side of the sanctuary.

"Got to," she replied. "You're not interested in hearing what they have to say?"

"Already know what they have to say."

"You do?"

"Hold onto your wallet and your mind."

Mingling with the rest of the visitors they ascended the staircase. At the top of the stairs he stopped abruptly, then moved to the side to get out of the way of the crowd. A sick hollow feeling was filling his head. Above him the copper roof loomed high above, threatening to swallow him. To his right the columns rose, taking on the personality of mighty creatures, intimidating him. He glanced in the direction of the park, then towards the crowd. Above the three sets of double doors hung a polished steel statue of Jesus nailed to a cross. Eva finally made it back across the stream of people to him.

"You ok?" she asked.

"These kinds of places give me the he-be-gee-bees. Let's get this over with." He shuffled towards the far left door. She followed.

Posted at each door was a young man and woman dressed in smashing red suits. They stood erect and poised, hands crossed humbly in front of them. They nodded and greeted each guest they could make eye contact with. A current of warm air, stale with the smell of new carpet hit Stace at the door.

The main foyer was tiled in dark marble speckled with ivory colored swirls. The ceiling above was inlaid with different combinations of woods running in neat parallel lines around the corners. Eight chandeliers hung from the ceiling like spiders descending gold chain threads. Each one of them six feet in diameter and possessing hundreds of tiny lights reflected in tears of crystal. The inner shape of the sanctuary mimicked the crescent shape of the sanctuary's outer wall. To the right and left of the entrance doors were two massive oil paintings bordered in exquisite, gold dusted frames. On the wall, opposite the doors on the other side of the foyer, hung twelve full-sized paintings inspired by Biblical themes. Stace's eyes drifted upwards towards colored patterns reflected on the smooth white surface of the upper portion of the wall. He found the source of those reflections on the wall behind him. There, above the entrance doors was an enormous set of stained-glass windows running the entire length of the foyer. The center windows measured ten feet in height and they tapered with the wall like a smile until they were little more than three feet in height. There was just enough sunlight pouring in to bring out their colors and reflect these same colors across the foyer onto the opposite wall. Ten doors led into the floor of the main sanctuary. At each door stood a deacon, dressed in a white suit with white gloves. From unseen speakers soft organ music played and drifted over the mummers of voices and clatter of heels on the marble floors. When the song ended a woman's voice, smooth and inviting, told that the service would begin in a few minutes and would everyone please take a seat.

"Let's go sit in the balcony. That way, if people start dancing in the isles we can slip out of here with only minor embarrassment," he said.

She was powerless to resist Stace as he grabbed her by the hand and made his way to the double doors leading into the balcony where an usher stood blocking their way. She tugged at Stace's hand suggesting they just take a seat on the main floor. Stace persisted, moving closer towards the door with determination. When he got within ten feet the usher stepped aside and opened one of the doors.

"See what I mean," he said, stopping in the staircase. "Things are done subtlety around here."

"Let's at least take a seat in the front row," she said, taking charge and moving ahead of him.

This seemed appropriate to him, because only a handful of people were present in the balcony and it gave him plenty of space to feel comfortable. She walked towards the middle of the front row and took a seat as he plopped down next to her.

"How long has it been since you've been to a church service?" he whispered in her direction.

"I've never been to a church service."

He looked at her questionably. "Never? Unbelievable."

She leaned forward in the cushioned seat and peered over the rail far below where a blur of people moved through the isles looking for seats escorted by flashes of men in white. Others were leaning towards each other talking and embracing as if they were friends who'd not seen each other for years. Children were sitting compliantly next to parents. Directly below her, a little girl in a frivolous yellow dress with ruffles sat on her father's knee giggling at the faces he was making. Eva leaned back in her chair and bumped Stace's arm off the armrest between them. He let her take it. There was a piano melody playing somewhere, but she resisted the mood it sought to put her in. She decided then and there to face what had been winding her up all week.

She was pissed—pissed at the world. In fact, she had a list of all she was pissed at that ran like a resume of frustration. There was the paper, which passed onto her its' demands. Mr. Schwarz, who required her to perform the impossible at any given time. There was the CRM, whom she deemed as innocuous, but due to the urging of Mr. Schwarz she had to visualize them as radical and dangerous. Then Shelly screwed up the directions causing her to nearly miss the cut off to the ICC. And what of the ICC? Things seemed pretty peaceful around here, although Stace would like her to believe that demons stood at every door. Then there was the recording about the American—or Stace—that a week's worth of twisting through its various implications had gotten her nowhere. Finally, there were the confusing ramifications of her own life, which a few months ago seemed all in order, but now she was doubting the very purpose to which she lived. There seemed to be a thousand other things—"and why they hell won't they turn those damn heaters off!" she screamed in her mind.

"You're more apprehensive than I am," Stace said, noticing her fidgeting.

"I'm not apprehensive," she snapped back, looking directly at him.

"Then why do you look like you're about to go on a carnival ride?" Her hands were wrapped around the edge of the armrests, knuckles whitening and veins bulging.

"I do not." She folded her hands across her chest and turned away from him.

"Well, what do you expect?" she said into the air. "You're making it impossible for me to be objective."

"When did you take a liking to the ICC? I thought they were the bad guys."

"I don't know who the 'bad guys' are as you put it." Her lips tweaked. "I'm trying to see things straight."

Stace shut up. The more he said the worse things got. Something had changed in her, or something had surfaced he had never noticed before. He could work with the change. If there was a misunderstanding between them he might be able to clear it up. If she was reacting to the stress of her work, that would pass, but if this is the way she acted most of the time, than that would be much more difficult to overlook.

He back tracked in thought and considered the way he'd been acting and some of the things he had said. "Perhaps I've been a little abrasive," he thought…"No, I don't think so," he concluded after only a few seconds. "Abrasive or not, I know when I'm right."

He thought he knew a great deal about the nature of organizations like the ICC. His father was a prime example of someone caught in the powers some of these larger organizations can weld. After his mother died, he'd watched his father sink deeper and deeper into isolation. He did little more than go to work, come home, make dinner for Stace and Sam, watch TV and go to sleep. But all that came to an end when his father caught sight of a local church production on TV one Sunday morning. Everything changed. They all started attending church together. His father became completely absorbed in it. Church became his life and his life became that of his children's. He and his sister were compliant at first, but this changed when their father started dictating every event of their life as if an unseen spiritual war was raging around them. Eventually, they resisted those changes and gradually pulled away from his ideals.

At his father's request he attended a college sponsored by the church. He complied, mainly because his father was paying for it. But the atmosphere there was even more restrictive than at home. Surrounded by religion, Stace was able to witness first hand the formality of it. He saw that even religion had little power to restrain the darker passions of those around him, and he discovered it had even less power to control his own imaginations. He made an honest attempt at conforming, tried every ritual available to him, but these rituals did little more than change his actions without effecting his inner person. Consequently, he developed his own way of understanding the nature of spirituality. It was a process he was still investigating, but for the time being, it seemed to be working.

His theology centered around one focal point; which was essentially, that religion was a man made social order, which people used to find purpose in their lives by surrounding themselves in an endless cycle of rituals. Rituals he knew from experience, were mere habits that might change the outer actions and give the illusion someone was spiritual, but it had no power to change the inner man. Subsequently, he'd concluded them to be useless. He preferred a more honest approach in discovering the meaning of life and spirituality, and this was to recognize the human mind is a volatile and a creative organ. What a man or woman thinks is really what they are, and one would be much happier in accepting their thoughts as a continuing process of human growth, rather than a reflection of the impulses of devils and gods. Consequently, what Stace feared the most was an outside force attempting to control his thoughts with little more than promises of guilt, punishment, or reward.

His love for Eva was based on his perception that she was one who shared in his ideas, but if she was beginning to buy into the charade of the ICC, if she was beginning to spiral into the depths of having an outside force control her life—or worse—if she was demanding their happiness together might be contingent upon him giving up all that he stood for, then it could just not be.

"Eva, I need to ask you something. Something's changed in you. Are we starting to drift apart already?"

CHAPTER 33

▼

Poised like a coin sitting on edge, he waited for her response. Had the weeks they shared come to an end? He took off his coat, throwing it with a sense of defeat on the empty seat beside him. With resolution, he folded his hands in his lap and considered what he must do.

Eva turned and looked deep into his soul. It was like looking into the heart of the milky-way galaxy. Much of who he was she could see in its splendor; fragments of his personality shining through like the brightness of the stars. What she'd not been able to see, she imagined to be even more glorious than that which was visible. How quickly, with the emergence of a taped conversation—ambiguous at best—had her impression of him changed. It was as if a black cloud had drifted across the lens of her perception, concealing in an instant, all she thought was wonderful about him.

The existence of the tape had made her doubt the relevance of their love. A love she'd never experienced before, a love capable of unleashing within her both passion and freedom. She'd come to know him through the communication known only to lovers. It was an intimate knowing. The kind that carries more truth to it than cold hard facts. Even so, the tape existed. By two isolated and possibly irrelevant words, "an American," she'd learned the painful truth of doubt. If the love between them was real, than she deemed herself worthy and ready for that love, but if the doubt proved to be true, than she hoped she would have enough strength to live without his love. Much of her wanted to embrace him, to experience his love for her right then and there; as if the embrace could dispel her doubt; as if the expression of love could right any wrongs between them. When she came out of her thoughts she realized she'd been stroking the side of his face with her palm. She withdrew like the snap of a rubber band, for the action proved that her love for him was hopelessly infectious. She downplayed the gesture by toying with one of the buttons on his shirt.

He could see her confusion. The drop of her hand falling in mid-thought, prompted by an unknown. He could sense the desperate attempt on her part to discover something within him he'd not yet revealed. "What is it that you want from me?" He questioned softly.

She thought of asking him pointedly about the tape, but feared the response. She thought about lying to him by telling him she wanted nothing from him, but that would only add to her deception. She thought about taking the honest road and telling him everything, but the lingering doubt as to his involvement and the telling of what she knew might put her in danger. Yes, there were many things she could have said, but she said nothing, leaving him certain something irreconcilable had come between them.

On the far wall above the stage the silver fingers of a pipe organ blasted into the prelude of "*God Of Our Fathers*" in a majestic call to order. The audience was silenced. The communication between Eva and Stace immediately suspended.

From where they sat in the balcony the stage looked to be about forty feet across and twenty feet deep. It was raised off the main floor of the sanctuary five steps high and was covered with plush purple carpet the hue of ripened grapes. An imposing wooden podium sat center stage just behind a garden of flowers popping out of an over-sized ceramic vase. The podium waited lifeless, anticipating its moment in the spotlight. Directly behind the podium were seven wooden thrones, six of them identical in size and structure, made of wood with extended backs, and in the midst of them a seventh, parting the others by three on each side. This throne sat directly behind the podium was upholstered in gold colored velvet. Behind the thrones a choir loft rose sharply like a fattening staircase, attaching itself high on the back wall. Just above its top row, carved into the wall and contained by Plexiglas, was a baptismal chamber decorated with a painting of a mountainous scene complete with waterfall.

Surrounding the stage were many other implements of liturgy. To the left, another collection of seats, where rested various instruments of an orchestra such as violins, flutes, and horns, all waiting for musicians to tease them to life. Towards the right side of the stage were two pianos. One of them, a lacquered grand, filled most of the floor area and the other an upright, sat against the left wall just under the walkway running along side the choir loft. Directly behind the grand, against the far wall, was a three-tiered organ, and seated at it, wearing a shimmering white cape with a wide train wrapping around the legs of its bench, was an elderly man, hands gliding effortlessly over the zebra-colored keys, feet dancing across the pedals along the floor. The organist soon began another hymn, and Stace noticed movement in his peripheral vision.

Two doors, located on each side of the stage, swung open simultaneously on a single note struck by the organist. Out popped a stream of choir members dressed in flowing red satin robes accentuated with long white scarves encircling their shoulders and lapping their knees. In their right hands they clasped leather bound portfolios with sheets of the day's musical selections. They marched up the walkways towards the stage like soldiers, keeping time with the rhythm of the organist. Suddenly, the two men leading their respective columns turned towards the choir box at precisely the same time. The one on Stace's left, rotating to the left; the head of the other line, rotating to the right, both lines now marching headlong into each other with determination until the last possible point where they might collide, then a sudden halt by all members of the choir at precisely the same moment. A quick turn towards the center of the loft by the leaders of both lines started the whole procession moving again, then ascending the choir loft side by side with an equal number of singers breaking into their respective rows from bottom to top. Stace wasn't at all impressed with the display of precise pomp, for from the moment the doors first opened until the last member stood in place he'd studied their timing, looking for imperceptible faults until finally he found one…the twentieth row was missing one person.

The choir remained standing and when the pipes of the organ began billowing out the third hymn the angelic voices of the choir joined it. Once again the door under the left side of the choir loft opened and out poured the members of the orchestra. They were not dressed in robes but rather, their Sunday best. They were less precise than the choir members, but kept the rhythm, filling the empty seats awaiting them without any confusion. The third hymn ended and another began, saturating the audience with the full force of the organist, the choir and the orchestra combined, then another opening of a door by which seven men filed out. The three leading men dressed in black, followed by an elder dressed in white and behind him the remaining three dressed in black. They marched down the walkway and onto the stage, stood before a throne with heads bowed until the hymn ended in a lengthy sustain. A projection screen slipped out of a slice in the ceiling like a silver tongue. When it stopped, several verses of a song were projected onto it from an unknown source. The orchestra began singing and those who were regular visitors or members of the ICC began to sing the words. Within a few moments, even those who didn't know the song had picked up the rhythm and began to sing as well. The verses were soothing and melodic; their purpose, to unify the minds of the congregation into a singular spirit. Many in the audience were now standing, their hands stretched towards the heavens, gently swaying back and forth as if moved by the spirit of God. Stace was beginning to feel queasy again.

Eva, on the other hand, felt much of the resentment and confusion clouding her mind dissipating into the melodic atmosphere. The choral strains with their superb orchestration, combined with the voices of the congregation, electrified her skin. All of the various implements of the service seemed to have polarized every impure emotion and thought within her, aligning them into a single beam of pleasure. Her vulnerabilities vanished; fears floundered. She felt like a feather suspended and drifting in a spiritual sea. Impulsively, she moved her hand towards Stace, wrapping her arm around the bend in his wrist, driving the tips of her fingers between the knuckles in his hand. It was perhaps the most significant act of the day, which definitely signaled to him something was dreadfully wrong. He'd wanted her to reach out to him all day. He longed for the warmth of her touch! But now that touch seemed like the sting of frost on his tongue. He didn't bother to look at her. He knew the expression well. He tried to convince himself that he reaction really wasn't a big deal, but experience told him otherwise. Her heart was open to receive the seduction of the coming message and if he didn't put an end to it the experience might rewrite the direction of her life.

"Eva, let's get out of here."

"I can't."

"You can't or you won't?"

"I can't, and I won't...Stace, I've got to know for—"

She was interrupted by a woman standing directly behind them. The woman had obviously been overtaken by the emotion Stace had been fearful of seeing, jumping frantically around in circles and waving her hands into the air screaming, "I love you Jesus!" At one point she lost her balance and nearly fell over the seats in front of her. When she regained her balance Stace gave Eva an "I told you this kind of thing would happen" kind of look. Eva looked embarrassed. No sooner had the woman calmed down than three others in the balcony rose and began shouting along with the woman. This started a mummer of other voices rolling across the bottom floor and many others rose waving their hands, clapping, mumbling, and yelping. The decibels began rising. Suddenly the podium was ignited with a white beam from the ceiling. The orchestra increased in volume peaking the excitement, repeating the last refrain of the song amidst a suspended crescendo of spine tingling drum rolls and clashing cymbals. The entire audience erupted into unrestrained clapping until they finally became aware of the ignited podium. Moments later, complete silence.

"What about now? Haven't you seen enough?" Stace persisted.

She said nothing, giving his request great consideration, for the reality of the moment was beginning to sink in. Whatever her decision might have been it would have been too late to make it.

The reverend's transition from throne to podium was swift. The mark of a man with a vision who never had enough time to express it. Having reached his destination, hands firmly clutching the edges of the podium, the reverend first fell into a moment of quiet thoughtfulness, arousing the audience even more. While he hesitated, Eva reached for her purse and pulled out her tape recorder and fumbled with the play button.

"You won't need that," Stace said.

"Why not?"

"Because we can buy a video of the service after it's done."

She shoved the recorder back into her purse and gave him a cynical look.

The reverend stood in silence. Stace wasn't sure if he was unprepared or whether he'd been caught up in the moment and couldn't begin. He noticed the rest of the audience seemed suspended in apprehension as well. A moment later the reverend took his eyes off his Bible and looked out across the audience, then up into the balcony area into the eyes of everyone who'd grant him the pleasure.

"I would like to thank the angel in the balcony for her unbridled expression. It's always a pleasure to have the spirit of the Lord so wonderfully manifested before our eyes," he began, then paused, giving the audience an opportunity to acknowledge his appreciation. They clapped amongst themselves, but this subsided quickly, for they were anxious to hear what he had to say.

"Brothers and sisters in the family of Christ. There comes a point in the life of every Christian when the clear word of the Lord comes in a voice that is unmistakable. During these times, one is usually called on to make important decisions. This is also true for ancient ministers such as myself, for when we think we have nothing more up our sleeves to give to the Lord, He comes along and demands one more final gesture of our commitment.

"Many of you who sit in this sanctuary this morning have been with me for the past seventeen years. Some of you I've known even longer. I remember the past like it was yesterday, when you shared with me your dreams and I shared with you mine. Together our dreams rose up as prayers into the heavens and into the presence of God. He answered those prayers and by His providence established the International Christian Coalition. Through nearly two decades we have grown from a handful of believers who met in the humble home of the late Elder Kurstein, to this magnificent complex dedicated to the spreading of the Gospel."

Directly above his head the text of Luke 19:26 was projected onto the screen. He paraphrased the text to suit his purpose. "To those who have been given much, and those who invest in what the Lord has given, even more shall be expected and demanded."

The reverend stepped to the front of the podium and confidently descended the steps onto the main floor, then continued up the middle isle out into the congregation. A young boy in the fifth row walked to the end of the pew away from his parents to watch the reverend pass by. The reverend stopped for a moment and extended his hand to the young man. The boy reached out and took hold of it. It felt like his grandfather's hand; strong, yet wrinkled and spotted with specks of age.

"Do you believe in Jesus?" The reverend asked him.

"*Ja,*" the boy replied, smiling at the sound of his voice in the loud-speakers.

"Then you are one of the wisest young men I know."

The boy beamed and let him pass. He ran back to his parents and was promptly rewarded with a pat on his head by his father.

When the reverend had nearly reached the center of the isle he turned around. The house lights faded. On the screen a video presentation began. For the next twenty-five minutes the Reverend would lead the congregation through a film of the ICC's tremendous rise to power.

Eva shifted and sat on the edge of her seat. The presentation of facts momentarily dislodged her emotional connection to the service. She slipped into her investigation mode scrutinizing the information. Stace took this as a further sign of her interest in religion and became even more anxious.

He watched the video with distaste, resisting any impulse to accept the physical evidence of the ICC's providence, but was impressed by the filming nonetheless, especially the way the film crew had captured the construction of the ICC complex. The first ten minutes of the video was comprised of a series of rapidly moving sequences that took the viewer from the groundbreaking ceremony, through the construction phase of each building inside and out, and even the planting of the landscape. The reverend himself christened the event by slicing through the ribbon stretched across the entrance of the main sanctuary. The final minutes of the video told of the ICC's ministries around the world. A dizzying array of numbers, which only an accountant could fully appreciate, listed the number of souls saved by the ICC like a balance sheet. But as far as Stace was concerned it was not providence that laid the brick of the sanctuary or welded the exorbitant sheets of copper across its roof. It was money. Money from young families who, primed by feelings of guilt and hopes of financial security, committed a percent of their earnings. It was money from little old lady's investments and life insurance funds and money from the wealthy, which dwarfed those of the poor and came at no sacrifice. And perhaps most disturbing, though he had no way of proving it, money from those in power who had donated with the unspoken understanding that their generosities would be returned in favor. If there were any patrons of the ICC in the church that morning, they would soon realize they would never see any return of their investments. For the reverend was about to lay the ax at the root of the tree.

He strolled quickly back to the podium and by the time the house lights came up he stood firmly behind it.

"Brothers and sisters, since the death and resurrection of our Lord, the church of God has spread across the world. It began by one man, then twelve, then a few thousand during Pentecost, until the present. Even the ICC began with just a handful of people. In the last seventeen years it has reached or saved millions of sinners." His voice strained to a high pitch. When he ended on "sinners" there was a thunderous applause. In direct defiance of that applause, the reverend made the most profound revelation of his career. "The Lord has shown me that this cycle is coming to an end. The time of the Lord's appearing is at hand."

The audience fell silent, not because the claim was new by any means, but by the fact that he'd spoken it with such conviction. Many had heard of the second coming of Christ since they were children. It was old news, which only generated interest in those who were still fanatical about it. The older Christians could tell immediately who the fanatical ones were, because they'd once been fanatical themselves. So to hear the ancient Christian repeat the rumor as though he actually believed it...well, quite frankly, it frightened even the most sincere believers.

"Furthermore, the Lord has shown me that the final work will be completed by the ministry of the ICC."

There were a few isolated "amens" and clapping, but the audience was quickly silenced due to lack of support. They knew the work of the ICC was important, but claiming it was the ICC's responsibility to finish the work of God meant it was *their* responsibility to finish the work of God. The very thought scarred the hell out of them. Why the significant changes in life-style alone! would be astronomical. But there were a few individuals who heard the reverend's words with open ears. They were with him in mind and spirit, and not only included individuals in the sanctuary that morning, but it also included millions of viewers and supporters of the ICC around the world. It was to those individuals the reverend now addressed. He would accomplish this though a series of attacks and appeals designed to rip at the heart of all of his loyal followers.

He directed his first attack towards himself, claiming there were many times during his life as a Christian when he'd let the Lord down. Most specifically, that while anticipating the Lord had delayed His second coming he had many times fallen into a state of complacency and had gotten caught up in the pleasures of the world. This he claimed to be one of the Christian's greatest sins. For when a Christian gets caught up in the cares and pleasures of the world, it is then that they cease to labor for souls. "It's a vicious cycle and it's the devil's work," he yelled.

Stace thought the appeal to be a pathetic attempt on the reverend's part to win the audience's support; a calculated gesture to identify him with their present state of mind and make his appeal all the more powerful. Eva, on the other hand, looked upon him with pity. He seemed a frail old man. One who had devoted his life to a cause and had come up short. One who claimed that if he'd put forth a little more effort he might have been able to reach his goal. She misunderstood the passion to which he worked, but she could identify with working to obtain something and to have that something evaporate before her eyes.

The reverend fell silent again while the bright lights from the ceiling twinkled in the beads of sweat pouring down his cheeks. Slowly reaching into his back pocket and pulling out a white handkerchief, he dabbed his forehead and robust cheeks, dulling his skin into a clammy complexion. Taking a deep breath, he considered what he would say next.

He then spoke of men and women of influence, of their power, of their political ties and of their hopeless attempt to gain the favor of heaven with their association to the ICC. He was direct, attacking specifically those who gave large sums of money to the ICC. These were people who thought by mere association with the ICC they might be able to gain a certain degree of social respect. They were right of course, the ICC had become an influential political force within German and European politics. In addition, even non-supporters recognized the ICC ministry had been able to alter the social climate of Europe. So associating with the ICC was more than a ticket to heaven, it was a passport for the influential to earn a position within the world. "They are like vultures!" The reverend proclaimed. "I don't care how much money you've given to the ICC. I don't care what your position is. It will not save you in that great and mighty day of the Lord!"

Stace too was impressed, as well as indignant. In ten minutes time the reverend had completely ostracized probably thirty percent of his most avid supporters, but in the process, he'd gained the respect of hundreds of thousands of less influential viewers. Once again, his words had a cut and paste effect. They were devised to rid the reverend of the responsibility of further catering to the powerful and politically minded, while gaining more fanatical support from the common people who were more gullible and naive. Stace located each one of the five cameras positioned around the sanctuary, fighting off a sudden urge to pull their plugs.

Again the reverend thrust his chin into the air with sweat dripping down from his forehead stinging his eyes. He blinked and reached laboriously around his waist, yanking his handkerchief out again and frantically stabbing the corner of his eyes. In the audience a child began to cough. The reverend waited…While he waited, he reached towards the thick rim of the podium, took hold of it at both sides, braced himself, and started rocking gently back and forth. He looked towards the heavens again, up into the throne room of heaven itself. He imagined himself to be one of the chosen and searched with intensity for the invisible words to which he might lay claim to his position; words which he might propel his audience into action. The voice of the child fell silent—muffled—and he began again.

"I have been shown by the Lord that He has called the ICC to deliver the final message of warning to the world! In consequence of that, preparations must be made. There will be sweeping changes occurring within the ICC, changes that will separate the wheat from the chaff. There are many here who will not survive these changes. You are like wolves in sheep clothing. You shall be weeded out like weeds in a field! You know who you are…Then there are some here who are among the faithful. You are the ones who know separation from the world is of utter necessity! You will embrace these changes. You are the sheep whom the Lord calls and you hear his voice. You have always known salvation begins at the house of the Lord, and before the blessed event of his second coming there would be a time of great upheaval within the church. You must remain steadfast. You will be rewarded!"

He released his grip from the podium and paused for a moment. The arteries in his neck pulsed. Perspiration glistened again. He didn't bother to wipe himself. A deacon approached from the side with a cool glass of water. He acknowledged the gesture, but did not drink.

"Many of you know we have through the course of this ministry engaged most of our financial resources towards helping the poor and less fortunate. This has been a worthy cause, but the Lord has shown me this must cease. This is a time that requires great faith. What I have been shown is, it is not clothes or food or shelter that man needs now, but it is an undying reliance upon the word of the Lord for their sustenance. The same word that sustained Jesus during his forty days in the desert must also sustain the poor and needy."

A man in the balcony stood up. He made his way to the middle isle and walked towards the stairwell. Near the staircase another man and his family quickly followed. Down on the main floor, some brave woman seated near the middle also stood. They all scurried to the exit door and never looked back. "As I mentioned before, those who can't handle this pure revelation from God will be weeded out," the reverend remarked.

"The reason for this change in ICC policy is simple. The Lord has shown me it is time for all of our resources to go into proclaiming the distinct word of the Lord. With today's modern avenues of communication there is no reason why every living soul on this earth should miss hearing the good news of salvation. I've calculated that we are in a position to make this goal a reality. Today we have radios, television, voice communications, satellites, and the Internet available to us. They should be utilized to their fullest extent. That is why we propose to channel every *German mark* that we receive in this final push before the Lord's coming!"

"Preparation for this time must begin at the house of the Lord. This goes for me, as it goes for each one of you listening. This will be a time of great changes. Don't be discouraged if someone in your family or one of your friends decides not to join us in this final thrust before the Lord's appearing. For those who leave will be replaced by thousands of others who shall hear our message proclaimed from the mountains and satellites around the world!"

"And now brothers and sisters, I have much to consider…much to pray about. It's my desire to have a clear understanding of what it is the Lord demands from me. I ask for your prayers and support. I ask for your patience, during which time I will seek the Lord's will for His church. Will you as well, begin to prepare your hearts? Don't despair. In the coming weeks and months to come I assure you, you will see the mighty hand of the Lord work miracles in this sanctuary and in this land!"

CHAPTER 34

▼

What the?" Neil mumbled.

Tasha looked up from the dining room table towards Neil thrusting his hand into the air and crouching under the table behind the couch. She could see a tiny piece of yellow paper about the size of a quarter pinched between his fingers.

"What's this?" he yelled.

Tasha got up to get a closer look.

"Derrick!" he shouted down the hall.

"What!" Derrick yelled back as he came out of his room.

"Do you have any idea what this is?" He asked Tasha.

"No."

He asked her again with a look of suspicion.

"I don't Neil." She replied sheepishly.

"Let me take a look," Derrick said. He clasped the edge of the paper by his fingers as though it were fragile and held it up to the dining room light. Something was written across the back of it, but he couldn't quite make it out. *Phhhh…phhhh*. He blew the dust off it and held it up towards the light again. Upon closer examination the words, *heftplaster* were written diagonally across it over and over again. "Adhesive tape," he replied.

"I know what it is! Do you know where it came from is my question?" Neil asked.

"I've never used that stuff."

"What's it used for?" Tasha asked eager to appear concerned.

"It's double-sided Tasha. You stick something to it then you stick it to something else," Derrick replied.

"Where'd you find it?" He asked Neil.

"Right here under the printer. I ran out of printing paper and I was setting this ream of paper on the floor."

Derrick got down on his hands and knees and started checking around the floor. Neil lay across the floor on his back and looked underneath the table. It took him only a few seconds to find it. He reached over and slapped Derrick on the leg. Derrick looked over to see Neil pointing up into the corner of the table where the leg was bolted to the frame. With his fingers Neil reached up and pried the device loose.

"What's the problem?" asked Tasha.

"Shut up!" Derrick demanded.

They crawled out from under the table and walked into the dining room. Neil cleared a spot at the edge of the table and set the device down. They took a seat next to it and examined it as though it were a resurrected skeleton from the past. Tasha came around and sat next to Neil. She thought to ask what it was but kept her mouth shut. Instead, she just looked. What she saw was a tiny silver metallic object, circular in shape and about a quarter inch in diameter, with a black wire screen covering it. Through the screen she could see electrical circuitry. She was clueless.

Neil took a note pad out of his briefcase and pulled a pen out of his pocket clicking it open. After scratching a quick note, he flipped it around, laid his pen across it, and slid it over to Derrick.

"What do you think?" It asked.

Derrick looked at the note, picked up the pen and scribbled his response. "First rate," he wrote, sliding it back to Neil.

"Tasha?"—Neil wrote.

"Possibly."—Derrick.

"Doubtful."—Neil.

"I've never trusted her."—Derrick.

"I think it's the *Schwartz Monatlich*."—Neil.

"Could be right. How'd they get in?"—Derrick.

Tasha was mystified by their behavior. Neither one of them looked at her or spoke to her. All she could do was watch the volley of the note pad sliding back and forth between them. She reached the conclusion on her own the object was a recording device. Their strange behavior and the existence of the object itself was beginning to frighten her.

"Maybe Tasha let them in."—Derrick.

After reading Derrick's last note Neil thought long and hard. He couldn't believe it—didn't want to believe it—but couldn't think of any other explanation.

"Could be more of these. Do you want to take a look at this one more closely,"—Neil.

"No need. I won't find anything else I don't already know."—Derrick.

At this point they both looked over to Tasha. She read their expression as hostile.

"What?" She asked, tilting her head.

It took Neil and Derrick two minutes to find the other bugs and another thirty minutes of looking to make sure there were the only two. Neil was disturbed they'd located them within the phone receivers. He knew that at the very least, whoever had planted them had heard his conversation with Stautzen in the early hours of the morning. It meant the entire program might be in jeopardy.

Tasha thought she deserved an explanation. "What are those for Neil?"

Neil looked up to silence her one more time and saw she would not be silenced.

"Wait," he said, gesturing to her with an uplifted hand.

Neil took the three bugs and set them in the middle of a sheet of paper. Methodically, he began folding the sheet of paper into a tight little ball as though plotting their demise. Walking into the kitchen he snatched a roll of masking tape out of one of the drawers and started winding the tape over and over around the paper, ending up with a tape ball about the size of a baseball, sufficiently silencing the bugs. When he finished, he set the ball down on the table and looked over at Derrick then back at Tasha.

"What do you know about the *Schwarz Monatlich*?" He asked her.

It was not the explanation she was looking for. "The *Schwarz Monatlich*? What's that got to do with anything?"

"I want you to think real hard Tasha." His words came calmly, but his expression was sinister. He rolled the ball around on the table under his palm and stared at her. She'd never seen the look before.

"I've heard of the paper, but nothing more."

Neil looked down at the ball. His next question would come slow and deliberate. "Has anyone at the *Schwarz Monatlich* ever made contact with you?"

It was obvious to Tasha he hadn't believed her first response. She would articulate her next response so it would be much more simple for him to understand.

"No!"

Neil glanced at Derrick who sat disbelieving. Neil, however, was almost convinced of her innocence. As a token gesture to Derrick he pressed her again.

"Tasha…this is serious. Have you or anyone at the *Schwarz Monatlich* ever spoken to each other?"

Tasha flew out of her chair. It made a *gruff* sound as it slid out from under her across the wooden floor. She stood silent for a moment looking from one disapproving face to the other.

"No Neil! and you're scaring me. I told you I've only seen the paper around town and nothing else!"

She crossed her arms across her chest and turned towards the dining room window. She could feel their eyes burning through the back of her head. She felt like running to her room, but for some strange reason she stood frozen and unable to move. She might have been moved to cry if she knew exactly what to cry for. Her pupils spun frantically in the whites of her eyes looking for something to land on. Eventually they did, looking out the window and focusing on two boys playing soccer in the field behind their apartment.

Her movements, her expressions and the tone of her voice led Neil to believe she was innocent of what they suspected. He was a good judge of character, but this was only a partial reason for him to believe her. For he was in a strange way infatuated with her. It was a crazy type of infatuation, one like a father's love for a child, a man's lust for a woman, and all complicated by his own commitment to celibacy.

Confronting her however, had been necessary and he felt no need to apologize. He also knew he'd have to devise an explanation for her, one that would set her mind at ease and at the same time keep her out of the present dilemma which he and Derrick faced. So he sat quietly distilling in his thoughts and considering the problem, while she stood with her back against them looking out the window. What he forgot to do was anticipate Derrick's reaction.

Derrick had always known how Neil felt about her. He knew that some day Neil's dependence upon her would jeopardize the purpose of their ministry. She'd come between them many times before. His resentment towards her was keen, like the edge of a blade sharpened in stone, and he was convinced she'd participated in the planting of the bugs, if not directly then indirectly, by her own carelessness. There was only one time of day when the bugs could have been planted, in the morning, when either he or Neil were working. Either she had let someone into the apartment or she'd given someone opportunity to enter by leaving the apartment unoccupied. He looked up at her, her back turned defiantly against them, and saw in the corner of his eye her dog, Pauli. Eva walked Pauli in the park every morning and every evening, leaving ample time for someone to have come into the apartment. His conclusion to the matter was swift.

Leaping out of his chair he grabbed Pauli by the back of the neck. Yelping in terror Pauli awakened Tasha out of her confusion. As Tasha turned she could see Pauli twisting and kicking and Derrick hauling her up to his chest and wrapping his brutal arms around her neck immobilizing her. Then Derrick made a run for the door, but Tasha was quicker. She sailed around the table behind Neil and used his shoulder to propel her even faster. This brought Neil rising up out of his seat. Within a few seconds all three stood in a fixed position in front of the solid oak door leading out into the stairwell.

"Give her to me Derrick!" she yelled, eyes no longer shifty, but fierce and filling with tears.

"Derrick!" Neil commanded, clawing Derrick's shoulder from behind.

Derrick advanced another step towards the door.

Tasha felt a sharp pain smack her skull as her head hit the door. She would not let him pass. She had a firm grip on the handle of the door and was braced against another wall, but her grip failed her and she began slipping in her socks across the slick floor. Hopelessly, she sunk all the way to the floor, but never took her eyes off of Derrick. She was as much bewildered as terror stricken. In the three years she'd known Derrick she never seen him display such an expression of horrific potential.

Derrick didn't hear Neil call out to him the first time, nor the second. Now, the call of his name sounded in his soul as if it were rising like an echo from the depths of a bottomless well. When he finally did hear his name, he awakened out of his rage and realized where he stood and what he'd done. Tasha's face came into focus where she sat sobbing, huddled by the door, just a throat's grab away. The depths of her deep brown eyes now fully round, eyebrows raised, and lips tensely twitching.

"Tasha's got nothing to do with this!" He heard the roar of Neil behind him. At the same time he felt Neil's hands yanking him backwards by his shoulders. He looked down and saw he had a hold of Pauli by her ear and the side of her face, his grip so tenacious that the skin on her face was pulled out of position exposing her discolored fangs and her left eye lying buried under flesh. She panted heavily, but made no sound, as if a mere yelp would bring her destruction. Derrick let loose his grip and Pauli's skin fell back into place. She ran her long red tongue around the edges of her dry mouth and resumed panting.

Tasha saw Derrick return to coherence and quickly grabbed Pauli out of his arms and ran down the hall and into her room.

"What the hell's wrong with you?" Neil asked, spinning Derrick around by the shoulders.

"How do you know she's not involved? How do you know she didn't let one of them in?" Derrick persisted.

"Because I know," Neil replied, convinced.

"Jesus Chr—shit Neil! How long have those things been around?"

Neil left him at the door with his hands on his hips and went and sat down at the kitchen table staring at the object of their conflict. It looked like a crinkly dried pear. He grabbed a hold of it and hurled it into the kitchen. It slapped against the door of a cabinet with a solid thud, bounced off the counter and rolled along the floor, eventually coming to rest in the indentation left by the impact.

CHAPTER 35

▼

Sluggishly, like a snail slithering, tentacles raised towards the unknown, Neil crept down the hall and stopped before Tasha's door. He reached for the handle then abruptly withdrew. She'd never locked the door in the past. Now she had reason to. For the first time since they'd met nothing had ever come between them. That something now loomed as impenetrable as the solid door before him. Defeated, he turned and went into his room, plopped on his bed, tucked his hands under his head and gazed up into the ceiling into a long forgotten memory of Derrick. It seemed like ancient history, how swift and brutal Derrick had been, but time hadn't changed him. Neil sighed at the repeating cycle of his own life. He and Derrick had become friends when their world was dark and demons lurked in the streets as well as the halls of justice. It was a time when friends were earned not by word but by deed. They were the stuff of revolutionaries; those who trip through childhood and smash into adulthood by standing by their fathers and watching them wave banners of independence in crowded streets. Neil and Derrick would later beat those banners into weapons and be given ample opportunity to become the best of friends in deed.

As all motivation to fight for freedom is derived from a spiritual seed, so too, Neil and Derrick found themselves fighting in battles of more gargantuan concerns than simple political skirmishes. Christianity provided them an inexhaustible source of reasons to live and die, despite the fact they were now free to worship as they willed, and the fall of the Berlin wall was only an example of just how persuasive the mass of human wills could be. But time, materialism and imperialism, had a profound effect on them in the new world they encountered in the Unified Germany. They had laid their physical weapons aside and redirected their zeal towards building their own ministry. They did it though the power of the word. But desperation, will with opposition, soon resort to the use of force and Derrick's outburst with Tasha had brought that reality to light.

After an hour had passed Neil walked over to his desk. The necessary chore of notifying Stautzen about the discovery of the bugs would have to be done. He could only imagine the frenzy of paranoia that would invade Stautzen's mind. Stautzen never had the heart for the project in the first place. He'd probably flip. But Neil was a man of action and without further hesitation he picked up the phone and dialed Stautzen's cellular phone.

The sights and smells of Austin had been asleep for many hours and Stautzen himself was wrapped up in a state of comatose. How long it had been signaling he couldn't tell, but the sterile ring of his cellular phone was calling him back to the reality of his exile to America. He opened his eyes, found the light switch and looked for the sound. He crawled out of bed and found the phone in his suit jacket, which he'd taken off the night before and laid on the armrest of the sofa. How he missed the buzz of his own phone and the view of the Alps from his office! How he missed his country and the sound of his language!

"Stautzen."

"Neil?"

"*Ja,* we've got a problem."

Stautzen recognized the tone of urgency. He fell back on the sofa, fearing what he feared the most, and stared with glazed eyes at the faucet on the kitchen sink, sparkling in the diffused light coming from the lamp next to him.

"What kind of a problem?"

"Derrick and I found recording devices in our apartment tonight."

At first, his comment didn't register. He'd been in their apartment once before and it was full of equipment, most of which he couldn't name.

"You still there?" asked Neil.

"I'm just trying to figure out why someone would need to bug your apartment." He'd always suspected that Neil and the CRM were a little peculiar, but suspected no more.

Neil anticipated such a reaction and would have to be delicate.

"Any idea who did it?"

"I've got a pretty good idea."

"Who?"

"You just let me worry about that."

Stautzen got up and walked towards the living room window overlooking the parking lot three-stories down. He slid the window open and peered through the dusty screen. The parking lot was full with the exception of a few spaces towards the back. He saw no movement. Not a soul. In the apartment building across the lot he saw only one sign of life, beyond the drawn curtains flickered the subtle blues of a television. The fact that he saw no movement didn't alleviate his fears. People in the business of watching other people shouldn't be seen. "All right, then we're pulling the plug on this right now."

"We're not pulling the plug."

"If those bugs have been there since our last conversation then someone else knows about the program."

"They know nothing. They have a computer company's name, which specializes in building security programs and they've got the voice of two people discussing the purchase of such a program. We're no different than a business. We have confidential information that needs to be protected. Nothing unusual about that."

"And you're not the least bit concerned?" Stautzen was fishing for reassurance.

"From a legal standpoint no. Last I heard circumstantial information obtained by illegally planting bugs is still illegal and inadmissible in court."

"Provided it wasn't the authorities that planted them."

"It wasn't. I told you, I know the organization that did it and that's not your concern."

"Then what the hell is my concern?"

Neil took a deep breath. "Your concern is to see to the project's completion. As far as everyone is concerned you're just the consultant from the ICC who is lending his expertise to build a security program."

"But it's no security program."

"Sure it is. The program is being built around a perceived threat, just like any other program. Understanding this threat necessitates designing it around certain realistic parameters. If, and only if the program is used without the security aspect of it in place, then it becomes questionable. But I thought we all understood—for the sake of what we're striving for—that we can't be expected to confine ourselves to all the limitations of the law"—he stopped short."

Stautzen didn't respond. Who was Neil to question his commitment?

Neil took his silence as an affirmation of his acquiescence. "Is the program still on schedule to be completed by the end of October?"

"*Ja.*"

"Then we're shooting for an execution date of November 8th." Neil found a notepad and a pencil on his desk and jotted down the words, "Execution Mandatory—Nov. 8."

"Have you spoken with the reverend? Is he aware of this little snag as you describe it?"

"It's not a snag and no, I haven't. I see no need to sound an alarm. I recommend you say nothing to him as well. He's got other problems of his own to focus on at the moment."

"So he's given the sermon and set things in motion?" Stautzen questioned.

"This afternoon. I watched the broadcast."

Having worked with the reverend for many years Stautzen knew the reverend's sermon must have served up a severe blow to his unsuspecting flock.

"So you see why the projects still a go?" Neil stated flatly.

"Yes. There will be no turning back."

"Exactly. Now, have you found out any more about the other members of the team?"

"Only that they were contacted just weeks before the program was due to start. All selected by Fred Watson himself through a confidential process. Which means—"

"It eliminates the probability they have any connections with the *Schwarz Monatlich*." Neil concluded. "And what about the company man?"

"Forstein?" Stautzen questioned.

"He's been with Trojan Security the longest correct?"

"Going on four years."

"How long has he known about the program?"

"According to Mitch Pruitt even less time than the others."

"No way he could have known about it beforehand?"

"Not according to Pruitt." Stautzen thought for a moment. "Still doesn't mean he's not involved. He's had a couple of weeks to contact all kinds of people. We're safer to assume he is connected to the *Schwarz Monatlich*."

As Neil listened to Stautzen he jotted down the name "Forstein" below his previous note. He also wrote down the name "Burtman" next to it and drew an arrow between the two signifying the possible connection between the two."

"I don't see the logic. Forstein works for Trojan Security. Why would he risk his job by going public with the program?" Stautzen asked.

"I didn't say he was going public, but he's the only explanation as to why the *Schwarz Monatlich* would be suddenly interested in us. I suspect he's feeding information about the program to the American here, who is in turn passing that information on to one of the reporters at the paper. Neil scribbled "/American" after Burtman's name on his notepad and added a question mark.

"This is getting to be a fricken nightmare Neil! What am I supposed to do?"

"Up to this point you've just asked Pruitt a few questions correct?"

"*Ja.*"

"Then I think it's time you make Pruitt aware you're concerned about Forstein."

"And if he asks why?"

"Tell him what you want, just don't mention anything about the paper's investigation here."

Stautzen was silent as he considered how he was going to approach Pruitt. Neil broke the silence. "If you have to call me for some reason, let it ring here twice and hang up in the middle of the third ring. I'll call you back on your cellular."

"Anything else?"

"Just let me know if you find anything out."

"All right."

Upon hanging up the phone Neil reviewed the notes he jotted down on the notepad. He tore the note off the pad and rolled it up into a little ball. For the longest time he sat at his desk considering his options. He rested his feet on the steel support beams of his office chair and leaned back, juggling the note ball from one hand to another. His seat groaned with every flick of the wrist as he swayed gently from side to side. His most pressing problem at the moment was what to do about Tasha and Derrick. He was convinced of Tasha's innocence. Her loyalty to the CRM was without question, but then, she never knew what they were really about. She'd become indispensable to the everyday workload of the ministry. Furthermore, they would need a third person to watch the apartment. At least one of them would have to be there at all times. He caught the paper ball in his left hand, stopped rocking on the chair, held his breath and listened…some stirring in Derrick's room, but Tasha was deadly quiet. It suddenly occurred to him Tasha might be capable of doing something stupid to herself. Derrick's actions had scared the hell out of her. For the past few years she'd become totally dependent on the two of them. If she somehow felt she'd lost that support…he spun out of his chair and reached for the door. At the same time he tossed the paper ball towards the wastebasket on the floor next to his desk. The ball hit the plastic rim, bounced against the wall then onto the floor and rolled to a stop along the baseboard.

Pauli lay curled up on Tasha's pillow, paws hanging over the curl and folded with sophistication. Over her forearms she rested her weary head, but had yet to drift asleep. Her black dilated eyes swayed back and forth like a mirrored pendulum, keeping pace with Tasha as she moved back and forth between the dresser and closet. At the knock on the door her ears shot up.

"What do you want?" Tasha asked, setting a jar of lotion down on the dresser.

"It's me. I wanted to see if you were all right."

"Go away!"

He considered the tone of her response and paused before replying. "I'm not going away until I see you're ok."

She felt a sense of relief at his persistence. Pride and anxiety had prompted her to hastily start filling her suitcases, but she didn't want to leave. What she really wanted to do was talk. She knew Derrick would make no attempt to apologize, so she expected Neil to mediate on his behalf. She'd been waiting for his knock at the door, which had taken much longer than she'd expected. The longer it took for Neil to come the slower she began to pack. An hour ago she was flinging everything into the suitcases. They were both nearly full. Seeing them full meant she'd have to make good on her intention to leave, but she had nowhere to go. So with reluctance and yet, expectation, she unlocked the door and returned to her task without looking at him.

He sat down in the chair by her bed and noticed she'd been crying. But that must have been a while ago. The tears were long gone and only the swelling remained. He looked at the suitcases and three dresses strewn across the bed, then watched her fiddle with the cosmetics on her dresser. She had changed to a long soft dress with a floral design, which hung straight down to the floor after catching the curve of her delicate breasts and hips. On her feet she wore a pair of leather sandals. She drifted from the dresser, to the closet, then back to the dresser in search of something, knees now slightly bent, as she peered into her bottom drawer. He could see it was empty, but she remained there confronted by its emptiness. After a moment she rose and shuffled to the closet again, taking nothing from it, before walking back to the dresser. There she picked up the jar of facial cream and walked towards the bed to pack it. Neil rose out of his chair and prevented her. She complied with his gesture by wobbling to a stop just inches from him. His action surprised even himself. Her endless fidgeting was driving him crazy.

She stood before him with her head dangling towards the floor, shoulders drooped, back slumped in the weight of her thoughts. He looked down onto her head into the part of her short black hair as it cut a white line across the middle of her scalp. The heat of her body rose up into his face, and her aroma moved him. He could see only the tips of her eyes under her eyebrows. They were empty of hope. He raised his hands up around her shoulders, but held them suspended and away from her as if her body was as hot as fire. He'd never touched her before and questioned his own weakness for having desired to do so now. The choice to embrace her, however, was not his, for she collapsed into his chest. Involuntarily, he wrapped his arms around her. She wept quietly for sometime, the wetness of her tears eventually reaching his chest through his shirt.

"You believe me don't you Neil?"

"I believe you," he said without hesitation. "Just where were you planning on going?"

"No place I guess."

"Good, because I don't want you to leave."

She looked up into his eyes searching for truth to his words.

"I've known Derrick for a long time Tasha. I know he can be a little harsh. I wish I could tell you more but I can't."

"Neil, I don't want to know anything. Don't explain anything to me. Just promise me one thing."

"I'll try. What is it?"

"Promise me you'll keep him away from me."

Neil fell silent and tried to reassure her with a smile.

She looked at his smile and into the eyes expressing it. The assurance she was looking for was not there. She knew it was a promise he couldn't keep. She backed out of his arms and walked towards the door, turned off the light, then set the lock on the handle. Shocked by the sudden darkness, he heard her walk over to the bed, grab hold of the suitcases, and flip them over the side of the bed, where they landed with a muffled *flop* on the floor. Suddenly she was directly in front of him, her hands delicately clawing their way from his stomach up towards his chest. She took a step forward and forced him over the edge of the bed. He knew what she was doing, but couldn't believe it. From underneath the crack in her door, weakened rays of artificial light invaded the room, just bright enough to pass through the airiness of her cotton dress and reveal the sharp outline of her form. What was she thinking? Her face showed no details. It was obscured in shadow. The beat of his soul awakening, he watched as she lifted her hands above her head and placed them around her neck. A tug of hand…a quick jerk with the other…two straps cutting lines across the pale wall behind her. When her hands fell to her side her dressed followed effortlessly to her waist, where it hung motionless. She twisted in the light and it drifted the rest of the way to the floor, curling around her sandals. Like eager fingers the light wrapped around the features of her body, revealing highlights of egg-white virgin breasts curling into focus and the jutting roundness of her hips curving inward. The oblong swirls of nipples and navel now suddenly dark as chocolate. The fold of her womanhood richly suspended in the fine lines of her panties.

A possessive sensation was stirring within him commanding him to sit up and take hold of her, but the sensation was immediately overtaken by the raw chill of wilderness. Still he watched. She stepped out of her dress and for a brief moment he caught the profile of a breast, round and elegant, capped with a square hardened nipple. She crouched down for a moment loosening her sandals, kicking them aside. The wilderness he had found himself in was becoming a frightful place. Shadows lurked and the musty aroma of that wilderness was overtaking him. The fire in his groin was becoming unbearable. She was relentless. Her hands rose above her waist, thumbs catching the strings of her panties. She slipped them over her hips and pressed them down over her thighs. He glimpsed the dark soft curls through the hollow, then the fall of her panties to the floor. She was an angel! But no!

Moving over the edge of the bed she straddled herself over his knees and felt the warmth of his thighs through his slacks and the coldness of the bedspread below her knees. The contraction of her nipples iced over in a sea of tingle as she crawled over him slowly like an arched cat. His expression, confused, almost frightened. She tried to ignore it, tried to use her weakened skills of flirtation to change it into something more wanting. Positioning herself above him, she tipped her head down and kissed him softly on the lips. They were like paper. She tried again. Construction paper. Letting her legs slip out from underneath her, she pressed the full warmth of her form across his petrified body. She sensed his arms rise above her. Would he have her? They came to rest in the small curve of her back, then with apprehension, slide over the rise and fall of her open hips. When he reached the back of her inner thighs he abruptly stopped. She held her breath in suspense. Without warning he flung her off of him.

"What are you doing?" he asked, sitting up without looking at her.

She clutched at the bedspread and tried to pull it over her, but it gripped the mattress and would not yield. He stood up facing the door and tucked in his shirt. She didn't answer. He walked across the bedroom floor and stopped at the door. Tasha's naked form lie huddled on the bed. A moment later she was sucked into darkness.

Neil staggered back into the dining room. Nothing had changed since the bugs had been found. All the lights were on, the computer was running and the printer was still waiting for a fresh ream of paper. He paced back and forth between the couch and the dining room table. "Yes!" He surmised, having resisted the temptation offered by Tasha. For a moment the victory appeased him, but soon came frustration and with it, anger. He considered the whole episode morally base; an action he'd prided himself in being too holy to engage in. Yet, he couldn't hide the fact that he wanted her. He coveted her passion from the very depths of his being. But he couldn't have her, couldn't partake of the pleasure, because he'd given his life to the work of his ministry. His absolution from the lust of the world would in the end have his own reward. This he believed, yet that belief had not been able to curb the desire of his flesh. This bewildered him. Had he not been promised the power of God would allow him to overcome such evils? But this promise had not reached its fulfillment. In fact, it didn't even seem to have put a dent in his desires. If anything, his abstinence had only fueled that lust. He shuttered to think a woman such as Tasha was living under his roof. She was a vile creature! A prostitute of passion! And he would have no relationship with her other than on a spiritual level. He must avoid her at all cost, lest she bring him down. "And that son of bitch Derrick! What an idiot!" Derrick's outburst had exposed Tasha's carnal nature and made him the target. It must not happen again. Not bothering to knock, he lunged through Derrick's door with wrath bursting from his lips.

"What the hell did you think you were doing?"

His outburst caught Derrick by surprise, but Derrick's mind had been revolving around the incident for the past hour. He was quick to respond.

"You should have never let her come here Neil. I tell you she's no good!"

"You might have blown it tonight." Neil countered.

"How? By getting rid of her before everything gets in full swing?"

"She's never been apart of this until tonight. She's never had a reason to question what we're about. Now she does. You put that doubt in her mind and now we can't be entirely sure what she'll do next."

"All the more reason to let her go. Let's be free of her before she blows the whole thing."

"No. I'm not going to just dump her on the streets."

"Then she's your responsibility, but I swear Neil, if she does anything to jeopardize this project she will have to go!"

They were silent for a few minutes, with nothing but the sound of their panting filling the room.

"Now, what are we going to do about the investigation?" Derrick persisted. He had his own ideas and was looking for concurrence from Neil.

"We do what we have to do, as we've always done."

"They must not be allowed to interfere with the program."

"I know," Neil responded.

"So what do we do?"

"We wait."

"Until when? Until they have all the information they need?"

"They don't have much."

"They have enough to justify their suspicions, which means, they won't stop until they've exhausted their resources. And if the American here is connected in any way with Trojan Security, then they may already have all the information they need."

"I doubt that's the case."

"Neil, where's your head? All it will take for them to effectively shut this down is to leak one article to any of their media connections. Hell, real or not, a simple editorial just mentioning the possibility of such a program could be enough. Look Neil, I've never questioned your authority until now. Tasha's got your head spinning and you're not thinking too clearly. We need to do something to get them off our backs."

"And I say we wait. This isn't Berlin."

"You bet it's not. The stakes are much higher now. You've been in charge of this ministry from the start Neil and I've supported you, but you may have forgotten I'm just as much a part of this as you are. If you're not capable of making rational decisions then I'll have to make them for you."

Neil took his eyes off the floor and burned them into Derrick's memory. "You wait. Do you understand? You wait until we both agree on what to do."

Derrick didn't concur, but ended boldly. "I'll give you two weeks. If you haven't come up with some reasonable options then something will have to be done. Now do you understand?"

CHAPTER 36

▼

She looked as if she'd been sucking on lemons. She was plump, cranky, in her late sixties and didn't have a clue as to what the word hospitality meant. Eva argued with her for what seemed to be five excruciating minutes. Stace knew they were talking about rooms and something to the effect of there not being one. Eva was insistent, but the woman more so, but in the end she handed Eva a registration form.

Stace and Eva had spoken little during their drive to the dinky Tudor-style bed and breakfast, propped up on the corner of a not so busy avenue on Munich's southern edge. The inside, however, was much nicer than its outside appearance. It had been remolded in the antiquated decor of German style about two hundred years distant with a flavor of aristocracy. He guessed the place had once been a home before its conversion. Next to the check-in desk was a dining area were several other guests sat for dinner. Their apparel reflected their opposing lifestyles and the odor of sausage and spicy mustard drifted in the stale air.

The woman waddled out from behind the counter and with little more than *"ugh,"* and invited Stace and Eva to follow her upstairs. Stace carried the bags, a backpack over his shoulder, gym bag with a change of clothes in one hand and Eva's overnight bag in the other. Halfway up the sliver of a staircase he got stuck. He backed down a step, turned sideways, thrust his gym bag out ahead of him, and proceeded. No hint of the evening meal had seeped upstairs. From beyond the cheery yellow wallpaper, the odor of wet wood, like the smell of a tree trunk decaying in a mountain meadow, filled his nostrils. He followed the two up another staircase and onto the third floor. The old woman opened the first door on the right and waited for her guests to pass though. Eva took the key from her. He dropped his load on the bed and fell onto a couch against the wall.

"Rather quaint don't you think?" he asked her. She plopped down next to him without looking around. He double-checked the accommodations. "Sure, it's a little old, but tolerable. Looks like they've done some recent covering up. What's this?"

Eva looked around him to his side of the couch. "A refrigerator."

"No kidding. Anything in it?" he asked, while opening it up and checking for himself. "It's full! You want anything?"

"Not hungry. But be careful how much you eat. We'll have to put it on the bill in the morning."

"Figures," he thought to himself. He pulled out a bottle of coke and a bag of peanuts, opened the bag and tossed a peanut in his mouth, rolling it around on his tongue. Sweet and sour, coated in sugar and salt, not unlike the vibrations he'd getting from Eva all day.

He decided he'd made a complete fool of himself earlier in the day. "Should have kept my mouth shut," he thought to himself. He'd broken one of his most treasured values. That people should be free to make their own decisions, especially when it came to religion. If people needed religion and if it gave them a sense of purpose, then by all means! let them use it, even if that someone was Eva. There was no doubt in his mind the service had been orchestrated perfectly. Each component had been carefully thought out and executed to bring about the most satisfying spiritual sensations. He chuckled to himself, remembering the few times even he had dropped his guard, and had to admit there were parts of the service he enjoyed, but that all came to a crashing end at the beginning of the sermon. Reverend Eisner knew how to work the crowd. He was a real showman. When the hearts of the people were softened and exposed, he reached down into their chests and yanked them out. Today the reverend had proposed an ultimatum for his followers; they could survive by following *his* understanding of religion; or they could think for themselves and be damned. But Stace's main concern rested on the woman next to him. Where was her head?

She was at present, trying to find it. Throughout the week everything had swirled together and hardened like an enormous pile of tangled twine. She'd picked at it constantly throughout the week, freeing one strand, disengaging another, and now it appeared her confused state of being had begun to disentangle itself. Her mind was beginning to isolate her fragmented thoughts into patterns, then patterns to forms, and from forms into three distinct yet intermingled situations. Together they had no specific order of significance, but they would all have to be resolved. One of them had to do with her position at the paper. Would she keep it or would she follow her heart into unknown territories? Much of that decision depended on the second; who was the man sitting next to her? Did they have a future together? The last situation had to do with having a spiritual point of reference in her life. Just exactly where was she going to obtain those answers? Who would she trust to give them to her?

Stace finished the bag of peanuts and crumpled the cellophane wrapper in his hands. It sounded like shattering plastic across linoleum tile, but not half as annoying as the unbearable silence he'd been sharing with Eva since the ICC's service.

"Eva, you really need to help me out here."

"What do you mean?" she asked without looking at him.

"I would like to know if I've done anything to upset you."

"It's complicated."

"Then how can I help you? I miss the Eva I knew last week."

He watched the corner of her lips curl upwards, but her eyes didn't share in the humor. "I'm still the same Eva."

"You look the same. Then maybe it's me. I've become the stranger."

She didn't answer. He downed the last of the coke and set the bottle on the top of the fridge. The light filling the windows had dipped from dusk to blackness. Shadows clung to the corners of the room and oozed down towards the floor. The ceiling closed in from above. The old home groaned with the sounds of guests creeping about like ghosts up and down the staircases.

He stood up and turned on the light. "I'm going to get some fresh air." He checked for a pack of cigarettes in his coat pocket. "Do you want to come?"

"Not now. I think I'll take a warm bath instead."

"Perhaps I should stay then. You might need some help," his voice pleaded.

"No." Then as an after thought she added, "but don't stay away too long."

She listened to the sound of his footsteps creak across the foyer and down the stairs. She rose, walked into the bathroom and started a bath. In the corner cabinet she found a jar of bath suds, opened the top and poured a generous portion into the running water. The aroma of wild raspberries moistened with steam rose up to greet her as the water turned a delicate shade of pink. The mirror above the sink began to fog. She went back into the room and slipped out of her clothes then returned. After closing the door she tipped the toes of her right foot into the water, letting out a sigh of pleasure and pain. She brought her other foot over the edge and stepped inside. A numbing sensation of fire surrounded her ankles. She reached over and turned off the tap. Silence once again filled her night. Steam continued to rise above the settling waters. Every so slowly, she eased down into the water and laid her head against the back of the tub. When she was accustomed to the heat she drifted even further down until nothing but her face, the tips of her breasts, and knees were left un-submerged. Closing her eyes she told herself over and over everything was going to be all right.

How much time had passed she didn't know. The water had chilled and the bubbles vanished. She was interrupted by the sound of the door as Stace came back inside the room. She heard the door of the refrigerator open and close and the *slush* as he fell back into the couch. She rose. Sheets of raspberry scented water slipped off of her body producing an orchestration of *plinks* and *plunks* rippling the surface. She took a towel off the rack and patted herself dry before the mirror. The fog had cooled, leaving a collection of beads across the silvery mirror. She took the edge of the towel and cleared the condensation, then looked at the woman standing before her and considered her happiness. Without a second thought she wrapped the towel around her damp body, synching the edge in a knot between her breasts and stepped out into the room.

Stace watched her glide across the floor and stop directly in front of him with the most puzzling expression he'd ever seen. She leaned over and rested her hands on his knees. Steam clung to her presence. Her bosom hung ripe with the aroma of berry.

"You are simply—"

"*Shish!* No words please."

He was no fool.

CHAPTER 37

▼

The following Monday Eva flew off to work with the same sense of reckless abandonment to which she'd spent the weekend with Stace. Surrounded in the steel cocoon of her Opel she sped along the A-66 into Frankfurt as if she were the only one alive in the world, hugging the far left lane, whipping past slower moving traffic to her right. Over the weekend she'd completely disregarded the object of her work and it felt good. She'd succeeded in laying all her fears and concerns aside. And that felt good too. She'd tasted the secrets of her own desires. She would not be tamed. This of course, was totally contrary to the attitude of professionalism to which she normally composed herself. By force of habit she looked into her rear view mirror into the flashing lights of a sleek BMW, which had pulled up five feet off her rear bumper. Her speedometer read 132 Km/h. Not fast enough. She pulled into the right lane to let it pass. At the *Schwarz Monatlich* her boss and the others were expecting a good report. What the hell was she going to offer them?

No doubt, they would question her about the infamous Stace Manning. Who did he work for? What did he know about the program? Why did he come to Germany? Ruben would be at his desk fumbling with a pencil. Mr. Schwarz would be standing nearby with his hands resting on his round hips shifting his weight from side to side and calculating. Shelly would be holding a stack of papers to file and sitting on the edge of Eva's desk like she always did when they were discussing matters of the male species. They would all be starring at her as if they were expecting a detailed report. Would she would tell them that she loved the man? Hardly. She would for the first time in her life put something ahead of her work and devise a reason to elude their questions.

If that didn't strike enough of a blow to their confidence in her, the absence of answers to the other questions they would ask surely would. For what could she tell them about the ICC? It had been the first time she'd ever set foot in a church and what she'd discovered was something far less threatening then any of Mr. Schwarz's imaginings, or Stace's sarcastically motivated fears. Would she tell them never had she experienced an atmosphere in which complete strangers could come together laying all their prejudices and vices at the door? How her flesh tingled and her spirit reached up to something greater than herself? How she'd never heard such beautifully orchestrated music, which yanked at the very fabric of her being? Hardly. She would tell them the reverend was a charismatic facilitator of dissension. She would tell them how he had the power to breathe life into the hearts of children one moment and in the next moment rain terror upon the heads of their parents. She would tell them if he was an impostor, then he was an impostor to only the fools who wished to believe him. This too, would be a lie, but it would buy her more time. The confrontation however, would have to wait.

At the last moment she suddenly decided to visit her parents at the *backerei*. Seeing them always had a way of bringing her back in touch with what mattered most in life. Her parents enjoyed one of those fantastic romances, which matured with age like a fine wine. In all of Eva's life she'd never witnessed anything more than a brief disagreement between them. Their tenderness and love towards each other affected everyone who came in contact with them. The reassurance that such love and trust existed in the world was something Eva needed far more than an interrogation at the office.

The bell over the front door rang as she stepped inside, but her mother was too busy to notice her. Three other customers were standing in front of the glass display shelves and she was ringing up another customer at the register. Without hesitating, Eva moved around the side of the counter and started assisting those who waited to make their selections.

"Eva! What a nice surprise!"

Eva walked over to her. "It's good to see you too mama. You stay there at the register and I'll help the folks at the counter."

Leda smiled and walked back to the register. Eva watched her out of the corner of her eye. She was as busy as she'd always been, but she never lost her patience and courtesy no matter how busy the work got. It reminded Eva of the days when she attended the university and would help her mother out in the mornings before classes started. After she began working at the paper her parents had never hired anyone to take her place. She knew it was because they couldn't afford the help. She hated having to leave them and move on with her life, but they were insistent. Now, she realized how much she'd missed helping them out. She missed the sounds; like the silver bell above the door *chiming* when customers arrived, or the *chings* of the cash register opening and closing. She missed the smells; like the aroma of sugar and cake frostings, of yeast mingling with heat in the ovens, of maple, nuts and molasses, of sugar glaze coating spilling over plate sized cinnamon rolls.

"Hello father!" Eva yelled, poking her head through the kitchen door.

He barely heard her. The two mixers in the corner were spinning flour into dough at high speed. "Eva! How are you?" he asked, looking up momentarily from a cake he was frosting.

"Fine!"

"Are you staying?"

"For a little while."

"Good."

Thirty minutes later the crowd thinned down and she sat at the table along the wall waiting for her mother to finish with the last customer at the register.

"It's so good to see you again Eva. Thanks for the help."

"I enjoyed it."

Her mother sat down in front of her on the stool and propped herself up by the wall. After wiping the beads of sweat off her forehead with a damp cloth, she tucked a loose strand of hair back up under her hair net and sighed with exhaustion.

"Why haven't you ever gotten any one to help you since I left?"

"It was your father's idea."

"But the *backerei's* paid off. Surely you can afford the help now."

"Perhaps," said her mother, not wishing to disclose why they couldn't yet afford the help.

"I'll talk to father about it," Eva insisted.

"No please don't. There are only a few hours in the morning when it gets a little busy. After that it settles down and your father and I are able to handle it."

Her mother daubed her forehead again. "So what brings you around?"

"Can you believe it? I got a ticket for running the yellow light on the corner."

"Who got you? The *polizei* or one of the cameras on the pole?"

"The camera of course."

"You say the light was yellow?"

"I'm sure it was yellow."

"You should give them a call. I hear from the neighbors the timing might be a little off. A lot of people are getting tickets around here that shouldn't be."

"I'd rather not mess with it."

"You didn't come all this way to tell me you got a ticket did you?"

"No. Actually, I came to ask you a favor."

"A favor? Of course."

"I have someone I'd like you and father to meet."

"The American?" she asked sitting up and leaning over the table towards Eva.

Eva thought her expression comical. Something in the range of serious excitement followed by a dreamy look of poetic wonder.

The bell on the door chimed. A little boy about twelve walked in.

"Wait," her mother said raising a hand. "Don't go anywhere."

She bagged a loaf of bread and rolls for the lad and added a chocolate chip cookie.

"Thank you, Mrs. Burtman," he said and sailed out the door.

"*Auf wiedersehen!*" she yelled after him and hurried back to the table, sitting on the edge of her seat.

"Do you love him?" she asked expectantly.

"*Ja*...I think I do."

Her mother relaxed against the wall again with an air of hapless wonder. Her daughter was in love. She sighed and smiled, then quickly sat back up. "We must tell your father."

"Let's wait," Eva replied, but it was too late, Leda had dashed into the kitchen. The door leading into it *squeaked* as it swung back and forth. It didn't stop swinging before her mother returned pulling her father by his apron.

"Tell me it's true Eva," he said, clutching a cloth stained with oil and wet batter.

"It's true," she said rising.

Her father walked over to her and gave her a huge hug. He was warm as the ovens and the aura of cinnamon hung around him.

"I'm happy for you," he said. "When do we get a chance to meet him?"

"Actually, I was hoping I could bring him over for dinner on Wednesday night."

"This Wednesday?"

"Is that a problem?"

"No, of course not," her mother said, taking her husband around the arm and smiling as she looked up into his face.

"About 8:30. Will that be all right?"

"That will be just fine," her mother said.

Eva looked at her parents standing side by side, her father beaming with satisfaction and her mother clutching his forearm mirroring his delight.

The bell chimed again and in walked a young woman.

"I should let you go now," Eva said reaching for her bag on the table. "You sure you don't need anymore help mother?"

"Naw, you go on now and take something with you for your friends at the paper."

She shoved a bag into Eva's hand with insistence.

"Wednesday night then Eva," her father said, backing into the kitchen door and disappearing.

Eva smiled. She turned to the glass counter and took out a dozen or so pastries and shoved them into the bag.

At the *Schwarz Monatlich* the situation was just as she'd expected. Mr. Schwarz, Ruben and Shelly were all seated around Ruben's desk waiting for her to arrive. She came in and set the bag of pastries down on her desk. No one said a word to her and she started running through the lies she'd rehearsed.

"They found the bugs," were the first word's spoken.

She leaned back into her chair indifferent to the revelation, but soon the significance sunk in.

"How do you know?"

Shelly walked over to the CD machine. "I went through the weekend recordings this morning. What you're going to hear is the last conversation the tapes picked up."

She watched Shelly flip the machine on and she tried to put the fragments of the conversation into perspective.

"What the?"—Man's voice.

"What's this?"—Same man's voice.

"Derrick!"—Neil's voice.

"What."—Derrick.

"Do you have any idea what this is?"—Neil.

"No."—Tasha.

"I don't Neil."—Tasha, insistent.

"Let me take a look."—Derrick. Pause. *"Phhhh…phhhh!"* Pause. "Adhesive tape."

"I know what it is! Do you know where it came from is my question?"—Neil.

"Never used the stuff."—Derrick.

"What's it used for?"—Tasha.

"It's double sided Tasha. You stick something to it then you stick it to something else. Where'd you find it?"—Derrick.

"Right here under the printer. I ran out of printing paper and I was setting this ream of paper down on the floor."—Neil.

Long pause.

"What's the problem?"—Tasha.

"Shut up Tasha!"—Derrick.

Long pause.

"What?"—Tasha, obviously upset.

Long pause.

The next thing heard on the tape was indecipherable fumbling sounds, whispers of voices, footsteps across hardwood floors, then the sharp sounds of crunching paper, growing quieter and quieter until reaching a muffled hollow hum like the sound of space in a giant sea shell.

Shelly switched off the machine.

"Does Alfred know about this?" Eva asked.

"I called him this morning," said Mr. Schwarz.

"So that's it. They know everything," She said sinking back into her chair. "If they were up to anything at all then you can bet there's no evidence of it around."

"Which is why we must work fast," Mr. Schwarz said quickly before they lost their morale.

"What's the point?" Eva blurted out, lifting her hands in a display of defeat. "From day one I've never understood the purpose of this investigation."

Mr. Schwarz rose out of his chair and squared off with Eva in an expression demanding no word of authentication. Shelly checked for Eva's response. Curiously enough, Mr. Schwarz hadn't fazed her.

He turned towards Ruben, "Tell Eva what you found out over the weekend, it might change her perspective."

Ruben looked up at her apprehensively.

"On Friday I contacted the *Berliner MorganPost* and spoke with *de* Editor of *de* paper there in Berlin. I asked him if he'd ever run across either Derrick Sachs or Neil Usher. He said they'd scan their computers and find what they could. By the end of the day he faxed me two articles that had been written by his father during *de* earlier years of *de* paper. Both articles connected Derrick Sachs with an organization known simply as *De Menschen*."

"People—the people?" Eva verified." What kind of a name is—"?

"Let him continue Eva," said Mr. Schwarz.

"Both articles spoke of *de* organization as one of a slew of underground movements existing during the 80's. Derrick Sachs was listed as a possible suspect in one of *de* articles. At the time he was under investigation for arson. Seems he might have set fire to the city courthouse. He was later acquitted."

He paused from his notes and looked at Eva. She seemed disinterested. "Now all of *dis* is virtually useless. It was a long time ago...."

She suddenly took interest. "But he was acquitted right?"

"Correct."

"That doesn't eliminate the suspicion. Never has, never will," Mr. Schwarz added.

Ruben continued. "There's more. Seems that *de* current editor, Boris Ulricht, spoke to his father Max that Friday about my questions.

The elder Ulrich began *de* paper just after WW II, retired in 1989 and then he—."

"Get to the point Ruben."

"Yes sir."

"Now what he told me you won't find in any public records, so searching them is useless, but he told me that he and a member of his staff during the 80's had an on-going investigation of *De Menschen*. Despite all of the information they'd gathered on *de* movement they could only legally publicize *de* two articles in question and—"

"—Ruben!"

"I'm getting there sir. Ulrich referred to *de* movement as one of those 'sleeper' movements. Although they were smaller and less vocal than other organizations around *dat* time, he believed *dey* were responsible for no less than thirty percent of all *de* terrorist related activities that occurred during the 80's in and around Berlin. While other organizations were sponsoring public sit-ins and non-violent demonstrations, the *Menschen* was busy setting fires to public buildings, planting car bombs, mail bombs, and as far as Ulrich was concerned, they were personally responsible for at least two assassinations of public officials. More curious is *de* fact *dat* no time did they ever claim responsibility for their terrorist activities. Ulrich only discovered their existence during an investigation of another group."

Ruben paused again to gauge Eva's reaction. She had turned to face him now, listening to every word.

"What Ulrich feared most about *de* group was they had some twisted religious motivation behind their actions. He swears to this day they were responsible for *de* assassination of Hans Lofter. Hans Lofter was working in the cabinet as the Secretary of Urban Development. He also owned a construction company. Through his office he was able to successfully divert large government contracts towards his own enterprises."

"Where do the *Menschen* fit in?" Eva asked.

"Hans Lofter didn't bother to conceal his actions. Ulrich believed too many other government officials had their hands in his pocket, so they overlooked much of what he did. Lofter was also an outspoken atheist. He justified his actions and *de* policies of his administration to his own warped sense of philosophy."

"Was he a white-supremacist?" Eva asked.

"Not exactly. He had many people working for him in either his office or at his company who were far from what one might call purely white. Color or nationality was not an issue with him."

"What was?" Eva asked.

"Atheism. Within a few years Lofter had successfully weeded out any person working under him who had any religious ties. Got rid of *dem* all."

"How'd he do that?"

"Through extensive background investigations and whatever means he had at his disposal."

"And nobody stopped him?"

"Not until *de Menschen* stepped in. It seems a handful of those who had worked for Lofter had been trying for years to get someone high enough in *de* government to hear them. Ulrich didn't supply me with any names, but one of *de* individuals he let go made contact with someone in *de Menschen*. Within a few weeks Hans Lofter was found shot to death outside his home in Berlin."

"Did the authorities ever discover it was the *Menschen* who'd made the hit?" Eva asked.

"Ulrich believes they knew it was the *Menschen*, but the way Ulrich describes it, *de* authorities, as well as many other people, were glad to have him out of the way."

"So nothing was done?"

"*Noting*, but one more thing, Ulrich was familiar with both Neil Usher and Derrick Sachs. Whether they were with *De Menschen* or another organization is unclear. When the wall fell in '89 they disappeared. Ulrich knew both of them immigrated into western Germany, but what became of them he didn't know."

"But we do know what's become of them, so we pick up where Ulrich left off." Mr. Schwarz turned towards Eva." We take it from here."

"Now, what did you find out about the ICC and Stace Manning?"

The question hit her like a bolt of lightning. Ruben had given the group a detailed report. Would her pack of lies hold up to the scrutiny? It would have to. She told them the ICC was just what they expected, an organization run by a charismatic leader who had more concern for his personal glory than for his followers. Her revelation of Stace was even less descriptive. "As far as Stace is concerned, I haven't found any discrepancies in his story. He seems to be what he says he is. In fact, he's entirely antagonistic towards any religious organization. Much more than I expected him to be."

"That doesn't say much. A lot of people oppose organized religion," said Mr. Schwarz.

"Those were my thoughts. If he's working for an outside source it doesn't seem to me he'd go around advertising his personal perspective of the ICC."

"I'd still expect him to have an opinion, even if it's offered to siphon information from you," said Mr. Schwarz."

"He didn't even want to go to the service," Eva offered in Stace's defense.

"Could have been just a tactical maneuver if he knew you had to go anyway…" Ruben added.

Eva remembered for a moment all of the photos Stace had taken of the compound. He took pictures of practically everything, even the satellite dishes. This seemed rather odd to her at the time. Having thought about Stace's overall response towards the service she said to Ruben and the others, "I still think his feelings towards the ICC were genuine."

"Perhaps they were. How many times have you investigated an organization you didn't like? Ruben asked.

Eva didn't answer.

"The question is, who does he work for?" Mr. Schwarz stated.

"Why does he have to work for anybody? He's not the only American in Frankfurt. There are thousands of them here. Just because I met up with him doesn't mean he's connected with our investigation."

"You may be right Eva, but I'd suggest you don't get too involved with him on a personal basis," Shelly said.

"Best you keep your distance," Ruben added.

"At least until we've completed our investigation and we know he's not involved," said Mr. Schwarz.

Eva sat up in her chair and lifted her hands above her head. "I'm confused, I thought you wanted me to find out what I can about him, to flush out any information. Now you're asking me to stay away from him?"

"I'm just asking you to be careful Eva. Use your judgment. If you can find out what he's up to than good. If you can find out he's got nothing to do with Trojan Security or with the ICC, or with any other organization, than that's even better," Mr. Schwarz said finally taking a seat.

"We care about you Eva and we just don't want to see you get hurt," Shelly said pleading with her.

"I appreciate your concern," Eva said, settling back into her chair, while each one of them glanced at her with their own depth of concern. She felt uncomfortable with their stares and had to say something to get them to turn away. "You all know me. When have you ever known me to let my guard down?"

"Never," said Mr. Schwarz without hesitation.

For a moment or two they just sat there. A truck rolled by on the street and the windows along the wall buzzed, followed by the sound of more cars and the clops of shoes along the sidewalk. Eva watched the sounds and shadowy forms pass by. She wondered where they were going or where they were coming from. She envied the way they carried on with their lives without any clue of the injustices she had to consider on a daily basis. One particular shadow drew her attention, just the simple form of a woman wearing a long skirt passing across the widows. A woman that could have been her and for just a moment, Eva wondered what it would be like to just get up and leave. Leave her briefcase on the desk; leave the in-box full of urgent, insignificant forms and itinerary; leave the Post-It notes requiring her immediate attention right where Shelly had stuck them on her computer monitor; leave it all behind and take a long slow walk into another life....

"You mind if I have one of these?" Ruben asked.

Eva awoke from her daydream to see Ruben leaning over her desk ripping open the bag of pastries she'd brought.

"No." When she looked back up the woman was gone.

After Ruben opened the bag, Mr. Schwarz walked over to her desk and grabbed one. Then Shelly walked over looking at Eva with those wonderfully searching eyes of hers that possessed both a knowing and at the same time a supple wanton curiosity. True to form, she delicately picked out the tiniest donut she could find.

"Does anyone want some coffee?" Shelly asked.

"I'll have a cup if you don't mind," Eva replied.

"So where do we go from here?" Ruben asked.

Mr. Schwarz spoke up. "To begin with, find out everything you can about Neil and Derrick before the wall fell. Brainstorm. What's the CRM all about?" Mr. Schwarz twisted in his chair and spoke to Shelly at the coffee pot. "You give him a hand Shelly." He turned to Eva. "You've gotten a good start on the ICC. See what you can find out about their financial accountabilities. I want to know where their money goes and if it goes towards any anything political."

"As far as I know it's not illegal to donate money towards political parties in Germany."

He said nothing. Eva recognized the implications.

Shelly walked over and set a cup of coffee before Eva. "What about the program at Trojan Security?" Eva asked.

"I was getting to that. Somehow, The ICC, the CRM and Trojan Security are connected. It's obvious that at least the CRM knows we're on to them."

"Or worse," Eva added.

"They could take the bugs to the *polizei*," Shelly said.

"I doubt it." Mr. Schwartz said. "Whether or not they've got something to hide they're not going to draw unnecessary attention to themselves. It's safe to say we've got more pull with the *polizei* than they do. But, just in case, Alfred is on his way over here to pick up this equipment. I don't want it around if they do come knocking."

Mr. Schwarz had set to thinking. The rest of them enjoyed the short break until he spoke again. "Someone has got to make contact with Tasha."

"What makes you so sure she's willing to give us information?"

"Well, she's only been with Neil and Derrick a few years. It's possible she has no idea of their past history in Berlin."

"Then I'd say she's pretty damn stupid," Rubin injected.

"Perhaps not," Mr. Schwartz added. "If you were Neil or Derrick would you go around advertising your past?"

"Not exactly, but what about now? Surely she knows all about the program and what they're up to now?" Shelly said.

For the first time that morning Eva offered her insight, letting the others know she was back with them. "Let's assume she does know about the program, but not about Neil and Derrick's past, we might be able to convince her to cooperate with us."

"How do we know she's not as dangerous as they are?" Ruben added.

"We don't, and if they found the bugs they have enough reason to retaliate already."

Suddenly the air was thick with potential hostility. It still seemed ironic to Eva given the religious tenor of the groups involved.

"Eva's right," Mr. Schwarz said rising out of his chair again. "We don't have the luxury of time. We've got to find out what the program's all about and she may be our only hope. She'll either talk or she won't."

"And if she doesn't? Ruben asked.

"Then we've lost nothing," Eva concluded.

Mr. Schwarz shifted his feet and straitened up, which was an indication to the others he'd made a decision. "It's settled. Ruben I want you and Eva to—"

"I think it would be best if I contacted her own my own," Eva interrupted.

Ruben looked up from his desk feeling a little resentment at being left out. "Why?"

"I don't want to intimidate her…yet. If she is as we hope she is, not entirely caught up with them, than what I tell her will be frightening enough. I want her to feel she's in way over her head, and I want her to know we're here to help her swim. I just think that's better done woman to woman."

Mr. Schwarz was about to speak but Ruben interrupted him." I know, I know. It's worth a try. I don't have a problem with it."

CHAPTER 38

▼

Days before Eva and the rest of the *Schwarz Monatlich* staff had debated the coincidental emergence of Stace Manning, Derrick had implicated him without question. Derrick was convinced he was working jointly with the paper's investigation of the CRM and nothing could persuade him to believe otherwise, not even Neil, whom he now believed to have surrendered his sense of duty to Tasha. Neil had always been the one who made the decisions between them when it came to the direction of the CRM and had usually been the man to carry those details out. But the present crisis, which in Derrick's estimation was the most significant crisis of their lives, would have to be handled by him.

Throughout the week until Wednesday, he'd been following Eva like a hound follows scent. She'd yet to make contact with the American, but knew she would in time. She'd done little more than go back and forth to work with one exception; this morning she'd made a sudden and mysterious trip to an obscure *backerei*. Determining why'd she gone to that particular *backerei* hadn't been difficult. A cast-iron sign written over the entrance in cursive letters read, *"Burtman's Backerei."* Its owners were obviously, someone in the family.

He had a great deal of time to consider the course of action he must take if he hoped to divert the paper's investigation off the program.

Nothing must stand in the way of its implementation. He deemed his own life as expendable, cherishing with twisted logic the notion that the greater the sacrifice on his part, the greater his reward would be in the kingdom to come. If he was expendable, certainly those who opposed his plans were expendable. His world was full of demons lurking around every corner in human form. He knew exactly who they were. They were those who disagreed with him. His bedfellow was terror and its offspring—intimidation. For intimidation is the tool of terrorists, chiseled by insecurity and randomly dispensed by the terrorist for all of the injustices they perceive others to have done to themselves.

Later that evening his watch ticked 6:17 p.m. He was seated in Neil's car a comfortable distance from the entrance of the paper, when he was disrupted in his thoughts by the emergence of Eva on the sidewalk. She got into her Opel and he followed her home. At 7:53 she reappeared under the porch light and got back into her car. He followed her at a distance as she zigzagged through *Hochst* then onto an obscure road leading into an area of open fields dotted with isolated homes. At the aqueduct she took a right and decreased her speed. He did likewise. When she parked in front of a house at the end of the street he remained at the opposite end and waited. His days of surveillance finally paid off. When she got back into her car she was accompanied by the American. He followed them back into *Hochst* where they made a brief stop at a flower shop. The American got out and returned about five minutes later with a bouquet of flowers. When they parked in front of the *Burtman's Backerei* a few minutes later, he pulled into a slot just up the road. From his rear view mirror he watched them get out of the car and go to the front door of the *backerei*. Deciding to get a closer look, he got out of the car and walked along the sidewalk on the other side of the street. The embankment to his left was covered with brush and dwarfed trees, providing a cloak of darkness. The road along his right side was lined with a solid row of parked cars. When he was nearly opposite them, he darted into the cover of the embankment and clung to the side of a tree trunk. Within a few moments the downstairs light of the *backerei* came on and a woman appeared from a swinging door in the back. She walked around the shelves to the front door and let Eva and the American in.

After opening the door, Eva's mother greeted them and let her eyes wander over Stace, finding him pleasantly handsome and flushed with embarrassment. She gave Eva a hug and kissed her on the cheek, while Stace noticed their similarities. They almost mirrored one another in likeness, as if Eva were looking into her future reflection and Mrs. Burtman in turn, looking into the reflection of the woman she once was. They shared the same-boxed jaw and delicate chin, as well as their delightful mannerisms. Following their embrace, Mrs. Burtman stood back to observe him more closely, as though she was trying to ascertain whether or not he was fitting enough to share in her daughter's company.

"So you're the one I've heard so little about," she said, turning a wink towards Eva.

Stace reached out and took her extended hand and handed her the flowers with the other. She let go of his hand and inhaled their aroma. "Thank you so much," she said, obviously pleased.

She handed Eva the bouquet and took hold of his arm. "Now, let me give you a quick tour of the place." She pulled him around the shelves and gave him a rundown of the front room. Eva followed behind them with a look of chagrin. Mrs. Burtman turned off the light switch to the front room and pulled him through the swinging door into the kitchen. She flipped on the light. The kitchen was tiny, clean and well equipped, but he was more interested in her expressions as she talked, for they would be Eva's expressions in the years to come.

He liked what he saw. She was every bit as formidable as Eva, radiating a certain strength of character which awakens admiration. Given her age, she appeared to be much calmer than her daughter. With the calmness, however, was something disturbing. Something along the lines of defeat or perhaps, resolve. Was this what Eva was fearful of loosing, of becoming? He refused to consider the negatives. He could only guess her mother had lost through the years a bit of her fire and passion for life. She'd settled in...aged...but the fire was still there, declared though her expressions and liveliness as she tugged him around the bakery.

"But I suppose you've seen enough of this place haven't you?" she suddenly asked, having made a full circle around the kitchen and back to the door where Eva waited patiently. Reluctantly, Leda let loose her grip of his arm, reaching up to check strands of slivered gray hair that were loosely tied into a bun at the base of her neck. Before he could respond, she'd opened the door leading up to the apartment. An imposing figure stood at the top of the staircase waiting for them. Dwarfish, yet stout, he had a chest as round as a barrel of dough, arms like an ape and was dressed in dark slacks and an indistinguishable colored shirt with a collar. He shoved a meaty hand into Stace's, and shook it vigorously.

"Stace, it's nice to meet you."

"Likewise."

"We're all ready to eat so let's just have a seat at the table," Mrs. Burtman said.

Stace followed her into the dining room. Oddly enough, the table was set for five.

Outside, still hidden in the brush across from the *backerei*, Derrick flipped up the collar on his coat and synched the top button. He shoved his hands into his jean pockets and shifted his numb feet from side to side. Other than a few casual glances at the nearby intersection, his eyes had never left the building, darting between two faintly lit windows on the second floor. After forty-five minutes, not even a shadow had passed in front of them. He had the whole place photographed in his memory within five minutes of his arrival and the rest of the time was spent warding off his frustration and the chill.

To the left of the *backerei* was a shop that doubled as a clock and jewelry store. Next to it was a restaurant. There were other shops standing around the corner to the left, but he couldn't discern what they were. On the right side of the *backerei* was an alleyway and beyond the alleyway other rows of homes and apartments were crammed together in typical Frankfurt form. Just a few cars had turned off the busy intersection onto the quiet street in front of the bakery, so when Derrick saw a utility van swing around the corner he followed it in his line of sight. It looked vaguely familiar as it slowed and approached, and he tried to make out the logo on the side panel in the light from the corner post. "There it is!" *Frankfurt Bundespost*, the company logo of the telephone company. The van took a hard left into the alleyway and parked with its tail end overlapping the sidewalk. His curiosity peaked to suspicion. "A last minute repair?" Derrick questioned. The bright red taillights went dim and the engine puttered to a stop. Moments later, the shadow of a man appeared, but the darkness of the alley obscured his face. The man went to the back of the van and cracked the doors open, only to reach inside to check the locks on both doors. He closed the doors and rattled the handle. The slight movements and uniform of the man struck Derrick as someone he'd seen before, recently in fact. Dark gray overalls, medium build, crop of dark hair, protruding nose, even the way he checked the locks on the door. The young man stepped onto the sidewalk and walked towards the *backerei*, where he stopped, reached into his pocket and pulled out a cigarette. He slipped it between his lips and struck a match. His face was momentarily set aglow in the yellow light of the match and in an instant Derrick recognized him as the same technician that had parked in front of him at the *Schwarz Monatlich*. What were the odds? Million to one? Telephone man at the *Schwarz Monatlich*, same man at the *Burtman's Backerei* after hours. Derrick reasoned with himself, "Now, technicians know the basics around communication wiring. Some even possess advanced degrees in electrical engineering. One thing's for certain, all of them know how to get into an apartment with little suspicion." The man stood on the sidewalk and glanced up and down the street, then over in Derrick's direction. The cigarette sailed from his hand sending orange embers shattering in sparks across the asphalt. He reached for his keys and went inside. The connection had settled in Derrick's mind. The *Schwarz Monatlich*, the American and the technician were working together, and now the three of them were meeting in the upstairs apartment of this obscure *backerei* in *Hochst* to discuss what? How to plant more bugs? How to get more evidence against the CRM? The program? Derrick had no way of knowing, but he was positive of one thing, they weren't baking cookies.

They had all moved into the living room when Mrs. Burtman heard the door at the bottom of the stairs open. "Ah, here's Alfred now."

Alfred crept up the stairs and into the foyer. Stace looked around the wall as he stepped into the living room anxious to greet him. Alfred immediately set his eyes on Stace with a look of complete dissatisfaction. They were cold disbelieving eyes that froze Stace's tongue. Only Mrs. Burtman caught the exchange.

"You two have met?" she asked Alfred.

"*Ja*," he grunted.

Alfred took a few steps forward looking questionably at Eva and shook Stace's hand for show.

"Save any for me?" Alfred asked looking at the set table.

"It's on the stove," Mrs. Burtman said.

Alfred didn't waste any time.

"I'll give him a hand," Eva said rising off the couch.

Stace sat back down. The Burtman's sat across from him on the other side of the cramped living room, their two cushioned armchairs separated by an end table with a lamp and a stack of magazines. Above them hung a menagerie of family photos hung in no particular order. He glanced nervously back at the Burtmans, who looked anxious for conversation, then back into the kitchen. Alfred was leaning against the counter and Eva was standing directly in front of him. She was speaking too softly for him to hear, but he could tell by her gestures and the way Alfred was forced back against the counter they were arguing about something.

"Eva says you're a photographer," Mr. Burtman said suddenly.

"Yes," he replied without filling in the details, glancing back into the kitchen.

"What brought you to Germany?" asked Mrs. Burtman.

Stace turned to face her. "Adventure I guess. I like the arts and renaissance history and I figured Germany was right in the middle of it. I like the fact that within a few hours you can travel to almost anywhere in Europe."

"So you've been to some other countries then?" she asked.

Whatever Eva and Alfred were discussing in the kitchen was over. Eva leaned against the opposite counter with her hands folded across her chest. Alfred poured himself a glass of wine from a bottle on the counter and walked over to the dinning room table.

"Actually, no. I really haven't had the time to. Eva and I went to Munich last weekend, but that's the furthest south I've been." After he said it he wished he hadn't.

He glanced up at Eva as she came back into the living room. She managed a tense smile. He wished they were alone.

"You didn't mention your trip to Munich Eva," her mother said leaning forward in her chair.

She glanced at Stace with an "I shouldn't leave you alone" look.

"It was work related mother. Part of an investigation I'm working on involving a religious organization based down there." She looked across the room into the dining room and into Alfred's wary expression. "Nothing serious Mom," she added.

"Are you a religious man Stace?" Mr. Burtman asked.

The question surprised him and he was unprepared to answer it. Eva beat him to it. "I asked him the same question once."

"And?"

"I can safely say he's not fanatical about it."

Mrs. Burtman leaned further out in her chair around the lamp and looked at her husband. "I guess you could say it was religion that brought us together," she said. Her smile was elegant and Stace knew there was an inside story to it.

"So what are your plans for the future?" Mr. Burtman asked him.

Stace looked at Eva hoping for help, but she had nothing to offer him. "I try and leave that open. I'm taking it one day at a time."

Mrs. Burtman looked at Stace with an expression that seemed to demand a more elaborate answer. Stace conceded.

"What I'd like to do at some point is work for myself."

"Like a business you mean?" asked Mr. Burtman.

"Sort of. Something related to the field of photography. I'd like to have my own studio someday."

"Would you go back to America to do that?" Mrs. Burtman asked concerned.

"That was my original plans. But I like it here in Germany and I've thought about staying. On the other hand, it would be easier for me to set up shop back in the states."

"Why's that?" Mr. Burtman asked with interest.

"I'm more familiar with what's required to start a business in the states."

"Well, I don't know about the states, but I do know a lot about setting up a business in Germany. Perhaps we could sit down sometime and I can tell you what's involved."

Stace looked at Eva, who seemed neither pleased nor displeased with the suggestion. "I'd like that. It would at least give me some ideas."

Without hesitation and disregarding his own comment to wait until a more appropriate time, Mr. Burtman proceeded to discuss with Stace some inside information on how he might be able to start a business in Frankfurt. Within minutes they were down to the details. Eva sat idly by watching her mother watch Stace, who hung on his every word as if she were extracting clues of his character out of a mountain of dull conversation. Her expression was entertaining in itself. Meanwhile, Alfred had finished eating and without saying a word went into another room.

"Mother," she said, while her father was in mid-sentence discussing the sales tax rates that might be applicable to a photography studio. "Let me help you clear the table before it gets too late."

"Why? Are you leaving soon?" Then suddenly understanding Eva's suggestion she got out of her chair.

"We can't stay late tonight," Eva said after they'd walked over to the table.

They picked up a handful of dishes and took them into the kitchen. "I think he's delightful," her mother said.

"There's a lot I don't know about him."

"I don't think you can know everything there is about a person."

"It's just so confusing."

"How so?"

"For one thing he's an American. The only things I know about him are what he's told me."

"Is there some reason you have to distrust him?"

"Not from my point of view, but my friends think I'm moving too fast."

"Perhaps you are. As much as I'd like to see you get involved in a serious relationship it doesn't hurt to think things through carefully. You have a lot of time, unlike your father and I. We had to make some quick and painful decisions."

"You two seem very happy together," Eva said.

"We are. Mrs. Burtman set down the plate of roast on the counter and turned towards her daughter. "I just want you to be happy Eva. Finding someone you love and who loves you is just a start. So don't be afraid to take your time if you need to."

Eva crossed her hands and leaned against the refrigerator. "But I'm afraid if I take too much time then I'll miss the opportunity."

"There's always that risk. That's why it's important to follow your intuition. It's the only way to look ahead when there are no facts to rely on. Does Stace care for you as much as you care for him?"

"I think he does."

"Then he knows as much about you as you know about him?"

"That's a difficult question to answer."

"Does he know what kind of work you're involved in?"

"He knows, but he doesn't know all the details."

Mrs. Burtman leaned against the counter opposite her daughter and with all the motherly persuasive tone she could muster said, "Then I'd suggest you make no serious commitments until he does."

"And what if I can't tell him, or he doesn't want to wait until I can tell him?"

"Then he's not right for you, or you'll have to make a decision about your work."

Eva sighed and looked towards the couch where Stace and her father were still engaged in conversation.

"I think in some ways the decision to marry daddy was easy for you."

"If you mean I didn't have the conflict of a profession like you do, yes, but you forget when your father and I married we had no idea how we were going to survive and where we were going to live. You on the other hand, have that all worked out."

"I hadn't looked at it that way."

"It sounds to me that the real conflict might be your work."

"It is. That's what's kept me going through all these years and now it's just not as important to me as it once was."

"Then find something you'll enjoy that will free you up to have other things in your life—like men," her mother concluded with a smile.

"You make it sound so simple."

"Because it is."

Eva watched her mother take a few steps towards her. She wiped her hands on her apron and reached up to touch Eva's face. "Look Eva. I don't know why it is you have to be so serious about what goes on in this world. You and Alfred got that from your father. Take my advice, life's short and by the time you reach forty you'll have wondered where it went. Sooner or later you're going to have to think of yourself and not what other people want from you."

"Perhaps."

"I think you understand what I'm talking about."

Meanwhile outside, still hidden from view, Derrick made the decision to return to his apartment. For three days he'd been following Eva around and this evening he'd been rewarded for his diligence. He'd been able to connect the *Schwarz Monatlich*, the American and the telephone technician together. He was certain he had sufficient evidence to awaken Neil out of his complacency and to the seriousness of the threat. Perhaps the *backerei* was their safe house where they met to discuss their plans. Maybe, it was where the American made contact with his associates in Texas. If they kept any records of their activities it was probably here. It was the perfect front. If he were to strike anywhere this would be the place to do it.

CHAPTER 39

▼

Thursday morning snapped open with a hint of winter to come. Eva was out the door by 6:45. After parking her car along *Hugelstrasse* down the street from the CRM's apartment, she crossed the street and slipped into the park through a side gate. The park, situated between two long rows of apartment buildings, had once been leased to the 5th Army Brigade, but after the fall of the wall in 1989 and the subsequent withdrawal of most American troops, it was returned back to the Germans. Far longer than it was wide, the spacious greens stretched for what seemed to be at least 2 km, with a cement path meandering through it, connecting several clusters of playgrounds where children climbed intricate rope mazes. Poplars and maples were also sprinkled about, providing shaded areas in the summer for family picnics or respites for lovers. But this morning there would be no shade, not for reason that the morning was young and crisp, but rather, because the leaves of the trees had just recently fallen. Once a jogger had passed, Eva found herself alone and took a seat on a bench near the playground closest to the apartment. In her bag was a three-page summary consisting of two photocopies of the articles that Ruben had obtained from the *Berliner MorganPost,* and a one-page synopsis drafted hastily by Shelly of Neil and Derrick's history in Berlin. She hoped the evidence, would be intimidating enough.

She checked her watch at 7:43. Tasha walked her dog in the park every morning and evening and with the delay Eva was growing impatient. Was it possible she had come too late?

Hiding just off to the side of one of the apartment buildings behind Eva, was Derrick, leaning up against the white plaster, eyeing her movements with suspicion. He woke long before Eva did and was waiting for her outside her home when she left that morning. Her conduct perturbed him. What could she hope to accomplish by sitting in the park across the street from their apartment? Tasha and Neil were both in the apartment and would not be leaving soon. Since the discovery of the bugs they'd been extra cautious, making sure at least one of them was in the apartment at all times. It might be a long morning. He waited. She waited. At 8:45 she stood up. He ran back to the BMW and followed her without incident around Frankfurt the rest of the day.

Friday morning bloomed as crisp as Thursday and Eva woke earlier and was out the door by 5:20. Traffic was non-existent. This morning Derrick had missed her. After checking Eva's house and not seeing her Opel he drove to Stace's place then the *backerei* She was nowhere in sight. He thought next of driving to the paper, but at the last moment decided on a hunch to return to the park. Driving along *Hugelstrasse* he spotted her car and her seated at the same bench as the morning before. Taking the next turn around, he parked and dashed to his previous hideout along side the apartment, taking a few moments to catch his breath. Huge rolls of steamed air billowed from his lungs dissipating into the brittle air. Once again, he knew neither Tasha nor Neil had plans to go anywhere that day. It might be another long day.

No sooner had the thought passed when he spotted Tasha setting that stupid little dog of hers down at the beginning of the walkway into the park. He looked quickly at Eva, who didn't seemed to have noticed, or was pretending to be inconspicuous. Pauli ran ahead of Tasha looking for just the right spot. Tasha followed her from a distance, walking as though she'd just awakened, oblivious to everything except the cold, hands shoved desperately into the pockets of her black wool coat. Derrick pushed himself off the building and moved to get a better view. It was obvious to him the two were there to meet, but Eva seemed hesitant to make contact and as far as he could tell Tasha still hadn't noticed her.

Tasha was now almost perpendicular to Eva, about fifty yards away, and Eva was well aware of her approach. Her plan was to wait until Tasha had passed and then creep up behind her. After a few moments Tasha walked so far that Eva could hardly make out the profile of her face. She rose quickly. Through the night the grass had gathered a thick, frosty crust. It crunched under her feet as she walked, leaving a trail of darkened green patches. When she reached the walkway Tasha suddenly stopped. Eva stopped too. Tasha bent over and picked up a branch that had fallen from a tree. Pauli had joined her and was hopping up and down on her hind legs waiting for Tasha to throw it. Eva watched Tasha lean back and heave the stick out into the center of the park. Pauli pranced after it, tiptoeing through the freezing grass as Tasha walked on down the sidewalk. Eva took advantage of the distraction and walked briskly up the path to catch up with her. Ten feet away she slowed, then settled into a pace along side her.

"Excuse me…Tasha?"

Tasha turned to her, shaken by the sound of the stranger's voice appearing out of nowhere.

"*Ja?*"

"Sorry I startled you."

"Do I know you?"

"No. We haven't met. My name is Eva Burtman," she said extending her hand out in Tasha's direction, who took hold of it cautiously. "I'm with the *Schwarz Monatlich.*"

Tasha halted and took a step back, dropping Eva's hand.

"What do you want?"

"Just a minute of your time," Eva said, looking as entreating as possible.

Tasha looked over Eva's shoulder towards her apartment then glanced around the park. "I don't have time. I have to get back."

The fine lines of Tasha's eyes swelled and her rich brown pupils grew sharp. They darted quickly about the park without stopping long enough to focus on anything. Then she turned around in the direction of her dog that was spinning in circles looking for the stick. It was the reaction Eva was hoping for. Fear might be unpredictable, but it can be manipulated. She looked like a frightened little child.

"It will only take a few minutes. I'm here to help. Let's take a walk." Eva gambled with the directive, but it worked.

"I really shouldn't be talking to you," Tasha said, then continued with a disjointed comment, "what makes you think I need help?"

Eva left her question unanswered. The dog had found the stick and was dragging it sideways up the path towards them. "She's cute, what's her name?"

Tasha pulled a short leash out of her pocket. When the dog approached and stood still, she snapped the hook on its collar. "Pauli."

Eva bent over and stroked Pauli on the back of her head, along her back and down the length of her tail. Pauli shifted towards Eva, tugging against the leash and feverishly wagging her tail. "I have a shepherd at home," Eva said, standing back up.

"Look I really need to get back," Tasha said, taking a step in the direction of her apartment.

"Wait!" Eva said, gently taking a hold of Tasha's coat. "I've had the last three days to think about what I was going to tell you when I finally met you, and I was hoping it might have gone a lot smoother than it has, so let me just come right out and say why I'm here. We have reason to believe that Derrick Sachs and Neil Usher were involved in at least two political assassinations back in the eighties."

Tasha looked at her with an expression mingled of disbelief and confusion. The leash she'd been holding popped out of her hands. Pauli took the cue and darted off towards a row of hedges nearby. "I don't believe you. Why are you telling me this?"

"They were part of an underground movement called the *Menschen*, a right wing extremist group. The authorities in Berlin tried to catch them for years, but were never successful."

Tasha stumbled a few steps backwards, driving her hands into her pockets. She turned a full circle then stopped to face Eva again. She glanced over Eva's shoulder in the direction of her apartment again. "I don't believe you."

Eva could see by her expression that Tasha had no clue of Neil and Derrick's past and if those details were hidden from her it was possible other things were being kept from her as well. "You really don't believe me do you? You have no idea about the kind of men you are living with do you?"

"Why are you telling me this?" Tasha asked a second time. Her terror seemed extraordinary to Eva, almost as if she was afraid of something much more than the information Eva had in her purse.

"Wait a minute," Tasha said suddenly, "you're from the paper right?"

"Yes." Eva replied calmly. Tasha's memory was fragmenting. She called for Pauli and started walking in the direction of her tinkling tags near the hedges.

"Wait Tasha!" Eva called after her.

"I don't want to listen to you," Tasha mumbled without turning around.

Eva decided to gamble. She was running out of options.

"Do you realize you could be connected with anything they may have done during the time you've lived with them?"

Tasha had reached the hedges and snatched Pauli up in her arms. Eva caught up with her. "We know the CRM is in the process of building a computer program. We don't know exactly what it's about, but we've got a hunch it's not good."

Tasha looked back at her apartment nervously, but the fear in her eyes seemed to be replaced by curiosity.

Eva continued. "We know the program is being built as we speak by a computer firm in the United States. We also know an organization called the International Christian Coalition is involved. We believe that Neil and Derrick are working with both of them and suspect they've been hired to take care of any problems that might arise by the implementation of the program...are you hearing me all right?"

"I don't know anything about any program."

Given the nature of Derrick and Neil's violent history and the political pursuits of the ICC, we believe this program to be highly dangerous. When we have enough evidence of this we'll be turning that information over to the *polizei*. Now, we know you've been working hand in hand with the CRM for years, so you'll be implicated along with them."

"But I don't know anything!" she burst out.

Eva knew she'd finally gotten Tasha's attention and looked sympathetically into her eyes. "Let's sit for a moment," she said, leading Tasha over to a nearby bench. When they took a seat Eva pulled out a white legal sized envelope, pulled out her information and laid it on Tasha's lap.

"This first article links Derrick to an arson investigation. No one could prove anything, but it's believed he burned down the city courthouse." She flipped the article over to the second page. "In this next article you'll find information about what the *Menschen* did in Berlin long before you met Neil and Derrick."

"You said assassinations!"

"I know. The original Editor of the *Berliner MorganPost* followed the developments of the *Menschen* throughout their history. He swears Derrick was personally responsible for the murder of Hans Lofter. He can't prove it. I can't prove it, but you've at least got to be suspicious."

Tasha was no longer looking at Eva. Her eyes were fixed in space and on a recent memory of Derrick.

"Tasha...you with me?"

"I heard you."

"Now this final page is a list of the details we know about them so far."

"How do I know you didn't just make all of this up?"

Eva didn't give Tasha anytime to read through the information. She folded the papers back up and shoved them into the envelope and handed it to Tasha. "You take this with you. There's nothing here those two aren't aware of, but I wouldn't tell them you have it."

She took the envelope and rammed it into the inner breast pocket of her coat.

"I could be wrong Tasha, but I don't think you're mixed up in all of this mess. Unfortunately, what I think's not important. The authorities will assume you're guilty of something. They're not going to believe you were totally oblivious to what's been going on."

Tasha jumped off the bench and turned towards Eva. "Why for Christ's' sake are you telling me all of this? What do you want from me? If you've got all the information you need then—"

"We don't have all the information we need," Eva confessed. "We'll get it one way or another, but we're running out of time. We have reason to believe the program's near completion. We'd like to stop it before that time, because after it's implemented it will be too late. I know this all sounds crazy to you right now, but you must have suspected something."

"Nothing. I told you. I know anything."

"Surely you must have heard or seen—"

"All I do is copy tapes. I put them into packages and send them out. I do a little of their computer work…some bookkeeping—that's all."

"We could really use your help. Without it, well, who knows? And unless you help us out…."

Tasha sat back down on the bench. Pauli was wandering aimlessly in the sand under the swing set nearby. Tasha was oblivious to her whereabouts, staring at a spot in the grass in front of her. She was quiet for a long time.

"I just don't know," she whispered finally. Eva watched the steam from her breath roll over the top of her head.

"We don't have much time," Eva said.

"I wouldn't even know where to start looking. I don't know what to look for. And if they caught me…" she mumbled pathetically, "if they catch me…." Suddenly she sat up and looked around for Pauli. Sighting her under a nearby tree she called to her in a barely audible tone. Pauli walked compliantly over to the bench and stood in front of her. Tasha bent over and stroked Pauli on the head. Pauli looked up into her face and wagged her tail. Tasha smiled tensely as though she'd just discovered some irony in life.

"Look I really need to get back now," she said.

Eva sighed. "All right," she said, then reached into her wallet and pulled out a business card and handed it to her. It was a long fifteen seconds or so before Tasha took it out of her hand. "I have two numbers. This one is for the office and the other is my cell number. Call my cell first and if I don't answer leave a message or a number where I can reach you. I'll call you right back. I promise."

Tasha stood up and started back towards the apartment without saying a word.

Derrick witnessed the encounter between her and Eva with a keen sense of indignation boiling in his bones. He'd told Neil the woman couldn't be trusted and now he had verification of that fact. Would Neil believe him? He had to believe him. He thought the exchange between the two as just one of many, and he wondered how long the two had been working together. Was it possible Tasha had been deceiving them all along? Anything seemed possible now. Everything was in jeopardy. Feeling oppressed from every direction, he knew from past experience there was only one way to stop the oppression, and that was, to stop the oppressors.

With steam snorting out of his mouth and nostrils he watched Tasha walk towards the apartment and when he was sure Eva had left, he headed across the street. When he entered the apartment and slammed the door shut, Tasha had not yet made it to her bedroom. Neil was sitting at the table reading the paper and drinking a cup of coffee when he heard the slam and saw Derrick whizzing by the table. He dropped the paper and leaped to intersect him.

Seizing her by the shoulder, Derrick spun Tasha around and thrust his hand into the breast pocket of her coat for the envelope. Tasha wrapped her arms around her breasts.

"What's going on?" Neil demanded.

Derrick pulled his hand out of her coat and took a step backwards. She fell against the wall in an attempt to get as far away from him as possible.

"Why don't you ask her?"

Neil looked a Derrick, then Tasha. It seemed a repeat of an earlier confrontation and he was getting tired of the pattern. "What's this about?" He flipped on the hallway light and it lit up Tasha's horror stricken face. She couldn't speak.

"Ask her about the information she has in her coat pocket she just got from Eva Burtman in the park."

Neil gazed at her in disbelief.

"Go ahead. Ask her how long they've been meeting in the park across the street. How many months Tasha? How many years?"

She was still backed against the wall clutching her coat.

"Is that true?" Neil asked her.

Her eyes twitched between the two. She was without answers and full of questions. She didn't know where to begin, or when it would all end.

"Let me see what you have," Neil demanded.

Without hesitation she reached into her pocket, pulled the envelope out and laid it in Neil's outstretched hand. She managed to utter a few words. "I swear to God, Neil, I don't know what's in there. I...I was walking Pauli and she came up to me. I've never seen her before in my life—"

Neil stopped her rambling with an uplifted hand. He pulled the hand back out of her face and with one continuous motion flipped open the triangular flap of the envelope and pulled out its contents. Derrick took a step in his direction and the two stood side by side examining the first page.

Tasha checked their reaction. Neil remained calm and passionless. Balls of muscle twitched in Derrick's cheeks. Neil flipped over to the second article, then giving it only a few seconds flipped to the last page. It was obvious to her they were acquainted with the contents. On the third page Derrick shuffled in closer and Neil tipped the page in his direction. Neil finished scanning it before Derrick and looked at Tasha.

"Seems you know everything now doesn't it?"

Derrick finished reading and joined Neil in staring her down. Her tongue felt swollen and lodged in her throat.

"And that presents us with a serious dilemma," Neil continued.

Tasha's fear forced her tongue loose. "I'll leave. I'll pack my things right now and I'll go. You've got to believe me, I don't know anything and I don't want to know anything. You'll never see me again. I promise." She spoke deliberately and with determination, but her actions testified to her lack of courage. She couldn't move, partly for fear they would stop her, so she just waited, hoping they'd agree to her arrangement.

"I'm afraid that's impossible now," she watched Neil say, and coming from him she knew the decision was final.

"You see Tasha, you don't know everything, but everyone seems to think you do, which means of course, you're with us whether you like it or not."

Derrick looked crossways at Neil. "Are you crazy?" he thought to himself, but didn't say a word.

"Not that you'll find anything here you might be able to use against us," Neil continued. "We've kept you out of this from the beginning. These articles mean nothing! old news! past history!" he yelled, flipping the articles about in front of her face. She turned sideways avoiding has taunts. "Everything important is up here," he said, rapping the papers against his head.

"You can't keep me here!" She blurted out.

"Miss, you have know idea what we can do." Derrick yelled back. She didn't dare imagine what he meant.

"You're right of course. We can't force you to stay. In fact, you're free to go right now if you like." Neil took a step backwards.

Derrick remained in place and glanced at him with a look of profound bewilderment. "What the hell are you thinking about Neil?"

Neil turned decisively towards him and snapped, "she knows nothing Derrick!

He walked back into the dining room and tossed the papers on the table near his cold cup of coffee. Derrick followed.

"We can't let her stay Neil! And we sure as hell can't let her leave either."

"So what do you want to do Derrick?" He took a seat at the table in front of his paper, arms folded in a tense sort of way and waited for Derrick to respond.

"Well?"

Derrick said nothing. Tasha had slithered on her feet to her door and took hold of the handle. She cracked it open, but waited…listening.

"This isn't the 80's and we're not in Berlin Derrick."

Derrick stood on the opposite side of the dinning room table facing him. He wanted to say something but held his breath instead. "The stakes are higher. I thought I'd made that point," he said finally, with force.

"And we are a hell of a lot smarter now aren't we?"

Derrick clenched his teeth. Muscles popped.

"Well, aren't we?"

Still silence and his expression hadn't changed. Neil grew concerned. He leaned across the edge of the table and palmed his hands on the open newspaper that crinkled in his grip. "Look. We were extremely lucky back then and that kind of luck doesn't last long." He dropped his voice to a near whisper. "We are both lucky we're sitting here and not rotting away in some German prison."

"Luck has nothing to do with it."

"Luck has everything to do with," Neil replied, raising his voice up a couple of notches. "What do you call it then?"

"Providence."

"Providence?" Neil blurted out then dropped his voice again. "You call killing people and getting away with it providence?"

"Yes I am. We did it for the cause, for what we believed in and we won didn't we?"

"We were young and stupid Derrick and lucky enough to have gotten away with it. They came damn close to getting us on the second one, and lucky for us they didn't have a clue about the third."

Derrick's expression grew from frustration to one of painful desperation. "I thought you believed in what we did!"

Neil raised his voice along with Derrick. "I did."

"And now?"

"Now is different. I'd like to believe we've learned from the past."

"Now is *not* different. Nothing has changed except the level of intensity. We're still fighting for the same things. We did what we had to do then and we succeeded and survived. Now the objective is much more defined and it seems to me our actions should match the importance of the objective."

Neil leaned back in the dining room chair and folded his arms across his chest, searching for a reason to believe what Derrick was saying. He looked at him as though the longer he looked the clearer the solution to their problem might be and got lost in the magnitude of the moment.

Derrick walked over to the dinning room window and peered outside. The morning had cleared, but a storm was brewing in his soul. He turned and walked to the edge of the hallway. Tasha was still standing in front of her door. He knew she'd been listening and what they were about to discuss she could not hear.

Her eyes met his. In the four years she'd known Derrick she'd never seen him wear such a compassionless face. Neither hate nor love was in his eyes, or any resemblance they had shared in any friendship whatsoever. She would have rather seen his anger. She would have preferred some verbal abuse or even another physical assault. That would have at least been conclusive. What she saw in his eyes was something far more disturbing than anything she might have imagined, and she backed into her room to escape them.

After hearing her door shut firmly, Derrick returned to his spot across the table from Neil and took a seat.

"She needs to go doesn't she?" Neil asked Derrick in a sudden switch of authority. He was not looking for an answer. He was looking for the courage to do what he knew had to be done.

Derrick leaned over the table so that he was only a few feet away from Neil and whispered his next words. "She not only has to go, but she has to disappear Neil."

Neil's fingers began to twitch. He lifted his arms off the paper, folded his hands, and set his chin on his fingers.

Derrick continued, "and since we've been forced into this situation we also need to keep in mind the situation with the *backerei*."

Neil was unresponsive, but Derrick could sense his mind was at least turning in the right direction. "We have to nip this in the bud Neil."

"I know! I know," Neil spoke up, coming to life.

"Then we're agreed?"

CHAPTER 40

▼

If the first call from Neil to Stautzen in Austin regarding the discovery of the audio devices in the CRM's apartment had given Stautzen a scare, the second call from Neil revealing a possible leak about the program to the European press by Tasha was more than his feeble mind could handle. He called Pruitt immediately.

"I can understand your concern, but relax," Pruitt said. "We expected some problems." Pruitt was in his bed and his wife was stirring beside him.

Stautzen thought Pruitt didn't sound half as concerned as he should be. "We need to meet."

"When?"

"Now."

"All right. There's a Dunkin Donuts just off of Research between Mopac and the Arboretum. Know where it's at?"

"Not exactly."

"You can't miss it. Exit at the Arboretum and take the turn around. I'll meet you there at 9:00."

"What about Fred Watson."

"I'll hear what you have to say and if I think he needs to know then I'll talk with him."

Pruitt waited a moment over a short pause.

"Ok," Stautzen agreed.

Pruitt hung up the phone and looked at the alarm clock on the nightstand. 7:45. "Christ," he mumbled and crawled out of his bed.

"You going somewhere?" his wife asked.

"I have to, but it won't take long."

By 8:50 Stautzen had finished two cups of coffee when Pruitt's Jaguar pulled up between two pickup trucks in the dinky parking lot. Pruitt came inside, acknowledged Stautzen who sat in the farthest booth in the corner, but got a cup of coffee and a dozen donuts before joining him. He sat down and opened the box up.

"Care for one?" he asked.

"Not hungry."

Pruitt took out a glazed donut, swallowed nearly half of it and resealed the box to take home. Stautzen waited for him to wipe the frosting from the corner of his mouth.

"I wouldn't worry about it. Like I said on the phone this morning, we expected something like this to happen and we've taken all the necessary precautions."

Stautzen filled him in on his conversation with Neil and asked, "just how are you going to prevent an investigative paper from finding out about a program of this magnitude?"

"We're not."

Stautzen sighed in frustration and leaned back against the hard bright orange bench.

Pruitt finished the donut and slid it down his throat with a sip of coffee. "You don't seem to remember the dynamics of the program."

"Then refresh my memory. Tell me why I don't need to worry."

Stautzen's unnecessary excitability rattled him. "Very well, but first you tell me how you think the program is going to be implemented. Then I'll tell you if you've left anything out."

Stautzen crossed his arms in front of him and looked out the window. He watched as a man with a black cowboy hat steered a muddied and stretched 4X4 pickup, with huge tires and a massive grill guard, out of one of the slots. He didn't want to play Pruitt's game, but did anyway.

"Very well. Your team develops the program based on the objectives of the ICC. As I understand it, there will be some flexibility to the program. That is, it will be designed so the ICC will be able to use it as a tool in their evangelism. As the needs of the ICC change and the intensity of the messages has to be adjusted, the program will allow for that."

"That's correct. The program is going to be undoubtedly, the most psychologically manipulative program ever created. It's limited of course, in that it's designed to work though the Internet, but what the hell? By the last current estimates nearly one forth of the world's population accesses it." Pruitt eased out a smile of satisfaction. "Your production and publication avenues have the potential to reach most of the rest of the modern world. So that covers just about everyone. When we're though with it you'll be able to program short or instructional phrases into the program. Depending on how persuasive you make those messages and how well they fit into the ICC's combined evangelistic thrust, will determine the outcome."

"And all we have to do is plug in a few key phrases?" Stautzen asked skeptically.

"Exactly. Listen…it's designed to work in conjunction with your current evangelistic capabilities. It's not going to do everything for you."

"But will it be effective?"

"Oh, it will be effective." Pruitt leaned across the table towards him. "Think of it as an advertising tool but fifty times more efficient. You'll have thousands of converts crawling out of the woodwork to go anywhere the ICC wishes to lead them and they won't have the slightest idea why they're suddenly so interested in Christianity. They'll be tuning into your satellite broadcasts, Reverend Eisner's books will be sell-outs all over the world, people will be flocking to your services in Munich, and let's not forget those donations, The ICC will be generating revenue faster than it can spend it."

Stautzen leaned into the booth with greedy expectancy, his fears enjoying a short reprieve. "I guess what I'm really concerned about is the ability of the program to be traced. Now we've got the paper snooping around and also a certain American who seems to be working with the paper in their investigation."

"An American? Why haven't you told me this before?"

"I'm telling you about him now. I just found out about him a few days ago."

"Your people don't know what he's up to?"

"No."

"What's his name?"

"Don't know that either. We're concerned he might be working along with someone on the team."

"Impossible. None of them have any connection to ICC and they've only known about the program for the short time we've been working on it."

"What about Rick Forstein?"

Pruitt settled into his seat and gave the suggestion some thought. "I've known Rick going on four years now. He's a company man. He's had even less time to know about the program than the others. How long has the paper and the American been working together in their investigation?"

"That's uncertain. Neil Usher only stumbled across him a few weeks ago."

Pruitt took a serious look at Stautzen and sucked in a mouthful of air. The bottom edge of his paper coffee cup spun on the table between his fingers. "You haven't told me everything have you?"

Stautzen looked out the window considering the question. A burgundy colored Chevy Caprice pulled up into the slot left by the pickup. "The ICC's a big organization Pruitt. Its ministry stretches around the globe. It uses other people's money to fund its evangelism and programs and because of this from time to time it has been the object of careful examination. You name them, we've been looked at with some degree of scrutiny by dozens of private and governmental organizations."

"Well there you go! This could be just another group looking into your activities, but what about Neil's group?"

"There might be something there."

"Is it possible that the paper, with the help of the American of course, might be looking into Neil's group?" Pruitt looked for the expression in Stautzen's face that would give him an indication he might be right. Uncertainty lurked in the cavities of Stautzen's eyes. "Or is it possible the paper is doing a joint investigation of the ICC and his group?" Still uncertainty. "Am I safe in assuming there's an investigation going on by the paper which also involves Trojan Security?"

"All of the above. We don't know what to think yet, but we're taking care of it."

"I certainly hope so for your sake."

Pruitt reopened the box and took out another glazed donut. He took a bite and set it on a napkin. "More coffee? he asked Stautzen before sliding out of the booth.

Stautzen looked at him quizzically, "No."

Pruitt walked over to the coffee machine, filled his cup and walked back to the booth. He sat down and took a few more bites of his donut, then opened two packs of sugar and slowly swirled them around in the cup. Stautzen waited in aggravation.

Pruitt looked up at him and spoke as though he knew what was on his mind. "There are two reasons why I'm *not* concerned with this investigation. First of all, Trojan Security is prepared to defuse any criticism of the program no matter who that criticism may come from. We've spent more time considering how we might be able to cover ourselves than we're spending on the actual program. Mr. Watson in particular has been running this around in his head for several years now. So we're covered. Secondly, I'm really not alarmed about any ghosts in Neil's closet or in the closets of the ICC for that matter. I suspect if you've been able to stave off the wolves for this long then all of you should be able to handle the pressure of using the program. Mr. Watson of course, might be concerned if the ICC suffers any loss to its impeccable reputation, but frankly, what you folks do with the program after we create it will be entirely up to you. It will be in your hands."

"Aren't you worried the paper might make a connection between Trojan Security and the ICC, or even Neil's group?"

"No, because there already is a connection remember? Trojan Security is building a security program, plain and simple. That's what we do. As far as the members of the team are concerned they believe they're building a security program and nothing more. The fact that we might use real life scenarios to build the program, such as building the program around the purposes of the ICC makes no difference legally."

"So what happens after the program is put to use and the paper finds out about it?"

"Again, you don't understand the dynamics of the program," Pruitt said bluntly. "It will not be detectable once it's inserted into the system. With only a few simple instructions the program can be sent to its intended destinations though any phone booth located on any street corner in the world. Once it has been unleashed into the Internet, manipulating the program, such as changing the on-screen messages, will take only a few additional key strokes. Now, the responsibility of how the system is used should fall under one person to minimize the risk. I understood you're going to be that man."

"That hasn't been determined yet," Stautzen said, suddenly realizing he didn't want to carry the ball. "Just for the sake of hypothesis, what if I, or the person who's responsible for implementing the program gets caught before they're able to get it into the system? Surely they'll be able to make the connection then."

"Perhaps, but we've already thought that through."

"You have?"

"Don't underestimate us."

"So how are you going to get around this?"

Pruitt took a sip of his coffee and hesitated. This was information he couldn't reveal, discussed at length between he and Mr. Watson exclusively. It was to be their own method of escape should any part of the program be compromised. Stautzen's current emotional fortitude notwithstanding, there was no way Pruitt was going to reveal the information to him.

Both Pruitt and Watson knew the possibility existed that at some point the program might fall into the wrong hands. If that happened, their defense would be someone copied and stole the program without their knowledge. It was a simple alibi really, but one which provided a lot of suspects and possibilities. They had worked out an elaborate structure of exactly where the blame for the breach could be put. First on their list would be the program's lead designer, Rick Forstein. He would be the most likely candidate, since he knows all the intricate details of the program. Pruitt himself had created a detailed plan to ensure the authorities would be led directly to him. Second on their list was Jean Thompson. Her distinguished military history had given her ample time to brush up against many individuals in both reputable and disreputable positions of power, such as people with large sums of money who would pay to have the program in their arsenal. The more irrefutable the better, it would keep the authorities sidetracked for years. Third on their list were other inconsequential participants like Dr. Loran and the others on the team, who were all substantially paid for their expertise. The last fall-guy on their list was Stautzen himself. The likelihood of him stealing the program for his own purposes would be unquestionable. He consulted in the creation of the program and had been instrumental in focusing the overall design of the program to the goals of the ICC. After seeing the potential of the program to increase converts, after realizing the potential of new converts to increase their donation base, after recognizing the program would greatly extend the global and political influences of the ICC; Stautzen could be viewed as the one who stole and implemented the program to increase his own position and power. As if that weren't enough, and to clear any doubt Trojan Security had intended to use the program for any means other than as a security program, they would proceed in the creation of the actual security program. Building security programs was after all, what they did. Pruitt could think of a thousand reasons for delaying the progression of that aspect of the program, effectively stalling its creation for years.

"You still haven't answered my question," Stautzen asked when no response from Pruitt was forthcoming. "How are you going to get around it when they find out about the severity of the program and start questioning people?"

"What you must remember is that this program is a gift from Mr. Watson personally to the ICC. He stands to gain zero out of the venture. Therefore, what occurs with the program in-between the time we build the secondary security program is out of our hands. All of the risk will be in your hands and the ICC. Not to mention any other people you choose to involve."

Pruitt checked for Stautzen's reaction. It was obvious his response had shaken something lose in him. "You knew from the start you would be the one to hand carry the program back to Germany. When you leave here you will be one of only three individuals who know how to operate the program. Whether or not you choose to pass that responsibility onto someone else is up to you."

"Wait a minute…how'd we get down to three individuals? What about the others?"

"No one except you, Rick and Jean will know exactly how to run the program. That's for security reasons. The program will come with other security measures dealing specifically with how to first access and initiate the program. The security measures are designed to allow only four people to run the program. You and the others, then a forth person to give you an option of choosing another person."

"Why not the others?"

"Believe me, you don't want anyone else to know how to operate it."

"What about you?"

"Neither I or Fred Watson will know how to run the program."

Stautzen leaned back in his seat again, lifted his cup of coffee to his lips and drank in the last cold dregs. Pruitt finished his donut and coffee and gave him time to think. He waited for any additional questions to arise, but Stautzen seemed to be satisfied at the moment. If Pruitt didn't know any better, it seemed as if Stautzen actually liked the idea of being the only one in Germany who would know how to run the program. He looked down at his watch poking though the sleeve of his sweater then back to Stautzen. "If you don't have anymore questions I'm going to take off. Family day you know...."

"Yeah, sure," Stautzen replied drifting off into thought.

CHAPTER 41

▼

Had it not been for the late President Johnson the town would have remained just a hick of place, worthy of only a black dot on the state map of Texas. Since Johnson's reign, however, they'd changed the name of the place to Johnson City and had been milking the name for dollars ever since. There was his boyhood home, the ranch, and the sprawling country park established in honor of him just outside of town. These three tourist attractions kept the town afloat, for it was not yet large enough for a McDonald's to root.

Rick downshifted into third and Jean was looking over his shoulder at the Dairy Queen passing by. A mile up the road he took a left and they headed down main-street. Just a couple blocks up the road was a quaint roadside park. He pulled onto the side street next to it and cranked down the top of his Miata. Typically Texas, the weather had been cool last week, would be warm for a few more days, then would turn cold again next week. Today was glorious. Once back on the road, he took another left where a bronze colored Texas recreational sign pointed the way to President Johnson's boyhood home in white reflective letters. The Miata drifted along at a comfortable 35 mph under yellowing pecan trees and decade old homes splashed in white, nearly all of them set back in shaded grassy yards surrounded by waist-high picket fences. What set President Johnson's home apart from the others was location. It had a block of town all to itself. It was just as tiny as all the other homes built during the same period, but more adequately maintained with visitation fees, and every half hour a tour was conducted of the inner home by polished and articulate National Park representatives, who rotated tours. Rick and Jean were early for the next tour, so they took a stroll around the home examining the aspects of the small estate.

There was nothing special about the house itself, but somehow the memory of the boy who once lived there brought significance to its commonness. The whitewash on the side...had the President once painted it? The lilac bush at the corner of the house in the back...did he hide his toys under it? Adjacent to the house was a rectangle garden wrapped in a low fence to keep the deer and rabbits out. Rows of cool weather vegetables were still growing in it like peas, radishes, lettuce and tomatoes. Surely he must have broken a sweat digging up weeds in it? Nearby, was an outhouse that hadn't been used in decades. Tourists now used the modern facilities just across the yard. Naturally, there was a barn and a few smaller buildings wrapped in fencing for livestock. Beyond the barn stretched a wooden windmill stretching halfway up into the trees. The water pump below it was still active. Aside from these features the rest of the grounds consisted of smooth green grass growing under the ever-present pecan trees, Texas Ash trees that had already lost their leaves, and a few scattered scrub oaks holding tenaciously onto their dead brown leaves. The state had gone to some length to make the estate appear as it might have during the time the President had lived there.

They had spoken little during the hour-long drive up from Austin. In the back of their minds both of them were aware their time together would be coming to an end. They'd been working side by side on the project for weeks now, flirting with the possibilities of sharing an intimate moment with each other. The pressure of that moment had reached its peak.

It happened before he knew it. He'd thought of doing it many times before but hadn't, and perhaps by some subconscious imperative in which the body responds to an unspoken desire, he reached out and took Jean's hand. He didn't dare look into her face, but sought her reaction to his gesture in the slight impulses of her hand and within a moment after taking it felt her fingers curl around his palm. Her grip was slight, disclosing a mutual and reciprocating affection. She didn't look at him either, instead, she let her eyes chase the leaves rolling along the grass.

He'd fought for weeks to avoid the contact, but now he felt powerless to resist his own desires, which to him seemed sinister and all the more exciting. At home, his wife Julie would be doing what she normally did on Sundays, light housework, perhaps running a few errands, or spending time with their daughter. Under normal circumstances he would have been right there with them, sharing and tending to the insignificant details of life, but still enjoying their moments together. He rather liked the kind of marital chastisement some men might find oppressive. And for the most part, he and Julie had enjoyed a life which up to this point was like a glassed over Texas lake, serene and peaceful. Little did he realize somewhere lurking in the coves there existed a suffocating stagnation, threatening to ripple the entire surface of their marriage. Which is why his attraction to Jean was so disturbing, for it was loaded with potentially disastrous ramifications, yet at the same time brilliant with new expectations, similar to the emerging sun at sunrise warming the heart with the promise of new beginnings.

Jean knew full well the hand that had taken hers would be the same hand that would caress the contours of her face in one significant expression of good-bye. As a woman who followed the path of career, affection had often come in the form comings and goings. When she was young, she'd resented the limitations of such affections. As she matured she'd learned to accept them as reality. Now, with age looming around the corner, she'd adjusted to their ebb and flow like the life cycle of a perennial wild flower, which blooms in glory during the spring and dies in vain with the coming of winter. She'd never experienced commitment from a man and thus took affection wherever she could find it, regardless of circumstances. She knew Rick was married and knew he would never leave his wife, but that didn't stop her from cherishing the moment. She had used all of her powers to lure and seduce him. She would take whatever affection from him she could seize. In the end, she would move on just like all the other times in her life and try to forget.

After the tour of the Johnson's boyhood home, they drove another forty minutes into the town of Fredericksburg. Here, Admiral Nimitz, a once brilliant commander had been born in a shack across the street from the modern museum now bearing his memorabilia. They drove into the heart of town by way of Main Street, lined with century old buildings remodeled into quaint, German-style shops and restaurants. Rick pulled into a slanted parking space in front of a Dulcimer shop. They spent the rest of the morning walking hand in hand over the bricked sidewalks window-shopping. There were candle shops filled with neat rows of curling candle castles sitting on polished glass shelves. There were a variety of arts and craft stores, each one divided up into neat cubicles stuffed with homemade dolls, ceramics and wooden thingamajigs. Ice cream pallor's, bakeries, and bookstores were frequent. Art galleries popped up about every fifth store. They spent a few minutes sampling Texas wines in a wine tasting room and left with a bottle of Chardonnay, feeling silly, and looking for the best German restaurant they could find. After lunch they headed out of town. Rick took a right a mile down the road and pulled into the parking lot of the Peach Tree Bed and Breakfast.

He killed the engine and squinted out the windshield. Unlike how he reached out and took Jean's hand earlier in the day, this move had been planned, though not discussed, so he sat quietly for a few moments listening to the sound of passing cars behind him. A minute passed and he'd heard no objections from Jean, so he turned to her with a rather serious but playful look and said, "Wait here, I'll see if they have any rooms."

Five minutes later he came out of the office and drove around the back to room seven on the bottom floor. He hopped out of the car before her, as she sat patiently waiting for him to open her door. Without a word spoken he led her into the room buzzing with the sound of the air-conditioner in the window.

No sooner had they entered the motel room, when a white four door Chrysler belonging to the Trojan Security Corporation pulled to the far end of the building, turned around, and backed underneath the skimpy shade of a giant 200 year old scrub oak with a good view of door number seven.

CHAPTER 42

▼

Tasha didn't venture out of her room for the rest of the day. That suited Derrick just fine, since it would be easier to watch her. When she finally did come out, shortly after the sun set on Saturday evening to walk her dog, Derrick went with her. He followed her from a distance into the park, sat at a bench until Pauli had taken care of business, then followed them back to the apartment. She stayed in her room the rest of the night.

Tasha had never gotten the chance to read through the information Eva had given her, but whatever it contained she concluded to substantiate Eva's words. She feared for her life. They would not let her stay indefinitely. They would not let her go. So whether she stayed or went they were sure to haunt her, and if what Eva had told her was true, they would do more than just haunt her.... She fought sleep with her light on, pacing the floor at times, looking out her window, rummaging through her things, packing then unpacking—anything just to keep moving. She'd locked her door, but that wouldn't stop Derrick from entering. At 1:10 a.m. she cracked her door open and discovered the apartment in darkness. She'd not eaten all day nor had Pauli. The door to Derrick's room was open and no doubt he was awake and lying on his bed listening for her. She closed the door.

By 5:00 in the morning she was desperate with hunger. Still, she remained in her room. At 7:45 Derrick and Neil were awake and whispering in the kitchen. Pauli had been standing at the door of her room for the past hour waiting for her walk.

"I don't trust her Neil. For all we know she could have planted more bugs," Derrick whispered. "Just to be on the safe side you should use an outside line if you have to make any more calls."

"I need to take off for a few hours. Watch her." Neil said.

Without hesitation Tasha threw on her coat and hooked Pauli's leash. She would not be left alone in the apartment with Derrick. She grabbed her wallet and shoved it into her coat pocket. They were standing at the end of the hall when she came rushing out of her room and darted between them.

"Where do you think you're going?" Neil asked.

"Where does it look like I'm going?" she asked, holding up the end of Pauli's leash.

Derrick followed her as she descended the stairs.

She walked along the path into the heart of the park and didn't look back. At a playground in the center of the park she sat down on a bench in front of an enormous contraption with triangular ropes knotted together into a huge maze that looked like a giant spiders web. She felt safe here. Two children were already stuck in the web like frantic bugs. A woman holding a baby was sitting on a nearby bench nursing her baby. Behind her boys were picking teams for an impromptu soccer game. She turned and saw Derrick behind her, met his gaze and turned away.

By 11:00 the sun had melted the frost on the grass into sparking drops saturating the ground. Tasha could no longer see the steam in her breath. Pauli had been running around all morning and now lay curled up beneath her feet. The boy's soccer game was in full swing, the maze was crawling with children and the benches around her had filled with parents. The tension in her stomach and mind were mounting. She felt dizzy for lack of food and recalled there was a convenience store near the *U-Bahn* station down the street. She looked towards Derrick. He was no longer seated on the bench. She found him propped against a tree in the far corner of the park near the street. "I must look repulsive," she thought. She'd thrown her coat over yesterday's clothes and hadn't combed her hair since…well, she couldn't remember. She reached up and patted it into some kind of order and wiped the sleep from her eyes. Rolling her tongue over her teeth she wished she had a toothbrush. After snapping the leash on Pauli's collar she stood up awkwardly. Not having moved for a few hours, the cold had stiffened her limbs and her leg had fallen asleep. It tingled in pain and for a few moments was utterly useless. She took a few steps forward and looked around. No one seemed to notice her except Derrick, taking a few steps away from the tree. At that point she could care less about him. She pretended to head back towards the apartment, but at the last moment turned on the sidewalk and headed for the corner store.

At the entrance to the store she grabbed two apples out of box and set them in a basket she took from a stand near one of the registers. She was grateful the store was nearly empty. The cashier was too busy to notice her. She was dealing with two children who had just laid out a handful of assorted candies on the counter and were counting their change. She picked out a half-pint cup of drinkable yogurt and a tin of spreadable cheese. On another isle she grabbed a box of crackers. Passing a refrigerator with tall glass doors she spotted an assortment of juices and soft drinks and snatched out a liter of orange juice. She was hoping to find a treat for Pauli, but the store had none. There was some canned dog food, but she'd have to go back to the apartment to get an opener. She walked towards the refrigerator and found a package of sausage. After paying she headed to the park. While crossing the street Pauli's leash got caught up in the plastic bag and knocked one of her apples out. It landed on the sidewalk with a *thump* and rolled out into the street. An Audi flew by and squished it under its front wheel, plastering the curb with green chunks. "Shit!" A cluster of kids giggled behind her.

In the park she took a bench underneath a group of stripped poplar trees and ripped open the box of crackers and dipped one into the container of cheese. The cheese was cold and hard and the cracker so brittle it snapped in half, leaving her to pluck it back out of the cheese. With fingers covered in crumbs she opened the yogurt and chugged it down. Half satisfied, she looked at Pauli sitting on her hind legs in front of her wrapping her long pink tongue around her muzzle over and over.

"Sorry girl."

Reaching into the bag she pulled out the sausage and ripped a slit in the clear plastic bag with her teeth, then squeezed a link out. Pauli danced on her hind legs and snatched it out of Tasha's hand swallowing it whole.

She looked over he shoulder and found that Derrick had plopped himself down on a bench. In a few short weeks she had learned to despise the man. They'd never been close. He'd always seemed untouchable and obscure and now she knew why. She shuddered in the thought she'd lived with the stranger for so long. Glancing in the direction of the apartment she guessed Neil had finished what he needed to do and was probably back at the apartment and working on another sermon. Her mind flashed back to a few nights back when she so foolishly opened herself up to him. She had never felt so naked in her life. The deception chilled her to the bone.

And she could not find God anywhere. She watched the children crawl through the webs of the maze in the distance. They giggled and laughed and chased each other over the mesh. He was not there. A little boy was juggling a soccer ball past a swarm of boys on the opposite team towards a goal. God was not there either. A woman was pushing a stroller with her infant wrapped snugly in blankets protected from the cold. A soft breeze was blowing through the poplar branches high above her head. The sun was warm and bright. The heavens were endless. Clouds rolled across the sky like puffs of cotton balls whipped in a deep blue sauce. Everything around her seemed to breath life; to everything there seemed a purpose—except for her.

What she knew about God was what Neil had told her. His God was exacting and demanding of the utmost in discipline and dedication; a God of rewards and punishments, who forgave, but would never forget. His kingdom would consist of those who followed his preachers to the letter. There was an acute sense of order to Neil's vision of God. She'd latched onto that vision, which gave her life purpose and meaning. It was the only version of God she had known and she'd worked side by side with Neil and Derrick living that vision out in her own life and now, through no fault of her own, she was suddenly swept into the world of darkness. She could think of only two explanations for the change; either God was not of the character to which Neil described Him, or there was no God.

She traveled back into her mind looking for the point of deception, looking for the exact moment she felt the courage to believe and the ignorance in which to follow. What she was hoping to find was a significant spiritual event that would let her continue to believe God was still with her, some point where she could legitimately claim God had breached the dimension of reality to lead her in the right direction. The search was hopeless. What she knew about God was nothing more than a series of ill-interpreted circumstances…nothing more than everyday events that had been glorified to the point of mysticism.

Who could she blame for such a deception? She'd followed God to the best of her ability, but He had let her down. Had she not done everything right? And if everything was so wrong now, why wasn't God telling her what to do now? It seemed far easier to simply blame herself, or at least question that she'd ever done things right. If she'd never done things right, then perhaps she was just an idiot…just one of the un-savable…the non-chosen ones. What a fool she'd been to have ever hoped God cared enough about her to keep her safe and protected! Surely, if He *was* alive, He would at least had the courtesy to correct her actions, or the decency to tell her she wasn't chosen in the first place! But He kept his mouth shut.

Her outlook turned from shadows to universal blackness. If God was the kind of God Neil said He was, then she wanted nothing to do with Him. If He was the God of rewards she'd been told He was, but rewarded her in this pitiful manner, then she would rather make her own mistakes. She would rather do what she thought was right and screw up without Him. It would be easier that way. For above all she was still scarred to death of meeting Him one day and when that time came she'd rather not be pissed off at Him. Somehow it was easier to just believe He existed, but didn't really care about people. That way she could still acknowledge that He had the authority to do whatever He wanted and in the end she could still bow down to Him with a flimsy excuse like, "Oh well. I tried, and I never heard a peep out of you anyway...."

Whether she knew it or not, she had a decision to make and the choice she was making was to never be the victim again. She would help Eva if she could. If there was any information in the apartment she would find it. She would do anything to right the injustice of what Neil and Derrick had done to her. She would be free of them one way or another, even if she died trying.

Sunday evening drifted into the night leaving no opportunity for Tasha to do what she needed to do. Derrick was watching her every move. He posted himself in the living room and watched television until 2:30 in the morning. Neil had busied himself at the kitchen table then retired to his room at about midnight. She spent the evening in her room trying to stay awake with Pauli. She knew if she was going to find anything it would be in Neil's room. Sometime after 3:00 she fell asleep on her bed and jumped to the sound of scratching on her bedroom door shortly after 7:00. Pauli needed her walk. She jumped out of bed and cracked her door open. The dining room light was on and the local news was pouring out of the television in the living room. She combed her hair and threw on her coat. Derrick was asleep on the couch as she passed by and Neil was in the kitchen fixing breakfast. She slipped out the door and walked Pauli downstairs. Before she reached the bottom flight of stairs she heard the apartment door open behind her and knew it was Derrick. After walking Pauli in the park she came right back.

After a shower she reached the conclusion she'd be better off assuming the posture they expected her to take. It would be the only way to keep them off her back and maintain her dignity as well, for she would not cower around the house like a frightened little animal any more. She would eat breakfast, feed her dog, and begin working like she'd done for the past three years. If they stopped her, she would decide what to do from then. When she came out of her room she discovered Derrick was gone and Neil was busy working in his room. She made herself breakfast and started a fresh pot of coffee. Halfway though her eggs and toast she heard Neil's footsteps down the hall and looked up towards him with the most stoic face she could muster. He sat down across from her at the table and was the first to speak.

"Derrick and I have decided you'll stay for a while."

She took a sip of her coffee then looked up at him. "Why? So you can keep watching me?"

He was taken back by her resolve, but not intimidated. "Yes."

"And whose idea was it really?"

"It was my decision."

"So I suppose I should thank you then."

"We are not the enemy Tasha."

"And neither am I. I've done nothing wrong and you're treating me like a prisoner." She took her plate into the kitchen to get away from him.

He got up and followed her. "You're not a prisoner. You're free to go anytime you like."

"That's reassuring. You know I have nowhere to go. Besides, you and Derrick just want to make it easier on yourselves. The closer I am the better you can watch me."

"Derrick doesn't trust you."

"And you do?"

He remained silent, thus speaking his mind.

She swung around to the sink and noisily scrapped the eggs off her plate then flipped on the garbage disposal to drown him out. "This is not going well," she muttered to herself. Recomposing, she took a deep breath and walked to the coffee pot. If she were going to maintain the illusion she gave a damn about him and his cause she would have to try much harder.

"Do you want a cup of coffee?" she managed to ask.

He hesitated for a moment. The question caught him off guard.

"*Ja*, you can pour me a cup."

She poured it strait up, black no sugar.

"I told you a few nights ago, that was the first time I ever met that woman from the paper. She snuck up behind me. If you and Derrick got something else going on you don't want me to know about, then I really don't care."

"We still have to take the necessary precautions."

"Then take them. I've been with you for over three years. I've always believed in this ministry. I've always believed in you. Can you think of any other reason I'm here and not somewhere else?"

Neil remained silent. She took his silence as another affirmation of his distrust in her.

"Good. Now is there any reason I shouldn't use the computer?"

"I'm not sure what you mean."

"Because I've got work to do and if you've got something in the files I shouldn't see then tell me now before Derrick comes back home and goes ballistic again."

"Like I said, there's nothing in the apartment for you to find."

She flipped on the computer then walked over to the dubbing machines.

"What about here? Anything I shouldn't touch" Any part of a sermon you don't want me to review?"

Neil looked bewildered and almost found her demeanor humorous. "I said—"

"I know what you said. Then we both have nothing to worry about do we?"

She didn't wait for him to answer. She walked over to the computer and set her coffee beside the keyboard.

"Have you finished the sermon for next week's service in *Adelsried*?"

"Excuse me?"

"The sermon. You know, the ones you write up on the weekend and I type in order for you to proof read so I can re-type them."

"Not yet."

"I see. Then I'll work on last month's newsletter, then start processing last week's sermon for distribution. Will that be ok?"

"Yeah, that will be ok," he said, and walked down the hall into his room.

When she heard his bedroom door close she wrapped her face in the palms of her hands and fought back the tears.

Lunch came and went and the clock ticked 4:30. Neil came out of his room twice, once to use the restroom and another time to make a sandwich. Tasha was too nervous and upset to be hungry. She'd decided earlier she would make a great dinner, nothing too extravagant, but still something out of the ordinary they would hopefully appreciate. She shut the computer down and went into the kitchen.

She beat the steaks tender then marinated them in a special sauce. She peeled the potatoes, sliced them, then mixed them up with cheese and spices and poured them into a casserole dish. She put the dish of scalloped potatoes into the microwave and set the steaks under the broiler. Then she set to work on the salad and dressed it in a glass bowl. She opened the broiler, turned over the steaks, set the table, went back into the kitchen and heated a can of creamed corn. When the buzzer went off she took the potatoes out of the microwave and set them on the table. She checked the steaks. Another five minutes and they'd be done. She leaned up against the counter in the kitchen and tried to gather herself together. She could not even imagine sitting down with the two and eating. The buzzer went off and she finished the last of the preparations. She walked down the hallway and knocked on Neil's door.

"*Ja?*"

"Dinner's ready."

"Start without me."

With a sense of relief she walked back to the table and ate as fast as she could before he came out. She'd almost finished when she heard his door open. He looked at the table for a moment then sat down.

"Derrick won't be home until later," he said without looking up.

She knew what to do with his food.

"After Pauli eats I'm going to walk her in the park."

Neil looked up from his plate. He thought about it for a moment then said, "ok."

Tasha went to her room and put on her coat. She grabbed the leash and secured the hook around Pauli's collar, then stood at the door for a brief moment fully expecting Neil to say something, but he didn't. "You feel like a walk?" she asked him.

He gave it a quick thought." No, you go ahead. I've got some work to do."

Once across the street Tasha, looked earnestly for Eva. The last thing she needed was another surprise visit. She could only imagine Derrick lurking behind a tree or in the nearby bushes. He and Neil had probably planned for her to be alone again just so she would make another mistake. She had no idea what they were up to, so without even going into the park she stood at the sidewalk and let Pauli walk herself in the yard. When Pauli came running back they went back upstairs. Once inside, she cleaned the kitchen and put all the papers back on the table just like they were before she cleared the table. Then she went to her room and waited.

Derrick returned around 9:15. She heard him sit down at the dining room table and scarf down his dinner. The television clicked on and she knew it might be another long night. She waited. At one point Neil came out of his room and he and Derrick talked. She could almost make out the details of their conversation, something to the sound of, "calling the states later," but she couldn't be sure. She passed most of the time sitting on the edge of her bed thinking and listening and thinking more about what information she might be able to find and where it would be located in Neil's room. To complicate her problem she didn't know what to look for, if and when she had the opportunity to look. Perhaps he kept some old photos, or a secret computer disk. Perhaps he had a file stuffed away with some papers, or maybe even an address book.

At 11:30 the television was still blaring away at a steady drum. She cracked the door to her room open. Neil's light was still on. She walked down the hall. Derrick was stretched out on the couch. She didn't have the courage to see if he was awake or not. She went into the kitchen, turned on the light and poured herself a glass of milk, walked back to the beginning of the hallway, looked over at Derrick again and noticed he hadn't stirred while she was in the kitchen. Either he was awake and didn't want to see her or he was asleep. She had to find out. Timidly, she tiptoed around the back of the couch where his feet were. When she reached the end of the couch she could see his eyes were closed and his head had awkwardly fallen into the gap between the armrest and the couch cushion. She stepped closer to get a closer look. A horrible thought leaped into her mind. What if he woke up and discovered her staring into his face? She snapped back. If he wasn't asleep, he was doing a good job of faking it. She shuffled past him and went back to her room.

Leaning against the headboard of her bed she guzzled her milk. Pauli lay curled up beside her with her head against Tasha's leg. Tasha stroked her head over and over without giving it any thought. As the clock ticked on she flipped over in her mind the things they'd said and done to her. Things she'd just brushed aside at the time without giving them much thought. She'd worked like a dog for them without pay.

Hell, she was a mother to them! And they were like two brutal sons who lacked even the common courtesy to thank her for cooking them dinner. She was not the woman she was three years ago. She had them to thank for that. Back then she was full of life, but they'd changed all that.

Half an hour passed in which she wavered between fear and apprehension, wondering if the time ever presented itself would she have the courage to search Neil's room? She thought about the clip of conversation she'd heard between them earlier. Neil would have to go out to make a phone call. Why he would have to leave the apartment to do it she didn't know, but it would give her time. That is, if Derrick was still asleep on the couch.

"Shit!" She muttered, suddenly jumping off her bed and bolting towards the door. Pauli popped onto her squatty legs and looked at her quizzically. She flipped off the light and walked back to her bed. "How stupid of me," she said, falling back against the headboard. The soft blue light from the television made its way down the hall and crept underneath her door. She watched the subtle faint patterns reflecting against the hard wood floors, painting the edge of her bed and the side of her dresser in a flickering glow. Another hour passed. It was 1:00 a.m. She had given up all hope Neil would leave and the thought relieved her. She closed her eyes.

Ten minutes later, she was startled by the sound of his creaking door. Terrified, she tiptoed to her door and heard his footsteps slip down the hall and stop in the living room. The television went silent and the apartment went dark. The front door opened without a creak and clicked shut. There was a shuffle in the foyer and the sound of shoes in the stairwell. A moment later, came the groaning of the outside door. Where he went from there was a mystery, but she guessed to the nearest phone, which was about a three-minute walk down the street. She could allow herself only five minutes time. To make matters worse she could not risk turning his light on. His room faced the street and if he happened to look up he'd know she was snooping around.

She turned on her light, opened her door and let the light from her room fall across his door. She walked halfway down the hall to make sure Derrick was still asleep. As near as she could tell he was. She crept back down the hallway and carefully opened Neil's door. The diffused light outlined his desk, a bookshelf and the end of his bed. The right side of the room was in shadow, the closet in the corner, inky. She decided the best thing to do would be to grab his briefcase and take it back into her room where there would be enough light to check the contents. It was open on his dresser. She closed the top of the briefcase, lifted it off the desk gently and shuffled back to her room. She'd wasted two minutes.

Thankfully, the case was in order. She went through the file pockets in the lid of the case first, reached in and pulled out two manila folders. One was full of accounting information about the financial status of the CRM. Neil did the books himself and everything was certainly in order. For the most part the file consisted of the last two months worth of balance sheets. Nothing there. She put the file back in the way she found it and looked into the other file. There she found several letters of correspondence from Joseph Stautzen of the ICC. She'd met Stautzen just once and looked for anything in the letters that might be incriminating. They were worthless. Behind the letters was a neatly computerized schedule of the next three months preaching dates and the cities they would be traveling to. Tasha had the schedule memorized. It was the same one she consistently updated in the computer. Next, she looked through the bottom of the case where she found another schedule in a black binder that was basically used as a back up for the printed version. She looked through the address book in the back and saw nothing of use. Mostly business numbers to companies like those that did their printing and mailing services. Other numbers listed the head elders in all the locations where the CRM had converts. There were a few miscellaneous numbers of people she didn't know, but she didn't have a copy machine handy. There was a note pad with a few Biblical verses scribbled on it along with about four sheets of notes for an up-coming sermon. The smaller pockets held nothing of significance; a calculator, a pocket full of pens and pencils lined up in perfect order, another pocket of business cards and miscellaneous receipts which had yet to make it to the receipt box. She put everything back in the case the way she thought it had come out and quietly ran it back into his room. After setting it on the desk she backed up into the doorframe and held her breath. Derrick was still breathing heavily, a car passed along the street. Still no sound of Neil yet.

She looked around the room searching for a place with enough light to look into next. She couldn't even make out the titles of the books on the shelf. The closet was not an option. Neither were his dresser drawers. She ran around the side of his bed and slipped her hand between the mattress and the box spring, checking all the way around the bed by driving her arm deep into the center as far as possible and came up with nothing. She went back to the door and took another hard listen. She was getting desperate and time was running short. At the desk she tried to open the top drawer. It was jammed. She bent over and found the drawer had a lock. No way she would be able to see what was inside short of asking Neil for his keys. She stood up and noticed the trash can on the floor beside the desk and decided to take a gamble. Bending over to pick it up, she felt it was full, but still had the presence of mind to gather up several other rolled up balls of paper around it along the baseboard. She tossed them into the can and dashed to her room, frantically spreading half the papers from the can all over her bed. "Damn! Too much noise." She thought, stepping into the hallway to listen.

Footsteps coming up the stairwell! She panics, turning around twice in the hallway not knowing what to do. Coming to her senses she grabs the wastebasket and fluffs up the remaining papers inside to make it look full, runs it back into Neil's room, backs out and closes his door. In her room she looks back and spots a sheet of paper that has fallen to the floor. She scrambles on her knees and reaches out into the hallway to get it, just as the front door clicks open. Ever so quietly she closes her door, suddenly realizing she's got a bed full of Neil's trash and if he ever found out about it she'd be out on the streets before sun up. She reaches down, takes hold of the door handle and with her thumb gently presses the lock.

Neil had not yet closed the door when he heard the spring on her lock snap into place. There was only one sound like it in the world and at 1:45 in the morning it might as well have been an air horn from a truck echoing down the hallway. He cocked his head and closed the door, then walked to the couch to see if Derrick was stirring. Not a twitch. His suspicions rise as he sees the light from Tasha's room go off and the hallway grow dark. At her door he stops and listens, little realizing that she is curled in the corner with her back against the door peering into the darkness of her room desperately trying not to breathe. Not hearing a sound, he goes into his room and turns on the light, taking an immediate assessment to make sure everything's in order. His eyes scan the doors of his closet, the bed, his bookshelves, his briefcase, then finally his desk. Nothing seems to be out of order. He moves to the desk and checks the top drawer. It's secure. He sits down at his chair and examines the contents of his briefcase. Everything is as he'd left it. He leans back into his chair and sighs.

When Tasha was sure it was safe she scurried across the floor to the chair in the corner. Pauli jumped onto her lap and curled in the seam of her thighs. Tasha just sat there, eyes fixed on the shimmer of the pale light from Neil's room seeping underneath her door. About a half hour later her room went black and she sat there for another fifteen minutes until she finally got the courage to turn on her light. She moved to her bed and pulled back the comforter. The sight of Neil's trash on her bed revolted her and she sat down next to it feeling an overwhelming sense of defeat. She began picking up the pieces of paper one by one. Some of them were whole pages without crinkle, some of them just bits and pieces of notepaper and tightly wadded balls full of useless information. She was methodical in her approach and before long had a stack of paper growing beside her in a neat little stack. Those which were rolled into balls she very carefully and quietly unraveled until they were fully opened, then with two hands she would smooth them out on the mattress and read them. About two thirds of the way through the pile she opened up one of the smaller balls of paper and ironed it out with her fingers. The lead on the paper had faded and it was difficult to read in the soft light coming from the lamp. She held it up before her face and muttered its contents.

Execution Mandatory—Nov. 8.
Forstein—Burtman/American?

CHAPTER 43

▼

When Eva's cell phone chirped with a new incoming message she and Stace were standing at the counter of the *Kriftel* Cafe on *Nuegasse* in *Hattersheim* eating hamburgers for lunch. She licked the ketchup off her fingers and flapped her hands together to dust off the sesame seeds. Derrick was just down the road in Neil's car. She heard the muffled beep of her cell phone deep down in her bag.

"Important?" Stace asked, as she checked the number.

"Could be." She snatched her cell phone and her bag. "I'm going to step outside and make a quick call."

Stace nodded and took a bite.

She'd been hoping her contact with Tasha had been successful, but the LCD number written across the window of her phone from the call she'd just missed didn't look familiar. Once outside, she walked around the corner of the building and dialed the number.

The receiver picked up on the other end. "Tasha?"

Tasha looked out of the windows of the canary colored phone booth, her eyes darting here and there, wondering where Derrick was. In her other hand she clutched a wadded piece of notepaper.

"Tasha?" Eva questioned louder.

"Eva?"

"Are you ok?"

"I…I'm scarred Eva."

"Where are you?"

"At a phone booth on the corner."

"At *Escherscheimer* and *Hugelstrasse?*"

"*Ja.*"

"Where's Derrick?" Eva asked, stepping out onto the sidewalk in front of Kriftel's and looking down the street.

"I don't know. He took off earlier this morning."

"What about Neil?"

"In the apartment."

Stace took another bite of his hamburger and watched Eva pace by the front window on the sidewalk a few times.

"What did you find out?"

Tasha squeezed the slip of paper in her pocket.

"I don't know, I mean…I'm not sure what it means."

"What?"

"I can't do it Eva. They're watching me. I don't know where Derrick is, but he's probably hiding right around the corner."

"What did you find Tasha?" Eva pressed.

"Just a note. A note I found in Neil's trash last night. I looked through his briefcase…it was dark—I didn't have any time."

"Listen, Tasha, take a deep breath."

Eva took another look down the street then walked around the side of the building. "Now tell me, what did you find?"

Tasha took another look out the windows of the phone booth and languidly pulled out the note. She pressed it up against the front of the telephone to straighten it out. The letters were hard to read and she leaned forward to get a better look.

"Execution Mandatory—Nov. 8. Forstein—Burtman/American… What does it mean Eva?"

Eva fell silent for a few moments trying to decipher the meaning of the note. Execution of what? Of whom? The three people on the list? No way. We're talking about a peaceful Christian organization here.

Possibilities…think Eva! Execution of the program? Could that be it? Possible, entirely possible. But what about the names? Forstein, me, and the American—Stace? "Shit."

"What's wrong Eva?"

"Nothing. Just give me a minute. I'm thinking—"

"I haven't got a minute. He could be anywhere."

Forstein. I've heard that name before, but where? Eva looked down at the ground. A chip of concrete was wedged in the dirt. She moved her shoe over it trying to jar the memory of the name Forstein loose. The American…Stace? She kicked frantically at the chip. Just a piece of it sticking out, the majority of it lodged deep in the dirt. She dug the tip of her shoe into it. She came at it backwards with the heel. It was starting to budge.

Stace had almost finished his sandwich and was wondering what was taking her so long. He looked out the side window where he could see the top portion of her body jerking about, phone pressed against her ear, hair hanging down and blowing about. "Who was she talking to?"

"You still there?" Tasha asked.

"*Ja*, still thinking."

The fact was she didn't want to think about it. She stopped kicking the stone and looked into the window at Stace. His back was turned towards her. Any mention of an American had always centered on him. Mr. Schwarz thought he was involved. Shelly and Ruben highly suspected him. She had tried to deny the question of his involvement even existed. Each time it popped up she would bury it. Now it was back, back with a vengeance that threw a black sheet over his head. "Who the hell was he? What was he *really* doing in Germany?" She looked back down at the stone and attacked it again. The name Forstein popped back in her head. She tried to remember where she'd heard it, analyzing every conversation she had with Stace, taking each phrase one by one and looking for the source. Her thoughts finally went as far back as the swimming pool where they'd met. She gave the stone one final kick and broke it free. There would be no turning back.

"Tasha, you stay put. Don't go back to the apartment. I'm coming to get you."

"But—"

"Just stay put. I want you to hang up the phone and walk into the store. I'll be there in ten minutes."

"Ok."

Stace finished his sandwich and reached for a napkin. He wiped the grease off his hands then grabbed the flimsy paper cup beside him. Wrapping his lips around the straw he turned towards Eva. Not in the side window, nor out the one in the front. Outside, he looked to the left and then to the right in the direction of the car and caught the tail end of it whizzing off down the road.

The decision to follow Eva instead of staying and watching the American was an easy one for Derrick. He'd watched her talking on the phone then watched her run to her car. She drove right past him and he could see the intensity in her eyes. She was up to something. He made a u-turn in the street and followed her from a comfortable distance. On the A-66 into Frankfurt he could barely keep up with her. He suspected she was heading towards her office, but at the last minute she took a left onto *Escherscheimer* and went north towards his apartment. He waited two cars behind her as she sat in the lane waiting to make a left onto *Hugelstrasse*. The traffic had come to full stop for the *U-Bahn* train and he had to wait. A minute later it was off and running south into Frankfurt. The train hissed as it picked up speed and moved past his window. The arrow turned green and Derrick followed her across the tracks. Without notice she suddenly pulled up along side the curb in front of the convenience store and stopped. He drove by and watched her enter the store, then found a space on the side of the road at the next block. He left the car running and with the power control adjusted the positioning of the right mirror so he could get a view of the sidewalk and the entrance of the store. He gripped the steering wheel with both hands and waited.

In the store Eva scanned from right to left looking for Tasha and thought she spotted the back of Tasha's head in the far left corner near a frozen foods refrigerator. She shot down the isle and discovered her standing in front of the glass doors cradling a plastic basket half full of groceries. Pauli sat on the floor next to her.

"Doing some shopping?" Eva asked to relieve the tension as she approached. Tasha turned towards her with a frazzled look missing the intent.

"What's happening at the apartment?" Eva asked.

"Neil and Derrick saw us meet. They took the envelope away from me right after I came home from the park," she said quivering, her eyes dark and sleepless.

"Did they hurt you?"

"Not exactly, but I'm willing to trust you at this point. I can't believe I've lived with them for over three years and never suspected anything. Never had an idea what kind of people they were."

"It's not always easy to tell those kinds of things about people Tasha. It's not your fault. They've been able to fool a lot of people for a long time." She was speaking at Tasha, but not to Tasha. She was speaking to herself and thinking of Stace. "Can I see the note?"

Tasha set the basket down on the floor and pulled the note out of her pocket. Eva uncurled the edges and read for herself the same words she'd heard over the phone. Somehow, having the hard copy of the message in hand seemed more forbidding. She hated to have to press Tasha for more information, but she needed more to go on.

"Do you think there's any more information in the apartment that might help us out?"

Tasha looked at Eva with a look of astonishment. "I told you on the phone I can't. If Neil ever finds out I even went through his trash—"

"I'm not going to ask you to look anymore," Eva interrupted her. "In fact, you're not going back to the apartment."

"I'm not?"

"No. It's too dangerous for you there."

"But I've got no place else to go."

Eva could see her trepidation building. Tasha started shuffling from side to side. Pauli moved out of the way so she wouldn't get stepped on.

"I know a safe place where you can stay for a while."

"But my clothes, all my things."

"Don't worry about that either. We'll get your things as soon as we can."

She stopped fidgeting. It was time to re-ask the same question. "Do you think there's anything else in the apartment that might help us?"

"The only other place I can think of might be in Neil's desk drawer, the top drawer. It was locked when I tried it."

"You also said something about his briefcase on the phone."

"There was nothing in it, paperwork, balance sheets, sermon notes, stuff like that. He had an address book in it, but I don't think it would be much help to you."

"Ok. Now let's see if we can't get you and…" Eva looked down at Tasha's dog on the floor, "what was her name again?"

"Pauli."

"That's right. I remember now. You and Pauli out of here. Are you hungry?"

"*Ja*, starved."

"Me too. I missed lunch. How about fresh hot apple fritters?"

"Apple fritters?"

"Yeah, I know a great place to get some."

The image Derrick witnessed in the rear view mirror of the BMW didn't compare to the surprise awaiting him when he followed Eva and Tasha to the *Burtman Backerei*. All his suspicions were suddenly confirmed. Tasha was supplying the *Schwarz Monatlich* with information. Just how long she'd been doing it and what information she'd given them he could only imagine. Everything was coming into focus and he knew it had to be done.

"*Guten tag* mother," Eva said as she and Tasha walked into the *backerei*.

"Hi Eva! I'll be right with you." Her mother looked up from behind the counter.

"Have a seat Tasha." Eva gestured to the wooden bench sitting against the wall near the front door. Eva sat beside her.

Tasha looked around the *backerei* nervously. She clutched Pauli tightly in her lap. "Why are we here?"

"My parents own this *backerei*. I grew up in the apartment upstairs."

"They still live here?"

"*Ja*, with my younger brother Alfred. You've seen him once, but I don't think you would remember. When I moved out about five years ago my father converted my room into an office. There's a nice comfortable couch up there where you can take a long, hard nap."

"Nap?" Tasha said jumping forward.

"*Ja*, sleep. You look like you haven't had any rest for the past two or three days."

"But I can't stay here!"

"Yes you can, and you are."

The customer Leda had been taking care of stopped briefly at the door in front of them. She tucked her bag of bread loaves under her arm and adjusted the shawl she was wearing over her head. The bell above the door chimed as she went out. A cool gust of wind blew in under their feet. Pauli dropped her ears and nearly fell off Tasha's lap shaking herself. Leda came out from around the counter. Eva stood up to meet her and Tasha watched as they pecked each other on the cheek.

"I'd like you to meet a friend of mine mama."

Tasha set Pauli down on the floor and stood up. Leda took one look at Tasha's frazzled expression and extended a warm hand towards her. She exchanged a quick knowing glance at her daughter. Tasha timidly took her hand.

"Tasha is helping us with one of our investigations. I would like her to stay here for a while until we get everything all wrapped up."

"No please! I don't want to inconvenience you." Tasha took a step back, reached down to the floor and picked Pauli up as if she were ready to leave.

"Nonsense," Leda said promptly. "You're not the first person Eva has brought over to stay with us and I doubt you'll be the last."

Tasha looked at Eva with a look of appreciation and hope. "Are you sure I won't be any trouble?"

"That depends," Eva said.

Her mother reached over and slapped Eva on the shoulder. "Don't pay any attention to her," she said to Tasha.

"Depends on what?" Tasha asked apprehensively.

"Truth is my mother and father could use a little help. I spent many years behind this counter and helping in the kitchen. When I left they refused to hire anyone to replace me. I'm sure mama will tell you its got something to do with money or not being able to find anyone who could do the job well enough."

"All true," her mother said. She stood with her hand folded across her pasty white apron, one foot stretched out in front of the other, looking as if she knew exactly where the conversation was heading.

"Anyway, they could use some help around here."

"I'd be more than happy to help out anyway I can."

"*Gut*. It's settled," Leda said. "Now you two run upstairs and get situated. Don't forget to introduce Tasha to your father in the kitchen."

Once upstairs, Eva gave Tasha a tour of the tiny apartment, which ended in her father's office.

Tasha looked around at the family portraits on the wall dating as far back as three generations. The old desk in the corner was cluttered with receipts and accounting books. On the large wall over the couch was a framed and embroidered cloth of an antiquated farm scene.

"It took my mother three years to finish it. She did it in her spare time. Father had it framed for their thirtieth wedding anniversary. I spent over twenty years of my life in this room." Eva reached over and touched the faded yellow wall below the frame. "When I was sixteen my brother and I painted it this color. Well, not this color exactly, it's faded quite a bit. You should be comfortable here." Eva walked over to a wooden chest in the corner. She opened the doors wide to see what was inside. There were a few coats hanging in it that were pushed to one side. Wire hangers dangled from the beam running across the top. She opened each one of the three drawers at the bottom and found they were full of unfinished sewing projects, patterns still wrapped in their paper wrappers and yards of fabric in various colors and textures. She closed the drawers and swung the two doors closed.

"But your father, won't he mind me intruding?"

"He would never tell me, but I think he was happy when I moved out and got a place of my own. He waited the longest time to convert this into his little sanctuary." Eva stroked her fingers along the front of the desk. "But don't worry. He only spends a little time in here each evening. Mostly just to do the books, then he goes into the living room and sits beside mama to read or watch television."

"I'd still feel better if I was staying with you," Tasha said from the couch.

"I know you would, but you'll be safer here. I've acquired a lot of enemies in my days at the paper and I'm sure most of them know where I live—not to mention Derrick. I made the decision a long time ago that I would not live in fear. That's a risk I can take, but one I won't take with you."

Tasha looked at her with wandering admiration. She contrasted what she saw in Eva with the impression she had of herself. Her head began to droop and she pulled strands of snarled hair up behind her ears, then leaned her tired head against the back of the couch and closed her eyes.

Eva looked at her for a few moments. Her innocence was becoming. She deserved much more happiness than her exhausted expression portrayed. Eva knew she'd risked a lot in getting the note and she determined she'd make it up to her in some way. She slipped out the door and went to the linen room closet. On the bottom shelf she found a stack of old blankets and took out a thick wooly one that she remembered curling up with in the living room when she was younger. In the living room she took a pillow off the couch. When she returned to the room Tasha had drifted into a light sleep. Eva sat down beside her. Tasha opened her eyes.

"Sorry, I must have dozed off. Where's Pauli?"

"Right here, lying on the floor."

"I haven't thanked you enough."

"It's me that should be thanking you."

"For what?"

"For the information."

"But it's just—"

"A scribbled note that has more information on it than you realize."

"I have to take off now Tasha. I want you to relax and take a long nap. My parents won't be upstairs for another four hours or so and Alfred won't be home until late tonight. I'll run by my place sometime today and pick you up some clothes. You look like a size eight."

"Good guess."

"Well, I'm a ten, so you should be ok for a few days.

"All right."

"I'll see you later this evening."

"How is she? her mother asked when Eva came back downstairs.

"Resting, finally."

"She looks like she has been though a lot."

"She has. I've got to run to work now, but I'll be back later this evening."

"I'll make sure she's comfortable."

"Thanks."

"Just about to page you Eva," Mr. Schwarz said as Eva walked into the office.

"Stace called looking for you," Shelly said from across the room interrupting him.

"What'd you tell him?"

"Told him you weren't here. Was I supposed to tell him something else?"

"No. If he calls back tell him I'm not here again."

Shelly had heard that tone before in Eva's voice. She stopped pecking on her keyboard. Mr. Schwarz and Ruben looked up at her waiting for elaboration.

"Seems you were right. It looks like Stace is involved with the program after all," she said, tossing the crumpled note onto her desk. It teetered for a moment on a sharp crease like a seesaw. Her eyes burned into it.

Shelly walked over to her desk and picked up the note. She uncurled the edges and read it, then looked down at Eva with a deep sense of regret, but Eva didn't notice. Her eyes were still fixed on the spot where the note was moments before.

"What does it say Shelly?" asked Mr. Schwarz walking towards them.

She extended the note in his direction and he snatched it out of her hand and read it through twice.

"I'm sorry Eva," he said.

Ruben took it out of his hands.

"We were all hoping it wasn't true," Shelly offered for support.

"I know," Eva said after a brief pause. She turned her head towards the door to avoid their glare.

Mr. Schwartz knew better than to emphasize the importance of the note. It was clear on all their expressions that the investigation was taking a dark turn. "We do have a bit of good news," he began after a moment. "Shelly was able to get some information on Trojan Security."

Shelly jumped in. "Since I've already told them I'll give you a brief rundown Eva. Finding the company wasn't too much of a problem. They're based out of Austin, Texas and have subsidiaries in a few other locations across the US. They even have a European branch in Heidelberg. When I got the number I spoke with their Director of Marketing, Brad Winston. Told him I needed a program written for my company and a friend had given me their name." She took a seat in the empty chair in front of Eva's desk. "Mr. Winston took it from there telling me all about Trojan Security, how long they've been around, the type of programs they build. I just kept milking him for more information. Trojan Security is in the business of designing corporate computer security systems. About eighty percent of the programs they build are designed to guard against industrial espionage. Bigger companies as you know rely on the Internet and other e-commerce services to exchange information. This information is always susceptible to hackers, so they build security programs that will stop that information from leaking into the wrong hands. I told him that was exactly what I was looking for and gave him a fictitious story about my business. Then I pressed him a little, said I'd heard they were building a program for the ICC and I was interested in having a similar system designed for my company. He seemed at a loss for a moment, then said although he was not at liberty to reveal their clientele, he could definitely substantiate they were not doing any work for the ICC. If they were he'd know, since he oversees the contractual agreements on every company they hire on with. I pressed him even further, saying I was certain they were, and since my interest was in obtaining a similar program to the ICC's, that perhaps I'd better check around with some other companies. A few seconds later he had me patched to another office where I spoke with another man, Mitch Pruitt. And here's where the conversation got interesting. He gets on the line and the first thing he asks me is what's my name and who I was representing. Then he asked me where I was calling from and where I'd gotten my information. Of course, I lied, but I don't think he believed me, because he got real polite and told me I'd been misinformed, Trojan Security was not building a program for the ICC and he'd never heard of them before. I pressed him, but he was insistent. That's as far as I got."

"So whatever *de* program is they're building it's hush-hush," Ruben said.

"Not necessarily," said Mr. Schwarz. "My guess is due to the nature of their business they would keep information about their clientele and the programs they're building secret. Nothing illegal about that."

"So it's a dead end," Ruben concluded prematurely.

"Not necessarily," Mr. Schwarz said again, with the same sense of intuition as before. "We know they're building a program for the ICC. That's a given. The audio conversations we've recorded and the note Eva has bear witness to that fact. We also know they're exhibiting a great degree of paranoia over this program. The ICC is going through very drastic means to deter anyone from knowing about it. We know this because the CRM is involved. Their previous history in Berlin tells us there's more to this than just the ICC wanting to keep evangelistic secrets."

"So where does Stace Manning fit in?" Eva asked. "Seems to me he's either with the ICC or the CRM."

"Why would he be tagging along with Eva?" Shelly asked.

"Perhaps he's working for one of those groups. If they've got something to hide like *de* evidence suggests, and if they know we're watching them, then I would think having a man on *de* inside would be beneficial to them. Stace might simply be keeping an eye on us and informing them of what we're doing," Ruben said.

Shelly glanced over at Eva to test her reaction. Ruben's comment hit her hard.

"Let me see that note again Ruben." Mr. Schwarz asked.

Ruben took it off the desk and handed it to him. They others looked at him as he studied the note more carefully. He paid particular attention to the word "American," followed by the heavily penciled question mark.

"What are you looking for?" Ruben asked.

"I'm just trying to figure out the meaning of the question mark."

"Let me see," said Eva.

"Seems to me it's possible that the ICC or the CRM may not know who the American is. The other possibility is, they know who he is, but they're guessing what he's up to," Mr. Schwarz said.

"You mean he may not be informing them of what he's up to?" Ruben asked.

"Either that, or he's not with them at all."

Eva twisted her head towards Mr. Schwarz then at the others. "What is it? Is he with them or not?" She shrunk down into her seat.

No one dared speak except Mr. Schwarz. "I think we can all agree on one thing; Stace Manning is involved with this investigation in one way or another. Who he is with and whose side he's on is still uncertain."

His words pounded in Eva's mind. He was dead right. Stace was involved. But how? She would now have to go with her instincts. She would have to break all ties with him. She would have to block him out of her mind and stay focused on the task at hand. She also knew she'd have to disclose to the others the one piece of information she'd been holding out on them. She glanced at the note again, searching for a reason to disbelieve what she knew to be true. She flipped the note onto her desk and sat up in her chair.

"There's one more thing about the note I haven't told you," she said.

They turned toward her with disbelief. Mr. Schwarz seemed the most perturbed. He opened his mouth eager to speak, but quickly shut it, waiting for Eva to explain.

"Forstein and Stace are connected," she stated flatly.

"Connected?" Mr. Schwarz asked quizzically.

Eva looked at each one of them in turn, hesitant to connect the name Stace with Forstein again. "Connected, and not just because their names are written on the same piece of paper. She stood up and walked around the side of her desk. "When I first met Stace at the *frie-bad* he told me a long story about his college days."

"A story?" Shelly asked.

"Yeah, a story Shelly. You know, one of those things people tell you about themselves that you want to believe is true."

Shelly shut her mouth. It was obvious that Eva was speaking out against the hurt. Mr. Schwarz tried to help her through it. "Do you believe the story?"

"I did at the time."

"And now you don't?" questioned Ruben.

She threw her hands into the air looking for some support to her thoughts. "Look, I don't know what to believe at the moment. I'm only trying to tell you that in the story Stace mentioned the name Forstein, and now, well...here their names pop up together on the same crumpled sheet of paper."

Mr. Schwarz turned his chair towards her desk and leaned across it. "Perhaps you should tell us this story," he firmly suggested. "Shelly, get Eva a glass of water will you."

She proceeded to tell them about the events surrounding the Marbel Art Exhibit. She went into as much detail as she could recall and was surprised she'd remembered as much as she did. She explained to them how Stace was working on a series of photographs for the exhibit and that Forstein—she couldn't remember his first name—had been in charge of the committee that oversaw the work to be displayed at the exhibit. Stace had worked for many months on his photographs. The exhibit was to be covered extensively by the local media and a nationally recognized art gallery in the city was to display the winning entries from each category. Stace expected no glitches in being able to present his work and felt he had a better than average chance of being noted as one of the most prominent artists. "The way he put it to me, he was fully expecting the exhibit to launch his career."

"And let me guess, they pulled the plug on him," volunteered Mr. Schwarz.

"Something like that. At the last minute the committee met and disqualified his photos from the exhibit."

"And this Forstein guy orchestrated the whole thing?" Shelly concluded.

"Stace never said he did, but I got the impression he holds Forstein personally responsible. He may even blame Forstein for the course his life took after the exhibit."

"What do you mean?" Mr. Schwarz asked.

She thought about the question for a few moments. "I guess you could say he's kind of drifter. It's almost as if he's incapable of locking onto something specific in his life." After she'd spoken, the words churned in her mouth like the taste of a moldy bread. It was the first time she'd ever verbally denied she disliked him.

Ruben sat at his desk spinning a pencil in the palms of his hands. "Did he ever say why he came to Germany?"

"*Ja*, something about wanting to see the world." Eva said, swallowing the taste.

"Sounds pretty flimsy to me," Ruben added.

"I guess it does," Eva concluded.

"Question is Eva, do you think he may still hold a personal vendetta against Forstein?" Mr. Schwarz asked.

"It's possible," Eva said without hesitation.

"More like probable!" Ruben interrupted. "Seems to me there are a whole lot of interconnected circumstances to his story."

"Then he's acting alone?" Shelly questioned.

"No. He's tied too much into the investigation to be working alone or on his own. He knew about Eva and the paper and our investigation. If he's connected to Forstein he's connected to Trojan Security. The note also suggests he might even be tied up with the CRM or the ICC." Mr. Schwarz concluded by rubbing his face in his hands and shaking his head.

Eva offered another alternative. "It's possible he works for another outside source we're still not aware of and still may have personal reasons of his own for getting back at Forstein."

"I would say that makes him a little unpredictable." Ruben began and Shelly finished, "and dangerous."

Mr. Schwarz looked at Eva. "I know I told you before to stick with him and see what you could find out."

"And now you want me to stay away from him—right?"

"Yes."

"Consider it done."

CHAPTER 44

▼

Just when the demons of extremism had entered Derrick's mind was a mystery, but he took those demons with him on a chilly night on November third to the *Burtman's Backerei*, along with a lighter and a small syringe full of gasoline. When he pulled the van along the curb just beyond the *backerei* at 2:45 in the morning, he knew at least four people were present in the upstairs apartment; the telephone technician, who had planted the bugs in their apartment, the older woman and her husband, and his primary target Tasha.

The nature of his terrorism had changed since his days in Berlin. An assault rifle with an isolated and untraceable bullet would have been much quicker and painless, but now his targets were more numerous and his objectives more defined. He had decided since the *backerei* was a safe house, it probably contained incriminating information about the CRM and the ICC. He'd caught Tasha with two articles dating back to his time in Berlin, so the *backerei* probably also contained a host of other files, disks, photographs, or other evidence detrimental to them. No bullet could eliminate that kind of evidence, so his preferred choice of terrorism was one of mass destruction. He also understood the possibility there were others, other than the four asleep in the apartment upstairs, who knew how he used to get rid of those who got in his way, so he would have to make it appear as though what he was about to do was an accident, or better, an act of God. And he kind of liked the ring in the latter idea. For surely all those who opposed God and stood in the way of Derrick's work would ultimately perish in fire. In his estimation it would be a "mercy killing."

His first task was to get inside the *backerei*. For this he was well equipped. The door to the *backerei* was over forty-five years old and the locks on the door were standard, a dead bolt and a worn lock in the door handle. He'd kept most of his tools of the trade from his previous years, amongst which was a set of variously shaped steel rods and plates that could easily pry open the outdated locks. He knew from a visit earlier in the week when he went in to the *backerei* to buy a loaf of bread that the *backerei* possessed no visible security system, so once inside he would have the time to do what he needed to do.

He stepped out of the van and walked the short distance towards the intersection where the *backerei* was located, glancing around to make certain no one was watching him. Having walked past the *backerei,* he stood at the corner for a moment peering down the cross street. When he turned back around he noticed a fast approaching car from beyond the intersection coming in his direction. The headlights of the car were bouncing on an off like a flickering candle from the bumps in the road. He thought for a moment of doubling back into the darkness of the alley between the corner of the *backerei* and the service van, but that would look suspicious now. He looked up at the lights of the intersection and noticed they'd changed to red. He suspected the car would stop at the light, but it increased its speed and sailed through the light, then past him. When he could no longer hear the car he turned around and walked back to the door.

After jimmying the locks he slowly opened the door. The bell above the door tingled slightly before he muffled it with his hand. The front room to the *backerei* was much darker than the street. He took a few steps away from the door waiting for his pupils to adjust to the blackness, then crept around the corner of the counter and walked behind the register heading for the kitchen door. He cracked it open—

eereeek—then stopped and listened. When he was certain there was no sign of movement in the upstairs apartment he cracked the door just enough to slip inside. A barely perceptible hint of blue light drifted in from a window located high on the wall towards the alley. It had been ions since the window had been cleaned. A film of grime covered the outside and a thick layer of flour dust covered the inside. After a brief moment he could make out the large stainless steel tables in the center of the kitchen, as well as the half-moon shapes of overturned bowls on the shelf against the wall. Other than that, everything else was shrouded in darkness.

He reached for the lighter in his coat pocket and spun the dial. A tiny flame about the size of a thumbnail erupted and the aromas of the kitchen were temporarily obscured in the smell of butane. He held the lighter high above his head like a miniature torch and looked for his target. What he was searching for was a wall socket, one preferably located down near the baseboard and on the inside wall. He found one located close to the stairwell, which was ideal for his purpose, because if the fire gutted the staircase first there would be no method of escape for the occupants upstairs. The bottom socket had an electrical cord running up into it, but the top socket was empty. He dropped to his knees and ran his hands along the wall. He felt just what he was hoping to feel, a smooth surface of paint and underneath it wooden panels. No doubt the framework under the panels was also made of wood and more than likely stuffed full of insulation filled long before fire-retardant insulation was used. He put the lighter down and reached inside his coat pocket for the syringe full of gasoline. He pulled it out and held it with the tip towards the ceiling. With the other hand he reached up and pulled off the rubber cap from the tip. He spun the dial on the lighter. Very carefully, he inserted the tip into one of the two round openings of the socket and slowly squeezed out the gasoline, completely saturating the electrical connections and the surrounding insulation inside. Then, holding the lit flame in front of the opening he squeezed out the remaining gasoline in the syringe so that it acted like a

touch, driving in through the opening and instantly setting aflame anything that had been soaked with gasoline. Some of the gasoline from
the syringe sprayed across the fixture and ran down the wall. The
kitchen erupted with light, but only for a moment, for it quickly
burned off. He waited, hoping the flames within hadn't suffocated.
With an isolated tip of his finger he touched the plastic fixture and
quickly snapped back. He flipped open the lighter and looked at the
wall. The outside coating of paint was shimmering as it melted and
two trickles of smoke were escaping from the holes of the socket like
snake tongues. When he heard the sound of wires popping he knew
he'd succeed. He backed out of the kitchen, out of the lobby and out
into the street. He didn't wait to see the results and was just passing
under the *U-Bahn* tracks near the *Ginnheim* tower when Pauli first
became aware that something was dreadfully wrong.

The fire spread quickly. Within ten minutes flames were devouring
the insulation in the walls just inches from where Tasha was asleep on
the couch. From there they progressed upwards, licking the insulation
lying across the wooden beams in the musty attic. From its point of
origin it also spread horizontally, steadily advancing towards the corner
of the wall by the stairwell and spreading to the frames within that
wall. Shortly thereafter, the joists of the stairs themselves caught fire,
followed immediately by the entire staircase.

At first, Pauli sniffed the foul odor and opened her eyes to the eerie
darkness of a smoke filled room. She took another deep breath and
sneezed. She sneezed again and stood up trying to shake the feeling
free. Her head was spinning. She couldn't see across the room to
Tasha, so she whimpered and walked in the direction she remembered
the couch was located at. She came face to face with the wall on the
opposite side of the room and sneezed again, lifted her head up and
yelped. She heard Tasha stir then cough and she ran across the room
towards the sound where she found Tasha's arm hanging over the edge
of the couch. She nudged it and barked, sneezed, then barked again.
Within the fog of Tasha's mind she heard the barking echoes and the

damp hot steam of Pauli's tongue in her fingers and woke up. The hot pungent odor of wood and chemicals seared her nose and she began to cough. When she opened her eyes it seemed as if they were full of butter, then came the burning and watering. She rolled over and sat on the edge of the couch clutching for her pillow and coughing uncontrollably. An eruption in her stomach filled her mouth with the remains of the evening meal. She puked on the couch and wiped the strand of saliva hanging from her mouth. When she found the pillow she fell onto the floor where the smoke was less dense. She could also see the flicker of yellow flames attacking the bottom of her door. She swung her arms wildly calling for Pauli, who yelped again as Tasha's arm caught her in the ribs and knocked her over. Tasha grabbed her by the front leg, yanked her into her arms then crawled towards the door. She fell against the inner wall cradling Pauli in one hand and the pillow in the other, ramming it against her face and trying desperately to breathe through it. The cling of moisture saturated her body and she became aware of the heat lashing like claws at her skin. Through the thin cotton shorts she was wearing she felt the sting of the hot hardwood floors pricking her skin. She shifted fanatically trying to transfer the pain and for the first time, realized she might die.

"*Aaaagh!*" Alfred awoke to the sound of her terror, "*thump... thump....thump!*" and the hollow pounding on her door. He opened his eyes to the sparkle of reflected flames ricocheting around the walls of his room and the crackle of fire outside his door. He flung his comforter onto the floor and stumbled over to the door.

"Mom! Dad! Wake up! He screamed, with his hand on the door feeling for flames though the wood. "Mom! Dad" he yelled at the top of his voice.

"Alfred help me!" Tasha yelled.

"Wait Tasha!" He yelled to her, then ran over to his dresser and threw on his boots, grabbed a beer bottle and something else, and went back to the door and cracked it open. Rising heat rushed past him throwing his hair back. The stairwell was entirely swallowed in flames caressing the wall and ceiling like molten electricity feeding swirling colors of white and blue tips. He forced the door open further and threw the beer bottle at his parent's room across the hall. The bottle landed with a solid *thump* on the hollow door, bounced across the floor and rolled into the stairwell where it disappeared into the flames. The Burtman's jumped when the bottle hit the door. Mr. Burtman looked into the orange fog suffocating the room and heard the walls sizzling with bubbling paint. The smoke from the paint was rising like a fluid white blanket, filling the ceiling above him with intoxicating fumes. He heard a second loud thud against the door and yelled to Alfred.

"Alfred! We're awake!"

Alfred fought off the heat searing his eyelashes and hair. "It's in the stairs dad. We can't get out that way!"

Mr. Burtman was standing just a few feet from the door when the bottom of it ignited. Suddenly, tongues of flames like party streamers began swirling up it. He threw himself backwards and began to cough.

"Dad!"

"I hear you!"

"You'll have to jump out the window!" Alfred yelled. "Use the sheets. Tie them to window frame. I'll jump down and run around the front to help you!"

Alfred listened for his father's response, but heard none. "Dad!" he screamed louder.

"We're going! What about Tasha?"

"Tasha! Did you hear me? You gotta jump out the window."

She had drifted into a state of shock. The floor was beginning to burn now and she tried to stand, but the smoke was hanging low in the ceiling and she fell back to the floor deliriously. She screamed and jumped at the *thrap* that hit her door after Alfred threw a book at it.

"Tasha! The window! Jump out the window!" Alfred listened for a response but could no longer wait.

She wiped the water from her eyes and squinted into the thick smoky blackness. Across the room she could see the sharp perpendicular edges of light from the window cutting through the smoke and falling onto the floor. She dropped the pillow and fell onto her hands and knees cradling Pauli in her left arm. No sooner than she started crawling did the door turn into a sheet of flames like orange foam behind her. She scrambled frantically as the flames from the door leaped onto the wall above the couch. By the time she reached the window the door and the staircase wall erupted sending flaming witch's fingers across the ceiling.

Alfred ran back to his window and spun the crank ferociously. Taking hold of the center beam he crawled over the ledge, tittered on his stomach and dropped his feet over the edge. His boots scuffled against the red brick looking for a firm footing. Peering into the darkness below he searched for a clear spot to land in the yard then pushed off, lunging backwards and sailing fifteen feet onto the grass below. His feet hit first, then he felt a sharp pain near his right elbow as his arm helped to break the fall. Stunned, he lay there for a few moments watching shadowy smoke billow out of his window and over the edge of the roof. He shook his head violently back and forth, shaking himself out of his stupor, then got up and ran towards the alley before stopping at the corner near the back of his van. Looking towards the front of the *backerei* he saw the hands of his father tying a sheet onto the window beam, then glancing up above him he saw Tasha's face poking out of the bottom of her window grasping for air.

"Tasha!"

Choking…she didn't hear him.

"Tasha!" he yelled louder. She looked in his direction. "Jump! Jump onto the van!"

Directly under her window was his van, parked about five feet from the edge of the building. It would be about an eight-foot drop to the top of the van and from there she could easily make it down to the ground. He looked up towards his parent's window and saw his mother's feet poking through. "You *gotta* jump Tasha!" he yelled one last time and ran to help his parents.

"That's it mom. Just ease your way on over," he said as his mother came out the window. She was barefoot and her nightgown flapped about in the soft breeze. Mr. Burtman was leaning out of the window above her, his hands tucked up under her shoulders suspending her as she groveled to take hold of the sheet.

"Now hold on tightly Leda, I'm going to ease you on down."

"Don't!" she pleaded.

"I have to. Now trust me. Alfred's below if you fall. You've got to slide down."

She gripped the sheet tenaciously and Mr. Burtman released his grip. Alfred watched from below as she dropped a few feet towards him, banging up against the wall and flipping around like a fish on a plate. She looked down in terror. Alfred braced himself for her eminent fall. "Slide down mom! When you get to the end let yourself fall. I'll catch you!"

She panicked and looked back up towards her husband. "Slide down Leda. I'm right here. Alfred's below you. You'll be ok."

Slowly, she eased open her fingers and her weight pulled her down towards the ground. Her robe snagged against the brick-face of the building as she dropped and cinched up around her waist. Her bare feet and ankles cut against the sharp edges of brick and mortar, but she didn't notice the pain. Finally, she reached the end of the sheet.

"Now just let go mom. I'm right here," Alfred said.

Her arms were raised tightly around her head and she tried to look down. She couldn't see Alfred but she could see the ground nearby and knew she was much closer to it than before. Her feet were still ten feet above the sidewalk, but she knew from here she could survive the fall. And she had to hurry. Her husband was still in the room.

"Alfred!" She screamed.

"Right here mama, jump!"

She thought about it for another few seconds. "All right. I'm coming," she yelled and let go.

Alfred caught her around the hips as she dropped. To help break the fall he fell backwards and let her fall across the top of him. Again, a sharp pain radiated through his right elbow and down his wrist as he hit the pavement. She rolled off him and onto her knees.

"You all right Alfred?" she pleaded, looking into his eyes and shaking him by the shoulders.

He looked up into her face and then beyond her as his father started climbing out the window. "I think so," he mumbled and tried to stand, but his head spun and he fell backwards. He ran his hand across his arm and felt a stub of bone breaking the skin. His father would be on his own.

Tasha was desperate for alternatives and solutions and coughing profusely. Tears were oozing out of her eyes in a steady stream. She kept blinking and scratching at them frantically. The top of the van seemed miles away, the heat behind her excruciating. Pauli yelped and squirreled around in her arm. She could not hold onto her any longer. Lifting Pauli in both hands she eased her out over the windowsill. Without hesitation she tossed her feet first onto the van. Pauli landed with a hard smack and rolled over. Tasha pinched the tears out of her eyes to see if she was ok. Within a moment Pauli got up and started barking at her. "She made it!" Tasha thought with hope, knowing what she must do. She squinted and held her breath as she climbed into the window box. A sharp pain cut into the arches of her feet as she stood on the thin metal rails. She opened her eyes but could no longer see. The stink of burning hair stuffed her nose and the rush of black smoke roared like a freight train over her head. She tried to remember the position of the van and just how far she needed to jump. When she thought she had the memory in focus she jumped.

For a brief moment there came the sensation of weightlessness and the cool night air slipping around her burnt skin. That sensation was short-lived. The sheet of metal capping the van seemed to rise up to meet her. A brief sense of relief followed when she realized her feet had made contact with the van, but then came the horror of imbalance as she sensed she'd missed her target. She stiffened, hands flailing out-wards as her body lunged backwards towards the brick face of the building. The last thing she remembered was the split-second crump as her head hit the wall, the taste of blood on her tongue and a thickening numbness in the back of her head.

CHAPTER 45

▼

She left him stranded at Kriftel's Cafe on Tuesday. He was irked at her disappearance, but unsuspecting, considering the type of work she was in. When he called the *Schwarz Monatlich* she was never in the office. He fully expected a call and an explanation by Wednesday evening, but none came and his tolerance gave way once again to irksomeness. She wasn't answering her pages and she was ignoring her phone. By Wednesday night he was really pissed. By Thursday morning he worried about her safety, so he called her office again. Shelly assured him she was ok and that she'd pass along the message that he called again. By Friday he'd about had enough and stewed all day long trying to decide just how tactful he was *not* going to be when he finally confronted her. If he was going to see her he would have to find her and the first place to look would be at her house on *Loreleistrasse*. If he caught her before 7:00 in the morning she'd probably be home.

He'd been up since 4:15 and waited until 6:00 to take the short thirty-minute walk to her home. He cut through *Kurmainzer Stadtpark* and encountered no less than three companies of American troops from the 32nd Signal Battalion out of McNair *Kasern*. In the soccer fields adjacent to the park one company was in the midst of a game of American style kill-the-man-with-the-ball game. They looked like dirtied scrambled eggs in their yellow sweat suits. He walked along the crushed gravel pathway winding its way through the park in swooping curves, until he approached the beginning of the enormous pond. Ducks squawked at his arrival sending the birds into a tizzy above him. Across a cement bridge arching over the neck of the pond he passed a floating barge of lily pads. In the frosted grass to his right another company of American troops squirmed on their backs doing sit-ups. He could barely make out the rhythmic calls of the company First-Sergeant that walked amongst them. The sun was just awakening somewhere, painting the entire scene into an impressionists' version of morning. The sky was a deep pink-magenta and the park, a mirage of romantic greens with just the right amount of morning mist to set the imagination on fire, but he didn't let that get in the way of his emotions. This morning he determined he would settle his relationship with Eva one way or another. After passing the pond, he took a ninety-degree turn to the right around a sculpture garden where two bolder sized cement statues of sea lions reclined. From their mouths protruded short copper tubes, which to his knowledge never spat water, the pond they sat in was empty. Approaching the main path that arched in a sweeping incline towards *Konrad Glatt Strasse*, he heard the rumble of another company of troops. Above the thunder of their steps rang a growing cadence lead by an E-7, who belted out the first stanza and the company sang the refrain like a polished men's chorus:

> They say that in the Army.
> They say that in the Army.
> The food is mighty fine.
> The food is mighty fine.
> A chicken rolled off the table.
> A chicken rolled off the table.
> And killed a friend of mine.
> And killed a friend of mine.

Oh what a day what a day what a day to fight a waroooor...
Oh what a day what a day what a day to fight a waroooor...

Stace wished that they'd all go shoot themselves.

Once he got past McNair *Kaserne* the noise died down and settled into the normal early morning conversations of last second good-byes as people left for work and children started walking to school. As he rounded *PeterBied Strasse* and looked down *Loreleistrasse* he could see Eva's orange Opel parked out in front of her home. Moments later, he unhooked the black gate at the walkway leading up to her apartment, took a deep breath and composed himself. To his surprise he noticed he was no longer angry. He entered the first door then the second and knocked sharply on her door. Sheeba gave a few deep barks and came to the door sniffing. The sound of her jingling tags and muzzle bounced under the door. If his knock hadn't gotten Eva's attention, Sheeba's bark surely should have. He waited. The jingle of Sheeba's tags disappeared. "Was she still asleep?" he thought to himself. "Then I'll wake her up." He knocked louder this time. Sheeba barked returning to the door, her voice hollow, deep and penetrating. He waited more. Now he didn't know what to do. "She probably still doesn't want to talk to me, but I'm here to stay." He knocked again with more determination. This time the door behind him opened and he turned to see the head of Mrs. Elderich poking out of the door clutching the collar of her white robe.

"Didn't mean to wake you, but I need to speak with Eva."

"She's not here."

"Where is she?"

"You didn't hear? It was on the news this morning. Her parent's *backerei* burned down last night."

"You're kidding?" he said walking to her door.

"*Ja.* You just missed her. Her brother came by about thirty minutes ago and took her to the hospital."

His mind flashed back to a week and half ago when he had dinner with her parents. Mrs. Burtman's face surfaced in his mind like a portrait floating on water. "Are they all right?"

"Alfred looked pretty bruised up. He had a towel wrapped around his arm and was bleeding. I think her parents are ok, but there was someone else in the apartment that was injured. Can't remember the name though…Tash…Tabitha…I'm really not certain."

"Do you know what hospital they went to?"

"The University hospital, It's where they take the most serious cases."

Stace was at a loss. "Do you now where it's at?"

"In *Niederrad*, by the *Niederrader* Bridge. Near where the autobahn crosses over the river.

"Thanks," he said moving towards the outer door.

"Ask about her for me will you?"

"I will."

Forty-five minutes later he reached the hospital. It was not as easy to find as Mrs. Elderich had said. The hospital was set-off from the road with only a small sign marking the entrance. It looked like the sterile offices of a Social Security building or an elementary school set in a cluster of trees. The main building was low and flat consisting of adjacent one-story segments fashioned in cement and held together by industrial sized windows. He walked down the tree-lined road beyond a parking lot and noticed a two story building on the left. Guessing it might be the main building he walked over to it, passed through the double doors and immediately knew he'd guessed wrong. He rehearsed some broken German in his mind and stopped at the first open door on his right. In the dull office a man sat behind a desk looking over papers.

"Are you looking for the hospital?" the man asked looking over the rim of his glasses as if he'd done it a thousand times before.

Stace understood the words "looking" and "hospital." A simple "*ja*" sufficed.

The man walked him back down the hall. He opened the door and stepped outside, then gestured with his free hand towards the gray flat building.

"Intensive care?" Stace asked, but he'd already gone inside.

The hospital was even more ominous than it appeared from a distance, lacking any modern details. Stace judged it was built sometime around WWII, with the understanding bombs would probably destroy it before construction could be completed. Its cement construction was solid, but decades of winters and summer rains had transformed its smooth sandy-colored complexion into a lunar landscape riddled with holes and leaking decades of grime. He stepped inside the two sets of double doors to an equally less impressive interior, most noticeable of which was the floor. Even after the dawn of modernization they'd not bothered to tile it. It had been left as cement and through the years had worn itself smooth. He stood for a moment just inside the doors groping for direction. After scanning the options and hearing not a whisper of life, he squinted and looked down the long hallway in front of him. At the end of the hallway was a wooden table, which in the distance looked like it belonged in a dollhouse. Behind the table sat a woman. She was not moving and seemed more like a photograph, rather than a real person. He took a deep breath and prepared for the journey. His tennis shoes squeaked unmercifully in the full minute it took to reach her. The elderly woman behind the table rose at his approach and suddenly coming to life.

"May I help you?" she asked, after the last squeak.

"*Ja*. I'm looking for the intensive care unit."

"She replied in perfect English, "you're here."

He glanced at the fat double doors to his right.

What bothered him most at the moment was the absence of smells. The lack of antiseptic and cleansing aromas in particular led him to believe he was standing in an empty well-swept warehouse. It evoked no memory of a childhood visit to the emergency room, where just the odor of hospital escaping out of its doors made him queasy. "And where was everyone?" He'd not even seen another visitor, much less anyone walking around in lab coats. Even a parked gurney along the wall would have been soothing to him, but there was nothing, no doctors, no nurses, no technicians.

"Are you sure?" he asked.

The woman glanced to the doors on her left. "Yes, just through those doors."

"I'm looking for the Burtman's."

"Who?" she asked with a puzzled expression, reaching for her clipboard listing the patients.

"The Burtman family."

She glanced at the registry. It consisted of four patients. "I'm sorry, there's no one here by that name."

He was at first relieved then skeptical. "Are you sure? I was told they were injured in an early morning fire," he said raising his voice.

"Sir this is the intensive care unit. It's not the burn unit. Most of the patients here are suffering from head injuries," she stated factually, "but I've just come on shift."

He watched as she looked over the other two clipboards in front of her.

"We had one person arrive early this morning. Her name is not Burtman however."

He was at a loss. He'd been trying to figure out all morning who the other woman was who'd been in the *backerei* at the time of the fire. "Was it possible she was the woman who had been admitted earlier?"

"If the people you're looking for are in this hospital, more than likely they came in through the emergency room. Would you like me to check?"

"Please," he replied impatiently, as if she should have thought of it hours ago.

She switched to German. "This is Margaret Fletcher in 1-C. I have a visitor whose looking for some patients. They may have been admitted under the name of Burtman. Could you check for me? *Danke*," she said after a lengthy pause.

She looked at the man pacing in front of her relieved she might have information to send him away. "Sir, the Burtman's were admitted earlier in the morning. You'll be happy to know their condition is stable and they've been moved to a step-down unit."

A sense of relief flooded through him, but he still wondered about the other woman. "What's the name of the person who was admitted to intensive care this morning?"

"I'm sorry sir, but I'm not at liberty to give you that information," she said, sitting down with an air of finality.

"Can you at least tell me how she is doing?"

"I'm sorry sir, I'm not—"

"I know, you're not at liberty," he interrupted.

"Yes sir." She rearranged her clipboard and the phone and noticed the visitor hadn't moved. "Is there anything else I can do for you?" she asked.

"Some directions would be helpful."

CHAPTER 46

▼

Eva deeply regretted her decision to not answer her phone that fateful morning. Her first call had come at 4:45. Thinking it was Stace she refused to answer it. At 5:15 it rang again, then at 6:00. Because of her decision, she'd not been there when her parents needed her the most, and it forced Alfred to have to come and pick her up. When she saw him she was sick with despair.

He was a pitiful sight. What he wore had been borrowed in haste from a neighbor; used jeans, a tee shirt, and an old brown corduroy coat far too large for him. He'd refused medical treatment at the hospital and the sling the paramedics wrapped around his arm was bleeding through. When Eva looked through the peephole of her door she saw first his rumbled hair, a bruise above his right eye and the blood soaked gauze of his propped up arm.

Upon reaching the hospital she went immediately to see her parents who where sharing the same room. They were awake but unable to speak through the oxygen masks, and she could tell by their tired expressions and nods they would be all right. Her next task was to get her brother Alfred taken care of. She took him back to the emergency room where they were holding his file and waiting for his return. He collapsed in a wheel chair and they rolled him into an examination room. X-rays taken earlier that morning showed a compound fracture in his left forearm. He would be in surgery within the hour. After inquiring the whereabouts of Tasha, Eva made the long walk through the quiet maze of corridors and swinging doors until she passed unchecked into the intensive care unit. She had come in haste and now the thought of seeing Tasha stopped her.

She froze for a moment just inside the double doors and looked down the short hallway. From the first two doors on the right she could hear the daily sounds of the unit like things buzzing and bleeping, the voice of a mother reading a story to a silent listener, the swish of water from a nurse or two trying to give a patient a bed bath. A child's voice moaned then let out a string of obscenities. She listened for any indication of Tasha's presence, but heard none. Taking a few steps forward she peaked in the first door. The two beds on the right side of the room were occupied by young children, which looked to be under the age of ten. In the bed nearest the door lay a young girl, propped up with pillows, her face pointed towards the door, a white blanket tucked neatly under her arms. Her head was entirely wrapped in gauze except for her face, which seemed as though it were about to pop out of the head dressing, but her eyes were swollen shut. Seated beside her on a chair was her mother. She hadn't noticed Eva and continued reading the nursery rhyme as though her daughter understood every word. A young boy occupied the other bed. He was naked and his head was shaved. Two nurses in light colored jumpsuits were washing his legs. The young boy turned towards Eva with effort, as through he'd noticed her two minutes earlier and was just now getting around to looking at her. The right side of his face smiled as he grinned and let out an exaggerated sneer. The left side of his face hung unresponsively. The nurse facing the door noticed this and looked up towards Eva then back down at the boy.

"What is it Henry? You see someone? Oh my! And you're all naked. You'd better hide before she sees you!"

He grinned and snorted even louder then turned his head in the other direction trying to hide. Eva moved on past the first door, but one of the nurses who had been bathing the boy came to greet her.

"May I help you?"

Eva turned around startled by her voice. "Yes. I'm Eva Burtman. I'm looking for Tasha Matyastick."

The nurse gently tipped her head back as though she'd been expecting her. "I'm very sorry about the fire and your parents. How are they doing?"

"You know?"

"Yes, but not much. My name is Ruth," she said extending a hand. "I know there were others who arrived along with Tasha and that—are you and Tasha related?" she quickly asked before disclosing any information.

"I'm a friend of hers."

She took a step back questionably.

"Probably the only friend she has at the moment," Eva quickly added.

"I see. Do you know the whereabouts of her family?" Ruth asked.

"No, I'm afraid I don't."

"It's important we locate them as soon as possible."

"Can I see her?" Eva asked anxiously.

Ruth thought for a moment before answering. "Sure," she said endearingly. "She's in the room down the hall."

She followed Ruth apprehensively with her hands thrust deep into her jean pockets. Another nurse seated just inside the door stood up when Ruth entered the room. Eva froze outside the door.

"Tasha has a visitor," Ruth said to the other nurse.

Eva took a step forward.

"Hi. I'm Bridgett." The other nurse said and handed Eva a white cotton facemask. "You'll need to put this on. Are you sure you're up to this?"

"I think so," Eva replied, her soft voice muffled by the cotton mask.

Ruth smiled with her eyes. "All right."

Tasha lay face down on the hospital bed, which had been cranked flat with only the head portion elevated. A gauzy, white cotton blanket covered her up to the bottom of her shoulder blades. Her arms had been carefully placed beside her and raised upwards, so that her hands rested beside the pillow. Her head had been shaved, exposing a paper-white complexion dabbed with sprinkles of black hair stubble. The only visible injury at the moment was a three by four inch patch of bandage located on the back crown of her head. A plastic tube protruded out of it. Around the bandage was a bright orange residue of iodine, which had been swathed in haste on her head leaving long trails down her neck and across the side of her face like the stain of rusty water on porcelain. Eva shuffled along the side of her bed and looked into Tasha's face. Contorted by the force of her weight on the pillow, it was noticeably swollen, like she'd suffered an allergic reaction to a bee sting. Her eyes were filled with a translucent milky substance. A wheeze came with every laborious breath, which could be heard through the foggy clear rubber air mask feeding her lungs. Eva fell back into one of the two chairs near the bed. She propped her elbows on her knees, then her face into her hands and mumbled though her cotton mask, "What happened? What's wrong with her?"

Nurse Ruth took the seat beside her and explained as much as she knew. The emergency room at the University hospital was well equipped to handle most severe cases of trauma, except in cases like Tasha's, so they'd called in an additional physician by the name of Helmut Gurlict, a notable neurosurgeon with extensive experience in treating head injuries. He arrived around 5:30 that morning looking much the same way he always did, which is to say his frosty roughly cut hair might have been combed or uncombed, but his goatee was as sharp and defined as ever. Upon examining the patient's burns and CT scans, he immediately decided against opening Tasha's scull to relieve some of the pressure mounting in her cranium. The surgery would be too risky. She'd been in a coma since the fall and any additional trauma to the injured area might push her over the edge. Tasha's first and second degree burns were not life threatening, but extensive. They ran from the back of her calves, up her thighs and across her back. There was the risk of possible infection and the likelihood that if she were to awaken the pain produced by the burns would cause the pressure in her brain to increase. His recommendations where therefore, simple and hopefully, effective.

While nurses attended to Tasha's burns, Dr. Gurlict drilled a tiny hole through the cranium and inserted a monitoring device just below the surface. The device was held to her scull with a few strips of tape. The device had but one function, to monitor the increase in swelling. Blood was rushing into the damaged area, yet at the same time the additional pressure within her skull would affect the normal supply of oxygen to the brain, thus running the risk of killing millions of cells. Time and additional CT scans in the weeks to come would begin to show just what permanent injury had resulted and the extent to which other areas of the brain were affected by the decreased lack of oxygen. Her coma was a mixed blessing. On the one hand, there was no indication of when she might wake up from it and on the other hand, it afforded her comfort from the pain. For if the brain were tasked to perform any other function, such as reacting to the pain and increasing pressure in the brain, it might cause more permanent damage.

The implement inserted into her skull was also attached to a monitoring device about the size of a shoebox. There were five simple dials on the left hand panel and an alarm button. To the right of the dials was a dark green window with digitized lime-green numbers. Two numbers preceded a decimal point followed by another number. Any numerical reading above 87.5 called for an immediate response. They also hooked up an IV to the back of her left hand, which fed her with fluids and antibiotics. To her chest they taped electrodes to monitor the rhythms of her heart. At various points on her head they attached additional electrodes, which ran up to a separate machine that measured how electrical impulses were being processed by her brain. Initial tests run by this machine showed a considerable delay in the time sequence between stimulation and reaction. This was expected, since the accident had just occurred, but in time it was hoped the delay would become normalized. Tasha was also suffering from smoke inhalation. Her brain at the moment required a generous supply of oxygen in order to heal, so they strapped a partial facemask over her mouth and nose forcing oxygen into her lungs.

Eva looked with despondency at the series of electrodes, tubes and wires, twisting up over her head and running into no less then five various machines and monitoring devices. "Will she be all right?" she finally asked Ruth.

"It's too early to tell and I'm not going to lead you to believe otherwise. What I can tell you is she is stable at the present time, which is a good sign she'll recover."

"What about her head injury?"

Nurse Ruth signed with reflection and turned to Eva. "She suffered a severe blow to her head during the fall. Injuries of this nature typically take a long time to heal. The initial CT scans show severe trauma."

"What does that mean?"

"It means that Tasha may lose some of her normal functioning capabilities."

"Will it be permanent?"

"That too is difficult to tell. In most cases the brain is able to reroute and relearn these functions. For children, that process is much quicker. For adults, depending on the severity of the injury, full recovery is unlikely. But I'll be quick to add the brain is an amazing organism. In almost every case I've seen there have been some genuine surprises. Look, why don't I leave you two alone for a while? Stay as long as you like. If you've got any other questions I'm sure Nurse Bridgett can answer them for you. Don't hesitate to call me if you need me."

CHAPTER 47

▼

The cause of the fire was still uncertain. At the moment, firemen from the first two of the three responding units were in the process of rolling up hoses and securing their equipment. The district fire chief was writing his report. An insurance representative was on site gathering information. Reporters were asking questions from neighborhood witnesses still lingering behind the yellow plastic band of security tape. An arson investigation team was kicking through the soggy ashen mud, gathering scraps of information, taking detailed photographs and trying to reconstruct how the fire started and spread.

Eva was intelligent enough to know that while she may have been responsible for Tasha being in the *backerei*, she was not responsible for the fire. Instinct also told her the fire was no accident. Regardless of whether the arson team concluded the fire had been caused by an electrical failure or an "act of God," would make no difference to her. She knew the fire had been deliberately set by the CRM. The only questions in her mind was which one of them did it and why. If the fire had been set in retaliation for the paper's ongoing investigation, then why strike at the *backerei*? The location of the paper would have provided a much better target. She could only conclude the intended target had been Tasha and with that in mind the terrorists had succeeded. Either Neil or Derrick had set the fire and instinct led her to believe it had been Derrick, but intelligent guesses based on instinct and experience could never bring retribution and justice. The system demanded hard facts in order to convict.

How or if Stace was involved with the fire, or to which agency or group he belonged to, was no longer up for question. The seriousness of the incident had reaffirmed her vigilance and brought her abruptly back to the gravity of the situation. It was not the time for emotional commitments and entanglements, and certainly not the time to be defused or purposely distracted from her investigation. In fact, she couldn't help but wonder if the emergence of Stace into her life had been to do exactly that, to distract her from her investigation of either the ICC or the CRM. Which meant of course, anything he'd said or done to her had nothing to do with whether or not he actually cared about her.

She pulled her sweater tightly around her and leaned forward into her chair. Although it hurt deeply, she took another long look at Tasha, drilling Tasha's predicament into her mind. The event was transforming; like a chameleon changes the color of its skin to suit a threat, Eva was able to transform all of her anger into the clear and perfect tint of determination.

Within fifteen minutes Stace had been able to locate the whereabouts of Mr. and Mrs. Burtman and had been refused the right to visit them. The nurse behind the desk would only give him a general statement as to their condition. Stace was aware Alfred had also suffered injuries and inquired about him. The nurse placed a few calls for him and told him that Alfred was in the emergency room being prepped for surgery. If he was there, then Eva was probably with him. He found his way into the emergency room where the nursing station had already been advised he was on his way over. Stace took a quick glance at the waiting room for Eva, but she was not there. Two young men sat on a nearby couch in front of a glass coffee table. One of them looked up at Stace and continued scribbling in his notepad. The other man appeared to be sleeping with his head cocked back and a video camera nestled in his lap.

"I'm looking for Alfred Burtman," Stace said stepping up to the chest-high counter.

"I'm sorry, but Mr. Burtman is in surgery," the nurse said.

"Can you tell me why?"

"Are you a relative or a friend of the family?"

"What difference does that make?" Stace was getting tired of the run-around.

The nurse pressed the question with silence and an inquiring look.

"I'm a close friend of the Burtman's. I learned about the fire just an hour ago and I'm just trying to make sure everyone is all right."

This seemed to satisfy the nurse's requirements. "Mr. Burtman is going to be just fine sir. He has a fractured arm that we're going to set. He'll probably be in surgery for about an hour and then a few hours in recovery. When he wakes up we'll ask if he'd like to have any visitors."

Stace was grateful for the information. "Thank you" but he needed more. "Do you know if his sister was here? I'm trying to find her."

The nurse responded quickly, "I'm sorry, I just came on shift and haven't seen anybody else."

"What about any of the others?"

"Other who?"

"Nurses and Doctors. Surely someone here can tell me if they've seen his sister or not."

"Sir, it's 8:50. Shift change occurs at 8:00. We haven't seen anyone else."

Stace was frustrated, but polite. "All right. I appreciate the information."

"Not at all sir."

"Just one more thing," he pressed. "The Burtman's were also admitted with another woman. Do you know anything about her?"

The nurse glanced down at her paperwork. She herself had just come out of the briefing room where the night shift gives a quick run down on the evenings activities. Her notes of the briefing were strewn in front of her. "Sir, if you're not a relative, I can't supply you with that information."

"You can't even tell me anything about her condition?" he asked raising his voice. The young man with the notepad glanced towards the commotion.

"No sir."

Stace backed away from the counter then stepped through the set of double doors leading outside. He'd been running around all morning trying to locate Eva without success. He'd not found out anything about the young woman. Eva would not have gone into work. Her entire family was in the hospital. She had to be around somewhere. "Maybe she's gone to the cafeteria to get a cup of coffee," he thought. With that in mind, he turned around and ran right into the young man with his notepad. Behind him towered the lanky man with long hair and a video camera hoisted unto his shoulder. A tiny red beacon light flashed signifying the camera was rolling.

"I couldn't help notice you were asking about the Burtman family."

"And you are?" Stace asked looking into his eager brown eyes behind perfectly circular wire-frame glasses.

"Daniel Talbot with the Frankfurt Post. Do you mind if I ask you a few questions?"

"Yes I do," he said turning around.

The reporter turned to his cameraman. "Turn that thing off." Then faced Stace. "How's that?"

"Better, but I've still got nothing to say."

"All right, then off the record. You said inside you were a friend of the Burtman's and you're looking for Alfred's sister."

"True. What does that have to do with you and me?"

"Nothing. I just thought you'd like to know where she is," he said starting to walk away.

"Wait a minute!"

The reporter stopped and turned around.

"I could use a little help at this point."

"Thought so," the reporter replied. He looked at his notepad for verification of his facts. "I got to the *backerei* at about 4:45 this morning. Mind you, after all the excitement had passed. Witnesses said the Burtman's crawled out of their window. Can you believe that? Tied a sheet to the window frame and hung out over the ledge."

"What about the young woman?" Stace asked trying to speed him along.

"Her name's Tasha Matyastick. She threw her dog out onto the van and then jumped out herself. Quite a story! On her way down she must have hit her head on the side of the *backerei* or the edge of the van. She was the first to leave the scene. Paramedics said they doubt she'd pull through."

"Where's she now?"

"In intensive care."

"Intensive care? Are there two?"

"No. First floor in the main building. She a friend?" The reporter asked, pulling his pen out of his pocket again and flipping his notepad about.

"Never heard of her."

The reporter capped his pen and shoved it back into his pocket. "They won't let you see her you know."

"Now what about Eva?"

"She brought her brother Alfred back to the emergency room a little while ago."

"Do you know if she left the hospital?"

"Doubtful. She left the emergency room though the inside doors leading into the main part of the hospital."

"Do you know where she might have been headed?"

"Not for sure, but I suspect back to intensive care to see her friend."

Stace stood there motionless for a few moments retracing the run-around he'd been through all morning. The thought occurred to him that while he was arguing with Margaret the receptionist outside of intensive care, Eva had probably been inside the unit all along.

The reporter had just about reached the doors leading back into the emergency room. Stace called back after him, "thanks for you help."

He nodded and walked inside with his cameraman following him like a dog on a leash.

Margaret was looking over a new recipe in the German edition of *Bon' Appetite* when she heard the familiar squeak of tennis shoes coming up the corridor towards her. She looked up over the top of the magazine to see if her assumption was true and slipped a pencil into the pages to hold the spot in her magazine.

The long walk back to the intensive care had given Stace time to cool off. He'd been prepared to confront Eva earlier in the morning at her home and now he was at a loss for words. He knew trying to reconcile their friendship would have to wait. His biggest concern was how she was holding up given the circumstances she was facing. He was quite certain she was in the unit and in a few minutes would be facing her for the first time in a week. The situation called for extreme sensitivity.

"Good morning again sir," Margaret greeted him without getting up out of her chair.

"Yeah, good morning," he replied and managed a faint smile. "I was told in the emergency room Eva Burtman is here in the unit."

Margaret looked down at her patient roster again as a formality, "I'm sorry, she's not listed as a patient."

Stace took a deep breath and tried again. "She would be a visitor. Her friend was one of the victims in last night's fire."

"I see." She looked down at the visitor's roster. "She's not on this list either."

"She might have arrived before you came on shift," he said calmly.

"That's entirely possible," she replied. "I'll step inside and check for you."

"I'd appreciate it. Tell her it's Stace."

She stepped into the hallway just as Nurse Ruth was heading across the hall.

"Ruth. There's a young man here who's looking for a woman named Eva Burtman."

"Is he a relative or friend of the patient?" Ruth asked.

"Neither."

"Then he has to remain outside the unit, but there is a Miss. Burtman here. You'll find her in there."

"Thanks Ruth."

Margaret took a few steps towards Tasha's room and greeted Bridgett at the door. With eyes conditioned to avoid looking at any patient in Tasha's situation, she quickly found Eva seated in the chair next to the bed. "*Verzeihung*, Miss. Burtman?" Eva looked up at the strange voice at the door. "You have a visitor."

"Who is it?"

"I believe his name's Stace."

"Who?" She couldn't believe her ears.

Margaret repeated the name. Eva heard it perfectly well the first time. "Tell him I don't want to see him."

"Very well."

"No wait! Tell him...tell him I can't come out right now and I'll call him at home tonight."

"All right Miss. Burtman," she said and returned to her post.

"Well?" Stace asked the moment she stepped through the doors.

"Mrs. Burtman is inside with a patient sir. Margaret repeated the message.

"Wait a second!" Stace pleaded, stepping towards her and preventing her from returning behind the table by stretching out his arm.

Margaret felt intimidated by the intrusion.

"Please. Please try one more time for me," he said desperately. "Just one more time and I'll leave, ok?"

Margaret frowned and looked at him. "What do you want me to tell her?"

"Tell her it's urgent, that it's very important I speak with her."

"All right. I'll give it one more try for you," she said, backing away from his arm.

"Thanks Margaret," he said as if they were old friends.

In a moment she was at the door to Tasha's room again. "I'm sorry to bother you again Miss. Burtman, but he says it's urgent."

She returned without a reply from Eva.

"Is she coming?"

"I have relayed the message to Miss. Burtman as you requested. You will just have to wait patiently and see."

He let out a long sigh and listened to the air pass through his nose and for the first time that morning noticed the chill in the air. He looked down the long corridor towards the front door. Through the windows lined along the length of the hall he could see a stiff breeze passing through the shrubs in the courtyard just outside the windows. Along the windows to the right, refracting rays of sunlight spilled in horizontally and bounced off the smooth cement floor onto the ceiling. The warmth called to him, so he walked over to the first window and lifted his face towards the sun. He could do nothing but wait. After a few moments had passed he dropped his glance. The sun had temporarily blinded him, filling his eyes with hot white circles. He backed out of the sun and checked his watch, then looked back outside. The beauty of the courtyard was deceptive. The picnic table resting under a tree in the middle of a green lawn looked cozy enough, but the brisk breeze rippling the windows in front of him told him otherwise. He checked his watch again. A full six minutes had passed and he doubted she was going to come out. Suddenly, he heard the double doors from the unit open.

He turned to see Eva stop and stand by them momentarily with her arms crossed in front of her. He took one look at the expression on her face with its distant eyes and knew he'd have to scrap everything he'd planned to say and just be there if she needed him. She dropped her hands to her side and slowly walked towards him. Her face grew more stern and ridged as she approached. She stopped about five feet from him and just looked into his eyes. It was a confusing look, a look that was at a lost for words.

"What are you doing here?" she asked.

It was a simple question, but her tone told him she resented his presence.

"I went to see you this morning and found out about the fire. I rushed over to see if you and your family were all right." He spoke with genuine concern hoping to melt the ice on her face.

"I don't want you to go near my parents." She crossed her arms back in front of her and shifted.

The comment knocked him completely off guard. He let go of the rail he was holding on to and took a step closer to her. She took a step back and held her hands up in front of her.

"Don't! I don't want you to come near me either."

He stopped his advance, utterly bewildered by her posture and choice of words. He took his eyes off her and tried to figure out what to say next. Moments seemed to pass into minutes.

"I don't understand Eva. One minute we're eating hamburgers and the next second you're gone. You won't return my calls, and now…now you're telling me you don't want me to help you." He knew his words came out strong, but they were the truth.

"It's pretty simple Stace. I have just figured you out. It took me a while, I had to find a few pieces to the puzzle, but now I've got a clear picture of who you are."

"What the hell are you talking about Eva?" He'd passed beyond being flustered and felt the sudden urge to defend himself.

"How long did you expect you could fool us—fool me?" she asked, throwing her hands up into the air.

"What the hell are you talking about Eva?" he asked with more force and clarity.

She took a deep breath and looked at him hard. For a split second he'd almost convinced her that he didn't know what she was talking about. But that was only for a split second. She quickly wised up.

"It's my job to know what's going on. How long did you think it would take me to discover what you were up to?"

He considered her question, but like the others it made no sense at all. Any comment would have been silly on his part, so he decided to just shut up for the moment.

"I bet you thought you could keep on distracting me from my investigation until it was too late didn't you?"

Stace kept his mouth shut.

"And when you'd accomplished what you intended to do you were just going to walk out of my life. Just disappear and never come back."

Eva brought her hands back around in front of her and bit her lip. She looked out into the courtyard beyond him. There was pain in her eyes, something desperate to which he knew he was innocent of, yet still felt entirely responsible for.

"So help me God Stace…" she began then stopped. Her words were deadly with intent. "If I ever find out you were responsible for this fire, or that you were even a part of it, I will personally dedicate my life to making sure you pay for it."

He cocked his head in disbelief, eyes widening and probing for an explanation for what she was saying, searching for some response that would put her back on track. He took another step forward towards her and she backed away.

"Ok. Ok!" he said. "I have no idea what you're talking about Eva. Absolutely none. I don't know how to answer you Eva. I don't know the first thing to say to you."

She took her eyes off the floor and looked at him again. "And I suppose you know nothing about Trojan Security, the ICC, or the CRM—or the program for that matter?"

"What the fuck are you talking about Eva?" he shouted. Margaret had been listening all along, but his swearing peaked her interest.

Eva pressed on. "And I suppose you don't know a guy named Rick Forstein either, do you?" she asked.

He spun around and grabbed the rail by the windows with both hands, looking momentarily at a handful of dead leaves swirling in the dirt in the corner of the building.

"Forstein," he thought to himself, "Rick Forstein? What the hell has he got to do with any of this?" He juggled the name around in his head. It was a name he'd tried to forget. "And where did Eva come up with it?" He wondered, and decided to ask.

"Where did you hear the name, Forstein?" he spoke to the window.

"You're now going to tell me you don't know Forstein?"

"Of course I know Forstein. Rick Forstein, but where'd you hear the name?"

"You told me all about him. The day you came up with that glorious story about where you came from and what you did before you came to Germany."

"At the *friebad*?" he asked. It was coming back to him. He'd forgotten, however, that he'd mentioned the name to her.

Eva didn't answer. She knew he was lying.

"Stace, I'm going to make this really clear for you and I'm only going to say it once...." She paused for a moment to gather the courage. He was still facing the window and she thought she better get it out. "I don't want to see you anymore. Don't come by the house, because I won't come to the door. Don't call or page me because I won't return your calls. I've got an investigation to finish. I know you and Forstein are involved with it and it's only a matter of time before I find out to what extent. So, you do what you need to do because I'm certainly going to do what I need to do." She finished what she was saying and walked straight back into the intensive care unit.

CHAPTER 48

▼

All the members of the team were present with the exception of Jean Thompson. Stautzen as usual, sat at one end of the conference table aloof and indifferent. He was the first to arrive and hadn't spoken to anyone. Dr. Loran sat in the chair to his immediate left and beside him, Davia Reese. The two exchanged small talk. Dr. Loran remarked that he would be happy to get back home and Davia spoke about going to visit her sister in New Hampshire before returning home to Phoenix. Rick Forstein sat on the opposite side of the table next to Jean's empty chair. On the table before him lay his leather bound briefcase. More than once he had leaned forward to brush the dust off it and now he sat composed and wondering why Jean was running late. The occasion should have been a happy one. Rick announced the completion of the program to Pruitt late yesterday afternoon. At Pruitt's request they were all gathered for what would be their final meeting together. At precisely 8:30, Pruitt arrived followed by Fred Watson. The others shuffled in their seats, but Rick remained steadfast. Pruitt took the seat beside Rick without the least bit of a greeting and they turned their attention to Fred Watson, who stood at the head of the table ready to speak.

"Ladies and Gentlemen, I would like to thank each one of you for your services to which you played a crucial part in designing this program and without your individual efforts," he stalled for a moment searching for words, "well, let's just say we couldn't have done it without you."

"As all of you know this program will now enter its second phase. That is, the designing of the secondary security system that will in essence, totally eliminate the possibility the work you've done actually gets put to use." He smiled at having said this and Dr. Loran chuckled. Watson got serious again. "Which I'm fully confident our own teams here at Trojan Security will be able to produce."

"I hope you don't find it too crass or awkward, but Mr. Pruitt here has your compensation checks in hand and I have an appointment in about ten minutes." He glanced at his watch. "Again, I thank each of you and have a safe trip back home."

"Where's Jean?" Rick whispered in Pruitt's ear.

"Pruitt turned the side of his face towards Rick and rested his chin on his palm. "Called this morning. Said she couldn't make it in."

Rick thought the comment peculiar, especially in light of what occurred at the Peach Tree Bed and Breakfast.

Pruitt stood up and pulled out several white envelopes out of his coat pocket. "I would like to add to Mr. Watson's thanks with something more concrete. Dr. Loran," Pruitt began, reading the name off the top envelope he was holding. Dr. Loran stood up. Pruitt handed him the envelope and shook his hand. "Best of luck to you."

"Davia Reese." She stood up. "Thanks so much for your help. Best of luck."

"Stoozen...Staupen?" Stautzen stood up. Pruitt smiled. "Just kidding Stautzen, you'all have got some funny names." Stautzen took the envelope without comment.

"And last but not least, Rick." Rick gave him a puzzled look. "I told you to expect this didn't I?" Pruitt asked.

"Well, yeah."

"You've earned it."

"Folks, you may stay a few minutes and say good-bye if you wish. Rick, meet me in your office in about fifteen minutes and we'll tie up some loose ends."

While Rick slipped the envelope into his briefcase Pruitt went around the room and shook everyone's hand. He ended with Stautzen and whispered something into his ear. The group rapidly dispersed. Stautzen left alone without any formal good-byes. Dr. Loran and Davia left together and Rick went back to his office.

Rick opened his office door to the sound of hollow space. With the exception of the phone on his desk and the battery run clock on the wall, every other piece of electronic equipment had been stripped from his office. Even his laptop computer was gone. He set his briefcase on the desk and snapped it open. The two CD's containing a copy of the program were still there, but he knew that because he'd put them there and hadn't lost sight of his briefcase since. What he was most concerned about was the secondary copy he'd made and slipped into the back file slot in the cover. He reached in with his hand and felt for them, but at that moment heard footsteps at his door. He shoved the disks back into the case and slammed the lid shut. There was a knock at the door, but Pruitt didn't wait for a response to enter. When Pruitt opened the door Rick saw three security officers standing in the hallway with their hands resting on their gun belts. Pruitt shut the door behind him. In his hand he cradled an eight by eleven inch manila envelope.

Pruitt casually strolled across Rick's office and took a seat on the couch possessing a silly smirk. Suddenly Rick felt warm and sticky. He followed Pruitt's lead by taking a seat behind the empty desk trying to retain his composure.

"Rick Forstein…" Pruitt said through the same smile, cocking his head to the left as if he'd just heard the name for the first time and was trying to decide whether he liked it or not. "I am surprised."

Pruitt relaxed into the couch and slapped the envelop across his lap a few times. The noise was irritating to Rick, a prelude to the contents.

"You know," Pruitt began again, "stealing programs is a felony offense in the state of Texas and every other state I believe."

Rick swallowed hard and adjusted his tie. He looked nervously at his briefcase. For lack of anything better to say he said," I don't know what your taking about."

Pruitt either didn't hear him or choose to ignore him. He slapped the envelope down a few more times on his knees. "By the way, how is Fredericksburg this time of year?"

Rick was painfully aware he was not in control of the conversation and never would be. His face swelled with sweat and he drove his thumb down into his pants to loosen his pants a bit. A slight pain cramped his chest.

"My wife and I—you know Caroline don't you? We usually wait until March or early April to head out that way. The spring rains have fallen by then and the roadside is covered with bluebonnets and Indian paintbrush. Beautiful sight really, but I suppose you had other scenery on your mind, eh?" Pruitt looked down at the envelope and smiled the same silly smile. "Yeah, you had other scenery in mind. "Of course, these photos don't really capture the entire naked beauty, but they tell the whole story nevertheless."

It occurred to Rick that Jean's absence was more than coincidental. Fact, she was probably on a plane right now headed God-knows-where. "Son of a Bitch!" he muttered.

"What's that Rick? Say something?" Pruitt asked looking at him.

Rick was tired of the game and met his glance. "You know, it really wasn't too difficult to figure out what we were building the program for."

"And what would that be?"

"For Stautzen and the ICC."

"You figure that out on your own Rick? Or did you forget that was decided before you even began the project?" Pruitt lifted a palm in mock sincerity.

"You have no plans on building a security program do you?"

"Of course we do, that was our original intent, remember? It's too bad you won't be the one to build it."

"Where's Jean?" Rick asked nervously.

"Like I told you this morning, she won't be in."

"She's been with you all along hasn't she?"

Pruitt chuckled and shrugged his shoulders. "Your imagination's quite active this morning. Like the others, her work is finished here. She knew that yesterday. As for where she is now I have no idea."

Rick didn't care anymore about appearing composed. He snapped open the top button of his shirt and slid his tie loose.

"Really nothing to get flustered about Rick," Pruitt said rising. "I'll tell you what, you give me the copies of the program and I'll let you see what we're keeping sealed in your employee file for future reference ok? We won't even press charges for making the extra copy of the program. And I'll make you an additional promise, you keep your imagination to yourself and I promise I will not personally deliver these photos of your Fredericksburg excursion to Julie. Sweet gal," he added for affect. "I'd sure hate to see her upset."

Pruitt walked over to Rick's desk and stood over his briefcase. He extended the envelope towards Rick. Rick could only muster a look of complete disgust. He opened his case and handed Pruitt the copies. Pruitt tossed the envelope on his desk.

"I think you'll find everything in order there; severance pay, a fairly nice recommendation written by me personally, despite your attempt to steal the program and of course, some wonderful shots. Oh, by the way, almost forgot. We've got other interesting encounters of you and Jean on video too. Those I'm afraid do require a little imagination, but the underlining tone is easy to see."

Rick glanced around the room looking for the locations where the video cameras might be and cursed his stupidity.

Pruitt headed for the door but stopped short. He didn't even bother to turn around. The inflection of his voice revealed the intensity of the entire encounter. "You've got ten-minutes to leave the grounds. After that, I'll have you arrested for trespassing."

As he left, Rick caught another glimpse of the security officers outside.

"You want us to keep watching him Mr. Pruitt," Officer Dublin said anxiously after Pruitt closed the door.

"Like a hawk. Don't let him out of your sight until I tell you."

"Yes sir!"

CHAPTER 49

▼

There are two priorities that hold a man in place. Without them he is like a feather drifting about in the whimsical winds of the universe. They're not extravagant priorities by any means, but justifications for existence. They are in essence, work and a good woman. A man can live with either one or the other at any given time, but to have both is to be one step beyond the gates of heaven.

Stace had neither.

He'd come to Europe hoping to enrich his life and reawaken his passion for his craft. A year spent in Germany hadn't brought him closer to that goal. He was still just a step ahead of poverty, developing blurry photos of images he'd seen over and over and over again. And he was a man just like any other man. That is to say, he wasn't just looking for great sex. What he wanted was what all men want, a woman to call his own. A woman with whom he could count on to always be *his* woman. A woman he could devote the best of himself towards enriching. He had thought—no hoped—that woman would be Eva. In his entire life he had never discovered a woman who could satisfy him on so many levels. She was the realization of all his expectations and a surrealistic version of his love utopia. His disappointment was severe.

By 10:00 a.m. he'd made it back to his apartment, but a transformation had taken place since he'd left it earlier that morning. It had been his home for over a year and now it seemed stranger to him than the first day he moved in. What had once been quaint and charming now seemed ugly and awkward. Nothing was familiar to him. The wooden floors were not tiled. The appliances in the kitchen were 220 volts and not 110. The wallpaper lining the hallway was old fashioned and the furniture in his bedroom, depressing. The toilet in the bathroom had a handle on the top cover and not on the tank where it should have been. No matter how many lights he turned on, the apartment was still dark and lonely. It was no longer home.

He walked into the bathroom and looked at his sorry excuse of a photo-lab. Everything in it could be replaced except for the developing machine. He unplugged it from the wall and carried it into the back room where he stored the rest of his equipment. The two boxes he'd unpacked all his junk in when he came were still where he'd left them, empty in the far corner. Without hesitation he started throwing everything back into them. The most valuable equipment, such as his camera bodies, lenses and other accessories, would fit into his large aluminum briefcase. The foam was already pre-cut to their shapes. That case he would hand carry on the plane. Most of the rest of his stuff he could fit into his two suitcases. What could not fit in either the boxes or his suitcases would have to stay.

He was not in the mood to see or speak to anyone and besides, no one would miss him when he left. For his landlords he would leave a note and call them when he'd settled back into his parent's home in Austin. They could keep the deposit. There would be last month's utilities bills they would have to pay and he didn't have the time or the energy to clean the place up. The company where he worked could forward his last check. They had a stack of applicants ready to fill his position. The only other business he needed to take care of was to close his bank account, but the banks were closed on the weekends. He had less than four hundred marks in his account and decided he would just go to a money machine in the morning and withdraw it. He had one piece of plastic, a visa, and it still had a sizeable credit limit on it, enough to buy the ticket for his way back to Austin.

He finished packing his equipment, sealing the boxes with masking tape, then went into the kitchen and wrote the note to his landlord. He apologized for his abrupt departure, "an emergency had come up," and would they please forward the boxes to his new address. He decided the rest of the packing could wait until evening. He went into the living room and booked a Sunday afternoon flight to Los Angeles with a connecting flight to Austin. After getting off the phone he walked over to his stacks of CD's and removed an ancient recording of Ozzy Osbourne's tribute to Randy Rhodes. It was over three decades old, a little early and heavy for his taste, but slipped it into the CD player anyway. He forwarded it to track eleven to a song entitled "*Goodbye to Romance*" and cranked it up. It sealed his mood into a cocoon of despondency and hopelessness.

Meanwhile, back in Austin, Rick had said goodbye to no one. He threw his briefcase and the box of his packed stuff into the trunk of his Miata and headed west on Research until it joined I-35, where he went north and headed towards Pfluggerville, then Round Rock, then up towards the metropolis of Dallas/Ft. Worth, with no particular destination in mind. He just needed to drive—drive hard and fast.

Trojan Security had screwed him and left him out to dry. Jean had betrayed him and disappeared on a flight with a check written in a handful of zeroes. He was no better than the rest of them and his bonus check would hold him for a few months. He could care-less about the program. As far as he was concerned people could believe what they wanted to believe. If they were stupid enough to be followers then let them follow. Let them fall right into the ditches along with their blind guides. The world was full of impostors, shamans, political messiahs and social pariahs. Rick was incubating a less constructive motive…he just wanted to get even.

He knew Stautzen was probably on a flight to Germany at that very moment. Finding him later at the ICC in Munich would not be a

problem. Simply wrestling the program out of his hands would do little. Stautzen would simply call Trojan Security and copies of the program would be expressed to him within a couple of days. He would
have to come up with a better plan.

In Hillsboro, he got off the interstate and pulled into a Wendy's
drive through for a drink. He doubled back on the access road, took a
right on the bridge that took him over I-35, and entered the freeway
going back towards Austin. He pulled into his driveway at 2:45 in the
afternoon and opened the garage door with his remote. He backed
Julie's Ford out of the garage, went into the garage, pulled the string
hanging from the ceiling, opened the trap door, unfolded the wooden
latter, and climbed into the attic.

"What are you looking for?" Julie called up to him. She was wondering why he hadn't come inside first.

"The suitcases."

He looked into the rafters of the roof and spotted them, four matching vinyl Samsonites sitting side by side on a sheet of plywood. He
took a couple of steps up the ladder and reached for the biggest one,
then backed it down the ladder where Julie was waiting for an explanation.

"I've got to make a quick trip to Germany," he said walking into the
house.

"Germany? Whatever for?" She followed him upstairs. His daughter
watched her father pass without a hug. She dropped down onto her
knees and climbed up the stairs.

"To work. We just completed the project and they're going to need
help getting it all set up." He started to lay the suitcase down on the
bed and Julie grabbed a hold of it.

"Wait a second. This thing's filthy. She went into the bathroom,
wiped the case clean with a washcloth and set it on the bed. "Where
exactly in Germany are you headed?"

"Frankfurt."

"You never mentioned you'd have to take a trip with this program."

"That's because most of the programs we build are for clients in the Austin area. There's always an on-site installation. I didn't expect to be going, so I never mentioned it."

"But can't someone else go?"

"No. I designed it. It's up to me to get it up and running."

She thought the tone of his voice peculiar, but said nothing as she took a seat on the couch across from the bed. He unzipped the case and started stuffing it with clothes.

"How long will you be gone?"

"Probably not more than a week."

Their daughter had finally waddled down the long hallway and into the room. She giggled and walked over to her father then held onto his leg for dear life. He reached down and pried her loose, lifted her up and kissed her forehead and sat down with Julie on the couch. "I know this is sudden, but it will only be for a few days. I really didn't know I'd be going until this afternoon."

"When do you have to leave?"

"Right away. Fact, I should have left this morning. One of the other members of the team has already gone ahead and I'm supposed to meet him there." He set his daughter back down on the carpet.

"Do you have reservations?"

"No. I was hoping you could do that for me."

"You'll need your passport. If I can just remember where I filed them…

"You didn't file them, I did. They're in the cabinet downstairs.

Julie got up. "Well, let me see if I can book you a flight."

"First class, if you don't mind."

Julie turned around. "First class?"

"Yeah. I've got some last minute planning to do and I don't need any distractions."

"All right. First class," she said and headed for the door. "Watch her Rick. She's starting to get into everything."

He glanced at his daughter who was walking along the dresser. She had one hand stretched along the top and was feeling for things to grab.

He finished packing his clothes and went into the bathroom for his personals. As an added measure he grabbed a spare suit from the closet and laid it over the rest of his things in the suitcase before zipping it up. Julie returned about ten minutes later. She looked at the suitcase standing upright near the door.

"Finished already?"

"Sure. Told you, short trip."

"Good thing. I've got you booked on a flight leaving at 6:50. You've got an hour layover in New York. You should get to Frankfurt sometime in the late afternoon tomorrow."

"Good work," he said kissing her on the cheek. He grabbed his suitcase and walked to the top of the staircase. "Tell you what, I'll go put this in the trunk. Why don't you get ready and we'll go out to eat before my flight. Threadgills if you like. You haven't started dinner have you?"

"It's 3:30 Rick."

"You're right," he said looking at his watch. "Good, then it won't be too crowded."

He left Julie upstairs and took his stuff out to the car. He'd forgotten about his box of stuff from the office, but slid it towards the backseat anyway and crammed his suitcase in. He reached for his briefcase and took out the envelope Pruitt had fired him with. God forbid Julie should ever see the contents. He shoved them into the briefcase and locked it.

Rebecca was sitting on the couch and kicking her feet. "Stay still honey," Julie said, trying to tie her sneakers. Rick sat down next to them and took the check out of his pocket.

"What's that?" Julie asked.

"My bonus and a bit more. It should ease the pain of me having to leave you for a few days."

He endorsed the check and handed it to his wife. She fell back on the floor and studied it carefully. "Is it real?"

"Of course it's real. Deposit it for me first thing Monday morning and don't forget to buy something special for yourself."

She checked for his signature on the back and slipped it into her blouse pocket. "Ok. I think I can do that.

CHAPTER 50

▼

No sooner had United Airlines flight 347 reached its cruising altitude of 33,000 feet over the Atlantic that the fate of Rick Forstein was decided. The calls originated from a pay phone at the Austin International Airport to Pruitt's cellular phone. Pruitt took the call on the deck of his home overlooking the winding Brazos River. Upon hanging up with the security officer from Trojan Security he placed a call to Stautzen's home in Munich and left a message with his wife for Stautzen to call him back upon his arrival in Munich. Later that day Stautzen returned Pruitt's call, understood the message and immediately placed a call to Neil, who then had a brief discussion with Derrick, who would be the last to know, but the first man called upon to rectify the situation. Rick Forstein would have no clue when he cleared customs at Frankfurt Main International that he would be instantaneously submersed into the world of the subversive.

Having consumed a generous portion of chicken-fried steak, homespun potatoes and a fresh ear of hot-buttered corn on the cob at Threadgills, Rick passed up the invitation for dinner on the plane and opted instead for a glass of white wine to calm his nerves. His frame of mind hadn't changed since his meeting with Pruitt earlier that morning. He was still consumed with a burning sense of vengeance. Had he

considered the implications of his plan he might have been able to pre-
serve some fragment of his future.

The hallways of Trojan Security were silent and dark when Pruitt
returned to his office shortly after speaking with Stautzen. Once inside,
he unlocked the bottom file cabinet to his desk and pulled out the photographs of Jean and Rick and took them over to the copy machine.
After slipping on a pair of cleaning gloves, he reduplicated the eight by
ten photographs into brilliant color representations of the originals. He
took the copies and placed them into another envelope then secured
the originals. Thirty minutes later he pulled his car up along the curb
of Dolan Street a few houses down from the Forstein's house. He
wasn't at all intimidated by the faint light falling across the street and
nearby homes originating from a nearby streetlight on the corner. He
got out of his car and casually strolled up the sidewalk, stopping at the
Forstein's mailbox for a brief moment formulating an impromptu
plan. The living room light was on, as well as the kitchen light downstairs. He walked up to the door and looked for signs of movement
through the inlayed windows in the front door. He saw none and slid
the envelope between the door and the doorframe, just above the
gold-plated handle. That way it would be sure to fall onto the welcome
mat as soon as Julie opened the door. He rang the doorbell twice and
strolled briskly over the manicured St. Augustine grass of the front
yard, disappearing down the street.

Julie was upstairs giving Rebecca a bath when she heard the chime.
"Shoot," she muttered to herself, wondering whom it could be at this
time of night. "Well, they'll just have to wait a minute won't they
Pumpkin." She finished rinsing her daughter's slippery nude body and
tossed a fluffy towel over her head and around her chubby little face.
"Now let's go see who that is." Stepping onto the tile of the foyer she
looked through the window in the front door. There were no shadows.
She flipped on the porch light and looked out the window in both
directions before reaching for the handle. One can never be too careful.
Seeing no one, she turned the handle on the door. Something fell onto

the mat and tumbled onto the cement patio. She peered out the edge of the door and noticed the manila envelope. She thought it rather odd and searched for the person who delivered it. There was no one in sight. After picking up the envelope she went back inside. Balancing it on the wooden railing at the bottom of the staircase she took her daughter upstairs to dress her and to put her to bed. When she came back downstairs she took the envelope into the dinning room and opened it.

Pruitt had arranged the five photographs in chronological order, so that they would reveal the illicit fling between Rick and Jean as a progression of an all-consuming affair. The first two photographs were black and white copies of select images off the video footage filmed in Rick's office. One of them captured Jean the moment she'd reached up and brushed the crumb off Rick's face. It was a tender gesture. The other black and white had been taken about a week later. Rick had come up behind Jean and was massaging her shoulders. The photo revealed Rick's hands slipping around the front part of her neck and gave the impression he was intending on reaching for more. Julie's mind flashed between bewilderment and rage. Suspicions she'd buried came to life in their most fantastic form. She wanted to believe the photographs were a cruel joke, but the evidence was unquestionable. Painfully, she flipped to the third photograph and her greatest fear was justified. The color photograph showed a frontal view of Rick and Jean strolling hand and hand across the lawn of the Johnson Estate. In the background were blurred impressions of tourists. Julie found it offensive in its boldness. She and Rick had themselves walked the same path a few summers ago. Here he was surrounded by strangers and showing the same degree of affection and warmth to another woman. The last two photographs she put side by side. The initial shock of opening the envelope had passed and it was time to see just how far they went. In the photo on the left, Rick had Jean backed up against a tree and engaged her in a passionate kiss. The photo on the right lacked any sexual nuances, but the implication was clear. Rick was escorting Jean through a pink motel door. The name of the motel was not revealed in the photograph, but Julie knew it was the Peach Tree Bed and Breakfast in Fredericksburg. She remembered it well because she'd logged the name in her daughter's baby book, for Rebecca had been conceived there.

She pushed the photos to the middle of the table abruptly and laid her head down on the table. Emotions swirled in her mind like a tornado. Never in her life had she been confronted with the sudden absence of trust. She felt as if she were falling through space at an ever-increasing speed. All around her images and memories of her life were flashing by. She reached out to grab a hold of them, but they were slippery and elusive. Some of the images were sharp, like the triangular pieces of shattered glass cutting though her soul. She fell deeper and faster losing all sense of time until she felt a sore spot forming in the middle of her forehead where her head was resting on her wrist. She turned her head on its side. A tear rolled across the bridge of her nose and hung for a moment on the tip of her nose. She got up and went into the bathroom. Warm water spun in the bottom of the sink. Cupping her hands she splashed some on her face. She reached with closed eyes for the hand towel nearby. The downy cotton had the aroma of a fresh home. She patted her face dry and opened her eyes to the broken woman standing in the mirror before her.

It was the face of a woman that no man desired. She'd aged ten years in twenty minutes. Her long blond hair was lifeless and without body, falling across her shoulders like straw. Her eyes were puffy and red. Darkened circles lingered below them. She leaned forward to check the lines on her face. They were still there, only deeper and longer and originating from areas where she'd never noticed them before. She stepped back to get a full look at her self. The bathroom scale upstairs had lied to her, she was much fatter than it told her she was. She looked for reasons to disbelieve what she thought about herself; looked for an excuse to disprove she was not as beautiful and desirable as before, but there were none. She could only find fault with herself. She desired only one thing, to run and hide from the man who'd caused her fall. If she were indeed the loathsome creature to him she now saw standing in the mirror before her, then she would spare him the task of caring for her. She would free him and perhaps, just maybe, she would regain some dignity for herself. She turned off the bathroom light and went to the phone. Her sister was home and on the way. She ran upstairs to pack.

Back in Frankfurt, Stace had decided sleep would be a mockery to his predicament. He was in the mood for self-pity and had good reason to be tormented. He wished to take full advantage of his sudden and inexplicable turn of fate in his life. Sleeping would rob him of his need to experience the full pain he wanted to go through. If there was a God and that same God was bringing him torment, then he'd just as soon go through the hell of it all and learn the lesson he needed to learn. That way, if he learned his lesson well, perhaps God would not permit him to go through the experience again.

He was packed by 10:00 that evening. Just inside his front door he'd slid the two cardboard boxes full of his things and attached the note to his landlord Mr. Summersheim on the largest box. Next to them were two suitcases bulging with whatever he could cram into them without any concern for order. Half of his clothes would remain hanging in the closet and in the dresser drawers. They wouldn't fit. Next to his suitcases sat his photography case. He spent the evening trying to watch television. When he bored of that he listened to the radio. At 2:00 a.m. he thumbed through old magazines and woke at 3:15 pissed he had the nerve to fall asleep. He hoped God wouldn't hold it against him. He went into the kitchen and fixed a pot of coffee. He made a sandwich with the last of the sliced ham and a dab of mayonnaise from a new jar. He ate in the silence of the living room. He'd not made reservations for the flight back to the states. His plan was to simply go to the airport and catch the earliest flight. He wanted to slip out early, so he wouldn't have to confront the Summersheims about his departure. He had time on his hands and didn't mind getting there a little early. There's no other feeling like watching a flurry of planes take off and land. It reeks of new beginnings, of comings and goings and Stace knew that regardless of how long he would have to wait, he could still find some comfort there. At 4:37 he called a cab.

The lanes of the autobahn were virtually empty. The next sizable town was Darmstadt about twenty-five kilometers south. Since it was Sunday, headlights were few and far between. The Mercedes taxi was standard around Frankfurt and Stace was refreshed by its comfort and speed. The driver got him to the airport in less than fifteen minutes and dropped him off at the international terminal. Stace gave him three twenty-mark bills and told him to keep the change.

He parked his suitcases near a bench and went to three airlines looking for the best deal. TWA and American Airlines were the most expensive. United Airlines offered the best rate. They had five flights leaving for the states that day. The earliest flight out was at 10:15, but that flight was already booked. Another flight left at 2:37, but that was booked as well. The next one leaving was scheduled to depart in the late afternoon at 3:20. It still had seats available. Stace purchased a seat by the window. "Probably over the wing," he thought. "So I won't be able to see a damn thing on the way home." Although it was early, he went ahead and checked in his bags. He sure didn't want to lug them around for the rest of the day. His aluminum photography case would stay right by his side where it belonged.

The next order of business was to find a cash machine and empty his account. He spent a couple of hours walking the gift shops after that, perusing though magazines and paperbacks. He finally decided on a short novel he could finish during the flight over the Atlantic. Once hitting the states he knew he'd never pick up the book again. He also bought a few magazines, *Life*, *Sports Illustrated* and a copy of *Glamour's* Germany edition. When he bought magazines, which was rare, it was always for the pictures and not for the articles.

By 11:30 he had climbed his way up to the forth floor of the terminal and into a tranquil lounge, taking a seat overlooking the main runway. Across the runway he could make out the sterile, gray buildings of *Rhein* Main Air Force Base. He counted no less than seven C-5's and ten of the latest versions of the Cobra attack helicopter, all lined up perfectly as if set in place with a giant hand. He called for a *Viesen* beer, not because he enjoyed it the most, but because of its pungent yeast flavor and alcohol content. Later he ordered a hamburger and fries. He finished his lunch and the waitress brought him another beer. Within an hour he'd devoured the magazines, memorizing every specific detail of each photograph contained within them. As usual, he admired a few, detested the rest and admitted his work was far better than that represented. After eating, he shifted his chair around so that he faced the window and his back faced the door. His posture spoke for itself. He didn't want to be bothered.

After a few minutes the clatter of dishes, glasses and small talk behind him merged into a distant drone. Jet liners took off with measured accuracy. From where he sat he could see a line of them waiting in taxing position at the end of the runway. Like clockwork, about every three minutes one would swing around and its nose would point down the endless cement runway. He couldn't hear the surging and thrust of their engines, but he thought he could make out the blur of their outline as they began to vibrate. Then, ever so perceptibly, they would lurch forward and increase their speed like a finch emerging into an eagle. They had broken well over 200 miles per hour when they slipped past his line of sight. He followed each one as they eased their noses upwards towards the sky. Once free of the ground the jets shot upwards like arrows. Behind each one a swirl of turbulence spilled out until they disappeared from beyond the edge of the window.

Having finished two beers, he discovered escaping his own thoughts was an impossibility. A year ago he'd left America under the false premise he was seeking adventure. Now that he was returning, he realized what he'd actually been doing was running. He didn't confront the rejection of his work at the Marbel Art Exhibit then and he was not confronting Eva's rejection of him now. Two more planes took off with uncanny predictability. Just when was he going to break his pattern of dealing with the everyday crises of life?

He tried desperately to understand his feelings for Eva, to find any possible explanation for her actions. Something beyond his control had set her against him. She was beyond reason. What had caused her to suddenly and erratically eliminate him out of her life? He tried to recall the exact words she said to him at the hospital. She said she had him "figured out." She said he was "fooling her…distracting her from her investigation." And that when he was finished doing what he was supposed to be doing that he was "just going to leave her."

"I've never had any intention of leaving her. I was in love with her—am in love with her," he thought. "So what the hell am I doing here?"

"I'll tell you what I'm doing here. I'm here because she's flipped out. I'm here because she's so wrapped up in her work she can't separate it from real life. Shit! How the hell am I supposed to get around that? When this investigation's over she'll start another. And who will I be then? It doesn't matter what I tell her. Doesn't matter how much a try and reassure her I love her and care for her. She thinks I started the fire. How the hell did she come up with that? Paranoia…that's what it is, paranoia. Sure, I may have walked into her life at the wrong time, but it's not like you plan these kinds of things."

"Perhaps it's just as well. I tried to warn her about the ICC. Tried to tell her they'd have her head all mixed up and she'd lose all sense of direction. She thinks I'm tangled up with them. Like I'm working for them or something. And something about another group, a program, then out of the blue she talks about Rick Forstein. Hell, I bet there's at least fifty Forstein's in the Frankfurt telephone directory alone. It's like Smith or Jones in the states. There's got to be thousands of them."

"Rick Forstein, you son of a bitch, doesn't matter where I go you're going to follow me around the rest of my life aren't you?"

"No! I'd have to say she was pretty clear about the way she felt about me. You can't love someone who doesn't love you. You'd be stupid to even try. I can work with insecurities, I can work with confusion, but I won't hang out the rest of my life hoping she'll come around some day. No. I just won't do it. She was as direct as she could be. She doesn't want to see me anymore. I can call and page her from now to eternity and she'd never answer me back."

He closed his eyes for a few minutes. The *viessens* had taken effect. Add to that his lack of sleep and he was becoming irrational. He couldn't wait to get on the plane, just slip the chair back a few inches and take a long hard nap. Maybe, if he slept long enough and woke up in the states, the whole affair would seem like a bad dream. He checked his watch. It was 2:14. He'd been in the lounge for nearly four hours. It was time to head downstairs.

In the terminal, lines had formed at the check-in counters and he was thankful he'd bought his ticket and cleared his luggage through earlier. Fact, the terminal had become quite a zoo. People from all over the world were zipping about in random chaos. He quickly found Terminal C, which led towards customs and into a three spoke complex housing the international departures and arrivals. After walking under the terminal sign, he looked down the long corridor. The end of it seemed miles away, but he could still see the preliminary security gates where he would have to unload his pockets and run his camera case through the X-ray machines. The corridor itself measured about thirty-five feet in diameter. Two conveyer belts ran from one end to the other. The belt on the right carried passengers towards the departing flights and the one on the left carried arriving passengers to the luggage claim area. They ran along the walls and were divided by a walkway about twenty feet across. The walkway was covered with a layer of light gray, non-slip rubber tiles. Only a few people chose to ignore the luxury of using the belts, opting instead to walk. Stace opted to ride and fell in behind a group of suits. He grabbed a hold of the handrail for support. The ride was kind of nice. It zipped by the walkers in the middle at twice their speed. There was only a trickle of passengers departing, but apparently a flight had just come in and the left conveyer belt was full of riders. He looked over in their direction as they zipped by. The movement made him dizzy and sick to his stomach. Now more than ever, he couldn't wait to get settled on the plane.

Suddenly his eyes noticed a young man in his late twenties. He was moving up the conveyer belt on the other side, but was still about thirty yards away. The face seemed familiar to him and for an unknown reason, disturbing. He rubbed his eyes and focused a little harder. He was nearly positive of the identification, but doubted the possibility. Perhaps it was just an illusion of circumstance. He'd been focusing on the name earlier and now he was seeing someone who resembled the very person he'd been thinking about. The figure passed by him and Stace turned around to check his backside. He couldn't believe what he was seeing. It had to be him! He looked towards the approaching inspection point then back at the young man. The man was disappearing fast. To double-check his hunch he'd have to do it now. People eyed him suspiciously as he leaped over the handrail, dodged a few people walking in the middle and leapt over the rail of the other conveyer belt. He could run to keep pace, which would attract obvious attention, or he could hop a ride. He opted for the latter and jumped over the rail. Then he inched his way up towards the young man until he came to a spot just ten feet behind him. He was now more certain then ever, he was staring at the back of the head of a man he once despised and now loathed. The conveyer belt ended and Stace continued following the man into the baggage claim area. As a precaution, he hid in the background hoping to get a clearer sight of the man's face.

Suitcases, olive green duffel bags and boxes of all sizes began sliding out of the center shoot and onto the steel carousel. The man stood with his back facing Stace, waiting for his luggage to pop out. There were a few times when the man turned his face to the side to look around. Stace caught site of his profile, but would need a better frontal view just to make sure. Finally the man bent over and retrieved his suitcase. As he turned around and started to walk, Stace finally got a good look. He was, beyond any doubt, Rick Forstein. It was too unbelievable to be true, but before Stace could decide what to do, Rick was immediately confronted by a stranger who'd slipped up behind him, a man who looked vaguely familiar to Stace as well, like he'd seen him in a photograph. And it was clear to Stace by the expression in Rick's face that the man who took hold of his arm was not at all expected.

CHAPTER 51

▼

The grip of a firm hand spun Rick around. "What do you want?" he asked shaking himself free.

"Mr. Forstein. I've been expecting you."

"And you are?"

"That's not important at the moment. What's important is you know I'm not the only one here."

Rick glanced around the baggage claim area. Passengers were shuffling to get their baggage, but no one looked suspicious. He looked right past Stace, who turned as he faced his direction.

"Well, I don't care who are."

"That's unfortunate. I'm sure Julie and your daughter would appreciate your cooperation."

Rick looked hard into the eyes of the stranger. "What did you say?"

"Just that for the moment they're safe." Derrick said with a sleazy smile. "Now, if you don't mind, there's a van waiting for us out front." Derrick took him by the arm and escorted him out of the terminal like an old friend into the late afternoon sunlight. Next to the curb in the waiting zone was a faded blue van. Derrick opened one of the back doors. "Excuse the accommodations. Now get in."

Stace had very little time to think and less time to act. He'd not yet put it all together, but knew now that Eva's mentioning the name of

Rick Forstein had not been without reason. Rick was involved with her investigation and he understood how she could have made the connection between he and Rick. Above the confusion of the moment hope was stirring within him that he might be able to reconcile things with Eva after all. Exactly how was uncertain, but it would begin by finding out what Rick was doing in Germany and what his role in Eva's investigation was. He walked out to the curb and flagged down a taxi.

"Where to?" the driver asked.

"Blue van," he said, pointing to the van as it was pulling away from the curb.

"*Ja?*"

"Follow it"

"*Verzeihung?*"

He gestured to the van again. "*Gehen sie,*" he managed to say.

"*Selbstverstandlich!*" the driver exclaimed.

Rick sat on the floor of the van leaning up against the rusted side panel as the tires whined with increasing speed. He knew they were on the autobahn, but had no idea which way they were heading. When they exited the autobahn, he bounced around trying to get a mental picture of each turn they made, but it was hopeless, he didn't know the city. He looked for points of reference to focus on out of the square windows in the back doors, but they only offered to him treetops and an occasional cluster of buildings.

"So, Mr. Forstein, what brings you to Germany?" The man in the passenger seat asked as if he already knew the answer.

"Seemed like a good time for a vacation," Rick replied.

The man in the passenger seat turned his head to the driver and grinned. The driver didn't respond. The van took a hard right and Rick looked out the back windows again. He caught sight of an enormous tower rising high into the Frankfurt city sky.

"No Rick. I don't think you came here for a vacation. If you were really going on vacation you would have gone some place warm like Mexico. Don't get me wrong though, Frankfurt's a nice city and all, but it's rather gloomy this time of year. Perhaps you had some other place in mind, like maybe...Munich. Yeah, I bet that's it. You were going to go skiing in the Alps, in which case, you picked a good time of year."

"What do you know about my wife?" Rick asked pointedly.

"Not much more than I've already told you. She's safe. Staying with her sister I believe."

Rick was getting annoyed with the way the man was toying with him. "Why would his wife be at her sister's house?"

"You're probably wondering how I know that aren't you? Or better yet, why she's even there?" the man asked, finally turning around in his seat and addressing Rick directly. "Seems that while you were on the flight over, Julie received a package from Pruitt. Next thing you know, sister comes over, helps her pack and they're on their way back to the sister's place. Ah, I wouldn't let it worry you too much Rick. Parting is such sweet sorrow don't you think?"

Rick felt the van slow down and make a couple of sharp left turns. He looked out the back window again and saw they were pulling in underneath a steel awning. A garage? The driver stopped the van and got out. Rick heard his footsteps disappear in the distance. The man in the passenger seat turned around again. "Now, were here, but let me lay down one simple ground rule. We just want to have a little talk with you. You're here on your own free will. If you were to say, suddenly run at this point, then no telling what might happen to your wife and your little girl. So, I'm going to let you out the back and then I want you to walk ahead of me upstairs like we're old friends. Can I trust you to do that Rick?"

Rick didn't answer.

"That's not a good sign Rick. Do I need to explain the ground rule to you again?"

"No," Rick said with disgust.

"Much better."

Stace's taxi pulled up on the side street in view of the back parking lot of the apartment. While counting out sixty marks he watched the two men enter the building. After paying, he walked across the street and stood at the entrance of the driveway near an old cement wall considering his options. Notifying Eva, or anyone else from the paper was out of the question. He could only tell them he knew the whereabouts of Rick Forstein, which they probably suspected he knew anyway. Calling the *polizei* would be worthless. They'd never understand the relevance of how he'd cornered the man who had screwed him over in college and who was now responsible for ending the relationship of his lifetime. Sure, he suspected something downright illegal was going on, but that was only because he knew the *Schwarz Monatlich* was investigating Rick Forstein and he still didn't have clue why.

"Rick Forstein," Stace muttered his name. "Rick Forstein," he said a little louder walking in circles. He'd heard stories of how people can cross the same pathways in life, like the story he heard of the two college professors who'd met in undergraduate school and wound up teaching at the same university in the later years of their life. But that kind of an event is understandable. Some people run in the same circles and it's inevitable they'll bump into each other again. But this was different. Why Rick Forstein? Why this skeleton in his closet?

Stace didn't believe in the notion of fate. To believe that you'd have to believe in a personal God and predestination. You'd have to believe the events of your life had been predetermined and even the most simple decisions have lasting ramifications or consequences. Quite frankly, it was so much easier for him to believe the random events of life are brought on by mere circumstance. Life is much more fair that way. There's no obligation to perform. It puts everybody in the same boat. Take the ride down Terminal C at the airport for instance. He could have been looking right instead of at the passengers arriving on his left. He could have been looking at the pretty stewardess standing just in front of the three guys in suits on the escalator. For Christ's sake, he could have sneezed and missed Rick altogether. But he didn't. He looked left and suddenly boom! life throws him onto an entirely different course.

He was growing tired of thinking about it. He could still catch a cab back to the airport and probably exchange his ticket for the next flight out. Forgetting about Rick had not been easy the first time around, but he could do it again. Forgetting about Eva would be much harder, but it could be done. All it takes is a little time and a diversion. Find something to occupy yourself with and time can pass rather quickly. You can postpone the pain until time has erased away any of its impact. At that point it becomes a memory and just a useful piece of information telling you what to do or what not to do the next time you're placed in a similar position. This sounded all well and good to Stace, but even so, he found himself wandering over to a nearby bus stop across from the apartment trying to devise a plan.

"Suppose I just go on up there and knock on the door. Just introduce myself. Say I'm an old friend of Rick's and just happened to know he was in town. That'll go ever well. Next thing you know I'm taking a ride in the back of the van—my last ride. Who were those guys in the van anyway? Definitely not the ICC, but maybe they're connected in some way to the ICC? Are they part of that other group? Unlikely, I'd hardly classify them as professionals. And why's Rick connected to them? They definitely weren't buddies. Maybe he's not associated with them. Maybe they just intercepted him at the airport. But it sure didn't seem like he was forced into going with them up to the apartment, which means, he's definitely involved, but with whom?"

The more he thought, the more confused he got. He had just a couple of names swirling around in his head that had little to do with him anyway. What he did know cut him deeply. Rick Forstein was a demon from the past, who had somehow managed to walk back into his life and destroy something much more meaningful than a potential career. Eva was convinced he and Rick were working together. As long as she thought that, Stace didn't have a chance with her. There seemed to be only one possible solution to his dilemma. He had to confront

Rick directly, alone, in a manner that Rick would be forced to confess his involvement.

He didn't know the area of town, but remembered passing a convenience store just down the street. He hoped it was still open, though he had only a faint idea of what he would buy when he got there. Convenience stores weren't in the market of selling items to be used for pernicious intent. He'd throw a plan together once he knew what he could buy. Behind him was the park. He walked into it a short distance and looked around. A few shadows were lurking about in the distance, but they didn't seem to be paying any attention to him. He darted into a thick covering of shrubbery high enough to swallow him whole. He set his camera case down and covered it with loose leaves and branches, then walked down to the store.

The woman behind the register tweaked her face slightly at the array of trivia he laid across the counter. Some of the items she'd forgotten the store carried. Thrown together with a hundred marks worth of groceries they might not have seemed unusual, but in and of themselves looked quite peculiar. There was; a roll of nylon twine, slightly thinner than a clothes line, a cheap eight inch kitchen knife with a black plastic handle, a package of woman's stockings, a roll of electrical tape and a plastic flash light with batteries.

"Will that be all?" she asked, eager to see him on his way.

"I certainly hope so."

Back in the cluster of shrubbery, he ripped open the plastic molding wrapped around the knife with his teeth. With the knife he opened the flashlight and batteries. He popped the two AA's in and was surprised to discover the damn thing actually worked. A minor victory in the scheme of things. Holding the flashlight in his teeth he set to work. First he modified the pantyhose by cutting the legs out and shoved the piece he was going to use in his pocket. He unrolled half of the ball of twine, cut it clean, rolled it up loosely, then forced the wad into his back pocket. The remainder of twine he put in his right coat pocket. The tape he put in his other pocket. He gathered up all the trash and stuffed it back into the bag, then shoved the knife into his pants pocket over his right hip, concealing its black plastic handle with the tail of his coat. On his way across the street he dumped the bag into a wire trash basket at the bus stop.

Finding the manager's apartment wasn't difficult. It was on the bottom floor with a sign on it saying, "Manager 1-A." However, what was required of him beyond that point was a ferocity to which he didn't possess. He'd have to fake it and hope he got away with it.

He knocked on the door and stood in front of the peephole.

"Who is it?" asked a woman.

He sees a shadow form in the peephole and he tries to look pleasant as the woman studies his face, while reaching with his right hand to grab the ripped up piece of pantyhose. "My name's Karl Morgan. I've come to see if you have an apartment available."

"*Ich verstehe nicht,*" she said, without so much as a jiggle on the door handle.

So much for minor victories. She didn't speak a word of English. "*Wohnung?*" He tried again.

"*Es tut mir leid,*" she replied.

It was time to get desperate. "*Helfen sie mir!*" he pleaded, a phrase he'd learned just in case of an emergency.

She hesitated for a moment, still peering through the peephole.

"*Helfen sie mir. Wohnung?*" he repeated, trying to sound less desperate and more civilized.

"*Augenblick mal,*" she replied. Light filled the peephole and the lock on the door turned. He ripped the stocking out of his pocket and rammed it half-cocked over his face, just barely slipping it under his chin when he heard the door crack and like a rhinoceros shoved his way inside. The woman let out a quick, but rather weak scream as she fell backwards over the armrest of her couch. He slammed the door closed, rushed around the back of the couch and capped her mouth shut.

"Shut up! I'm not going to hurt you!"

The comment had no affect. He'd just yelled at her in a language she didn't understand. He might as well have said, "I'd like to kill you now." Her eyes were white with terror, hot breath snorting out of her nostrils over his hand. He'd have to improvise.

He pulled the knife out from his pants flashing it in front of her face. She turned her head in its direction trying to scream. He moved the blade slowly over his lips and whispered, "*Shhhhh*," then waited a few moments until she calmed down. "*Ruhig*," he said calmly, finally remembering the word.

"Are you *allein*?"

"Alone" she understood, and nodded her head yes.

"*Wo ist schlussel?*"

She cocked her head in confusion, looking as if she expected him to ask or do something else.

"The Keys. *Schlussel!*" he repeated.

She understood him all right. She just couldn't talk with a hand forced over her mouth.

"*Nicht sprechen…shhhhh*," he said, returning the knife over his lips. Then ever so carefully he removed his hand. Once it was away she took a few sharp breaths and let out a whispery cry. Her face was as white as flour, except where the grip of his hand had left neat red lines across her face.

"*Gut*. Now the *schlussel*." He backed away from her to let her get up, but he latched onto her with his other hand and brought the knife around in front of her throat, having seen it done in the movies that way once before.

She moved towards the cabinet against the wall and he was right behind her. At this point she'd begun to sob. How he wished he could talk to her. Maybe sit her down on the couch and pour her a cup of coffee, then explain the whole misunderstanding to her.

She opened one of the cabinet doors and reached for the keys. He stepped in close behind making sure she didn't grab anything else to smack him with. He heard the keys jingle and he let out a sigh of relief, but when she handed him a ring of about twenty keys he shook his head in confusion. This would not do. It would take him all night to find the right one.

"3-B," he said. "*Drei B.*"

That much she understood. She took the keys out of his hand, pinched key 3-B in her fingers and handed him the set.

"*Danke.* Now, *Wo ist der toilette?*

For some reason this sent the woman into another state of panic. She backed herself up against the wall and her lips were beginning to quake. "*Shhhhh! Nicht sprechen!* he yelled, reaching for her face again. She swallowed both breath and scream.

"*Der toilette?*" he repeated taking a step back. She walked towards the hallway. When she got to the bathroom door she quickly turned around. Terror had returned and she'd begun to violently shake her head back and forth.

"*Halt!*" He yelled and grabbed a hold of her chin. "*Gehen,*" he commanded, pushing her into the bathroom. She took a few steps and turned to face him. He stopped at the door. "*Nicht sprechen.* Do you understand? *Nicht sprechen.*" She nodded her head in affirmation. Stace closed the door behind her and hoped she wouldn't do anything stupid. He had no idea what he'd do if she suddenly started screaming. He grabbed the roll of tape from his coat pocket and wrapped the end around the door handle. The linen door was right behind him. Working frantically, he spun a web between the two handles. It would be virtually impossible for her to get out without help. Before he left he found the two phones in the house and cut the cord with his knife.

"Tell us again why you came to Germany Rick," Derrick demanded upstairs.

"I've already told you—three times!" Rick said, rubbing his face in his hands. He sat on one side of the kitchen table and the two men sat on the other. Neil had not said a word to him yet and Rick wondered who was really in charge of the two. Rick was free to get up and move around, but he felt glued to his chair.

"You seem like a fairly intelligent man Rick. You should know the program is out of Stautzen's hands. Of course, we have no idea where it is. He tells us it was stolen from him on his drive down to Munich last evening. Can you believe it? Somewhere north of Stuttgart some thugs pulled him over and confiscate the CD's. Which is really quite a shame, because now we'll never know if the thing worked or not. He reported it to the *polizei*, but we all know they'll never find it."

"You expect me to believe that?"

Neil spoke up. "Of course not, you're too intelligent for that. Which brings us back to why you're here. Surely you know even if you got your hands on the program another copy would be sent out."

His tone lacked all of the sarcastic wit of the man sitting next to him and Rick judged he was the brain behind the two.

Rick looked at him. "Of course I knew that. Actually, I really hadn't made any plans. I guess I was hoping I could just reason with them, talk them out of using it."

Derrick glanced over at Neil and chuckled. Neil's face was motion-less and still fixed on Rick. Derrick regained a straight face and returned to Rick.

"Talk them out of it?" Neil questioned barely audible. He folded his arms across his chest and settled back into his chair. "You have no idea what you're up against do you?"

Rick said nothing.

"This is much bigger than the three of us. Much bigger than the ICC. Much bigger than anything you've ever imagined! There are lives hanging in the balance here. The salvation of souls is at stake. And you thought you were just going to stride on into the ICC and politely ask for the program back?" There was a rising crescendo to his words. They were disturbing, pulsating with fanaticism and spoken in the tone of a person absence of reason.

"Are you aware you're the only one standing in the way now?" Neil asked. His words were calm and decisive.

Rick looked over at him then at the other man, who now wore an eager smirk. He realized they had no intention of ever letting him go.

"Look, I admit it was a bad idea for me to come here. After all, what do I care what you do with the program?"

"That's right Rick, what do you care? Derrick asked.

"As far as I'm concerned, what you do is between you and Trojan Security—right. I mean it's just another security program anyway. That's what Trojan Security docs. There's certainly nothing wrong with that is there?" he asked groping for words.

"Right again," Derrick said.

"And we've gone to extreme measures to ensure everything's as it appears to be," Neil added.

"So, I'll just take the first flight back to the states and go about my business," Rick said quickly, hoping his request would sound reasonable.

Derrick smirked again and turned towards Neil. "What do you think Neil? He says he's willing to forget about the whole thing."

"I think you can't expect a leopard to change the color of his spots," Neil replied.

"My thoughts exactly," Derrick said suddenly standing. And just as he stood the front door flew open.

CHAPTER 52

▼

Derrick turned to see the madman rushing towards the dining room table. It took Stace only a split second to reach them, cutting through the air with wild knife strokes as if he had a room full of enemies to kill. Derrick slammed against the wall behind him, avoiding the arch of the knife.

"Back against the wall! All of you!" Stace shouted.

Rick fell backwards out of his chair and against the baseboard. Neil, with slightly more finesse, stood and backed up.

"Over there!" Rick blasted with another swing of the knife forcing Neil and Derrick into one of the corners.

"What do you want?" Derrick yelled. He was stalling for time, trying to see through the nylon wrapped over Stace's head. It was no use. His face was all contorted, nose smashed in, eyes all askew, hair matted over his forehead.

This was Stace's second act at intimidation in the past ten minutes and he was getting good at it. The image of Rick plastered against the wall also gave him satisfaction. "I said back up!" he yelled jumping towards Derrick and waving the knife just a foot from his throat. Derrick jerked his head back, slamming it into the wall behind him.

"Ok! I hear you."

Stace grabbed the edge of the table, throwing it back about five feet, sending sheets of paper across the floor.

"Now down on the floor—face first—both of you!" He thought they were moving a little slowly so he lunged back in their direction. "Now! I said." It took them only a second to drop, face down, side by side next to each other. He looked over to Rick to see if he was thinking about going anywhere. He wasn't. His arms were flipping about all over the place, his feet looking for a hold and that cringe on his face! Stace almost smiled.

He leaned over the two men's feet and poked the tip of the knife into the back of Derrick's thigh.

"*Yeaaah*! Shit! What you do that for?"

"Shut up! Just give me the keys to the van."

"It doesn't run," Derrick was stupid enough to say.

Stace drove the knife deeper and this time cut though his pants penetrating the skin.

"Damnit!" he yelled.

"Bull shit. I know it works!"

"All right!" Derrick reached into his front pocket for the keys then held them up above his head.

"You!" Stace said, taking a few steps towards Rick who still couldn't speak. "Take this rope and tie them up. Use it all up and make it tight. I'll be standing right over the back of you to make sure you do it right."

Rick took the rope from him and began to tie them up.

"Not like that you idiot! Do it like they do in Texas, like you're roping a calf. You know, feet first then the hands, then tie it all up in a bundle in a good strong knot."

Rick thought the reference to cattle roping in Texas a little peculiar, but did as he was told. When he finished a few minutes later the two were permanently immobilized.

"Good, but not good enough. Here's some tape. Use it!"

Three minutes later Rick was done. When he stood up Stace grabbed a hold of the back of his sports coat and rammed his face up against the nearby wall. He brought the point of the blade between Rick's shoulder blades. Rick arched his back avoiding the tip. "You can choose to ignore me or choose to cooperate. What do you choose?"

"What do you want me to do?" he asked though clenched teeth.

"You're going to walk downstairs and out to the van. I'll be right behind you with this reminder positioned just over your spine. Don't make it the last walk you take. Understood?"

"Yeah."

Stace pulled him away from the wall, forced him out the door and down the stairs. He stopped for a moment at the manager's door, pulling Rick back into the point of the knife. Hearing nothing at her door he shoved him through the hallway and out the back door. At the van he gave Rick the keys. You've got five seconds to open the door."

The first key fit the lock and Stace shoved him into the back. With some extra rope he tied Rick's hands and legs up behind his back and covered his head with an oily tee shirt he found lying near the base of the driver's seat. "Finally!" he said to himself while ripping the stocking off his head and jumping out the back into the cool night air. "I did it!" On the way out of the parking lot he tossed the apartment keys out the window.

A minute later Stace took a right onto *Hugelstrasse* then a left on *Ginnheimer Landstrasse*, past the *Ginnheim* tower. The sky was black and he could see the lights protruding out of the windows of its saucer-like observation deck. Human forms, cut out like silhouettes from a sheet of cardboard paper, looked pasted against the windows. Within moments he entered the A-66 traveling west and headed out towards *Eschborn* and his final destination, the *Taunus* Mountains in *Kronberg*. He'd been there once before with Eva under a different set of circumstances. The location would suit his purposes. He and Rick had a lot to discuss.

A thousand sordid thoughts had passed through Rick's mind since his abduction at the airport. He left Texas on the mistaken assumption he could get back at Trojan Security for the fool they'd made of him.

He cursed himself for proving they were right. He should have forgotten about the whole thing and gone on with his life. Now, everything was ten times worse than he could have imagined. His marriage was probably ruined. Julie had the photos in hand, but he quickly dismissed the thought. He was just hoping and praying she and his daughter would be all right. He'd take a broken marriage any day of the week just to know they were safe. Words came back to haunt him. "This is much bigger than anything you've ever imagined. There are lives hanging in the balance here. Whose life? Mine? My wife's? My daughter's? Who else?"

Stace exited the autobahn at the *Taunus* exit. The force of the turn flipped Rick over and he went bouncing across the rippled steel floor of the van. The tee shirt around his head provided him with some padding, but it stunk of burnt oil and dirt. Through it, he could hear the tires whining and picking up speed again. Momentum pulled him towards the back door and he knew they were traveling up hill.

"Where are you taking me? What do you want from me?" he yelled through the tee shirt and above the noise of the road. Stace ignored him.

"Do it like they do down in Texas, like you're roping a calf," the madman had said, like he'd been there before, like it was a part of who he was. "An American?"

"Did Trojan Security send you?" he yelled.

Still, no response.

"Tell them I'm ready to go back. Tell them I'll forget the whole thing. Tell them I appreciate all they've done for me and I'm willing to forgive and forget." Rick was desperate now and fumbling for reasons to stay alive.

Stace drove fast, but cautiously. If stopped, he would never be able to explain why he had a man tied up in the back. The *polizei* don't screw around.

This was the second time Stace had heard the name Trojan Security. Eva spit it out in the hospital and now Rick had mentioned it. Rick

Forstein was another name and then there was something about another group. "What was it? CRB, PRC?" He just couldn't remember. Where the two creeps he left tied up in the apartment part of that group? He also remembered a time not so long ago during his first visit to Eva's place. There was a stack of boxes near the couch where he was sitting. On the side of one of the boxes was the abbreviation, ICC. Eva also mentioned something about a program, which could mean just about anything. "How much did Rick know?" It was something he'd have to find out. Eva had dropped him under the assumption he was mixed up with one of them and he was damn sure not going to let something like that come between them. He cared far too much for her. If he could put the pieces of the puzzle together, she just might be willing to listen.

"Hey! You from Texas?" Rick asked.

"Shut the hell up will ya?"

"Sounds like you're from Texas to me. Tell Trojan Security I'—"

"I said, shut, the fuck, up!"

Rick shut up. Now he'd pissed him off.

The van made a few more rights and lefts and shifted into a lower gear. It was climbing at a much steeper rate now. Rick also knew by the winding turns that they were somewhere on an isolated mountain. He listened hard for any another signs of life like a car passing by, but they were alone. It was a worse case scenario. His life would come to an end thousands of miles from home and no one would ever find his body. He started to sob quietly, but willingly.

Stace shifted into second gear then first, thinking he'd missed the cut off to the parking lot where Eva had taken him before. The last kilometer turned into a five-minute trip. Rick tried to control his sobs, so the driver wouldn't know he was scared. Finally, the headlights streaked across a familiar sign and a few meters later the dirt road came into view. Stace took the left and parked in the deserted lot. The mountain forest was cold and black as envy. Only a fool would be up here after sunset, or a man such as Stace with a guest.

Rick felt a rush of cold air seep under his pant legs when the back door opened. "This is it," he thought. A firm hand slapped down on his leg and pulled him to the back. He heard a snip and felt his arms and legs fall free.

"We are going to take a little walk. Don't try anything stupid."

Rick said nothing. Stace heard what he thought to be whimpering and smiled. He was beginning to take some pleasure in his reversal of fortune. He shoved Rick in the direction of the path and lit the way with his flashlight. Rick stumbled and fell. Stace picked him up, then held onto his coat to guide him. It took them fifteen minutes to reach the crest of the hill. Rick had resolved that at any moment he might be pushed over a ledge, stabbed with a knife, knocked unconscious with a stone to his head, shot, or anyone of a dozen other scenarios. He'd begun weeping uncontrollably. Stace almost felt sorry for the bastard. But he also knew the more terrified Rick was the more he would be willing to talk.

At the top of the ridge Stace pushed him to the left and they followed the crest of the hill by weaving in and out of the mammoth pines standing like barrel chested warriors. The crest dipped downwards just as Stace remembered it did and he stopped. "Sit down!" he snapped, throwing Rick to the ground and up against a tree. Stace went around the backside of the tree and with the little remaining rope he had left wrapped it several times around Rick's chest and cinched him to the trunk. The restraint was far from adequate. Rick could have broken free easily, but he'd degenerated into a pathetic excuse of the man he once was. Stace stood in front of him for a moment admiring the depth he'd brought Rick to, then sat down in front of him.

He tried to remember Rick as the all around guy at Marbel University. Rick wasn't exactly the most recognizable man on campus, but he was popular and well liked. He carried himself with confidence and had the presence of a young man who might go places someday. "Was he married? Did he have a family? What kind of work did he do? Did he ever think about Stace Manning and what happened to him after graduation? Did he even care?" Stace wondered all of these things, excluding for the time being, the situation at hand. He tipped the flashlight towards Rick and over his ragged form. The tee shirt wrapped around his head was filthier than he thought. He had forced it tightly over Rick's head in a hurry and now the neckline cut across Rick's mouth leaving some of his teeth and gums exposed. His expensive sports coat had been ruined in the grime and grease from the van floor. His wingtips were scuffed. If he only knew who sat in front of him. If he only knew who had the power now.

A full ten minutes passed before either one of them spoke a word. Rick was the first to speak. His words were slow and painful, spoken as if he really didn't expect an answer. "What do you want out of me?"

"Some information would be helpful," Stace said.

"I don't suppose you're going to let me go are you?"

"That depends on how helpful you are."

"Why should I believe you? If you're going to kill me anyway then why should I give you the satisfaction of answering your questions?"

As he spoke, Stace remembered the little nuances of his voice. It was much deeper now, laden with half sobs and drool, an indication of his grief.

"What do you know about my family?" Rick asked.

"I tell you what, you answer my questions and I'll consider answering yours. If you tell me what I want to hear I might consider letting you go."

Rick didn't answer, but he needed hope. If the man said he might let him go…then he might just let him go.

"Now, who do you work for?"

"You know who I work for, the same people you work for. That is, until you'all set me up the other day."

Stace leaned over and ever so slightly jabbed the edge of the knife into Rick's throat. Rick threw his head back against the tree trunk. "Are you at all interested in getting down from this mountain alive?" Stace asked, clenching his teeth and sounding as mean as possible.

Rick attempted to lick his lips and let out a wimpy "yes."

"Then answer my questions!" Stace snapped.

"All right."

Stace removed the knife and resumed his interrogative position.

"I work for Trojan Security."

"What do you do at Trojan Security?"

"I design computer security programs."

He couldn't remember what Rick's major had been, but by the sound of things that made sense.

"Where do you live?"

Rick cocked his head to the side as if the question seemed irrelevant. "I live in Austin," he said, as if he knew the man knew exactly where he lived.

Stace ignored the tone in his voice. He was entitled to some frustration. "Tell me about your family."

It suddenly occurred to Rick the man seated in front of him didn't work for Trojan Security. It was a frightening thought. He'd only just discovered the true nature of the likes of Pruitt and Watson, men he'd known for several years. And though he still thought them to be above the act of killing, they were not beyond hiring someone else to do it for them. "If this man doesn't work for Trojan Security then who does he work for? What's he capable of doing?" The unpredictability in the nature of Stace's questions made the man appear much more sinister than Rick had previously suspected.

"Why the sudden interest in my family?"

"Let's say I'm curious."

"I have a wife and a young girl."

"The perfect little family," Stace replied. "Who'd you marry?"

Rick repeated the question in his mind. "Who'd I marry? What kind of a question is that? A better question would be why'd I marry? But even that's a stupid question."

"Tell me her name," Stace demanded.

"Her name's Julie."

"Last name."

"Norvel…Julie Norvel."

"Ain't that special—and your daughter?"

"Rebecca. Now what do you know about them?"

"You tell me. How long have you been married?"

"About four years."

"How old is your daughter?"

"She's two. What does all this have to do with anything?"

"Don't you watch television Rick?"

"Yeah. Why?"

"Because if you did you'd know to keep your mouth shut. The smartest thing any hostage does in the movies is to tell the terrorist about his wife and family. He tries to be-friend the terrorist. That way, if the terrorist has any degree of compassion he might decide not to kill him. It's much harder to kill a friend don't you think?"

Rick realized he was being a fool. There was definitely something peculiar about this man.

"So tell me about Julie, about your daughter. Just how are things going Rick?"

"I met my wife in college. She's all a man could ever want, beautiful, intelligent, loving…she's the best thing that ever happened to me."

"You say that as if you're never going to see her again."

"If you were in my position wouldn't you think so?"

"I suppose you're right, things do seem a little up in the air right now. Funny how life has a way of flipping on you doesn't it?"

Rick didn't answer. He was trying to picture his wife's face and the last time he saw his daughter laughing.

"A bit ironic how you hope and dream…how you make plans and work to make sure those dreams come true, then somebody comes along and screws it all up for you. Makes you just want to run and hide doesn't it Rick?"

It actually made Rick feel like fighting, but he played along, "yeah, I guess it does."

"I'd even say you wish you were somewhere else then here, don't you?"

Rick didn't answer. The question didn't need a response. There was a psycho sitting in front of him. Someone with a past to reconcile. Someone willing to use a complete stranger to take out his frustration.

"You strike me as a coward Rick. I think if you had to make a tough decision, one that was obviously ethically and morally right, but knew you might personally suffer from making that decision, you'd fold. You'd go with the flow. You'd save your ass and your reputation. Wouldn't you?"

Rick was silent for a long time. Stace let him stew.

The fact was the psycho with the knife was right. He thought of no less than three specific situations in which he had saved his ass and let another person suffer as the result. He even recalled the decision he'd made at Marbel University. Some pervert had wanted to display pornographic pictures at the last public gathering of the University. Rick had sought advice from the most respected professor on campus, who advised him he couldn't ethically prevent the artist from displaying the work. But he'd gone with the flow. He sided with the committee and cast the deciding vote. "What the hell ever happened to that guy?" he wondered.

"I don't suppose you know what it's like to be rejected Rick, so let me explain the dynamics to you. First, you feel like running, so you do. It's a good thing really. Gets you out of the situation and away from the people who pissed you off. Cause you really feel like killing them you know. You even start dreaming of little scenarios. Start making plans on how you can kill them. Of course, if you're sane, which I am, you bury those thoughts, but you still find yourself thinking of more creative and intelligent ways to get back. You know, something much more civil, but just as cruel nevertheless. Then time begins to set in. You cool off. You stop dreaming about killing at night. You stop making plans through the day, but you see...the damage is done. You've got this scar in your life you feel is so grotesque that you still think you need to hide. Go somewhere where nobody knows you. Someplace where you can start all over again. Of course, this is all a part of the running. A year goes by, maybe two or three. You think about what happened sometimes, but it's like a bad dream now, like an event that never happened. But you can't doubt the evidence of it in your life. Can't hide from the concept you really are a coward, that you really don't have what it takes to make it in the real world. You look for reasons to disbelieve what you're thinking, but you can't find any, because you're nowhere. You're living in a dump, trying to make ends meet and you're not even close to being where you thought you'd be."

Stace paused for a moment to take a breath. He ran his sleeve across his forehead as if he'd worked up a sweat. "If you're lucky, like I was, something completely extraordinary happens. You're suddenly presented with the opportunity to set things right. To stop running. To get the monkey off your back."

"What do you think you'd do Rick, If you were in that situation? Would you have the courage to do what you needed to do?"

Rick thought quickly. Nothing in his life even resembled the situation the man was talking about. He agreed nevertheless, "I suppose I would."

"Would do what Rick? Keep running or have the courage to do what you needed to do?"

"I'd do what needed to be done. I'd do what I had to do to set it right."

"You have no idea how that makes me feel Rick to hear you say that."

Stace stood up. His legs were cramping and the chill was reaching his bones. Rick heard him rise and cringed as though he was expecting a blow from the knife. Stace smirked. He had him right were he wanted him. Rick's few hours of suffering had come nowhere near to what Stace had gone through over the past few years. He could suffer a little longer. Stace surmised it was high time for him to get down to business. He stared over the tall pine trees beyond the open meadow and into the sparkling lights of *Wiesbaden* far below.

"What do you now about the CRM?" Stace asked, startled he'd remembered the abbreviation.

Rick looked up under the confines of the mask he was wearing looking for the direction of the voice. "I've never heard of them before."

"Never? Hard to believe."

"Maybe they work for Trojan Security. I don't know."

"And the two guys in the apartment, who were they?"

"Never met them before in my life, till one of them grabbed me at the airport."

Stace thought about this for a moment. "Do you suppose they're a part of the CRM?"

"It's possible." Rick was choosing his words.

"There's a religious organization headquartered in Munich called the International Christian Coalition."

"The ICC?" Rick questioned.

"Correct. Their influence reaches across the globe. What do you know about them?"

"I know their Executive Director, Joseph Stautzen."

"Now we're getting somewhere. How do you know him?"

"I met him in Texas a few months back. We were building a new security program and he came to the states to assist us with it."

"You are referring now to 'the program.'"

"Yes."

"And where is the program now?"

"The master copy is at Trojan Security. I thought Stautzen had the other copy. I came to Germany to get it back from him."

This puzzled Stace and he shined the flashlight at Rick's head. "Who told you to do that?"

"No one. I was on my own. Those two goons at the apartment told me someone stole it from Stautzen when he was driving back to Munich, but I don't believe it."

"All right, let's try a different question. "Why did you need to get it back?"

Rick thought to himself. "He's either playing games with me or he's got no idea what's going on."

Honesty seemed the best approach. "Because Trojan Security framed me. They set me up. I figured if I could get the program back I might be able to expose them. I could get back at them for what they did to me. If I'm lucky they've probably only ruined my marriage. They know where my family is. They've threatened to kill them if I don't cooperate."

"Who threatened you?"

"Those two knuckle heads in the apartment."

"That's an interesting story Rick."

Rick sat up and spurted out into the night air, "Well I don't give a fuck what you think. Because of you they probably think I'm still after the program. They probably think we're working together. So if they think we're working together to expose them, what do you think they're going to do to my family?"

Stace turned the flash light off and looked up above him through the treetops into the clear night sky. The stars were brilliant. He didn't know what to believe, or perhaps he didn't want to believe what he was hearing. Every time Rick opened his mouth the problem grew more complex. If Rick was telling the truth about his family then he might be right, and Stace's own actions might be putting Rick's family in jeopardy. This was an unexpected and unwelcome thought. If that were true, it meant they were both after the same thing. Both of them had a need to stop whatever the hell was going on. Rick had his reasons and Stace had his. Primarily, that he had to disassociate himself with Eva's investigation. He had to prove to her he was in no way connected to it. That he was not even remotely linked to anyone involved. That would be hard to prove, seeing that he was indeed, associated with Rick. They had a past together and now they were inexplicably thrown together into the same future. He hated Rick Forstein; blamed him for every rotten thing that had happened to him since graduation; hated him even more when he realized Rick had been responsible for taking Eva away from him. Now, he was supposed to believe he might be responsible for the fate of Rick's wife and child? It was overwhelming—inconceivable.

He walked over to Rick and sat down in front of him. There was really only one solution to the problem, a solution he hated to think about and one he doubted could even work, which was, they must work together. They must somehow reconcile their differences. They both wanted the same thing for different reasons and they both had plenty of reasons and energy to make it happen. But would it work?

"What do you know about the Burtman fire?"

"Nothing. I don't know any 'Burtman.' Why? What happened?"

"I lost the most important person in my life because of that fire."

Rick sensed a tender spot in his interrogator. A window into the man's soul. A possible reason for his abduction.

"Who was it that died?"

"No one, yet."

"I don't understand."

"The bakery belongs to the parents of the woman I love. She thinks I'm responsible for it. She thinks I work with the people who set the fire."

"It wasn't an accident?"

"It was *no* accident."

"Why would she think it was deliberately set?"

"Because she's an investigative reporter. She's made lots of enemies over the years. She's in the middle of an investigation of the ICC, the CRM, Trojan Security's program and you."

"Me? Why me?"

"You built the damn thing didn't you?"

"Not entirely."

Stace took a deep breath. "I think it's time you told me what this program is all about."

"You don't have any idea what the program's for?"

"No."

"Why should I tell you?"

"Let me put it to you this way. I hold you personally responsible for ruining my life. My only hope of putting it all together is with the information you have in that greedy little head of yours. I'm mad enough to kill you right now, the question is whether or not you're going to supply me with enough information to convince me I shouldn't."

"You come right to the point don't you?"

"I don't have the luxury of time right now and it seems to me you don't either. Seems to me any minute you waste puts your family closer to danger. If I let you go, you might just be able to do something about it. But that's going to depend on what you tell me."

Rick was quick to respond. "I was in charge of a team of four individuals brought in by management to assist me in creating the program. Each one of these people brought to the table various skills. One was a notable neurosurgeon. One was a linguist. Another, a woman, had worked for the US Government for years. She was an expert on informational warfare and the Internet. The other person was Joseph Stautzen with the ICC."

"What was the purpose of the program?"

"At first it was vague. Basically, our task was to design a program that would infiltrate the Internet with psychological messages.

"What kind of messages?"

"Undetectable ones to the human eye, but not to the human subconscious. Anyone who's looking at their computer screens when the messages appear will be instantly affected without their knowledge. But it was more than just messages, really more like brainwashing, there were some technical aspects to the program—"

"And you built this thing? What hole did you stuff your conscience in while you were doing this? Surely you must have known such a program would be highly illegal, not to mention unethical."

"That was not the main emphasis of the program."

"Explain."

"Trojan Security builds security programs. This particular program had two phases to it. The first phase was the one I've described. The second phase was to design a security program that would be able to seek out and destroy the purpose of the first program."

"Let me see if I got this…The first program was just a mock program. You built it so you could have something to go on to build the second program."

"Yeah, and we did our job right. We took everything into consideration. Without a doubt, in the wrong hands that program could effectively manipulate the minds of millions of individuals."

"You mean it could actually change the way people think?"

"Exactly. Hitler might have been able to conquer the world with it."

"I still can't believe you built the thing."

"Sure you can, think about it. Timing is everything in the world of business. The technology exists to build such a program. If we didn't do it someone else eventually would. Our motives were clear. We were to build a security program to ensure that if such a program ever was developed and used by someone else, then there would be a way to stop it."

Stace thought about the logic of this for a moment. "So the plan was to market and sell the security program all along?"

"That's what I thought."

Stace shined the flashlight into Rick's face again. "Don't stop there. That's what you thought, until what?"

"Until they set me up and pulled me off the program."

"Why would they do that?"

"Because they had no intention of ever building the security program."

"What do you mean?"

"Personally, I thought something strange was going on only a week after we started."

"Like what?"

"Like Stautzen. While were in the planning stages he railroaded through his idea the program should be designed around the mission of the ICC."

"Why the ICC?"

"He made it all sound so logical. The ICC is extremely influential and their mission is to convert souls to their way of thinking. They have everything in place to take advantage of such a program."

"He used reverse psychology?"

"Exactly. We were looking for the most fanatical and persuasive ideological power in which to design the program around. He suggested using the ICC as a working model."

"Smart."

Rick didn't respond.

"So let me guess. Stautzen and the ICC now have possession of the program."

"Yes."

"And it's designed to do one thing, bring them more converts?"

"Exactly."

"And you didn't see this coming?"

"Not until it was too late."

"And I suppose Trojan Security has tied up all the loose ends."

"Air tight."

"But surely the program must be detectable. If they were to use it on the Internet someone would notice it wouldn't they."

"No."

"What do you mean no?"

"Like I said before, we did our jobs right. A person would first have to know the messages were appearing on their screen, then they'd have to use some extremely sensitive monitoring or photographic equipment to detect it."

"What kind of equipment?"

"In the lab we used video cameras at first, but they were too slow. Later we developed a special program based on the other technical aspects of the program to help us see the impact of the program. But the only reason we found it was because we knew it was there in the first place and modified our detection methods with special equipment."

"So where do I get this equipment."

"You don't. You have to build it."

"What about using high-speed film and camera equipment?"

"You're kidding right? That would be a shot in the dark. You'd have to have twenty cameras all pointed at the same screen constantly clicking off pictures. It might take a few weeks, it might take years to get any kind of evidence."

"Ain't that the shit?" Stace mumbled. "What about electronically detecting the images?"

"All you'd be able to pick up would be frequency fluctuations and for the most part, you can't isolate frequency fluctuations. Once you're logged into the Internet the computer is in a continual state of fluctuations. You'd still have no proof."

"So there's no way to stop them from using the program?"

"Not unless you know where the program's at. It could be halfway around the world by now."

"It can be used anywhere?"

"Anywhere there's a phone line and a lap-top computer."

"That narrows it down to about ten billion locations."

"Like I said, we designed the program right."

"Do you have any idea when they were planning on using the program?"

"If I was them I would use it as soon as possible. I wouldn't doubt if it was already in the system even as we speak."

"So stopping them is out of the question."

"I would say so."

"But exposing them might not be"

Rick cocked his weary head up in the direction of the last words he just heard. He would like nothing better than to expose the whole bunch of them, the ICC, Trojan Security and most of all, Pruitt. "Just how do you suppose you're going to do that?"

"I'm not going to do it alone. You're going to help me."

Rick couldn't believe what he'd just heard.

"We?"

"Yes, 'we.'"

"But I have one more question for you before I let you go. I was told you cast the deciding vote. Is that true?"

"Vote?"

"Marbel University...the committee met...the ballot was cast. You broke the news to me personally. I just wanted to know if you cast the deciding vote.

"Stace...Stace Manning? Is that you Stace?"

CHAPTER 53

▼

Rick tried unsuccessfully to peer through the blackness of the shirt wrapped around his head groping for the familiar form. He could not believe the name he'd just spoken could be the same man he'd once known. A soft breeze blew through the pine trees above and he listened to the groan of the massive limbs like the moans of old men swaying back and forth. Before him spread the hollow sound of space, weaving though unfamiliar columns in a world absent of light.

"Does this help?" Stace asked, lifting the shirt off his head and holding the flashlight just below his face to illuminate himself.

It was the face of a phantom, a contorted image of the past coming back to haunt him. His eyes had to be playing tricks on him. He'd lived through a night of terror to which nightmares are spun from and if one could put a face to those nightmares, than this would be the face. It just could not be—but there he was; jaw line, nose, dark eyebrows looming over inset eyes, long spindles of hair dangling in curls below his shoulders. "Stace?"

"Where you expecting someone else?"

"From Marbel?"

"One in the same." Stace took the flashlight off his face and shined it into Rick's. There was horror, anxiety and confusion stretching across it like a canvass Van Goth might have painted.

"I don't believe it!"

"Believe it."

Rick was dumb-stuck. He looked around into the darkness to get a feel for where he was and what was going on. It was no dream. It was worse than a nightmare. He was sitting on the top of some fricken mountain in the middle of Germany with a ghost from the past. What was happening to his wife and child? Who were the two goons who grabbed him at the airport? Hell was unfolding around him. He struggled to free himself.

"Not so fast, the vote."

"For Christ sake Stace, that was years ago."

"I know. It was the highlight of my life. You don't forget things like that."

"It meant that much to you?"

"Yeah it meant that much to me!" Stace screamed and the echo drifted down into the valley below.

"I had no idea," Rick confessed.

That's because guys like you always have other things lined up. Contingencies. Networking possibilities. If one thing fails you've got something else to fall back on. Photography was my life. It meant everything to me. I may not have won the exhibit, but I had a good chance of winning. Things could have gone much differently for me."

"I'm sorry Stace. I really am."

"Sorry really doesn't cut it does it?"

Words were futile. Years of time hadn't erased the memory, another few minutes wouldn't help.

"I'd almost forgotten about you—you know? I almost had you erased out of my memory. Tell me its true. If you'd voted for me I would have been able to show—right?"

"I wasn't the only one who voted against you."

"But you didn't pull for me either did you?"

Rick fell silent and motionless.

"Didn't think so. The way I heard it, it was a tie. You cast the deciding vote. Tell me it's true!"

"It's true God damnit…it's true."

The wind picked up in the treetops and the calm of the night was replaced by a soothing whistling sound. It began as an almost imperceptible passage of air, built into an intense orchestration of noise, then slowed to a silence. Seconds turned into minutes. Rick shivered. His hands were numb from sitting on them. Five minutes passed, maybe ten, he didn't know. Stace stood with his back against him immobile as a granite statue.

"How'd you get mixed up with the ICC and the program?" Rick asked, breaking the silence.

"I'm not mixed up with any of it. I came to Germany for entirely different reasons and got stuck in the wrong place at the wrong time. Your name came up in Eva's investigation."

"Eva?"

"Eva Burtman. I met her at a swimming pool a few months back. She was curious about why I came to Germany. In the course of telling her my story I talked about the Art Exhibit and mentioned your name."

"And she put two and two together and assumed we were working together?"

"I don't know what she assumed, but yeah, she put two and two together."

"And here we are…."

"And here we are."

They both thought long about the irony of it all.

"Would it be too much to ask for you to untie me now?" Rick asked calmly. "That is, if you still don't have plans to kill me." He was looking for some humor in the situation. As far as he could tell Stace wasn't smiling. Stace flicked the flashlight back on and walked around the tree. With one sweep of the knife he cut him free.

"They would have killed you," Stace said calmly.

"The guys back at the apartment?"

"I'm guessing they also started the fire at the bakery. Eva's mother and father, her brother and her friend were in the upstairs apartment at the time. They barely made it out alive. Right now Eva's friend is lying in a coma in the hospital. They doubt she'll make it."

"So I owe you my life. Is that what you're trying to tell me?"

"I'm not trying to tell you anything, so don't flatter yourself. I did it for me."

Rick stood up wobbling like a newborn calf. He rubbed his wrists where the twine had cut into them. "You did a hell of a job in there. I must admit, you even had me convinced I was going to die."

"Good. You deserved it."

"I won't argue with that. You still want to get back at them?"

"Be honest with you, I just want my girl back. I don't give a damn about the program, or the ICC, or any other them."

"You don't care about what that program will do to people, how it might change things?"

"No. I guess I just don't have a save the world mentality. I don't care that stupid people want to follow stupid people. Guess I'm basically selfish. I just want my girl back."

"Well, I for one would like to turn the tables. Sons-a-bitches. I swear to God Stace, if they even breathe on my daughter I'll devote my life to—"

"Then it sounds like we've got work to do," Stace said starting down the hill.

"If they think you're with me Stace they'll be looking to kill you as well."

"I know. The thought has crossed my mind."

"So what do you plan on doing?"

"I've got some ideas, but first I want to get off this mountain."

"Where are we headed?" Rick asked, once they'd gotten on the autobahn towards Frankfurt.

"First thing I have to do is pick up my camera equipment. I left my case in the park across from the apartment building."

Stace took the autobahn as far as *Escherscheimer Landstrasse* then went north. He took a left onto *Lilienstrasse* and parked the van where three small streets came together at the far end of the park.

"I'll be about twenty minutes. You stay put."

"I'm not staying in this van. What if the police are looking for it?"

"I doubt the *polizei* are looking for it. The guys at the apartment wouldn't have called them."

"If it's all the same to you, I'd rather be as far away from the van as possible."

They got out and cut through a path leading into the park that ran next to a brick wall, then walked along the winding path through the park past a dozen park benches and playgrounds. When they passed the last playground, Stace looked up towards the apartment across *Hugelstrasse*. The apartment manager must have called the *polizei* for there was a squad car out in front. Its revolving lights spun across the white plaster of the wall behind it like a disco ball.

Stace stopped at the next park bench. "Tell you what, you wait here." He took out a piece of paper from his wallet and scribbled his address on it. He handed it to Rick with the keys to his apartment. "My case is just up that way. If I don't make it back take a cab to this address. Don't take the van there, but I shouldn't be more than five minutes."

"All right."

He left Rick at the bench and walked off the path into the grass. There was a long row of hedges running along the left hand side of the park and he followed them up towards the cluster of shrubs near the entrance of the park. As he got closer to the squad car he could see it was empty. All the lights in the manager's apartment were on. Three or four neighbors stood on the sidewalk just outside the front door, probably talking about all the excitement that went on. "The criminal always returns to the scene of the crime," Stace mumbled. "How true."

When he was about thirty meters from the shrubs the forms of two *polizei* officers passed through the doorway. The first one stood for a moment on the steps and looked out towards the park. Stace crouched close to the ground as his heart pumped away in his chest. He stood up and made a quick dash into the shrubs. After uncovering his case he peered through the thickets across the street. The *polizei* had walked to their car and were getting in. He waited. The dome light was on and he could see they were talking and looking over paper work. He waited five minutes then ten, frozen with indecision. Finally their light went off and they merged into the incoming traffic. After watching them disappear down the street he grabbed his case and trotted back to Rick.

"I was just about ready to leave. What were you doing?"

"I couldn't leave. The *polizei* were sitting in their car across the street."

"I thought you said they wouldn't call the police."

"They didn't. It was the manager. Might have had something to do with me borrowing the keys to the apartment upstairs and locking her in the bathroom."

Rick glanced at Stace. Time and circumstances can certainly change a man.

They made it to the van and got back on the autobahn heading south towards Darmstadt and the Airport.

"How much money you got?" Stace asked.

"About six-hundred and plastic."

"Good, cause I'm broke, and we're going to need a boatload lot of film. I'm assuming you have a lap-top somewhere in that luggage back there."

"I do. Why? What are you thinking about doing?"

The first thing we need to do is ditch this van and rent a car. Then we'll head back to my place."

"Do those guys know where you live?"

"Don't know, but that's a risk we'll have to take. First thing tomorrow morning I'm going in to work to pick up a few cases of high-speed film. I've got one phone line, but I haven't a clue how to get on the Internet. I'm hoping we can be all set up by 9:00 tomorrow morning."

"You're kidding right?"

Stace didn't flinch.

"How many cameras have you got?"

"Four."

Rick forced air between his teeth exaggerating a sigh. "Did you not hear me? I said it would take twenty cameras months to catch anything on film even if we could detect when the program is operating."

"You said it would take twenty cameras and a few weeks. I'm thinking positive."

"You're dreaming."

"Maybe."

"Why don't we just go to the police?"

"Two reasons. The first is because I know the paper hasn't wound up its investigation yet. I know Eva's work and a little about the tenacity of the paper she works for. If they haven't got enough information to bring a conviction, then the evidence isn't there. Which brings me to my second point. Hard evidence is the only thing that is going to put these people away. They have to use the program and we have to catch it somehow. Once we have that evidence we can go public and their whole scheme will come crashing down around them."

"How are you even going to get all that film developed?"

"I'll try and do some of it myself and hire the rest out. We'll move as fast as we can. In fact, it might not be a bad idea to pick up dozens of more cameras and tripods."

"A dozen more computers and phone lines wouldn't hurt either."

"The luxury of plastic."

"There's goes my bonus," Rick muttered.

"Tomorrow afternoon you're going to make contact with Eva and you're going to tell her everything you know. We need to work this from both angles. You've got more information floating around in your head then they've been able to collect in months. I can tell you they're pulling teeth right now."

"And what if they have me arrested?"

"Not a bad idea really. You ought to be arrested, since you built the program in the first place."

Rick looked out the window into the passing fields dissipating into darkness.

"They won't arrest you. We'll figure something out."

Stace merged into the scattered traffic flowing to the right then took the airport exit. After about a mile a highlighted sign over the road read, "*Abfahrt*." The sign announcing the departure terminal was followed immediately by another sign listing long-term parking. It would be as good a place as any to leave the van. It would be weeks before anyone became suspicious of it. After parking the van they walked back into the terminal and found a rental agency. Stace insisted they at least get a BMW. It would draw less attention. After renting the car Stace stopped by the terminal and made arrangements for them to return his luggage from the states. He loaded Rick's suitcase in the trunk while Rick made a quick phone call.

"Susan, this is Rick, is Julie there?"

Susan knew exactly what to say. "She's here Rick, but—"

"Thank God. Is she all right?"

"What do you mean is she all right? She got a handful of photos yesterday."

"I know, but she's ok?" She's there with you right?"

"They're both here, but she doesn't want to talk to you."

"Listen Susan, I don't have time to explain everything to you right now, but she's in danger. Trojan Security sent the photos to her as a way to shut me up."

Julie walked into the kitchen to ease drop. Susan covered the mouthpiece with her hand, "It's Rick."

"I don't want to talk to him."

"I think you should."

"Is that Julie?" Rick asked hearing a bit of the exchange.

"Yes, but—"

"She's in danger Susan and you could be to."

"He says you may be in danger. Something about the photos and Trojan Security. You'd better talk to him."

· Julie cocked her head to the side and walked across the tiled floor. Reluctantly, she took the phone and pulled it up to her ear as if it weighed a hundred pounds.

"Julie! Is that you? Let me here your voice!"

"It's me."

"Thank God you're all right! And Rebecca?"

"She's in the living room watching a video."

Rick looked out through the phone booth for a second then bounced his head off the glass in the booth.

"I know you got the photos and you're upset."

"Why Rick?

"I…I don't know Julie."

"Do you have any idea what you've done to me?"

Rick didn't respond. He had not considered her feelings through the whole affair and a mock attempt at it now would be useless.

"Do you have any idea how that changes things?"

"I know, I wasn't thinking…"

She sniffled and Susan went to get a tissue.

"Julie, I don't want to frighten you and I don't have time to explain everything to you right now. All I can tell you is that you and Rebecca might be in danger."

Having thought about how weak that must have sounded he spoke more directly. "Julie, you and Rebecca and your sister are in danger. I was met by someone at the airport who knew your name, knew you'd gotten the photographs and knew you'd gone to your sister's house. They threatened me Julie. Told me if I didn't cooperate with them something might happen to you."

"You're scaring me Rick. Who told you that?"

"The guys who took me from the airport. I've never seen them before. I think they're working with Trojan Security. They set me up Julie."

"Who set you up?"

"Trojan Security. The whole thing was a set up."

"And the afternoon at Peach Tree's…was that a set up?"

An excuse would only compound the problem. "Julie, I don't have time to explain everything."

"Where are you now?"

"I'm at the airport in Frankfurt."

"Are you coming back?"

"No, I can't come back yet."

"Why not Rick?"

"I can't explain it to you now Julie. You're going to have to listen to me. I know I've ruined things, but you've got to listen to me right now do you understand?"

"Yes," she replied, peering out the kitchen window across the pool and the backyard.

"What I want you to do first is call the police."

"The police? Why? What am I going to tell them?"

"Tell them you have reason to believe someone is trying to hurt you."

"Who Rick?"

"Someone associated with Trojan Security."

"Who Rick?"

"I don't know yet Julie, but that will at least get them over to Susan's place. So you need to call them now. Understand?"

"Yes."

"Don't wait Julie. Do it right after you get off the phone."

"Ok."

"The next thing I want you to do is go through the yellow book. There should be some numbers for bodyguards and private investigators. I want you to call some of them and see what you can find out.

When the police get there they should be able to help you find someone reputable. I don't care what the cost is, you hire the best people
you can find."

"All right Rick. I'll do it. But what about you?"

"Don't worry about me. I'm with an old friend. What we get done
here may affect how safe you are, so I need to stay here. Do you understand?"

"No Rick I don't understand. Why can't you just come back?"

"Because it won't help you right now. I have to clear things up here.
Right now you need to call the police and I've got to get off the phone
so you can do that."

"All right."

"I'm sorry Julie, I really am, but I promise. I'll call you back as soon
as I can ok?"

"Ok."

"Bye Julie—call them now."

"I will."

Stace was waiting outside the booth when Rick finished his phone
call.

"Are they safe."

"So far."

Stace slid the shifter into drive and they sped away.

CHAPTER 54

▼

Making a decision is like laying a cement foundation; once you've begun there's no stopping.

Before driving south to Munich, Stautzen had a meeting with Neil that lasted all but thirty minutes. During the meeting Stautzen had run Neil through the dynamics of the program and had designated him as the forth person who would have access to it. Stautzen had decided he wanted nothing to do with it and Neil was more than anxious to take on the responsibility of infecting the Internet with it.

The fact that Neil and Derrick had lost Rick the night before to the madman in the pantyhose mask was of little consequence to them. They knew the program would be unstoppable until a security program was built to stop it, and they also knew Trojan Security had no intention of building that program. If the program worked as well as it was anticipated to work, they could expect it to operate undetected indefinitely. As far as Neil was concerned time was on their side—not to mention God. Derrick understood his mission as well. There was no right and no wrong; there was the mission and his mission was to do what God had called him to do. The decision had been made to run the program and there was no looking back. If there were any more future obstacles in their path, that path would be made straight. If someone tried to stop them at this point, then it was up to God to take care of that problem. And if God needed a strong arm, Derrick would be more than willing to lend Him a hand.

It was November 8th, execution day, and thanks to Stautzen they had the program in hand. Neil and Derrick stayed awake through the night making plans. At 3:30 in the morning they hopped into Neil's car and traveled north towards *Bonames*. When they reached the village of *Nieder Eschbach* they went east another seven kilometers into the quaint village of *Nieder Erlenbach* and parked across the street from an Episcopalian church just off *Alt-Erlenbach*. The journey lasted only twenty minutes from their apartment, but they were a world away from Frankfurt. The town was rarely patrolled by the *polizei*.

Set in the red brick design of the sidewalk across from the church was a lone, dull yellow phone booth underneath a lofty sycamore. The streets were dark and secluded, not even the leaves were twitching. Neil took his briefcase into the booth while Derrick waited in the car as a lookout, just in case someone got nosy. They didn't expect any trouble and didn't find any. Neil was in and out of the phone booth in six minutes.

"Any trouble?"

"None whatsoever."

"Then everything's a go."

"This is where it all begins," Neil said somberly.

"The beginning of the end," Derrick replied.

They sat quietly for a moment, reflecting on all the events that had brought them to this point. It was to them the accumulation of a life's long dream and labor. Somehow it all seemed too easy, the sacrifices weren't nearly what they expected.

The virus instantly made its way through the intricate maze of wires and fiber optics, through 23,000 miles of space to distant satellites and back, and within moments was halfway around the world. It entered through one Internet provider and quickly swept into a dozen others. As each piece of e-mail was transferred and as more and more web pages were accessed for information the virus spread from country to country. Within thirty minutes it would spread into tens of thousands of homes, business, corporations, and governmental institutions. By the time they arrived back at the apartment it would begin randomly targeting computer screens around the globe simultaneously with undetectable, intoxicating messages.

Later that morning, at around 11:00 they packed up the car with a week's supply of personal items and everything essential to carrying out the business of the CRM. Munich was a short four hours away. The move was preplanned. Two large offices on the second floor of the ICC's administrative building had already been prepared for their arrival. They would move their base of operations out of Frankfurt, but more importantly, they would join forces with the ICC. They might loose a few converts in the transfer, but most of the CRM's supporters were already familiar with the ICC and its brand of faith. Neil had been prepping his churches for months with a barrage of sermons to ensure all of his disciples made the transition into the ICC without difficulty. Reverend Eisner would also be graced with a new right hand man in Neil, whom he'd come to admire for his leadership abilities and charisma, and now deemed him far more qualified for the position than Stautzen. Perhaps the only one who balked at the idea of the CRM merging with the ICC was Stautzen himself, but that could be expected, he stood as the only one who would lose the most.

In preparation for the increase in members and donations that would result from the inception of the program, the reverend had hired additional staff. Their purpose was mainly to analyze, record, and coordinate the various components of the ministry above and beyond the normal routine of day-to-day operations. Extra personal were called in to help in the audio and video departments and to make sure an adequate surplus of tapes would be stocked for future distribution. The publication department was beefed up. The ICC presses had been running non-stop for the past four weeks preparing pamphlets, booklets, flyers and most importantly, Reverend Eisner's best-selling book. Two accountants and a statistical expert were called in to monitor the increase in donations. Beside these key positions other areas were not left undone. Additional parking lot attendants and ushers were hired. The landscape received an extra work over. Although the live annual flowers were still doing well, silk snapdragons and pansies were ordered in to replace them. There would be no dead flowers on the grounds. In the buildings, floors were polished, windows cleaned and bathrooms sanitized. The parking lot lines received another coat of white reflective paint. The fountain was drained and the blue tile scrubbed and polished. The bronze statues of the twelve disciples in the fountain were scrapped clean of bird droppings. Two additional guards were hired for the front gate. The reverend left no stone unturned. When that great day of the Lord would come, the ICC would be ready for it.

The reverend himself had embarked on a daily routine of fasting and prayer. He searched his soul for any defects or deficiencies and found none. This was to be the Lord's finest hour and he would not disappoint him. He'd devoted decades to the Lord's work. Every hour he had delegated for Bible study…every hour he had crouched on his knees in earnest prayer…every sermon he had prepared had all led up to this moment. A new chapter in the history of mankind was unfolding and he'd been selected to be the mouthpiece of God. It was a humble and terrifying experience. One he felt honored to be a part of. Right and wrong no longer existed for the reverend. The same God, which had slaughtered thousands of heathen men, women and children to prepare the way for His people, would be the same God who would assist in the success of the program. It was certainly a small matter for Him. Ethics and morality no longer existed either. God had created both and He could suspend them. God was in no way expected to work around inadequately constructed man-made regulations. In this hour, His finest hour, He had every right to bend and break the rules, for He had created them. They were his toys and no one could take them from Him. Reverend Eisner was proud to be a part of such omnipotent power. And on Sunday it would all come together.

CHAPTER 55

▼

Beep…Beep…Beep! Beeped the monitor on the shelf above Tasha's head. Her legs were twitching, fingers jerking about aimlessly. Eva had been watching the monitor creep incessantly upwards for the past thirty-five minutes. When it sounded she leaped out of her chair and the nurse in the room came rushing over to press the reset button. The monitor crept up another notch to102.7. Any reading above 87.5 wasn't good. Each second the monitor registered a fraction of a point above 87.5 irreparable damage was occurring within Tasha's brain. She was hopeless to prevent it. The nurse walked calmly, but briskly out of the room and called for assistance.

A second nurse came in and lifted the oxygen mask off Tasha's face. She placed a long black rubber device over her mouth and nostrils and began pumping away on the balloon at the other end. The device was designed to force much needed oxygen into Tasha's lungs, a mechanical way of hyperventilating a person. "Come on Tasha. It's ok. Everything's all right. You just need to relax. Come on Tasha, be still, relax, relax." The nurse said. As she pumped she kept her eyes glued to the monitor. Tasha groaned and tried to pull her face away from the device. Her right arm slid across the sheet a few inches. Her legs twitched again. The monitor shot up another four points to 103.1. "Come on girl, relax. It's going to be all right. Take it easy. We've got some medicine for you that will make you rest for a little." The other nurse returned with a syringe and ran the medicine into the IV line flowing into Tasha's left hand. The other nurse kept pumping away. In a few minutes Tasha stopped twitching altogether. The nurse with the syringe went back to the cabinet and discarded the needle, then returned with a chart. Eva watched the monitor drop below 102. A few minutes later it was approaching 101.

"What's happening?" Eva questioned.

"She's waking up," the nurse with the chart said smiling.

"Waking up? That's a good sign isn't it?"

"Yes, that's a good sign."

"Then why did you put her back to sleep?"

"Because she's in a lot of pain right now, at least when she's awake. Her brain was responding to that pain with increased activity. That causes more pressure. Right now we just want to make her as comfortable as possible. The more comfortable she is the lower the pressure in her brain will be." The nurse could see Eva was entirely baffled with what she was saying and walked around the side of the bed to speak with her more directly. "Right now it's better that she remains unconscious. It's a very good sign she's waking up, but it's early and the pressure in her brain is still at dangerous levels."

"Is that procedure?"

"With these kinds of cases it is. The most important thing is to keep the brain relaxed so it can concentrate on healing. I can't promise you anything, but normally within a few days the pressure drops enough so we can allow her to wake up.

Eva fell back into her chair without a word considering the logic. She looked up at the monitor, which had dropped since the injection three points down to 99.4. She could only hope the nurse was right. The other nurse continued hyperventilating Tasha for another few minutes, then strapped the oxygen mask back on her face. Eva was once more left alone with Tasha to twist in her thoughts.

At 9:15 Margaret popped her head in the door and called across the room to Eva. "Mrs. Burtman, you have another visitor."

"Who is it?" Eva said rising.

"An older gentleman. Mr. Schwarz I believe."

"Tell him I'll be right out."

"Yes ma'am."

She stroked Tasha's hand and looked into her placid expression. The swelling still had her face contorted and puffed and Eva longed for even the slightest indication of the woman she once was. She left the room and went out into the corridor.

Mr. Schwarz was waiting just outside the door. "Here, I brought these for Tasha," he said, handing her a bouquet of flowers.

"Thanks. They're beautiful. I'll see she gets them."

"How's she doing?"

"She woke up about an hour ago."

"That's great!"

"But they put her right back to sleep. Has something to do with the pressure in her brain. They want her to keep sleeping until the pressure comes down."

"I see. Well, at least she's coming out of it."

"At this point I'll take it as a minor victory."

"Let's take a walk." Mr. Schwarz took her by the arm. They strolled halfway down the corridor towards the front entrance and stopped by the windows. "Have you found out anything about the fire yet?" he asked.

"*Ja*. They're fairly certain at this point it was deliberately set. They still have to run a few tests to be certain."

"Of course, we knew it was deliberately set, but it's good the arson investigation is proving that true."

"What did the *polizei* have to say?" she asked.

"Fortunately, we've got some friends in the department, otherwise they wouldn't even give us an ear. Normally, they'd wait for the arson team to determine something positive before they'd even consider looking into it. I spent about an hour this morning with Detective Macabre. I gave him all the information we had along with photographs of the CRM members."

"Is he a friend?"

"Yes, otherwise I wouldn't have bothered. All we have is a bunch of circumstantial evidence stitched together with intuition. He says he'll keep checking on the arson investigation. His hands are tied until they reach their conclusions. As far as the ICC goes, all the *polizei* can do is check with the Munich *polizei* to see if they've got anything on them. He said not to expect much. He did have something interesting to offer me though."

"What is it?"

"I told him we suspected Neil or Derrick as the two individuals behind the fire. We talked about where they lived and about how they'd been following you and Ruben around. Well, seems last evening two of their *polizei* units answered a call to the apartment building."

"Did he offer any details?"

"The manager called them with a complaint. She said a man came to the door at about 6:00 wearing a stocking over his head and waving a knife in her face."

"A burglar?"

"No. Didn't steal a thing, only the keys."

"Rapist?"

"Far from it. He just wanted her keys to get inside one of the third floor apartments—guess which one?"

"The CRM's."

"Right. Then he locked her in the bathroom."

"That's odd."

"It gets more strange."

"They found her keys in the back parking lot. The *polizei* questioned Neil and Derrick and they said they didn't hear a thing."

"Figures."

"Everyone else in the building was questioned and nobody saw or heard anything."

"So, someone breaks into the manager's apartment wearing a stocking, steals nothing but her keys, then leaves them in the parking lot on his way out."

"The *polizei* thought it might have been an old boyfriend or someone harassing her, but you and I know better. I was able to convince Detective Macabre that the fire on Friday night and last night's event are probably related. He said he'd look into it."

"What do you think happened there last night?"

"I think Neil and Derrick had an unwelcome visitor who was after something."

"Like the program?"

"Maybe, or information."

"Suppose they got what they were looking for?"

"Hard to tell. They sure aren't talking. Either way, it just complicates things more. Ruben still hasn't come up with anything substantial on the ICC. Shelly could only get so far with Trojan Security. What we know about them she has already told us. Then there's the CRM. We still haven't figured out how they play into all of this. The arson team may rule it as an arson, but proving they started the fire is an entirely different story. Even with the support of the *Berliner-Morgan Post* and the information they supplied us with, getting any kind of a conviction on the CRM is going to be next to impossible. For all we know the program could be just an accounting package for the ICC." As he spoke Mr. Schwarz looked dispassionately into the courtyard outside.

"You sound as though you're ready to give up," Eva said facing his profile.

He took his eyes off the courtyard and rested them on her face. "You know me better than that. I never give up. I was hoping to get something substantial by now and nothing is coming to the surface."

"But what about the fire? That's got to count for something."

"Of course it does Eva. Someone set that fire and everything points towards the CRM, but you and I have seen many people walk which should be rotting away in prison right now. It could have been set by an old enemy, someone who's waited a long time to pay you back."

Eva didn't respond. Mr. Schwarz was right. The fire could have been set by just about anybody.

"I just don't want you to get your hopes up," Mr. Schwarz said, putting his arm around her shoulder. They started walking back towards the unit.

"I'm well aware of how worthless intuition and circumstantial evidence can be."

"We need a break Eva. We need something substantial about either the nature of the program or how the ICC and the CRM are connected. Otherwise, we've got absolutely nothing and nothing doesn't pay the bills."

"Are you thinking about pulling the plug on this?" Eva asked, suddenly stopping.

"Not yet. I'm just saying if I don't get proof soon, I'll have to. We've got other projects we need to be working on."

Mr. Schwarz shook her shoulder and urged her back towards the unit. "Don't worry Eva. I know you want this resolved and I'm willing to hold out a little longer on it just to give you that opportunity."

"I appreciate that."

"Now I've got to head back to the paper. I'll let you know if anything comes up." Though it was not his custom and he certainly felt awkward in doing so, Mr. Schwarz leaned over and kissed her on the cheek. "You take care now," he said and turned to go.

"I will. Don't worry about me."

"I never worry about you Eva."

When Eva got back to Tasha's room her heart leaped, but not for joy. *Beep...beep...*not again," she thought. A new nurse sat at her post and thought nothing of it. Eva walked over to the bed and checked the monitor. It read 92.6. She listened closer and discovered the sound was originating from her cell phone inside her purse. She took it out and checked the number of the call she'd missed. She'd never seen it before.

She stepped outside the unit and dialed the number. "This is Eva Burtman, someone just called me from this number."

"I called you."

"Who is this?"

"Rick Forstein."

Eva didn't know quite how to respond.

"We need to talk," he pressed.

Eva smelled a set up. "About what?"

"About the program."

"What's your part in it?"

"I designed it. I came to Germany to try and stop it from being put to use. I was told by a reliable source you've been investigating the ICC, Trojan Security—"

"Who told you that?"

"I can't tell you, but I can tell you all you need to know about the program."

Eva was still cautious. "How do I know I can trust you?"

"You don't, and I don't know if I can trust you, so we're even. I'm trying to stop this thing before it gets out of hand. The last thing I need is to be picked up by the police by a tip from you."

"What do you propose?" she asked after a moment.

"That we meet. Just you and me."

"Ok. Where?"

"Someplace busy, the *Hauptbahnhof.* Just outside the main entrance there's a cluster of flags. Between the flagpoles there's a telephone booth. Can you make it there by 11:00?"

She checked her watch. "How about 10:30."

"Then make it 10:30."

She went back into the unit to collect her things. The door was closed and she entered with reservation. Two nurses were standing by Tasha's bedside. The blanket that had been covering her was folded neatly over the calves of her legs. She was naked except for large patches of gauze scattered over her back and legs. They were in the process of checking her burns and reapplying clean bandages. Eva hated to look, but she had to.

"How bad are they?" she asked the nurses.

"Some are worse than others. Her feet and calves have second-degree burns that will leave permanent scarring. The rest of the burns are relatively minor, just blistering of the skin."

Eva looked across Tasha's shoulder blades at an exposed area of charred flesh. One of the nurses was busy picking and cutting away at the dead skin. The other nurse was working on her calves and changing her dressings.

"Isn't that painful for her?"

"It would be if she was awake, but right now she doesn't feel a thing."

Eva reached for her bag. "I have to go for a few hours. If anything changes please call me."

"All right Eva."

"She'll be just fine, don't worry," the other nurse added.

The university hospital was about fifteen minutes from the *Hauptbahnhof*. Eva pulled her Opel into the parking lot out front and spotted the yellow telephone booth underneath the flagpoles. It was 10:15. She waited in the warmth of her car another five minutes then walked to the booth and waited another fifteen. At 10:35 a silver BMW pulled up along the curb. The horn beeped and the tinted window slid down. She thought nothing of it until the horn beeped again and she walked a few steps forward, bent over and peeped in the window. Behind the wheel was a handsome looking blond haired man around thirty, who could have passed as a European. He waved her closer with a hand. She walked cautiously to the curb.

"Hop in."

"I assume you're Rick Forstein?"

"Yes."

She got in the car and he drove out of the parking lot.

"You're not exactly what I expected."

"He glanced over towards her and noticed she was eyeing his rumpled coat.

"You'll have to forgive me. My arrival party was a little rude."

She looked out over the hood. "Where are we headed?"

"For a drive. How do I get back on the autobahn?"

"Going which way."

"Doesn't matter. I just want to keep moving."

"Then take a left."

"Here?"

"Here."

He swerved across two lanes of traffic and cut off a taxi. A horn faded in the distance.

"First trip to Frankfurt?"

"Yeah."

"Take the next left, *Kleyer Strasse*. It'll take you to the autobahn."

Neither one of them spoke until Rick had cleared the entrance ramp and was headed in a southerly direction.

"This will take you out towards the airport."

"Makes no difference to me." He checked his rearview mirror for the third time and was confident they weren't being followed.

"He loves you, you know."

Eva snapped her head towards him, but was unable to speak. Emotions flooded her mind. She turned her head and looked out the window for clarity.

"You should have seen him last night. He saved my life."

She looked back over to him wondering if they were talking about the same Stace Manning.

"I knew you two were in this together. Where are you taking me?"

"A drive. I told you that. When I have what I need and you have what you need, we'll head back. Point of fact, Stace and I were not in this together until last night. I haven't seen or talked with him since our college days."

"I don't believe you!"

"You can call it what you want; a quirk of fate, destiny, or just plain bad luck. Whatever it is, Stace has gotten the worst of it."

"I've got no idea what you're taking about."

"Of course you don't and even after I tell you, you still might not believe me."

She looked over the sloping hood of the BMW into the expanse of autobahn stretching far ahead. She'd spent the last few days groping over the shattered body of a new friend thinking of dozens a ways Stace had been involved with the fire and their investigation. Believing he was totally innocent would be extremely difficult. "Who do you work for?"

"I worked for Trojan Security up until Friday when they fired me. Gave me a twenty-five grand bonus to shut me up. Framed me actually, probably ruined my marriage and if I'm lucky, when I get back to the states my family might still be alive."

Eva searched his expression for verification to his story. His eyes never left the road, his body, rigid. They were passing everyone in sight.

"Maybe you'd better slow down."

Rick ignored her and merged into the right hand lane. A slower moving car drifted past them on the left.

"You'll get a ticket that way."

"I thought you could drive as fast as you wanted here?"

"You can in most places, but you never pass on the right."

Rick looked at her as if she was joking.

"If you're in the fast lane and someone's in your way flash your lights. They'll move."

Rick liked the idea. "I'll give it a try next time," he replied and pulled back into the left lane.

"Why'd they fire you? Why do they want to harm your family?"

"Because I know too much."

"You said they were blackmailing you?"

"In a rather dignified and professional manner, yes."

She thought about this for a moment. "So how does Stace fit into all of this?"

"Like I said, he doesn't, or didn't, up until last night."

"What happened last night?"

"He was on his way back to Austin—"

"To Austin? For what?"

"It's my understanding you didn't want to see him anymore."

It never occurred to Eva he would actually leave Germany. The thought of him being forever out of her life sickened her, even though she knew that was exactly what she had told him. "I never want to see you again," she remembered saying. A hollow emptiness filled her stomach.

"He was on his way to customs and I was just coming into Frankfurt. He saw me and followed me and thank God he did."

"Why, what happened?"

"Some goon grabbed me in the baggage claim area."

"What did he look like?"

"Gruff. Had wild black hair—not long, not short—just wild. Not too tall either. Told me he knew where my family was and if I didn't cooperate that…well, I don't even want to think about it."

"Then what?"

He dumped me in the back of a van. Another guy was driving—"

"Clean cut, short blond hair?"

"That's right, you know him?"

"I think so. Go on."

"They took me to an apartment and interrogated me for about a hour. Then suddenly this maniac comes in waving a knife, forces the other guys back into a corner and has me tie them up."

"Then you went back out into the back parking lot," Eva said filling in a detail to his story. "The maniac was wearing a stocking over his face."

"How'd you know?" he asked.

"Not important. Did you know who he was?"

"Not at first. I honestly thought the guy was going to kill me. He tied me up in the back of the van and blindfolded me. Then he drove me up into the mountains and tied me to a tree. Questioned me for what seemed a lifetime. I hate to say it, but when he finally took off my blindfold it was the most beautiful face in the world."

"And it was Stace?" she said, imagining the surprise Rick must have felt.

"I almost had a heart attack. You have to remember, I haven't seen him since college and we left as enemies. Even after I saw it was him, I still couldn't believe it. The son-of-a-bitch was still out to kill me. I really screwed him over at school."

A rest stop whizzed by on the right. "You're right," Eva said, "I don't believe it."

"Then I lost twenty bucks."

"Twenty bucks?"

"Twenty dollars. I bet Stace you'd believe me. He said you wouldn't. Why do you think I'm trying to explain this to you?"

"Because I told him to never call me again. Told him I never wanted to see him on this side of the earth."

"Exactly, and we don't have time to play that game. I'm nearly one-hundred percent certain the program is already out there doing its damage."

"Then maybe you better tell me about it."

"I'm not so sure I want to now."

"What?"

"Why should I? If you or whoever you work for is stupid enough to think Stace has got anything to do with this, I'm not so sure you're competent enough to handle what I've got to say."

"That's ridiculous!"

"Is it? How long have you been working on this?"

"Four months."

"And what do you know about the program?"

Eva thought about making something up, but that would have been pointless. She decided to repeat Mr. Schwarz's words, which he had spoken just that morning. "Nothing. 'For all we know it could be just an accounting program.'"

"Thought so."

"So what do you know about the CRM?"

Rick's mind went blank. Stace had just briefly mentioned the name to him last evening. "Nothing."

"Thought so. Did you know those two guys that grabbed you last night were part of a revolutionary underground organization in Berlin back in the eighties?

"No."

"Did you know they're presumed to have killed or assassinated at least two people and probably more?

"No."

"Did you know they tried to kill my family this weekend and that a close friend of mine is lying in a coma at the hospital right now as result of their handiwork?"

"I hadn't made the connection. No."

"One thing's for sure, you're lucky to be alive."

"Then you admit Stace might be on the right side of this?"

"I'll consider it. Now what about the program."

"First things first. I want to nail these guys worse than you do. I've got half the Austin police camped around my family right now and I want to make sure we still have a future together as a family. So, I'll work on putting together the evidence about the program and you work on getting all the dirty little facts put together about the ICC and the rest of those clowns. Fair enough."

"Fair enough, but our investigation's at a standstill."

"It won't be after I tell you what I know."

"I think I can work with that arrangement."

"You don't have a choice."

"I'm curious, where's Stace now."

"Can't tell you, but we're working together. We're hoping to have something before the ICC's Sunday broadcast. We expect you to do the same."

"This is Monday."

"I know what day it is, but you don't know how dangerous this program is. The longer it's out there the worse it's going to be. Whether or not we've got something or you've got something by Sunday is irrelevant. If we have enough evidence that would be great. If not, we'll embarrass the hell out of ourselves, but we still might be able to cause them damage. Either or, it has got to be Sunday."

Eva reached inside her handbag and pulled out her tape recorder. "Mind if I turn this on now?"

"No."

CHAPTER 56

▼

By Tuesday morning Stace and Rick had settled into a frantic routine that was getting them nowhere. Their set-up was far too inadequate to get the job done. They had one laptop, which had been running constantly since early Monday afternoon. They'd opened one Internet account. Facing the screen were three Nikons propped on tripods, two of them had auto-winders snapping off six frames per second. They spend hours snapping shots off the computer screen as fast as they could. Through all day Monday they'd accumulated over four hundred rolls of film. Stace decided developing them himself would be fruitless. He drove two-hundred of them to Stroff's. It was all they could handle for the day. They promised a speedy turn around and he could pick them up by close of business. The rest of the rolls he distributed to three other developing outlets. For an additional charge they could have them done by 7:00. It would have to do.

"This ain't going to cut it," Rick said when he returned just after lunch lugging a case of film. "We're going to need more equipment."

"Phone lines too."

"Already got it arranged. Five more lines. Should be in by 3:00 this afternoon, and by this evening we should be hooked up with another five Internet servers.

"You'll need more computers."

"I know. Do you know of a place where we can pick up used ones?" Rick asked.

"No idea. I don't use the things."

"Never mind. I'll find some."

"We'll need more cameras and tripods as well. Those I do know where to get." Stace said.

"Let's do this. I'll give you my card and you go pick up the cameras. When you get back I'll run and get the computers."

"Sounds good," Stace said as he headed for the door. "You keep shooting."

At 5:30 that evening all of the equipment had been purchased and the phone lines had been tapped into the apartment. Rick opted to buy five brand new IBM clones. They were skeleton grade, absent of any superfluous details, minimum capacity hard-drives and limited RAM. Their processors were slow, and their 56,000 K modems barely adequate. Rick figured that by buying them new he could return them within thirty days for a full refund. Receipts of the last two days of charges totaled over $18,000.

At 6:45 they were ready to do battle. The living room looked as if they already had. The coffee table had been pushed up against the stereo. The couch had been flipped around and moved to the center of the room. The space between the back of the couch and the coffee table looked like Christmas come and gone for a wealthy family full of teenagers. Towering above the coffee table and the back of the couch were half a dozen empty computer boxes, plastic bags and chunks of white Styrofoam. Settled amongst them were ten or so additional empty camera cartons and their fillers. For over twenty-four hours they'd been opening the cartridges of film and tossing the packaging near the balcony window. What started as a small pile in the corner was spilling out into the living room like water from an overflowing dike. Rick used one of the computer boxes like a shovel and scooped them up and tossed the box on the other side of the couch. He took another empty box and set it down near the cameras as a trash box.

They hauled the kitchen table into the living room and set it on the far wall against the shrunk. All six computers were placed on it as close together as possible. It took Rick only an hour to get them up and running and logged into their respective servers. Cables, power cords and extension cords ran all over the floor filling all the power outlets in the room. Extension cords ran down the hallway and into the bathroom. Opposite the computers, about five feet from the edge of the table, were thirteen cameras mounted on tripods. Each camera was pointed at the group of computers as a whole, so when one single shot was taken by any camera it would capture the images on all six computer screens. To compensate for lighting problems, Stace used the fastest film he could get his hands on regardless of whether it was color or black and white. Rick brought in a few lamps to give them extra light. He put one on the television and the other on a table near the door leading out to the hallway. Underneath the computers on the table was a pile of computer information manuals, pamphlets, warrantees, back up CD's of the operating systems, as well as informational pamphlets on how to operate the cameras. Neither Stace of Rick needed to consult them. They were simply tossed under the table in the shuffle of getting everything organized and ready to go.

The plan was simple, to shoot as many shots as possible. Only five of the cameras had auto-winders. For the most part, they moved from camera to camera, clicking and advancing the film as they went. When a roll was finished in one camera they'd simply toss it into the box. Every morning Stace was to take the film into the development companies and pick up more cases of film. After 5:00 each evening he would return to pick up the processed photographs. In the evening he would look over each photograph one by one to see if they'd managed to capture any image produced by the virus. They would work in shifts through the night, since the main objective was to keep the film rolling. There would be a lot of redundancy in their actions. Most of the photographs would look the same. The messages, if indeed the program had been set in motion, would be flashed on and off the screen in just the fraction of time it takes a person to blink. They would be lucky if just one of the cameras managed to isolate one of the images, even luckier if the image captured was readable. There was always the likelihood the image would flash on and off the screen so rapidly that even if they did manage to capture it, it would be nothing more than a blurred photograph. Which is precisely what happened.

It was late Wednesday evening, about 11:00, and Stace was seated on the far right side of the couch. To his left were three boxes of developed photographs. At his request, the companies he was using didn't bother to place each role of film they developed into individual packages. Instead, the developed prints were stood end on end, one right after the other and sandwiched tightly into each box. This would save Stace a great deal of time. On the floor at the end of the couch was an empty computer monitor box. On the bottom of the box was a two-inch stack of prints, which had already been discarded from the prints developed on Monday and Tuesday. Both days' cache had yielded nothing.

Stace reached for a handful of prints out of the first box and rotated them so they wouldn't capture the glare of the lamp just above his head. This next round of photographs would take more time. He now had six screens to look at in each photograph instead of one. It called for the utmost in patience and scrutiny. The odds of them finding anything were already slim. If he even blinked or rubbed his eyes he might inadvertently pass over the screen that had captured what they were looking for. To add to the mediocrity, the five by seven prints shrunk each one of the screens down to a dinky, square inch blob. Any words in those blobs above 42-inch pica were readable to his naked eye, anything less looked like jagged black lines speckled across the screen. He took out a magnifying glass from his top pocket and studied the first photograph. It took him all of ten seconds and was absolutely worthless. Without looking, he reached over the armchair with his right hand and tossed the photograph in the box. As he did this he picked up another photograph with his left hand from the stack on his lap. Again nothing. It was a pattern he repeated over and over again, like a two-armed robotics contraption built to perform four simple functions; lift photograph to face, pass magnifying glass over photograph, study photograph, discard photograph.

Rick's actions were no less monotonous, but much more energy consuming. He moved from camera to camera, taking shots, unloading and reloading film, tossing the film into the box behind him, and occasionally taking a break from this pattern to move each computer to different locations on the Internet.

Stace finished the first set of prints two hours later. He dropped the last photo in the box with disgust. "Shit!" he exclaimed standing up and rubbing the back of his neck.

"Nothing yet?"

"Nothing. I've got to get something to eat." He headed down the hallway and into the kitchen. Rick followed. They'd been at it since Monday. They'd slept little and eaten practically nothing. They fixed a couple of turkey sandwiches. Rick got the one with the heel. They grabbed a bottle of Coke out of the refrigerator and returned to the living room. Neither one of them spoke as they ate. Stace finished and lit a cigarette.

"This is really beginning to feel like a waste of time. Tell me again why we're doing this?" Rick asked. He took out a handful of chips and shoved them in his mouth.

"I guess I just don't see the difference." Stace finally responded, but not to Rick's question.

"The difference in what?"

Stace smashed his cigarette butt into the ashtray. "The difference between what the ICC is doing with the program and what the committee did with my work at the exhibit." He looked over at Rick to see if he was getting the point. The expression on Rick's face was like a plain sheet of paper.

"I submit a few photographs with only a partial rendering of the female form. People say the university is disgraced, the staff is in an uproar, students are offended and a committee is formed to make sure my work isn't exhibited. You cast the deciding vote against me. Then I bump into you after all these years and find out you've designed and built a computer program that has the power to alter human consciousness. A program that's now in the hands of one of the largest Christian organizations in the world, and they're prepared to use it as a psychological weapon to indoctrinate people in mass numbers. And all you're worried about is getting back at them for what they've done to you. That's pretty weak don't you think?"

"I never thought the ICC would actually use the program." Rick said defensively.

"Ah, that's right. It was a security program wasn't it?"

"That's right. It was!"

"And you never suspected at anytime what you were doing was incredibly dangerous, not to mention stupid?"

"No. It was a security program Stace. We had to build one phase of it before we could build the other." He'd been using the same logic for weeks now and it was beginning to sound even weak to him.

"Or did you just think since it was being targeted towards the ICC—a Christian organization—it would be all right?"

"Christianity's got nothing to do with it."

"It doesn't? Are you a Christian?"

"I am" Rick replied flatly.

"So, maybe you thought even if the program was to be used by an organization like the ICC, it probably wouldn't be all that bad would it? I mean, you do believe the world would be a much better place with more Christians in it don't you?"

"Not that it has anything to do with the program, but yes. Don't you?"

"I think the world would be a much better place if people were tolerant of other people's ideas. It's one thing to tell a willing person what you believe. It's entirely different to force people to believe what you want them to believe, or worse, getting people to follow what you believe through some type of psychological manipulation or fear tactics. I'd be more inclined to follow any religion that steers well clear of that garbage."

"Any religion?"

"Any religion, but since I haven't found any that do, I prefer not to subscribe to any of them."

"And that's your only criteria for deciding whether or not a religion is justified?"

"Not the only one, but it's a start. There're thousands of religions in the world. Every one of them is slightly different than the others. Seems to me, if God had one particular religion He favored it would be pretty obvious."

"There is only one, Christianity," Rick said. He wasn't sure if he really believed what he said, but he'd been defending the idea all his life.

"That's my point. The only thing religion can offer as a point of their legitimacy is what they teach. They claim to be special and different from all the others, and even go so far as to say they're the only religion that's valid, but the only thing they can offer in defense of that argument is doctrine. As long as religions are primarily concerned with trying to convince people why their particular brand of faith is better, then they've missed the most important point."

"Which is?" Rick asked. He was entirely at a loss.

"Actually, I can't say with any definiteness. It's only an idea I have, but come to think of it, the fact that it's just an idea is part of my point."

Rick glanced toward the computers hoping Stace would get to that point quickly. Stace was either bored, didn't care, or was going silly on him.

"Here's the thing," Stace continued, "God speaks to no person directly and yet we've got all these experts out there willing to tell the world they know exactly what God's thinking and want God wants them to do. People that are absolutely convinced they are favored by

God and they've got the answers. So, these people convince others to believe them and before you know it another religion is born."

"So you don't believe God talks to people, that He answers prayers and all that stuff?"

Stace thought about it for a moment or two. "No and yes. I think God speaks to people in more subtle ways. I think there are principles that exist, ways in which people should live and cooperate with each other. Tolerance is just one of those principles. It's the beginning to understanding. It allows everyone to accept the fact that when it comes to spiritual truth they might not have all the answers, and it just might be that someone else has some of the answers they're looking for. That's what makes an organization like the ICC so dangerous. They've got the power, influence and money to take advantage of people who are weak. People who are just looking for someone or something to follow."

"So if a person is a Christian or has some other religion, you think they're weak.

"I'm saying most people use religion like a driver's license manual, it's just something to tell them what to do and what not to do. Rules and laws come and go and exist only to help people get along with each other. I just think there's a common thread of principles that run through life, principles that may or may not have anything to do with religion. When the committee decided to pull my photo's from the exhibit they were acting on a perceived moral obligation and not by principle."

"The principle was in the nature of your photographs. You stepped over the line Stace."

"That was not principle. I offended someone's perception of right and wrong and they used their power and influence to stop me. The principle was whether or not I had a right to show my photographs."

"And what if you wanted to enter photographs that were more graphic? Where do you draw the line?"

"You draw the line on accessibility. You let people know what they're in for. If my photos were really all that offensive, then the public could have been easily told they might be offensive. Nobody was twisting anybody's arm to go to the exhibit. Nobody was going to be forced to look at my work. It's quite possible someone might have even enjoyed my work. Did you ever stop to think about that?"

The thought never even occurred to Rick.

"My work was condemned from the start based purely on its content."

"True."

"There was never any consideration given that what I had to share might have been important?"

"We're talking about three photographs Rick. Not about saving the world."

"We are talking about art. We are talking about one person having the right to express their opinion. Even if the whole world disagrees with that opinion, we still have to safeguard that right. I think anything creative and artistic in nature, anything that springs from the mind as a result of conscious thought and takes the form of expression, ought to be particularly safeguarded."

"Anything?" Rick stated.

"Everything artistic; books, paintings, music, photography, dance, theater, movies, everything."

"There should be no censorship whatsoever?"

"None, because art is the expression of the human predicament at its most raw form at a particular time in history. It's the energy from which all thought is formed and from what all actions spring from. You can't censor one aspect of it without inadvertently censoring the other."

"But what if what it expresses is obviously evil. What if someone acts on that idea and harms another person?"

"You're assuming evil exists independent of good."

"Are you trying to tell me good and evil are the same thing? Surely you aren't telling me that?"

"If you believe in the Bible and only One Supreme being they're one in the same."

"So you don't believe in the devil?"

"As far as a personal identity...no."

"What kind of an answer is that?"

"As far as if there's a creature roaming around the universe that is altogether evil, perhaps that's a possibility. I don't believe it, but perhaps it's true. But as far as whether that same being is totally responsible for evil, no. That I don't believe, because if I believed that, then I'd have to also believe evil is a power that exists which is independent of God. It's my understanding what makes God so powerful is the fact that He created everything. Am I right?"

"Everything but evil."

"So you believe a devil created evil?" Stace tested him.

"Yes."

"Then you believe the devil has the power to create?"

"I didn't say that."

"If he's responsible for evil than he must have created it."

Rick was at a loss for words. Stace continued.

"If he doesn't have the power to create than he must have gotten that power from someone else."

"I don't follow you."

"It's simple Rick. Either God created both powers, since every thing and every power originates from Him, or God gave the devil an evil power to play with. Which is it?"

"I've never really thought about it," Rick said not wanting to get into it.

"Well, if you believe God gave the devil the power to use evil, then you'd better be prepared to answer the question of why? Why would God allow all the evil and nasty things of life to exist? On the other hand, if you believe the devil created evil then you've got to answer the question of whether good is really more powerful than evil. Because it sure looks to me that evil is winning. The only other option is to believe God created both powers, both good and evil."

"And you think that's the best option?"

"If you want to recognize God as the creator; the only creature powerful enough to create everything that exists, it is"

"So why would He create evil?"

"I'm afraid that's not a valid question. Point of fact, evil exists. It was never created. If you believe God is the creator of all things and nothing was created before Him, then evil has always existed. Even if you believe God was once some glob floating around in the universe, you'd still have to believe everything that currently exists came from that glob. And if you can see that, then the only way to understand it is that whatever you describe as evil is also God."

"That's hard to swallow."

"Not really. It makes a lot of sense if you see the universe, or God, as comprised of spiritual principles rather than mere physical properties. Take love and hate for instance. They are principles. You can't have one without the other. You can't appreciate one without the other. One is not any more evil than the other. Most people think love is good and hate is evil. Ever known someone to experience any kind of pain or heartache from love?"

"It comes with the territory."

"And what about hate? Ever known something good to come about as a result of hate?"

"Seems I read somewhere God hates sin but loves the sinner." Rick replied.

"So even the Bible says God is capable of hating something. So what happens when a person hates something? What happens when you Rick, hate what Trojan Security has done to you?"

"You go after them. What do you think?"

"You mean you act on it."

"I guess so."

"And let's say we succeed at this, that we teach Trojan Security a lesson and pulverize the ICC's empire. We will owe it all to this power we call 'hate' won't we?"

"Hate. Justice. Anger. Vengeance. Call it what you want."

"Makes no difference to me either. But you still can't argue the point that the good intent we have was accomplished by what some would call 'evil motives.'"

"Your point Stace."

Stace could see Rick had grown weary of his words. "Perhaps he's just the kind of person that prefers looking over the driver's license manual for an hour or so each week."

"I'm saying there's more to right and wrong than what people perceive. There's more to it than people living by a set of standards and expecting the rest of the world to follow the same set of standards with nothing more than a flimsy excuse like 'what I believe is right and what you believe is wrong.' My work was rejected because of a false set of standards. Trojan Security has taken that a step further. They think they can force their standards into the heart of where people think. I don't think you understood the point at Marbel and I don't think you understand the point now."

"I'm helping you aren't I? Where would you be without the information I provided you? Where would you be without all this equipment?"

Stace decided to let the issue lay. "I guess I'd be sipping sun tea on my mother's porch in Austin about now." He grabbed another handful of photos out of the box and examined the first photograph, moving the magnifying glass slowly from the left to the right. There was something entirely unusual about the forth monitor in the line.

"Rick. I think we might just have something here...."

CHAPTER 57

▼

The Frankfurt Herald in its Sunday addition printed a three-paragraph article of the *backerei* fire. Officer Rossittener wasn't on duty that day nor was she ever on duty during the weekend. She worked as a traffic officer in the headquarters of the Central *Polizei* office at the *Konstablerwache,* just a ten-minute walk from *Hauptwache.* She sat alone at her dining room table, sunlight pouring through the widows and across the newspaper unfolded in her lap. She squinted her eyes, leaned over and drew the embroidered drapes closed, then glanced down at the article that had captured her interest.

The short news clip was at the top of the third page. Had it not been accompanied by a graphic black and white photograph, she might never have given it a second glance. The photograph was an after-the-fact shot taken shortly after the sun had risen of the once standing, *Burtman backerei* and home. There was nothing left. Caught in the photograph were firemen. Two were still wearing their flame retardant uniforms with wide brimmed hats facing backwards like duckbills. The fireman nearest the camera had discarded his coat sometime earlier and he stood on a giant pile of bricks that Officer Rossittener guessed might have been the front of the building, which had collapsed during the fire. Near this fireman were the remnants of some kind of cabinet structure. It was nothing more than a pile of twisted triangular shaped sheet metal. In the background, two burnt steel ovens stood immobile as bank vaults. The trees in the backyard were fried like year old Christmas trees left in their stands through summer. Only the brick sides of the *backerei* remained intact, this simple fact had probably kept the fire from spreading to the buildings beyond, which incurred only partial roof damage. A van in the alley looked like it had escaped most of the heat's intensity. It leaned noticeably to the left. Officer Rossittener pulled the paper closer to her face and discovered the two tires nearest the *backerei* had popped. She was relieved as she continued to read that all the occupants of the apartment upstairs had escaped. "Arson was suspected," the writer of the article concluded.

Officer Rossittener had never personally visited that particular *backerei*, but she was aware of its location and recognized the corner on which it stood. She had sixty-seven traffic cameras under her command, cameras mounted on traffic signals at various locations throughout the city. There were two such cameras hanging at that corner. In fact, she processed on average ten citations a week from those two cameras alone. It had been brought to her attention just recently that it was possible one of the cameras at that location was malfunctioning. The other camera, however, always captured the *backerei* in the background when taking pictures of traffic violators. "It will be interesting to watch the clearing of the debris and the rebuilding in the photographs," she thought to herself.

Her job was as predictable as the rising of the sun. With the exception of malfunctioning cameras, the cameras never lied. All of them were equipped with sensors and triggering equipment that performed two basic functions: to photograph speeding cars and cars that ran red lights. Every photograph captured the car's license plate number from either the front or rear angle. That number was then traced by computer to the owner, a fine was assessed and a paper copy was forwarded to the owner. Rarely was a traffic violation ever contested, for the *polizei* had a photograph with a stamp stating the exact date and time of the incident. The system provided an on-going source of revenue for the city, but more importantly, it freed up the unit *polizei* to concentrate on more serious crimes.

Later that same week on Thursday, Officer Rossittener was sitting at her desk reviewing the next stack of photographs that had arrived from the developers that morning. She was methodical in her approach, examining each photograph just as it came out of the package. Coding on the photograph told how severe the violation had been. Perhaps the occupant of the car hadn't been paying attention to the yellow light. By the time they passed through the intersection the light had turned red and the camera had done its work. As she reviewed each photograph she would turn her chair a quarter turn to the right to face her computer screen. Then she'd slide the photograph under a clipboard just above her computer monitor. Next, she'd enter the license plate number of the car into the computer and almost instantaneously a data base form would appear headed by the name of the owner of the car, as well as their last current address. Additional information printed on the bottom of the photograph listed the other particulars such as location, time and reason for the violation. She quickly entered that information into the database, and fines were automatically assessed based on the information typed in. When she was done she punched it through to the printer and the computer set itself up for another entry. About half way through the stack she slid a photograph up under the clip. She went through her steps, but hesitated when she saw the location of the photograph.

She leaned back in her chair and studied it. The time stamp read "November 6, 02:33." She quickly understood the photograph had been taken early Saturday morning. The code indicated the camera had photographed the rear license plate number after the car had cleared the intersection. In the photograph stood the *Burtman's Backerei*, just hours before it had burned to the ground. Officer Rossittener distinctly remembered reading arson had been suspected as the cause of the fire. It took her only a moment to recognize something suspicious. Near the front door of the *backerei* a man was walking towards the corner. The passing car's headlights put him in the spotlight at the exact time the camera had taken its picture. "Was it possible this man was the same person who set the fire?" she wondered. The newspaper had said the fire was started sometime between 1:00 and 3:00. She could see no visible signs of fire in the photograph as of 2:33, so it was likely the fire had been started sometime after that. "What was this man doing just outside the *backerei* at that time of the morning?"

She reached above her desk and took a binder from the shelf. The binder held in concise alphabetical order all the phone numbers of the various departments of the Frankfurt City Municipal Departments. She laid it across her desk and it took her only a few moments to find the Arson Investigation Department. The department had arrived at its own conclusions on Tuesday, based on physical evidence and a series of tests conducted both on site and in their labs, their conclusion was the fire had been deliberately set. They in turn forwarded their report to the Frankfurt *Polizei*. This procedure was dictated by policy. The responsibility of the Arson Investigation Department was to determine the cause of the fire. It would be up to the *polizei* to further investigate, arrest and prosecute if possible. It was highly fortuitous that Officer Rossittener had photographical evidence of a possible suspect. She was instructed to send her photograph to Detective Owens by courier.

When Detective Owens received the photograph he immediately took it to the photo-lab for enlargement. The enlarged photograph of the suspect was then scanned by the computer for possible identification. While the photograph was in the lab Detective Owens placed a called to Detective Macabre, who'd contacted him earlier in the week after a visit from a reliable friend, Mr. Schwarz.

"You say the photo was taken early Saturday morning around 2:30?" Detective Macabre questioned Detective Owens.

"2:33 to be exact."

"And the image of the man in the photo is clear?"

"Every detail."

"Can you fax a copy of that over?"

"We're getting a larger photo made up as we speak, but you don't need to wait. The photo's been logged into the department's computer."

Detective Macabre fished through the department computers and within a couple of minutes had a clear eight by ten photo of the man standing just outside the *backerei* front door. He took it back to his desk and laid it next to the photographs provided to him by Mr. Schwarz, positively identifying the man as Derrick Sachs. Finding Mr. Sachs was now a priority.

At the ICC complex in Munich, Stautzen gave three sharp knocks on the reverend's open door before proceeding into his office.

"What's the word Joseph?" the reverend asked gazing out of his windows overlooking the fountain area. The silk flowers had been planted in the bedding areas and his eyes were taking in the pleasant display of reds, subdued pinks and brilliant yellows. The fountain was sparkling, the apostles glistening, and the outstretched arms of Christ in the boat seemed to anticipate the coming Sunday as much as the reverend himself.

"The reports are in. The numbers are low, but promising. I think the program's beginning to have an affect."

"Publishing?" the reverend asked turning around and walking towards his desk.

"Up seven percent since Tuesday."

"What about the audio and video department?"

"About the same. Most of the calls we've been getting are requests for additional information."

"Internet hits?"

"Up eleven percent. That's the best indication we have the program's working."

"Donations?"

"They're lagging, but that's to be expected. Donations usually reflect the amount of information we send out, allowing time for people to digest what they read."

Stautzen saw the reverend was satisfied with his verbal summery of the report. He laid it down on the reverend's desk and decided to add a bit more to it. "Everything is ready for Sunday. We've gotten two additional confirmations from television networks to carry our weekly broadcast, both of them in Central America. Neil's created a new homepage for our Internet address. Of course, the satellites always carry the broadcast around the world, but it will be interesting to see the increase in numbers from those who randomly view the broadcast this Sunday. Mayor Baxter has still not called to confirm, nor has any of the other government officials we sent invitations to."

"They are a proud bunch...may take some time. People in their position always want to make sure the train is headed out of the station before they're willing to jump on board."

"Yes sir."

The reverend took a seat behind his desk and stroked his beard a few times. "Overall, I'd say that's not bad is it Joseph?"

"No sir. Much better than I anticipated."

"Faith, Joseph. It's all a question of faith." The reverend smiled and drifted momentarily into a lapse of contentment.

Stautzen waited patiently by the front of his desk for any additional instructions.

"That's good work Joseph. Keep everyone on their toes and let me know if anything changes. That'll be all."

"Yes sir."

CHAPTER 58

▼

The first visitors to arrive at the ICC complex were Mr. and Mrs. Karl Montclair. They arrived promptly at 7:30 a.m., well in advance of the 9:00 meeting. They'd driven in from France the day before where they lived in a border town between France and Germany. Mr. Montclair had been writing a letter to his son on his computer on Wednesday. Upon completing the letter he sent it out over the Internet to his son via e-mail. For some unexplained reason he suddenly felt the urge to drive into Paris and find a bookstore. He didn't need to write the name of the book down he was looking for, because oddly enough, the title seemed permanently etched on his mind. Without any assistance, he found the religious section and located Reverend Eisner's bestseller. This was a simple task, for the store clerks had just that morning restocked the shelves with the book. Apparently, every copy of the book on the shelf had been sold out the previous day. By the time Friday evening rolled around Mr. Montclair had completed the book and called the toll free number on the jacket seeking additional information. The ICC promised they would send information out promptly and advised him their next broadcast could be viewed on television that Sunday morning, but that wasn't good enough for him. He inquired about the location of the ICC and where the services were held. Being retired, it was not beyond his reach to spend Saturday driving into southern Germany. He loaded up the camper Saturday morning and he and his wife took off towards Munich.

Before the Monticlair's had gotten out of their camper a Volkswagen van pulled into another slot of the main parking area. The owner of the van, a Mr. Hertzfeld, lived in Stuttgart. He was accompanied by his wife and two young children, as well as a friend he'd been able to talk into coming with him. Like Mr. Montclair, Mr. Hertzfeld was not exactly sure why he was there. He worked for European Airways as a ticket sales representative at the Stuttgart Airport. The three computers located just below the counter top at the check-in area where he worked were on twenty-four hours a day processing ticket sales and coordinating arrival and departure times. Any communication between the Stuttgart and Frankfurt terminals of European Airways was done through the Internet and Mr. Hertzfelt spent a great deal of his time accessing information from Frankfurt Main International. Sometime Tuesday evening, long after he had arrived at home and his thoughts had been given time to settle, he'd been talking to his wife in their upstairs bedroom and suddenly a telephone number popped into his head. He didn't recognize the number, but it stuck in his mind and wouldn't go away. He called the number. The voice of a young woman on the other end told him he'd reached the International Christian Coalition. He wasn't in the slightest bit interested in what they had to say, but was compliant when the woman suggested she'd send information his way. Saturday mornings mail brought two pamphlets outlining the details of the ICC. Normally, he wouldn't have opened the envelope, but immediately sat down on his couch and read through both pamphlets.

The next car to pull in the slot to Mr. Hertzfeld's van belonged to a member of the ICC. There was nothing unusual about his presence there. He simply came week after week as a matter of routine. And so it went throughout the next hour or so with the parking lot attendants ushering cars into the next available slot with their bright-orange flags. Those who came were either members of the ICC or were visitors attending services for the first time. By eight thirty the parking lot was nearly full. The security guards at the front gate had logged in over 475 cars, 125 more than any previous weekend. For the first time they had to concern themselves with where they were going to put any additional visitors once the parking lot had reached maximum capacity. Arrangements were made to have them start lining up along the entrance road and if that didn't suffice, they would have to park on the grass lining the road out front.

Those that were members of the ICC quickly made their way into the sanctuary. Visitors were in less of a hurry. Most of them took a casual walk over the inlayed brick of the park, admiring the flowers that looked so real, and becoming familiar with the compound by using the brochures given to them at the main gate. Some visitors took a few minutes to relax on the benches, waiting for the services to begin. Many more stood around the fabulous fountain with the imposing forms of Jesus and his disciples. The air was still and the mist created by the tiny fountainheads was mystifying. Like a fog the mist floated along the surface of the water and up around the calves of disciples, which made it appear as though they were actually walking on water. The path leading up to the sanctuary was trickling with people, who upon entering under the massive columns of the sanctuary were at once taken in by the exquisite paintings and the detail in the stained-glassed windows. The ushers inside were ill prepared for the hordes of people that huddled within the main foyer.

John Petr, the head deacon on duty that morning, stood his post in the foyer near the front entrance, so he could be readily available should any of the other deacons need his assistance. The second deacon to approach him that morning said the exact same thing the one preceding him had said. "Where did all these people come from?" the young man asked in passing, stopping only long enough to draw a bewildered expression from John.

"I have absolutely no idea," John said without looking at him, his attention fixed on the multitudes and the giant Victorian style clock hanging on the opposite side of the foyer.

Stace himself was sitting on the main floor in the third row from the back near the isle. He'd been there since 8:05. On the pew next to him was a hymnal he'd taken out of the rack in front of him to hold a spot for Rick. He was glad he did. All morning people had been rapidly filling into the pews around him and by now they were all packed in like toothpicks in a box. He informed the elderly woman seated next to him he was holding the spot for a friend, but he still had to keep his hand on the hymnal for she kept invading the spot every time someone else filed into his pew.

"Where have you been?" Stace asked when Rick finally arrived as the audience was quieting down in anticipation to the start of the service.

"It took me a while to find the projector."

"Did you make the switch?"

"Barely. How's it coming?" Rick asked looking down at the sheet of paper Stace crinkled in his left hand.

"I'm nervous as hell."

Rick turned around in his seat and glanced at all the exits. He turned to the front again and studied the back of the heads of everyone around him.

"Who are you looking for?" Stace asked. "You're making me even more nervous."

Rick looked back at the exits again then settled into his seat. "No one in particular. I just wanted to make sure no one saw me."

"Why, did you have some trouble with the slides?"

"No."

"Then settle down will you?"

Since it was only Stace's second visit to the ICC's worship service, he was unaware of the heightened sense of anxiety in the audience, or perhaps he was too preoccupied with his own fears thinking about what he was planning to do. Aside from the fact that there were hundreds of more visitors to the service than at any previous time, there was yet, an aura of uneasiness hanging in the air like the still gray haze lingering in the summer skies of Texas, which foretell of a possible tornado. There was the usual amount of joyful greetings taking place and the casual exchange of conversation between friends. Women hugged and kissed each other on the cheeks. Men exchanged handshakes gingerly, a sentence or two spoken between them before they moved on to find a seat. Toddlers stood in the pews facing the myriad of faces behind them, giggling and cooing. Elderly couples sat silently holding each other's hands. Children, who always find church service far too stoic for their intemperate natures and who would normally be reading quietly in the pew or coloring a scene out of their coloring books, seemed more excited. It may have been that they too sensed something far more interesting was going to take place than at any previous service. But all of this went unnoticed to Stace. He took the church bulletin out of the pew pocket in front of him and rehearsed the appropriate time in which he would make his move.

At exactly 9:00 the organ pipes, fixed like giant irregularly cut stalks of bamboo on the wall above the stage, billowed across the auditorium and into the balcony, sufficiently silencing the audience. Children were encouraged to take their seats, toddlers were turned around and set on parent's laps, all eyes turned to the front, and those which had still been lingering in the isles or near the exits moved quickly to find a seat to avoid embarrassment.

"Who are you looking for?" Stace asked Rick again, noticing he was still fidgeting about.

"No one. I'm just amazed at the numbers of people here." He leaned over to Rick and whispered, "was it like this when you came the first time?"

Stace glanced around. The last time he'd come the ground floor had been filled to capacity like today. No difference there. Above his head hung the ceiling of the balcony so he couldn't see the people in the balcony. The only difference I see is there are two extra thrones up front. The last time there were only six."

"Well, if you ask me, something's definitely up. Personally, I find the mood in this place a little discomforting."

"Spooky is the way I'd put it."

At that point the organist kicked in with the second stanza of "*Oh God Our Help In Ages Past.*" It was an octave higher, volume piercing to the effect that it rippled goose bumps across the skin, rather like the trumpeting of a bugle blast ushering a call to arms. At that point the choir entered, marching as it were with their weaponry of psalm and song, single file, all in step, towards the audience then abruptly turning in unison and filling up the choir loft. This came unexpectedly to Stace. He anticipated their entrance to come during the second hymn. Consulting the bulletin again he found everything was in order. The service had just been speeded up. When he looked for the reason why he saw the bulletin announced several changes that would require more time. The last choir member took his seat at the very top of the loft and the hymn ended. There was a brief interlude of silence and the second hymn began. The choir door opened again and out flowed the entourage of the elite, heads bowed presumably in an act of humility.

"I don't fucking believe it," Stace mumbled irreverently.

Rick looked quickly at the stage and discovered the reason for his outburst.

The eight men stood like representations of deity; piously positioned in front of their thrones for a moment as the organist concluded the hymn. Rick had no idea who six of them were, but he instantaneously recognized, even from the distance where they sat, that the two on the far left were the two men who had abducted him at the airport. The organist quieted the hymn down with a sustaining note that seemed off the low end of the scale and all eight men humbly sat down.

"This is getting more and more interesting," Rick whispered.

Stace was suddenly consumed in a state of trepidation. "What have I gotten myself into?" he thought, as the hordes of people around him blurred and disappeared, as if he'd just entered the suffocating confines of a closet. He started having second thoughts, doubting he had the courage to proceed as he'd planned. "Would he be stopped before he ever reached the podium? If he made it to the podium would the two goons on the end jump out of their seats to silence him? Would the elders and deacons be summoned and carry him out of the sanctuary like a madman?" There were at least two-thousand people in the building and millions more scattered around the world watching the telecast. To what degree of utter foolishness was he willing to succumb? No doubt, they would try and stop him, so how much could he possibly hope to get out?

He returned to his senses when a man at the podium called out the name, Reverend Jeremiah Eisner. The other introductions had been completed, while he was groping in the darkness of his thoughts. There would be no song service. The heart of the service had begun. No time to think at this point, only time to react. He glanced at the bulletin again and noted for the third time the reverend had been allotted forty-five minutes to speak. The next item on the bulletin was entitled, "Slide Presentation." "Would it follow the sermon? Was it a part of the sermon?" No time to think now, only react. He lifted his head towards the ceiling at the fifteen-foot crease where the silver projection screen was locked into position. "When would it be lowered? And when the first slide was projected onto the screen and they realized something was dreadfully wrong, what would they do? What would he do?" Rick was fidgeting next to him again. "What the hell for?" He decided not to ask.

The reverend began…"Brother's and sisters in the family of Christ, distinguished guests, Mayor Baxter, your lovely wife, and to the millions of viewers around the world, 'this is the day that the Lord has made, let us rejoice and be glad in it!'" The audience erupted out of their seats amidst a frenzy of applause and "hallelujahs!" Hands waved into the air like parallel cobras swaying to the piped music of an Indian enchantress. "Praise Jesus!" and more "alleluias!" were heard here and there in the sea of people.

"'Eyes have not seen nor ears heard, the wonderful things God has prepared for those who love him.'" The reverend was indeed a crafts-man; his presence blessed with a mysterious power that impels men and women to gaze upon him as though their very life depended upon his words. The audience again erupted like a flame that could not be quenched. The reverend held firmly onto the sides of the podium, not in any attempt to gain balance, but rather, as if the grip itself was nec-essary to keep him grounded. His head was raised to the ceiling, the sharp line of his beard cutting across his neck like the arch of a snowy horizon. His face looked wounded and tortured with an unbearable sensation of pleasure and excitement. The moment was his. The audi-ence would not be calmed and he would not think of cutting them short. Moments passed into minutes, three, four, then five, before they finally began to settle down. Slowly the audience took their seats. The applause died to a quite roar, then to a trickle, and ended with the final clap of an old man seated on the front pew. The reverend lifted his hands towards the audience with palms facing down, as if to say he appreciated their homage, but he now wished to speak.

"I wish to tell you a story. It's about an old man named Nicodemus. A man possessed with the knowledge and wisdom of the ancients. Nicodemus was a Pharisee, a distinguished member of the Sanhedrin. Nicodemus wasn't just any Jew, for all Jews knew the scriptures in those days, but Nicodemus was a Jew who sustained himself solely by the word of God. He knew the scriptures well. He'd devoted his life to them. There was not one element of truth to which he was unfamiliar. None that is, except one. And that was the work of the Holy Spirit.

"Nicodemus came to Jesus one day in secret. For you see, Jesus had become an object of hatred for the members of the Sanhedrin and it would be extremely embarrassing—if not lethal—for anyone of them to seek counsel from the lowly carpenter of Nazareth. Strangely enough, Nicodemus had absolutely no idea why he was seeking out

Jesus. No clear idea why he would risk the exposure of being seen with Jesus. I dare say it is not unlike many of you seated here today. Not unlike thousands of you who sit in front of your television screen at this very moment in your life. You may not have any idea as to why you are here, or what prompted you to tune in to our broadcast today, but I have the answer to that mystery."

"Jesus was alone and sitting under an olive tree when Nicodemus found him. Jesus knew he was coming long before he arrived. He knew the answer to Nicodemus' questions long before Nicodemus considered he had any questions. They met underneath that olive tree in solitude, where only the slight sound of a soft breeze rippled through the leaves above them. Jesus talked to Nicodemus about being born again. Nicodemus questioned the logic in being born again. 'How is it that a man or woman can return back into their mother's womb and be born again?' Nicodemus wondered. Jesus answered his question much like he always answered questions, with an indirect statement. Jesus said, 'Listen to the wind and how it blows, for you do not know from which direction it comes or which direction it goes. And so it is with the Holy Spirit.'"

"I can imagine Nicodemus standing there looking up through the creaking branches and the spinning leaves of the olive tree, straining to see that invisible presence passing above him. Maybe he examined how the branches were bending. Maybe he looked for the peculiar way in which the leaves were spinning. How long did he stand there? I don't know, but I'm sure he stood there long enough to know Jesus was right. What Jesus told him was true. That there was an ache in his heart, a steady longing for things unexplained which he needed answers to."

The reverend paused for a moment to daub sweat from his forehead with a white handkerchief. The audience waited patiently.

"So how is it with you today? I suspect some of you here don't have a clue as to why you are here. What prompted you to get up this morning and take the drive out to our services? What did you hope or expect to find here? A mystery? You will find no mystery here, for it is the same Holy Spirit that moved the skeptical, but opened the heart of Nicodemus, that has brought you here today."

The reverend concluded his story with a long pause. Like all his actions it was calculated for affect. He was giving his audience time to process the story, to measure it with their experiences and to validate it. He waited a full two minutes before proceeding. "There is something I'd like to show you," he said finally, and out of the ceiling dropped the projection screen.

Stace's heart shut down for a split moment, then erupted into a swelling and throbbing volcano taking on a life all its own, forcing blood up through the arteries in his neck and into his head. His ears rang, but not enough to drown out the sounds around him. Quite the contrary, he acquired an almost immortal sense of hearing. He could hear the *humm* of the motor in the projection screen and the breath of every person in the auditorium. He could hear the terror in the voices of those who would undoubtedly seek to silence him. He even thought he could hear a voice telling him to run, to get the hell out of there, but ringing a note above everything else he heard was the clear, bell-like tone of what had to be done.

While the screen continued to fall the reverend went into a brief introduction of what the presentation was going to be about. He'd strolled away from the podium and was making his way down into the audience. The screen itself hung beyond the steps of the stage. It was impossible for those on stage to view the presentation, including the reverend, so by way of habit he would venture out in front of it so he could use each slide as a way to cue himself. After descending the stairs of the stage he made his way up the very isle Stace was sitting next to. He stopped about mid-point between the stage and the exit stopped facing the audience.

The reverend continued. "Several weeks ago we presented a slide presentation in which we outlined the history of the ICC. For those of you who had the privilege of seeing that presentation, I'm sure you felt a sense of pride and accomplishment for being involved with the ICC. We had some humble beginnings, but God has blessed us. This beautiful sanctuary in which you sit was built with the Lord's providence. 'To those in whom much is given, much is expected,'" he quoted from the Bible. "With that in mind, I followed up that presentation with a rather pointed message on what I think God was calling this church to do. It was not an easy message to swallow. I realize this, but neither is the truth sometimes. I ended with an appeal to you as members and viewers to examine your life and to put things into order, because I believe we are living in the last days. If I might be more direct, I think the Lord's second coming is at the door, even as we speak."

The screen locked itself into place with little more than a gentle sway and the projector was turned on. The first slide was nothing more than a title to the slide presentation.

Stace looked over at Rick and was about to speak. Rick interrupted his thought. "It's coming. Next slide."

"Since that time I have sought earnestly for the Lord's guidance. I have prayed for both wisdom and victory and the Lord has answered my prayers. If it's not too much trouble I would like to ask our visitors to stand at this time."

On the main floor about fifty visitors stood up from various pews around the auditorium. The reverend took a few steps back towards the stage, so he could look up into the balcony. Another twenty-five or so were standing silently in front of their seats. The rest of the congregation turned their heads and singled them out. Television cameras panned across the audience.

"I ask that you remain standing for a moment, because I'm certain there are more of you." At this point there was a noticeable murmuring within the auditorium. Those who were visitors and had remained seated grew self-conscious. It would have been better had they stood up in the first place.

"Shortly before the service started I was informed by the front gate the parking lot was filled to capacity. Some of you arrived a little late to find you had to park along the entrance road. Others had to park along the main street. That's a first here at the ICC and I think providential of what the Lord has in store for us. Our parking lot has never, even during Christmas or Easter services been filled. That tells me there are many more visitors in the audience, and I would just like to ask that you grant us the privilege of honoring you for the first time as our guests. Would you please stand?"

Almost instantaneously another three to four hundred people stood up, followed by a few stragglers. The reverend waited a few minutes until he was certain all of the visitors had stood who were going to stand. The cameras continued to pan across the audience and the reverend tipped back on his heels with a look of satisfaction and accomplishment.

"Ladies and Gentlemen this is unprecedented. Let's give them a big hand of appreciation." The audience erupted in applause and "hallelujahs." Many of the regular members got out of their seats and took a few moments to greet the visitors standing around them. Eventually, the applause died down. "This is nothing short of a miracle. But even so, it's just the beginning. I've known it was coming for a long time. If you would now direct you attention to the screen above I'll show you the reasons why are witnessing this kind of explosive growth."

The projector switched over to the next slide and the reverend continued. He didn't even bother to look up at the screen, having rehearsed the presentation thoroughly through the week.

"To begin with, we have merged with another Christian organization based in Frankfurt." The Reverend turned to the stage. "Neil Usher and Derrick Sachs, would you please stand at this time?" The two humbly rose. "It's not very often churches with different theological backgrounds can come together with the same mutual understanding." Neil was the first to notice an uneasy tension had drifted across the audience. Heads were turning between the reverend, the stage and the screen. Whispers could be heard above the imperceptible hiss of the microphones. The reverend didn't notice. "In the last ten years or so these two individuals have been steadily building a small army of Christian soldiers of their own. People like you and I who love the Lord and are willing to sacrifice. Who are willing to do what it takes to proclaim the glorious second coming of our Savior!" The whispers had grown into a disturbing rumble. Heads were still turning, but most of the audience had taken their eyes off the players on the floor and were gazing with a fistful of questions up at the projection screen. The reverend noticed the disturbance and was indignant he'd lost their attention. Only a fraction of them seemed to be looking at him now, so he followed the faces of the others upwards. This prompted the cameras to pan their cameras upwards as well. The studio engineer played along with it and sent the images on the screen around the world. Of the four shots Stace and Rick had managed to capture, this was the most clear and damaging of them all. Once Stace discovered it on the monitor, he had the image blown up and transferred to slide format. What started out as a barely readable image now ran across the fifteen-foot screen in letters two feet high. The first line read, "Reverend Eisner. Savior of the World!" The second line just below it, "Find Him. Follow Him!"

The reverend immediately understood the message as one in which he personally approved to be included in the program, but under no circumstances was it ever to be displayed in front of the public in this manner. He was quick, "Ladies and Gentlemen, someone has apparently decided to play a little joke on us this morning. If the projectionist would please advance the projector we'll get to the next slide."

The next slide on the screen was not as clear, but the words were just as large and the message equally damaging. "Book," read the first line. "Our Global Community," second line. Then "BUY IT!" printed in taller bold-faced letters on the third line.

The Reverend stumbled on his feet as he spun around to assess the impact of the second message. People were clearly talking now, no longer whispering, though there was so much of it going on he couldn't hear any specific comment in detail. "Next slide!" He blurted out in frustration. And there it was, simple and affective, "CHANNEL 47," and below it, "WATCH IT!"

"Turn it off!" the reverend screamed, but it was too late. If the messages were affective in their impact on the subconscious at lightning speed, they were overwhelming when displayed in letters two-foot high for minutes at a time. The cameras, by force of habit centered once again on the reverend, who had begun to turn in circles in the isle looking for either an explanation or a way out. He reached for his handkerchief in his suit pocket. Every eye was upon him and for perhaps the first time in his life he felt extremely uncomfortable in the limelight. Sweat collected in his cropped beard and across his forehead. A flush of embarrassment crept across his cheeks. His eyes jerked for a place to find rest away from the gaze of the multitudes. The choir was silent and motionless. The faces of the clergy seated on the thrones, who still had no idea what was going on because they couldn't see the screen, begged for enlightenment. The organist turned and faced the crowd for the first time in his life. Members of the orchestra reached for their instruments. They were always called upon at a moment's notice to smooth over the awkward moments of the service. The drummer, who was fiddling with his sticks, dropped one of them across the snare drum and broke the silence with a sharp, loud *pap*! The reverend daubed his lips with an already damp handkerchief and spoke.

"Brothers and sisters, I really must apologize for what appears to an obvious prank. Someone must have switched a few slides and inserted their own to disrupt our service."

Stace stood up about twenty-five feet from where the reverend stood and interrupted him. "It's no prank reverend and you know it!" he yelled. The camera to the front swung around and focused on the lunatic. It panned along with him as he stepped out into the isle and walked towards the teetering spiritual giant. The two deacons by the exit nearest Stace glanced at each other looking for an indication of what to do. The head elder, who had been seated next to Neil, stood up and walked to the podium. It wasn't the first time he'd been in that position. There were a lot of strange people in the world; kooks who made it their mission in life to make a fool of themselves on global television.

Stace stopped about six feet from the reverend, well within the reach of the reverend's microphone pickup. He knew it would be only a matter of moments before they would silence him. Spinning around to face the greatest portion of the audience, Stace spoke as clearly and loudly as possible. "What you have just seen are photographs I took off a computer screen." Out of the corner of his eye Stace saw Derrick quickly rise.

"Would the two deacons and a few of the elders please escort the gentleman outside so the service can resume the service," said the elder at the podium.

Stace glanced towards the exit and watched as two young men lurched down the isle towards him. Time was short. "The images came from a computer program created by the ICC to manipulate your minds." The audience erupted into a chatter of confusion and accusation. The two deacons reached Stace and seized him by the arms. "That's why many of you have no idea why you're here!" he blurted out at the top of his lungs.

The head elder at the podium attempted to regain control. "Could we be quiet? Please ladies and gentlemen. It's obvious we have a situation here that needs to be controlled. Deacons, escort the young man outside!" he commanded. Derrick had made it up the isle at this point. The two deacons turned Stace around and forced him towards the exit. Derrick followed right along behind them.

Suddenly, from the side door behind the orchestra, two *polizei* officers emerged followed by a man wearing a long tan overcoat. One officer remained at the door and the other officer escorted the man with the overcoat up onto the stage. Simultaneously, at each one of the exits on the main floor other officers emerged, stood in force and sufficiently sealed the exits. The two deacons that were escorting Stace out stopped abruptly in the isle. The head elder was so stunned by the presence of such a show of civil authority that he backed away from the podium and granted the man in the tan overcoat access to the microphone. Every camera in the auditorium swirled about in the futile attempt to capture what was going on. Their signals went by cables into the production room, where they were still being strung together by the production crew, and being sent out around the world.

"May I have your attention." My name is Detective Macabre. I'm with the Frankfurt City *Polizei*. The other officers here are with the Munich *Konstablerwache*. We apologize for disrupting your service. If I can have your full attention and cooperation, we shouldn't be more than just a few minutes." He raised his right hand to the back of the auditorium and flipped a quick gesture. Seconds later additional officers filed down the main isle and made their way towards the podium. At the bottom of the stage they split and panned outwards, lining up about five feet from each other, then faced the audience without so much as a twitch.

"I have a short list of names I'm going to read out. After I call your name I want you to come down to the stage and place yourself into the hands of one of these officers. Given the nature of the environment here, I expect no resistance. Should you find it necessary to resist, let me assure you the entire compound is secure." He reached into his coat pocket and pulled out a slip of paper, and laid it on the red velvet of the podium. A small reading light lit the five names.

"Derrick Sachs."

Heads and cameras turned isolating the man even before the officers had identified him. He looked around at all of the exits, but saw them blocked and secure. He looked at Stace, who stood just a few feet away. Hatred ripped though his mind. His fingers extended then contacted into solid fists, the only weapon available to him. He turned around and walked back towards the stage. His eyes met the first officer's eyes to the left of the stage and he never removed them. The gaze was in itself an act of defiance, stemming from a lifetime of repulsion towards any authoritative figure. He stopped just inches from the officer's face, stiff and snorting like a bull.

"Turn around," the officer commanded. Derrick stood his ground. Calmly, the officer walked behind him, cuffed him tightly and with a sharp nudge urged him towards the side exit.

Stautzen was sitting on the second throne from the right. He fully expected his name to be called next. In anticipation, he slid down into the folds of the throne and hadn't watched as they cuffed and escorted Derrick out. His eyes focused on a non-descript spot in the purple carpet in front of him. He dared not look at the audience and didn't have the courage to face his wife, who was seated in the first pew on the left hand side of the sanctuary.

"Neil Usher," came the second name out of the sanctuary speakers.

Neil slowly rose off his throne like a dethroned king. After standing, he instinctively adjusted his suit coat, even taking a moment to check the knot in his tie. His walk was proud though lifeless. He was promptly cuffed and moved along.

"Joseph Stautzen."

There it came. Just a name, but with its mention a world full of dreams and promises came crashing down around him. He buried his face in his hands and felt an earthquake of emotions rippling through his body. They rendered him powerless and he could not stand.

"Joseph Stautzen!" Detective Macabre said again. He looked over the audience in search of the man. He saw an audience full of faces all turned in one direction to a location behind him. He turned around to see why. Stautzen was incoherent with grief. "Will two of the officers please remove Mr. Stautzen out of the building."

The next name he read would be done in the same manner as the others, with no special tone or inflection, just a generic name on paper. "Jeremiah Eisner."

Up to this point in time the audience had been muted by incredulity. The fact that anyone at all was being led out of their sanctuary by *polizei* officers was enough of an intrusion in itself. So much had taken place within these Holy walls that just the impression that a crime had been committed by one of their own would never be erased out of their minds. But the reverend himself? Never mind the mysterious messages and the frantic cries of a wild-haired visitor. It was beyond comprehension. It threatened to suck the life out of hundreds of thousands of believers. It was just beyond believability. Every camera and eye in the room was fixed on the reverend. At any moment he would surely resist. Wouldn't he? Surely he would be quick to lash out with some kind of verbal assault that would put an end to the absurdity of it all.

"Reverend Eisner," the detective said again.

But the reverend seemed almost powerless to move. What was he thinking? What would he say? Only moments passed by, but it was more like hours to the faithful. And with each moment that passed the faith of the faithful evaporated like a thimble full of water nestled in desert sands. Several of the women in the audience were quietly sobbing, like the consensual sniffle of the elderly, who seemed to understand in the passing of time almost anything is possible.

The reverend finally took his eyes off the floor and looked at his flock. His expression was endearing, though certainly pathetic. It was the look of man who had worked his whole life to achieve only one noble goal, and who suddenly realized that just shy of victory it had slipped elusively though his hands. These were his people, his friends, his family. He could see in their faces that some still granted him the respect he'd earned from them over the years as their servant. These were the younger and idealistic ones, who simply couldn't accept the fact their spiritual leader had erred. "Perhaps they just wanted him for questioning," they thought, but the reverend gave no sign that was the case. No words of reassurance to comfort them he'd be back next week. He smiled too; an attempt at reassurance that came off looking like something had suddenly snapped inside him that could never be mended. He cast his eyes back towards the floor, his very lack of words an indication of his guilt. They cuffed him like they did the others after he'd shuffled down towards the stage. The cruel steel sound of metallic jaws synching around his plump wrists was amplified through the sanctuary speakers, for the audio man had yet to switch off the reverend's microphone.

"Rick Forstein."

Throughout the auditorium heads turned in search of the next man on the list. Stace was the only one who could identify him. He was standing in the isle just a few feet from where Rick was seated. The call of his name seemed unjustified. He had after all, played a big part in bringing the ICC down. And yet, he had after all, created the program in the first place. Stace was sure of one thing, he wouldn't be the man to point him out. Their lives had become mysteriously intertwined; connected in a mix-match of ideals and purpose that had triumphed for the cause of justice.

Detective Macabre was about to call his name out again when he noticed a lone figure rise out of his pew near the back. The man came out into the isle and stood before Stace face to face. It took the audience and the cameras a few moments to find him. Detective Macabre decided to be patient.

"You did it," Rick said. He was calm and hadn't lost any of his wit.

"We did it."

There was a slight hesitation, a pause of mutual respect in their demeanor.

"By the way," Stace said glancing around, "what do you know about all of this?"

Rick flashed a warm smile, one that was playfully sinister. "You'll have to ask Eva about that. I'll be tied up for a while."

Again, there was some hesitation; it was one of those moments in which thoughts fly back and forth without words; where silence does a better job of bonding friendships far faster than communication ever could. Rick extended his hand and Stace took it. He turned and walked down the isle towards the stage. Stace watched him. It wasn't a laborious walk. There was no hesitation whatsoever. An officer escorted Rick un-handcuffed through the side door.

"I'd like to thank you again ladies and gentlemen for your coopera-tion. Please accept the apologies of both the Frankfurt and Munich *Polizei* for disrupting your services." Detective Macabre exited the side door and the rest of the officers quickly cleared the sanctuary. Without delay the head elder returned to the podium. He summoned the minis-ter of music to lead the congregation in a hymn. The minister of music nervously picked out a random hymn and cued the organist to begin. As the organist played and he alone sang, the entire congregation left in mass exodus.

Stace preceded the crowd and made his way up into the loft where the audio/visual room was. He opened the door and found a young man still monitoring the television cameras on video screens. Three of the screens were focused on the exodus of the congregation and one screen on the man singing at the podium. All the images were still being processed in the adjacent studio for the world to see. The man at the chair paid him little attention to Stace, who simply walked over to the projector and pulled out his two slides. He would keep them purely for the sake of nostalgia. In they end, they would not provide much proof of the program's existence, that would come later, but they had served their purpose nevertheless.

Outside the room Stace took a seat in the loft awaiting the clearing of the building and the parking lot. Why the organist kept on playing was beyond comprehension. He finished a hymn and started another, then still another. Perhaps he just liked to play. Perhaps he knew it was his last opportunity to play the pipes. Perhaps he still thought there was someone in the auditorium who was willing to listen. Eventually, even the minister of music set down with his hymnal on one of the thrones behind him after everyone in the sanctuary had left, leaving Stace and the organist alone.

"Was it all worth it?" he wondered. How many souls around the world were at this very moment feeling the pain of disillusion and deception? Probably thousands of people, who had for years placed all their hope and faith in the ICC. What would these people do? Who would they turn to next? Would they have enough faith in themselves to realize they had the power to make their own decisions? That they had the freedom to think for themselves?

The organist was into his sixth hymn when Stace heard a voice behind him.

"I've been looking for you," Eva said.

He was startled, but didn't turn around.

She laid her hands on his neck and he could feel the warmth of her touch. It was a touch of reassurance. He closed his eyes as her hands moved down his neck and across his shoulders. "And now that you've found me..." he began, but let the sentence dangle.

"I was hoping we might be able to make that decision together."

He brought his hands up and took hold of hers. She sat down on the chair behind him and leaned towards him. He could feel her breath in his ears as she whispered, "I've made many mistakes in my life Stace. Misjudging you was by far my worst."

He was silent for a few moments, listening through a soft refrain played by the organist before deciding what to say next. "I suppose you had good reason too. I might have done the same thing."

"Even so, I was wrong and I'm sorry." She kissed his neck just behind the ear. The wetness of her lips electrified his spine.

"I quit my job Stace. I no longer work for the paper. This was my last investigation."

Now he turned to face her. Her work had been the most important thing in her life. Could he ever replace it? There were no tears in her eyes. She was far too determined and independent for such sentimentality.

"Why?"

"It was time. I nearly lost my family, and as it stands, I may still lose you."

Rarely does a comment carry with it such explosive implications. It was an appeal for forgiveness. It was an agonizing affirmation he was the most important thing in her life. It was a reaching for the hope of togetherness with no clear vision of the future. It was a blind declaration of her faith in him that left her completely vulnerable and exposed. But most importantly, it was the precise expression of her love he'd been hoping to hear.

He reached up and touched the outside of her face caressing her cheek. "You will never lose me," he whispered. He ran his fingers through her hair and around the back of her head, gently pulling her face towards his. Their eyes met, their cheeks gently touched and their lips joined to explore their new beginning and love for one another.

0-595-27009-3